KU-490-167

B.S.U.C. - LIBRARY
00217345

A Bernard Shaw Chronology

Author Chronologies

General Editor: **Norman Page**, Emeritus Professor of Modern English Literature, University of Nottingham

Published titles include:

J. L. Bradley
A RUSKIN CHRONOLOGY

Gordon Campbell
A MILTON CHRONOLOGY

Martin Garrett
A BROWNING CHRONOLOGY
ELIZABETH BARRETT BROWNING AND ROBERT BROWNING

A. M. Gibbs
A BERNARD SHAW CHRONOLOGY

J. R. Hammond
A ROBERT LOUIS STEVENSON CHRONOLOGY
AN EDGAR ALLAN POE CHRONOLOGY
AN H. G. WELLS CHRONOLOGY
A GEORGE ORWELL CHRONOLOGY

John McDermott
A HOPKINS CHRONOLOGY

Norman Page
AN EVELYN WAUGH CHRONOLOGY

Peter Preston
A D. H. LAWRENCE CHRONOLOGY

Author Chronologies Series
Series Standing Order ISBN 0–333–71484–9
(*outside North America only*)

You can receive future titles in this series as they are published by placing a standing order. Please contact your bookseller or, in case of difficulty, write to us at the address below with your name and address, the title of the series and the ISBN quoted above.

Customer Services Department, Macmillan Distribution Ltd, Houndmills, Basingstoke, Hampshire RG21 6XS, England

A Bernard Shaw Chronology

A. M. Gibbs

palgrave

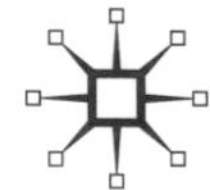

© A. M. Gibbs 2001

All rights reserved. No reproduction, copy or transmission of this publication may be made without written permission.

No paragraph of this publication may be reproduced, copied or transmitted save with written permission or in accordance with the provisions of the Copyright, Designs and Patents Act 1988, or under the terms of any licence permitting limited copying issued by the Copyright Licensing Agency, 90 Tottenham Court Road, London W1P 0LP.

Any person who does any unauthorised act in relation to this publication may be liable to criminal prosecution and civil claims for damages.

The author has asserted his right to be identified as the author of this work in accordance with the Copyright, Designs and Patents Act 1988.

First published 2001 by
PALGRAVE
Houndmills, Basingstoke, Hampshire RG21 6XS and
175 Fifth Avenue, New York, N. Y. 10010
Companies and representatives throughout the world

PALGRAVE is the new global academic imprint of
St. Martin's Press LLC Scholarly and Reference Division and
Palgrave Publishers Ltd (formerly Macmillan Press Ltd).

Outside North America
ISBN 0–333–63327–X

In North America
ISBN 0–312–23163–6

This book is printed on paper suitable for recycling and made from fully managed and sustained forest sources.

A catalogue record for this book is available from the British Library.

Library of Congress Cataloging-in-Publication Data
Gibbs, A. M. (Anthony Matthews), 1933–
A Bernard Shaw chronology / A. M. Gibbs.
p. cm.
Includes bibliographical references and index.
ISBN 0–312–23163–6 (cloth)
1. Shaw, Bernard, 1856–1950—Chronology. 2. Shaw, Bernard, 1856–1950—Characters. 3. Dramatists, Irish—19th century–
–Chronology. 4. Dramatists, Irish—20th century—Chronology.
I. Title.

PR5366 .A238 2000
822'.912—dc21
[B]

00–024437

10 9 8 7 6 5 4 3 2 1
10 09 08 07 06 05 04 03 02 01

Printed in Great Britain by Antony Rowe Ltd, Chippenham, Wiltshire

To Dan H. Laurence

Contents

General Editor's Preface

Most biographies are ill adapted to serve as works of reference – not surprisingly so, since the biographer is likely to regard his function as the devising of a continuous and readable narrative, with excursions into interpretation and speculation, rather than a bald recital of facts. There are times, however, when anyone reading for business or pleasure needs to check a point quickly or to obtain a rapid overview of part of an author's life or career; and at such moments turning over the pages of a biography can be a time-consuming and frustrating occupation. The present series of volumes aims at providing a means whereby the chronological facts of an author's life and career, rather than needing to be prised out of the narrative in which they are (if they appear at all) securely embedded, can be seen at a glance. Moreover whereas biographies are often, and quite understandably, vague over matters of fact (since it makes for tediousness to be forever enumerating details of dates and places), a chronology can be precise whenever it is possible to be precise.

Thanks to the survival, sometimes in very large quantities, of letters, diaries, notebooks and other documents, as well as to thoroughly researched biographies and bibliographies, this material now exists in abundance for many major authors. In the case of, for example, Dickens, we can often ascertain what he was doing in each month and week, and almost on each day, of his prodigiously active working life; and the student of, say, *David Copperfield* is likely to find it fascinating as well as useful to know just when Dickens was at work on each part of that novel, what other literary enterprises he was engaged in at the same time, whom he was meeting, what places he was visiting, and what were the relevant circumstances of his personal and professional life. Such a chronology is not, of course, a substitute for a biography; but its arrangement, in combination with its index, makes it a much more convenient tool for this kind of purpose; and it may be acceptable as a form of 'alternative' biography, with its own distinctive advantages as well as its obvious limitations.

Since information relating to an author's early years is usually scanty and chronologically imprecise, the opening section of some volumes in this series groups together the years of childhood and adolescence. Thereafter each year, and usually each month, is dealt with separately. Information not readily assignable to a specific month or day is given as a general note under the relevant year or month. The first entry for each month carries an indication of the day of the week, so that when necessary this can be readily calculated for other dates. Each volume also contains a bibliography of the principal sources of information. In the chronology itself, the sources of many of the more specific items, including quotations, are identified, in order that the reader who wishes to do so may consult the original contexts.

NORMAN PAGE

Acknowledgements

This book is dedicated to Dan H. Laurence, with admiration and affection. I am greatly indebted to him not only for the vast range and superb quality of his scholarly work on Shaw, but also for the generosity with which he has shared, in meetings and correspondence, unpublished information from his files and records, and drawn on his unique fund of knowledge to make numerous suggestions for additions and corrections to the work in progress. He should not be held responsible for any shortcomings in this book, but he has been a major contributor to the information it contains.

I am also deeply indebted to A. Norman Jeffares, doyen general of Irish literary studies, for his kind encouragement and support over many years. I am grateful to the General Editor of the Macmillan Author Chronology series, Norman Page, for kindly proposing the invitation to me to undertake the Shaw volume in the series, and for his advice and help during its development. I also thank Charmian Hearne for the commissioning of the volume, and Anne Rafique and Eleanor Birne for subsequent editorial work.

Research for the Shaw Chronology project was carried out with the aid of funding from the Australian Research Council and the Macquarie University Research Committee, and I am grateful to both those bodies for indispensable support. During the preparation of the Chronology I have been much indebted to the skilful work and helpful ideas of a number of Research Assistants: Penny van Toorn, Sue Kossew, Marcelle Freiman, Geoffrey Windon, Ed Wright, Liam Semler, Julie-Anne Tapper and Annette Wong. I have also continued to draw on the scholarly findings of two Research Assistants who worked with me on a previous Shavian project, Lyndy Abraham and Jeremy Steele.

In the course of research on this work, I have been helped by many other people, and I record my thanks particularly to: Ruth Amos, Tom Amos, Lawrence Aspden, Janet Birkett, Ron Bowles, Helen Boyd, Malcolm Brand, Lucy Burgess, Sarah Cobbold, the late Fred Crawford, Janet Crombie, Sue Donnelly, Tom Evans, Catherine Fahy, Ann Ferguson, Pat Fox, Nicholas Grene, Elizabeth Harrison, Michael Hughes, Michael Kenneally, Daniel Kevles, Noel Kissane, Adrian Le Harival, Frances McCarthy, Juliet McLean, Bernadette Masters, Dawn Melhuish, Leslie A. Morris, Rhoda Nathan, Christina Rowe, Margaret Nicholas, Carl Peterson, Graeme Powell, D. A. Rees, Michael Roe, Nancy Sadek, Marion Shaw, Barbara Smith, Robin Smith, Stuart Ó Seanóir, Anne Summers, John Telec, Eleanor Vallis, Annemieke Vimal, Tara Wenger, Melanie Wisener and Giles Yates.

Permission to quote from published and unpublished writings of Bernard Shaw has been kindly granted by the Society of Authors

(London), on behalf of the Bernard Shaw Estate. Permission to quote from unpublished correspondence of W. A. S. Hewins has been kindly granted by the University Librarian, University of Sheffield. Acknowledgement is also made to the following institutions for permission to quote from unpublished writings in their collections: the British Library; Archives Division, British Library of Political and Economic Science; Special Collections Department, Case Library, Colgate University; Rare and Manuscript Collections (Burgunder Collection), Carl A. Kroch Library, Cornell University; the Manuscript Department, Houghton Library, Harvard University; the National Library of Australia; the National Library of Ireland; the Harry Ransom Humanities Research Center, the University of Texas at Austin; Trinity College Dublin Library by permission of the Board of Trinity College Dublin; University College London Library; the University of Victoria Libraries.

Finally I thank my wife Donna, whose astute advice has helped in manifold ways.

A. M. Gibbs
Sydney, Australia
December 1999

List of Abbreviations

Agits	Bernard Shaw, *Agitations: Letters to the Press 1875–1950*, eds Dan H. Laurence and James Rambeau (New York: Frederick Ungar, 1985)
Auto1, 2	Bernard Shaw, *Shaw: An Autobiography*, 2 vols, selected from his writings by Stanley Weintraub (New York: Weybright & Talley, 1969, 1970; London: Max Reinhardt, 1970, 1971)
BL	British Library, Department of Manuscripts
BLPES	British Library of Political and Economic Science
Carlow	Carlow County Library
CJS	C. J. Shaw, *A History of Clan Shaw* (Chichester, Sussex: Phillimore, 1983)
CL1, 2, 3, 4	Bernard Shaw, *Collected Letters*, 4 vols, ed. Dan H. Laurence (London: Reinhardt, 1965, 1972, 1985, 1988)
CMS	Charles MacMahon Shaw, *Bernard's Brethren* (with comments by GBS) (London: Constable, 1939)
Cole	Beatrice Webb, *Beatrice Webb's Diaries 1924–1932*, ed. Margaret Cole (London: Longmans, Green & Co., 1956)
Cornell	Rare and Manuscripts Collection, Kroch Library, Cornell University
Court	Desmond MacCarthy, *The Court Theatre: 1904–1907* (London: A. H. Bullen, 1907)
CP1, 2, 3, 4, 5, 6, 7	Bernard Shaw, *Collected Plays with Their Prefaces*, 7 vols, ed. Dan H. Laurence (London: Bodley Head, 1970–4)
D1, 2	Bernard Shaw, *Bernard Shaw: The Diaries*, 2 vols, ed. Stanley Weintraub (University Park: Pennsylvania State University Press, 1986)
DBW1, 2, 3, 4	Beatrice Webb, *The Diary of Beatrice Webb*, 4 vols, eds Norman and Jean Mackenzie (London: Virago/ London School of Economics and Political Science, 1982–5)
Dent	Bernard Shaw, *Bernard Shaw and Mrs. Patrick Campbell: Their Correspondence*, ed. Alan Dent (New York: Alfred A. Knopf, 1952)
DHL	Dan H. Laurence, private communication

Drama1, 2, 3, 4	Bernard Shaw, *The Drama Observed*, 4 vols, ed. Bernard F. Dukore (University Park: Pennsylvania State University Press, 1993)
Dunbar	Janet Dunbar, *Mrs G.B.S.: A Biographical Portrait of Charlotte Shaw* (London: George G. Harrap, 1963)
Erv	St John Ervine, *Bernard Shaw: His Life, Work and Friends* (London: Constable, 1956)
Farmer	Henry George Farmer, *Bernard Shaw's Sister and Her Friends* (Leiden: E. J. Brill, 1959)
Guelph	Dan H. Laurence Collection, University of Guelph Library
Harvard	Houghton Library, Harvard University
Hend1	Archibald Henderson, *George Bernard Shaw: His Life and Works* (London: Hurst & Blackett, 1911)
Hend2	Archibald Henderson, *Bernard Shaw: Playboy and Prophet* (New York: D. Appleton & Co., 1932)
Hend3	Archibald Henderson, *George Bernard Shaw: Man of the Century* (London: New York: Appleton-Century-Crofts, 1956)
Hol1, 2, 3, 4, 5	Michael Holroyd, *Bernard Shaw*, 5 vols (London: Chatto & Windus, 1988–92)
Hyde	Bernard Shaw, *Bernard Shaw and Alfred Douglas: A Correspondence*, ed. Mary Hyde (Oxford: Oxford University Press, 1989)
I&R	Bernard Shaw, *Shaw: Interviews and Recollections*, ed. A. M. Gibbs (London: Macmillan, 1990)
Imm	Bernard Shaw, Preface to *Immaturity* (London: Constable, 1930)
Joad	C.E.M. Joad, *Shaw* (1949)
L&G	Bernard Shaw, *Shaw, Lady Gregory and the Abbey: A Correspondence and a Record*, eds Dan H. Laurence and Nicholas Grene (Gerrards Cross: Colin Smythe, 1993)
Lbib1, 2	Dan H. Laurence, *Bernard Shaw: A Bibliography*, 2 vols (Oxford: Clarendon Press, 1983)
Lgen	Dan H. Laurence, 'The Shaws and the Gurlys: A Genealogical Study', in *SHAW: The Annual of Bernard Shaw Studies*, vol. 18 (University Park: Pennsylvania State University Press, 1998), pp. 1–31
McNulty	Edward McNulty, 'Memoirs of G.B.S.' (ed. Dan H. Laurence), in *SHAW: The Annual of Bernard Shaw Studies*, vol. 12 (University Park: Pennsylvania State University Press, 1992), pp. 5–46
Morgan	Margery Morgan, *File on Shaw* (London: Methuen Drama, 1989)

NYPL	New York Public Library, Henry W. and Albert A. Berg Collection
O'D	John O'Donovan, *Bernard Shaw* (London: Gill and Macmillan, 1983)
OTN1, 2, 3	Bernard Shaw, *Our Theatres in the Nineties*, 3 vols (London: Constable, 1954)
P&P	Bernard Shaw, *Platform and Pulpit*, ed. Dan. H. Laurence (London: Rupert Hart-Davis, 1962)
Pearson	Hesketh Pearson, *Bernard Shaw: His Life and Personality* (London: Methuen 1961)
Pease	Edward R. Pease, *The History of the Fabian Society* (London: Frank Cass, 1963)
Peters	Margot Peters, *Bernard Shaw and the Actresses* (Garden City, NY: Doubleday, 1980)
Prefs1, 2, 3	Bernard Shaw, *The Complete Prefaces*, 3 vols, eds Dan. H. Laurence and Daniel J. Leary (London: Allen Lane, Penguin Press, 1993–97)
Rat	R. F. Rattray, *Bernard Shaw: A Chronicle*, rev. edn (Luton: Leagrave, 1951)
Ross	B. C. Rosset, *Shaw of Dublin: The Formative Years* (University Park: Pennsylvania State University Press, 1964)
SA	*Shaw Abroad – SHAW: The Annual of Bernard Shaw Studies*, vol. 5, ed. Rodelle Weintraub (University Park and London: Pennsylvania State University Press, 1985)
SCG	John O'Donovan, *Shaw and the Charlatan Genius: A Memoir* (Dublin: Dolmen Press, 1965)
SM	Bernard Shaw, *Shaw's Music: The Complete Musical Criticism of Bernard Shaw*, 3 vols, 2nd rev. edn, ed. Dan H. Laurence (London: Bodley Head, 1989)
SSS	Bernard Shaw, *Sixteen Self-Sketches* (London: Constable, 1949)
Texas	Harry Ransom Humanities Research Center, University of Texas, Austin
Theatrics	Bernard Shaw, *Theatrics* (Selected Correspondence of Bernard Shaw series), ed. Dan H. Laurence (Toronto, Buffalo and London: University of Toronto Press, 1995)
Tompkins	Bernard Shaw, *To a Young Actress: the Letters of Bernard Shaw to Molly Tompkins*, ed. Peter Tompkins (London: Constable, 1960)

Tyson	Bernard Shaw, *Bernard Shaw's Book Reviews*, ed. Brian Tyson (University Park: Pennsylvania State University Press, 1991)
Webb	Beatrice Webb, *Our Partnership*, eds Barbara Drake and Margaret I. Cole (Cambridge: London School of Economics and Political Science/Cambridge University Press, 1975)
Wein1	Stanley Weintraub, *Private Shaw and Public Shaw: A Dual Portrait of Lawrence of Arabia and GBS* (New York: George Braziller, 1963)
Wein2	Stanley Weintraub, *Bernard Shaw 1914–1918: Journey to Heartbreak* (London: Routledge & Kegan Paul, 1973)
Wein3	Stanley Weintraub, *The Unexpected Shaw: Biographical Approaches to G.B.S and His Work* (New York: Ungar, 1982)
Wein4	Bernard Shaw and Frank Harris, *The Playwright and the Pirate: Bernard Shaw and Frank Harris: A Correspondence*, ed. Stanley Weintraub (Gerards Cross: Colin Smythe, 1982)
Weiss	Bernard Shaw, *Bernard Shaw's Letters to Siegfried Trebitsch*, ed. Samuel A. Weiss (Stanford, CA: Stanford University Press, 1986)
Wisenthal	Bernard Shaw, *Shaw and Ibsen: Bernard Shaw's* The Quintessence of Ibsenism *and Related Writings*, ed. J. L. Wisenthal (Toronto: University of Toronto Press, 1979)

Introduction

This book aims to provide what might be described, in imitation of Shaw's title for his 1944 work, *Everybody's Political What's What?*, as 'Everybody's Shavian What Was When and Who Was Who'. In other words, the book presents a full chronology of significant events in Shaw's life, prefaced by an account of his ancestry and family, and followed by a 'Who's Who' of the most important of his associates during his long and multi-faceted career.

The project of creating a chronological account of the life and career of a figure such as Shaw poses a number of intriguing questions about biography, and about the procedure itself of describing a person's life in chronological form. In the middle years of the twentieth century, the long-running Australian weekly, *The Bulletin*, carried a readers' correspondence column, jovially and male-chauvinistically called 'The Other Fellow's Mind'. At the head of the column was always placed a drawing of a man with a magnifying glass, peering, as though into a cooking pot with the lid removed, into the horizontally bisected cranium of another 'person'. The image is a *reductio ad absurdum* of what is commonly seen as one of the main purposes of the biographical quest, the exploration and discovery of the secret mechanisms at work in the mind and spirit of the subject of enquiry. The problematical nature of the image becomes clear when we try to make it perform its emblematic functions. What *is* the magnifying glass, or what does it represent; what is being looked at with it; and why is the magnifying glass man behaving in this way in the first place?

Curiosity about the lives of writers has remained an enduring phenomenon in Western society, at least since the late Renaissance. In the English-speaking world, the writing of literary lives had its beginnings in the seventeenth century, with the work of such writers as Izaak Walton, Thomas Sprat and John Aubrey. In the following century, a new stamp of respectability and importance was given to this genre of writing by the publication, in 1779–81, of Dr Johnson's *Lives of the Poets*. The tradition has flourished ever since. During the latter part of the twentieth century, literary criticism and literary theory, from various political standpoints, have fought a persistent, but on the whole unsuccessful, battle against literary biography and the fetishizing of the author as subject. Despite numerous proclamations, the death of the author has not taken place. Biography, including literary biography, flourishes as never before, and interest in the person behind the book or play or film has if anything intensified. This is not to say that the problematical connections between life events and literary creations are widely understood.[1] Often reductive and oversimplifying connections are made, as they frequently have been in the case of Shaw.

But granted that biography seems here to stay as a human activity and pastime, what is it that we are peering into through its magnifying glass? In Shaw's opinion, expressed at the beginning of his late collection of autobiographical essays, *Sixteen Self Sketches* (1949), the only worthwhile subject of biographical enquiry in his own case – the proper point of focus for the magnifying glass – was his published work:

> ...all my happenings have taken the form of books and plays. Read them, or spectate them; and you have my whole story: the rest is only breakfast, lunch, dinner, sleeping, wakening and washing, my routine being just the same as everybody's routine.[2]

This statement is reminiscent of Oscar Wilde's declaration, through the medium of his character Gilbert, in 'The Critic As Artist', that criticism is the 'only civilised form of autobiography, as it deals not with the events, but with the thoughts of one's life; not with life's physical accidents of deed or circumstance, but with the spiritual moods and imaginative passions of the mind'.[3]

Admirable in some ways as the Shavian and Wildean platonic, or purist, ideals of biography may be, they create a Cartesian dualism about life and letters, event and mind, which ultimately breaks down. Once known, biographical information is very difficult to disentangle from the rest of our image of a writer. The 'story' of Wilde himself is indelibly affected by the events of his trial and imprisonment. Similarly in the case of Shaw, events, though never being of the kind which overtook Wilde, can be argued to hold a similarly important place in the meanings of his life and work. Nor, of course, can we discount the role of personal events in writers' lives in the shaping of their works, even though the connections need to be cautiously handled.

Shaw's 'Apology' at the beginning of *Sixteen Self Sketches*, coming as it does before his entertaining accounts of numerous 'happenings' which did not take the form of books or plays, belies the fact that he did have an extraordinarily eventful life in many ways. While some events, such as births, deaths and marriages, travels, dates of publication and first performances of works, meetings and public engagements, choose themselves as items for inclusion in a chronology, a large degree of choice arises in the case of other categories of event. For a writer, the first reading of a book, or coming into contact with a new set of ideas, can be as momentous an event as any other. Shaw tells us that his whole way of thinking about life was transformed when, in September 1882, he listened to a lecture by Henry George, the American author of *Progress and Poverty*. In his diary entry for 10 August 1889, Shaw records that, after his mother had bought him the score of Wagner's *Parsifal*, he 'spent a good deal of [his] time at the piano in consequence'. For the future author of *The Perfect Wagnerite*, this was an important event. In the present study, then, 'events' are broadly defined. The chronology aims at a record of significant events in Shaw's intellectual, emotional and creative life, and in the course of his relationships with other people, as well as occurrences which belong to the more public domain.

As a means of investigating a literary life, the chronology form has its own strengths and limitations. While a chronological account of a writer's life does not allow room for sustained investigation of, or reflection on, events, it can be claimed to have the potential of creating an almost uniquely graphic form of life-portrait, evoking the day-to-day experiences of the subject in ways that are difficult to achieve in a thematic or narrative biography. Chronologies strip things to essentials and often reveal juxtapositions and patterns of events in a life in a striking way. Shaw sitting down to write a flirtatious letter to Lena Ashwell in the afternoon of 1 June 1898, after his marriage to Charlotte Payne-Townshend in the morning of the same day, supplies one example. During the days before his marriage, the events of Shaw's Don Juan-like entanglements with members of the opposite sex often assumed the complexity of a French farce. At this time Shaw's life was filled with an extraordinary multiplicity of activities, as he juggled the claims on his time of literary and debating societies, Fabian Society meetings, lecturing commitments, various forms of self-education, writing and reviewing, friendships and amours. After his marriage, and as his fame grew, his life became if anything even more intensely packed with activities. Even when he was supposedly on holidays Shaw was prodigiously energetic and productive.

The instruments through which a writer's life can be investigated are many and various. As well as the works themselves, they can include: letters (by others as well as the writer), diaries, autobiographical writings, interviews, recollections of the writer by contemporaries, newspaper and periodical reports, archival records, legal documents, genealogies, local histories, documentary film and radio recordings, oral report, and general histories of various kinds. In the case of Shaw, all of these sources of information come in to play in great abundance. Shaw was a brilliantly entertaining and prolific correspondent, and is estimated by Dan H. Laurence, editor of his collected letters, to have written over a quarter of a million letters and postcards during his lifetime. In addition to the four volumes of the *Collected Letters*, there are numerous special collections of correspondence with individuals such as Mrs Patrick Campbell, Ellen Terry, Siegfried Trebitsch, and H. G. Wells. Laurence has added to the *Collected Letters* two further collections of Shaw correspondence, *Theatrics* (letters relating to the theatre) and a gathering of Shaw's letters to the press, *Agitations*. The Laurence editions of the letters, with their concisely written introductions and editorial notes, have been a major source of information in the preparation of this work. I have also drawn on correspondence still in manuscript and held in various locations around the world.

Shaw began keeping, largely in shorthand, a regular diary at the beginning of 1885, and maintained it until April 1897. He also made scrappy autobiographical notes during the period 1875–87. He made a resolve to resume his diary-keeping at the beginning of 1917, but this was kept for only a fortnight. Shaw's diaries were not written as literary journals, with extensive descriptions of people and events, or as essays in self-revelation and analysis. They are mainly records of engagements, meetings, purchases and expenses, visits to plays and concerts, negotiations with publishers, and so forth. They are nevertheless often enlivened by piquant and succinct summaries of events by Shaw, and they reveal an enormous amount about his life and activities during the London days before his marriage in 1898. The excellent, two volume, edition by Stanley Weintraub of the diaries, up to and including the 1917 fragment, with its copious and well informed notes, is a major source of the chronology for the periods they cover.

In addition to the diaries published in the Weintraub edition, there is a collection of forty-eight mostly pocket-size engagement diaries which Shaw maintained, irregularly, from 1877 to the year of his death in 1950. Along with the personal diaries, the engagement diaries are held, in accordance with Shaw's bequest, in the Archives Department of the British Library of Political and Economic Science. Information from these is supplemented by an 'Annuary', or annual digest of events, which Mrs Judy Musters prepared for Shaw during the Second World War, the original copy of which is held by Dan H. Laurence. A great deal of information relevant to the Chronology is also contained in the engagement diaries of Shaw's wife, Charlotte. These diaries, kept from 1874 to 1942, are held in the Department of Manuscripts in the British Library as Additional Manuscripts 63188A-63192N. The British Library also holds, as Additional Manuscript 56500, a diary of Charlotte Shaw for the years 1876 to 1919. This comprises a writing pad of one hundred and six pages of annual summaries of events, accompanied by a typed transcription (which contains a few substantive errors). Dan H. Laurence has privately communicated numerous suggestions for the Chronology from his own researches into the various diary sources and his personal card file of Shaw's lectures and speeches from 1882 to 1949.

As his international fame grew from around the turn of the nineteenth and twentieth centuries, Shaw became one of the most celebrated, commented upon and quoted literary figures of all time. With his gift for unusual and amusing ways of looking at things, and for pungent and witty articulation of ideas, he was a natural quarry for journalists and interviewers; and recollections of meetings with Shaw appear in countless autobiographies, diaries, journals, memoirs and collections of correspondence. A large selection of these forms of biographical information was published in my *Shaw: Interviews and Recollections* (1990), and I have been able to draw extensively on the research into newspaper collections and numerous other sources carried out by me and research assistants working with me in connection with that project. This book also draws on research over a long period of time into collections of Shaw manuscripts and other Shaviana in the United Kingdom, Ireland, America, Canada and elsewhere. The principal manuscript collections are shown in the List of Abbreviations, and others are indicated in the relevant places in the Chronology.

In preparing the Chronology, I have endeavoured as far as possible to draw on primary sources, or carefully assessed transmissions of them, rather than rely on secondary biographical narratives.[4] Though they often contain valuable and otherwise inaccessible information, the earlier biographical studies of Shaw by Archibald Henderson, Hesketh Pearson and St John Ervine have now been largely overtaken by later scholarship, as has an earlier, rather sketchy, attempt to produce a full chronology by R. F. Rattray, in *Bernard Shaw: A Chronicle* (1951). The biography of Shaw by Michael Holroyd though sometimes useful, is heavily, and generally without adequate acknowledgement, dependent on secondary sources, and is written with a novelistic approach to biography and a tendentious selectivity in the use of source material which often makes it unreliable as a work of reference. All of Shaw's major biographers leave much to be desired in terms of scholarly standards and procedures, and identification, use and acknowledgement of sources.[5]

The present work is intended both as a contribution to the Palgrave Author Chronology series and as a companion to another work in preparation, a thematic biography of Shaw, in which the emphasis will be less on the record of events and more on the connections between Shaw's life and his development and achievement as a creative writer.

Notes

1. Nor does it mean that the problems identified in the 'death of the author' literature have gone away.
2. Bernard Shaw, 'My Apology for this Book', *Sixteen Self Sketches* (London: Constable, 1949), 6.
3. Oscar Wilde, 'The Critic as Artist – Part 1', *Oscar Wilde*, ed. Isobel Murray (Oxford, New York: Oxford University Press, 1989), 261.

4. Sources of information are indicated in square brackets following the record of an event.
5. For a discussion of problems in Shavian biography, see A. M. Gibbs, '"Giant brain…no heart": Bernard Shaw's Reception in Criticism and Biography', *Irish University Review*, vol. 26, no. 1 (Spring/Summer 1996), 15–36. The curiously manipulative and misleading treatment of source material by Holroyd is considered in A. M. Gibbs, 'Bernard Shaw's Family Skeletons: A New Look', *Bullán: An Irish Studies Journal*, vol. 3, no. 1 (Spring 1997), 57–74.

Ancestry and Family

George Bernard Shaw (1856–1950), Nobel Prize-winning playwright, novelist, essayist, critic and political activist, was born in Dublin on 26 July 1856, and died at Ayot St Lawrence, Hertfordshire, England, on 2 November 1950. On his father's side, he was descended from a branch of a Scottish clan which, according to reasonably reliable accounts, had settled in Ireland from Hampshire in the late seventeenth century. His mother was a member of the Gurly family, landowners in Carlow and Galway, whose ancestry in Ireland has also been traced back to the late seventeenth century. In 1898, Shaw married Charlotte Frances Payne-Townshend (1856–1943) daughter of a wealthy Irish gentleman and his English wife, of Derry House, Rosscarbery, in County Cork. The marriage of George Bernard and Charlotte Frances Shaw was without issue.

The Irish Shaws

The clan of Shaws to which George Bernard Shaw the playwright belonged was probably involved in the late seventeenth-century establishment, and certainly prominent in the subsequent maintenance and administration, of the political, religious and social regime known as the Protestant Ascendancy in Ireland. Although the seventeenth-century history of the Shaw family in Ireland is more complicated, indeed confused, than some commentators admit, I think it is reasonable to accept the family tradition that the beginning of the line of Irish Shaws is traceable to a Captain William Shaw of Hampshire who is said to have served in the Williamite invasions of the 1690s, and, after the Battle of the Boyne, to have gained land at Sandpits, an area adjacent to the Earl of Bessborough's Demesne at Piltown, near Carrick-on-Suir, Co. Kilkenny.[1] Eighteenth-century gravestones at St Nicholas's Church of Ireland, now a Heritage Museum, at Carrick-on-Suir, confirm that Shaw families were established in that region from the early years of the century.

On 7 August 1689, a Captain William Shaw delivered to a Committee of the House of Lords in London his written 'Proposals for subduing those in rebellion in Ireland'. Captain Shaw's paper, which was read by the Committee on the following day began with the words: 'The Irish have from time to time been in rebellion ever since the conquest of that kingdom, and though they are a flattering people yet they can never be won by kindness, as sad experience has shown.' The prejudiced, but decisive, Captain Shaw outlined a detailed plan of action involving the dispatch of 'seven or eight nimble frigates' and 'some good ships of war, with 8,000 or 9,000 arms', to deal with the 'infatuated' Papists whose activities were presenting an unprecedented threat of revolt in Ireland.[2] The existence of Captain Shaw's paper has apparently gone unnoticed in family histories and Shavian biography, but there is a strong likelihood that this adviser to the British House of Lords in the events leading up to the Battle of the Boyne was the male progenitor of the Irish family of Shaws from which the playwright was descended.

During the eighteenth and nineteenth centuries several members of the Irish branch of the Shaw clan – as lawyers, bankers merchants, soldiers and MPs – rose to positions of great eminence in the social, political and judicial systems of the Ascendancy regime. Amongst them was Robert Shaw (1749–96), co-founder of 'Shaw's Bank' which later became the Royal Bank of Ireland. He held the office of Accountant General of the Post Office, and purchased Terenure Manor, Dublin. This side of the family was raised to the baronetage when Sir Robert Shaw (1774–1849) was created 1st Baronet of Bushy Park by George IV on 17 August 1821. He was a Colonel of the Royal Dublin Militia. As MP for New Ross in the Irish Parliament he voted against the Union, and he represented Dublin in the Imperial Parliament from 1804 to 1826. In 1796 he had acquired the large estate and imposing residence of Bushy Park House, Terenure, as part of his marriage dowry from Abraham Wilkinson.

Reversing fortunes of the kind which befell the house celebrated in Marvell's 'Upon Appleton House', Bushy Park House, once seat of stern Protestants, is now a Catholic Convent attached to Our Lady's School for Girls, Templeogue. Following the death of GBS's grandfather, Bernard Shaw of Kilkenny, his widow and eleven children were afforded rent-free accommodation in Roundtown Cottage in the grounds of Bushy Park, by the Second Baronet, another Sir Robert Shaw. Although he seems to have visited it on only one occasion, the house has a significant symbolic place in GBS's reconstructions of his childhood. The prosperous and powerful 'Bushy Park Shaws' were the point of contrast in his famous description of his immediate family's position in the social scale as belonging to a class of 'the Shabby Genteel, the Poor Relations, the Gentlemen who are No Gentlemen'.[3]

One of the most formidable members of the family in the nineteenth century was the Rt Hon. Sir Frederick Shaw, Privy Councillor, 3rd Baronet of Bushy Park (1799–1876), and younger brother of the benefactor of GBS's grandmother and her children. He was an epitome of the strongly pro-British pillars of Church and State establishment in the Protestant Ascendancy regime. Queen Victoria thought him extremely handsome.[4]

Sir Frederick was educated at Trinity College, Dublin and Brasenose College, Oxford and held the Office of Recorder[5] of Dublin from 1828 until his death. He was an MP for Dublin City and Dublin University, and made a Privy Councillor under Sir Robert Peel's government. In 1837 he gave evidence to a Select Committee of the House of Commons on behalf of the Sunday School Society for Ireland. His letters show him to be a crusty gentleman, with a strong sense of property rights. Bent with sciatica in his old age, he was still able to write a stern letter about his insurance policies and pecuniary interests. When he ran for a second term as MP for the University in 1847 he became the subject of a satirical and extremely hostile pamphlet, carrying the ironical title, *Reasons for Voting for The Right Hon. Frederick Shaw: Being A Familiar Address to the College Constituency,* a copy of which is in the National Library of Ireland. Borrowing techniques from Swift, the writer of this sarcastic document, which contained a whole range of reasons for *not* voting for the Rt Hon. Frederick Shaw, attacked especially Shaw's subservience to the British Imperium and his allegedly excessive salary claims.

Shaw's paternal grandparents and their children

Shaw's paternal grandparents were Bernard Shaw of Kilkenny and his wife Frances. Bernard Shaw of Kilkenny (1773 – 3 February 1826) was a descendant of Captain William Shaw, but not in the line of primogeniture. He was High Sheriff of Kilkenny, and later a Dublin notary and stockbroker. He married on 1 April 1802 Frances Carr (*c.*1782 – 9 May 1871), daughter of the Rev. Edward Carr, rector of Kilmacow near Waterford. Fine portraits of Bernard and Frances Shaw, by an unknown artist, are privately owned in Tasmania, and they are also represented in miniature portraits which are held in the Shaw Museum at 33 Synge Street, Dublin. Bernard and Frances Carr Shaw had 15 children, including, finally, one stillborn infant. The playwright's father, George Carr Shaw, was the eighth child of this family.

The two first children of the family died before reaching adulthood and the tenth child died in infancy. Four of the remaining children migrated to Australia, where two of them settled permanently. The four emigrants were as follows. Frances (1807–72) emigrated to Western Australia in 1830 with her husband Arthur Greene (c.1810–76) and her brother Edward Carr Shaw (1813–85). The vessel on which they travelled, the *Rockingham,* was wrecked on the coast of Western Australia at the place now named after it. The three then travelled on the schooner *Eagle* to Tasmania, where they began farming at Campania. The Greenes having returned to Ireland, Edward Carr

Shaw moved to the east coast of Tasmania where he established a property (still in Shaw family hands) 'Red Banks' at Swansea. The ninth child of the family, Robert (1816–?) migrated to Australia, but returned and settled in England. The last migrant was the thirteenth child, Walter Stephen (1822–85), who settled in Melbourne and worked as a clerk in a government auditing office. One of his sons, Charles MacMahon Shaw (1863–1943), a manager of a branch of the Bank of Australasia, and from 1923 to 1936, of the Metropolitan Golf Club, Melbourne, was the author of a book about the Shaw family entitled *Bernard's Brethren* (1938). Published with amusing and caustic annotations by GBS printed in red in the margins, *Bernard's Brethren* challenges the Shavian accounts of his family, and particularly Shaw's unflattering portrayal of his father.

The other sons and daughters of Bernard and Frances Shaw remained in Dublin. Three of the sons, William Bernard (Uncle 'Barney'), George Carr (the playwright's father) and Henry, became merchants, George Carr having been first a civil servant. Another son, Richard Frederick Shaw, became chief of staff of the Irish Valuation Office, and it was through his influence that the future playwright gained his first employment, as a clerk and later chief cashier at the respectable land agent's office of Uniacke Townshend. The fifth child of the family, Charlotte Jane (Shaw's Aunt 'Shah'), had a daughter who was to become the first celebrity in the family, the prolific novelist and journalist, Mrs Cashel Hoey. She introduced Shaw to Arnold White who offered him a job with the Edison Telephone Company in 1879. Her second husband, John Cashel Hoey, was Agent-General in London for the State of Victoria, Australia.

Shaw's attitude to the clan to which he belonged was highly critical. He disliked the family snobbery – 'we are a family of Pooh-Bahs – snobs to the backbone', he told his Australian agent, Henry Hyde Champion in 1912 – and their view of themselves as a dynasty like that of the Valois or Hohenzollern families.[6] Shaw had strong sympathies with English radical Protestantism – with the republicans Cromwell (from whom he claimed descent, erroneously as it turned out) and Milton, with Bunyan and the Quaker-born Tom Paine, and of course with the whole tradition of revolutionary non-conformism in England as represented by figures such as Blake and Shelley. But he detested the institutionalized Protestantism, with all its social trappings, of his youth in Ireland. In a well-known statement first published in 1898, Shaw described Irish Protestantism as 'not... a religion' but 'a side in political faction, a class prejudice, a conviction that Roman Catholics are socially inferior persons who will go to hell when they die and leave Heaven in the exclusive possession of Protestant ladies and gentlemen'.[7]

Yet despite his stated hostility towards his 'Family of Pooh-Bahs' and undoubtedly sincere dislike of their pretensions and prejudices, Shaw's own social manners (and eventual social position, as a kind of Squire of the village of Ayot St Lawrence, employer of full-time chauffeurs, housekeepers and other servants, and First Class traveller), his accent, circle of friends and acquaintances, and his marriage to the wealthy daughter of an Irish landowning family, complicate the account of his relation to his family background. The integrity of his lifelong dedication to attacking social inequalities and class prejudice is unquestionable. He was always ideologically and spiritually a friend of working-class people, and was completely without snobbishness in his personal dealings with them. But, even in his office-boy days in Dublin, he never became closely associated with people on the lower end of the socio-economic scale, and his own social background contributed in manifold ways to the shaping of the Shavian career and complex persona, more so perhaps than he himself would have wanted to admit.

The Gurly family

The Gurly family were members of the Irish squirearchy, landowners and attorneys-at-law in County Carlow, South of Dublin, who also held property in the West of Ireland. In the chancel of St Mary's Church of Ireland, Carlow, is an elaborate monument in late eighteenth-century neoclassical style erected by 'THO.^{S} GURLY ESQ.^{RE},/as an affectionate Tribute to the Memory of his Brother/BAGNEL GURLY Esq.^{RE} /and to Commemorate his many Virtues.' After enumerating his many qualities and his 'Social Virtue that sweetens and adorns private Life', the tablet goes on to record that Bagnel Gurly died in the 25th year of his age on 25 February 1796. The gentleman who commissioned this monument was Shaw's great-grandfather, Thomas Gurly (1760 – 14 April 1816), solicitor and registrar of Leighlin diocese. The Gurlys were a leading family in the Carlow district, descended from James Gourlay (or Gourly) (d.1691) of Wexford, who originally hailed from Cumberland and Chester. The Gurly (sometimes Gurley) family owned numerous properties in Ireland in the nineteenth century, and, like the Shaws, they were clearly prominent lay members of the Church of Ireland.

Shaw's maternal grandparents and their children

Shaw's maternal grandfather was Walter Bagnall (Bagenal) Gurly (1800–20 December 1885), second son of Thomas Gurly. He moved to County Mayo around 1855. When visited by his daughter, Lucinda Elizabeth Shaw, in 1857 his address was Kinlough, Cong, Co. Mayo.[8] He later, in 1868, moved to Oughterard, Co. Galway.

In a Carlow town valuation of tenements taken *circa* 1853, Walter B. Gurley [*sic*] is named as the lessor of twelve properties in Carlow and one in the Parish of Ballinacarrig. A number of these Carlow properties were inherited, reluctantly, by GBS on the death of his Uncle Walter John Gurly in 1899. The Carlow properties were mostly small tenement houses and yards, used as dwellings and offices, but they also included an impressive building known as The Assembly Rooms. These were originally used for social gatherings and entertainments, such as balls and concerts, of the local gentry. Subsequently the rooms had various uses. In the *c.* 1853 valuation the occupier is the 'Carlow Reading Club', and the building is called the 'News and Assembly Rooms', indicating that one of its uses was for newspaper reading.[9] The building had a period of use (1912–15) as a cinema, called the Picture House, and from 1923 it became the Carlow Technical College.[10] At the time of completion of the present book, it houses the Carlow County Library and Local Studies archives. From 1915 Shaw had entertained ideas of making a gift of the building for public use, but legal encumbrances prevented that at the time. In 1916 he attempted to have the building sold or let by his Carlow agent, Major William Fitzmaurice.[11] This plan was not satisfactorily concluded, and on 31 October 1919 the property was transferred to five trustees representing the Carlow Technical Instruction Committee. In 1945, Shaw completed his gift to Carlow town of his properties there, a special act of the Dail being required to effect the unusual procedure of municipalizing privately owned property.

Walter Bagnall Gurly married twice. He first married, on 29 December 1829, Shaw's maternal grandmother-to-be, Lucinda Whitcroft (1802–14 January 1839), daughter of Squire John Hamilton Whitcroft (1768–1843) of Highfield Manor, Whitchurch, Rathfarnam, a cotton manufacturer, landowner and pawnbroker, and Lucinda Davis of Dublin. On 25 May 1852 he married his second wife, Elizabeth Anne Clarke.

By his first marriage Walter Bagnall Gurly had three children. The first child was Lucinda Elizabeth ('Bessie') Gurly (6 October 1830 – 19 February 1913), Shaw's mother. The second was Walter John Gurly (1831 – 30 August 1899). Another child by this marriage died in infancy. Walter John Gurly was educated at Kilkenny College and was enrolled at Trinity College, Dublin on 15 October 1852. He entered medical school in 1854 and became a licentiate of the Royal College of Surgeons in 1863.[12] By 14 July 1881, after several years' service as a ship's doctor on the Inman Line, he set up practice as a physician at 200 High Road, Leyton, Essex, on the border of Epping Forest. He married Emily Jane Walton, without issue. Shaw described Walter in *Sixteen Self Sketches* as his 'Rabelaisian uncle', a rich source of ribald jokes and limericks, and regarded him, along with George Carr Shaw and the musical entrepeneur Vandeleur Lee, as one of his three 'fathers'.[13] During his early days in London, Shaw occasionally visited his uncle in Leyton, and the Gurly house was his refuge when he was ill with smallpox in the summer of 1881.

By his second marriage Walter Bagnall Gurly had six children, all daughters. Those who had a special connection with Shaw included Arabella ('Moila') (baptized 17 Aug 1856–1941) who, after being widowed young from her husband John Gillmore, resided with GBS's mother (her half-sister), Lucinda 'Bessie' Shaw, from 1898 until the latter's death in 1913. She later became a companion to Mrs Jane ('Jenny') Patterson, Shaw's lover in the 1880s and early 1890s. Arabella's daughter, Georgina ('Judy') (1885–1974), who married Harold Chaworth Musters in 1912, was Shaw's first full-time secretary from 1907–12. Another of Walter Bagnall's daughters by his second marriage, Georgina ('young Georgie') (*c.*1866–1911), was Shaw's favourite of all his aunts.[14]

Shaw's immediate family

The playwright's father, George Carr Shaw (30 December 1814 – 19 April 1885), was eleven years old when his father died in 1826. In 1838 he took a clerical post at the merchant firm of Todhunters where he remained for seven years.[15] Probably through the influence of the Rt Hon. Sir Frederick Shaw, Recorder of Dublin, he then (*c.* 1845) obtained a post as a civil servant in the Dublin Four Courts. When this post was abolished in 1851, he received a pension of £44 per annum. After brief periods of employment in ironmonger and corn merchant firms he sold his pension to a Mr Joseph Henry O'Brien for the sum of £500. With this capital he finally entered into a partnership with one George Clibborn in an already established wholesale corn, flour and cereals firm. Clibborn and Shaw had an office and warehouse at 67 Jervis Street and a mill (purchased in 1857) 'on the country side of the canal, at the end of a rather pretty little village street called Rutland Avenue'[16] in Dolphin's Barn, where Bernard Shaw was sometimes taken by his father to play as a child.

After the death of Walter Bagnall Gurly's first wife in 1839, the future mother of the playwright, Lucinda Elizabeth ('Bessie') Gurly (6 October 1830 – 19 February 1913), was placed in the care of her maiden aunt, Ellen Whitcroft, who was aided in this task by Bessie's uncle, John Hamilton Whitcroft, Ellen Whitcroft's brother. Aunt Ellen lived in Palmerston Place, Dublin, and under her care Bessie received an education in French, music and all the ladylike virtues. From 1839 to 1846 she studied piano at the music-teaching establishment of Johann Bernhard Logier, and has left a lively account of the Logier teaching methods. She had a mezzo-soprano voice which Shaw describes as being 'of extraordinary purity of tone',[17] and after her marriage became a leading amateur concert and opera singer in Dublin. She composed songs and, as a devotee of spiritualism and seances, produced some remarkable 'spirit' drawings, the originals of which are held in the art collection of the Harry Ransom Humanities Research Center at the University of Texas, Austin.[18] The impression is sometimes created that

Shaw and his mother had little to do with one another in their lives in London before Shaw's marriage. But Shaw's diaries record several instances of visits to plays with his mother, and their common interest in music must also have been a cause of frequent communion between them. It was his mother, Shaw records in his diary for 10 August 1889, who purchased for him, as the author-to-be of the classic essay, *The Perfect Wagnerite*, the score of *Parsifal*.

The marriage of Shaw's parents took place on 17 June 1852 at St Peter's Church, Dublin. The bridegroom is described as bachelor of 17 Lennox Street, Dublin, and the bride as spinster of Stillorgan. The minister officiating at the ceremony was the Rev. William George Carroll (d. 9 October 1885), the husband of George Carr Shaw's sister, Emily. The marriage was witnessed by the bride's father, W. B. Gurly and Geo. H. MacMullen.[19] According to GBS, who is the only source of information about the matter, the honeymoon was spent at Liverpool.

Shaw's account of his parents' marriage, the honeymoon and their subsequent relationship is highly suspect. He represents the marriage as having instantly proved to be a disastrous failure, ruined from the outset by his father's drinking habits and lack of success in business. This account, at least in relation to the early years of the marriage, is called into question (and in my view rendered untenable) by the content and tone of a substantial body of letters written by George Carr Shaw to his wife when she was staying with her family in Co. Mayo in the summer of 1857, one year after the playwright's birth. Shaw's representation of his family's economic circumstances is also open to question. Certainly in comparison with the Bushy Park relations, the George Carr Shaws were not rich, but neither did they live in poverty as the son stated. The playwright's portrayal of these matters in his autobiographical writings is examined in my 1997 essay, 'Bernard Shaw's Family Skeletons: A New Look'.[20]

George Carr and Lucinda Elizabeth Shaw had three children, Lucinda Frances ('Lucy'), Elinor Agnes ('Yuppy') and George Bernard. The latter was nicknamed 'Bob' or 'Bobza' as an infant, 'Sonny' as a young boy and 'GBS' when he became a famous figure. He disliked the name George, preferring to be called Bernard.

Lucinda Frances (Lucy Carr) Shaw (26 March 1853 – 27 March 1920) had, like her mother, a fine mezzo-soprano voice and enjoyed a successful career as a star performer in musical comedy and light opera, until forced into retirement by her contraction of tuberculosis *circa* 1898–9. She had a working knowledge of several languages, wrote translations of plays by Strindberg for the Adelphi Play Society, and tried her hand at translations of works by Ibsen and Bjørnson. She had a teasing, conspiratorial and affectionate sisterly relationship with Shaw, and followed his career with the closest interest and with great pride in his achievements. Her nicknames for him, in letters to others, were 'Der Beruhmte' (the famous one) and 'the Super One'. 'He and I', she wrote to her friend Janey Drysdale in the early 1900s after what she described as a delightful talk with her brother, 'are always two thorough blackguards when we get together alone.'[21]

Lucy worked initially in amateur productions under the direction of George Vandeleur Lee whom she came to dislike intensely, partly because of his unwelcome amorous advances toward her. She made her professional debut under the name 'Frances Carr' in the pantomime, *Beauty and the Beast,* at the Royal Park, Camden Town, on Christmas Eve 1879. She subsequently worked with the Carl Rosa Opera Company and the D'Oyly Carte Company. From the mid-1880s she was frequently on tour, leaving Shaw living alone with his mother. She married fellow actor Charles Robert Butterfield in 1887 and they divorced, after a long separation, in 1909. Shaw's lifelong friend Edward McNulty had a close friendship with Lucy which lasted long after her refusal to marry him in the late 1870s. Regarding their personal correspondence as 'sacred,' McNulty burnt it all on her death but kept in his Dublin home the Bechstein piano which she had bequeathed him and which Shaw arranged to be sent to him. By all accounts, Lucy was physically attractive, confident without being overbearing, clever and personable, outshining her shy brother in the early years. She is recalled in the characterization of Lalage Virtue in *The Irrational Knot* and Madge Brailsford in *Love Among the Artists*. From the time of his marriage, Shaw was financially assisting Lucy who was gradually being rendered an invalid by tuberculosis. Lucy's health deteriorated substantially after 1913, from which time she was cared for by Eva Maria Schneider, and died in her brother's arms at 5 pm on 27 March 1920 at Champion Cottage, Champion Hill, Camberwell, London.

Elinor Agnes Shaw (7 July 1854 – 27 March 1876), known in the family as 'Yuppy' and later 'Aggie', was described by Shaw's friend, Edward McNulty as 'a lovely, sweet-tempered girl with large hazel eyes and superb, reddish-gold hair which could be combed almost to her heels'.[22] A fine photographic portrait survives, but otherwise little is known about this sister of the playwright. She contracted tuberculosis, and died at the age of 21 in the Hospital Saint Lawrence at Ventnor on the Isle of Wight, where she is buried in a churchyard beneath a tombstone which carries the text from 1: 23 of St Paul's Epistle to the Philippians, 'To be with Christ which is far better.'

From 1866 to 1873 the Shaw family shared houses in Dublin and the nearby seaside village of Dalkey with the conductor and musical entrepreneur George Vandeleur Lee.[23] The speculation, enthusiastically developed by O'Donovan, Rosset and others, that Shaw was the product of an adulterous relationship between Lee and Bessie Shaw is based on very slight circumstantial 'evidence', and, while it is not possible to make categorical statements about the matter, on balance it seems unlikely to have any foundation in truth. Particularly in his old age, the playwright showed a strong family resemblance to male relatives in the Shaw clan. In a 1947 postcard written on receipt from Tasmania of photographs of the portraits of his grandparents, Shaw exclaimed about his grandmother: 'What a change the Carr nose and ears made!'[24] Both Shaw himself, and his paternal uncle Edward Carr Shaw, the emigrant to Tasmania, bear clear traces of those Carr features, and their general family likeness is apparent in photographs taken in old age. There is also a striking resemblance in some photographs between GBS and his Tasmanian first cousin, another Bernard Shaw, the eldest son of uncle Edward. Various comments by Shaw and others suggest that his mother had a very strong sense of propriety. According to Shaw, in a 1916 letter to Thomas Demetrius O'Bolger, his mother was 'one of those women who could act as matron of a cavalry barracks from eighteen to forty and emerge without a stain on her character'.[25]

In his autobiographical writings, Shaw wrote a good deal about his immediate family. But like that of many people, his interest in his more distant ancestry was spasmodic and his knowledge patchy. At times certain possibilities of connections between himself and famous historical figures would catch his imagination. He liked to think that his lineage could possibly be traced to the Scottish thane, Macduff, the slayer of Macbeth, and a suitable role model for a quixotic world-betterer. He was also interested in a theory that his family was related by marriage to Oliver Cromwell ('old Noll', as Shaw called him), a connection which many other Irishmen would not care to trumpet. The Cromwell connection depended on the assumptions that a Mary Markham who became one of Shaw's great-great-grandmothers was the sister of Bishop William Markham, Archbishop of York from 1777 to 1807, and that this Markham family was descended from Oliver Cromwell. Neither of these assumptions turned out to be correct. Bishop Markham had only one sister, Elizabeth, who died unmarried, and the idea that this Markham family ancestry could be traced back to Cromwell was shown to be erroneous by a family member, Sir Clements Markham. The Irish Mary Markham in the Shaw ancestry was a daughter of Bernard Markham of Fanningstown, Co. Kilkenny: this was likely to have been the way in which the name Bernard was introduced into the Shaw family pool of Christian names.[26]

One of Shaw's summaries of his Irish ancestry, made in a letter to his future biographer St John Ervine in 1936, is a factually flawed but, as usual with his comments about his family, entertaining statement. After declaring his descent from 'Macduff the Unborn, through his third son Shaigh', Shaw continues in sweeping style:

> I am also descended from everybody who was alive and fertile in these islands in the XVII century and earlier; but old Noll and Macduff are my selections.[27]

Who could argue with such poetic genealogical licence? When it came to discussions of his ancestry and family, Shaw did not often fall into what Oscar Wilde, in *The Decay of Lying*, deplores as 'careless habits of accuracy'.

Notes

1. Principal sources for Shaw's genealogy include Joseph Foster, *The Peerage, Baronetage, and Knightage of the British Empire for 1881: The Baronetage and Knightage* (1881), 560–1; CJS 206–40, 361–3; *Burke's Genealogical and Heraldic History of the Peerage, Baronetage and Knightage*, 103rd edn (1963), 2205–6. Dan H. Laurence provides a richly detailed account of the playwright's genealogy on both his father's and mother's sides in his 'The Shaws and the Gurlys: A Genealogical Study', *SHAW: The Annual of Bernard Shaw Studies* XVIII (1998), 1–31.
2. *The Manuscripts of the House of Lords, 1689–1690*, Historical MSS Commission, Twelfth Report, Appendix Part VI, vol. 2 (1889), 183. I am grateful to Mr Ed Wright for his discovery of this record while working for me as a Research Assistant.
3. See his recollections in Imm viii-xii; CP3: 6–9.
4. CJS 219.
5. A Recorder was a senior judge or magistrate of a city. According to the *Enyclopedia Britannica* of 1886, cited in the *OED*, 'The recorders of Dublin and Cork [were] judges of the civil bill courts in those cities.'
6. Shaw to Henry Hyde Champion, 17 November 1912, Texas (copy in La Trobe Library, State Library of Victoria).
7. Bernard Shaw, 'In the Days of My Youth', in T. P. O'Connor's magazine *M.A.P. (Mainly About People)*, 17 September 1898, pp. 324–5. This autobiographical essay was reprinted in revised form in *Shaw Gives Himself Away: An Autobiographical Miscellany* (1939), and in *Sixteen Self Sketches* (1949) where these quotations appear on p. 93 and p. 45 respectively.
8. Dan H. Laurence has suggested to me in private correspondence that 'Kinlough' in this address may refer to the name of a house or estate, which would overcome the confusion of it also being the name of a well-known fishing resort in nearby Co. Leitrim.
9. '*c*. 1853 Primary Valuation of Tenements', Act, 9 & 10 Vict., Cap. 110, Carlow County Library Local Studies Section.
10. B. O'Neill, 'The Old Assembly Rooms', *Carloviana*, vol. 1, no. 2, January 1948; L. D. Bergin and B. O'Neill, 'Shaw's Ties with Carlow', *Carloviana*, vol. 1, no. 4, new series (December 1956).
11. Unpublished letters of Shaw to Major William Fitzmaurice, 22 January 1916, 22 March 1916, 13 April 1916, 27 May 1916, 1 November 1916, 8 December 1916, Carlow County Library Local Studies Section. Also among the Carlow County Library papers is a copy of an advertisement which describes The Assembly Rooms as occupying a 'commanding site' and the building as 'inspiringly designed in the style of the classic revival of the eighteenth century, characteristic of the Irish Public buildings of that date; and the facade, with its flight of

seven massive granite steps at the main entrance, and the east window facing Dublin Street, gives importance and architectural interest to the edifice.' The view of the facade is now bisected with a traffic sign, indecorously placed on the footpath in front of the building.

12. For details of Walter John Gurly's youth and education see Ross 8.
13. SSS 14–16.
14. Dan H. Laurence notes that 'with the single exception of Constance... all the Gurly sisters and their offspring received financial assistance from Shaw as long as they lived' (Lgen: 8).
15. BL MS Add. 50710, fol. 25.
16. Imm x; CP3: 7–8.
17. SSS 14.
18. One of the finest of the drawings is reproduced as Item 584 in Dan H. Laurence, *Shaw: An Exhibit,* a Catalogue of an exhibition of representative Shaw materials held in the Harry Ransom Center from September 1977 to February 1978.
19. Ross 54.
20. A. M. Gibbs, 'Bernard Shaw's Family Skeletons: A New Look', *Bullán: An Irish Studies Journal*, vol. 3, no. 1 (Spring 1997), 57–74.
21. Lucy Shaw to Janey Drysdale Crichton, 24 July 1901, Texas.
22. McNulty 24.
23. See Who's Who section below.
24. Shaw to Edward B. Shaw, 10 November 1947 (private collection, Tasmania). Commenting on the ubiquity of one of these Carr–Shaw family features in a letter to Grace Goodliffe of 3 December 1942, Shaw declared: 'The Carr nose is now all over Australia.' Grace Goodliffe was a distant cousin of Shaw, being the third daughter of Sir Frederick Shaw (5th Baronet of Bushy Park), who married Major Guy V. Goodliffe [CL4: 652; DHL].
25. CL3: 356. O'Bolger was an Irish-born American, engaged in writing a Shaw biography. After supplying O'Bolger with a good deal of information, Shaw eventually refused to allow publication of the work because he considered its treatment of members of his family and himself to be tactless and offensive. (See CL3: 844–5.)
26. The demolition of the Cromwell claim is described in an informative article, 'Bernard Shaw's Ancestry: No Link with Oliver Cromwell', *Bath & Wilts Chronicle and Herald*, 28 April 1949.
27. CL4: 430.

Chronology Part I
1814–98

1814

December

30 (Fri) **Birth of Shaw's father, George Carr Shaw, eighth child of Bernard and Frances Shaw of Kilkenny.**

1821

August

17 (Fri) Sir Robert Shaw created 1st Baronet of Bushy Park during George IV's visit to Ireland.

1828

March

20 (Thu) Henrik Ibsen born in Skien, Norway.

1830

Presumed year of birth of George John (later 'Vandeleur') Lee, musical entrepreneur, conductor and theorist, who became closely associated with the Shaw family. [O'D 20; SCG 50–1]

October

6 (Wed) **Birth of Shaw's mother, Lucinda Elizabeth ('Bessie') Gurly, eldest child of Walter Bagnall Gurly by his first marriage.**

1839

January

14 (Mon) Death of Shaw's maternal grandmother, Lucinda Gurly.

1844

October

15 (Tue) Birth of Friedrich Nietzsche at Röcken in Saxony.

1845–50

George Carr Shaw leaves his job as a clerk at the merchant firm of Todhunter's. Possibly through the influence of Sir Frederick Shaw, MP of Bushy Park, Recorder of Dublin, he obtained a position at the Four Courts. [BL MS Add 50710A; O'D 9–10]

1848

Publication of *The Communist Manifesto* by Karl Marx and Friedrich Engels.

1849

January

22 (Mon) Johann August Strindberg born in Stockholm.

1851

George Carr Shaw receives a government pension of £44 per annum after his post with the Dublin law courts is abolished. He is subsequently employed for short periods at Haughton's, at Wilson's and at McMullen, Shaw & Co., all corn factors. (The Shaw of this last company was George Carr Shaw's younger brother Henry.) [BL MS Add 50710A; D1: 20–1; O'D 9; SCG 23]

1852

Foundation of the Amateur Musical Society, the main vehicle of Lee's musical career in Dublin. [O'D 21]

May

25 (Tue) Walter Bagnall Gurly marries his second wife, Elizabeth Anne Clarke.

June

17 (Thu) **Marriage of George Carr Shaw and Lucinda Elizabeth Gurly at St Peters Church, Aungier Street, Dublin, the Reverend William George Carroll, the bridegroom's brother-in-law, officiating.** [Register of Marriages, St Peters Church, No. 239; CL1: 133; O'D 15; SCG 19; Ross 54; Erv 14]

October

7 (Thu) George Carr Shaw enters a partnership with George Clibborn in a corn trading business, with offices at 67 & 68 Jervis Street, Dublin. George Carr had sold his pension to Joseph Henry O'Brien, who was associated with McMullen, Shaw & Co. and had a separate flour business, for the sum of £500. [BL MS Add 50710A; BL MS Add 50509; CL1: 133; SCG 23; O'D 9; Ross 61]

1853–7

Construction of the great circular reading room at the British Museum, a favourite haunt of Shaw during his early London days.

1853

March

26 (Sat) Birth of Shaw's elder sister, Lucinda Frances Shaw. [*Saunders's Newsletter and Daily Advertiser,* Dublin; O'D 15; Ross 72, 350]

1854

Foundation of the National Gallery of Ireland, soon to be frequented by the young Shaw, and later to become the receiver of his very generous bequests.

July

7 (Fri) Birth of the Shaws' second daughter, Elinor Agnes ('Yuppy'). [*Saunders's Newsletter,* 8 Jul 1854; DHL]

1856

Establishment of the Royal Irish Academy of Music.

July

26 (Sat) **Birth of George Bernard Shaw at 3 Upper Synge Street (later 33 Synge Street), Dublin.** According to information provided to the Shaw Museum, Dublin, Dr John Ringland, Master of the Coombe Lying-In Hospital, delivered the child after a difficult breech birth. A notice of the birth appeared in *Saunders's News-Letter and Daily Advertiser*, Dublin, No. 35, 649, on Monday, 28 July 1856, p. 3, col. 5 as follows:

BIRTHS

On the 26th inst., at 3 Synge street, the wife of George C. Shaw, Esq., of a son.

Shaw declared in a letter to Denis Johnston of 1 April 1938: 'I am an Irishman without a birth certificate.' In the same letter Shaw states that the records of St Bride's parish, where he was baptized by his Uncle William George Carroll, were transferred to the Four Courts after the abolition of the parish, and perished in the siege of the Four Courts building during the post-treaty troubles. [Shaw Museum, 33 Synge St, Dublin; Shaw to Denis Johnston, 1 Apr 1938, Trinity Coll. Dublin, MS 10066/287/2823]

September

23 (Tue) William Archer (1856–1924), translator of Ibsen, critic, essayist and close friend of Shaw, born in Perth, Scotland.

1857

January

20 (Tue) **Birth of Charlotte Frances Payne-Townshend (future wife of GBS) at Derry House, Rosscarbery, Co. Cork.** [Dunbar 25]

July–August

Bessie Shaw visits her father Walter Gurly at Kinlough, a village near Cong in Co. Mayo, taking Lucy Shaw with her and leaving the other two children, George Bernard ('Bob') and Agnes ('Yuppie'), in Dublin with George Carr Shaw, a nurse, and a maidservant named Sarah. Fifteen letters written by George Carr Shaw to Bessie during this period (17 July – 15 August) provide much information about the family at this time. [BL MS Add 50508; O'D 16]

July

17 (Fri) George Carr Shaw reports: 'Poor whiggedie whellow ['Bob'] was very sick in the stomach about 1 o'clock in the night, but he is all right and as brisk as ever this morning.' [BL MS Add 50508]

20 George Carr Shaw reports that 'the young beggar is getting quite outrageous, I left him this morning roaring and tearing like a bull'. [BL MS Add 50508]

24 'Bob flittered his hat to pieces yesterday and Nurse says I must get him a new one.' A replacement hat, a 'Tuscan' straw costing 10 shillings, is bought on GBS's first birthday two days later. [BL MS Add 50508]

28 George Carr Shaw reports that they are all 'getting on famously', that 'Bobza' and he are having 'walking matches together', and that he has taken the two children out for a ride in the perambulator, a mutually enjoyable experience. [BL MS Add 50508]

August

2 (Sun) George Carr Shaw reports that 'Bob spent some time in bed with me this morning.' [BL MS Add 50508]

5 George Carr Shaw expresses his appreciation to Bessie Shaw for writing so regularly, and says 'write away my honey or I will feel disappointed every morning that Bob does not stagger into me with a letter from you.' [BL MS Add 50508]

8 The one year-old Shaw has an accident, recorded by his father: 'Poor Bob had a narrow escape on Sunday morning – he was sitting on the kitchen table in charge of Nurse who merely she says stooped down to pick up something off the floor when he suddenly fell back and his head went slap through a pane of glass and against the Iron bar outside. miraculous [*sic*] to say he was not even scratched. had [*sic*] he

fallen with his face against the glass he would have been ruined.' He adds the message in this letter: 'I delivered your kisses to Yup and Bob but contrary to your instructions I fobbed a few for myself. You know how sweet a stolen kiss is!' [BL MS Add 50508]

1864

A choral and orchestral concert in honour of the Shakespeare Tercentenary establishes the Dublin Amateur Musical Society, with Lee as impresario-conductor, as a leading musical group. By this time Lee is using the Shaws' house for rehearsals and music lessons which meant that the house was periodically filled with his pupils, who, as GBS was to say in a 1916 letter, 'were almost all Catholics (and therefore from the point of view of the Shaw family unfit for human intercourse)'. [CL3: 369; O'D 27]

Sometime between 7 March and 3 December, Lee leaves his family house in Harrington Street and moves to 1 Hatch Street where he rents part of the multiple dwelling from the owner Mrs Anna F. Fraser. Probably in early 1867, the Shaw family take up residence with him at 1 Hatch Street, sharing the rent. [Ross 118–20]

January

20 (Wed) – 22 Shaw, aged $7\frac{1}{2}$, sees his first play, Tom Taylor's *Plot and Passion,* together with the pantomime *Puss in Boots, or, The Fairies of the Gossamer Grove* at the Theatre Royal, Dublin on one of these three days. In 1938 he recalls that he 'had to be removed forcibly from the theatre at the end because after the falls of the curtain three times in *Plot and Passion* I could not be persuaded that it would not presently go up again'. [Roy Nash, 'The Theatre Today and Yesterday According to George Bernard Shaw', *Manchester Evening News,* 6 Dec 1938; I&R 382–3; DHL; Theatrics xii]

1865

Lee organizes a music festival to coincide with the Exhibition in Dublin, featuring soloists from London. Bessie Shaw performed the roles of Azucena (*Il Trovatore*), Donna Anna (*Don Giovanni*), Marguerite (*Faust*), and Lucrezia (*Lucrezia Borgia*) in Lee's productions of those operas. [Hendl: 18; SM1: 49; Farmer 24]

c. **May 1** Shaw begins attending the Wesleyan Connexional School at 79 St Stephen's Green, less than a mile from Synge Street. This was the first of several periods of irregular attendance at the school during the years 1865–8. He had already been taught to read and to do arithmetic – although not division – by his governess, Miss Caroline Hill. He was to describe her as 'a needy lady who seemed to me much older than she can really have been... [who] punished me by little strokes with her fingers that would not have discomposed a fly...' He also wrote that 'The only other teaching I had was from my clerical Uncle William George (surnamed Carroll) who.... had two boys of his own to educate, and took me on with them for a while in the early mornings to such purpose that when his lessons were ended by my being sent to school, I knew more Latin grammar than any other boy in the First Latin Junior.' [Ross 178; SM1: 39–40; CL4: 726–8; Hend1: 16; Hend2: 49, 52; I&R 14–16]

June

13 (Tue) W. B. Yeats (1865–1939) born at Sandymount, Dublin.

1866

The Shaws move to Torca Cottage, Dalkey Hill, a house leased by Lee. In 1916 Shaw told Thomas Demetrius O'Bolger: 'we spent a whole year there, winter and all; and then we went to Hatch St, and used the cottage only in summer.' During this year Shaw attends James Frederick Halpin's Preparatory School at 23–4 Sandycove Road, Glasthule, near Dalkey. The Shaws omit attendance at church on Sundays while at Dalkey, and do not resume the practice on returning to Dublin. Shaw described the cottage at Dalkey as being '...high up on Torca Hill, with all Dublin Bay from Dalkey Island to Howth visible from the garden, and all Killiney Bay with the Wicklow mountains in the background from the hall door. Lee bought this cottage and presented it to my mother [Bessie Shaw], though she never had any legal claim to it and did not benefit by its sale later on.' Shaw recalls this period: 'When my mother told me we were going to live there I felt an intense joy that I have never felt since.' [CL3: 376; DHL; Prefs2: 196 n15; O'D 33; SM1: 37]

1867

Publication of Marx's *Das Kapital*.
Shaw is introduced to Gounod's *Faust*. [Theatrics xii]

September

19 (Thu) Lee takes Shaw to a performance of Verdi's *Il Trovatore*. Shaw recalls that when he asked 'What is that?' on hearing the sound of Manrico's off-stage serenade in scene two, he received the reply: 'A pig under a gate.' [*Everybody's* (London), 40, 11 Nov 1950; SM3: 768; Theatrics xii, xviii]

1868

January

The *Irish Evangelist* reports that Shaw received 'a first place in English, in writing' in the Christmas 1867 examination. The *Irish Evangelist* had previously (Aug 1867) reported Shaw's receipt from the School of Certificates of good conduct. Evidently forgetting the latter, in a postcard to Willie Cullen of 12 May 1938, Shaw emphatically declared that he never got a school prize for good conduct: 'But I believe I got into the lists twice as first class in English Composition.' [DHL; Shaw postcard to Willie Cullen, 12 May 1938, Colgate University Library MS]

28 March or 3 April

Shaw sees Dion Boucicault's *The Corsican Brothers* (a play adapted from the novel by Alexandre Dumas) with T. C. King in dual roles as Louis and Fabien del Franchi. [DHL; Theatrics xii; I&R 383]

November 1868 – January 1869

For some period between 1 November 1868 and 31 January 1869, whilst the family stayed at Torca Cottage, Shaw again attended the James Frederick Halpin Preparatory School near Dalkey. [SSS 22; Ross 182]

1869

The Voice: Its Artistic Production, Development and Preservation by George J. Lee is published in Dublin.

February

1 (Mon) On Lee's advice, GBS is sent to Central Model Boys' School in Marlborough Street, Dublin. Because the school was in theory undenominational, but in fact Roman Catholic, Shaw remembered his admission there as a source of 'shame and wounded snobbery'. He remained there for less than a year, refusing to return after September, when he was transferred to the Dublin Scientific and Commercial Day School. Shaw records that the reading lessons in history at the Model School 'ignored Ireland and glorified England', and that he always 'substituted Ireland for England in such dithyrambs'. [SSS 22–3, 28; Auto1: 53; Prefs 2: 296 n15; Erv 29; Ross 183–9; Rat 19]

19 Death of Sir Robert Shaw, 2nd Baronet of Bushy Park. Shaw records making his only visit to Bushy Park on the occasion of the funeral. The baronetcy passes to Sir Robert's brother, Sir Frederick Shaw.

September

11 (Sat) Shaw leaves Central Model Boys' School. School roll states 'No reason given.' [Ross 185]

October

30 (Sat) An indented deed of appointment, agreed to by Walter Bagnall Gurly, George Carr Shaw, and the beneficiaries, defines the terms of distribution of the estate of John Whitcroft, maternal grandfather of Bessie Shaw and her brother Walter John Gurly. £2500 was assigned to Walter John Gurly, and £1500 to Bessie. Her portion, 'for her sole and separate use and free from the debts control or engagements of her husband', was to be paid to her in annual instalments of £100. Contrary to some accounts, no separate provision was made for Bessie's children. [Registry of Deeds Office, Kings Inn Dublin (Book 1869, 37 35); Ross 66; CL1: 133]

Late 1869

GBS is sent to the Dublin English Scientific and Commercial Day School, corner Aungier and Whitefriars Streets, about half a mile from 1 Hatch Street. He stays two years, until October 1871, by which time he has become joint head boy with a school fellow named Frank Dunn. Shaw meets his close childhood friend, Matthew Edward McNulty, at this school. McNulty records the formation of a 'Shakespeare Club' at the school, alleging that in playing the part of Ophelia in *Hamlet*, Shaw 'for some reason best known to himself, persisted in walking about on his toes and delivering his lines in a shrill falsetto which changed the play from tragedy to farce.' Contradicting McNulty's account of the 'Shakespeare club', Shaw wrote: 'All invented. The duel scene in Romeo & Juliet was our only achievement.' [SSS 28; Prefs2: 196 n15; Ross 200; McNulty 5 n1, 11–12]

1870

Barry Sullivan's first theatre tour to Dublin. Sullivan's tremendous energy and stage presence make a profound impression on the young Shaw, who sees him perform Hamlet and other roles at the Theatre Royal. [Prefs 1: 20 n7, 3: 73–4; I&R 150–1, 306]

April

18 (Mon) Shaw sees Sullivan's *Hamlet*, with a local Ophelia [Faucit Saville] who reduces him to 'paroxysms of laughter'. [Prefs3: 74 n10]

June

9 (Thu) Death of Charles Dickens.

Autumn

Shaw attends evening freehand classes at the Royal Dublin Society School of Art, probably from before October until at least February the following year. [BL MS Add 50710A]

1871, 1872, 1873

Shaw has season tickets for art exhibitions at the Hibernian Academy and the Dublin Exhibition. [BL MS Add 50710A]

1871

Operas produced by Lee for the Amateur Musical Society at the Theatre Royal and the new Gaiety Theatre are taken on tour to Cork and Limerick. [SCG 129–30]

A diary note by Shaw in this year refers to an infatuation he had with a dark-haired woman he refers to as 'Calypso'. 'Calypso' is the title of an early Shaw drawing of a nude female figure, and the name 'Calypso' recurs in an early untitled poem by Shaw, beginning with the line 'Hail, Folly! And flourish, Delusion', where, in company with Queen Mab and Yolande, Calypso is condemned as a 'blackeyed enslaver'. The relationship was resumed in 1875, by which time, the poem indicates, the woman had married. Shaw's diary notes for this year also refer to 'The L*** Episode', presumably a relationship with another girl or woman, of which he writes: '"But food for mirth and mocking." But they laugh best who laugh last. First acquaintance concluded in 1871.' [BL MS Add 50710A; D1: 26; BL MS Add 50719 (Calypso sketch); BL MS Add 50720 (Calypso poem)]

c. 1871

At about this time George Carr Shaw becomes a teetotaller in fact as well as in principle when, according to Shaw, 'he fell down on our doorstep in a fit which gave him a thorough fright, and made him understand that he was destroying himself'. [CL4: 479]

January

10 (Tue) J. Martin, a school tailor who lived in a lane off Fishamble Street, is paid eighteen shillings to make Shaw a suit. [BL MS Add 50710A]

April

16 (Sun) J. M. Synge (1871–1909) born at Rathfarnham, Co.Wicklow, Ireland.

May

15 (Mon) Shaw sees Henry Irving play Digby Grant in a performance of James Albery's *The Two Roses*, in a London production on tour to Dublin. [DHL; Prefs3: 76]

October

Shaw leaves the Dublin English Scientific and Commercial Day School. [Ross 200]

November

1 (Wed) Shaw commences employment as an office boy at a land agent's office, Uniacke Townshend and Co., 15 Molesworth Street, Dublin, at a starting salary described by Shaw in *Sixteen Self Sketches* as £18 a year and in the Preface to *Immaturity* as 18 shillings a month. He was introduced to this 'highly genteel firm of Irish estate agents' by his uncle, R. Frederick Shaw, Chief of the Land Valuation Office. [SSS 30; Imm xxxi; Prefs3: 24; CL1: 22; Ross 218.]

December

At this time George John Lee begins to advertise his concerts under the name 'G.V.Lee', the initial V standing for Vandeleur. O'Donovan argues that Lee's adoption of the name was an assertion of his claim to be the natural son of Colonel Crofton Moore Vandeleur, MP, JP, DL, of Kilrush House, Kilrush, Co. Clare, and 4 Rutland Square, Dublin. [SCG 47–51; Ross 226–7]

1872

Lee organizes a series of concerts for the International Exhibition, reconstituting the Amateur Musical Society as The New Philharmonic Society. [SCG 74]

Summer

Shaw spends the summer holidays at Newry with Edward McNulty, who had been transferred to the Newry Branch of the Bank of Ireland. In his fourth year of service with the Bank, 1874–5, McNulty was re-transferred to Head Office in Dublin and resumed his association with Shaw on a regular basis. [McNulty 13–14, 17]

September

19 (Thu) Lee purchases the lease of Torca Cottage which, until this point, he had only rented. Records show George Carr Shaw as tenant of Torca Cottage from 1866 to 1875, although it appears that Lee took legal responsibility for it. [Ross 224–6, 356; SCG 74]

November

27 (Wed) Shaw recorded his weight as being 9 stone 1 pound. He continues to check his weight periodically: it was 10 stone 2 pounds in 1884. [BL MS Add 50710A]

1873

February

When the Head Cashier at Uniacke Townshend absconds, Shaw fills his position first on a temporary basis, then as a permanent appointee at a salary of £48 a year. [SSS 31; CL1: 22; Imm xxxi–xxxii; Prefs3: 24–5; I&R 28 n6]

March

31 (Mon) Lee and his partner Richard Michael Levey mount an operatic production comprising two acts of Bellini's *La Sonnambula* and a compressed version of *Lucrezia Borgia* at the Theatre Royal, Dublin. Lucinda Carr Shaw 'distinguished herself' as Amina in *La Sonnambula*. [CL1: 8; SCG 76; SM1: 51; *Irish Times* 1 Apr 1873; Farmer 24–5]

April

14 (Mon) Lee and his group perform *Il Trovatore* at the Theatre Royal with Charles and Annie Cummins as Manrico and Leonora, and Bessie Shaw, who 'staggered under bouquets', as Azucena. McNulty describes Bessie as 'being the leading amateur singer of Dublin and her home the popular resort of musicians'. [SCG 76, 135–6; Dublin *Evening Mail*, Apr 1873; McNulty 18]

May

14 (Wed) Lee is the conductor at the New Philharmonic performance of Mendelssohn's *Athalie* to open the 1873 Exhibition. [SCG 76–7, 84, 138–41 (cites *The Daily Express*, 15 May 1873)]

15 *The Irish Times* of 16 May records the departure on the previous day of a Mrs Shaw for Holyhead. As Rossett suggests, this may have been Bessie Shaw travelling to London to make arrangements for her permanent move there the following month. [Ross 240]

26 Lee's last concert in Dublin, given by the 'Amateur, Musical and Dramatic Society' at the Antient Concert Rooms, before he abandons his Dublin musical career and sails to London by 4 June. His leaving Dublin is alleged to have been the result of a row and Lee's 'unmasking' as an imposter by his rival, Sir Robert Prescott Stewart, then Professor of Music at Dublin University. [SCG 69–73, 77–8]

June

17 (Tue) Bessie Shaw, accompanied by her younger daughter, Agnes, leaves Dublin to settle in London, taking lodgings at 13 Victoria Grove SW. In his memoirs, Edward McNulty writes: 'Mrs Shaw decided to live in London with her children, leaving her husband to manage or mismanage his affairs in Dublin. But, as a matter of fact, wife and husband parted good friends and remained so until he died. Agnes the youngest [*sic*] and most delicate went first with her mother. Lucy (who was the eldest) and George Bernard remained with their father in Dublin until their mother had made a home for them in London.' [Ross 240; *The Irish Times*, 18 Jun 1873; McNulty 20]

August

Foundation in Liverpool of the British National Association of Spiritualists. From 1875, it is housed at 38 Great Russell Street. Bessie Shaw was a practising spiritualist (holding seances, and creating 'spirit drawings') and Shaw himself took a close, if sceptical, interest in the subject. [I&R 411–12; Texas: Art Collection]

26 (Tue) *The Irish Times* of 27 August records the departure of a Mrs Shaw on this date. Probably Bessie Shaw had returned briefly from London and was now departing with Lucy, leaving Shaw in lodgings with his father. [Ross 240]

1874

March

Bessie Shaw again returns briefly to Dublin to sell up the Hatch Street furniture and install her husband and son in lodgings at 61 Harcourt Street. While living at Harcourt Street, Shaw befriends Chichester Bell, cousin of Graham Bell (inventor of the telephone). [CL1: 7, 2: 504–5; I&R 9 n2]

September

8 (Tue) After initially lodging in Ebury Street in London, Lee sells his interest in the cottage on Torca Hill, Dalkey to Julian Marshall, for £300 and subsequently rents No. 13 Park Lane from Marshall. [SCG 85, 149]

1875

February

24 (Wed) Shaw writes to his mother intervening in a dispute with Lucy over another production by Lee of Bellini's *La Sonnambula*. 'Lee is ruined you say. My dear mother, the same calamity has

occurred on an average three hundred & sixty five times a year, during my experience of him. Get up the Sonnambula, *stop worrying Lucy*, act like sensible people (if possible) and you will have your Amina [the heroine, played by Lucy] all safe enough, I believe... [Lucy] doesn't complain of being ill used, she simply states the case, which is confirmed by my old experience, of the usual unbusinesslike, wearisome rubbish, & vituperation of everybody and everything, which is inseparable from Lee's "acting management".' [CL1: 11–12; SCG 86]

April

3 (Sat) Shaw's first publication appears in the correspondence column of *Public Opinion*, a London weekly news digest. He denounces revival meetings held in Dublin by American evangelists Dwight Lyman Moody and Ira D. Sankey, and publicly declares his atheism. The letter was reprinted in the same journal on 8 November 1907. [Auto 1: 77, 298; CL1: 13; Hend1: 11; Rat 24–6]

April(?) – May

Shaw renews the acquaintance of 'Calypso'. See above, 1871.

1876 – year of Shaw's move from Dublin to London

Shaw's fragmentary diary notes for the years 1876 to 1879 make cryptic references, in astrological terms of ascent or eclipse, to what are presumably new flirtations or infatuations – he terms them 'episodes' – with girls or women whom he names 'Terpsichore', 'La Carbonaja' and 'Leonora'. Weintraub suggests possible identifications. Lucy Shaw's biographer, Henry George Farmer assigns to 'before or in 1876' a letter from Lucy to Shaw, written while the latter was still living with his father in Dublin. She asks Shaw to tell 'Par' that a pair of boots bought for her have arrived and that they are 'delightful, enchanting, ravishing to a degree'. She confides that she is sending another of her stories to V. (S.?) Lile for publication, and seems to have been successful in this already. She says that she expects £2.2.0–£3.3.0 – for what she describes as her 'exceedingly commonplace and occasionally vulgar' latest story, 'The Lady Help'. She intends to buy 'Mar' a new dress with the money. She reports that she and Lee are now 'bitter enemies... frostily civil to each other's faces, and horribly abusive behind backs'. [D1: 34–5; Farmer 31; Lucy Shaw to Shaw, *c.* 1876, Texas]
Publication of Richard Wagner's *Der Ring des Nibelungen*.

February

29 (Tue) Shaw submits his letter of resignation at Uniacke Townshend, to take effect from the end of the following month. He gives as

his reason his feeling of having too little to do in the less responsible position of 'general clerk' he has been given to make way for one of Townshend's relations to take over the head cashier's job. [CL1: 14, 22; Imm xxxii; Prefs3: 25; Rat 26]

March

27 (Mon) Agnes Shaw dies of tuberculosis in the Hospital Saint Laurence, at Ventnor on the Isle of Wight, aged 21. She and her mother (Bessie) had been staying at Balmoral House, a guest house on the Esplanade at Ventnor (not a sanitarium, as assumed by most commentators) since 3 March. [DHL; Isle of Wight *Mercury*, 3, 10, 17, 24, 31 Mar 1876; Isle of Wight District Registry Office HB 216843]

30 Agnes Shaw is buried at Ventnor, the Reverend W. W. Whelan officiating. A gravestone, which carries a text from St Paul's Epistle to the Philippians, 1: 23: 'TO BE WITH CHRIST WHICH IS FAR BETTER', was erected at Shaw's direction many years later, possibly during the First World War. Photographic portraits of GBS and Lucy Shaw at Ventnor, taken some time after the funeral, are extant. [DHL; Ross 276–9]

31 Shaw leaves his post at Uniacke Townshend.

April

1 (Sat) Shaw leaves Dublin for London, boarding a ferry at the North Wall Quay on the Liffey in Dublin. Arriving at Euston Station in London from Holyhead, he took a 'growler' (four-wheeled cab) to his mother's lodgings at 13 Victoria Grove S.W. He remains in London on 2–3 April, then travels to Ventnor on the 4th, to join his mother and sister. [DHL; D1: 29; Imm xxxii; Prefs3: 25; CL1: 6, 17]

May

3 (Wed) Shaw returns to London from Ventnor. Shortly after settling in, Shaw asks his mother to teach him singing, and Lucy helps him with the piano by playing duets with him. During May, he sees Squire and Marie Bancroft and Ellen Terry in a revival of Tom Robertson's *Ours*. [D1: 30; DHL; Pearson 52; Farmer 33]

September

Shaw studies Excise in preparation for entry by examination into the Civil Service. [D1: 30; CL1: 17]

November

Shaw gives up Civil Service study and begins ghost-writing for Lee as music critic on *The Hornet*. O'Donovan states that 'between 29 November 1876, and 28 March 1877, he ghosted

18 articles for Lee at a guinea apiece'. [D1: 30; SCG 88; Morgan 7; I&R 3]

December

Shaw sees Ellen Terry in Tom Taylor and A. W. Dubourg's *New Men and Old Acres* at the Court Theatre. [DHL]

16–28 Charlotte Payne-Townshend, Shaw's future wife, records in her diary for 16 December that she is 'getting on with Guitar'; on 18 December that she 'got some books of Guitar Songs'; on the 21st that her father gave her a Latin lesson in the morning; and on the 28th that she 'had a splendid ride on the sand in the morning.' [BL MS Add 63188A, fols 80–2]

1877

August

Early At this time a development or incident occurred in his relation with 'Calypso' which Shaw described as 'The Catastrophe, or the indiscretion'. [BL MsAdd 50710A; D1: 26]

September

26 (Wed) Shaw's last piece of ghosted music criticism for Lee in *The Hornet*. [Lbib 344; Ross 285–6 suggests the ghost writing for Lee may have continued until May 1878]

November

25 (Sun) Birth of Harley Granville Barker.

1878

During this year Shaw studies 'French, harmony and counterpoint', the latter two supervised by J. M. Crament, composer and organist at Brompton Parish Church. [D1: 30, 35–6 n4]

January–February

Shaw writes his unorthodox sketch, 'A Practical System of Moral Education for Females', which was published posthumously in 1956 as *My Dear Dorothea: A Practical System of Moral Education for Females Embodied in a Letter to a Young Person of That Sex*. [Lbib1: 269–70; Laura Tahir, '"My Dear Dorothea": Shaw's Earliest Sketch', *SHAW: The Annual of Bernard Shaw Studies*, vol. 9 (1989), 7–21; Texas]

February

Shaw begins writing a profane Passion Play in blank verse, under the working title, 'The Household of Joseph'. He abandoned the work at the end of Act II, Scene 2. [Lbib1: 326–7; I&R 119]

March

21 (Thu) Shaw receives a letter from Mrs E. A. Collier (evidently a hostess and friend of Shaw in his early London days) with a medal of the Virgin Mary enclosed. Concerning the medal Shaw notes that he: 'agreed to wear for 6 mths & discarded it accordingly 21/9/78.' The medal, which he kept all his life, is held in the British Library. [BL MS Add 50508; CL1: 20]

July

Novelist Elinor L. Huddart writes to Shaw, thanking him for his criticism of her novel *Cheer or Kill*. This marks the beginning of an extensive correspondence and platonic friendship lasting until 1894. Only Elinor's letters survive. [BL MS Add 50535, 50536]

15 (Mon) Shaw receives a letter from one Laura Willock, inviting him to come and meet some 'very sweet and pretty girls'. [BL MS Add 50508]

Autumn

Shaw begins a first novel, *The Legg Papers*, soon abandoned. [CL1: 21–2]

October

29 (Tue) Letter from Pakenham Thomas Beatty to Shaw from Dundalk to say that he is sending his first book of poems, *To My Lady and Other Poems*, to Shaw c/o Mrs Collier at 20 Brompton Square, London W. [BL MS Add 50530; CL1: 20]

November

Shaw is introduced to a representative of the Imperial Bank, South Kensington, presumably regarding possible employment, 'without result'. [D1: 30; Peters 4]

Winter 1878–9

Shaw becomes acquainted with James Lecky, who shared his interest in music and from whom he 'gained his earliest knowledge of philology'. [CL1: 34–5; Erv 86]

1879

Throughout the year, Shaw submits essays to various publications; only two are accepted. He writes the first draft of his novel *Immaturity*.
Publication of Henry George's *Progress and Poverty*.
Publication of Ibsen's *A Doll's House*.

January

5 (Sun) Shaw makes the acquaintance of the Lawson family, who live at Carlton House, Cheyne Walk, on the Chelsea Embankment. He is subsequently invited to Sunday evening at-homes with this artistic family. His hostess, Mrs Elizabeth Lawson, was the mother of the landscape painter Cecil Lawson and Malcolm Lawson, musician and conductor. In his 1921 Preface to *Immaturity* Shaw describes his 'agonies of shyness' over his visits to the Lawson house. Mrs Lawson's at-homes are recalled in *Immaturity* itself and in Act 3 of *Pygmalion*, where Mrs Higgins's at-home day in her flat on the Chelsea Embankment (in which one of the decorations is a large landscape by Cecil Lawson) is the scene of Eliza Doolittle's sensational social debut. [D1: 35 n5; Imm xli–ii; Prefs3: 34]

February

22 (Sat) Shaw's unsigned and unpaid for essay, 'Opera in Italian' is published in the *Saturday Musical Review*. [CL1: 21]

March

5 (Wed) Shaw begins writing *Immaturity*. [D1: 30; Imm xxxvii; Prefs3: 29; Erv 64]

14 James Lecky invites Shaw to tea, mentioning a Polish friend called Szczepanowski, a name Shaw later uses for the female Polish acrobat in his play *Misalliance*. [BL MS Add 50508]

April

Shaw sees Henry Irving in a revival of Bulwer-Lytton's *The Lady of Lyons* at the Lyceum Theatre. [DHL]

September

G. R. Sims (1847–1922), the editor of *One and All*, accepts Shaw's article 'Christian Names' for publication. The 15 shillings Shaw received for this piece was the first payment for a literary work submitted in his own name. Sims failed to acknowledge further contributions sent to him by Shaw. [CL1: 21, 38]

28 (Sun) The first draft of *Immaturity* completed. [D1: 30; Erv 64]

George Carr Shaw writes to Bernard, thanking him for his 'grand letter', and showing interest in his writings. [BL MS Add 50508]

October

Shaw meets Dr Kingston Barton (1854–1941), a physician of St Bartholomew's Hospital. They become close friends, and Shaw uses him as a consultant about medical subjects touched on in his second novel, *The Irrational Knot*, and as a confidant about

	the Shaw family's drinking habits. In this month, he begins to visit J. Kingston Barton regularly, nearly every Saturday night, at his lodgings in Gloucester Road. [CL1: 35–7; BL MS Add 50710B; Lgen 25–8; D1: 27–9, 30]
11 (Sat)	Publication of 'Christian Names' in *One and All*. [Lbib2: 523]

November

Early	Shaw's first visit to the home of Lady Wilde in Park Street. He may have been invited on the basis of being Lucy Shaw's brother, as she was then popular with Oscar Wilde and his brother Willie. [D1: 31, 35 n9; Farmer 42; Harris 263]
5 (Wed)	First revision of *Immaturity* completed. [D1: 30]
8	Shaw submits the MS of *Immaturity* to publishers Hurst and Blackett. They decline it the following week. [D1: 30; CL1: 24]
13	Shaw thanks Hurst and Blackett for reading *Immaturity* and requests them to forward the MS to Kegan Paul & Co. [CL1: 24; D1: 31]
14	Shaw begins working at the Edison Telephone Company, persuading property owners to allow the company to erect structures to support telephone wires on their rooftops. He works on commission at half a crown for each consent. While employed at the Edison Telephone Company he spends Saturdays at the British Museum. [D1: 31, 36; CL1: 21, 25; Erv 66; Peters 4; Hol1: 77, 80]
25	Kegan Paul & Co write a letter to Shaw rejecting *Immaturity*. [BL MS Add 50508; D1: 30–1]

December

24 (Wed)	Lucinda Carr Shaw makes her professional stage debut in the role of Primrose in the pantomime *Beauty and the Beast* at the Park Theatre, Camden Town, London. [DHL; *The Shavian*, Sep 1960, 29]
29	Shaw sends *Immaturity* to Richard Bentley & Son. [D1: 31]
31	Shaw submits a letter of resignation to Edison Telephone Company after obtaining only one commission in six weeks. In response, the Company puts him on a salary of £40 per year. [CL1: 25]

1880

During this year Shaw attempts to place *Immaturity* with various publishers and, in December, finishes his second novel *The Irrational Knot*. In May/June, John Morley, editor of the *Pall Mall Gazette*, having encouraged Shaw to submit articles, rejects his offerings, and tells Shaw he should get out of journalism. In October, Shaw joins the Zetetical Society and begins his colourful career as a public speaker. After a promotion in the Edison Telephone Company in February, Shaw resigns from the job in July.

January

2 (Fri) A postcard sent to Shaw from Hogarth Road and signed C. G. B. says: 'Quite alone. Turn up when you like. At home tonight & tomorrow night.' [BL MS Add 50508]

8 Rejection of *Immaturity* by Richard Bentley & Son. [BL MsAdd 50508]

*c.*13 Shaw sends *Immaturity* to Macmillan. [D1: 31]

15 Shaw responds to the rejection of *Immaturity* by Richard Bentley & Son. ('You cannot possibly regret the unfavourable result more than I do.') [CL1: 26]

Mrs Lawson invites 'Mr Carr Shaw' (i.e. GBS) to 'a little dance' at her home, Carlton House, Cheyne Walk, Chelsea, SW. Shaw's elegant refusal includes the excuse that he does not know how to dance: 'I should be an envious and gloomy wallflower, and in your house an unhappy guest would be an anomaly.' [BL MS Add 50508; CL1: 28–9]

31 Macmillan sends Shaw their reader's mixed report on *Immaturity*, suggesting revision: 'A 3 vol novel. I have given more than usual attention to this M.S., for it has a certain quality about it – not exactly of an attractive kind, but still not common. It is the work of a humourist and a realist, crossed, however by veins of merely literary discussion. There is a piquant oddity about the situations now and then and the characters are certainly not drawn after the conventional patterns of fiction. ...On the whole, I doubt much whether it would catch public fancy.' [BL MS Add 50508; CL1: 26; Charles Morgan, *The House of Macmillan (1843–1943)* (London: Macmillan, 1944), 119]

February

1 (Sun) Shaw writes to Macmillan explaining his reluctance to revise *Immaturity*. [CL1: 26]

3 Macmillan rejects *Immaturity*. [CL1: 27]

c. 6 Shaw sends *Immaturity* to Chapman & Hall. They reject it – according to St John Ervine on the curt advice, 'No', of novelist George Meredith as their reader. [D1: 31; Erv 64]

c. 18 The Edison Telephone Company promotes Shaw to Head of the Way-Leave Department at a salary of £80 per year plus commissions. [CL1: 25; D1: 31]

March

5 (Fri) George Bentley, editor of *The Temple Bar* rejects 'The Brand of Cain' and returns the MS marked with advice for revisions, which Shaw declines to make. [CL1: 29]

17 Shaw sees Geneviève Ward in Herman Merivale and F. C Grove's *Forget-Me-Not* at the Prince of Wales's Theatre. [DHL]

24 Shaw submits *Immaturity* to Blackwood & Sons. [CL1: 34]

April

7 (Wed) Shaw writes his first theatre review, '*The Merchant of Venice* at the Lyceum', with detailed comments on Henry Irving's Shylock and Ellen Terry's Portia. This review, which refers to a production which opened on 1 November 1879 remains unpublished until its inclusion in Bernard Shaw, *The Drama Observed*, ed. Bernard Dukore (1993). [Drama1: 3–11; DHL]

May

17 (Mon) Shaw sees a revival of T.W. Robertson's *School* at the Haymarket Theatre, with an all-star cast of Squire and Marie Bancroft, Johnston Forbes-Robertson, Marion Terry, Arthur Cecil, H. B. Conway and Henry Kemble. [DHL]

22 John Morley suggests that Shaw come to see him the following week to discuss Shaw's contributing to the *Pall Mall Gazette*. [CL1: 30]

June

Shaw begins writing *The Irrational Knot*. [CL1: 37]

2 (Wed) John Morley declines to use Shaw's review of *George Vanbrugh's Mistake* but requests that he submit other articles. [CL1: 31]

5 The Edison Telephone Company having merged with its rival, Bell Telephone, gives its employees a month's notice. Shaw declines the offer of reinstatement in the newly formed United Telephone Company. [CL1: 25; Erv 67; Rat 35]

13 Shaw submits an essay 'Exhausted Arts' and a review of Henry Irving's production of *The Merchant of Venice* to John Morley at the *Pall Mall Gazette*. [CL1: 31]

14 Morley returns Shaw's two articles, finding them 'not quite suitable for this paper'. He recommends that Shaw get out of journalism, 'a most precarious, dependent, and unsatisfactory profession' for all but the very few who have 'the knack'. [CL1: 32]

July

5 (Mon) Shaw resigns from the Edison Telephone Company. [CL1: 25–6, 32–3]

22 Shaw applies for a job as a clerk at R. F. White and Son of Fleet Street. [CL1: 33]

September

2 (Thu) Letter to Shaw from his father with a postal order for 30 shillings. [BL MS Add 50508]

22 Shaw writes to Blackwood & Sons inquiring as to whether they have reached a decision about *Immaturity*. [CL1: 34]

28 Blackwood & Sons reject *Immaturity*, after initially accepting it according to Shaw: 'Blackwood actually accepted and then revoked.' [Imm xxxviii: Prefs3: 30; CL1: 34; Erv 64]

October

24 (Sun) Shaw writes to the Secretary of the Zetetical Society to obtain information about joining. The Society was formed in 1878 'to furnish opportunities for the unrestricted discussion of Social, Political, and Philosophical subjects'. [CL1: 34–5]

25 Shaw formally accepts nomination for membership of the Zetetical Society. [CL1: 35]

28 Probably on this date Shaw attends for the first time, and speaks at, a meeting of the Zetetical Society, where a few weeks later he makes the acquaintance of Sidney Webb. His participation in the Zetetical Society debates mark the beginning of his career as a public speaker. (In SSS and D1, Shaw incorrectly states that he joined the Zetetical in the winter of 1879.) [CL1: 34–5, 47; I&R 39; SSS 56–7, 65; D1: 31, 33]

November

29 (Mon) Shaw seeks Kingston Barton's professional advice about dipsomania, fainting and death with a view to portraying Virtue Lalage (Susannah Conolly) as authentically as possible in *The Irrational Knot*. [CL1: 36]

December

Shaw finishes his second novel, *The Irrational Knot*. In a typescript preface of March/April 1946 to the manuscript of this novel, when he presented it to the National Library of Ireland, Shaw wrote of this second novel: 'It is interesting to me as marking a crisis in my progress as a thinker. It carried me as far as I could go in Rationalism and Materialism; and when, having finished it, I was carried by my daily task of five pages into a third novel entitled *Love Among the Artists*, I found that I had come to the end of my Rationalism and Materialism.' In answer to a question from Thomas Demetrius O'Bolger in March 1915, he had earlier said that this novel 'really gives the summing up of my Dublin culture. After that I deliberately threw over my intellectual integrity, so to speak, and took the unreasonable instinctive man for my theme.' [D1: 31; National Library of

	Ireland MS; Laurence Collection, Guelph, TS '66 Years Later'; Auto1: 96, 317–18; Harvard, b Ms Eng 1046.9]
15 (Wed)	Henrik Ibsen's *The Pillars of Society* produced at the Gaiety Theatre, in William Archer's translation. Dan H. Laurence notes that this was 'the first recorded production of Ibsen in England'. [CL1: 291]
23	The Shaws move from Victoria Grove to first-floor rooms at 37 Fitzroy Street, WC1, within easy walking distance from the British Museum which Shaw had now begun to frequent a good deal. [D1: 31; CL1: 37; Farmer 46]

1881

At the beginning of this year Shaw begins his first experiment with vegetarianism. He does some ghost-writing for Lee, and in May, begins his third novel, *Love Among the Artists*. In October he joins the Dialectical Society. He spends another frustrating year sending manuscripts to publishers without result. He contemplates migration to America. During the year H. M. Hyndman, Marxist leader of the Social Democratic Federation, and future political debater with Shaw, publishes his influential booklet *England for All*.

January

	A diary note records the beginning of Shaw's first experiment with vegetarianism: 'Became a vegetarian, and remained so until June.' [D1: 31; Auto 1: 300 n12]
	Shaw ghost-writes for Lee on an unidentified project. [CL1: 40]
3 (Mon)	Second revision of *Immaturity* completed. After being refused by ten publishers ('an eleventh, Sampson Low, declined to even read it') *Immaturity* remained unpublished until 1930, when it appeared as the first volume in the Constable Collected Edition of Shaw's works. [Lbib1: 183; CL1: 21]
	Shaw receives Macmillan's letter of rejection of *The Irrational Knot*: 'A novel of the most disagreeable kind. It is clearly the work of a man with a certain originality, a courage of mind. There is nothing conventional either about the structure or the style; & the characters have a curious flavour & "sapidity" about them. But the thought of the book is all wrong; the whole idea of it is odd, perverse & crude. It is the work of a man writing about life, when he knows nothing of it, & thinks incongruously of it. The irony is too remote, & it is of a starved kind – not rich nor humorous. So far as your publication is concerned, it is out of the question. There is too much of adultery and the like matters.' [BL MS Add 50509]

4 Shaw requests Macmillan to forward the MS of the *Irrational Knot* to Blackwood & Sons. [CL1: 37]

January–June

As well as reading daily at the British Museum, Shaw spends three nights a week visiting the house of the Alsatian singer Richard Deck to learn French and help Deck improve his English. [D1: 31; CL1: 18]

March

A diary note indicates that Shaw had contemplated migrating to America, probably at the suggestion of the Bell family, at about this time. [D1: 32]

10 (Thu) Letter from Elinor Huddart with comments on *Immaturity*. She doesn't like the novel's characters Miss Woodward ('a very low type of fashionable flirt') and Smith: 'You may think he is like you but one never knows oneself, and I am sure he is not. He behaves like a prig.' [BL MS Add 50535 781 B]

25 Pakenham Beatty invites Shaw to Sunday lunch, asking him to bring 'some M.S. with you, a good wholesome refreshing murder for instance, to enliven the dullness of the seventh day'. [BL MS Add 50530]

27 Letter from Elinor Huddart includes comments on Blackwood & Sons' rejection of *The Irrational Knot*: 'The title itself is... a challenge flung in the face of society, heralding, no doubt, a raid against its dearest prejudices.' [BL MS Add 50535 781 B]

28 Letter from George Carr Shaw to Shaw, chiding him for not writing: 'You are an illnatured cur that you would not once in a while say 6 or 12 months drop me a few lines... What about your second book – I think it will take if it only gets into proper hands... Tell the Mar I got her letter yesterday... Lucy is in great demand here – I think she must soon be turning her face towards London.' [BL MS Add 50509]

29, 31 Pakenham Beatty invites Shaw to join him on a visit to the Lyceum Theatre to see Tennyson's *The Cup*. They will travel in a Brougham 'chariot' (i.e. one-horse closed carriage). [BL MS Add 50530]

May

19 (Thu) Shaw begins writing *Love Among the Artists*. [D1: 31]

25 Shaw contracts smallpox and is confined to his room for three weeks. [D1: 31]

29 Letter from Huddart about Shaw's illness: 'Cheer up, you are a man, and someday the world will acknowledge your genius.' [BL MS Add 50535 781 B]

Mid-June–October

Shaw recuperates at his Uncle Walter Gurly's place at Leyton, Essex, where he continues working on *Love Among the Artists* and labours to improve his shorthand. During this period he records that he temporarily 'resumed meat eating'. [CL1: 38; D1: 31]

July

14 (Thu) Richard Bentley having rejected *The Irrational Knot*, Shaw requests Smith, Elder & Co. to read the MS. [CL1: 39]

August

6 (Sat) Shaw writes to John Manger Fells from Leyton, re-submitting himself for election to the Philosophical Section of the Zetetical Society. 'My readiness to consider and decide questions of Metaphysics, Logic, Psychology, Political Economy, Jurisprudence and Ethics, and indeed all questions whatever, is not, I trust unknown to the Committee of the Z.S.' [Cornell 4617 Box 10]

23 Referring to his smallpox as 'a thing of the past', Shaw undertakes to deliver his first paper, 'On what is called The Sacredness of Human Life, and its bearing on the question of Capital Punishment', to the Zetetical Society. [CL1: 39; I&R 415–16]

Lee proposes that Shaw ghost-write a third edition of *The Voice*. The next day, Shaw agrees but does not complete the commission. [CL1: 40]

Letter from Pakenham Beatty reporting the birth of his son. [BL MS Add 50530]

September

Shaw resumes his correspondence with Edward McNulty. [D1: 32]

7 (Wed) Pakenham Beatty reports that he and his wife have named their son Albert William Hengist Mazzini, the last name being a salute to the Italian revolutionary republican and liberal Giuseppe Mazzini (1805–72), also remembered in the naming of Mazzini Dunn in Shaw's *Heartbreak House*. [BL MS Add 50530]

17 Pakenham Beatty tells Shaw he is about to take boxing lessons from 'the scientific Ned Donnelly', (boxing instructor at the London Athletic Club). The letter includes a jocular command that 'O'Balzac' Shaw be set on 'eight white she asses' and carried to 'our palace of Philbeach' to view the one-month old Beatty child. [BL MS Add 50530]

19 Pakenham Beatty sends Shaw a copy of a book by Donnelly on self-defence. [BL MS Add 50530]

October

Shaw joins the London Dialectical Society. [D1: 32, 54]

Shaw answers various employment advertisements without success, and resumes his regular Saturday evening visits to Kingston Barton. [D1: 32]

2 (Sun) Shaw returns from Leyton to London. He resumes his vegetarian habits and his daily reading schedule at the British Museum. [CL1: 41; D1: 32]

October–November

Shaw explores the possibility of publishing *Immaturity* at his own expense. [CL1: 42–3]

December

18 (Sun) Shaw submits a copy of his paper on Capital Punishment to Pattie Moye of the Zetetical Executive. [CL1: 44]

23 Pakenham Beatty invites Shaw to 'partake hoff ha leg hof mutton & turnips' on Christmas Day. [BL MS Add 50530]

1882

Early in this year Shaw meets and falls in love with Alice Lockett. In April he begins writing his fourth novel *Cashel Byron's Profession*. In September he attends a lecture by Henry George, author of *Progress and Poverty*. During the year he applies unsuccessfully for various writing positions. The Shaws move from 37 Fitzroy St to an apartment at 36 Osnaburgh Street, NW.

January

Shaw suffers what he calls 'a light attack of scarlet fever' (which Lucy Shaw had also contracted) and returns to Leyton for a period of convalescence with his Uncle Walter John Gurly, who places him under 'a species of quarantine'. During this period Shaw completes the first draft of *Love Among the Artists*, and revises *The Irrational Knot*. [CL1: 47–8; D1: 32]

17 (Tue) Shaw submits *Love Among the Artists* to Richard Bentley & Sons, saying that 'It contains none of the more objectionable features of my previous composition – no radicals, dipsomaniacs or disreputable characters of any kind; but plenty of high art, of which the public seems to be fond at present...' [Shorthand draft letter to Richard Bentley, transcribed Barbara Smoker, Texas]

February

Introduced by her older sister, Jane, Shaw meets Alice Mary Lockett, at Leyton. This begins a stormy love affair which lasts until 1885. References to the relationship occur in Elinor Huddart's letters to Shaw of 26 March and 17 April, 1882. Shaw's earliest surviving letter to Alice is dated 9 September 1882. [D1: 32; BL MS Add 50535; CL1: 62–4]

2 (Thu)	James Joyce (1882–1941) born in Dublin
8	Shaw travels to London to deliver his first paper at the Zetetical Society, on the subject of capital punishment. [CL1: 47; D1: 32]
Mid	Richard Bentley & Son reject *Love Among the Artists*. [CL1: 48]

March

Shaw sends *The Irrational Knot* to America, seeking a publisher, but reports in July that it was 'refused on the score of morality'. He begins ghost-writing a book on singing for Lee. [D1: 32]

Mid	Shaw returns to London. [D1: 32]
19	Emily Gurly, wife of Shaw's Walter John Gurly, writes to Shaw saying, inter alia: 'Alice [Lockett] appeared *once* looking blooming for I fear you have...made a deep impression.' [Emily Jane Gurly to Shaw, 19 Mar 1882, BL MS Add 50509, fol. 155]
26 (Sun)	Letter from Elinor Huddart: 'I have got the life of Goethe you mentioned.' [BL MS Add 50535 781 B]

April

Shaw earns his Zetetical Society subscription money by working at Leyton for one week in the election of Poor Law guardians (a job secured for him by Emily Gurly) during which time he continues his relationship with Alice Lockett. Alice subsequently takes singing lessons each Thursday from Mrs Shaw, GBS seeing her to her train at Liverpool Station. [D1: 32; BL MS Add 50509, fol. 155; Peters 16, 18]

12 (Wed)	After attending an amateur boxing competition with Packenham Beatty, Shaw begins writing *Cashel Byron's Profession*, which he drafts in shorthand. [D1: 32]
22	Shaw and his mother (Bessie Shaw) move from 37 Fitzroy St to an apartment on the second floor, with a room on the third in which Shaw slept, at 36 Osnaburgh Street, NW, a more respectable address. [D1: 32, 52; CL1: 49; Farmer 46]

May–June

Acting as rehearsal pianist, Shaw assists Lee in preparing an amateur operatic performance of Gilbert and Sullivan's *Trial by Jury*, and scenes from Gounod's *Faust* and Verdi's *Il Trovatore* in aid of the Fund for the Relief of the Distressed Ladies of Ireland. The performance takes place at Lee's home, Londonderry House, Park Lane on 1 July. At Lee's request, Shaw writes a review which is published anonymously in the *Court Journal* on 8 July 1882. [D1: 32; CL1: 40–1; SM1: 193]

July

Shaw works on *Cashel Byron's Profession*. Having failed to find an American publisher, Charles Bell returns *The Irrational Knot* to Shaw. [D1: 32]

9 (Sun) Letter from Elinor Huddart commenting on some dazzling shirt studs given to Shaw by Lee (who she thinks has florid taste). [BL MS Add 50535 781 B]

24 Shaw responds to a Miss Ethel Southam's advertisement in the *Daily News* for a copyist to work on the manuscript of a novel. [CL1: 49]

31 Having examined Ethel Southam's MS, Shaw begins advising her on technical and practical aspects of novel-writing, placing particular emphasis on dialogue and character development. [CL1: 50–3]

August

5 (Sat) Letter from Elinor Huddart: 'Friendship is better than love.' [BL MS Add 50535 781 B]

24 Still searching for work, Shaw replies to an advertisement for a 'paragraphist' on an unidentified provincial weekly. In his letter he describes himself as an 'earnest and energetic gentleman, capable of writing satirical articles and descriptive reports. My politics are those of an atheistic radical with no very strong attachments to any established party.' [Shaw to C. Payne, 20 Aug, 1882, Texas; DHL]

September

5 (Tue) Shaw hears the American Economist, Henry George, speak on Land Nationalisation and Single Tax at the nonconformist Memorial Hall in Farringdon Street, later declaring this to be a momentous event in his career: 'He struck me dumb and shunted me from barren agnostic controversy to economics.' He proceeds to read George's *Progress and Poverty,* and joins the Georgite Land Reform Union where he met James Leigh Joynes, Sydney Olivier, Henry Hyde Champion, and the Rev. Stewart Headlam. [D1: 32; Auto1: 113; I&R 32; CL1: 18, 2: 489; Hend1: 47–8]

October

2 (Mon) Shaw applies unsuccessfully to Joshua Hatton, editor of Colburn's *New Monthly Magazine*, for a position as 're-write man'. [CL1: 53]

26 November 1882 – 5 January 1883

During this period, the Huddart–Shaw correspondence is dominated by discussions of spiritualism. Elinor relates how she frightened herself with an experiment in which she hypnotized a girl. The girl went into a deep trance, becoming 'as pale as death' and difficult to wake, but later reported being conscious of Elinor's will for her to speak. This is echoed in Ellie Dunn's hypnosis of Mangan in Shaw's *Heartbreak House.* [BL MS Add 50535]

December

4 (Mon) George Carr Shaw sends a postal order for 10 shillings, writing: 'There is no use expressing my opinion that it would be well if you get something to do to earn some money – it is much wanted by all of us.' [BL MS Add 50509]

28 First surviving letter to Shaw from his future inamorata, Mrs Jenny Patterson. The letter concerns a meeting with Shaw's mother. [BL MS Add 50544]

Shaw applies unsuccessfully for a position at the Smoke Abatement Institute. [CL1: 54]

1883

During this year Shaw completed *Cashel Byron's Profession*, and from July to December wrote his fifth and final novel, *An Unsocial Socialist*. Early in the year, he began reading Karl Marx's *Das Kapital* in the French translation by Gabriel Deville. 1883 was almost certainly the year of the first meeting of Shaw and William Archer, whose recollection of first seeing Shaw reading Marx and Wagner in the British Library is probably assignable to February/March 1883. Meetings of the Fellowship of the New Life, an organization from which the Fabian Society developed, began in October.

January

Shaw works on *Cashel Byron's Profession*, assists Lee as a rehearsal accompanist for a later cancelled production of Gilbert and Sullivan's *Patience*, and attends debates at the Zetetical and Dialectical Societies, and at the Social Democratic Federation. [D1: 32]

7 (Sun) On Lee's recommendation, Shaw applies to Francis Hueffer, the editor of the *Musical Review*, for work as a musical critic. [CL1: 55]

18 Shaw having submitted a sample of his work ('Music for the People') to Hueffer, the two meet for an interview, which soon erupts into a dispute. [CL1: 56]

20 Joshua Hatton of *The New Monthly Magazine* commissions Shaw to write an article. [CL1: 69]

February

Shaw begins reading Marx's *Das Kapital* in Gabriel Deville's French translation. [BL MS Add 50710 A; Letter of Dan H. Laurence to Peter Whitebrook, 24 Mar 1991, Special Collections, Cornell University]

Early Shaw completes *Cashel Byron's Profession*. [CL1: 59]

17 (Sat) Marriage of Edward McNulty to Alice Maud Brennan. George Carr Shaw, with whom McNulty has maintained friendship, acts as a witness. [BL MS Add 50710; D1: 22; SCG 80]

19 Shaw writes a vehement defence of 'Music for the People', and Hueffer eventually accepts the article for publication. [CL1: 56]

February–March

Probable time when Shaw came to William Archer's notice in the Reading Room of the British Museum. Archer records his first impression of Shaw, as a young man with 'pallid skin and bright red hair and beard' whom he noticed 'day after day, poring over Karl Marx's *Das Kapital* and an orchestral score of Wagner's *Tristan und Isolde*.' The precise date and circumstances of their meeting are unclear. Archer had supplied Shaw with materials for the play which was to become *Widowers' Houses* by August 1884, but they almost certainly met in 1883. Late in his life, Shaw wrote that he had been introduced to Archer by Henry Salt, but according to Dan. H Laurence the introducer was more likely to have been Salt's brother-in-law J. L. Joynes. [I&R 87–8; CP1: 37–9; Letter of Dan H. Laurence to Peter Whitebrook, 24 Mar 1991, Guelph]

March

Lucy Shaw has her first major stage engagement in a revival of Offenbach's *Belle Lurette* at the Avenue Theatre, London, going on tour with the company later in the year, playing in the chorus and small parts. [Farmer 50–1]

9 (Fri) William Laffan, London agent for Harpers of New York, expresses interest in seeing the MS of *Cashel Byron's Profession*, but the MS is still with Richard Bentley. [CL1: 59]

10, 17 Publication of 'Music for the People' in two parts in Hueffer's *Musical Review*. [CL1: 57]

14 Death of Karl Marx in London where he had lived in obscurity for 34 years.

17 Shaw and Pakenham Beatty enter the Amateur Boxing Championship, but neither is selected to compete. [CL1: 20; I&R 194]

20 Note to Shaw from Lee about Shaw's payment as an accompanist: 'Would you accept a guinea for 4 visits a week to Mrs. Bell to try over her songs – at any time that would suit you an hour each.' [SCG 90]

May

25 (Fri) Having been told by Shaw that as a child he was allowed to roam about alone at the age of 5 or 6, Elinor Huddart says in a letter: 'How tame my childhood looks beside yours.' [BL MS Add 50536]

31 Richard Bentley returns the MS of *Cashel Byron's Profession* which Shaw submits to Harper & Brothers. [CL1: 59–60; BL MS Add 50510]

July

9 (Mon) Shaw begins writing *An Unsocial Socialist* (first entitled *The Heartless Man*). [CL1: 78; Morgan 70; Erv 111; Rat 44]

24 Shaw receives Harpers' letter rejecting *Cashel Byron's Profession*. (They later, in 1886, publish the work in their Harper's Handy Series.) [CL1: 61; Lbib1: 5]

September

6 (Thu) Shaw applies unsuccessfully to H. Sutherland Edwards for work as a musical critic on the *Pall Mall Gazette*. [CL1: 62]

October

24 (Wed) First fortnightly meeting at Edward Pease's rooms in Osnaburgh Street of the Fellowship of the New Life, out of which the Fabian Society later develops. [Pease 29; Erv 123; Hend 2: 139]

30 Shaw asks Joshua Hatton to pay for his article 'C. H. Bennett and Co.' in the *New Monthly Magazine*. [CL1: 69]

November

1 (Thu) Shaw finishes the first draft of *An Unsocial Socialist*. [CL1: 78; Erv 111]

26 After Bentleys' hesitant rejection of *Cashel Byron's Profession*, Shaw invites George Bentley to read it personally and judge its quality for himself. [CL1: 74]

December

13 (Thu) Shaw is proposed for membership and accepted into the Bedford Debating Society, which had its opening meeting earlier in the year, on 11 May. [DHL; D1: 33]

15 Shaw finishes revising *An Unsocial Socialist*. [CL1: 78]

1884

In May of this year, Shaw attends his first meeting of the Fabian Society and joins it in September. A fortnight after joining the Society, he delivers his first Fabian Tract, 'A Manifesto', which is published in October. During the year *An Unsocial Socialist* is published serially in *To-Day*. From January to July he works on a glossary and index for the works of Elizabethan poet Thomas Lodge. In August he begins collaborating with William Archer on the play which was to become *Widowers' Houses*. Quarrelling with Alice Lockett, briefly flirting with, and writing verses to, a new 'flame,' Katie Samuel, and continuing his relationship with Mrs Jenny Patterson were amongst his other activities this year. H. M. Hyndman begins the regular Sunday evening lectures in the coach house attached to William Morris's Kelmscott House at Hammersmith.

January

4 (Fri) At a meeting of the Fellowship of the New Life, the Fabian Society is formed. [Pease 33; A.M. McBriar, *Fabian Socialism and English Politics, 1884–1918* (1962), 3; Rat 46; Erv 124]

29 Shaw writes to A. S. Smith, Secretary of the Hunterian Club, Glasgow, about the task he has been given by Dr F. J. Furnivall of supplying an index and glossary for the Club's new edition of the works of the Elizabethan poet, Thomas Lodge. Later in 1884 Shaw records in his diary that he 'wasted the year deplorably' on this work. He completed most of the index, but did not finish the whole task, and in July 1885 requested that it be taken over by the Shakespearean scholar Thomas Tyler. [CL1: 79–80, 95, 112, 135–7; D1: 33, 53]

February

29 (Fri) A speech by Shaw on Shakespeare's *Troilus and Cressida*, containing an extensive analysis of the play, which Shaw sees as exemplifying Shakespeare's 'pessimism', is read in his absence to the New Shakespeare Society. [Drama1: 11–30]

March–December

An Unsocial Socialist (after being rejected by conventional publishers) is published serially in *To-Day*, a new 'Monthly Magazine of Scientific Socialism' edited by J. L. Joynes and E. Belfort Bax. This publication leads to Shaw's meeting William Morris. [Lbib1: 11; D1: 33]

March

15 (Sat) Shaw's letter on economics headed 'Who is the Thief?' published under the pseudonym 'G.B.S. Larking' in *Justice*, the journal of the Social Democratic Federation. [CL1: 81; D1: 61]

April

25 (Fri) Shaw attends a meeting of the Browning Society where he makes a speech during the discussion of James Cotter Morison's paper on 'Caliban upon Setebos'. Shaw's speech is published in the Society's *Monthly Abstract of Proceedings*. [CL1: 87; Drama1: 30–1; Wein3: 124–5]

28 A letter from Elinor Huddart implies Shaw had become attracted to Eleanor Marx Aveling. [Peters 32]

May

Annie Besant hears Shaw speaking of himself as 'a loafer' and, missing his irony, reproaches him vehemently in the *National Reformer*. He writes a charming letter to her in reply. [Peters 38; Annie Besant, *An Autobiography* (1939), 402]

Shaw rehearses *Don Giovanni* at Lee's and is strongly attracted to Katie Samuel, who was playing Donna Anna. In a comparison with Shaw's other youthful flirtations, Dan H. Laurence has observed that, 'While the others sought awkwardly to have the last word, Katie wielded the one weapon she instinctively recognized was capable of wounding and disturbing him – silence.' [Dan H. Laurence, 'Katie Samuel: Shaw's Flameless Old Flame', in *SHAW: The Annual of Bernard Shaw Studies*, XV (1995)]

1 (Thu) Chapman & Hall reject *Cashel Byron's Profession*. [BL MS Add 50510]

4 Shaw's delivers a lecture on Socialist themes, entitled 'Thieves', at the Invicta Working Men's Club, Woolwich. [CL1: 81, 87, 88; I&R 40]

5 Shaw sends the report of his Browning Society lecture to the Society Secretary for publication in its *Monthly Abstract of Proceedings*. [CL1: 87; Lbib2: 524]

16 Shaw attends his first meeting of the Fabian Society. He has previously attended meetings of H. M. Hyndman's Social Democratic Foundation, before finding a more congenial group of Socialists in the Fabian Society. [Pease 40; CL1: 18; Hend2: 155; Rat 48]

22 Shaw reads a paper entitled 'The Socialist Movement is Only the Assertion of Our Lost Honesty' to the Bedford Debating Society. [D1: 54]

July

7 (Mon) In a letter to Alice Lockett, Shaw mentions that, in annoyance with her, he has had 'for consolation a long walk with Mrs Chatterbox' (i.e. Mrs Jenny Patterson). He responds tartly to her charge that he treats her as a baby, giving her 'lumps of sugar'. [CL1: 90; Peters 28]

8 Alice complains about Shaw's 'cruel letter', and says 'I have a decided objection to being sugared, and hope you will keep your sweets to yourself.' A spirited correspondence, alternating between expressions of affection, and exasperated declarations that the affair is over, continues, with Alice frequently anticipating Eliza Doolittle's defiant manner towards Higgins in *Pygmalion* in outbursts to Shaw such as that in a letter of 20 November 1884: 'Ha! Ha! Don't care a snap for your sage advice. I screamed laughing at your letter, put it on the floor, danced on it till the plates rattled on the shelf.' [BL MS Add 50510; CL1: 62–76, 89–100, 142–3, 157–9]

August

8 (Fri) Letter from George Carr Shaw to Shaw which reports that Robert Brabazon is going into a lunatic asylum – 'It is not

improbable that I shall follow him there soon... I hope that fellow [Pakenham Beatty] is not still annoying Lucy.' [BL MS Add 50510; CL1: 150–1]

15 Letter from George Carr Shaw to Shaw (with a postal order for £1 and a message 'sending the same to your Mar') praises, with some qualifications, the character of 'Smilash' alias Sidney Trefusis, in *An Unsocial Socialist,* misspelling the name as 'Slimash'. [BL MS Add 50509]

18 From this date until 18 November 1884, Shaw worked intermittently on the first draft (in shorthand) of the work which was to become *Widowers' Houses,* his first full-length play. The plot materials, suggested to Shaw by William Archer, were derived from Émile Augier's play *La Ceinture Dorée.* The first working title of Shaw's work, *The Way to a Woman's Heart,* was changed to *Rheingold,* and subsequently to *Rhinegold.* After writing two acts and a substantial part of Act 3, Shaw temporarily abandoned the project on 18 November. He resumed work on it in 1885, 1887 and again in the Summer and Autumn of 1892 when he completed the play (in holograph) as *Widowers' Houses* on 20 October. [BL MS Add 50594; D1: 106–7; D2: 839–40; I&R 120–4; CP1: 36–8]

29 In a letter to Shaw, George Carr Shaw apologizes for his misspelling of 'Smilash', saying it was a slip of the pen: 'I know and like the name too well to make any mistake about it.' [BL MS Add 50509]

September

5 (Fri) Shaw formally joins the Fabian Society, and a fortnight later delivers Fabian Tract No. 2, 'A Manifesto'. [CL1: 18; Erv 128; Hend2: 155; Rat 48]

October

Publication of Shaw's first Fabian tract, 'A Manifesto'. [Lbib1: 3]

Publication of Philip Wicksteed's critique of *Das Kapital* in *To-Day,* to which Shaw responds with a defence of Marx in the same journal. These debates with Wicksteed, pursued both in print and at meetings of the 'Economic Circle' founded by Charlotte Wilson, which meet at the home of Henry R. Beeton in Belsize Square, have a profound influence on Shaw's political and economic thought. In 1904 Shaw calls Wicksteed his 'father in economics'. [I&R 43–4; CL1: 168; D1: 33]

20 (Mon) Shaw lectures on 'Competition' at the Queen's Bench Coffee House in Southwark Bridge Road. [D1: 57]

21 Shaw sends the MS of a short story, *The Brand of Cain,* to the publishers Hawkes & Phelps, but the MS is lost in transit or mislaid by the publisher, never to be found again. [CL1: 110]

23 Emma F. Brooke, friend of Charlotte Wilson and later a member of the Fabian Executive writes to Shaw consoling him about rejections of his novels, and telling him: 'your vegetarianism is bad for your health and... beef and beer are urgently necessary for you.' [BL MS Add 50510]

31 Henry Hyde Champion asks Shaw to carry out editorial work on *The Co-operative Commonwealth* by Danish-born American Laurence Gronlund, an invitation he accepts. The book is published in May 1885, although Gronlund's dissatisfaction with Shaw's edition provokes him into releasing his own 'authorised and copyright English edition' in July 1886. [Lbib1: 483–4; CL1: 101–2, 112]

November

21 (Fri) Shaw plays a piano duet with Kathleen Ina in a Social Democratic Federation 'art evening'. [CL1: 139; R.Page Arnot, *William Morris: The Man and the Myth* (1970), 221 n1]

December

Shaw searches for a publisher who will put out *An Unsocial Socialist* in book form. [CL1: 102]

27 (Sat) Alice Lockett writes to Shaw saying that their correspondence 'closes with the year'. Shaw and Alice corresponded several times in later years, and the romantic interest between them remained alive until at least 22 December 1885. [BL MS Add 50510; CL1: 157–8]

1885

This year is, in many ways, a year of firsts in Shaw's writing and journalistic career. Shaw's first article of music criticism is published in *The Dramatic Review* in February, followed by his first article of dramatic criticism and first book review in May. In April, *Cashel Byron's Profession* is serially published in *To-Day* while *The Irrational Knot* is serially published in *Our Corner*. Also during this month Shaw's work is published for the first time in America. In June, Shaw begins his regular 'Art Corner' column for *Our Corner*. In January, Shaw is elected to the Executive Committee of the Fabian Society and throughout the year, he is heavily involved in political activities, lecturing and attending lectures and meetings several times a week. In addition to his hectic schedule of writing, lecturing and attendance at meetings, he also manages to indulge in various romantic interests. In January of this year, Shaw becomes interested in May Morris, and also begins visiting Annie Besant. In February, his relationship with Jenny Patterson becomes increasingly intimate. He subsequently celebrates his 29th birthday by losing his virginity to her. This tempestuous relationship continues throughout the year while the romance with Alice Lockett fades. Also during this year, Shaw's father, George Carr Shaw, dies alone in Dublin and Shaw's grandfather, Walter Bagnall Gurly, dies in Carlow.

January

The second clash between Shaw and Philip Wicksteed in the pages of *To-Day*. [CL1: 168]

Having been accepted into William Morris's family circle, Shaw becomes interested in May Morris. [I&R 54; D1: 114; Hol1: 223; May Morris to GBS, 5 May 1936, Texas]

2 (Fri) Shaw is elected to the Executive Committee of the Fabian Society. [Pease 44; Rat 51]

5 Shaw lectures on 'The Iron Law of Wages' at the Blue Ribbon Hall, Westminster. [D1: 55]

11 Shaw says that he 'was to have lectured at St. John's Coffee House, Hoxton, but found no audience there in consequence of W. Morris being round the corner lecturing'. [D1: 55]

18 Shaw lectures on 'Laissez Faire' to the Labour Emancipation League in Stepney. [D1: 56]

21 Shaw lectures on 'Socialism' (and its achievement by Fabian permeation tactics) to the Dialectical Society, where he meets Annie Besant. To his astonishment she defends his arguments against opposing speakers, asks him to nominate her to the Fabian Society, and invites him to dine with her. [D1: 56]

22 Shaw receives an encouraging reader's report on *An Unsocial Socialist* from Macmillan & Co., who have nevertheless rejected it. [CL1: 113–14]

30 Shaw appears, in the role of Stratton Strawless, in a Socialist League production at Ladbroke Hall of Simpson and Merivale's play *Alone*. The cast also includes Edward Aveling, May Morris, and Eleanor Marx Aveling. [D1: 54, 57; CL1: 114–5; Peters 32–3] Earlier on this day Shaw had delivered his 'first major address (as a Fabian Society delegate) to a formal public gathering' at the Industrial Remuneration Conference held at the Prince's Hall, Piccadilly. The full text was published in the proceedings of the Conference and in *The Commonweal* in March. [D1: 57; Lbib2: 525; Pease 44–6]

31 In the evening, Shaw makes his first visit to Annie Besant's house in St John's Wood. [D1: 57; Peters 39]

February

1 (Sun) Shaw lectures again on 'Competition' at the Grantham Coffee House, Old Kent Road. [D1: 57]

7 Shaw makes a 'disagreeable but somewhat forcible speech' at a meeting of the Socialist League. [D1: 58]

8	Publication of Shaw's first article of music criticism, 'Herr Richter and His Blue Ribbon', in the second number of *The Dramatic Review*, a journal started by an Irishman, Edwin P. Palmer. His position as musical critic for this journal was procured for him by William Archer. [D1: 53; SM1: 208–13; Lbib2: 525]
10	First mention of Mrs Jenny Patterson in Shaw's Diary. She had visited the Shaws at 36 Osnaburgh Street. 'Mrs Patterson here in the evening. Got a letter from V.L. [Vandeleur Lee], and went out late to see Mrs. P. to a bus, and to call on L.' From this date, Shaw's Diary begins to reflect an increasing intimacy with Jenny Patterson. She attends lectures with him, they take walks together, he visits her home at 23 Brompton Square, she frequently visits the Shaws at 36 Osnaburgh Street, where she was taking singing lessons from Mrs Shaw. [D1: 59 ff.]
14	Shaw begins revising *The Irrational Knot* for serial publication in *Our Corner*. [D1: 61]
15	Shaw lectures again on the 'Iron Law of Wages' at the Perseverance Hall, then sits up till 2 a.m. writing to Edward McNulty. [D1: 61]
16	Shaw works at the first instalment of *The Irrational Knot*, and offers *An Unsocial Socialist* to Swan Sonnenschein for publication. [CL1: 116; D1: 61]
20	Shaw delivers a paper on 'Money' at a Fabian Society meeting. [D1: 63]
21	After having visited the *Dramatic Review* offices and the printers Shaw returns home to find 'Mrs Patterson here [at 36 Osnaburgh Street]... Sat chatting and playing and singing until past 21 [9.0 p.m.] when [I] put her into a cab with her dog and went off to [Kingston] Barton's.' [D1: 63]
22	Shaw lectures on 'The Iron Law of Wages' at the Socialist League. [D1: 63]
23	Swan Sonnenschein agree to publish *An Unsocial Socialist* and Shaw requests that they send him a contract. [CL1: 117]
25	Shaw refuses to assign Swan Sonnenschein the copyright on *An Unsocial Socialist* indefinitely, as their standard contract requires, but states his willingness to lease them exclusive rights to the book for five years with provision for renewal. [CL1: 116–17]
26	Shaw lectures on 'Socialism' at the Liberal and Social Union, and complains to the editor of *The Dramatic Review* that his article on a choral performance of Shelley's *Prometheus Unbound* has neither been published nor paid for. [D1: 64; CL1: 118]

27 After a two-hour ride with Belfort Bax on a tandem bicycle, Shaw lectures at a meeting of the Croydon Social Democratic Federation on 'The Iron Law of Wages'. [D1: 64]

March

Publication of Shaw's article 'What's in a Name? How an Anarchist might put it' in the first number of *The Anarchist*, leads many to believe mistakenly that Shaw is an anarchist. In April this article becomes the first work of Shaw's to be published in America. [Lbib2: 525; CL1: 109]

1 (Sun) Shaw completes an instalment of *The Irrational Knot* for publication in *Our Corner*, and lectures on 'Competition' at Perseverance Hall. [D1: 65]

2 Shaw receives his cheque from *The Dramatic Review*, but returns it because the article has not been printed. Lucy Shaw is at home with her mother and brother until March, but later leaves to go on tour. [CL1: 121; Farmer 52]

9 Shaw's cousin, Robert ('Robbie') Carroll (son of the Rev. William George and Emily Carroll) arrives on a visit to the Shaws at 36 Osnaburgh Street. He makes a return visit in August–September 1886. Robert Carroll (wrongly identified as 'Carl' in the diary) was one of the few family relationships Shaw maintained. [DHL; D1: 67–8]

11 Shaw first meets Grace Gilchrist (a young socialist who later, in 1887 and 1888, develops a passion for him) at a gathering at her home where he reads his abstract of a chapter from *Das Kapital*. Sidney Webb, Sydney Olivier and Edward Pease also attended this gathering. [D1: 68; Peters 37–8, 419 n11]

15 Shaw dines with Packenham Beatty and records that there was 'chaffing about his flirtation with Lucy'. [D1: 70]

16 What is probably Shaw's first written reference to Ibsen occurs in a letter to William Archer. He had been reading a translation of a Swedish play, and said: 'It smells of Ibsen.' [CL1: 127; Wisenthal 5]

20 Shaw is present when Sidney Webb delivers his first paper at a Fabian Society meeting. [D1: 71; Erv 129]

25 In his diary, Shaw writes: 'Imploring letter from Glasgow about Lodge index. Desperate resolve to get up early–to buy an alarum clock.' [D1: 72]

27 Shaw replies to the main speaker at a Browning Society lecture on 'Mr Sludge, the Medium'. [D1: 72]

29 Shaw lectures on 'Private Property, Capital and Competition' at Kelmscott House, then has supper with William Morris. [D1: 73]

April

Cashel Byron's Profession began to be published serially in *To-Day* (a shilling magazine edited by Belfort Bax, James Joynes and Hubert Bland) until March 1886. [Lbib2: 526; D1: 53]

The Irrational Knot begins serial publication in Annie Besant's socialist magazine *Our Corner* until February. [Lbib2: 526; D1: 53]

1 (Wed) Shaw delivers a speech on 'Cooperative production' at the Dialectical Society. [D1: 74]

5 Shaw lectures on 'Thieves' to the Clerkenwell Social Democratic Federation. [D1: 75]

6 Shaw sends a signed agreement to Swan Sonnenschein concerning the publication of *An Unsocial Socialist*. [CL1: 130]

8 Shaw attends a 'Karl Marx meeting' at Hampstead. [D1: 75]

11 First publication of Shaw's work in America, an unauthorized reprint of 'What's in a Name? How an Anarchist Might put it' in the anarchist Benjamin Tucker's Boston weekly, *Liberty*. [Lbib2: 525; CL1: 109]

12 Shaw attends a mass meeting in Hyde Park supporting the eight-hour day. [D1: 76]

13 Shaw notifies J. L. Mahon, secretary of the Socialist League, that he will not speak at the League's anti-Sudanese War meeting and will not submit to being referred to in League handbills as 'Comrade Shaw'. He attends a boxing competition in the evening. [CL1: 131; D1: 76]

19 **Shaw receives a telegram with news of George Carr Shaw's death at his lodging house at 21 Leeson Park Ave, Dublin**. Lucy Shaw, in Dublin at the time, does not attend his funeral, nor do any other members of the family. Edward McNulty provides an account of his death. The Shaws receive about £100 from George Carr Shaw's life insurance policy, but must now do without his weekly 30 shillings remittance to them. [CL1: 132–3; D1: 54, 78; I&R 9 n2; McNulty 22–3]

20 Shaw writes in his diary: 'Mrs. Patterson at home when I got back – wasted all evening.' Shaw also writes to his uncle in Dublin, Richard Frederick Shaw, to ascertain what money might be realized from his father's estate. [D1: 78; CL1: 132]

23 Having received no reply from Uncle Frederick concerning the family finances, Shaw writes again. Uncle Frederick's replies are scrawled between the lines of this letter. He was in charge of the estate, and it was at his suggestion that George Carr Shaw had drawn up a will. Uncle Frederick states that he will remit money to the family. [BL MS Add 50511; CL1: 132–5]

26 Shaw is introduced to G. W. Foote of the National Secular Society at William Archer's house. [D1: 80]

27 Shaw leaves a symphonic concert to visit Mrs Patterson. 'Found her alone, and chatted until past midnight.' [D1: 80]

May

1 (Fri) Persuaded by Shaw, Sidney Webb joins the Fabian Society. Webb's friend Sydney Olivier joins at the same time, and later introduces Graham Wallas to the Society. During this month Mrs Annie Besant also became a member. [A.M. McBriar, *Fabian Socialism and English Politics, 1884–1918* (1962), 4; Rat 52; Pease 46; Hol1: 174, 176]

2 Publication of Shaw's first piece of drama criticism for *The Dramatic Review*, an unsigned review of performances by an amateur group at St George's Hall of Robert Browning's *A Blot on the 'Scutcheon* and Shakespeare's *Comedy of Errors* [Drama 31–2]

4 William Archer introduces Shaw to Henry Arthur Jones. [D1: 81]

5 Shaw calls at the Avelings' house to discuss a projected reading of *Nora*, a translation of Ibsen's *A Doll's House* by Henrietta Frances Lord. The reading takes place on 15 January 1886. [D1: 81]

13 Around this time, Shaw seems to have recommended that Pakenham Beatty read George Moore's novel *A Mummer's Wife*. In response to this, Pakenham Beatty sends Shaw a list of 'damages' claimed against Shaw for having 'induced the aforesaid Pakenham Beatty to read *A Mummer's Wife*'. These 'damages' included 'Injury to morals £1 000 000, Injury to Digestion £1000, Injury to Intellect £100 000 000.' [Guelph]

14 Shaw speaks on 'Vegetarianism' at a Bedford Society meeting. [D1: 84]

16 Publication of Shaw's first book review (passed to him by William Archer) in the *Pall Mall Gazette*. Shaw subsequently contributes 111 book reviews to this periodical until Christmas 1888. The first review was of a 642-page novel *Trajan* by Henry F. Keenan, which is commended as likely to be popular with readers who like 'plenty of such exciting incidents and highly coloured scenes as will not wear out their thinking apparatus too rapidly', but 'they must be persons whose time is of comparatively small value'. [Tyson (1991), 20; Lbib2: 527; I&R 28 n13; D1: 53, 84]

17 Shaw lectures at the Woolwich Radical Club on 'Thieves'. [D1: 85]

22 Shaw finally obtains a publishing agreement with Swan Sonnenschein. [D1: 64; Rat 53]

25 On this day, Shaw records in his diary: 'Went to Mrs. Patterson to dinner. [Henry Eugene] DeMeric [a surgeon] was there, and we three spent the evening singing etc.' [D1: 86]

June

Shaw begins a regular 'Art Corner' column reviewing all the arts in Annie Besant's *Our Corner*. He continues this until September 1886. [Lbib2: 527; D1: 53]

7 (Sun) Shaw lectures on 'Driving Capital Out of the Country' at Kelmscott House. [D1: 89]

10 In his diary, Shaw writes: 'Found Mrs. Patterson here when I came home. Lost night's work in consequence. Went home with her by train. Walked back.' [D1: 90]

14 Shaw attends a lecture by William Morris. [D1: 90]

16 Final meeting and supper of the Karl Marx Society. [D1: 91]

18 Shaw records in his diary that he 'spent the evening with Wicksteed going over his Jevonian curves'. [D1: 91]

19 Shaw orders a new suit of clothes from Jaeger's store, to be paid for with money from the insurance on his father's life. The new clothes form part of a hygiene programme, designed to allow the body to 'breathe,' which involves eschewing bedsheets and all non-animal fibres. His Jaeger suits become a distinctive mark of Shaw's public persona. [D1: 91]

26 Shaw attends a meeting of the Psychical Society and walks Jenny Patterson home. [D1: 93]

30 Shaw collects his new clothes from Jaeger's and wears them to a meeting of The Women's Protective and Provident League. The next day, Shaw writes in his diary: 'Slight cold from wearing Jaeger.' [D1: 94]

July

3 (Fri) Shaw attends a Fabian Society meeting and walks May Morris home. [D1: 94]

4 Shaw calls on Mrs Patterson twice; finding her at home on the second visit, he stays until 1 a.m., recording later: 'Vein of conversation decidedly gallant.' [D1: 95]

9 First meeting of the Men and Women's Club, founded by London University mathematician Karl Pearson, for discussion of a wide range of subjects relating to human sexuality and gender roles. The Club was probably the model for Shaw's comic invention of 'The Ibsen Club' in *The Philanderer*. [Judith R. Walkowitz, 'Science, Feminism and Romance: The Men and Women's Club 1885–1889', *History Workshop: A Journal of Socialist and Feminist Historians*, no. 21 (Spring 1986), 37–59; A.M. Gibbs, ' "Giant Brain... No Heart": Bernard Shaw's

Reception in Criticism and Biography', *Irish University Review*, vol. 26, no.1, (1996), 24–7]

10 Jenny Patterson declares her passion for Shaw, but he is '*virgo intacta* still'. [D1: 96; CL1: 151]

18 Shaw purchases French letters, anticipating a consummation of his relations with Jenny Patterson. Returning home he examines them and is 'extraordinarily revolted'. He later endures 'forced caresses' at Jenny Patterson's house before going to Lady Wilde's. Returning later he finds Mrs Patterson not at home. [D1: 97; CL1: 151]

19 After visiting the Salts at Tilford, Shaw calls on Jenny Patterson, but is too late to see her. [D1: 98]

22 Shaw attends a talk by Laurence Gronlund and carries on a discussion with him almost single handedly for nearly two hours. [D1: 98]

26 Shaw celebrates his 29th birthday with 'a new experience', the loss of his virginity with Jenny Patterson. [D1: 55, 99; Peters 30]

29 Finding Jenny Patterson waiting when he returns home, he walks her to Brompton Square where he stays until after midnight. Hereafter he visits Jenny Patterson several times per week. [D1: 100]

30 Shaw attends a Socialist League choir meeting, walking with May Morris afterwards. [D1: 100]

August

Shaw begins contributing periodically to *The Magazine of Music*. [D1: 53; Lbib2: 528]

3 (Mon) Shaw writes a detailed account of his affair with Jenny Patterson to Edward McNulty, and later wrote 'a rather fierce letter' to Jenny herself. Sidney Webb tells Shaw of a recent disappointment in love. [D1: 101]

4 Shaw resolves to 'begin new *Pilgrim's Progress* at once', an intention apparently not carried out. [D1: 101]

9 With Archer, Shaw hears Hyndman lecturing in Regents Park; in the evening Shaw lectures on 'Socialism and Scoundrelism' at Hammersmith. [D1: 103]

10 Shaw purchases an unconventional one-piece knitted woollen suit from Jaeger's. [D1: 103]

14 Shaw reads the second volume of *Das Kapital* in German with Sidney Webb and has nightmares that night which he attributes to drinking lemonade. Writing to Graham Wallas on 17 August, Webb says 'I have begun to teach German to G.B. Shaw, the embryo-novelist. He knows "and" and "the" only. We began Marx, *Kapital*, vol. 2 – not the easiest of books. We read 2 pages in 2 hours, accompanying each word with a philological disser-

	tation.' [D1: 104; *The Letters of Sidney and Beatrice Webb*, ed. Norman MacKenzie, 3 vols, (1978), 1: 93; I&R 44]
23	Shaw attends William Morris's lecture 'What is to become of the Middle Classes?' [D1: 106]
24	Shaw hears rumours that Eleanor Marx and Edward Aveling may part. [D1: 106]

Autumn

The Dramatic Review ceases to pay Shaw but he keeps up his contributions anyway until early 1886 [D1: 53; CL1: 121]

September

6 (Sun)	Shaw attends a lecture in Hammersmith, supping afterwards with William Morris. [D1: 109]
13	Despite an attack of influenza, Shaw attends his usual Sunday night lecture at Hammersmith. [D1: 111]
16	Shaw agrees to serve on the Dialectical Society council. [D1: 111]
18	Shaw attends a Fabian Society meeting where Webb lectures on 'Socialism and Economics'. [D1: 112]
20	Shaw attends a Socialist League meeting in Hyde Park before travelling to Hammersmith with May Morris and others to hear a lecture by William Morris. [D1: 112]
21	Shaw learns of William Morris's arrest for 'obstructing traffic' while addressing a meeting in Dod Street. Morris acts as a voluntary martyr in the Socialists' free speech campaign. [D1: 113]
23	Shaw attends a meeting at Stepney Green to plan a Free Speech protest demonstration the following Sunday, Shaw agreeing to speak, be arrested and go to gaol if necessary. [CL1: 139]
27	Shaw speaks at the Socialists' free speech demonstration at the Burnett Road docks, and later at a Socialist League gathering in Hyde Park. The Home Office having backed down on the issue of public meetings and free speech, Shaw is not arrested. He visits Kelmscott House in the evening with the intention of seeing May Morris. [D1: 114]

October

2 (Fri)	Shaw attends a Fabian lecture by Rev. Charles Marson on 'Christian Socialism'. [D1: 115]
3	Busy juggling relationships, Shaw records in his diary that: 'Alice Lockett called... After tea went to South Kensington and called on J[enny] P[atterson]'. [D1: 116]
8	A letter from Shaw to Alice Lockett indicates that she wants their relationship to continue. Shaw refuses her proposal for a meeting with a cry of 'Avaunt, sorceress'. After saying 'lovemaking grows tedious to me – the emotion has evaporated

from it', Shaw rhetorically concludes this letter with the statement that when love has gone from him he is remorseless: 'I hurl the truth about like destroying lightning.' [CL1: 142–3]

10 Shaw hears William Morris lecture at the Working Men's College in Ormond Street. [D1: 117]

11 Shaw speaks in Hyde Park for the Socialist League in the afternoon, and at Hammersmith in the evening on 'The Attitude of Socialists toward other Bodies'. He sups afterwards with the Morrises. [D1: 117]

16 Shaw chairs a Fabian meeting at which Walter Crane speaks on 'Art'. [D1: 118]

18 Shaw attends a Socialist League meeting at Hyde Park and proceeds afterwards to Hammersmith to hear William Morris lecture, but leaves before the end. [D1: 118]

19 Shaw still disputing with Swan Sonnenschein over payment for 'The Miraculous Revenge', published in March in *Time*. [CL1: 143]

21 Shaw lectures on the 'Division of Society into Classes' at a Socialist League meeting at 13 Farringdon Road. [D1: 119]

25 Shaw delivers a 'very dull and bad' lecture on 'Competition' at the Woolwich Radical Club. [D1: 57, 120]

28 Shaw lectures again on 'Driving Capital Out of the Country' to the North London branch of the Socialist League. [D1: 89, 120]

29 Following a meeting of the Psychical Research Society, Frank Podmore dares Shaw and three other members to spend the night at the supposedly haunted Ivy House in Wandsworth. Shaw later records in his diary: 'Slept there. Terrific nightmare.' [D1: 121; CL1: 187]

30 Shaw attends a Browning Society meeting where he makes an extended reply to painter and writer John Nettleship's lecture on 'Browning's Development as Poet or Maker'. [D1: 121]

November

1 (Sun) Shaw lectures on 'Socialism and Individualism' at the National Secular Society. [D1: 122]

8 'Tremendous heckling successfully answered' at Shaw's Hammersmith Club lecture on 'Socialism and Radicalism'. He repeats this lecture on nine subsequent occasions. [D1: 123]

18 Shaw takes the chair at a Dialectical Society meeting, and later attends a Fabian Executive meeting. [D1: 125]

22 For his first provincial lecture, at the Secular Hall in Leicester, Shaw lectures again on the subject of 'Socialism and Scoundrelism'. [D1: 54, 103, 126]

24 Shaw begins attending meetings of an 'economic circle' at stockbroker Henry R. Beeton's home at 42 Belsize Square, Hampstead.

This group evolved from the Hampstead Historical Society formed in the Autumn of 1884 by Charlotte Wilson for study and discussion of Marx and Proudhon. Shaw recalls attending some of the meetings of the Hampstead Historical Society in Mrs Wilson's home in 1885, before the venue changed to the Beeton house. Mrs Wilson was one of the first women students at Cambridge, an anarchist and a prominent early Fabian. The discussion group, the members of which included Sidney Webb, Philip Wicksteed and London University Professors of political economy, H. S. Foxwell and F. Y Edgeworth, was to become the British Economic Association. [D1: 54–5, 126; I&R 42, 43]

25 Shaw lectures at the North London Branch of the Socialist League on 'Socialism and Radicalism'. [D1: 126]

26 Shaw attends a meeting of the Bedford Society, at which higher education for women pioneer, Dr Sophie Bryant, spoke on 'The Sentiment of Nationality as Rational and as Righteous'. Bryant was to become, from 1895 to 1918, headmistress of the North London Collegiate School for Ladies, where Lucinda Elizabeth Shaw became singing mistress in January 1886. [D1: 127]

27 In his diary, Shaw records how he 'saw the great burst of falling stars [the Leonid meteor showers]'. [D1: 127]

29 Shaw lectures on 'Socialism and Radicalism' at the Eleusis Workmen's Club in Chelsea. [D1: 128]

December

2 (Wed) Shaw chairs and contributes to discussion at a Dialectical Society meeting where W. A. King lectures on 'The Celibacy of the Richer Classes' (an unwitting preview of Shaw's marital relationship). [D1: 128]

7 Shaw attends a performance of Pinero's *Mayfair*. [D1: 129]

10 Shaw lectures on 'Art' at the Bedford Society. [D1: 130]

12 Shaw returns William Archer's cheque for one pound, six and eightpence, sent to pay Shaw for 'intellectual property'. Archer's column had drawn on ideas expressed by Shaw during a tour the two had recently made of London's galleries. [CL1: 145–6]

13 Shaw visits Lee. [D1: 130]

14 Archer having returned his cheque to Shaw, Shaw promptly re-returns it, accompanied by a letter disputing the validity of Archer's concept of intellectual property. [CL1: 146–7]

16 Shaw attends a Dialectical Society meeting. He begins preparing *The Irrational Knot* for serial publication. [D1: 131]

17 Shaw attends a lecture on Shakespeare at a meeting of the Royal Society of Literature. [D1: 131]

18 Shaw attends a Fabian Society lecture by Annie Besant on 'How to Nationalize Accumulated Wealth'. In a letter to Andreas

Scheu (an Austrian revolutionary and close friend of William Morris), which he commenced writing on December 17, Shaw described this lecture as a sign that radical Socialists were drifting towards the Fabian Society, and jokingly predicted that the latter would 'rise resplendent as the Salvation Army of Socialism'. [D1: 131; Shaw to Andreas Scheu, 17 December 1885, Internationaal Instituut voor Sociale Geschiedenis, Amsterdam; DHL]

20 Death of Shaw's maternal grandfather, Walter Bagnall Gurly in Carlow. [Lgen 20; D1: 132; O'D 97]

Shaw lectures again on the 'Division of Society into Classes' at a Social Democratic Federation meeting. [D1: 119]

22 Alice Lockett writes to Shaw (on notepaper carrying a mourning border): 'Humph! So you think that I am so fond of you that I shall send you my photograph by return of post.' She absolutely refuses. This letter probably marks the conclusion of the Shaw–Lockett romance, but they kept in touch for many years, and Alice borrowed money from Shaw during the First World War when her husband Dr Sharpe was in military service. [BL MS Add 50511; DHL]

23 Shaw reaches an oral agreement with Henry Champion to publish *Cashel Byron's Profession* in a 1/- edition of 2500, with an author's royalty of 1d. per copy. [D1: 132–3]

Late 1885

Bessie Shaw finds new employment as a teacher of singing in high schools. [D1: 54]

Shaw begins reading German once a week with Sidney Webb. [D1: 54]

1886

Shaw's routine of attending meetings, lectures and performances, and writing lectures, articles and reviews remains basically the same as in the previous year, except that his appointment as art critic for *The World* necessitates more frequent visits to the galleries. He is also writing art notes for *Our Corner*, book reviews for the *Pall Mall Gazette*, and musical criticism for the *Dramatic Review*. Enjoying intimate friendships with Annie Besant, May Morris and Edith Bland, and frequent correspondence with Alice Lockett, Shaw attempts (unsuccessfully) to shift relations with Jenny Patterson onto a platonic footing. Letters to him in the summer of this year from Patterson and May Morris show he had been expressing a preference for friendly companionship to the toils of possessive love (a theme reflected in his play, *The Philanderer*). For self-improvement, he works his way through Ollendorff's book of German language lessons, and buys an alarm clock with the object of starting work earlier in the day. He attends numerous meetings of the Fabian, Dialectical, Social Democratic Federation, Socialist League, Bedford, Browning, Shelley, Psychical and Hampstead Historical Societies.

January

Bessie Shaw appointed as choir and singing teacher at the North London Collegiate School, where she remains until her retirement in 1906. Before that she had taught at the Clapham High School. [CL1: 228]

4 (Mon) After having procrastinated for months about buying an alarm clock, Shaw now complains about the clock disturbing his sleep. 'Set the new alarum clock to wake me at 8, which it did after keeping me awake all night dreaming of it'. [D1: 137]

6 In a letter to Shaw, Jenny Patterson writes: 'My dearest I shall not go away now... I love you... when you come let it be fairly early so I may get to sleep before 2 a.m.' [BL MS Add 50544]

9 Following a visit to Jenny Patterson's, Shaw records in his diary: 'Went to J[enny] P[atterson's]. Revulsion.' [D1: 138]

10 Shaw lectures at the Hammersmith Radical Club on 'Socialism and Scoundrelism'. [D1: 138]

12 Shaw and the *Vanity Fair* journalist and novelist Tighe Hopkins (the latter 'bent on seduction') try to outstay each other at Jenny Patterson's house, but Hopkins must leave first to catch his train. [D1: 138; CL1: 195]

15 Shaw plays Krogstad in a private reading of Henrietta Frances Lord's translation of Ibsen's *A Doll's House* (entitled *Nora*) at the Avelings' house in Great Russell Street. In his Preface to *The Irrational Knot* (a work he described as 'an early attempt on the part of the Life Force to write *A Doll's House*') Shaw said that at the time of this reading he 'concerned himself very little about Ibsen', and that his interest in him was not awakened until later when William Archer translated *Peer Gynt* to him *viva voce*. Of the 1886 reading he recalled that he 'chattered and ate caramels in the back drawing-room (our green-room) whilst Eleanor Marx, as Nora, brought Helmer to book at the other side of the folding doors'. [Prefs1: 184; Auto1: 96, 301 n16; Wisenthal 5–6; Wein3: 48–9]

24 Shaw lectures again on the 'Division of Society into Classes' at the Walmer Castle Coffee Tavern. [D1: 141]

27 Shaw lectures again on 'Laissez Faire' at the Socialist League meeting. [D1: 56, 141]

31 Shaw lectures at Kelmscott House on 'Exchange, Fair and Unfair'. [D1: 142]

February

William Archer persuades Edmund Yates to appoint Shaw as art critic on *The World*, an appointment he holds until early 1890. [CL1: 145; I&R 28, 88; Wein3: 54]

2 (Tue) Shaw records in his diary: 'Archer proposes that I shall take over *The World* art criticism.' [D1: 143]

7 Shaw visits Jenny Patterson's house where, on her return from a theatrical tour, Lucy Shaw is laid up with pleurisy. Mrs Patterson nurses her for three weeks. [D1: 145; Farmer 54]

8 'Black Monday' demonstration against unemployment in which John Burns, Henry Hyde Champion, and H.M. Hyndman are arrested. [D1: 145; Hend 2: 206; Shaw's Fabian Tract No. 41, 'The Fabian Society: Its Early History', 8]

10 Publication of Shaw's first item of art criticism in *The World*. [Lbib2: 533; D1: 143]

21 Shaw attends a mass meeting of the unemployed at Hyde Park. [D1: 148]

23 Shaw records that he 'Received a copy of *Cashel Byron* printed at last'. This first issue of a Shaw novel in book form was published by Henry Hyde Champion's The Modern Press. It was 'printed from corrected and revised stereos of the original setting for the journal *To-Day*'. [D1: 148; Lbib1: 4]

24 Shaw again lectures on 'Laissez Faire' at the Hammersmith Radical Club. [D1: 56, 148]

26 Shaw defends Andrea del Sarto's artistic achievement at a meeting of the Browning Society. [D1: 149]

March

7 (Sun) Shaw's first meeting, at Jenny Patterson's house, with future playwright Alfred Sutro. [D1: 151]

Shaw lectures on 'Socialism and Scoundrelism' at St John's Temperance Hall, Edgeware Road, to an audience of about 150 people. [D1: 151]

10 At the Shelley Society's first open meeting Shaw shocks staid ears by proclaiming himself to be 'like Shelley, a Socialist, Atheist and Vegetarian'. Sitting on the platform at the meeting, playwright Henry Arthur Jones remarks in an aside to T. J. Wise: 'three damned good reasons why he ought to be chucked out'. [SSS 58; CL1: 145; I&R 45–6; Doris Arthur Jones, *The Life and Letters of Henry Arthur Jones* (1930), 221]

In the afternoon, Shaw goes to tea at William Archer's house to hear R. L. Stevenson's opinion of *Cashel Byron's Profession*. Stevenson had written to Archer to say he found the novel to be replete with 'strength, spirit, capacity, and sufficient self-sacrifice, which is the last chief point in a narrator. It is all mad,

mad and deliriously delightful.' In a parenthesis, Stevenson added 'I say Archer, my God, what women!' [D1: 152]

Shaw writes his only surviving letter to Jenny Patterson (about Pakenham Beatty's attentions to Lucy Carr Shaw, and saying in a PS that he has an 'unbroken array of engagements right up to the 23rd [of March]'). [CL1: 151–2]

Jenny Patterson writes to Shaw on this day, saying: 'You are absolutely free to do as you please. I resent you discussing me with your women friends. I can imagine your way of doing it.' [BL MS Add 50544]

13 Jenny Patterson takes Lucy Shaw to her second home, Chandos House, at Broadstairs to recuperate from her pleurisy. Bessie Shaw joins them in the second week of her stay. [Farmer 54–5]

19 Annie Besant and Frank Podmore are elected to the Fabian Society Executive Committee, bringing its membership to seven (Shaw, Sidney Webb, Edward Pease, Hubert Bland and Charlotte Wilson being the other five). Shaw keeps company almost daily with Annie Besant at this time. [Pease 53; Peters 40]

30 Jenny Patterson (in a letter dated 1 April but postmarked 30 March 1886) calls Shaw a 'monster of ingratitude' for sending only a postcard to thank her for her gift of violets hand-picked by her. [BL MS Add 50544]

April

4 (Sun) Henry Sparling tells Shaw of his love affair with May Morris. [D1: 158]

5 Bessie Shaw and Lucy Shaw return from Broadstairs, too late in the season for Lucy to obtain a theatrical engagement. [Farmer 55]

15 In a teasing letter to Shaw, Jenny Patterson says he must have some new clothes, and wishes he would come to Broadstairs to offer a sight of 'the coming man'. [BL MS Add 50544]

May

Letters from Jenny Patterson contain repeated complaints of Shaw's 'cruelty' and declarations of her devotion to him during their 'nearly ten months of intimacy' (11 May). [BL MS Add 50544]

(Michael Holroyd's suggestion, based, as he says, on 'meagre evidence', that Jenny Patterson may have had a miscarriage at this time, is disputed by Fred D. Crawford. [Hol 1: 251; Crawford, *Victorian Review*, Spring 1989])

5 (Wed) Letter from May Morris to Shaw applauding his resolution to maintain their relationship on a basis of comradeship rather

than lovemaking, but promising to send a photograph of herself, as requested by him, nevertheless. [BL MS Add 50541]

7 Shaw attends the Shelley Society's private production of *The Cenci* at the Grand Theatre, Islington, to which the Lord Chamberlain has refused a licence on the grounds that it will deprave the audience. [CL1: 154; D1: 168]

8 A letter from Jenny Patterson indicates his relationship with socialist Grace Black had commenced by this time: 'Of course if you care so much for Miss Black or Miss anyone else and not care for me you will do nothing but pain me.' In the following year (25 May) Grace Black admitted that she was in love with Shaw. [BL MS Add 50544]

9 Shaw writes to Jenny Patterson that their 'future intercourse must be platonic'. [D1: 168]

13 Having received Shaw's letter, a distraught Jenny Patterson calls on Shaw. After 'much pathetic petting and kissing' Shaw placates Jenny Patterson. [D1: 169]

15 Shaw calls on Jenny Patterson where he finds that his mother and Lucy are already visiting. In his diary, Shaw records: 'Slight scene [with Jenny Patterson] in consequence of my refusing to budge from our new platonic relations.' [D1: 169]

16 Shaw lectures again on 'Socialism and Individualism'. [D1: 170, 122]

17 Jenny Patterson to Shaw: 'I have done for you what I have done for no other: loved you with all my soul and body.' [BL MS Add 50544]

June

Shaw publishes an unfavourable review of *The Cenci* in *Our Corner*. [Lbib2: 535; CL1: 155]

1 (Tue) Shaw reads a paper on 'Unearned Income' to the British Economic Association. [D1: 55]

*c.*11 Jenny Patterson reports that she has been ill and can't afford a doctor. [BL MS Add 50544]

26 Shaw spends the day and 'a memorable evening!' at Vandeleur Lee's house with fellow Fabian, Edith (Nesbit) Bland. On this day he records 'I discovered that she had become passionately attached to me. As she was a married woman with children and her husband my friend and colleague she had to live down her fancy. We remained very good friends.' [D1: 34, 179]

27 Shaw resumes sexual relations with Jenny Patterson. [D1: 180]

July

5 (Mon) Evidently responding to Shaw's desire for friendship rather than love, Jenny Patterson writes: 'Goodnight my love. My friend

and lover. I am content that there are no barriers between us – that you have taken me back. I will try to make you content with me be my friend when you will My lover when you will– but let the friend be first.' [BL MS Add 50544; CL1: 151–2]

21 Shaw attends a performance of Pinero's farce, *The Schoolmistress* at the Court Theatre. [D1: 186]

August

10 (Tue) Shaw writes to Andreas Scheu to show off his newly acquired prowess in German, and ends the letter in French. [Shaw to Andreas Scheu, 10 Aug 1886, Internationaal Instituut voor Sociale Geschiedenis, Amsterdam; DHL]

11 Shaw begins revising *An Unsocial Socialist* for printing by Swan Sonnenschein. [D1: 190]

19 In a letter to Alice Lockett, Shaw outlines his theory of human unoriginality: 'at least nine tenths of me is a simple repetition of nine tenths of you'. [CL1: 158]

26 Shaw finishes revising *An Unsocial Socialist* and dispatches it to Swan Sonnenschein. He also begins revising *The Irrational Knot* for *Our Corner*. [CL1: 159; D1: 194]

29 Lee's last preserved letter to Shaw shows his feelings to Shaw to be warm and friendly. [SCG 93]

30 August – 6 September

Shaw's cousin, Robert Carroll, again visits the Shaws in London. Shaw and he spend time on 1 September 'playing and singing', and attend a Promenade Concert at Covent Garden on 3 September. [D1: 195]

September

14 (Tue) First mention of Oscar Wilde in Shaw's Diaries, as one of a group of people at the house of novelist and historian Joseph Fitzgerald Molloy. Shaw's acquaintance with Wilde probably began at least as early as November 1879. [D1: 198]

17 The Fabian Society carries Annie Besant's motion that Socialist organizations should come together to form a political party. Instead of promoting unity, however, stormy debate preceding the vote widens the existing rift between collectivists (Shaw, Besant, John Burns, and the Social Democratic Federation) and anarchists (led by William Morris and Charlotte Wilson). [D1: 198–9; G. B. Shaw, – *The Fabian Society: Its Early History* (1892), 12–13; Pease 67–8; Auto1: 135–6]

18–22 Shaw is troubled with specks on his vision. [D1: 225]

25 Lucy Shaw is engaged as 'Phyllis' in the company of the popular comic opera *Dorothy*, by B. C. Stephenson and Alfred Cellier, at the Gaiety Theatre, with her future husband, tenor Charles

Butterfield, who played 'Tom Strutt', under the stage name Cecil Burt. Shaw attended a matinée of this production on 4 December 1886. [Farmer 55–6; D1: 218; DHL]

October

1 (Fri) Shaw's lecture on 'Socialism and the Family' outrages the Fabian Society. [D1: 202]

5 Jenny Patterson writes to Shaw: 'You are a man of stone without either feelings or passion.' [BL MS Add 50544]

10 Shaw delivers a revised version of his earlier lecture on 'Competition' at Morris's Kelmscott House. [D1: 57, 204]

17 Shaw sends revised version of *An Unsocial Socialist* to Swan Sonnenschein. [CL1: 160]

27 Shaw finishes revising the proofs of *An Unsocial Socialist.* [D1: 208]

November

5 (Fri) Annie Besant proposes the formation of a Fabian Parliamentary League. [D 1: 210]

6 Shaw plays Chubb Dumbleton in a copyright performance of Edward Rose's *Odd to Say the Least of It!* at the Novelty Theatre. [D1: 211; Wein3: 49]

9 Shaw participates in a prohibited Socialist rally at Trafalgar Square, and lectures at the British Economic Association on 'Interest: Its Nature and Justification.' [D1: 55, 211]

25 Lucy Shaw, in the company of Harry Douglas Butterfield, brother of Charles, visits her mother (Bessie Shaw), upon which occasion Charles is acknowledged as her fiancé. [Farmer 56]

27 **Lee suffers a heart attack and dies while preparing for bed.** Shaw later (Feb 1916) told O'Bolger: 'He had no relatives; and his possessions passed, I presume, to the young lady who had rescued him from the entire loneliness in his latter days', a housemaid who, Shaw relates, had been exposed trying to pass for a member of the musical society at one of Lee's 'at homes', a difficulty which led to the disbanding of Lee's musical group at the house in Park Lane. [SCG 94; CL3: 359–60]

30 Actor-singer Hayden Coffin tells Lucy of Lee's death three days previously. She hurries to inform Shaw. In the 1935 Preface to *London Music,* Shaw was to claim that 'The postmortem and inquest revealed the fact that [Lee's] brain was diseased and had been so for a long time.' O'Donovan points out that 'A post-mortem was made, and the cause of death was found to be extensive heart disease.' On searching for further post-mortem details he finds that records are missing, and that there is no available evidence to support Shaw's assertion of Lee's death

from brain disease. He also points out that 'Lee's alleged father, Colonel Vandeleur, died of brain disease.' ('Softening of the Brain, 3 years certified' from Col Vandeleur's death certificate). Dan H. Laurence conjectures that Shaw may have mistakenly applied the latter information to Lee, or else was attempting to exculpate Lee 'for questionable behaviour during his last years in London'. [D1: 217; SM1: 50; Auto 1: 194, 305; SCG 94–6; Farmer 57; Prefs 3: 335 n11; DHL; Erv 63]

Late 1886

Shaw becomes close to Annie Besant, but never becomes sexually involved with her: 'During this year my work at the Fabian brought me much into contact with Mrs Besant, and towards the end of the year this intimacy became of a very close and personal sort, without, however, going further than friendship.' [D1: 136]

December

5 (Sun) Shaw lectures at Kelmscott House on 'Illusions of Individualism'. [D1: 219]

8 Letter to Shaw from Jenny Patterson contains jealous comments about Grace Black, who she considers is poaching on her preserve. [BL MS Add 50544]

11 Recuperating from a cold, Shaw 'took a sort of holiday' from writing and reading. [D1: 220]

12 Shaw lectures at the Hammersmith Club on 'Socialism and Malthusianism'. [D1: 220]

14 Shaw 'did not get up till 10. Seem to be relapsing into bad habits.' [D1: 221]

16 Shaw quarrels with Jenny Patterson. [D1: 221]

25 Shaw begins writing a new conclusion to *The Irrational Knot*. [D1: 223]

26 Shaw finishes *The Irrational Knot*. [D1: 223]

27 Shaw is introduced to the Russian Anarchist, Peter Kropotkin. [D1: 224]

31 Harpers in New York publish *Cashel Byron's Profession* in their Handy Series. A rival publisher had already pirated the novel in June 1886. [CL1: 61; Lbib1: 5]

1887

Shaw's earnings in 1887 derived from literary criticism for the *Pall Mall Gazette*, art criticism for *The World*, and the serial publication of *The Irrational Knot* and *Love Among the Artists* in *Our Corner*. He continued to attend the same society meetings except that in July he joined the Charing

Cross Parliament ('a mock parliament of Socialists, founded by Annie Besant, which met weekly from June to September 1887') whose Friday meetings curtailed his attendance at meetings of the Browning and New Shakespeare Societies. Shaw continued his sexual liaison with Jenny Patterson, although he saw her far less frequently than Annie Besant, with whom his relations remained platonic.

January

7 (Fri) Jenny Patterson writes concerning a pair of slippers she has had made for Shaw: 'Your slippers are waiting for you. So come for them.' This episode is probably recalled in the drama arising from Eliza Doolittle's care of Henry Higgins's slippers in Act 4 of *Pygmalion*. [BL MS Add 50545]

12 James R. Osgood, Harpers' London representative, informs Shaw that the Harpers' Handy Series edition of *Cashel Byron's Profession* is out in America. He offers Shaw a £10 honorarium for the book. [CL1: 161]

13 Shaw attends a 'boxing show' at St James's Hall with J. L. Joynes. (Dan H. Laurence points out that D1: 233 incorrectly assumes that Shaw took Joynes's son to the show. Joynes was not married, and did not have a son.) [DHL; D1: 233]

16 Hampered by a severe cold, Shaw lectures at 13 Farringdon Road on 'Some Illusions of Individualism'. The next day, Shaw records in his diary: 'Voice gone.' [D1: 234]

22 Shaw attends a performance of Arthur Wing Pinero's farce *The Hobby-Horse*. [D1: 235]

25 Shaw reads, for review in the *Pall Mall Gazette*, Samuel Butler's *Luck, or Cunning?*, an anti-Darwinian treatise and polemic that profoundly influenced his thinking on evolution. He continues his reading of the work on 17 and 28 February and 1, 2 and 5 March. On 7 and 8 March he writes the review which was published in *The Gazette* on 31 May 1887. [D1: 236, 243, 246–8]

February

Swan Sonnenschein publish *An Unsocial Socialist*. Shaw immediately urges them to take over the British publication of *Cashel Byron's Profession* from the Modern Press, which they do not do. [Lbib1: 10; CL1: 159, 162]

6 (Sun) Shaw lectures at a Social Democratic Federation meeting in Blackfriar's Road on 'Socialism and the Bad Side of Human Nature'. [D1: 240]

7 The Shaws receive a month's notice to quit 36 Osnaburgh Street because the landlord is planning to sell the house. [D1: 240]

8 Shaw agrees to represent the Socialist League in a debate with Charles Bradlaugh of the Secular Society, scheduled for 20 March.

	(The debate was cancelled, Bradlaugh having been advised to back out.) Shaw also attends a performance of Pinero's *Dandy Dick* at the Court Theatre. [CL1: 164; D1: 240]
9	Shaw writes to the secretary of the Socialist League to give warning that he will not be bound by the League's manifesto in his debate with Charles Bradlaugh. [CL1: 164]
13	Shaw lectures to the Social Democratic Federation on 'Exact Definitions of Socialistic Terms' at Phoenix Hall; he gives a second lecture at Farringdon Road on 'Dangers and Fallacies of Individualism'. [D1: 241]
15	Shaw is notified of the Socialist League's intention to debate Bradlaugh in print as well as orally, with E. Belfort Bax as the League's representative in the print forum. [CL1: 164]
16	Shaw chairs a debate between the Secularist G. W. Foote and the Socialist Annie Besant. [CL2: 762]
20	Shaw lectures in the morning at Cleveland Hall on 'Driving Capital out of the Country'. In the evening he lectures at the West Marylebone Working Men's Club on 'The Attitudes of Socialists Towards Other Propagandists'. [D1: 243]
21	Shaw donates about 70 books to the Kyrle Society, an organization which worked to improve the living conditions of the working classes. [D1: 184, 244]
22	Shaw revises Annie Besant's draft of the Fabian Parliamentary League manifesto. [D1: 244]

March

4 (Fri)	Shaw vacates 36 Osnaburgh Street, but since the new rooms at 29 Fitzroy Square, Bloomsbury, are not yet habitable, he stays for two and a half weeks (till 21 March) with J. Kingston Barton at 2 Courtfield Road, South Kensington, and then moves in to 29 Fitzroy Square. [D1: 228, 247, 253]
7	Lucy Shaw goes on tour with *Dorothy*, this time in the title role, opening at Cardiff on this night, and proceeding to Birmingham, Nottingham, Newcastle upon Tyne, Blackpool, Liverpool, Dublin, Glasgow, Edinburgh and Hull. [Farmer 57–8]
10	Shaw lectures at a meeting of the Westminster Radical Club on 'The Meaning of Socialism'. [D1: 249]
12	Shaw attends the opening night of *La Traviata* at Covent Garden. [D1: 250]
13	Shaw lectures on 'Socialism and Radicalism' at the Chiswick Liberal Club; and on the same day debates with the Rev. F. W. Ford (in place of Charles Bradlaugh) at South Place Chapel, on the proposition 'That the Welfare of the community necessitates the transfer of the land and existing capital of the country from private owners to the State'. [D1: 250]

18 Jenny Patterson follows Shaw as he walks Annie Besant to her bus. [D1: 252]

21 The Shaws move into their new apartment at 29 Fitzroy Square. [D1: 253]

22 Shaw lectures on 'The Working Day' at Culvert Hall, Battersea. [D1: 253]

27 Shaw has another uncomfortable encounter with Jenny Patterson. He records in his diary: 'Began a letter to Mrs Besant. J[enny] P[atterson] came in. Reproaches.' [D1: 255]

April

3 (Sun) Shaw lectures on 'Some Illusions of Individualism' at the Labour Emancipation League. [D1: 257]

10 Shaw lectures at Kelmscott House on 'The Rent of Exceptional Ability'. [D1: 258]

11 Shaw addresses a mass meeting at Hyde Park protesting the Irish Coercion Bill. [D1: 259]

26 Lucy Shaw receives 'a tremendous ovation' and an excellent review as Dorothy at the Gaiety Theatre, Dublin. [Farmer 58]

May

2 (Mon) Having failed to gain satisfaction from Swan Sonnenschein's editors over the publication of *Cashel Byron's Profession*, Shaw writes direct to the proprietor of the firm, William Swan Sonnenschein. [CL1: 167]

3 William Swan Sonnenschein informs Shaw that he cannot at present republish *Cashel Byron's Profession* but that he will consider including it in their series of cheap reprints scheduled to commence in autumn. (A revised second edition was eventually published by Walter Scott in the spring of 1889.) [CL1: 167; Lbib1: 6]

4 In a debate over the warring interests of members of the Fabian Society, Shaw argues unsuccessfully that the Society should be disbanded. [D1: 266]

7 Shaw attacks H. M. Hyndman's Marxist theories in a letter published in the *Pall Mall Gazette*. [Lbib2: 540; CL1: 168]

10 On this day, Shaw recorded that 'Alice Lockett called... we got back on the old terms in less than five minutes.' [D1: 268]

11 An unpleasant scene with Mrs Edith Bland occurs after she insists on coming with him to Fitzroy Square. His mother (Bessie Shaw) being absent, Shaw insists she leave the house as being alone with him would compromise her. [D1: 268]

Publication of Hyndman's rebuttal of Shaw's attack in the *Pall Mall Gazette*. [CL1: 168]

12 Shaw again attacks Hyndman in the *Pall Mall Gazette*. [CL1: 168]

14 Shaw begins writing his sixth novel, but abandons it a month later. The text is published posthumously in 1958 as *An Unfinished Novel* edited by Stanley Weintraub. The novel draws on his relationship with Edith Bland. On 31 August 1889, Shaw wrote to Tighe Hopkins: 'Some time ago I tried novelizing again, and wrote a chapter & a half: but I could not stand the form: it is too clumsy and unreal. Sometimes in spare moments I write dialogues.' [Cornell 4617 Box 10; D1: 229, 269; Lbib1: 273]

16 Publication in the *Pall Mall Gazette* of Hyndman's angry rejoinder to Shaw. [CL1: 168]

21 Shaw speaks at a second anti-Coercion Bill demonstration at Victoria Park. [D1: 271]

24 *The Pall Mall Gazette*, having declined to publish a third letter from Shaw attacking Hyndman, prints a letter from Annie Besant which convincingly promotes Fabian socialism over Hyndman's doctrinaire Marxism. [CL1: 168]

28 Shaw replies to two letters written to him on 24 and 25 May by Grace Black, in the second of which she had said: 'I guessed you would think I am in love with you. So I am, but that has nothing to do with my letter.' [BL MS Add 50511; D1: 272]

31 Publication in the *Pall Mall Gazette*, under the title 'Darwin Denounced', of Shaw's review of Samuel Butler's *Luck or Cunning?* [Tyson 277–8; Lbib2: 540; CL1: 300]

June

8 (Wed) Shaw writes a passionate plea to William Stead, editor of the *Pall Mall Gazette*, to use his paper to fight social injustice and promote nationalization of land and capital. [CL1: 170–4]

12 Shaw lectures at Kelmscott House on 'Socialist Politics'. [D1: 276]

14 Other commitments cause Shaw to abandon the new novel begun on 14 May. [D1: 221, 342]

15 Shaw seconds Rev. Stewart Headlam's move to disband the Dialectical Society. The move is defeated. [D1: 277]

21 Shaw records that he 'went down to Piccadilly Circus via Shaftesbury Ave. to see the Procession [for Queen Victoria's Golden Jubilee]'. [D1: 279]

July

3 (Sun) Shaw becomes a member of Annie Besant's mock Charing Cross Parliament, later serving on its Socialist 'government' as President of Local Government. The 'government' took office

on 15 July, with Henry Hyde Champion as Prime Minister and First Lord of the Treasury. [Lbib1: 13; D1: 274, 229]

18 Shaw sees Sarah Bernhardt playing in Sardou's *Theodora* at the Lyceum. [D1: 285]

25 Shaw begins the writing of a story 'The Truth About Don Giovanni', eventually published under the title 'Don Giovanni Explains' in his *Short Stories, Scraps and Shavings* in 1932. (The tale, which clearly reflects Shaw's amatory entanglements of the time, is erroneously included as an autobiographical work in Auto1: 164–5.) [D1: 287]

August

1 (Mon) Shaw completes the writing of 'The Truth About Don Giovanni'. [D1: 289]

7, 14, 21 Serial publication in the *National Reformer* of Shaw's review, 'Karl Marx and *Das Kapital*', of the first English translation, by Samuel Moore and Edward Aveling (ed. Friedrich Engels), of Volume I of Marx's *Kapital*. [Lbib2: 542; CL1: 168]

18 Shaw declines to write further 'European Correspondence' for the American journal *The Epoch* after the editor requests that he write on topics such as 'how English swells who have nothing to do pass away their time'. [CL1: 174]

20 Suffering from a bad cold made worse by the draughty theatre, Shaw attends a special rehearsal for the autumn tour of *Dorothy* with Lucy in the title role. Afterwards he went home, wrote to Jenny Patterson and 'sang a lot in spite of the cold. Very roupily.' [D1: 293]

30 Shaw begins writing his Preface to *Love Among the Artists* for *Our Corner*. [D1: 295]

September

Finding the British Museum too full of distracting acquaintances, Shaw moves his work-base to the top floor of 29 Fitzroy Square. [D1: 228]

3 (Sat) Shaw resumes work on *Rhinegold*. [D1: 107, 296]

25 Shaw lectures at Kelmscott House on 'Choosing a Career Nowadays'. [D1: 301]

October

2 (Sun) Shaw lectures on 'Practical Socialism' at the Chiswick Liberal Club. [D1: 302]

4 Shaw delivers a longhand copy of the first two acts of *Rhinegold* to William Archer. [CL1: 175]

6 Shaw reads the first two acts of *Rhinegold* to William Archer who 'received it with great contempt'. Archer was 'utterly contemptuous of its construction' and during the reading of Act 2 'fell into a

deep slumber', whereupon Shaw 'softly put the manuscript away and let him have his sleep out.' [D1: 304; Shaw, 'How William Archer Impressed Bernard Shaw', in 'Preface' to William Archer, *Three Plays*, 1927, repr. in Shaw's *Pen Portraits and Reviews*, 1931]

14 Shaw speaks at a free speech meeting at South Place urging the release of the Chicago anarchists. [D1: 306]

29 Shaw begins writing Fabian tract No. 6, published as 'The True Radical Programme', and urging taxation of unearned income, an eight-hour working day, nationalization of the railways, and votes for women. [D1: 310]

November

2 (Wed) Shaw hears Joseph Mazzini Wheeler lecture on 'The Social Experiment at Oneida'. [D1: 311]

13 Shaw participates in the 'Bloody Sunday' demonstration in Trafalgar Square. Socialist and Anarchist bodies protesting against the government's Irish policy and the right to free speech in public places are broken up by police and the Foot Guards and Life Guards. Although Socialists such as H. M. Hyndman, John Burns, and R. B. Cunninghame Graham are arrested, the protesters win a moral victory, securing the right of free speech in Trafalgar Square. [CL1: 177; D1: 315; I&R 402; Hol1: 184–5; Bernard Shaw, *The Fabian Society: Its Early History* (1892), 9–10]

15 Shaw has a 'tedious quarrel' with Jenny Patterson over Annie Besant. [D1: 315]

20 Shaw attends a 'Free Speech' meeting in Hyde Park before proceeding to Trafalgar Square where police patrols discourage further gatherings. [D1: 317]

22 After the violence of Bloody Sunday, Shaw writes to William Morris, 'I object to a defiant policy altogether at present.' [CL1: 177]

28 Shaw proposes to William Swan Sonnenschein a new edition of *An Unsocial Socialist* with a preface added, and suggests he also consider publishing *Cashel Byron's Profession*. [CL1: 179]

November–December

Love Among the Artists serialized in *Our Corner*. [D1: 313; Lbib1: 46]

December

10 (Sat) The autumn tour of *Dorothy* is suspended for the Christmas recess at Bath. Lucy Shaw and Charles Butterfield make their way to London for their wedding on the 17th. [Farmer 58–9]

15 Mrs Cashel Hoey, cousin of GBS and Lucy, and successful novelist, calls on Lucy to congratulate her on her upcoming wedding. [Farmer 59]

17 **Lucy Shaw marries Charles Robert Butterfield at St John's Church, Charlotte Street.** Shaw prepared refreshments ('whisky and cake') for the wedding-guests at 29 Fitzroy Square, but he dined at the Wheatsheaf, his favourite vegetarian restaurant, and 'did not get to the church until the ceremony was over'. Georgina Sime thought that his absence from the ceremony 'made a crack in his sister's heart'. [D1: 229, 324; Farmer 59, quoting Sime and Nicholson, *Brave Spirits*, 154; SSS 150]

18 Shaw lectures at the Farringdon Hall on 'Choosing Our Parents'. [D1: 324]

23 Annie Besant and Shaw return the letters they had written to one another, and Annie reproaches him for his treatment of her. According to Hesketh Pearson, Shaw told him that she had drawn up a contract 'setting forth the terms on which they were to live together as man and wife', without her divorcing her husband who was still alive. There is no other evidence of this contract. Despite their continued professional cooperation, their close personal attachment comes to an end at this time. [D1: 34, 230, 325; Pearson 114]

24 While Shaw is out, Jenny Patterson calls and finds Annie Besant's returned letters on his table. She reads them and steals nine. Writing at 2 a.m. on Christmas Day she describes herself as 'the most miserable woman in London'. [BL MS Add 50545; D1: 326; Peters 44]

25 On Christmas morning, Jenny Patterson turns up at Shaw's door. Shaw records: 'Was awakened by J[enny] P[atterson] knocking at my door. She came about the letters.' Shaw retrieves and destroys the letters she had taken the previous day. 'Reading over my letters before destroying them rather disgusted me with the trifling of the last two years or so about women.'[D1: 230, 326]

27–29 Shaw writes the 'Sidney Trefusis' Postscript to Swan Sonnenschein's proposed cheaper edition of *An Unsocial Socialist.* [D1: 327]

29, 31 Shaw negotiates further with Swan Sonnenschein over *Cashel Byron's Profession* and the second edition of *An Unsocial Socialist.* [CL1: 179]

31 Shaw sees the New Year in with Jenny Patterson at her request. [D1: 328]

1888

Shaw's sexual relationship with Jenny Patterson (of which she leaves an eloquent testimony on 23 February) continues, as do their quarrels, and various relationships with other women are recorded. Early in the year Shaw has his first meeting with W. B. Yeats, and in the summer he first sees Janet Achurch on stage. He suffers from bouts of ill health (colds and various aches) and depression during this year. His journalistic earnings for the year amount to £150. He delivered 73 lectures, all for no fee.

January

1 (Sun) Shaw reads a reprinting of William Blake's 'The Marriage of Heaven and Hell' in the arts-and-crafts quarterly, *The Hobby Horse*. [D1: 334]

13 Shaw attends a séance at 'Mr Deakin's, 63 St. Peter's Rd, Mile End'. He found it 'a paltry fraud'. [D1: 338]

15 After visiting Dublin, Bessie Shaw brings her half-sister Georgina ('Georgie') Gurly to London. On 24 May 1888, Georgie returned to Carlow for a few months. She came back to live in London on 27 September 1888. Sometime following this Georgie seems to have become Jenny Patterson's live-in companion. [DHL; D1: 339]

Shaw meets his former idol, Alhambra dancer Erminia Pertoldi, the model for Mlle Bernadina de Sangallo (later renamed Erminia Pertoldi) in *Immaturity*. [D1: 339]

19 Shaw is appointed to write political leaders on *The Star*, newly founded by T. P. O'Connor. In a letter to Hubert Bland on 31 December 1887, Shaw had written of his imminent involvement in *The Star*, and revealed some misgivings about it: 'I have seen [T.P.] O'Connor, and am not so sanguine as I was about the paper.' [CL1: 183; D1: 340; University of Victoria, BC MS; DHL]

20 Publication of Shaw's first identifiable writing in *The Star*. [Lbib2: 546; D1: 340]

23 Shaw resumes work on his novel abandoned in June the previous year. Five days later (28 January) he again abandons the project, ending his career as a novelist. [D1: 342–3]

February

1 (Wed) Shaw lectures at Kelmscott House on 'Socialism and Economics'. [D1: 344]

5 Shaw lectures at the Secular Hall, Leicester, on 'Practical Socialism', returning to London the following morning. [D1: 346]

9 Shaw tenders his resignation from his editorial position on *The Star* to T. P. O'Connor: 'Dear Chief, This is my resignation... though what is to become of you and Mass^{ghm} [H. W. Massingham] when you have no one to guide you through the mists of sentimental Utopianism is more than I can foresee.' [I&R 88–9; CL1: 183–5; D1: 347]

10 O'Connor accepts Shaw's resignation, but arranges for Shaw to write occasional signed articles and notes for *The Star*. [D1: 347]

12 Shaw has his first meeting with W.B. Yeats at Kelmscott House. Shaw records this meeting in his diary: 'An Irishman named Yeats talked about Socialism a good deal. I lost my train and walked home, Yeats accompanying me as far as High St.' Yeats reported the meeting to Katherine Tynan: 'Last night at Morrises I met Bernard Shaw, who is certainly very witty. But like most people who have wit rather than humour, his mind is maybe somewhat wanting in depth – however, his stories are good they say.' [D1: 348; *The Collected Letters of W.B. Yeats*, ed. John Kelly and Eric Domville, vol. 1, 1865–1895, 50]

18 Shaw lectures on 'Socialism: Its Growth and Necessity' at a meeting of the Cambridge Fabian Society, and is given a sovereign to cover his expenses. [D1: 350]

20 Shaw returns all but the cost of his third-class rail fare to the secretary of the Cambridge Fabian Society. [D1: 350;CL1: 186]

23 Jenny Patterson writes to Shaw: 'Be as ardent as you were last week... I adore to be made love to like that. It takes my breath away at the time & leaves oh such a memory behind.' [BL MS Add 50545]

25 Shaw meets R. B. Cunninghame Graham for the first time at Kelmscott House.
Shaw also performs (under the pseudonym 'I. Roscius Garrick') with May Morris and Ernest Radford in Ada Radford's sketch *The Appointment*, an entertainment organized to support the Bryant and May Strike Fund. [D1: 352; Wein3: 51]

April

1 (Sun) Emma Brooke takes Shaw to task ('heaped abuse on me') about his relationship with Grace Gilchrist. He and Emma Brooke exchange letters about this on 4 April and spend almost a whole day discussing it on 12 April. On 24 April he 'wrote a letter to Miss Brooke about the Gilchrist affair which took up all the afternoon.'[D1: 362, 363, 365, 369; Erv 157–8]
In the evening, departing from his usual practice of writing his lectures on note cards, Shaw 'delivered an incoherent lecture at Battersea on nothing in particular'. [D1: 362]

14 Shaw makes the acquaintance of 'a pretty girl named Geraldine Spooner' with whom he becomes involved. Geraldine Spooner later became a member of the Fabian Society. Shaw's attentions not leading to matrimony, she married fellow Fabian, Herbert Wildon Carr in December 1890. She described Shaw as 'a strange and very wonderful looking man, tall, and thin as a whipping post, with a massive head.' He was 'different to every-

	body... because one side of his face was Christ-like, although the other was Mephistophelian.' [D1: 366]
	Instead of performing, Shaw joins the audience of a second Socialist League production of Ada Radford's *The Appointment*. [CL1: 106; D1: 366; Wein3: 51]
16	Shaw spends the day at the British Museum, 'Revising and making an important addition to the next instalment of *Love Among the Artists* for *Our Corner*.' [D1: 367]
22–23	Visiting Kate and Henry Salt at Tilford, and taking a Sunday walk to Gallows Hill on Hindhead, Shaw twice gets drenched by rain. This occasions Shaw's wry entry in the Diary : 'I have had a change of air and a holiday; and I have no doubt I shall be able to throw off their effect in a fortnight or so.' The visit was also the subject of a humorous article, 'A Sunday in the Surrey Hills', about the drawbacks of rural life, in the *Pall Mall Gazette* on 28 April. [D1: 369; I&R 260]
29	After lecturing in the morning on 'Old and New Radicalism' at the Bethnal Green Liberal and Radical Club, a fatigued Shaw gives a 'poor lecture' on 'Copyright' at Kelmscott House in the evening. [D1: 371]

June

5 (Tue)	Shaw first sees Janet Achurch on stage at the Olympic Theatre, playing Hester Prynne in a matinée copyright performance of Edward Aveling's adaptation of Nathaniel Hawthorne's *The Scarlet Letter*. Aveling appears on the programme under his theatre pseudonym 'Alec Nelson'. [D1: 382; DHL; Peters 56]
11	Shaw accepts Sutton & Co.'s invitation to write a book on Socialism for their University Economics Series. He works on it sporadically for three years with a working title, *Technical Socialism*. A second draft of this work, which remained unpublished in Shaw's lifetime, is included in Louis Crompton's edition of Shaw's unpublished essays, *The Road to Equality* (1971) under the title 'Capital and Wages'. [Lbib1: 327; CL1: 190; D1: 384]
24	Shaw speaks on Clapham Common for the Battersea Branch of the Social Democratic Federation on 'Socialism and Selfishness'. [D1: 388]
29	Shaw seconds a motion to dissolve the Browning Society on the grounds that it is hindering the poet's reputation rather than enhancing it. The motion is soundly defeated. [D1: 390]
30	Shaw's 'first speech at an ordinary political meeting', a public meeting against Coercion. [D1: 390]

July

7 (Sat) Jenny Patterson complains of his disregard for her, and says she will not write again. [BL MS Add 50545]

15 Shaw lectures at Kelmscott House on 'The So-called Period of Apathy 1851–1870'. [D1: 395]

22 Shaw speaks at a Social Democratic Federation demonstration in Hyde Park against the Sweating System. [D1: 396]

Late Shaw helps Annie Besant and others raise and distribute money to the striking Bryant and May match-girls. [D1: 394]

August

Shaw accepts Havelock Ellis's invitation to write a book on rent and value for his Contemporary Science series, but their negotiations break down over payment and Shaw never writes the book. [CL1: 190; D1: 404]

2 (Thu) – 13 Jenny Patterson stays at 29 Fitzroy Square, hindering the pace of Shaw's work. She also pries into his private letters while he is out. [D1: 399–402]

13 Shaw chastises T. P. O'Connor for refusing to publish his article on the Report of the Pan-Anglican Synod on Socialism. [CL1: 192]

14–18 Shaw stays at William Morris's Kelmscott Manor in Oxfordshire. [D1: 402–3]

19 Shaw lectures at Walham Green for the Socialist League on 'Socialism and the Bishops'. [D1: 403]

26 Shaw lectures at the West Kensington Park Radical Club on 'Anarchy and the Way Out'. [D1: 405]

September

2 (Sun) Shaw lectures on 'Ferdinand Lassalle' at the Deptford Liberal Club. [D1: 408]

4 Shaw submits the MS of *Cashel Byron's Profession* to Fisher Unwin. [CL1: 193]

7 Shaw delivers an invited lecture in Bath on 'The Transition to Social Democracy' to the Economics Section of the British Association for the Advancement of Science. Shaw described himself to the distinguished audience as 'a live Socialist redhot "from the streets"'. The lecture was published in *Our Corner* in November 1888, and in *Fabian Essays in Socialism*, c. 1–5 December, 1889. [I&R 57–8; Lbib1: 486–7, 2: 552]

8 A favourable report of his lecture of the previous day is published in *The Star*, but Shaw claimed in a letter of 16 September that he had been 'maligned and misrepresented in the report'. [D1: 409; CL1: 195]

14 Shaw remonstrates with the subeditor of the *Pall Mall Gazette* over the 'parcels of rubbish' he is asked to review. [CL1: 194–5]

15 Shaw delivers an impromptu lecture on Social Democracy at a Dalston Reform Club meeting. [CL1: 195]

16 Shaw delivers an impromptu lecture on Social Democracy at a meeting of the Southwark Branch of the Social Democratic Federation. [CL1: 195]

19, 20 Shaw writes two pseudonymous letters to *The Star* in an attempt to join in the public debate on Christian morality provoked by the Jack the Ripper murders. The letters were not printed. [CL1: 197–9]

20 After hearing the high church Bishop of Rochester preaching 'Blessed are the poor' at a meeting sponsored by the Guild of St Matthew, Shaw writes a satirical pseudonymous report to *The Star*, but the editor elects not to print it. [CL1: 199–201]

21 Shaw's conventional 'correspondent's report' of the Bishop of Rochester's talk is published in the *Pall Mall Gazette*. [CL1: 199]

23 During the afternoon, while Shaw is at home working on a Fabian paper, Jenny Patterson makes another dramatic appearance. Shaw records in his diary: 'J[enny] P[atterson] came, raged, wept, flung a book at my head etc.' [D1: 415]

24 Shaw congratulates 'Jack the Ripper' for rousing public interest in the 'the poor and the disinherited' inhabitants of London's East End. [D1: 414]

October

5 (Fri) Shaw lectures on 'The Economic Aspect of Socialism' at a Fabian Society meeting. [D1: 418; CL1: 195]

20 Jenny Patterson complains that Shaw thinks of her as 'a sucking baby does of its Mar when its hungry'. [BL MS Add 50545]

November

6 (Tue) – 8 Shaw attends the National Liberal Federation Conference in Birmingham. 'A Growl from Mr. Shaw' in *The Star* (12 Nov 1888) records his disappointment in the conference. [D1: 430; Lbib2: 552]

10 Having apparently received a charming letter from Shaw, Jenny Patterson declares: 'I never loved you better than I do now and you know it.' This is her last surviving letter to Shaw. [BL MS Add 50545]

11 Shaw attends a meeting at Hyde Park to commemorate 'Bloody Sunday' and the execution of the Chicago anarchists. [D1: 432]

18 Shaw lectures at the Secular Hall in Leicester on 'The Economic Basis', returning to London the following day. [D1: 435]

19 Shaw writes to Fisher Unwin, 'No more novels for me. Five failures are enough to satisfy my appetite for enterprise in fiction.' [CL1: 201]

26 At 32 years of age, finding that he had replaced his mother on the 'rate book', Shaw votes for the first time in his life, at a School Board election. [D1: 437]

28 Shaw lectures at Kelmscott House on 'The Practical Bearings of Socialism'. [D1: 438]

December

9 (Sun) Shaw lectures the Rotherhithe Liberal and Radical Club on 'The Social Democratic Program', and the Bow Liberal Club on 'Rent and Interest'. [D1: 442]

11 Shaw considers the Deptford Radical Association's request that he or some other Fabian candidate run for a seat on the County Council. [CL1: 202]

16 Shaw lectures at the Progressive Association on 'National Wealth and National Morals'. [D1: 445]

19 Shaw complies with August Mann's request that he identify himself after favourably commenting on the conductor in *The Star*. [CL1: 203]

20 Shaw lectures at the Communist Club on 'Purchasing Power as a Social Force'. Previously on this day, at the British Museum, he viewed drawings by Louis-Maurice Boutet de Monvel (probably including those of Joan of Arc dressed as a page) and looks at Adolphe Julien's *Richard Wagner, sa vie et ses oeuvres* (1886). During the night he suffers a recurrence of a toothache in his left lower jaw. [D1: 446]

23 Shaw lectures at Walham Green on 'Socialism and its Rivals' and at the Gladstone Radical Working Men's Club and Institute on 'Radicalism of the Liberal Party'. [D1: 447]

24 Shaw and Sydney Olivier walk a marathon 26 miles, during which they are twice drenched in heavy downpours. [D1: 447]

1889

Shaw records feeling 'nervous, depressed, and in unsatisfactory health in general as far as my nerves were concerned' in the early months of the year. With the spring, however, he recovers his usual 'capital working condition and... good spirits'. He embarks on his first visit to the continent. In summer he meets and falls in love with Janet Achurch who is playing Nora in Ibsen's *A Doll's House*. In February his first notice as 'Corno di Bassetto', writer of the 'Musical Mems' column in *The Star*, is published. During this year Shaw's journalistic earnings amount to £197.6.10. He delivers 74 lectures.

January

1 (Tue) Shaw's discussions with the Deptford Radical Association continue, with Shaw extremely dubious about running for a seat on the county council. [CL1: 203–4]

2 *The Star* sends Shaw a review copy of Madame Blavatsky's two-volume work, *The Secret Doctrine*. Shaw forwards the book to Annie Besant who is immediately won over to the doctrines of theosophy. Shaw himself was probably influenced by Blavatsky's esoteric doctrines in the creation of *Heartbreak House* and *Back to Methuselah*. [D1: 455; A.M. Gibbs, *'Heartbreak House': Preludes of Apocalypse* (1994) 77–80]

28 Having undertaken to edit *Fabian Essays in Socialism*, Shaw calls on Fisher Unwin to arrange publication. [CL1: 190; D1: 463]

30 Shaw lectures at the Brixton Liberal Association on 'The Politics of the Party of Progress'. [D1: 463]

February

3 (Sun) Shaw lectures at Kelmscott House on 'National Wealth'. [D1: 465]

5 Shaw delivers a paper before the Church and Stage Guild entitled 'Acting, by one who does not believe in it; or the place of the Stage in the Fool's Paradise of Art'. Afterwards, Shaw reports: 'Audience could not make head or tail of the paper'. The paper is published in the *Church Reformer*, March 1889 and in *Platform and Pulpit. Bernard Shaw*, ed. Dan H. Laurence (1961). [D1: 465; CL1: 215; Lbib1: 287; P&P]

9–10 Shaw visits Cambridge to lecture on 'The Economic Basis of Socialism' at King's College. Goldsworthy Lowes Dickinson, Fellow of King's College, records that 'at lunch next day [Shaw] described inimitably his Irish relations, especially an uncle who thought he was in Heaven, and hung himself up in a basket from the ceiling dressed in gauze.' [D1: 466–7; CL1: 182; I&R 56–7, 264–5; *The Autobiography of G. Lowes Dickinson and Other Unpublished Writings*, ed. Dennis Proctor (1973), 144–5]

'On their way south on the 10th February, the theatrical coach in which [Lucy and Charles Butterfield, on tour again with *Dorothy*] were travelling was linked up with the same train in which G.B.S. was sitting on his way back from a lecture at Cambridge. Yet neither party was aware that the other was on the same train until they met at the London platform!' [Farmer 67]

12 Shaw executes the agreement with Walter Scott for the publication of *Cashel Byron's Profession*. [D1: 468]

15 Shaw's first notice as 'Corno di Bassetto', writer of the 'Musical Mems' column in *The Star* published, Shaw having taken over

from E. Belfort Bax as music critic. [Lbib2: 555; D1: 463, 468; CL1: 183; Auto1: 306; I&R 85]

16 H. W. Massingham and Shaw play an elaborate spirit rapping and table turning hoax on Belfort Bax. Shaw later recorded in his diary: 'I have not laughed so much for years.' [D1: 469]

24 Lucy and Charles Butterfield have lunch at Fitzroy Square on their way to Wales via London, but are gone before Shaw's return home from lecturing on 'Rent and Interest' at the United Radical Club and Institute, Hackney. [D1: 472]

March

13 (Wed) In the afternoon Shaw is introduced to the Norwegian composer Edvard Grieg at a rehearsal of Grieg's *Peer Gynt* music by the Philharmonic Society at St James's Hall, Piccadilly. Grieg was visiting London with his wife, Madame Nina Hagerup Grieg, who played duets with him and sang his songs 'with unrestrained expression'. Shaw found 'a certain quaintness about the pair'. His reviews of Grieg's conducting of the *Peer Gynt* Suite and of a Grieg concert at St James's Hall appeared in *The Star* on 16 and 21 March 1889, and he contributed a 'Special Correspondence' article on the *Peer Gynt* concert to the Oslo paper *Dagbladet* on 18 March. [D1: 452; SM1: 576–86]

In the evening Shaw lectured on 'Shelley's Politics' to the Shelley Society at University College. [D1: 452]

21 Shaw withdraws *Fabian Essays* from Unwin Brothers over their handling of a union wage dispute in the print shop, and hands the printing job to Arthur Bonner, son-in-law of Charles Bradlaugh. [CL1: 283]

22 Shaw addresses the Women's Committee of the Chelsea Liberal Association. [CL1: 205]

23 Shaw's need to earn a living by writing causes him to decline an invitation from the Battersea Social Democratic Federation to run for Parliament in the seat of Battersea. [CL1: 206; D1: 481–2]

April

7 (Sun) Shaw records that he 'had a few words' with Henry George at the house of the Fabian Christian Socialist minister, the Rev. Stewart Duckworth Headlam [D1: 487–8]

17 With Sidney Webb, Shaw embarks on his first visit to the continent. 'I spent the night in my berth, squeamish and sleepless but not sick.' [D1: 490; CL1: 208]

18 Shaw visits Antwerp ('like Limerick, only duller') before proceeding to Rotterdam, Mechlin and Brussels. He records the first

	stage of his travels in a letter to William Archer from the Hotel de Vienne, Brussels. [CL1: 208]
19	Shaw spends the day sightseeing in Brussels. [D1: 491]
20	Shaw travels from Brussels to the Hague and Amsterdam. [CL1: 208; D1: 491]
21	Shaw spends the day sightseeing in Amsterdam, attending a Dutch production of Ibsen's *A Doll's House* in the evening. [CL 1: 208; D1: 491]
22	Shaw and Sidney Webb make a day trip from Amsterdam to Utrecht and back. [D1: 492]
23	Sidney Webb and Shaw travel from Amsterdam via Haarlem and Leyden to Rotterdam, where they board the boat back to Harwich. 'I sat on deck all night and was sick myself once.' [D1: 492; CL1: 208]
24	Shaw arrives back in London. [CL1: 208]

June

4, 7, 12	Shaw assists the French Socialist and journalist Jules Magny with his translation of 'The Transition to Social Democracy' for the August and September issues of *La Revue Socialiste*. [CL1: 211, 213, 214–15]
7 (Fri)	Shaw, accompanied by his mother (Bessie Shaw) and William Archer, attends the first performance of Ibsen's *A Doll's House* at the Novelty Theatre, produced by Charles Charrington, with his wife Janet Achurch playing Nora. Shaw's unsigned review of this performance, 'A Play by Henrik Ibsen in London', was published in the *Manchester Guardian* the next day. He wrote that Janet Achurch brought her 'charm, her magnetism, and her instinctive intelligence' to the role. [CL1: 213–16; D1: 508–9; Peters 55–6]
10	The *Penny Illustrated Paper* rejects Shaw's third weekly contribution and terminates its agreement with Shaw to write articles. [D1: 509]
11	Shaw sees *A Doll's House* a second time. [D1: 510]
12	Shaw meets Else and Hedwig Sonntag at the home of Sydney Olivier. Else Sonntag was a pianist and Shaw was to take German lessons from Hedwig in 1891. [D1: 452, 510; SM2: 117, 640]
16	Shaw sits next to Janet Achurch at the *Doll's House* celebration dinner at the Novelty Theatre. 'Interesting young woman.' [D1: 512; CL1: 215]
17	Shaw writes a facetiously adoring letter to Janet Achurch, wooing her with copies of *Cashel Byron's Profession, An Unsocial Socialist* and a copy of his lecture 'Acting, by one who does not believe in it'. In the same letter he recalls his mother's comment

about Janet on the first night of *A Doll's House*: 'That one is a *divil*.' [CL1: 215–16; D1: 512]

20 Shaw attends *A Doll's House* again, sitting in the box arranged for William Archer's wife, Frances, and apparently offending her by 'going on about Miss Achurch'. [D1: 513–14; Peters 59]

21 Shaw writes an extravagant love letter to Janet Achurch (allegedly 'by kind permission of Charles Charrington Esquire') in which he mentions her forthcoming tour to Australasia: 'The world has vanished: the gardens of heaven surround me... Away with you to Australia – for ever, if you will.' [Theatrics 3; Shaw to Janet Achurch, 21 Jun 1889, Texas]

24 Shaw pays his first visit to the Charringtons. [Peters 60]

27 Shaw takes Jenny Patterson to see *A Doll's House*. [D1: 516]

29 On train journeys in London, Shaw 'worked at the plan of the play which has come into my head'. The unfinished work, entitled *The Cassone*, was partly inspired by tensions in his relations with William and Frances Archer, and his feeling that Archer was losing his creative freedom in his marriage with Frances Archer, whose conventional attitudes seem to have been upset by Shaw's infatuation with the married Janet Achurch. [D1: 517,534; Peters 62, 421 n27; CP7: 533]

June–October

Shaw revises proofs of the Fabian Essays. [D1: 507ff.]

July

2 (Tue) Shaw attends a debate on 'Single Tax vs. Social Democracy' between Henry George and H. M. Hyndman. [D1: 518]

5 Shaw sees Janet Achurch and Charles Charrington off at Charing Cross for their tour of the Antipodes, from which they did not return until the spring of 1892. [D1: 518; CL1: 215]

25 Shaw leaves for his first Bayreuth Wagner Festival. While he is away Lucy, who is on summer recess, stays with Bessie at 29 Fitzroy Square. [CL1: 217; D1: 525; Farmer 67]

27 Shaw arrives in Bayreuth via Cologne, Würzburg and Bamberg. [D1: 526]

28 Shaw is obliged to break his vegetarian regime at the World Inn above the theatre at Bayreuth: 'Dined at the restaurant, eating some salmon in the absence of anything more vegetarian.' He catches sight of William Archer and *Liverpool Courier* art critic Edward Dibdin at the theatre and has supper at a café with them afterwards. [D1: 526]

August

1 (Thu) Shaw leaves Bayreuth for Nuremburg on the 11 p.m. train arriving at 1.10 the following morning. [D1: 527–8]

2 Shaw travels to Frankfurt in the evening. [D1: 528]

3 Shaw travels back to Cologne via Castel, Mainz, Coblenz and Bonn. [D1: 528]

4 Shaw returns to London. [CL1: 217; D1: 529]

10 Shaw records that his mother has bought the score of Wagner's *Parsifal*, and that he 'spent a good deal of [his] time at the piano in consequence.' [D1: 530]

14 August – 14 September

Strike of the London Dockers, led by John Burns, which initiated protracted agitation for the eight-hour working day. [Pease 83–4]

August

18 Shaw speaks on Clapham common on 'Socializing London'. [D1: 532]

28 Sitting in Regent's Park, Shaw writes dialogue for *The Cassone*, which he now describes as 'a comedy which I have planned and which has been in my mind since the Achurch–Archer incident'. [D1: 534]

31 Shaw tells Tighe Hopkins of his aim to 'incarnate the Zeitgeist': 'My business is to incarnate the Zeitgeist, whereby I experience its impulse and universality, and it experiences the personal raptures of music ~~and copulation~~ [*sic*].' [Shaw to Tighe Hopkins, 31 Aug 1889, Cornell 4617 Box 10; CL1: 222 (omitting crossed out words)]

September

2 (Mon) Shaw tells Tighe Hopkins of his necessary self-conceit as an artist: 'Never fear: my comedy will not be unactable when the time comes for it to be acted, though perhaps it may be obsolete by then. I have the instinct of an artist; and the impracticable is loathsome to me.' As a playwright he needs to create not only 'the comedy' but actors, manager, theatre and audience. 'Somebody must do these things – somebody whose prodigious conceit towers over all ordinary notions of success – somebody who would blush to win a 600 nights run at a West End Theatre as a duke would blush to win a goose at a public house raffle – some colossal egotist, in short, like

Yrs in hot haste

GBS'

[Theatrics 5; Cornell 4617 Box 10]

7 Accompanied by William Archer, Shaw sees Lucy Shaw (Butterfield) playing the lead in the 789th performance of *Dorothy* at Morton's Theatre, Greenwich. His review in *The Star* on 13 September laments the fate of the cast as 'young

persons doomed to spend the flower of their years in mechanically repeating the silliest libretto in modern theatrical literature.' Describing his sister with critical detachment, he wrote: 'Dorothy herself, a beauteous young lady of distinguished mien, with an immense variety of accents ranging from the finest Tunbridge Wells English (for genteel comedy) to the broadest Irish (for repartee and low comedy) sang without the slightest effort and without the slightest point, and was all the more desperately vapid because she suggested artistic gifts wasting in complacent abeyance.' [D1:537; SM1: 778–83]

13–27 Edward McNulty and his wife visit London. [D1: 539–43]

October

3 (Thu) Shaw lectures to the Bloomsbury Socialist Society on 'Socializing London'. [D1: 545]

18 Finding the work both unsatisfying and unprofitable, Shaw asks Edmund Yates to let Lady Colin Campbell (Irish-born journalist and separated wife of one of the sons of the 8th Duke of Argyll) take over as art critic for *The World*. [CL1: 225–6; D1: 550]

20 In response to Shaw's resignation letter (18th October), Yates replies 'I have no idea of loosening my hold on you' and offers Shaw a retainer of £1 per week over and above his former payment for signed notices. Shaw nevertheless begins to wind down his art reviewing. By the middle of November he is only filling in when Lady Colin Campbell is unavailable. [CL1: 226; D1: 550, 552, 558]

22 Shaw spends the day working on the *Fabian Essays*. He completes the revision late in the afternoon and sends them off to the publisher. [D1: 551]

November

3 (Sun) Shaw lectures to the Social Democratic Federation on 'Democracy, False and True'. [D1: 555]

12 Shaw lectures to the Socialist League at Leicester on 'Radicalism and Social Democracy' returning to London the following day. [D1: 558]

15 Shaw is introduced to Samuel Butler. [D1: 453]

16, 23, 30 Shaw publishes critical articles on John Morley in *The North London Press*. [D1: 559, 561, 563]

18 Writing to Hubert Bland, Shaw says that if 'a man is to attain consciousness of himself as a vessel of the Zeitgeist', he must 'do what he likes instead of doing what, on secondhand principles, he ought'. In this letter Shaw describes his mother, Bessie Shaw, as 'a hearty, independent and jolly person'. [CL1: 228–9]

26 In a letter to the editor of the *Truth* (which had recently reported on a male brothel frequented by members of the aristocracy), Shaw calls for the decriminalization of homosexuality among consenting adults, and for a more rational discussion of sexual matters in the press. (The letter, rejected by the *Truth*, is published in CL.) [CL1: 230–2]

December

Publication of *Fabian Essays in Socialism*, edited by Shaw, who contributes two essays, 'The Basis of Socialism: Economic' and 'The Transition to Social Democracy', both recently published in *Our Corner*, as well as the preface. The book is a best-seller, and resulted in a great expansion of membership in the Fabian Society. [Lbib1: 487; Pease 88]

8 (Sun) Shaw lectures for the St Pancras Social Democratic Federation on 'The Working Day'. [D1: 567]

17 *The Star* 'Mainly About People' section reports that GBS's art columns are soon to be replaced by those of Lady Colin Campbell whose 'dark eyes and witching dresses will not atone for the absence of the famous harmony in snuff-colour with which Mr Shaw used to enliven Academy picture shows'. [D1: 569]

24 Shaw departs London to spend Christmas and New Year with Jenny Patterson at her Broadstairs house. [D1: 572; Pearson 143–4]

1890

During this year Shaw writes his final *Star* article as 'Corno di Bassetto', begins writing musical criticism for *The World*, and delivers to the Fabian Society the lecture which was to be published in 1891 as *The Quintessence of Ibsenism*. He collaborates with Jules Magny, who translates and arranges publication of some of Shaw's essays in *La Revue Socialiste*. He meets Beatrice Potter (Webb) for the first time, and begins his relationship with Florence Farr (Emery). During this year, Aunt Kate Gurly moved in with the Shaws, residing with them until at least 1897. Shaw's journalistic earnings for the year amount to £252.

January

3 (Fri) Shaw returns to London from Broadstairs. [D1: 576]

8 Publication of Shaw's last signed art review for *The World*. First meeting of Beatrice Potter and Sidney Webb, apparently at the house of Margaret Harkness. [Lbib2: 564; D1: 577; DBW1: 319]

16 Ernest Parke, proprietor of the *North London Press* is jailed for a year for libel against the Earl of Euston, an aristocrat implicated

in the Cleveland Street male brothel scandal. Shaw writes Parke's leading articles for the *North London Press* without remuneration until the paper merges with the *People's Press* in early March. [D1: 563, 580]

18–20 Shaw visits Bristol to lecture to the Sunday Society on 'Socialism in Real Life'. [CL1: 235; D1: 580–1]

25–27 Shaw visits Nottingham where he lectures twice on the same day (Sunday 26th) at the Secular Hall on 'Historical Abandonment of Laissez-faire' and 'True Radical Policy'. 'Talked all day – about 15 hours of it... Terrible tongue work.' [D1: 583]

28 Writing to Charles Charrington, Shaw declares that: 'My next effort in fiction – if I ever have time to make one – will be a play.' [CL1: 241]

February

2 (Sun) Shaw lectures at Sydney Hall, Battersea, on 'Class War'. [D1: 586]

5 In a letter to T. P. O'Connor, showing that he thinks his remuneration is inadequate, Shaw threatens to resign as 'Corno di Bassetto', *The Star's* music critic. A letter to H. W. Massingham of 28 February indicates that *The Star* payments for his expenses were seriously in arrears. Despite his resignation threat in February, he continued *The Star* 'Musical Mems' articles until May 1890. [CL1: 241, 243–4]

8–10 Shaw visits Leicester to deliver a Secular Society lecture on 'Socialist Individualism'. [D1: 588]

17 After attending a ballet performance at the Alhambra Theatre, Shaw is intercepted by a policeman while leaping along the carriage way round the railing at Fitzroy Square. The policeman joins in the competition, as do the early morning postman and the milkman. [D1: 590]

March

Publication (after a sell-out of the first edition) of the second impression with corrections of *Fabian Essays in Socialism*. Concerning this, GBS wrote to Karl Pearson on 24 March 1890: 'I have just seen your review of Fabian Essays in *The Academy*; and the fact that it is the only notice the book has received which is of any real importance only deepens the reproach which attaches to you for not being one of the authors instead of the critic... It is true that our campaigning gives us a touch of the barrack room in our conferences; but are you sure that your plan of excogitating socialism, hermit fashion, all to yourself, has not worse drawbacks?' [Lbib1: 486–7; GBS to Karl Pearson,

24 March 1890, Pearson Papers, University College London; Pease 88]

7 (Fri) Shaw calls on Horace Voules, Editor of *Truth*, to discuss his appointment as art critic. [D1: 595]

14 Shaw purchases his first typewriter, a second-hand Bar-Lock, from H. W. Massingham. [CL1: 376]

20 Shaw begins to write art criticism for the *Truth*, where he spends 'one season only'. [Lbib2: 566; D1: 595–6, 597; I&R 27, 29 n21]

April

3 (Thu) – **8** Shaw visits Paris where he attends the Opéra, the Comédie Français, and a Joan of Arc operatic work by Jules Barbier, with music by Gounod, starring Sarah Bernhardt. His caustic remarks on this work, and on Paris as a cultural centre, appeared in *The Star* on 11 April: 'Paris is what it always has been: a pedant-ridden failure in everything that it pretends to lead.' Having experienced a rough crossing back from Calais, as he had before, Shaw began his column: 'I am strongly of opinion that the Channel Tunnel should be proceeded with at once.' [CL1: 248; D1: 605; SM2: 20–7]

27 Shaw finds Pakenham Beatty 'just recovering from delirium tremens', caused by drinking. [D1: 611; CL1: 250]

May

4 (Sun) Shaw delivers a speech at the Eight Hours International Demonstration in Hyde Park. [D1: 613]

7 Shaw sees, and is impressed by, Florence (Emery) Farr playing the part of Amaryllis in John Todhunter's play *A Sicilian Idyll*. [D1: 614; SM2: 64]

14 Shaw accepts the position as musical critic on *The World*. [D1: 617]

15 O'Connor accepts Shaw's resignation from *The Star*. [CL1: 241]

16 Shaw, as 'Corno di Bassetto', publishes his last music column in *The Star*. O'Connor gibes at GBS in the editorial acknowledging his resignation. Under the pen-name 'GBS', he begins as music critic on *The World*, edited by Edmund Yates. His first article appears on 28 May. He continues in this position until 1894. [Lbib2: 568; Hol1: 237; Wein3: 3]

Shaw recalls: 'Interview with Voules [editor of *The Truth*] rather a fighting one. He wants me to puff [Frederick] Goodall, [a Royal Academy artist whose work Shaw disliked] and in the end I told him he must get another critic.' [D1: 618; CL1: 251; I&R 27, 29 n21]

19 In a letter to J. Stanley Little, Shaw writes: '*Truth* is quarrelling with me because I don't admire Goodall!!! My connection with

	the paper may not survive the language I have used in consequence.' [CL1: 251]
24	Shaw writes 'a long and strong letter to Horace Voules about the *Truth* affair before dinner'. Shaw has effectively resigned. [D1: 620; I&R 29 n21]
27	Shaw lectures at the Somerville Club on 'The Industrial Competition of Women and Men'. [D1: 620]
28	Publication of Shaw's first article of musical criticism in *The World*. [Lbib2: 568]

June

4 (Wed)	Shaw begins writing the Ibsen paper for the Fabian Society, which later becomes *The Quintessence of Ibsenism* (1891). [D1: 623]
6	May Morris visits Shaw who is at home working on an article for *The World* and his paper on Ibsen. [D1: 624]
14	May Morris marries Henry Halliday Sparling. According to Shaw in a 1936 reminiscence of his association with Morris, 'William Morris as I knew Him', this marriage constituted an astonishing and entirely unexpected end to a 'Mystical Betrothal' between himself and May Morris to which he fancied she had silently assented one night at Kelmscott House: 'suddenly, [Shaw wrote] to my utter stupefaction... the beautiful daughter married one of the comrades.' Lucy Shaw (Butterfield), in a letter of 24 July, 1901, told her friend Jane Crichton Drysdale that May Morris had always been madly in love with Shaw, and that her object in divorcing Sparling in 1898 was to give Shaw the chance of marrying her. [D1: 634; Prefs3: 283–5; Texas]
17	Jenny Patterson visits Shaw. They have 'a long talk' over tea. Shaw later writes in his diary: 'It looked like a breaking off.' [D1: 627]
18	After going to a musical recital at Steinway Hall, Shaw visits William Archer who reads *Peer Gynt* to him all afternoon. He arrives home in the evening to find Jenny Patterson waiting for him. [D1: 627]

July

5 (Sat)	Shaw writes Fabian Tract No. 13: 'What Socialism Is'. [D1: 632]
18	Shaw delivers a two-hour paper 'The Quintessence of Ibsenism' at St James's Restaurant, as part of the Fabian series 'Socialism in Contemporary Literature'. Edward R. Pease records of this 'high water-mark in Fabian lectures' that 'the effect on the audience was overwhelming. It was "briefly discussed" by a number of speakers, but they seemed as out of place as a debate after an oratorio.' The same evening Sidney Webb introduces Shaw to Beatrice Potter. [D1: 575, 636]

26 Herbert Burrows of the Social Democratic Federation attacks Shaw in 'Socialism of the Sty' in *Justice*. [CL1: 254]

29 Shaw and Webb set out for a holiday on the continent. [CL1: 253]

August

10 (Sun) After visiting Brussels, Cologne, Coblenz, Bingen (by Rhine steamer from Coblenz), Mainz, Frankfurt, Munich, Oberammergau, Stuttgart and Strasbourg, Shaw and Webb return to London. [CL1: 253; D1: 639]

24 Shaw lectures at Kelmscott House on 'Idealism'. [D1: 644]

Shaw goes down to Merton Abbey, and meets Florence Farr (Emery) for the first time. Shaw recalls this meeting in a letter of 6 January 1891 to Janet Achurch, in which he says Florence 'met me one day at a picnic at William Morris's factory at Merton Abbey, and astonished me by asking would I play the Stranger in the Lady from the Sea if she succeeded in getting up a performance. She said that as I had a red beard she thought I would look the part in a pea jacket. I pleaded ineptitude and declined.' [DHL; D1: 644]

September

Shaw negotiates with the Walter Scott Publishing Co. over new editions of *Fabian Essays*. [CL1: 259–60]

10 (Wed) Busy with a number of projects, including helping to organize the Birmingham Fabian Society, Shaw writes to fellow Fabian, Edward Deacon Girdlestone, 'I am so at my wits' end with the pressure of work'. [CL1: 261]

20 Shaw leaves London on a lecture tour of the Midlands during which he gives 13 lectures in 13 days. [CL1: 261–2; D1: 651–5]

25 Shaw rebukes Bland, Olivier and Wallas for submitting to an unfavourable agreement with Walter Scott over *Fabian Essays* without consulting other contributors to the volume. [CL1: 265]

October–November

'In October and November 1890, we find [Lucy] and her mother (Bessie Shaw), together with the latter's half sisters Kate and Georgie Gurly – both very musical says Mrs Georgina Musters – being taken to the operas *Les Huguenots*, *La Gioconda*, and *Rigoletto*, by G.B.S.' [Farmer 73]

October

3 (Fri) Shaw returns to London after his lecture tour. [CL1: 261]

4 Shaw works on contributions for the Christmas issue of *The World* then goes to the Private View where he has 'a long talk with Florence Emery [Farr]'. He returns home to have tea with

Jenny Patterson. When she leaves, he secretly follows her. [D1: 614, 655]

11 Florence Farr accompanies Shaw to the first concert of the season, after which he persuades her to get up a performance of Ibsen's *Rosmersholm* (instead of *The Lady from the Sea* as she has planned). She intrigues him to the extent that he misses another appointment. [D1: 657; Peters 69]

16 Shaw spends the day at the Grosvenor Gallery. In the evening he looks through his newly purchased volume of Grove's *Dictionary of Music* then goes to visit Jenny Patterson who 'was angry and jealous about F[lorence] E[mery Farr]'. [D1: 659]

November

Annie Besant resigns from the Fabian Society to pursue her interests in Theosophy. 'Gone to Theosophy' was Edward Pease's succinct summary of her career change. She did not, however, abandon her interest in the cause of Socialism. [CL1: 273; Pease 98]

9 (Sun) Shaw lectures on 'Eight Hours' at the Paddington Radical Club and the 'Working Day' at the Upholsterers' Club. He records in his diary that he went 'to bed with a decided toothache, which alarmed me; but I slept in spite of it until nearly noon on Monday. Am driving myself too hard.' [D1: 666]

15 Shaw's 'first really intimate conversation' with Florence Farr. [D1: 668]

19 Publication of *The Salt of the Earth* (as the Christmas extra number of *The World*). Shaw contributed some pages on Socialism to this collaborative 'novel', but described the work in a letter to John Burns as having 'nothing to enliven its doglike trash except a description of you'. [CL1: 271; D1: 633; Lbib2: 570–1]

20, 27 Shaw publishes two letters in *The Star* in response to the cry that 'Parnell Must Go'. [CL1: 274]

23 First meeting of the Hammersmith Socialist Society which, led by William Morris, had split from the Socialist League on 21 November. [Hend2: 279; Fiona MacCarthy, *William Morris: A Life for Our Time* (1994), 583]

December

16 (Tue) 'Disunion' and incipient 'moral chaos' in the Fabian Society cause Shaw to advocate the drafting of a Fabian manifesto. [CL1: 276]

Late Shaw and his mother go to visit Lucy and her husband 'at Denmark Hill, where they lived with Mrs Robert Butterfield'. [Farmer74]

1891

Early in this year Jenny Patterson leaves for a three-month tour of the Near East. In her absence Shaw develops his relationship with Florence Farr, and first meets American-born actress, novelist and playwright, Elizabeth Robins. During the summer Shaw takes German lessons with Hedwig Sonntag. In September *The Quintessence of Ibsenism* is published, and Shaw tours Northern Italy with a party organized by the Art Workers' Guild. In October he delivers a paper to the Fabian Society which is to be published in 1893 as a Fabian Tract, 'The Impossibilities of Anarchism'. After her return from the East, tempestuous scenes arise out of Jenny Patterson's jealousy of Florence Farr. Jenny departs for a six-month tour to Australia at the end of the year.

January

3 (Sat) – 5 Shaw visits Bristol where he lectures to the Bristol Sunday Society on German socialist and political journalist, Ferdinand Lassalle. [D1: 310; D2: 685]

6 Shaw in a letter to Janet Achurch records that he 'lately went up to Hampstead to give a private reading of the Ibsen paper [*The Quintessence of Ibsenism*] to Karl Pearson and his newly wedded wife [Maria Pearson, nee Sharpe]'. Karl Pearson, Founder of the Men and Women's Club in 1885, and Maria, the Club secretary, were both keen Ibsenites. Maria Sharpe's paper, 'Henrik Ibsen: His Men and Women', was presented at one of the final meetings of the Club and published in the *Westminster Review*, vol. 131 (1889), 626–49. In the same letter Shaw states that he is 'not married, nor likely to be', and confesses to being dissatisfied with things of merely intellectual interest: 'I want the noblest poetic beauty in sights, sounds, relations, and what not.' He refers to himself in this letter as 'Mephistopheles Shaw'. [Shaw to Janet Achurch, 6 Jan 1891, Texas]

9 Jenny Patterson leaves, with Georgina Gurly, on a three-month tour of the Near East, mainly visiting Egypt and Palestine. During her absence Shaw develops his relationship with Florence Farr. [D2: 686–7; Erv 164–5; Peters 71]

14–15 Shaw debates in the Hall of Science on the eight-hour day against G. W. Foote, President of the National Secular Society. [Auto1: 119, 302; D2: 688; Hend2: 169]

21 At William Archer's house, where he stayed longer than he intended, Shaw meets Elizabeth Robins, who was about to play Mrs Linde in *A Doll's House*. [D2: 689]

25 Shaw lectures to the Liverpool Socialist Society on the 'Evolution of Socialism' and 'Alternatives to Social Democracy'. [D2: 691]

January–February

Shaw writes to Clement Shorter, editor of the *Illustrated London News*, offering his services as a music reviewer and critic and saying that he is 'free for art criticism this season'. He upbraids Shorter for his disparagement of Olive Schreiner's *Dreams*: 'The book is a treasure.' [CL1: 280–1]

February

4 (Wed) Shaw visits 'for a while' the third inaugural performance at the Royal Opera House of Sir Arthur Sullivan's operatic version of Sir Walter Scott's *Ivanhoe*, of which he had earlier seen the opening performance on 31 January 1891. Lucy takes the other seat allotted to him as critic. On the same day, Shaw's highly critical review of Sullivan's opera is published in *The World*. [D2. 692–3; SM2: 253–60]

6 Shaw begins coaching Florence Farr in her part as Rebecca West in the upcoming performance of *Rosmersholm*. [Peters 73]

8 Shaw lectures at Yarmouth on 'The Evolution of Socialism' and 'The Landlord's Share'. [CL1: 283]

22 Shaw's invited address to the National Secular Society on 'Progress in Freethought', in which (he recalled in a 1908 letter to G. K. Chesterton) he 'proceeded to smash materialism, rationalism and all the philosophy of Tyndall, Helmholtz, Darwin and the rest of the 1860 people into smithereens', enrages the Society, and dispels any idea of his becoming their possible leader. [CL2: 761–2]

23 Shaw attends the opening matinée performance of *Rosmersholm*, starring Florence Farr. [CL1: 283]

Shaw participates in a rowdy discussion of Ibsen's *Ghosts* at a meeting of the Playgoers' Club, defending Ibsen, and attacking *Daily Telegraph* critic Clement Shorter. [CL1: 287–8]

March

H. W. Massingham is elected to the Fabian Society and its Executive. A valuable ally as a year later he becomes assistant editor of the *Daily Chronicle*. [Pease 109]

4 (Wed) Fabian business and journalistic jobbing leave Shaw 'without a moment for literary work'. [CL1: 284]

13 Ibsen's *Ghosts* performed at the Royalty Theatre as the inaugural production of J. T. Grein's Independent Theatre Society. [CL1: 285; D2: 705; Erv 241; Peters 75]

16 Shaw begins revising his paper of the previous summer into the longer essay, *The Quintessence of Ibsenism*. *The Quintessence* reflects current controversy about Ibsen, and also bears marks of Shaw's relationships with Florence Farr and Jenny Patterson. [D2: 706; Wisenthal 16; Peters 75–7, 87–8]

19 Shaw sends the *Our Corner* version of *Love Among the Artists* to Fisher Unwin, and facetiously proposes that he also publish the essay on Ibsen. [CL1: 286]

30 To Charles Charrington: 'N.B. I am in love with Miss Farr; but for Heaven's sake do not tell Mrs Charrington.' [CL1: 288]

30 March – 3 April

Shaw devotes all of Easter to *The Quintessence of Ibsenism*. [CL1: 290; D2: 709]

April

12 (Sun) Returning to a topic of 1885 lectures, Shaw talks on the 'Iron Law of Wages' at Leighton Hall, Kentish Town. [D1: 55; D2: 712]

16 Shaw records his completion of *The Quintessence of Ibsenism*: 'Finished the Ibsen MS in great excitement.' [D2: 713]

20 In company with his mother, Shaw attends the first performance of *Hedda Gabler* in London, produced by Elizabeth Robins and Marion Lea, with Elizabeth Robins playing Hedda. Having seen the production again on 30 April, he is haunted by the image of Robins, as Hedda, 'giving Lövborg the pistol with love in her eyes'. [CL1: 291; D2: 714; Theatrics 5–7; Peters 78]

22 Shaw replies to Fisher Unwin's proposal to publish a volume of his musical criticism that it would be better to 'leave [Corno] di Bassetto to rot peacefully in his grave'. The manuscript of *The Quintessence of Ibsenism* is in the hands of the publisher Walter Scott. [CL1: 293]

23 Shaw lectures at Wolverhampton on 'The Capitalists' Share'. [CL1: 295; D2: 715]

24 Shaw lectures at Hanley on 'Distribution of Wealth – the Capitalist's Share'. He also has his first ride on a bicycle. [CL1: 295; D2: 715]

26 Shaw lectures the Camberwell Branch of the National Secular Society on 'Freethought, Old and New'. [CL1: 300; CL2: 761]

27 At his first meeting with Jenny Patterson since her return from the East, she creates a 'fearful scene' over his relationship with Florence Farr. He arranges to meet Florence the following day, saying that 'the hart pants for cooling streams'. Throughout the remainder of the year, Shaw's diary records many fierce quarrels with Jenny Patterson. [CL1: 295–7; D2: 716]

May

3 (Sun) Shaw speaks at a Labour Day Demonstration in Hyde Park to promote the eight-hour working day. In the evening he lectures on 'Alternatives to Social Democracy' at the Southwark and Lambeth Social Democratic Federation. [CL1: 298; D2: 718]

June

3 (Wed) Shaw writes to Hedwig Sonntag requesting that she give him lessons in German. He calls on her to arrange this on 6 June. His Diary records regular attendances at classes during the summer. [D1: 727]

19–21 Enfeebled by a recent bout of influenza, Shaw visits Broadstairs with Jenny Patterson. [D2: 732]

August

3 (Mon) Shaw resumes writing *Technical Socialism* for the University Series. [D2: 744]

15 Shaw receives an advance copy from publisher Walter Scott of *The Quintessence of Ibsenism*. [D2: 747]

19–22 Shaw visits the Salts at Oxted in Surrey. [CL1: 306; D2: 748–9]

28 August – 6 September

Shaw makes a lecturing tour of the provinces. [CL1: 306; D2: 750–2]

September

Publication of *The Quintessence of Ibsenism*, in a printing of 2100 copies. [Lbib2: 16–17]

16 (Wed) Shaw embarks on a tour of northern Italy with the Art Workers' Guild. Sydney Cockerell and Emery Walker are amongst his fellow tourists. In order to have his dietary principles understood by Italian hoteliers, Shaw had to travel as 'a devout Catholic under a vow to abstain from flesh, wine and tobacco'. [D2: 755–7; I&R 211–13; Pearson 136]

October

4 (Sun) Shaw returns to London from Italy which 'seems to me a humbug… a show and nothing else.' [CL1: 311]

6–8 Shaw visits Birmingham to hear William Morris's address on the Pre-Raphaelites at the Municipal Art Gallery. [CL1: 313]

16 Shaw speaks on 'The Difficulties of Anarchism' to the Fabian Society, the paper subsequently published as Tract No. 45, 'The Impossibilities of Anarchism' (1893). The paper is a revised version of 'A Refutation of Anarchism', first published in *Our Corner* in summer 1888. [Lbib2: 548]

19 October – 31 December

In 18 separate appointments Shaw has substantial dental repairs. Shaw's extensive experience with dentists is reflected in the first scene of *You Never Can Tell*, composed in 1895–6. His unusual attitude towards going to the dentist is recorded in a letter to Charles Charrington of 1 March 1895, where he says that his 'favourite remedy' for headaches and sickness was 'the excavation of another tooth. To sit in an easy chair, hypnotised by keeping my mouth wide open, and soothed by the buzzing of the drill as it flies round inside my head, all the time watching another man working hard, is extraordinarily restful to me.' [D2: 760–78; CL1: 489]

October

19 — Shaw lectures at Halifax, returning to London the following day. [CL1: 314; D2: 760]

25, 26 — Shaw quarrels with William Archer over his 'Open Letter to George Bernard Shaw', a critique of *The Quintessence of Ibsenism* to be published in the November issue of the *New Review*. [CL1: 314]

November

1 (Sun) — Shaw lectures to the Secular Society in Leicester. [CL2: 761; D2: 763]

2 — Shaw lectures to the Oxford University Russell Club, returning to London the following day. [D2: 764]

7 — Shaw writes a slanderous letter to William Archer but sends it by accident to Frank Harris, editor of the *Fortnightly Review*. [CL1: 320; D2: 765–6]

8 — To Shaw's relief, Jenny Patterson leaves for Ireland. [D2: 766]

9, 10, 13 — Shaw continues arguing with Archer, the focus of their dispute having shifted to the question of critical bias. [CL1: 321–3, 324–9]

December

4 (Fri) — Having returned from Ireland, Jenny Patterson invades Fitzroy Square and makes so fearful a scene that Shaw must leave his room 'by main force' and escape to the British Museum until the coast is clear at home. 'The scene upset me much.' At about this time Jenny leaves on a trip to Australia and is away until 16 June 1892. Shaw's diary records he wrote letters to her on 14, 18 and 28 of the month. [D2: 772–3, 775, 777, 779, 826; Peters 96]

5 — Lucy Shaw (Butterfield)'s tour as 'Dorothy' ends at the Pavilion Theatre, London. She is staying at Fitzroy Square for the week's performances in London, after which she returns to her 'second home' with the Butterfields at Denmark Hill. At some time in this period Lucy separated from her husband, Charles. [Farmer 76–9, 81]

1892

Early in this year Janet Achurch and Charles Charrington return from their tour of Australia and New Zealand and revive *A Doll's House* at the Avenue

Theatre. In February, Shaw delivers a Fabian Society paper subsequently published as 'The Fabian Society: What it has done, and how it has done it'. In February–March, he sits for Bertha Newcombe's (lost) portrait, 'G.B.S., Platform Spellbinder'.† In the lead-up to the July General Election, he works on the *Fabian Election Manifesto*, and campaigns in Bradford for Fabian candidate Benjamin Tillett. In July, he rediscovers and resumes writing *Rhinegold* (*Widowers' Houses*) which he finishes revising in October. The play is performed by the Independent Theatre Society in December. Towards the end of the year Shaw begins a lengthy stay at the Hammersmith house of May (Morris) and Henry Sparling.

January

10 (Sun) Shaw lectures for the Social Democratic Federation in Brighton. [D2: 784–5]

17 Shaw speaks at a Free Speech demonstration at the Social Democratic Federation Hall in the Strand. He averts the possibility of arrest by convincing the Free Speech Committee (made up of representatives of several Socialist groups) that it would be better to hold a series of meetings just within the legal limit in numbers, instead of one large, defiant, illegal demonstration. [D2: 787]

February

6 (Sat) Shaw reads 'The History and Present Attitude of the Fabian Society' at the first sitting of the first Pan-Fabian Conference, at the Essex Hall. The paper is subsequently published as 'The Fabian Society: What it has done; and how it has done it', Fabian Tract No. 41. [CL1: 343; D2: 790, 792; Pease 106]

10 Shaw is commissioned by the Shelley Society to do the casting for a new production of *The Cenci*. [D2: 793]

14 Shaw lectures in Bristol on 'Social Limits of Individual Liberty', returning to London the following day. [D2: 794]

20 Shaw lectures at Oxford where he is 'ragged' during his first talk at Magdalen College by students (led by Simon Joseph Fraser, later 14th Baron Lovat) sealing the room in which he was lecturing from without, and 'wrecking the adjoining chamber by a vigorous bombardment of coals, buckets of water and asafoetida'. Shaw lost his gloves, umbrella and hat, and escaped under attack from water bombs from the situation. A 'new tall hat' was sent 'with Best Wishes from three Oxford Ladies who admire Mr. Shaw'. The President of Magdalen, Sir Thomas Herbert Warren, wrote a letter expressing regret at the rude

†The portrait is reproduced in various places, including, Shaw's *Sixteen Self Sketches*, 1949, opp. p. 56, with the additional caption 'Portrait by Bertha Newcombe, spell-bound', and as a frontispiece in *Platform and Pulpit. Bernard Shaw*, ed. Dan H. Laurence (1961).

behaviour of the students. Shaw wrote a humorous piece about this aggressive prank, ironically entitled 'Revolutionary Progress at Oxford', in the *Pall Mall Gazette*, 22 February 1892. [D2: 796; BL MS Add 50512; Agits 22–3]

24 February – 31 March

Shaw sits for Bertha Newcombe while she paints the three-quarter portrait, 'The Platform Spellbinder'. [D2: 798–9, 809; Peters 96]

March

13 (Sun) Shaw spends the day correcting proofs for *The World* and preparing a 'fresh set of notes for my lecture, as I accidentally tore up the Battersea ones'. In the afternoon, he lectures on 'The London County Council Elections and their Lessons' for the Kentish Town branch of the Social Democratic Federation. [D2: 804]

April

2 (Sat) Shaw visits 'Hadleigh', William Booth's 800-acre farm colony at Benfleet in Essex, established as a model alternative to city living. [D2: 810]

6 Shaw attends a performance of Wilde's *Lady Windermere's Fan* which, having opened on 20 February 1892, ran for 197 performances. [D2: 810–11]

19 Janet Achurch and Charles Charrington revive *A Doll's House* at the Avenue Theatre. In the course of severe criticism of Achurch's playing of Nora, Shaw concedes that her 'comprehension of the part is extraordinary', and that she 'make[s] it live in the most glowing, magnetic way.' [CL1: 337–8]

24 Shaw declines to write a political article for the Socialist League *Commonweal*, which has fallen into the hands of the Anarchists. [CL1: 339]

26 Shaw speaks on Women's Suffrage at St James's Hall, London. [CL 2: 493]

May

7 (Sat) Shaw makes his first visit to Janet Achurch since her return from Australia and New Zealand. [D2: 815]

14–16 Shaw visits the Salts at Oxted. He works on the *Fabian Election Manifesto* for the July General Election. The manifesto advocated direct political intervention through the formation of a working-class political party. [D2: 816–17]

28 Shaw spends an afternoon alone with Bertha Newcombe at Cheyne Walk. [D2: 821]

June

	Shaw continues with his work on the *Fabian Election Manifesto*. [CL1: 341–2; Lbib1: 19–20]
4 (Sat) – 7	Shaw visits the Salts at Oxted. [D2: 823]
16	Shaw returns home from a concert to find Jenny Patterson awaiting him. This is their first meeting since her departure the previous December for Australia. [D2: 826]
19	Shaw's first letter to Ellen Terry. The famous Shaw–Terry correspondence begins to blossom fully three years later, in 1895. [CL1: 342; D2: 827]
24	In compliance with Ellen Terry's request for advice about her protégée, Elvira Gambogi, Shaw attends a performance by the young singer at the Lyric Club. The singer's performance was overshadowed for Shaw by a recitation of 'superb artistic power' given by Ellen Terry at the same concert. [D2: 828–9; CL1: 342; SM2: 669; Erv 286]
	Shaw attends the Rev. John Trevor's lecture on 'The Labour Church in Relation to Life'. Trevor, a Unitarian Minister, was the founder in 1891 of a labour church in Manchester. (A 'William Morris Labour Church' is one of the features of Andrew Undershaft's model village, Perivale St Andrews, in the last act of *Major Barbara*.) [D2: 828–9; CP3: 162]
28	Shaw lectures in Dover, returning to London the following day. [D2: 830]

July

1 (Fri)	Shaw reports to Ellen Terry that he is 'up to [his] eyes in the [General] election', and needs to travel to Bradford the following day to employ his 'spouting propensities' on behalf of a Fabian candidate. [CL1: 346–7]
2–3	Shaw campaigns in Bradford for Benjamin Tillett, a Fabian candidate and founder of the Dockers' Union. This General Election signalled a major turning point in Fabian policies of political intervention. Six Fabians stand as candidates, though only J. Keir Hardie is elected. Another socialist (for whom Shaw campaigned), John Burns of the Progressive (Trade Union) Party is also elected. [CL1: 347, 355–6; Pease 112–14]
5	Shaw chides Ellen Terry for squandering her enormous talents on trivial 'charades'. [CL1: 348–9]
12	Shaw protests to the Social Democratic Federation that their attacks on the Fabian Society undermine the Socialist cause. [CL1: 349–51]

23 Marriage of Beatrice Potter and Sidney Webb. [DBW1: 371]

27 After strolling in St James's Park with Florence Farr before it was time for her to go to the theatre, Shaw visits Jenny Patterson for the first time since her return from Australia. Later the same evening he rejoins Florence Farr. [D2: 838–9]

29 Shaw rediscovers *Rhinegold* (the play which was to become *Widowers' Houses*) and resumes work on 'the comedy' the following day. Jenny Patterson urges him to make a collection of his articles for *The World* which she offers to paste up for him. The collection becomes BL MS Add 50961. [D2: 839]

August

Labour and Progressive Party gains at the election cause Shaw and Webb to jockey the Fabian Society into a favourable position in the post-electoral political arena. [CL1: 358–66]

4 (Thu) Shaw is involved in the Shelley centenary celebrations. [CL1: 352–3]

7 Shaw lectures in Manchester, returning to London the following day. [D2: 842]

16 Shaw tells Alma Murray 'it is impossible to get [*The Cenci*] licensed', explaining that the major obstacle is the opposition of the licenser of plays, E. F. S. Pigott, Earl Lathom. This episode marks the beginning of Shaw's long history of warfare with stage censorship. [CL1: 361]

October

20 (Thu) – 21 Shaw alters the title of his play, *Rhinegold*, to *Widowers' Houses*, and finishes it by inserting a new scene near the end of the second act. J. T. Grein accepts the play for the Independent Theatre. [D2: 863; CP1: 36; I&R 122–4; Peters 99; Hol1: 280]

November

1 (Tue) The 'unbearable' smell of paint and the disruption of redecoration and repair of Fitzroy Square drive Shaw to ask May (Morris) and Henry Sparling to have him to stay at 8 Hammersmith Terrace 'for a few nights'. The visit lasts until mid-January. Shaw's Diary records frequent playing of duets and outings to various places with May during this period. In 'William Morris As I Knew Him' (1936) Shaw described this *ménage à trois* as initially 'probably the happiest passage in our three lives', but as eventually creating intolerable tension. [D2: 867–93; Auto1: 166–9]

14 Commencement of rehearsals of *Widowers' Houses*, under Shaw's direction (though nominally by Herman de Lange), at the Mona Hotel, Covent Garden. However, not enough of the

cast turned up to make the rehearsal worthwhile. [D2: 871–2; DHL]

25 First rehearsal of *Widowers' Houses* with the full cast. [D2: 875]

December

5 (Mon) Shaw's close supervision (and continual interruption) of the rehearsals for *Widowers' Houses* annoys the director and distracts the cast. Shaw agrees to stay away from rehearsals so that the cast can learn their lines. [Peters 103; D2: 878]

9 *Widowers' Houses*, performed by J. T. Grein's Independent Theatre Society, opens at the Royalty Theatre, Soho, with Florence Farr playing Blanche Sartorius and comic actor James Welch (who was later to create the roles of Major Petkoff in *Arms and the Man* and The Waiter in *You Never Can Tell*) playing Lickcheese. After the performance, Shaw addresses the audience on Socialism. [CP1: 36; I&R122–43; CL1: 372; Pearson 186–7]

12 Shaw makes some alterations to *Widowers' Houses* for the following day's performance. [D2: 880]

13 *Widowers' Houses* given its second and final scheduled performance. [D2: 881]

14 William Archer's review of *Widowers' Houses* in *The World* draws a sharp response from Shaw in a postcard of the same date in which he calls Archer a 'sentimental Sweet Lavendery recluse'. [CL1: 373]

21 Shaw begins a Christmas visit at Kelmscott House. [D2: 882]

24 Shaw spends the Christmas period at Hammersmith with the Morrises. [Peters 105]

25 Shaw finishes four days of collecting and pasting into an album the 130 press cuttings, of reviews and notices, relating to *Widowers' Houses*. [CL1: 374; D2: 883]

29 Shaw returns to the city from Kelmscott. [D2: 884]

1893

During this year Shaw completes the second and third of his three *Plays Unpleasant – The Philanderer* and *Mrs Warren's Profession*. He also began writing the first of the four *Plays Pleasant – Arms and the Man*. Keir Hardie becomes the first Fabian to be elected to Parliament in the July General Election. Beatrice Webb is elected to the Fabian Society. Shaw's tangled relations with members of the opposite sex continue unabated, and he is deeply impressed with the acting and physical charms of Mrs Patrick Campbell, whom he sees acting in Ibsen's *Ghosts* in January and creating the role of Paula in Pinero's *The Second Mrs Tanqueray* in December. *The Second Mrs Tanqueray* was one of a cluster of 1893 plays in English which treated the theme of the 'woman with a past', two other works on the subject being Shaw's *Mrs Warren's Profession* and Wilde's *A Woman of No Importance*. Shaw's journalistic earnings for1893 amount to £310.

January

	William Morris instigates a Joint Committee of Socialist Bodies, made up of Fabian, Social Democratic Federation, and Hammersmith Socialist Society delegates. [CL1: 388]
3 (Tue)	Shaw attends a concert with May Morris (Sparling), and later has tea with her, Lucy and Kate Gurly, at Fitzroy Square. That night he tries out a new pair of skates bought the previous Christmas, paying sixpence for admission to the Grove Park skating pond, and arriving after 9 p.m. 'so that my awkwardness was not observed in the dark'. [D2: 890]
5	Shaw stays at the Sparlings' house at Hammersmith all day working on the appendix to *Widowers' Houses*. [D2: 891]
6	After dinner Shaw goes skating with May Morris (Sparling) for two and a quarter hours at Grove Park. [D2: 891]
11	Shaw proposes a plan to permeate Labour Party groups, and to supplant Liberalism by Progressivism in country areas. It is probable that this proposal was made on 12 January at a preliminary meeting in Bradford of Fabian delegates to the Labour Party conference. [D2: 893; CL1: 377]
12	Shaw leaves the Sparling house at Hammersmith to travel to Bradford. [CL1: 374]
13–14	Shaw represents the Fabian Society at the founding conference of the Independent Labour Party at the Labour Institute, Peckover Street, Bradford. His credentials for attendance having been challenged, Shaw 'promptly took up a strong enfilading position in the gallery', but was admitted to the conference the following day. [D2: 893–4; I&R 62–3; J. Sexton, *Sir James Sexton, Agitator: Life of the Dockers' M.P.: An Autobiography* (1936), 128–30; Pease 101; Henry Pelling, *The Origins of the Labour Party 1880–1900* (1965), 122]
16	Shaw returns from Bradford to London, resuming his room at Fitzroy Square, but staying overnight periodically at the Sparlings' where his intimacy with May continues, despite his relationship with Florence Farr. [D2: 894]
26	Shaw sees Mrs Patrick Campbell playing the part of Mrs Alving in a private performance by the Independent Theatre Society of Ibsen's *Ghosts* at the Athenaeum Theatre, 72 Tottenham Court Road. [D2: 898; Miriam A. Franc, *Ibsen in England* (1970), 102; Peters 108]

February

4 (Sat)	During an eventful day and night, Shaw interviews Elizabeth Robins who threatens to shoot him if he publishes anything of

which she does not approve. (The interview was not published.) Late in the evening, Jenny Patterson bursts in upon Shaw and Florence Farr at the latter's apartment, instigating a violent quarrel. Shaw later adapts this incident for inclusion in Act I of *The Philanderer*. The episode appears to have marked the end of the relationship with Jenny Patterson as far as Shaw was concerned, but diary entries suggest that she persisted with her claims on his affection until at least July 1896, though Shaw carefully avoided any actual encounter with her until 1898. [D2: 902–4, 909, 959–60, 973, 979, 989, 1003, 1134; CL1: 379–81; DHL; I&R 314, 316 n3; Peters 109]

19 Shaw lectures to the Liberal Club in Lincoln on Labour politics. [CL1: 382]

20 With William Archer, Shaw attends a performance of Ibsen's *The Master Builder*. [CL1: 382]

28 Shaw writes to Oscar Wilde, saying he has not yet received a promised copy of Wilde's *Salomé* ('Salomé is still wandering in her purple raiment in search of me'), and that he hopes soon to send Wilde a copy of *Widowers' Houses*. In this letter, Shaw depicts himself, Wilde and William Morris as being involved in a common cause against English Puritanism and Censorship. As writers partly on the periphery of English society they have a special educative role: 'when I say we, I mean Morris the Welshman and Wilde and Shaw the Irishmen; for to learn from Frenchmen is a condescension impossible for an Englishman.' [Theatrics 8–9]

March

3 (Fri) After seeing dramatic performances by Janet Achurch and Elizabeth Robins, Shaw writes congratulatory letters to both actresses. [CL1: 384–6]

14 Shaw buys a notebook in which to write his 'new play' (*The Philanderer*). [D2: 914]

28 March – 4 April

Shaw spends Easter with the Salts at Oxted. [D2: 918–20]

March

29 Shaw begins writing *The Philanderer*: 'After breakfast went up to the Common by Rickfield Rd. and selected a spot on the West Heath, near the orphanage, where I lay down and got to work on the new play which I resolved to call *The Philanderer*.' In the evening he plays duets with Mrs Salt. [D2: 918]

April

1 (Sat) Shaw goes on a picnic to Herbert Rix's half-built new house with the Salts, M. B. Williams and the Adamses. Herbert Rix was

a member of the Fellowship of the New Life. Francis William Lauderdale Adams was a novelist and poet who contracted tuberculosis and suicided only a few months later because of his worsening health. Following Adams's death, Edith Goldstone Adams, an Australian and a former actress, worked at promoting his verse drama, *Tiberius*, for publication. Shaw helped out in this endeavour, seeing Mrs Francis Adams fairly frequently until the time of her re-marriage in early 1894. In a letter to Shaw (21 December 1893), Mrs Francis Adams wrote: 'Delightful windbag of a genius... So you thought I was a good study for you? Beloved of my soul you haven't got to the bottom of your study by any means. Sometimes I *fancy* (only fancy) you're a bit of a liar yourself.' In Shaw's play, *The Doctor's Dilemma*, Mrs Francis Adams seems to have become the 'study' for the character of Jennifer Dubedat. [D2: 919, 968, 970, 972, 974, 976–7, 979, 1008; BL MS Add 50513]

19 Opening performance of Oscar Wilde's *A Woman of No Importance* at the Haymarket Theatre. Shaw records that he went to see the play, which ran for 113 performances, with Graham Wallas on 26 May 1893, but found the theatre closed for the evening. There is no record that he saw the play, but his knowledge of it is attested by brief but respectful references to it in theatrical reviews. [D2: 938; Drama1: 268; Drama2: 462]

24 Samuel Butler lectures to the West Central branch of the Fabian Society on the topic 'Was the Odyssey Written by a Woman?' [D2: 926; I&R 273–4; Rat 92–3]

May

Publication of *Widowers' Houses* by Henry and Co. in association with J. T. Grein of the Independent Theatre but, without effective marketing, the edition sold only 150 copies. [CL1: 423–4; I&R 97–9; Lbib1: 23]

1 (Mon) Publication by Shaw, Hyndman, and Morris of the manifesto of the Joint Committee of Socialist Bodies. [Lbib1: 492; CL1: 388]

4 In a letter to Lady Colin Campbell, Shaw praises Oscar Wilde for 'teaching the theatrical public that "a play" may be a playing with ideas instead of a feast of sham emotions compounded from dog's eared prescriptions'. In the same letter he declares that 'there are only two literary schools in England today: the Norwegian school and the Irish school'. [Theatrics 9–10]

June

5 (Mon) After a performance of *Hedda Gabler* which he attends with May Morris (Sparling), Shaw declares to Elizabeth Robins: 'I have

flattered you beyond the utmost appetite of the next vainest woman in the world... What have I ever done to you that you should so brutally shew your mistrust of me?... I cannot help being in love with you in a poetic and not in the least ignoble way.' He also brags to her that 'I have finished another play [*The Philanderer*]... Aha! I do not know how to write for the stage, do I not? We shall see, injurious Elizabeth, we shall see.' [CL1: 397]

7 Shaw discards the third act of *The Philanderer* on Lady Colin Campbell's advice. [D2: 946]

12 Upon reading *The Philanderer* to Hedwig Sonntag, Shaw discovers it is far too long, and sets about cutting and revising. [D2: 944]

21 Shaw attends a German class at '70 Cornhill'. His Diary records several German class attendances during the rest of the summer of 1893. [D2: 948]

22 Shaw begins writing a new third act for *The Philanderer*. [D2: 949]

27 Shaw completes *The Philanderer*, but the play is not presented until 20 February 1905. (A copyright reading was held on 30 March 1898.) [CP1: 134]

Mid-1893

Gladstone's Liberal government set aside the Fabian-inspired 'Newcastle Programme' of reforms, betraying the Fabians and revealing the weakness of their policy of permeation. [Pease 111–17]

July

20 (Thu) Shaw recommends the withdrawal of the Fabian Society from the Joint Committee of Socialist Bodies. [CL1: 388]

August

4 (Fri) – 14 Shaw and 60 other British delegates, including Sydney Olivier, attended the International Socialist Congress in Zurich. Olivier recalls Shaw's exploits as 'an insatiable swimmer' in the 'frigid Rhine', the 'impetuous Aar' and in the lake at Zurich during this journey. Shaw wrote about the conference ('from a special correspondent') in *The Star*'s 8–12 and 14 August editions. [D2: 961; I&R 196; Lbib2: 585]

17 Lying under the trees in Richmond Park, Shaw writes to William Archer about various subjects, including Pinero's *The Second Mrs Tanqueray*, 'a copy of which, printed for private circulation', Archer had lent him the day before. Pinero's play was among the works which influenced Shaw in the composition of *Mrs Warren's Profession*. [D2: 962; CL1: 400–2]

18	Again in the Park, Shaw contemplates the idea of working on 'a new play', but 'no ideas came'. In the evening he and Florence Farr visit the Earls Court Exhibition and Water Show at St James's Park, try the water chute together and take iced drinks. [D2: 962]
19	Shaw spends a leisurely day, strolling up to Hampstead and bathing and lunching there, before meeting Florence Farr and spending an afternoon reading papers, talking and dozing on the Heath. [D2: 962]
20	Shaw begins writing his third play, *Mrs Warren's Profession*. Earlier in the day he had been reading a childhood favourite *The Pilgrim's Progress* which he said 'still retains its fascination for me'. [D2: 963]
26	Shaw begins a three week stay with the Webbs at 'The Argoed' in Monmouth, during which he helps them revise their *History of Trade Unionism*. [D2: 964; CL1: 403–5; Webb 36; Peters 118; Morgan 8]
28	Shaw visits Beaufort Castle. [D2: 965]
29	Shaw visits Tintern Abbey. [D2: 965]
30	Shaw tells William Archer: 'I have finished the first act of my new play [*Mrs Warren's Profession*], in which I have skilfully blended the plot of The Second Mrs Tanqueray with that of The Cenci.' [CL1: 403]

September

4 (Mon)	Shaw tells Janet Achurch he has half finished the second act of *Mrs Warren's Profession*. The dramatic narrative of the play is indebted to Guy De Maupassant's story *Yvette* which Janet had suggested as providing promising material. She was simultaneously writing her own play based on this story, entitled *Mrs Daintree's Daughter*. [CL1: 403–4]
18	Shaw returns to London from Monmouth. [D2: 968]
19	Shaw begins drafting a Fabian Political Manifesto, which, co-authored by Sidney Webb, was to be published in November under the title 'To Your Tents, O Israel'. [D2: 968; DBW2: 40–1]
26–27	Shaw visits the Salts at Oxted, returning for a further visit on 1–2 October. [D2: 970, 972]

October

11 (Wed)	Shaw reads *Mrs Warren's Profession* to Janet Achurch. [D2: 975]
13	Shaw reads the Fabian Manifesto to a private business meeting of the Society in order to secure approval to publish it in the *Fortnightly Review*. [D2: 975]
16	Shaw meets Frank Harris at the *Fortnightly Review* office. [D2: 976; Harris 125–6]

November

1 (Wed) Publication in the *Fortnightly Review* (under the signature 'The Fabian Society') of 'To Your Tents, O Israel!' the Fabian manifesto written by Sidney Webb and Shaw. This attack on the Liberals provokes H. W. Massingham to resign from the Fabian Society, and his paper, the *Daily Chronicle*, to become hostile to the Fabians. [Lbib2: 586; DBW2: 40–1; Pease 115–17]

2 Shaw records in his diary that he has 'Finished the play' [*Mrs Warren's Profession*]. Shaw later revises the end of the third act. [D2: 982; CP1: 230; Peters 122]

5 Shaw dines with H. W. Massingham, disillusioned Fabian and editor of the *Daily Chronicle* who had recently attacked the Fabian Society in his paper. [CL1: 407]

6 Shaw 'spoke recklessly, without tact or temper, and probably did more harm than good' at the London Liberal and Radical Union council meeting. [D2: 983; CL1: 407]

7 On his way to see Florence Farr who, he has just learnt, has been offered £500 to produce Ibsen's *Wild Duck*, Shaw and May Morris 'forgot to get out of the train'. [D2: 983; Peters 123]

10 Shaw moves that the Fabian Society withdraw from the Joint Committee of Socialist Bodies. The motion is carried. [D2: 984]

14 In a letter to Elizabeth Robins, Shaw says he wishes she were 15 years older so that she could play Mrs Warren in his recently completed *Mrs Warren's Profession*. [Theatrics 10–11]

26 Shaw begins writing his fourth play, *Arms and the Man*. Originally entitled *Alps and Balkans*, the play is intended for Florence Farr, who has been granted £500 by Abbey Theatre patron Annie Horniman to promote a dramatic season at the Avenue Theatre in London. However, the play is not completed by the time Florence Farr is ready to open in late March. [D2: 989; Peters 124; CL1: 413; Hol1: 197, 199]

December

2 (Sat) Shaw visits the Charringtons where 'an orgy of play-reading over which we all made merry' takes place including Shaw's reading of what he has written so far of *Arms and the Man*. [D2: 992; CL1: 409]

3 Shaw lectures on 'How We Become Atheists' to the Pioneer Reform Association. [CL1: 408]

4 Alice Lockett, now Mrs William Salisbury Sharpe, visits Shaw. [D2: 992]

11 Shaw attends a performance at St James's Theatre of Pinero's *The Second Mrs Tanqueray* in which Mrs Patrick Campbell, 'a very attractive person', plays Paula Tanqueray. [D2: 995]

12 Shaw outlines the casting requirements of *Mrs Warren's Profession* to J. T. Grein presumably for a proposed production by the Independent Theatre. But Grein considers the work too risky, and it is not presented until 5 June 1902. [CL1: 412–13]

17 Shaw lectures on 'The Political Situation' at the Eleusis Club in Chelsea. [CL1: 408–9]

22 Shaw, Graham Wallas and the Webbs begin a three-week Christmas visit to 'The Argoed'. [D2: 998; DBW2: 40]

1894

In April of this year, Shaw's *Arms and the Man* opens at Florence Farr's Avenue Theatre. In August he writes his last column of music criticism for *The World*, and is subsequently offered the post of dramatic critic for Frank Harris's *Saturday Review*. The first performance of *Arms and the Man* at the Herald Square Theater, New York, on 17 September, with Richard Mansfield playing Bluntschli, marks Shaw's debut as a playwright in America. In the final months of the year he begins and completes *Candida*.

January

Shaw revises and enlarges 'To Your Tents, Oh Israel!' into Fabian Tract No. 49, *A Plan of Campaign for Labour*, one of the most controversial documents ever published by the Society. [Lbib1: 25; CL1: 419]

10 (Wed) Shaw returns to London from 'The Argoed'. [D2: 1005]

29 Shaw declines an invitation to stand as a parliamentary candidate in Chelsea. [CL1: 419]

February

14 (Wed) Reading three of the parts, Shaw assists with a copyrighting performance of Janet Achurch's *Mrs Daintree's Daughter* at Ladbroke Hall, Notting Hill. [D2: 1013;Wein3: 51]

March

17 (Sat) At Sergius Stepniak's house, Shaw meets a former Russian admiral, Esper Aleksandrovich Serebryekov, who advises him on the Balkan setting for *Arms and the Man*. [D2: 1019; I&R125–7; Theatrics 12]

21–29 Shaw visits the Salts at Oxted. [D2: 1021–2]

29 Shaw attends the opening of John Todhunter's *A Comedy of Sighs* and W. B. Yeats's *The Land of Heart's Desire*, the inaugural performances of Florence Farr's season at the Avenue Theatre. (Dr John Todhunter was the son of the owner of Todhunter's ironworks in Dublin where Shaw's father was employed from 1838. His play was a failure, and was replaced on 21 April by Shaw's *Arms and the Man*.) [D2: 1022; Peters 124–6]

30 Shaw finds Florence Farr and her acting manager Charles Helmsley in despair about the Avenue Theatre season, and contemplating production of his *Widowers' Houses*. After dissuading them from that he goes to the Embankment Gardens and puts the finishing touches on *Arms and the Man*. [D2: 1023]

April

11 (Wed) Commencement of rehearsals of *Arms and the Man*, supervised by Shaw, with Alma Murray playing Raina and Florence Farr as Louka. [D2: 1024; Peters 127]

20 In one of a series of admonitions about her diet and use of stimulants, Shaw writes to Janet Achurch, saying he wishes she had a good vegetarian cook, or that he could get Mrs Besant to 'make a Theosophist' of her. The Brahminical regimen had been a complete success with Mrs Besant. [Shaw to Janet Achurch, 20 Apr 1894, Texas]

21 *Arms and the Man* opens for 50 performances in a Shaw–Todhunter–Yeats season at Florence Farr's Avenue Theatre in London, replacing Todhunter's unsuccessful *Comedy of Sighs*. Florence Farr played the part of the fiery maidservant, Louka. A single boo amidst cheers and laughter at the end of the play provoked Shaw's famous response: 'I assure the gentleman in the gallery that he and I are of exactly the same opinion, but what can we do against a whole house who are of the contrary opinion.' The booer was future critic R. Golding Bright. Yeats (whose wording of the response is that quoted above) declared that 'from that moment Bernard Shaw became the most formidable man in modern letters'. The Prince of Wales and Duke of Edinburgh, who also attended, declared the author 'mad' and 'a crank'. [CP1: 388; W. B. Yeats, *Autobiographies* (1955), 281–4; Hend3: 427; CL1: 447; D2: 1025–6.]

22 Shaw participates in a debate at the Playgoers' Club on 'Criticism, Corruption, and the Remedy'. Janet Achurch also attended, standing up at the end to denounce herself publicly as a failure. [CL1: 432; Peters 136; I&R 59–60]

24 Shaw addresses 'a most private letter' to Janet Achurch fiercely reproaching her for displaying a 'want of reverence' for her own genius by calling herself a failure at the Playgoers' Club. He has two sorts of feeling for her, 'one is an ordinary man-and-woman hankering after you', the other deriving from his 'very strong sense of artistic faculty and its value', and his great respect for her 'power as an actress'. [Shaw to Janet Achurch, 24 Apr 1894, Texas]

25–26 Shaw attends the London Reform Union Poor Law Conference. [D2: 1026]

May

11 (Fri) Dropping in on a performance of *Arms and the Man*, Shaw is appalled to find the cast has lapsed into mechanical, uninspired acting. [Peters 132; CL1: 435]

19 *The World* editor Edmund Yates dies from a massive heart attack at the Savoy Hotel. [Peter Whitebrook, *William Archer: A Biography* (1993), 169; Auto1: 221]

30 Shaw resigns from his position as music critic on *The World*, but the new editor persuades him to stay on until the autumn recess. [CL1: 436–7; D 2: 1031; Peters 132]

June

9 (Sat) Shaw issues to Richard Mansfield a licence to produce *Arms and the Man* for one year in North America. [CL1: 441–2]

July

2 (Mon) Writing to Edward McNulty about the earnings of *Arms and The Man*, Shaw says: 'I have taken the very serious step of cutting off my income by privately arranging to drop *The World* business at the end of the season; and now, if I cannot make something out of the theatre, I am a ruined man; for I have not £20 saved; and Lucy and Kate Gurly (my mother's half sister) are now members of the family. I am about to begin the world at last.' [CL1: 447–8]

8 Last letter from Elinor Huddart, saying, *inter alia*: 'I am not mad most noble Festus.' [BL MS Add 50537]

16 Shaw departs for Bayreuth, stopping at Darmstadt, Würzburg and Nuremburg. [CL1: 450]

17 Shaw travels to Darmstadt especially to view Hans Holbein's 'Meyer Madonna'. As 'Corno di Bassetto', Shaw writes an article about this visit, 'Pursuing Holbein's Madonna', which remains unpublished until 1989. [*Bernard Shaw on the London Art Scene*, ed. Stanley Weintraub (1989), 363–6]

26 Shaw returns to London from Bayreuth. An elderly Fabian, Henry Hunt Hutchinson, commits suicide. His bequest to the Fabian Society of a large portion of his estate is used by Sidney Webb to found the London School of Economics. [D2: 1051; CL1: 304,450; DBW2: 56]

1 August – 4 September

Shaw visits the Salts at Tilford, coming up to London in the last ten days of August to attend rehearsals for the provincial tour of *Arms and the Man*. [D2: 1041–2]

August

8 (Wed) Shaw's last column of music criticism in *The World*. He expresses great relief to leave music criticism behind, having

'written a long article on the subject every week for seven years'. [Lbib2: 591; CL1: 460; CL1: 448; D2: 1041]

September

Frank Harris buys the *Saturday Review*, and probably at about this time invites Shaw to take the post of drama critic. [Frank Harris, *Contemporary Portraits*, 4 vols (1915–24), 2: 3–8; I&R 90–3]

5 (Wed) Shaw embarks on his second tour of Italy with the Art Workers' Guild. [D2: 1043; CL1: 454; I&R 212]

17 Shaw's American première. *Arms and the Man* opens at the Herald Square Theater in New York, with Richard Mansfield playing Bluntschli. Hailed by the critics, the play runs initially for 16 performances, returns to the bill later in the season, and remains in the Mansfield repertory for several years. [CL1: 441; Peters 139]

23 Shaw returns to London from Italy, having visited Basle, Pallanza, Milan, Florence, Pisa, Genoa and Como. [D2: 1043–4; CL1: 454]

October

2 (Tue) Having returned to the Salts' at Tilford, Shaw begins writing *Candida*, with Janet Achurch in mind for the leading female role. [D2: 1044; Peters 137–8]

15 Shaw completes Act I of *Candida*. [D2: 1045]

27 Shaw finishes reading Buckle's *History of Civilisation in England* (1857–61), which with Marx's *Kapital* leaves a 'permanent mark' on his mind. [CL1: 456]

29 Shaw embarks on a week-long lecture tour of northern England. [CL1: 458]

November

5 (Mon) American and British royalties on *Arms and the Man* amounting to some £340, Shaw opens his first bank account, at the London and County Bank, which later becomes the Westminster, the Oxford Street branch of which Shaw used until the year of his death. [D2: 1057; CL1: 447; DHL]

6 Shaw completes Act II of *Candida*. [D2: 1048]

8 'Trennung' (parting) from Florence Farr. Shaw and Florence Farr have ceased seeing each other regularly since the closing of *Arms and the Man*, although she has begun divorce proceedings against Edward Emery at Shaw's urging. [D2: 1048] Years later, Shaw was to write to Hesketh Pearson and Clifford Bax about Florence Farr. To Pearson (30 July 1939) Shaw wrote: 'She attached no more importance to what you call love affairs than

Casanova or Frank Harris'. To Bax (9 August 1940) '...you have some letters I wrote to the late Florence Farr. I am surprised to learn that I wrote any; for I saw so much of her that our intercourse was viva voce and not literary.
PS How the dickens did you get hold of them?... Florence claimed 14 lovers. Were you the fifteenth?' [Pearson 118; Shaw to Clifford Bax, Texas]

December

2 (Sun) Shaw lectures on 'The Limits of Social-Democracy' at Kentish Town. [D2: 1051; CL1: 466–7]

3 Shaw attends a private reading of William Archer's new translation of Ibsen's *Little Eyolf*. [CL1: 467]

4 Shaw calls on Frank Harris and settles his appointment to the position of regular theatre critic on the *Saturday Review* at £6 per week. [D2: 1052; CL1: 460]

7 Shaw finishes writing *Candida*, but could not get anyone to produce it in London with Janet Achurch in the leading role. [D2: 1052; CL1: 473, 478, 486]

15 Shaw runs unsuccessfully for a seat on the St Pancras Vestry. [D2: 1053; I&R 68]

22 Shaw takes a vacation at Folkestone with Graham Wallas, returning to London on 29 December. He writes to Janet Achurch saying he will begin a new play shortly, 'the last [*Candida*] having been so happily inspired by you'. [D2: 1053–4; CL1: 471]

28 On the eve of his new posting as dramatic critic on the *Saturday Review*, Shaw expresses his determination to 'educate the public into wanting' his plays. [CL1: 473]

1895

In January of this year, Shaw commences his appointment as theatre critic for the *Saturday Review*. On 5 January, at a performance of Henry James's play *Guy Domville,* he meets H. G. Wells. From 6 January, he begins taking regular Sunday lunches with the Webbs. He learns to ride a bicycle, which becomes a regular pastime (a famous bicycle collision between Shaw and Bertrand Russell occurs during Shaw's summer holiday with the Webbs). In May, he first sees the 'thrilling' 19-year-old Lillah McCarthy playing Lady Macbeth. He completes the first draft of *The Man of Destiny*, and begins writing *You Never Can Tell*. He drafts petitions in support of Oscar Wilde during his prosecution and imprisonment on charges of gross indecency. He resists the recommendation of 'everybody' that he should marry Bertha Newcombe.

January

1 (Tue) Having been 'fairly forced' by Harris, Shaw takes up his duties as theatre critic on the *Saturday Review*. Janet Achurch accompanies him on his first assignment, Sydney Grundy's *Slaves of the Ring*, but her public deportment leaves so much to be desired that Shaw puts her into a cab at the end of the second act. [D2: 1059–60; CL1: 472; Peters 141; Shaw to Janet Achurch, 3 Jan 1895, Texas]

5 The same day as his first piece of dramatic criticism appears in the *Saturday Review*, Shaw meets H. G. Wells (who was then at the beginning of a brief appointment as theatre critic for the *Pall Mall Gazette*) at a performance of Henry James's *Guy Domville* at St James's Theatre. [Lbib2: 591; H. G. Wells, *Experiment in Autobiography*, 2 vols (London, 1934), 2: 539–41; H. G. Wells, 'Bernard Shaw', *Daily Express*, 3 November 1950; I&R 269–70]

6 Shaw has Sunday lunch at the Webbs' house, a custom he keeps up throughout the year. [D2: 1059]

8 Shaw continues his reproaches about Janet Achurch's drinking habits. He points out that he himself survived nine years of 'unbroken failure and rebuff', but weathered it all 'penniless, loveless, and hard as nails', and without recourse to stimulants. He doesn't want to become her 'private temperance lecturer', and recalls an incident which took place at Kensington Gore in which, he says, Janet hurled a bus conductor 'from his perch into the mud, beating him with [her] gloves, jumping on him, and leaving him for dead because the fare had been raised...' [Shaw to Janet Achurch, 8 Jan 1895, Texas]

22 Shaw attends a dinner organized by Sidney Webb where Fabian and ILP members – MacDonald, Smith, Hardie, Mann, and Pease – aimed at enhancing cooperation between the two Socialist groups. [Webb 121]

February

4 (Mon) Writing to Edward Pease, Shaw notes that: 'no less than ten evenings this month are already booked for public orations alone.' [CL1: 482]

14 Shaw declines Clement Shorter's offer to write for *The Illustrated London News*. [CL1: 482–3]

22 Shaw offers Richard Mansfield *The Philanderer* and *Candida*. [CL1: 486–7, 487–8]

March

While attending one of Frank Harris's *Saturday Review* staff lunches at the Café Royale, Shaw is present when Oscar Wilde

	asks Harris to testify (at the hearing of his libel suit against the Marquess of Queensberry) to the 'high artistic character' of *The Picture of Dorian Gray*. Harris and Shaw vainly warn Wilde to drop the charge and flee the country. [D2: 1060; Hyde xii-xiv; Richard Ellman, *Oscar Wilde* (1987), 415–16]
1 (Fri)	Shaw speaks on 'Slaughter House Reform' at the Humanitarian League Conference. Writing to Charles Charrington, Shaw complains: 'I have had to work until I became sick – positively and literally sick – this week.' [D2: 1068; CL1: 489]
2	Publication in the *Saturday Review* of 'Down with Censorship!', a critical obituary by Shaw of E. F. S. Pigott, the recently deceased licensor of plays. [Lbib2: 592; CL1: 488; DHL]
3	Shaw lectures on 'The Fabian Society' to the Camberwell branch of the Social Democratic Federation. [CL1: 493]
4	Shaw lectures on 'The Fabian Society' to a social group in Hampstead called The Argosy. [CL1: 493]
13	Although rushing to get scripts and music scores for *Candida* ready for Janet Achurch to take to America the following day, Shaw goes to a Fabian Executive meeting then attends the opening of Pinero's *The Notorious Mrs Ebbsmith* at the Garrick Theatre. His review notes that Mrs Patrick Campbell is 'a wonderful woman', but dismisses the play as 'a piece of claptrap'. [D2: 1069; CL1: 495; Drama1: 283–7; OTN1: 59–66]
16	Janet Achurch departs for America to play in Richard Mansfield's production of *Candida*. Over the next weeks, Shaw attempts to mediate in the quarrels between Janet Achurch and Mansfield, who disliked her intensely. [CL1: 500ff.]
23	In a letter to Janet Achurch, Shaw writes of the recreative powers of religion 'which sanctifies all life and substitutes a profound dignity and self-respect for the old materialistic self.' [CL1: 505]
29	W. A. S. Hewins is appointed as Director of the London School of Economics, which Sidney Webb is 'slowly and quietly' establishing with the Hutchinson bequest. Graham Wallas had already declined the position when asked by Sidney. Temporary premises are found at 9 John Street, Adelphi. [DBW2: 71–2]
30	Copyright reading of *Candida* at the Theatre Royal, South Shields. [CP1: 514; I&R 130; Rat 104]

April

3 (Wed)	Shaw learns that Mansfield has decided to withdraw *Candida*. He sends off a volley of letters to Janet Achurch and cables to Richard Mansfield over the next several weeks. [CL1: 513ff.]
5	Publication in *The Realm* of self-drafted interview '*Candida*: a Talk with Mr Bernard Shaw'. An exchange about his disregard

for conventional plot in the play sets a pattern for numerous comments by Shaw on his dramatic practice:

'And then what happens?'
'Some conversations. That's all.'
'Absolutely nothing more than that?'
'No more than that. But such conversations!'
[*The Realm*, 5 Apr 1895; I&R 130–2]

10 Beginning of a week's Easter holiday at Beachy Head, Eastbourne with the Webbs. Shaw learns to ride a bicycle. [D2: 1073–4; I&R 214; DBW2: 72]

16 Shaw cables to Mansfield withdrawing his permission to produce *Candida*, and demanding that the MS be returned to American play-agent Elizabeth Marbury. [CL1: 519–20]

17 Shaw returns to London from Beachy Head. [D2: 1075; CL1: 519]

18 Mansfield cables: 'Since you insist will produce *Candida*.' Shaw replies: 'Withdrawal final.' [CL1: 521]

May

3 (Fri) Shaw complains to Janet Achurch about her not writing to him. He declares that unless he receives a letter in the mail the following day, 'F.F. [Florence Farr] shall be Mrs Bernard Shaw at the earliest date thereafter permitted by statute.' (Florence Farr was also away, in the Channel Islands and at Basingstoke playing Esther Eccles in T.W. Robertson's *Caste*.) [CL1: 532]

9 Shaw sees Lillah McCarthy give a 'highly promising performance' of Lady Macbeth in an amateur production by the Shakespeare Reading Society at St George's Hall, which he reviews in the *Saturday Review*, 25 May 1895. [D2: 1078; Drama2: 348–53; OTN1: 126–33; Peters 278]

10 Shaw begins writing *The Man of Destiny* in Regent's Park. [D2: 1079; CP1: 606; CL1: 539]

16 To Janet Achurch, Shaw writes: 'It is no use: marriage is a damnable thing, root and branch. If I were married to you, I should be jealous of everybody; and I should be the only person of whom nobody else would be jealous.' [Shaw to Janet Achurch, 16 May 1895, Texas]

25 Oscar Wilde convicted on the charge of gross indecency and sentenced to two years' imprisonment with hard labour. According to Mary Hyde, Shaw shortly afterwards drafted a petition for Wilde's release, but was unable to obtain enough signatures. [Hyde xix]

June

Janet Achurch returns to London. [CL1: 534]

1 Publication in the *Saturday Review* of Shaw's article 'Sardoodledom', Shaw's celebrated satirical attack on the

mechanical devices of the well-made play, as demonstrated in the plays of Victorien Sardou, whose plays *Fedora* and *Gismonda* were under review. [Lbib2: 594; OTN1: 33–40; Drama2: 354–9]

July

8 (Mon) From 'The Argoed', Monmouth, where he is holidaying with the Webbs, Shaw reports to Janet Achurch that 'the new play [*You Never Can Tell*] is not coming'. He resumes writing *You Never Can Tell*, initially entitled *The Terrestrial Twins*, in December 1895. [CL1: 539; D2: 1059–60; CP1: 668]

16 Shaw goes to William Archer's to meet Gilbert Murray, then a professor of Greek at Glasgow University. Archer had recently read the manuscript for Murray's play, *Carlyon Sahib*, and had invited Shaw and Murray to discuss the play. [D1087–8]

31 July – 21 September

Shaw holidays with the Webbs at their holiday house 'The Argoed', in the Wye Valley in South Wales. Despite their mutual esteem, Shaw finds life in close proximity with Beatrice Webb a strain, her nature being 'hostile to mine'. He expresses a complex mixture of envy and horror at the Webbs' physical and intellectual intimacy. Bertha Newcombe is in love with Shaw at this time, but the feeling is not reciprocated. [D2: 1088; CL1: 539, 545–6, 548–9, 554, 558–9; I&R 214, 277–8; DBW2: 79–82]

August

24 (Sat) Shaw finishes the first draft of *The Man of Destiny* (with Richard Mansfield in mind in his characterization of Napoleon). [CL1: 546; D2: 1089; CP1: 606]

September

1 (Sun) Shaw and the Webbs cycle to Cardiff, where they attend a Trades Union Congress and Fabian Executive meeting before returning to 'The Argoed' on 7 September. Beatrice Webb recalls the journey to Cardiff in her diary for 9 September 1895: 'Sidney, Shaw and I left... about ten o'clock on our cycles, rode through the exquisite valley of Raglan, Usk to Newport, thence along the coast to Cardiff, our first long ride (forty miles) arriving at the great Park Hotel hot, dusty and pleasantly self-complacent with our new toy and its exploits.' [D2: 1090; DBW2: 80]

9 Shaw declines Fisher Unwin's invitation to publish his plays. [CL1: 556]

12 Shaw has a spectacular bicycle collision with Bertrand Russell, whose knickerbockers are 'demolished' in the accident. [CL1: 558–9; D2: 1091]

21–23 Shaw travels by train and bicycle to London, via Bath, Salisbury Plain, Stonehenge, Andover and Basingstoke. [D2: 1091; CL1: 560]

October

4 (Fri) Shaw lectures on 'The Political Situation' at a Fabian Society meeting. [CL1: 545]

29 Janet Achurch falls ill with typhoid fever, causing Shaw much concern during November and December. [D2: 1059–60]

November

28 (Thu) Shaw dispatches the completed MS of *The Strange Lady* [i.e. *The Man of Destiny*] to Ellen Terry, calling it his 'beautiful little one act play for Napoleon and a strange lady'. [CL1: 565, 572]

December

Shaw resumes work on *You Never Can Tell* after a break of several months. [D2: 1088; CL1: 583; CP1: 668; Peters 177]

1 (Sun) Shaw lectures in Battersea on 'The Political Situation' to the Labour League. [D2: 1099; CL1: 563]

2 Shaw reads *Candida* to the actor manager Charles Wyndham at the Criterion Theatre, but Wyndham rejects the play. [CL1: 630]

13 Shaw declines a challenge (addressed to 'our friend, the enemy, G. Bernard Shaw, Fabian') from feminist 'new woman' Amy Constance Morant to a debate on 'The Place of Woman in the Community'. [CL1: 574–5]

15 Shaw sends Charles Charrington £10 to assist with expenses caused by Janet Achurch's illness from typhoid fever. [CL1: 579–60; D2: 1101]

23 Shaw chastises Janet Achurch who, recovering from her illness, is returning to her old 'brandy and soda... morphia injecting self'. Sergius Stepniak is killed by a train while crossing the tracks at Chiswick. Shaw helps set up a fund for his widow. [CL1: 582; D2: 1116]

1896

On 29 January of this year Shaw meets his future wife, Charlotte Payne-Townshend at the London home of Beatrice and Sidney Webb. They become 'constant companions' during a late summer holiday with the Webbs in Suffolk. Shaw becomes impatient with Florence Farr's increasing interest in occultism and their relationship falters. His correspondence with Ellen Terry flourishes. He completes *You Never Can Tell* and *The Devil's Disciple*.

January

14 (Tue) Shaw laments a drastic haircut carried out with ‘an instrument like a lawnmower’ which reduces his auburn locks to ‘a little [grey] wiglike oasis on the top’. [CL1: 585–6]

28 ‘[R]are scenes’ with Florence Farr as she takes leave of Shaw on her way to France for a brief visit. Shaw has not availed himself of the opportunity for marriage opened up by Florence’s recent divorce. [D2: 1117; CL1: 591]

29 Beatrice Webb introduces Shaw to Charlotte Payne-Townshend. Charlotte wrote in her Annuary for the year 1896: ‘Returned to London 4 Jan. Went a good deal to School of Medicine and saw the Webbs now and then. Met G.B.S. first time at Webbs 29 Jan. School of Economics beginning. Took flat Adelphi Terrace.’ [DBW2: 99; BL MS Add 56500; Dunbar 117]

February

4 (Tue) Shaw completes the first act of *You Never Can Tell*. [D2: 1118–19]

5 Shaw dines with Richard Burton Haldane, H. H. Asquith, and Arthur Balfour. [CL1: 587]

March

Shaw begins a series of negotiations (at times through Ellen Terry) with Henry Irving over *The Man of Destiny*, and with Charles Charrington and Janet Achurch over *Candida*. [CL1: 582–3, 608–14, 615–18, 620–7, 633–5, 641; D2: 1127]

7 (Sat) Shaw calls on William Terriss, actor-manager of the Adelphi Theatre, probably to discuss Terriss’s request for a Shaw melodrama, which led to the creation later in the year of *The Devil’s Disciple*. [D2: 1122,1127]

20 Shaw’s first reference to his future wife, Charlotte Payne-Townshend: ‘$^{\circ}$Miss Payne Townshend At-Home to London School of Economics lectures.’ (A superscript circle which he used up to this point in his diaries to indicate unkept engagements appears at the beginning of this entry.) Shaw meets with Archer in the British Museum Reading room, looks at a bicycle, and drops in on an art show instead. [D2: 1124; Dunbar 117]

30 March – 17 April

Shaw stays with Graham Wallas, his sister, and his niece at Stocks Cottage, Aldbury, ‘a lonely cottage on a remote hillside’ near Tring (returning to London to carry out his reviewing assignments). The Webbs and Charles Charrington also visit. By the 13th, Shaw has completed Act II of *You Never Can Tell*. The following day he makes a scenario for *The Devil’s Disciple*. [D2: 1125–7; CL1: 618, 620–1, 624–5]

April

Publication in periodical *The Young Man* of 'What is it to be a Fabian?: An Interview with Mr. George Bernard Shaw' by journalist Percy L. Parker, in which Shaw declares that 'a Fabian is a Socialist who is not a Socialist... we do not want in the Fabian Society a man who has got economic theories, or a social creed, to which he wants to square the world and human nature... We want a man who keeps his eye definitely on certain concrete reforms which we want to bring about.' [*The Young Man* (London), vol. X, no. 112 (April 1896)]

11 (Sat) Shaw reviews Thomas Common's translation of *Nietzsche contra Wagner*, the first volume of a proposed, but not completed, Collected Works of Nietzsche, in the *Saturday Review*. [CL1: 620; Drama2: 567–72; OTN2: 92–8]

May

18 (Mon) Shaw completes *You Never Can Tell*, his first play intended for the West End. [D2: 1130; CP1: 668]

July

13 (Mon) While riding his bicycle in Pall Mall on his way to see Florence Farr, Shaw is run down by a bolting horse pulling a railway van. He escapes with bruises only, but his bicycle is mangled into 'an amazing iron spider'. [CL1: 636; D2: 1134]

19–22 Shaw attends the annual Bayreuth Wagner festival. [D2: 1135; CL1: 633]

27–31 Shaw attends the International Socialist Congress at St Martin's Town Hall, London, a 'hideous fiasco' according to Beatrice Webb. [Webb 13; D2: 1136; CL1: 614; I&R 277]

1 August – 17 September

The Webbs and Charlotte Payne-Townshend rent Stratford St Andrew Rectory near Saxmundham, Suffolk, and invite Graham Wallas (whom Beatrice intends for Charlotte) and Shaw as houseguests. Wallas arrives four days late, by which time Shaw and Charlotte have become, in Beatrice Webb's words, 'constant companions'. Shaw spends the mornings writing and the afternoons cycling. He gives epistolary directions to Ellen Terry who is to play Imogen in Henry Irving's upcoming production of *Cymbeline* at the Lyceum. [DBW2: 101; CL1: 642ff.; D2: 1137; CP2: 51]

August

22 (Sat) Shaw writes to Charles Charrington about the casting of Gloria in *You Never Can Tell*: 'Janet [Achurch] would not do, because she would wipe the floor not only with Dolly, but probably with the play as well – Winifred [Emery] would quite certainly

play Gloria ten times over sooner than let her have such a chance... But Elizabeth [Robins]... would develop the proud, opinionated, unpopular side of Gloria – in fact, she would *be* Gloria.' [Theatrics 18]

28 Shaw tells Ellen Terry of his intentions regarding Charlotte: 'I am going to refresh my heart by falling in love with her.' [CL1: 645–6]

September

Sponsored by writer and art connoisseur More Adey, and probably drafted by Shaw, a petition urging Oscar Wilde's early release is prepared but, like the petition of mid-1895, it founders through lack of a sufficient number of signatures. [Hyde xxi; H. Montgomery Hyde, *Oscar Wilde: The Aftermath* (1963), 43–5]

7 (Mon) Shaw gives Janet Achurch a lively account of life on holiday with the Webbs in the leased Rectory in Suffolk: 'I am up to the neck in infidelities and villainies of all kinds. If the walls of this simpleminded rectory could only describe the games they have witnessed, the parson would move, horrorstricken, to another house. The nucleus of the party is Webb, Beatrice, myself and Miss Payne-Townshend, an Irishwoman with an income of about £5,000 a year (as I guess), who has been, so far, able to take care of it and herself, to see the world, to shun matrimony, and finally to get herself attached, as munificent patroness, to the London School of Economics, on the upper floors of which she will reside when she returns to London...' [Shaw to Janet Achurch, 7 Sep 1896, Texas; Peters 187–8]

10 Shaw begins writing *The Devil's Disciple*. [D2: 1137; CP2: 51]

21 Shaw, Charlotte and the Webbs arrive in London, having cycled from Stratford St Andrew via Felixstowe, Harwich, Braintree, Hertford and St Albans. [D2: 1138; CL1: 654; Peters 189; Dunbar 123]

22 Shaw attends the opening of *Cymbeline* at the Lyceum with Ellen Terry playing Imogen. After the play Henry Irving announces the plays for the coming season, but Shaw's *The Man of Destiny* is not among them. [CL1: 661, 665; D2: 1138]

23 Shaw asks Henry Irving for permission to submit *The Man of Destiny* to other managers. [CL1: 667]

26 Shaw has a meeting with Henry Irving at the Lyceum, and Irving retains *The Man of Destiny*. Ellen Terry, planning to attend the interview, gets as far as the office door before losing courage and fleeing from what would have been her first meeting with Shaw. [CL1: 669–70; Peters 184–5]

October

2 (Fri) Shaw confesses to Ellen Terry, 'I, too, fear to break the spell... [fear] materialising this beautiful friendship of ours by a meeting'. [CL1: 672]

3 Death of William Morris.

4 Shaw lectures on 'The Respectability of Socialism' at the Hornsey Socialist Society. [CL1: 672]

5 Shaw writes to Ellen Terry: 'I am at my wits' end – telegrams every five minutes asking for articles about Morris... Happy Morris! he is *resting*... I am beaten, tired, wrecked.' [CL1: 672–3]

9 The first rumblings within the Fabian Society of dissatisfaction with the 'Old Gang'. Ramsay MacDonald moves that Shaw's Tract No. 70, the 'Report on Fabian Policy', be withdrawn. But the motion is defeated 108–33. [CL1: 674]

12, 14 Shaw's letters to Florence Farr ('lost wretch') reveal his increasing irritation at her interest in 'exoteric Egyptology'. Florence's small book, *Egyptian Magic,* had just been published. In his letter of 14 October he warns mankind to 'beware of women with large eyes, and crescent eyebrows. And a smile, and a love of miracles and moonshees.' [CL1: 674–5, 679]

26 Charlotte Payne-Townshend and Beatrice Webb travel to Manchester to attend a conference of the National Union of Women Workers, after which Charlotte travels to Ireland. Shaw misses her companionship, and writes to her frequently in tones at once more prosaic and more intimate than the ostentatious gallantries addressed to his other female correspondents. [CL1: 686, 687–92]

November

1 (Sun) Publication in the periodical *The Chap-Book* (Chicago) of 'George Bernard Shaw', a written interview based on questions submitted to Shaw by the author and journalist Clarence Rook. This interview, containing much autobiographical material, begins with Shaw's statement: 'Even after twenty years London has hardly caught my tone yet.' [*The Chap-Book* (Chicago), vol. v, no. 12 (1 Nov 1896); Lbib2: 601; I&R 22–9]

2 Shaw travels to Bradford to campaign for Keir Hardie in his unsuccessful candidature for the seat of East Bradford. [CL1: 688]

4 While Charlotte is away in Ireland, Shaw writes to her almost daily. Unlike the abrupt notes that Shaw had previously sent Charlotte, his letters have now become long and intimate. 'I want to tell you lies face to face – close... P. S. I have a curious fancy to go to Derry without going to Ireland – by long sea or

	balloon or something, & spending just one evening there with you.' [CL1: 692]
6	Ellen Terry urges Shaw to propose marriage to Charlotte. [CL1: 696]
7	Shaw warns Charlotte: 'Don't fall in love... From the moment that you can't do without me, you're lost, like Bertha.' [CL1: 697]
8	Shaw writes to Grant Richards about the plays which Richards was to publish in 1898 as the two-volume *Plays Pleasant and Unpleasant*. Shaw was doubtful about the success of this venture and called Richards 'crazy to think of printing his plays'. [CL1: 698; I&R 97–9]
9	To Charlotte: 'I will contrive to see you somehow, at all hazards: I *must*; and that "must," which "rather alarms" you, TERRIFIES me... how I should like to see you again for pure *liking*; for there is something between us aside and apart from all my villainy.' [CL1: 699]
10	Charlotte returns to London. After seeing her, Shaw writes, 'Forgive me this one night of selfish *blessedness*. I really was happy. You always surpass my expectations.' [CL1: 686, 700].
12	Shaw departs for Paris to see a production of *Peer Gynt*. [CL1: 697; D2: 1142]
13	Shaw leaves Paris for London where he is scheduled to attend two Fabian meetings later the same day. [CL1: 697]
16	Shaw continues corresponding flirtatiously with his confidante Ellen Terry, 'heartwise Ellen... who knows how to clothe herself in that most blessed of all things – unsatisfied desire'. [CL1: 702]
23	*Little Eyolf* (in William Archer's translation) opens at the Avenue Theatre, with Janet Achurch, Elizabeth Robins and Mrs Patrick Campbell in the three female roles. Shaw's review of this production, with a cast including what he described as 'the three best yet discovered actresses of their generation', appeared in the *Saturday Review* on November 28. [CL1: 683; Drama2: 705–11; OTN2: 256–64]
30	Shaw reports to Ellen Terry that he has completed *The Devil's Disciple*. He has never tried melodrama before, and is anxious to have her opinion. [CL1: 705]

December

2 (Wed)	Shaw lectures on 'The Jevonian Theory of Value' at the Economics club. [CL1: 707]
4	Janet Achurch learns that Mrs Patrick Campbell has underbid her for the lead in *Little Eyolf*, in the production to be taken over from Elizabeth Robins by a commercial theatre syndicate. The rivalry between the two actresses causes fighting and bit-

terness among London's Ibsenite groups. [CL1: 708; Peters 203]

5 On Shaw's instructions, Charlotte rescues Janet from an afternoon of brandy drinking at the Solferino Cafe between the matinée and evening performances of *Little Eyolf*. [CL1: 709–10; Peters 203]

8 In the production of *Little Eyolf* at the Avenue Theatre, Stella Campbell replaces Janet Achurch in the role of Rita Allmers, and attracts Shaw's ridicule (in his *Saturday Review* criticism on 12 December, 'Ibsen Without Tears') for a 'reassuring and pretty' performance which 'succeeded wonderfully in eliminating all unpleasantness from the play'. [Drama2: 717–23; OTN2: 271–8; CL1: 713; Peters 204]

10 Shaw takes Charlotte to see Ellen Terry playing in *Cymbeline* at the Lyceum. [CL1: 713]

30 Shaw completes *The Devil's Disciple*. [CP2: 51]

1897

In February of this year, Shaw has his first personal meeting with Mrs Patrick (Stella) Campbell, with whom he has a serious love affair many years later (beginning in June 1912). His frequently confessional and autobiographical correspondence with Ellen Terry continues, and his relationship with Charlotte Payne-Townshend develops, under the watchful eye of Beatrice Webb. He accepts the offer of Grant Richards to publish *Plays Pleasant and Unpleasant*, and the first public performances of *The Man of Destiny* and *Candida* take place in summer. At a meeting in September with Stella Campbell and Forbes-Robertson, he conceives an idea for a play which eventually becomes *Pygmalion*. In October Richard Mansfield mounts the first professional production of *The Devil's Disciple*, and then takes the play on a successful tour of the mid-West. Income from the New York season and the tour constitutes Shaw's first major financial success as a playwright. 'I roll in gold', he reported to Ellen Terry on Christmas Eve.

January

5 (Tue) Lucy Shaw (Butterfield) plays the part of Kitty in a production of Sir Charles Villiers Stanford's *Shamus O'Brien* at the Broadway Theater, New York. The company then toured America. [Farmer 92]

8 Shaw tells Mrs Richard Mansfield *The Devil's Disciple* is 'just the play for America', but her husband is 'the last person in the world to whom it would be of any use offering it'. [CL1: 717]

9 Shaw travels to Manchester to lecture to the Ancoats Brotherhood on 'Repairs and Alterations in Socialism' on the following day. [CL1: 715]

11 Shaw returns to London. [CL1: 715]

31 Shaw writes ecstatically about Ellen Terry's performance the previous evening in W. G. Wills's play *Olivia*: 'Beautiful, beautiful – I cried like mad... After the play I wrote you a note begging you to let me come round and kiss you just once...' [Theatrics 23]

February

18 (Thu) First personal meeting between Shaw and Mrs Patrick Campbell: Shaw reads *The Devil's Disciple* to her and Johnston Forbes-Robertson. [CL1: 684; D2: 1158]

19 Shaw settles an agreement with Cyril Maude for a proposed production of *You Never Can Tell* at the Haymarket Theatre in the West End. [D2: 1158; CL1: 750; I&R 134]

20 Shaw completes the stage business of *The Devil's Disciple*. [D2: 1158]

March

9 (Tue) Beatrice Webb visits Bertha Newcombe, who gives a bitter account of her relationship with GBS: 'her five years of devoted love, his cold philandering, her hopes aroused by repeated advice to him (which he, it appears, had repeated much exaggerated) to marry her, and then her feeling of misery and resentment against me when she discovered that I was encouraging him "to marry Miss [Payne-] Townshend". Finally, he had written a month ago to break it off entirely.' [DBW2: 110–11]

14 Shaw lectures at the East Indian dock gates on 'The Use of Political Power'. Charlotte has taken to attending his political lectures, and is becoming embarrassed about her enormous wealth. [CL1: 733]

16 Shaw travels to Manchester to see Janet Achurch play Cleopatra to Louis Calvert's Antony. His scathing critique of Janet's performance appeared in the *Saturday Review* on 20 March. [CL1: 736; Drama 3: 803–8; OTN3: 76–83]

25 Shaw spends a tantalizing evening at the opening of Henry Arthur Jones's *The Physician* at the Criterion, where Ellen Terry is also present in the audience. [CL1: 737]

By 27 Shaw has decided to accept Grant Richards's offer to publish his plays. [CL1: 739–40]

April–June

The Webbs and Charlotte Payne-Townshend take a cottage at Tower Hill on the North Downs near Dorking, Surrey. Shaw remains based in London but visits them frequently. [CL1: 729–74, DBW2: 111]

April

9 (Fri) Shaw reads *You Never Can Tell* to the Haymarket company. Realizing the play is too long, Shaw decides he has to 'spoil it to suit the fashionable dinner hour' by cutting it. [CL1: 740; Peters 214–15]

12 Shaw commutes between Dorking and London, where he is closely involved in rehearsals of *You Never Can Tell*. [CL1: 742–3]

17 Bram Stoker, Henry Irving's business manager, informs Shaw that Irving has decided not to stage *The Man of Destiny*. [CL1: 747]

Under the pseudonym 'Cashel Byron', Shaw plays the Reverend Anthony Anderson in a copyright performance of *The Devil's Disciple* at the Bijou Theatre. [Peters 215; Wein3: 51; CL1: 757]

29 Exasperated with Cyril Maude and the Haymarket manager, Frederick Harrison, and refusing to make the changes to the play they want, Shaw withdraws *You Never Can Tell* from the Haymarket. [CL1: 750]

May

Shaw turns from the 'silly visionary fashion-ridden theatres' and plunges back into political affairs. As well as writing his weekly drama column in the *Saturday Review*, he attends two Fabian meetings and two Vestry meetings per week, and helps the Webbs revise their book on Industrial Democracy. [CL1: 770]

3 (Mon) Inaugural performance of the New Century Theatre, a rival to the Independent, established by William Archer, Elizabeth Robins, H. W. Massingham, and Alfred Sutro, in order to promote experimental drama. [CL1: 740]

8 Beatrice Webb records in her diary some censorious reflections about Shaw and his philanderings, and their effect on Charlotte: 'Silly these philanderings of Shaw's. He imagines that he gets to know women by making them in love with him. Just the contrary... His sensuality has all drifted into sexual vanity, delight in being the candle to the moths, with a dash of intellectual curiosity to give flavour... And he is mistaken if he thinks that it does not affect his artistic work...Whether I like him, admire him or despise him most I do not know. Just at present I feel annoyed and contemptuous.

For the dancing light has gone out of Charlotte's eyes – there is at times a blank haggard look, a look that I myself felt in my own eyes for long years... [Shaw] has a sort of affectionateness too, underneath his vanity. Will she touch that?' [DBW2: 114–15]

10 Shaw urges Henry Irving, who has been procrastinating about whether to produce *The Man of Destiny*, either to release the play, or go ahead with it. [CL1: 755–6]

11 Ellen Terry informs Shaw that Henry Irving intends to stage *The Man of Destiny* on a double-bill. [CL1: 760]

12 A Shaw letter to Ellen Terry indicates that Henry Irving has returned *The Man of Destiny* to Shaw, who resolves to have no further dealings with him. [CL1: 760–1]

13 Shaw expresses to Ellen Terry his continued hopes that she will act in a play of his, but not with Henry Irving: 'Your career has been sacrificed to the egotism of a fool... Nevertheless you shall play for me yet.' [CL1: 762–3]

15 Publication in the *Daily Mail* of Shaw's full account of his negotiations with Henry Irving, got up in the form of an interview and passed to the press through R. Golding Bright. [Lbib2: 604; CL1: 762]

18 Shaw becomes a member of the Vestry of the Parish of St Pancras, a predecessor of the St Pancras Metropolitan Borough Council. He served as vestryman and borough councillor until 1903. [I&R 68–70; H.M.Geduld, 'Bernard Shaw, Vestryman and Borough Councillor', *The Californian Shavian*, no. 3, vol. 3 (May–Jun 1962); CL1: 746, 754]

24 Still at Dorking, Beatrice Webb reports in her diary on Shaw and Charlotte Payne-Townshend: 'Charlotte sits upstairs typewriting Shaw's plays. Shaw wanders about the garden with his writing-book and pencil, writing the *Saturday* article, correcting his plays for press or reading through one of our chapters. With extraordinary good nature he will spend days over some part of our work, and an astute reader will quickly divine those chapters which Shaw has corrected and those which he has not.' [DBW2: 115–16]

26 Shaw's first St Pancras Vestry meeting. [CL1: 768]

June

11 (Fri) Shaw tells Ellen Terry that he had 'a devil of a childhood...rich only in dreams, frightful & loveless in realities.' [CL1: 773]

July

1 (Thu) First public performance of *The Man of Destiny*, at the Grand Theatre, Croydon, under the direction of S. Murray Carson. [CL1: 772, 779; CP1: 606]

13 Shaw apologises to Charlotte Payne-Townshend for the hurt he has caused in rejecting her proposal, made at Dorking, that they should marry. In a letter to Ellen Terry of 5 August, Shaw describes his reaction to the proposal as follows: 'Down at

Dorking there was a sort of earthquake, because she [Charlotte] had been cherishing a charming project of at last making me a very generous & romantic proposal... When I received that golden moment with shuddering horror & wildly asked the fare to Australia, she was inexpressibly taken aback, and her pride, which is considerable, was much startled.' [CL1: 783–4, 792]

27 With the announcement of Graham Wallas's engagement and subsequent marriage in December, Shaw becomes the only unmarried member of the Fabian 'Old Gang'. [CL1: 790]

30 First public performance of *Candida*, in Aberdeen, as part of the Achurch–Charrington Independent Theatre tour. Shaw wrote to Ellen Terry (14 July 1897): '...Charrington is taking out a *Doll's House* tour; and he's going out to try *Candida* on the provincial dog'. Janet Achurch played Candida, Charrington played the Reverend Morell. [CP1: 514 ;CL1: 675, 782]

Early August – late September

The Webbs, Shaw and Charlotte spend seven weeks at 'The Argoed' in Monmouth. Shaw works relentlessly throughout their 'holiday' preparing his plays for the printer. [CL1: 790, 803; Webb 53; DBW2: 122–3]

August

Shaw joins the Society of Authors. He writes to Henry Arthur Jones on 12 October 1897, about the need for 'some sort of an organisation' of playwrights 'with a view to getting a *minimum* price established for plays'. [CL1: 812]

September

8 (Wed) After referring to Mrs Patrick Campbell as a 'rapscallionly flower girl', Shaw tells Ellen Terry of his plan for a play in which Forbes Robertson will be a 'west end gentleman' and Mrs Patrick Campbell 'an east end dona'. Fifteen years later (1912) this plan comes to fruition in the form of *Pygmalion*. [CL1: 800–3]

Shaw writes to Richard Mansfield about various theatrical matters, and reproaches him for turning down *The Man of Destiny*: 'I was much hurt by your contemptuous refusal of The Man of Destiny... because Napoleon is nobody else but Richard Mansfield himself. I studied the character from you, and then read up on Napoleon and found that I had got him exactly right.' [Theatrics 24–7]

October

1 (Fri) First professional production of *The Devil's Disciple* at the Harmanus Bleecker Hall, Albany, New York, for one

performance after some strenuous negotiations between Shaw and the actor-manager Richard Mansfield. It then opens at the Fifth Avenue Theater, New York City where it runs for 64 performances before being taken by Mansfield on a successful tour of the mid-West in the spring of 1898. Shaw reaps £2000 from the venture (£700 from the New York season and £1300 from the tour), making it his first major financial success as a playwright. [CL1: 806; Hend2: 375]

Early — Charlotte's sister, Mary Stewart Cholmondeley, is staying with Charlotte. Mary's intense dislike of Shaw at this time makes it difficult for him and Charlotte to see much of each other. Charlotte also visits her sister in Leicester during this period. Shaw frets about her absence in a letter to her of 15 October. [CL1: 809–10, 814]

November

4 (Thu) — With the royalties from the first week's performances of *The Devil's Disciple* in America, Shaw is 'richer than ever I was in my life before – actually £314 in the bank'. [CL1: 821]

December

3 (Fri) — Shaw declines Charlotte Payne-Townshend's invitation to join her and Mrs Lucy Phillimore (social worker and wife of Fabian Society member and St Pancras Vestryman Robert Charles Phillimore) on a short trip to Dieppe. [CL1: 826]

5 — Probably annoyed by his response to the invitation, Charlotte leaves for Dieppe without informing Shaw. [CL1: 826]

7 — Unaware that Charlotte has left the country, Shaw dispatches a curt note to her: 'Secretary required tomorrow, not later than eleven.' [CL1: 826]

9 — Shaw warns Janet Achurch that unless she controls her drinking, he will no longer support her professionally or privately – 'farewell farewell farewell farewell farewell.' [CL1: 828]

24 — Shaw records his author's fees for the New York run of *The Devil's Disciple* at £850: 'I roll in gold.' [CL1: 831]

1898

In March, Charlotte travels to Italy, leaving Shaw querulous about his loss of her company and secretarial help. She does not return until 1 May. While Charlotte is away, Shaw is afflicted with a painfully swollen ankle: an operation in May reveals a bone infection. Suffering from overwork, and a generally run-down condition, Shaw gives up his theatre reviewing for the *Saturday Review*, handing over to his successor, Max Beerbohm on 21 May. On the morning of 1 June of this year, Shaw and Charlotte Payne-

Townshend are married in a London Registry Office.† After the marriage, the Shaws took houses in Haslemere and Hindhead in Surrey, remaining there until the summer of 1899. During the combined convalescence-honeymoon (in the course of which he compounded his health problems with further injuries), Shaw works on *Caesar and Cleopatra* and *The Perfect Wagnerite*. Copyright performances of *You Never Can Tell*, *Mrs Warren's Profession* and *The Philanderer* take place early this year, and on 19 April Shaw's first seven plays are published in the two-volume work, *Plays Pleasant and Unpleasant*.

Following Shaw's marriage and his move to Adelphi Terrace, Arabella Gillmore (Bessie Shaw's half-sister) and her daughter, Georgina (Judy) move into Fitzroy Square with Bessie. Judy becomes Shaw's secretary from 1907 until her marriage in 1912 while Arabella continues to live at Fitzroy Square until Bessie's death. Following this, Arabella succeeds her sister Georgie as Jenny Patterson's live-in companion. [DHL]

January

5 (Wed) Shaw writes to Ellen Terry: 'I never stop working now.' [CL2: 8]

15 Publication in the periodical *The Vegetarian* of a talk in which Shaw explains when and why he became a vegetarian, and states. 'I am a vegetarian, as Hamlet puts it, "after my own honour and dignity".' [Raymond Blathwayt, 'What Vegetarianism Really Means. A Talk With Mr. Bernard Shaw', *The Vegetarian*, 15 Jan 1898; I&R 400–3]

February

13 (Sun) Shaw attends the 14th annual dinner of the Playgoers' Club at the Hotel Cecil, where he acknowledges a toast to 'The Press' in an after-dinner speech. [CL1: 830; CL2: 9–10]

March

7 (Mon) In a letter to Charles Charrington, responding to one of his and Janet Achurch's numerous requests for financial assistance, Shaw records a number of his own recent expenses, including a payment of £21 to Lucy Carr Shaw. This is an instalment of a regular allowance which Shaw provides her with until her death in 1920. [CL2: 12]

† The Shaw marriage was probably unconsummated, though this is questioned by Charlotte's biographer, Janet Dunbar. [Dunbar 175–6] In the chapter 'To Frank Harris on Sex in Biography', Shaw states of his marriage that 'as man and wife we found a new relation in which sex had no part', and implies that one reason for their abstaining from sex was that the partnership was one in which the couple had 'passed the age at which the bride can safely bear a first child'. [SSS 115] Nevertheless, the early days of the marriage seem to have been a particularly happy period for both Shaw and Charlotte.

12 Charlotte Payne-Townshend travels to Italy, accompanied by Mrs Lucy Phillimore, to make a study of Rome's municipal administration. Kate Salt substitutes as Shaw's secretary until her return. [CL2: 14, 16; I&R 171; DBW2: 153]
Shaw learns that the Examiner of Plays, G. A. Radford, has refused a licence for the copyright performance of *Mrs Warren's Profession*, scheduled for 30 March. Shaw subsequently makes radical expurgations to obtain the licence. [CL2: 11, 13–14, 30]

23 Scheduled copyright performance of *You Never Can Tell* at the Victoria Hall, Bayswater. [CL2: 11; CP1: 668]
The Webbs depart for a tour of America and Australasia which lasts until December. The absence of the Webbs, and of Charlotte Payne-Townshend, leaves Shaw feeling 'detestably deserted' in London. [CL2: 21, 27; DBW2: 358–9]

24 Shaw lectures on 'Flagellomania' to the Humanitarian League in Essex Hall, published in *Humanity* in May 1899 and subsequently pirated by Charles Charrington who publishes it in Paris as a preface to a pornographic work, *Records of Personal Chastisement*. [Lbib 1: 39–40, 424, 2: 611; CL2: 19]

30 Copyright readings of *Mrs Warren's Profession* and *The Philanderer* at the Victoria Hall (Bijou Theatre). [CL2: 11; CP1: 134]

31 Shaw tells Charlotte Payne-Townshend of Grant Richards's interest in 'a Nibelungen handbook for the coming Ring cyclus'. In response to Richards's suggestion, Shaw produced a study of Wagner, published on 1 December 1898 as *The Perfect Wagnerite*. [CL2: 25]
Suicide of Eleanor Marx on finding out that her common law husband Edward Aveling has secretly married Eva Frye the previous year. When Shaw hears about the suicide he writes a weary and melancholy letter to Charlotte: '...At home, piles of letters – one from you – and the news of Eleanor Marx's suicide... Massingham wants [me] to write about her. *I* want to write about Aveling; so conclude to hold my tongue...' [CL2: 26; Peters 244]

April

5 (Tue) Shaw writes to Charlotte: 'Wrote article. No secretary. Weary at the end. Slamming the typewriter is furious nervous work... Lonely – no, by God, never – *not* lonely, but detestably deserted.' Eleanor Marx was cremated that afternoon. Shaw did not attend. [CL2: 27]

7 Shaw sends Charlotte Payne-Townshend a graphic account of being put under general anaesthetic for a dental operation, and, feeling exhausted and deserted, complains: 'Oh Charlotte,

Charlotte: is this a time to be gadding about in Rome!' [CL2: 27–8]

8 — Shaw tells Charlotte Payne-Townshend he has notified Frank Harris that he will hand over his position as drama critic on the *Saturday Review* to Max Beerbohm at the end of the season. [CL2: 28]

11 — Shaw to Sidney Webb: 'I live the life of a dog – have not spoken to a soul except my mother & the vestry since you left'. [CL2: 29]

19 — Publication of Shaw's *Plays Pleasant and Unpleasant* in two volumes simultaneously by Grant Richards in England, and Herbert S. Stone in Chicago. [Lbib1: 33–6]
For no apparent reason other than that he pinched his instep while lacing his shoe the previous week, Shaw's left foot suddenly swells to enormous size. [CL2: 32]

21 — Shaw reports to Charlotte Payne-Townshend on his foot and general condition: 'Locomotion now very excruciating... foot now as large as the Albert Hall... Am a fearful wreck.' [CL2: 32–3]

23 — While undergoing treatment for his foot, Shaw begins the composition of *Caesar and Cleopatra*. [CL2: 35–6]

26 — Sidney Webb writes to Shaw from Washington, saying 'as far as we can make out, every city here contains a few enthusiasts who read everything signed G.B.S., and take the *Saturday Review* for that purpose'. He reports on a favourable reception of Richard Mansfield's production of *The Devil's Disciple* in Washington. [*The Letters of Sidney and Beatrice Webb*, ed. Norman MacKenzie, 3 vols, 2: 62]

May

1 (Sun) — Charlotte Payne-Townshend is expected to arrive at Victoria Station at 7.30 pm. Shaw hobbles to Adelphi Terrace to meet her, but finds to his dismay she was not on the train. [CL2: 38]

2 — Shaw receives an apologetic and concerned letter from Charlotte Payne-Townshend: 'Well, here I am anyway now! Yes: I *might* have telegraphed: it was horrid of me. I am a wreck, mental & physical. Such a journey as it was!... My dear – & your foot? Shall I go up to you, or will you come here, & when? Only tell me what you would prefer. Of course I am quite free – Charlotte.' [CL2: 38]

9 — Dr William Salisbury Sharpe, attended by his nurse and wife, Alice Sharpe (née Lockett – Shaw's former love), perform an operation on Shaw's foot revealing a bone infection. [CL2: 35, 42, 50–1; Peters 246–8]

21 Publication of Shaw's 'Valedictory' in the *Saturday Review*, announcing with a complimentary flourish that Max Beerbohm will replace him as theatre critic: 'The younger generation is knocking at the door; and as I open it there steps spritely in the incomparable Max.' [Lbib2: 609; CL2: 42–3; Drama3: 1059–61; OTN3: 384–6]

23 Shaw to Grant Richards: 'I am going to get married... Keep this dark until I have done it.' [CL2: 44]

30 W. A. S. Hewins reports to Sidney Webb the forthcoming marriage of Shaw and Charlotte Payne-Townshend, and their search for a place in which Shaw can convalesce: 'You have probably heard from other sources that Shaw and Miss Payne-Townshend are going to be married... Miss P.T. is very busy nursing Shaw and looking for some "bowery hollow crowned with Summer seas" where he can recover his strength. She told me about it only a day or two ago. I was not greatly surprised.' [W. A. S. Hewins to Sidney Webb, 30 May 1898, BLPES]

June

1 (Wed) a.m. **Shaw and Charlotte Payne-Townshend marry at the Registry Office in Henrietta Street, Covent Garden**. Shaw described himself on the occasion as 'altogether a wreck on crutches and in an old jacket which the crutches had worn to rags.' Witnesses were Graham Wallas and Henry Stephen Salt. According to Shaw's account, the officiating Registrar first assumed that the tall, well-dressed Wallas was the bridegroom, and that Shaw himself was 'the inevitable beggar who completes all wedding processions'. [Hend3: 418; CL2: 46–7; Dunbar 175; Peters 251]

p.m. Shaw writes a note to Lena Ashwell from 29 Fitzroy Square:

Dear Miss Lena Ashwell,

This morning I hopped into a registrar's office and got married, and then hopped back & found your letter. If it had only come a post earlier, I think I should have waited on the chance of something fatal happening to Mr. Playfair in the course of the next forty years or so. [Texas]

Expressing opinions about Shaw which she was later to revise, Charlotte's cousin, Edith Somerville (author of *Irish RM*) writes in letters after the marriage: 'he is distinctly somebody in a literary way, but he can't be a gentleman and he is too clever to be really in love with Lottie, who is nearly clever, but not quite'; and that 'Charlotte seems perfectly happy and delighted with her cad, for cad he is in spite of his talent.' [Maurice Collis, *Somerville and Ross: A Biography* (1968), 127–8; I&R 171]

2 An amusing account of the wedding, written by Shaw himself, is published as an unsigned 'scoop' in the 'Mainly About People' column of *The Star*. [Lbib2: 610; CL2: 46–7]

10 Shaw and Charlotte set up house at 'Pitfold', near Haslemere in Surrey. The house is described by W.A.S. Hewins as 'very pleasant... an old farm house converted into a dwelling for well to do people.' Shaw 'rests' by working furiously on *The Perfect Wagnerite*. [CL2: 52; W.A.S. Hewins to Sidney Webb, 22 Sep 1898, BLPES]

17 Shaw adds to his health problems by falling downstairs and breaking his left arm near the wrist. [CL2: 48]

Summer Shaw writes to Sidney Webb that he and Charlotte 'have been amusing ourselves during the summer with a kodak.' Shaw had begun experimenting with photography in the 1880s but it was around this time that photography became a serious hobby for Shaw. [CL2: 67, 281; I&R 200–2]

July

27 (Wed) Shaw's second operation on the foot, performed this time by an eminent bone specialist, Dr Bowlby (who forgot that he was also supposed to operate on Shaw's arm). [CL2: 56; Hol2: 4]

August

20 (Sat) Shaw dispatches the MS of *The Perfect Wagnerite* to Grant Richards and spends the next months seeing it through the press. [CL2: 58]

September

Mid Shaw and Charlotte visit Freshwater on the western end of the Isle of Wight. [CL2: 65; Pearson 211]

22 W. A. S. Hewins tells Sidney Webb of his cycling visits to the Shaws, and reports on Shaw's health: 'I have been as often as possible to Haslemere to see the Shaws, and last week also to Freshwater where they are staying at present. Shaw does not seem to make much progress. At Haslemere I thought he looked much better in general health than before his illness. But last Friday at Freshwater he certainly looked very bad... The most serious drawback is his vegetarianism. Cannot someone convince him of his unreasonableness about it?' [W. A. S. Hewins to Sidney Webb, 22 Sep 1898, BLPES]

October

13 (Thu) Writing to Charles Charrington, Shaw reports having sprained his ankle by twisting his 'long disused foot' while trying to mount his bicycle. He is working hard on *The Perfect Wagnerite*, and having trouble with the writing of *Caesar and Cleopatra*: 'I

can make no headway with C[aesar] & C[leopatra]. Can't get any drama out of the story – nothing but comedy and character.' [CL2: 64–5]

18 Shaw writes a long letter to Sidney Webb from Pitfold, reporting, amongst other things, on: the fuss being made about his vegetarian habits and their alleged threat to his life, on having his leg massaged by a nurse, Dorothy Kreyer ('a rather good-looking young woman... fortunately not of an ardent temperament') and of his and Charlotte's experiments with photography, one of the results being a portrait of himself, taken by Dorothy Kreyer, and published in *The Academy* on 15 October, with the inscription 'The Dying Vegetarian'.

November

Early Shaw sees Dr Bowlby again in London, to be told the foot needs further rest. [Shaw to Henry Arthur Jones, 2 Dec 1898, BL MS Add 50561; CL2: 70]

*c.*12 The Shaws move from 'Pitfold' to a larger house, 'Blen-Cathra', near Hindhead. [CL2: 70; I&R 272]

Late Shaw returns to Bowlby, demanding that he amputate his toe rather than subject him to further inactivity. Bowlby advises Shaw to keep the toe and be patient. [Shaw to Henry Arthur Jones, 2 Dec 1898, BL MS Add 50561]

December

The Webbs return to England. [CL2: 71]

1 (Thu) Publication of *The Perfect Wagnerite*. Lucy Shaw sends a copy to Janey Drysdale for Christmas. [Lbib1: 37; CL2: 58; Farmer 116]

9 Shaw completes *Caesar and Cleopatra*. [CP2: 159]

Chronology Part II
1899–1925

1899

During this year, copyright performances of two of Shaw's *Three Plays for Puritans, Caesar and Cleopatra* and *Captain Brassbound's Conversion,* are held in March and October respectively, and in September the other play in this group, *The Devil's Disciple,* has its first British production. In April, Shaw's famous correspondence with Mrs Patrick (Stella) Campbell begins, with a note from him inviting her to lunch. Shaw's 'Rabelaisian' uncle, Dr Walter John Gurly, dies at the end of August while the Shaws are holidaying in Cornwall. Soon afterwards the Shaws take a cruise aboard the *Lusitania,* an experience which Shaw dislikes intensely. In early November they move into Charlotte's flat at 10 Adelphi Terrace. The first presentation of *You Never Can Tell* takes place on 26 November, in a production by the Stage Society at the Royalty Theatre.

January

28 (Sat) Shaw is one of the two principal speakers at a 'Peace Crusade' meeting held in Hindhead Hall and chaired by Sir Arthur Conan Doyle. The meeting is in support of a Disarmament Conference which followed a proposal made by Tsar Nicholas of Russia in the fall of 1898 for a 'pause in the development of European armaments'. [CL2: 73; Agits 51–4]

March

Shaw's foot and general health show signs of improving. [CL2: 83]

15 (Wed) Copyright performance of *Caesar and Cleopatra* by Mrs Patrick Campbell's London company at the Theatre Royal, Newcastle upon Tyne. Mrs Patrick Campbell played Cleopatra and Nutcombe Gould played Caesar. [CL2: 84; CP2: 159; Hend2: 490, Hend3: 455]

April

12 (Wed) Shaw's first letter to Mrs Patrick Campbell, inviting her and Johnston Forbes-Robertson down to 'Blen-Cathra', Hindhead, for lunch: 'Mrs Shaw will be delighted to see you.' [CL2: 84–5; Dent 3–4]

May

5 (Fri) Shaw drafts the scenario of *The Witch of Atlas* (subsequently titled *Captain Brassbound's Conversion*) for Ellen Terry. [CL2: 92]

14 Shaw begins writing the dialogue for *Captain Brassbound's Conversion*. [CL2: 92]

26 Shaw delivers his first lecture to children in a tiny schoolhouse in Surrey. The rather subversive lecture, on 'Animals', is received by the children with 'peals of laughter'. The occasion is witnessed by poet Richard Le Gallienne. [*Farnham, Haslemere*

and Hindhead Herald, 3 Jun 1899; Richard Le Gallienne, *The Romantic '90s* (1926), 143–6; I&R 280–1]

July

7 (Fri) Shaw completes the dialogue for *Captain Brassbound's Conversion*, having also written reviews and articles on Morris, Wagner, Nietzsche and British censorship since the early summer. [CL2: 92]

Late William Pember Reeves, Agent-General for New Zealand, a Fabian, develops diphtheria while on a weekend visit to the Shaws and the house is placed under quarantine for three weeks. [CL2: 93]

August

3 (Thu) After reading *Captain Brassbound's Conversion*, written expressly for her, Ellen Terry decides 'I couldn't do this one'. [CL2: 96]

4, 8 Shaw tries to persuade Ellen Terry to change her mind about *Captain Brassbound's Conversion*. [CL2: 96–9]

15 The Shaws rent a house at Ruan Minor, Cornwall, for one month of sea bathing, during which Shaw helps Charlotte learn to swim, as he tells Graham Wallas in a letter of 24 August: 'we have at last got away to this place, where I swim twice a day, taking a turn on the surface on each occasion for my own amusement, and another underneath in the capacity of a life preserver for Charlotte, who is learning to swim with nothing between her and death but a firm grip of my neck. The sea being the only element I enjoy exercising in, I am putting up muscle & rather straightened myself up.' [CL2: 99–100]

30 Shaw's Uncle Walter Gurly dies, leaving Shaw his heavily mortgaged Carlow estate. 'My infernal uncle has died; and the Carlow estate has descended on me like an avalanche.' [Shaw to Graham Wallas, 9 Sep 1899, BLPES; CL2: 101–2]

Late Lucy Shaw is diagnosed as having tuberculosis. This brings her singing career to an end. [Farmer 122]

September

14 (Thu) Shaw and Charlotte leave Cornwall and return to London on the overnight train. [CL2: 101]

21 Shaw and Charlotte leave for a six-week cruise of the Mediterranean (calling at Tangiers, Malta, Constantinople, Athens and Crete) on the SS *Lusitania*, which Charlotte thinks a success, but Shaw dislikes. He tells playwright Edward Rose (25 September): 'this is a godless cruise with godless people… an accursed place, this floating pleasure machine' and to Sydney Cockerell (17 October) Shaw writes: 'It is a guzzling, lounging,

gambling, dog's life.' (The experience of this cruise probably influenced Shaw's portrayal of Hell in his forthcoming work, *Man and Superman.*) [Charlotte Shaw to Grant Richards, 5 Oct 1899, Texas; CL2: 103, 111]

26 First British production of *The Devil's Disciple* at the Princess of Wales's Theatre, Kennington. [CL1: 772; Pearson 200]

October

10 (Tue) Copyright performance of *Captain Brassbound's Conversion* at the Court Theatre, Liverpool, with Ellen Terry and Laurence Irving (Henry's son) playing the leading roles. [CL2: 101]

11 Outbreak of the Boer War, sparking controversy in the Fabian Society over Britain's foreign policy. As an outcome, and with Shaw's involvement, all members of the society were asked to vote Yes or No to the question: 'Are you in favour of an official pronouncement being made now by the Fabian Society on Imperialism in relation to the War?' It was decided 259 to 217 that no action should be taken. [CL2: 115–16, 118–19; Pease 128–30]

21 Shaw writes to actress Beatrice Mansfield (who seems to have requested one of Shaw's plays for a matinée season) about *You Never Can Tell*: 'There is no difficulty about You Never Can Tell except the difficulty of getting it acted. The end of the second act requires a consummate comedian; and that comedian has never been available... everybody wants to play the waiter.' [Theatrics 32–4]

30 The Shaws return from their cruise, and move into Charlotte's flat over the London School of Economics at 10 Adelphi Terrace, where Beatrice Webb finds them happily settled: 'Charlotte and Shaw have settled down into the most devoted married couple, she gentle and refined, with happiness added thereto, and he showing no sign of breaking loose from her dominion.' [CL2: 115;Webb 189; I&R 173; Peters 264]

November

Early Shaw moves his belongings into Charlotte's place at Adelphi Terrace, although he retains his Fitzroy Square house for his mother, and to qualify him to serve in the St Pancras Vestry. [I&R 428; Theatrics 31]

26 (Sun) A single performance of *You Never Can Tell* by the Stage Society at the Royalty Theatre. [CP1: 668; Morgan 3; Peters 265]

December

11 (Mon) At Hindhead, Shaw delivers his first lecture on the subject of 'Garden Cities', from the Chair, after a lecture by Garden City projector Ebenezer Howard. [CL2: 118–19]

16 Shaw lectures on 'Socialism and the Universities' to the University of Wales Fabian Society at Aberystwyth, where he stays over Christmas and New Year. [CL2: 120–8; Pearson 240]

1900

Shaw's most important creative activity in this year is his commencement in May of an outline of the 'Don Juan in Hell' scene – a dream-like philosophical conversation and debate between the Devil and Shavian transformations of principal characters in Mozart's *Don Giovanni* – of the third Act of *Man and Superman*. This becomes the first major sounding in his writings of the theme of Creative Evolution, a system of ideas which Shaw comes to proclaim as his religion. He is also much preoccupied with international and local politics, writing the Fabian Election Manifesto, *Fabianism and the Empire*, in August, and being re-elected, as the Progressive candidate, a member of the St Pancras Borough Council. From May to October, he and Charlotte rent 'Blackdown Cottage' at Haslemere, Surrey. On 16 December, he at last meets his epistolary confidante and loved friend, Ellen Terry.

January

24 (Wed) Having recently consented to the Stage Society's request to perform *Candida*, Shaw declines William Archer's offer to include a Shaw play in the New Century Theatre's upcoming season. [CL2: 136]

February

9 (Fri) Ellen Terry having decided not to leave Irving and do *Captain Brassbound's Conversion*, Shaw determines to send the play into the market place to attract the highest bidder. [CL2: 147–8]

23 Shaw lectures to the Fabian Society on 'Imperialism'. [CL2: 88]

27 Shaw and Edward Pease are appointed as representatives to a conference cooperatively organized by the Socialist societies and the Parliamentary Committee for the Trade Union Congress. The conference results in the formation of the Labour Representation Committee, established to coordinate the activities of the trade unions, the Social Democratic Federation, the Fabian and the Independent Labour Party. [Pease 148–9]

March to April

Despite Shaw's attempts to smooth discord within the Fabian Society, J. Ramsay MacDonald and J. F. Green resign from the Fabian Executive over the Boer War. The Society also loses some two dozen other active members including Henry Salt and Mrs Pankhurst. [CL2: 116]

March

11 (Sun) Shaw lectures at the Albion Hall on 'Modern Scientific Credulity'. [BL MS Add 50703]

May

Shaw begins outlining the third act 'Don Juan in Hell' scene for *Man and Superman* (provisionally titled *The Superman, or Don Juan's great grandson's grandson*). (The full play was composed between July 1901 and June 1902.) Scenario reprinted in *SHAW: the Annual of Bernard Shaw Studies*, vol. 16 (1996), 202–9. [CL2: 5, 275; CP2: 491]

22 (Tue) Shaw addresses the Annual Meeting of the National Anti-Vivisection Society at the Queen's Hall. [*The Zoophilist*, 1 Jun 1900 (verbatim report)]

May–October

Shaw and Charlotte rent 'Blackdown Cottage' at Haslemere, and Shaw divides his week between there and London. Sidney and Beatrice Webb are house guests there for a time. [CL2: 165ff.; DBW2: 177]

June

10 (Sun) Harley Granville Barker impressed Shaw in the Stage Society's production of Gerhart Hauptmann's *Friedensfest* (translated by Janet Achurch and Dr C. E. Wheeler under the title *The Coming of Peace*). Shaw agrees with Charrington that Granville Barker would suit the lead role in the Stage Society's upcoming production of *Candida*. [CL2: 169–72; Hol2: 91]

c. 29 Shaw lectures to the Christian Social Union on 'The Housing of the Poor'. [*The Times* (London), 30 Jun 1900]

July

Throughout this month, Shaw is 'working like mad sixteen hours a day' on Vestry and Fabian business, seeing his plays through the printers, and supervising rehearsals of Forbes-Robertson's production of *The Devil's Disciple*. [CL2: 179]

1 (Sun) First London production of *Candida* by the Stage Society, with Harley Granville Barker as Eugene Marchbanks and Edith Craig as Miss Proserpine Garnett. [CP1: 514; I&R 130; CL2: 171, 178; Hend2: 386]

30–31 Shaw attends a conference sponsored by the Sanitary Institute on working-class housing. [CL2: 179]

August

Shaw drafts *Fabianism and the Empire*, the Fabians' Election Manifesto. [CL2: 181]

31 (Fri) Shaw completes *Fabianism and the Empire*. [CL2: 182; Pearson 240]

September

26 (Wed) Shaw writes to Grant Richards: 'The Manifesto has passed: all is well save its shattered author.' At 3 a.m., after making the revisions requested at the Fabian meeting the previous night, Shaw

despatches the document to Richards for printing. He then returns to the task of preparing *Three Plays for Puritans* for the printer. [CL2: 185–6]

October

28 (Sun) Shaw invites Ellen Terry to play in the Stage Society's private performance of *Captain Brassbound's Conversion*. [CL2: 188]

Late Shaw campaigns for re-election as a Progressive candidate in the Borough of St Pancras elections. [CL2: 188]

November

First unauthorized edition of *Love Among the Artists* published in America by H. S. Stone, albeit with Shaw's approval. In a letter to Stone dated 4 October 1899, Shaw wrote, 'I make no grievance of my old failure to secure American copyright, and see no reason why, because you now publish my copyright books, you should be cut off from the non-copyright ones which are open to your competitors in business. If you ever want to "pirate" them, go ahead: I shall be only too glad if you find it worth your while.' [CL2: 108–9; Lbib1: 45–6]

1 (Thu) The London Government Act replaces London's 42 vestries with 28 metropolitan boroughs, each with a mayor and council. Shaw and fellow Progressives were elected to all six seats on the newly created St Pancras Borough Council in the South Division. Over the next three months, he campaigns to have the Rev. Stewart Headlam and Graham Wallas elected to the London School Board, and to have Sidney Webb and R. C. Phillimore elected to the London County Council. [CL2: 187–8, 190–1]

3 Shaw declines Ellen Terry's suggestion that she play in the Saturday matinée performances of *Captain Brassbound's Conversion* and in Henry Irving's Lyceum productions in the evening. [CL2: 191–2]

7 Shaw refuses the Charringtons' request to do a production of *Candida* at the Comedy Theatre. [CL2: 198]

December

Early Shaw is plagued by casting problems for the upcoming production of *Captain Brassbound's Conversion*. [CL2: 199]

16 (Sun) *Captain Brassbound's Conversion* first presented by the Stage Society at the Strand Theatre. Shaw and Ellen Terry talk face to face for the first time after more than five years of regular correspondence. Following the meeting their correspondence lapses. Even though correspondence is resumed 15 months later, lasting until March 1920, it has now become sporadic. [Hend2: 385; Peters 272; Ellen Terry to GBS, 10 Dec 1902, *Bernard Shaw*

and Ellen Terry: A Correspondence (1931), 285–6; BL MS Add 43802]

17 — Shaw departs from London to spend Christmas at 'Piccard's Cottage', St Catherine's, Guildford, Surrey, a country retreat he and Charlotte use periodically from mid-November1900 to mid-April 1902, and which succeeds 'Blackdown Cottage', Haslemere, as their regular country residence. [CL2: 205–6, 236]

Christmas

Lucy Shaw is at Cliftonville to improve her health but finds the weather too severe, so shortly takes GBS's advice and travels at his expense to a continental spa. [Rat 145; Farmer 135]

1901

Shaw writes *The Admirable Bashville* during January of this year, and on 15 January *Three Plays for Puritans* is published. A copyright reading of *The Admirable Bashville* at Victoria Hall (Bijou Theatre), London is held in March. Shaw and Charlotte tour France during April and May, and on 1 May, the first performance of *Caesar and Cleopatra* is staged in America. In July of this year, Shaw works on a scenario for *Man and Superman*. *The Admirable Bashville* is published by Grant Richards on 23 October, and the proposed production of *Mrs Warren's Profession* is obstructed because fears of censorship have made it difficult to find a venue for the production.

January

Shaw commences composition of *The Admirable Bashville, or Constancy Unrewarded* (a blank verse version of his novel, *Cashel Byron's Profession*) to forestall the mounting of unauthorized dramatizations of the novel in the US. In the preface, Shaw wrote, 'It may be asked why I wrote *The Admirable Bashville* in blank verse. My answer is that the operation of the copyright law of that time (now happily superseded) left me only a week to write it in. Blank verse is so childishly easy and expeditious (hence, by the way, Shakespear's copious output), that by adopting it I was enabled to do within the week what would have cost me a month in prose.' [CP2: 431–3; CL2: 217]

6 (Sun) — Shaw writes to actor Frederick Kerr, responding to his request that Shaw write a play for him: '...for the last eight or nine years I have written a play whenever anyone asked me to – ten in all. Not one of these plays has been produced by the people for whom they were written: in fact except for a few scratch matinees, a provisional tour... a flutter at a suburban theatre... &c &c, they have not been produced at all.' [Theatrics 42]

15 — Publication of *Three Plays for Puritans*. [Lbib1: 46; CL2: 190, 412]

22 Death of Queen Victoria. Shaw uses the occasion to argue for more sanitary funeral arrangements. [CL2: 216]

February

2 (Sat) Shaw sends the manuscript of *The Admirable Bashville* to the publisher, Grant Richards, for inclusion in the revised edition of *Cashel Byron's Profession*. [CP2: 432; Lbib1: 7]

March

All the old members of the Fabian Executive who had offered themselves for re-election are returned, and the two vacated places are filled by anti-imperialists. [CL2: 116]

13 (Wed) Copyright reading of *The Admirable Bashville* at the Victoria Hall (Bijou Theatre), London. [CP2: 432]

22 Samuel Butler sends Shaw the MS of *Erewhon Revisited* with a note mentioning that Longmans refused to publish it. [CL2: 223]

28 Shaw introduces Samuel Butler to Grant Richards, who subsequently publishes *Erewhon Revisited*, as well as a revised edition of *Erewhon*, and a posthumous edition of *The Way of All Flesh*. [CL2: 224]

April

7 (Sun) Shaw and Charlotte leave London to tour France for four weeks. [CL2: 226]

May

1 (Wed) First American (amateur) production of *Caesar and Cleopatra* by the Anna Morgan Studios for Art and Expression at the Fine Arts Building, Chicago. [Morgan 36; CP2: 159]

11, 18 Publication in Frank Harris's periodical *The Candid Friend* of Shaw's two-part interview 'Who I Am, and What I Think'. The interview – effectively an extensive autobiographical essay – comprises written answers by Shaw to questions submitted by Harris. Revised versions were published in *Shaw Gives Himself Away* (1939) and *Sixteen Self Sketches* (1949). [*The Candid Friend*, vol.1, no.2 (11 and 18 May 1901); *Selected Non-Dramatic Writings of Bernard Shaw*, ed. Dan H. Laurence; Lbib2: 1965; I&R 29–35]

Summer Shaw and Harley Granville Barker join the management committee of the Stage Society. [Hol2: 95]

June

28 (Fri) Shaw chairs a general meeting of the Stage Society. [CL2: 227]

30 Shaw lectures to the South Place Ethical Society on 'Twentieth Century Freethinking'. [CL2: 227]

July

2 (Tue) Shaw begins mapping out the scenario for *Man and Superman.* [CP2: 491]

6 Publication in Frank Harris's periodical *The Candid Friend* of an article by Edward McNulty entitled 'George Bernard Shaw as a Boy'. The numerous inaccuracies in this article are shown by internal evidence and Shaw's marginal comments on the original typescript in the Currall Collection at the Royal Academy of Dramatic Art. [*The Candid Friend,* vol. 1, no. 10 (6 Jul 1901); *The Shaw Bulletin* [later *Review*], vol. 2, no. 3 (Sep 1957), 7–10; I&R 17–21]

19 July – 28 August

Charlotte installs Shaw in Studland Rectory at Corfe Castle in Dorset. [GBS to Beatrice Webb, 24 Jul 1901, BLPES; CL2: 229]

July

24–30 Shaw writes the script for Sidney Webb's participation in the public debate on British Imperialism. [CL2: 230–5]

September

16 (Mon) First written communication from Mrs Patrick Campbell to Shaw. [Dent xvi]

21 *The Times* publishes Shaw's 'Smallpox in St Pancras', the first in a series of letters published over the next two years alerting the public to London's appalling sanitation and health conditions, and warning them that vaccination is no substitute for better housing. [Lbib2: 615; CL2: 237]

October

8 (Tue) Shaw completes his scenario for *Man and Superman.* [CP2: 491]

19 In a letter to Shaw, W. B. Yeats tries to persuade Shaw to visit Dublin: 'I write to urge you to come over & see our "Theatre" this year... Come over & help us to stir things up still further'. [BL MS Add 50553]

23 *The Admirable Bashville* is published by Grant Richards. [Lbib1: 7]

November

Siegfried Trebitsch, a young Austrian writer, armed with a letter of introduction to the Shaws written by William Archer, visits Shaw at Adelphi Terrace and offers to act as his translator and agent in Europe. Trebitsch describes Shaw's appearance on this first meeting as that of 'an amiably mirthful giant'. [CL2: 277–7 (date 1900 corrected to 1901 in CL3: 927); Weiss 3; Siegfried Trebitsch, *Chronicle of a Life,* trans. Eithne Wilkins and Ernst Kaiser (1953), 123; I&R 173–4]

7 (Thu) Having seen Mrs Patrick Campbell in *Beyond Human Power* at the Royalty Theatre in the afternoon, Shaw writes to congratulate her on her 'really great managerial achievement'. [CL2: 239]

9 Shaw lectures to the Ancoats Brotherhood, Manchester on 'The Ideal Citizen'. [*Manchester Guardian*, 10 Nov 1901]

20 Shaw speaks on Zionism at an Article Club dinner, following a lecture by Israel Zangwill on 'The Commercial Future of Palestine'. [DHL; *Jewish Chronicle*, 22 Nov 1901]

22 Shaw thanks Mrs Patrick Campbell for the photograph she has sent him, and expresses his admiration of her beauty and talent. [CL2: 240–1]

30 Provoked in part by actor-manager Lily Langtry's indignant objection to a suggestion that *Mrs Warren's Profession* be staged at her Imperial Theatre, Shaw writes to Golding Bright on the fate of the play: 'There has been no difficulty whatever with anyone, save only the Censor and Mrs Langtry, on the score of the play's character: quite the contrary... The sole obstacle to the performance of the play is the intimidation of the Censor and his absolutely autocratic power.' Bright publishes Shaw's views on censorship in the *Daily Express* on 3 December. [CL2: 241–3]

November–December

The Stage Society cannot find a venue for their proposed production of *Mrs Warren's Profession*. Theatre managers will not stage Shaw's unlicensed play for fear that their own licence might be revoked. [CL2: 241–3]

December

9 (Mon) Beatrice Webb reflects on the Webb–Shaw association: 'the sort of partnership that exists between GBS and ourselves, based on a common faith and real good fellowship, is of the utmost advantage to both, we supplying him with some ideas, and he, on crucial occasions, enormously improving our form.' [DBW2: 225]

1902

In January of this year, Shaw writes the Preface to *Mrs Warren's Profession*. The play itself is produced for the first time (privately) on 5 January at the New Lyric Club. In March, the Shaws meet Siegfried Trebitsch, and the German translation of his plays is begun. In April, the Shaws' lease on Piccard's Cottage expires, and a lease is taken on a house at Maybury Knoll, Woking. 12 May sees the first public production of *Captain Brassbound's Conversion* at the Queen's Theatre, Manchester. Shaw spends the summer by the sea at the Victoria Hotel, Holkham, Norfolk. In September he makes a brief visit to Bruges to see a Flemish art collection. On 14 December, the first (amateur) production of *The Admirable Bashville* is staged at the Pharos Club, London. Shaw completes *Man and Superman.*

Early — H. G. Wells takes Shaw to meet Joseph Conrad, who is affronted when Shaw alleges that his father [George Carr Shaw] 'drank like a fish'. [Desmond MacCarthy, *Shaw* (1951), 213–17; I&R 287–8]

January

Shaw writes a preface, 'The Author's Apology', to a deluxe edition of *Mrs Warren's Profession* to be published separately by Grant Richards late in March. [CL2: 261]

5 (Sun) — First production of *Mrs Warren's Profession* (produced privately to avoid the Censor), by the Stage Society at the New Lyric Club. [CL2: 250; Hend2: 392; Morgan 18]

24 — Shaw lectures to the Fabian Society on 'The English Drama', as part of the Society's series on 'The Social Tendencies of the Drama'. [CL2: 261]

February

10 (Mon) — Shaw lectures on 'County Council Politics' at the Central Reform Club. [DHL]

15 — Shaw attends an amateur production of *Candida*, performed at Cripplegate Institute. The production was directed by Millicent Murby, a fellow Fabian. [Theatrics 44]

March

Introduction of an Education Bill in Parliament leads Webb and Shaw to prepare two new Fabian Tracts (Nos 114 and 117) proposing 13 amendments of the Bill, 11 of which are adopted in the London Education Act of 1903. [Pease 145–6; CL2: 378]

Early — Siegfried Trebitsch visits Shaw, proposing that he translate Shaw's plays into German, thereby 'conquering the German Stage for him'. Trebitsch chooses *The Devil's Disciple, Candida* and *Arms and the Man* for translation. [Weiss 3]

31 — The Treaty of Vereeniging is signed, marking the end of the Boer War.

April

Expiry of the Shaws' lease on 'Piccard's Cottage', Guildford. They subsequently rent a house at Maybury Knoll, Woking. [CL2: 236, 277]

5 (Sat) — Ellen Terry again declines to play Lady Cicely. [CL2: 272; Peters 283, 437 n17; *Ellen Terry and Bernard Shaw: A Correspondence* (1931), 289–90]

10 — Shaw writes an undertaking to 'refer any manager or publisher who may apply to me before the first of April 1903 for permission to translate, publish or produce any of my published plays

in Germany or Austria' to Siegfried Trebitsch. This would become a lifelong collaboration. [Weiss 4, 7]

12 Production of *Captain Brassbound's Conversion* at the Queen's Theatre, Manchester, directed by Charles Charrington, with Janet Achurch as Lady Cicely Waynflete. [Morgan 39]

13 Publication in *The Manchester Guardian* of a lengthy interview with Shaw about *Captain Brassbound's Conversion* and other theatrical topics, Shaw being described as 'one of the chief of dramatic critics and one of the best known playwrights of the time'. ['Mr Bernard Shaw on Plays', *Manchester Guardian*, 13 May 1902]

29 Shaw hears Yeats speak at Clifford's Inn, Fleet Street, on 'Poetry and the Living Voice', followed by Florence Farr 'cantilating' poetry to her lyre. [Peters 293]

June

Shaw completes *Man and Superman*. [CP2: 491; CL2: 275]

19 (Thu) Shaw addresses the Vegetarian Congress, London. [DHL]

26 Shaw begins negotiations through Siegfried Trebitsch with German and Austrian theatre managers. [CL2: 277ff.]

Summer

Arthur Balfour succeeds his uncle, Lord Salisbury, as Prime Minister. The Webbs cultivate Balfour's friendship between 1902 and 1905, but the Fabians' 'free trade' pronouncements help bring about Balfour's political demise. [GBS to Edward Pease, 30 Sep 1903, cited in Joad 171–2]

July–September

The Shaws spend summer by the sea at the Victoria Hotel at Holkham in Norfolk. Shaw revises *Man and Superman* throughout the summer, planning to publish it as a book rather than as a play for performance. [CL 2: 280]

August

9 (Sat) Coronation of Edward VII.

31 Shaw writes to Henry Arthur Jones, complimenting him about the play, *Chance the Idol*, which Jones has recently read to him and Charlotte, and which is about to open at Wyndham's Theatre with Lena Ashwell in the cast. About Ashwell, he remarks that: 'Lena is a squawker; but she is a squawker of genius.' About Holkham he reports: 'This isn't a bad place, cheap and simple, remote and slow, no annoyances and no conveniences of civilisation.' [Doris Arthur Jones, *The Life and Letters of Henry Arthur Jones* (1930), 220–1]

September

20 (Sat) Shaw makes a brief visit to Bruges to see a Flemish art collection. [CL2: 283]

November

7 (Fri) Shaw is still 'at work revising the *Superman*. It will be a longish job'. [CL2: 284]

12 Shaw refuses Max Beerbohm's request that he lecture to the Playgoers' Club. [CL2: 286–7]

December

Ellen Terry again declines to play Lady Cicely. [Peters 283]

14 (Sun) First (amateur) production of *The Admirable Bashville* at the Pharos Club, London. [CP2: 432]

1903

On 24 February of this year the first (amateur) American production of *You Never Can Tell* at the Studebaker Theater, Chicago takes place, and a day later *The Devil's Disciple* (*Ein Teufelskerl*) becomes the first German-language performance of a Shaw play. In May, *Candida* has its first public American production by the Browning Society of Philadelphia, and *The Admirable Bashville* has its first professional production by the Stage Society at the Imperial Theatre, in London. *Man and Superman* is published in Britain in August, and from August to October the Shaws visit Scotland, staying at Springburn, Strachur and making a short trip to Glasgow in early October where Shaw delivers a few lectures.

January

The Shaws spend the second week of January at the seaside at Cromer in Norfolk with the Webbs and the Wallases, to whom he reads *Man and Superman*. Beatrice Webb describes it as 'quite the biggest thing he has done. He has found his *form* ... a combination of essay, treatise, interlude, lyric – all the different forms illustrating the same central idea, as a sonata manifests a scheme of melody and harmony.' [CL2: 298–9; Webb 256]

12 (Mon) Trebitsch has a contract with the director of the Raiemund Theatre in Vienna to stage *The Devil's Disciple*, and is negotiating with other theatres to stage *Arms and the Man* ('Helden') and *Candida*. [CL2: 300]

15 Shaw writes to Siegfried Trebitsch on the subject of translation: 'unless you repeat the words I have repeated, you will throw away all the best stage effects... Half the art of dialogue consists in the *echoing* of words – the tossing back & forwards of phrases from one actor to another like a cricket ball.' [Weiss 36]

25 Shaw lectures on the 'Superman' in London. This is his first public pronouncement on the subject after commencing the play *Man and Superman* in 1901. He returned to the topic in a lecture on 16 February 1906. [DHL]

February

H. G. Wells joins the Fabian Society. [Pearson 249; Pease 164]

The Stuttgart publishers, Cotta, bring out *Drei Dramen*, Trebitsch's translations of *The Devil's Disciple*, *Candida* and *Arms and the Man*. [CL2: 287; Weiss 7]

Shaw sits for artist (Sir) William Rothenstein. [DHL]

24 (Tue) First (amateur) American production of *You Never Can Tell* at the Studebaker Theatre in Chicago, by the pupils of the Chicago Musical College School of Acting. [Hend2: 404; Morgan 31]

25 First German-language performance of a Shaw play, Trebitsch's translation of *The Devil's Disciple* (*Ein Teufelskerl* – Devil of a Fellow) which opens in Vienna at the Raiemund Theatre. The play closes after only four performances. [CL2: 305; Hend2: 417; Weiss 8, 47]

March

15 (Sun) The first staging of Shaw's work in Germany – *Helden* (*Arms and the Man*), translated by Trebitsch and produced by the Freie Volksbühne (Independent People's Theatre) – performed at the Metropol Theater. [Weiss 44–6: Morgan 22]

23 Shaw sends the manuscript of *Man and Superman* to the printer, and lectures on 'Darwin' to the Fabian Society in the 'Prophets of the 19th Century' series. [DHL]

10 April – 4 May

The Shaws tour Italy, visiting Parma, Perugia, Assisi, Orvieto, Siena, Genoa and Milan. [CL2: 320]

May

Following Chamberlain's tariff speech 'Free Trade versus Fair Trade', divisions arise within the Fabian Society. While Sidney Webb favours free trade, Shaw agrees with Chamberlain that tariffs are necessary. Shaw is given the job of canvassing opinions of members of the Fabian Society throughout Britain. [CL2: 368, 370]

18 (Mon) First public American production of *Candida* – a piracy – by the Browning Society of Philadelphia. [Hend2: 406; Morgan 28; DHL]

29 Shaw talks on 'Some Confessions of a Borough Councillor' at the Caxton Hall, Westminster, under the auspices of the Lecture Agency. A *Times* report says 'In a more serious vein Mr. Shaw dwelt on the necessity of having women councillors, and argued eloquently for the municipalization of rates.' [*The Times* (London) 30 May 1903; DHL]

June

After nine months of unsuccessful negotiations with American publishers, Shaw sends *Man and Superman* to an American printer to secure his American copyright in time for the appearance of the British edition. [CL2: 336]

1 (Mon) The Shaws make the first of several visits to explorer and author of *In Darkest Africa*, Sir Henry Morton Stanley and his wife in Surrey during Stanley's last illness. [DHL]

7 First professional production of *The Admirable Bashville* by the Stage Society at the Imperial Theatre, London, directed by Shaw and Harley Granville Barker. [CL2: 326–7; Hend2: 429; Morgan 41]

29 Copyright performance of *Man and Superman* at the Victoria Hall (Bijou Theatre), Bayswater. [CP2: 491; I&R 139]

Summer

Early Shaw signs with Archibald Constable to publish *Man and Superman,* an agreement of a few lines on a sheet of writing paper that was to last for the rest of his life. This also entails a severance of his relations with Grant Richards. [CL2: 337–8, 412; Hol2: 68]

July

14 (Tue) Last performance of Ellen Terry and Henry Irving together at the Lyceum. [Peters 284]

23 Dining with the Webbs, Prime Minister Arthur Balfour calls Shaw 'the finest man of letters today'. [DBW2: 289]

August

1 (Sat) The Shaws begin a two-month visit to Scotland, staying in Springburn, Strachur, except for a few days in Glasgow in early October. At Strachur, 'you can write as much as you like – indeed there is nothing else to do.' He attends political meetings there on 4 and 7 August. [CL2: 340, 348]

11 Publication of *Man and Superman* by Archibald Constable in Britain. [Lbib1: 52-3]

12 Formal registration of an American edition of *Man and Superman,* arranged by Shaw through University Press, of Cambridge, Mass. However, this edition was not actually issued by Brentano's until 1 June 1904. [CL2: 335, 366; I&R 86; Lbib1: 53]

Autumn

Shaw authorizes Augustin Hamon to translate his plays into French. [CL2: 512–14]

October

2 (Fri) Shaw delivers a lecture, 'Is Free Trade Dead or Alive?', to the Glasgow Fabians. [CL2: 375; Weiss 64]

4 Shaw lectures to the Glasgow branch of the Independent Labour Party on 'Socialist Unity'. [CL2: 375; Weiss 64]

7 Reflecting in London on the 'degrading exhibition' of his recent successful speech-making in Glasgow, Shaw remarks: 'All that prodigious expenditure of nervous energy... leaves one empty, exhausted, disgusted.' Shaw registers his increasing frustration at the interference of his political duties with his playwriting. [CL2: 375; Weiss 63]

November

19 (Thu) Première of Trebitsch's translation of *Candida* performed at Dresden's Königliches Schauspielhaus. [Weiss 66]

December

8 (Tue) First fully professional American production of *Candida* at the Prince's Theater, New York, directed and acted by Arnold Daly. [Morgan 28; Weiss 67]

11 Despite initial reluctance, Shaw expresses his willingness to contest a seat on the London County Council. [CL2: 378]

28 Shaw writes to Violet Vanbrugh, trying to entice her into the role of Ann Whitefield in *Man and Superman*: 'The part of Ann is no ordinary leading lady's business. Where is the person who can be this cat, this liar, this minx, this "something for which I know no polite name"... and yet be perfectly irresistible and perfectly dignified?' [Theatrics 47]

1904

In February of this year *The Common Sense of Municipal Trading* is published. After campaigning for election to the London County Council, Shaw is defeated in March 1904. He withdraws from local politics and soon afterwards begins his partnership with Granville Barker and Vedrenne at the Royal Court Theatre. Towards the middle of the year, the Shaws tour Italy and in June – the month *Man and Superman* is published – Shaw begins to write *John Bull's Other Island*, which he completes in August. Shaw also writes *How He Lied to Her Husband* between 13 and 16 August; a play which has its copyright performance on 27 August. The Shaws visit Scotland, staying at Alness, Rosemarkie, from August until October. *John Bull's Other Island* receives its first production by the Vedrenne-Barker company at the Court Theatre in London in November. *The Man of Destiny*, *Candida* and *How He Lied to Her Husband* were all produced in New York during this year. W. B. Yeats and playwright Lady Gregory found the Irish National Theatre Society.

1903–4

J. H. Leigh, the proprietor of the Court Theatre at Sloane Square, engages Harley Granville Barker as a director. Through Granville Barker, Shaw's plays are 'given a home' at the Court

Theatre. [C. B. Purdom, *Harley Granville Barker* (1955), 20–1; CL2: 389]

January

4 (Mon) Shaw writes to American critic and author James Huneker, 'I spend the whole slack holiday time in a mad race to get abreast of my correspondence'. [CL2: 395]

22 Shaw's draft of *Fabianism and the Fiscal Question*, Tract No. 116, compiled from the opinions on the tariff question of Fabian members all over the country, is evaluated at a Fabian Society meeting. Graham Wallas resigns after his motion that the tract remain unpublished is defeated. [Pease 160]

February

Publication of Shaw's book *The Common Sense of Municipal Trading*. [Lbib1: 56]

Shaw campaigns for election to the London County Council in the constituency of St Pancras. [CL2: 403; Erv 369]

10 (Wed) First American production of *The Man of Destiny* at the Carnegie Lyceum, New York, directed by Arnold Daly. [CL2: 396; Morgan 26]

March

5 (Sat) Shaw and his fellow Progressive candidate, Sir William Nevill M. Geary, Bart., are defeated by two Moderates at the London County Council election for South St Pancras (the constituency he had represented for six years on the Borough Council). Shaw withdraws from local politics. [CL2: 410; DBW2: 318–19]

31 *Fabianism and the Fiscal Question: an Alternative Policy* is published. Shaw is credited with drafting the work though, as he states in the preface, 'its authorship is genuinely collective'. An earlier version of this tract, in a letter written by Shaw, had already appeared in September 1903 and had been cyclostyled for circulation to the Executive Committee. [Lbib1: 55, 62]

April

16 (Wed) The première of Trebitsch's translation of *Arms and the Man* (*Helden*) at the Deutsches Schauspielhaus in Hamburg. [Weiss 31]

25 The Shaws give up their rented cottage, 'Maybury Knoll' in Woking. [CL2: 414]

26 April – 10 May

On Harley Granville Barker's initiative, six matinées of *Candida* are presented at the Royal Court Theatre. These mark the beginning of a three-year partnership between Shaw, Granville Barker and Vedrenne which launches Shaw's work into public consciousness. As well as helping finance the Court venture, Shaw handles publicity and supervises casting and rehearsals. An exacting but considerate director, he annotates the actors' scripts with musical directions as to pitch, pacing, rhythm, timing and volume. [CL2: 360; 389–91; Morgan 9]

April

29 Shaw attends the annual Stage Society dinner at the Café Monaco. [CL3: 451]

1 May – 10 June

The Shaws tour Italy, visiting Turin, Pisa and Rome, before returning to London via Geneva. [CL2: 416]

May

25 (Wed) Shaw visits the Sistine Chapel with the famous French author, Anatole France. [DHL]

June

Archibald Henderson writes to Shaw stating his intention to write his biography. Over the next several years, Shaw collaborates with Henderson, supplying generous quantities of autobiographical information. [CL2: 425]

Publication of a second impression of *Three Plays for Puritans* incorporating revisions of the text. [Lbib1: 48; CP2: 51]

1 (Wed) Publication of the first American edition of *Man and Superman* by Brentano's. This edition ran to 2000 copies. A previous printing (12 August 1903) was for copyright purposes only, and consisted of two unrevised proofs. [Lbib1: 53; CL2: 366]

12 Shaw again invites Ellen Terry to play in *Captain Brassbound's Conversion* at the Court Theatre. [CL2: 420]

17 Shaw begins writing *Rule Britannia*, later entitled *John Bull's Other Island*. There is evidence that Shaw had been contemplating a play of this kind since early 1900. In June 1903, Shaw wrote to Yeats, 'I have it quite seriously in my head to write an Irish play (frightfully modern – no banshees nor leprechauns) when I have finished a book I now have in hand on the succulent subject of Municipal Trading'. The idea created by Shaw in his 1907 Preface to the play that it was commissioned for the Irish National Theatre and subsequently turned down has been discounted. [GBS to Yeats, 23 Jun 1903, Cornell Box 10; CP2: 806; CL2: 423, 452; L&G x–xi]

29 Shaw asks Ada Rehan whether she would be interested in playing Lady Cicely in *Captain Brassbound's Conversion*. 'You were in the author's mind when he wrote the play.' [CL2: 423–5; Peters 285, 437 n19]

July

2 (Sat) The Shaws lease a larger house, the 'Old House', at Harmer Green, Welwyn, Hertfordshire which Shaw describes as 'a gem'.

	[*Ellen Terry and Bernard Shaw: A Correspondence* (1931), 297–8; CL2: 414]
	Shaw reads *Captain Brassbound's Conversion* to Ada Rehan. [Peters 285; CL2: 423-5, 429–30]
8	Ada Rehan declines Shaw's terms for *Captain Brassbound's Conversion*. [CL2: 433]
9	Shaw invites Ada Rehan to name her own terms, but to no avail. Rehan departs for America where she later falls ill and is prescribed a year's rest from the stage. [CL2: 433–4; Peters 285]
20	Shaw contracts with Arnold Daly to produce his plays in America. [CL2: 573]
26	Shaw tells Ellen Terry about his negotiations with Ada Rehan. [CL2: 436]

August

Early	The Shaws begin a two-month visit to Scotland, staying at Alness, Rosemarkie – 'a hole on the N.E. coast' – and Edinburgh, returning to London on 4 October via North Berwick. Shaw complains to Harley Granville Barker: 'Oh these holidays, these accursed holidays!' [CL2: 443; Weiss 72]
1 (Mon)	Alvin Langdon Coburn and Frederick Evans visit Shaw at the 'Old House', Harmer Green, where Coburn takes the first of his many photographic portraits of Shaw. Shaw was able to supply numerous items of photographic equipment, and offered the bathroom for use as a makeshift darkroom. [*Alvin Langdon Coburn: Photographer: An Autobiography* (1966), 26–8; I&R 202–3; CL2: 435–6]
13–16	Shaw writes a curtain-raiser for Arnold Daly, *How He Lied to Her Husband*. [CL2: 443; CP2: 1030]
23	Shaw finishes the first draft of *John Bull's Other Island*. [CL2: 423, 444]
27	Copyright reading of *How He Lied to Her Husband* at the Bijou Theatre (Victoria Hall), Bayswater. [CP2: 1030]
31	Shaw writes to Yeats: 'Is there any modern Machinery in I. L. Theatre? For instance a hydraulic bridge? ... I should like to know what I can depend on in the way of modern appliances.' [CL2: 452]

September

7 (Wed)	Shaw sends the final draft of *John Bull's Other Island* to the typist. [Shaw to Yeats, 7 Sep 1904, *Sotheby's Catalogue*, 25 Jul 1978, 330; Hol2: 83]
26	First performance of *How He Lied to Her Husband* at the Berkeley Lyceum Theatre, New York, directed by Arnold Daly. [CP2: 1030; Morgan 51]
Late	The Shaws return to London from Scotland. [CL2: 443]

October

The Irish National Theatre Society, meeting to discuss the production of *John Bull's Other Island*, expresses misgivings about the play. Several months of negotiations with Shaw follow. [CL2: 452–3; Hol2: 88–91]

4 Actor and stage-manager W. G. Fay writes to W. B. Yeats about *John Bull's Other Island* saying 'I think it is a wonderful piece of work' but that it would be difficult to cast in Dublin. [BL MS Add 50553, fol. 146]

5 W. B. Yeats writes a three-page letter to Shaw about *John Bull's Other Island*, in mostly complimentary terms. He adds that J. M. Synge has read the play and 'thinks it will hold a Dublin audience', but suggests some cuts. [BL MS Add 50553, fols. 144–5]

18 Beginning of the Vedrenne–Barker management of the Court Theatre. [CL2: 389; Pearson 232]

November

1 (Tue) First production, in six performances, of *John Bull's Other Island* by the Vedrenne–Barker company at the Court Theatre. [CL2: 389, 445, 458; CP2: 806; Morgan 48; DBW2: 350]

10 Beatrice Webb brings the Conservative Prime Minister, Arthur Balfour, to see *John Bull's Other Island*. He likes it so much that he sees it five times, bringing with him two leaders of the Liberal Opposition, Campbell-Bannerman and Asquith. [DBW2: 350; Hol2: 99]

16 Publication in *The Tatler* of an 'interview' with Shaw – compiled from pre-written 'answers' he supplied – by author and journalist Clement Shorter (founder of *The Tatler*) about the reception of *John Bull's Other Island*. An accompanying full-page photograph, taken at Adelphi Terrace, of 'Mr. George Bernard Shaw – Novelist, Journalist, and Playwright' carries a caption in which he is described as 'one of the most subtle and one of the most brilliant and original writers of our age'. [C. K. Shorter, 'George Bernard Shaw – A Conversation Concerning Mr. Shaw's New Play', *The Tatler*, no. 177, 16 Nov 1904; also cited in I&R 134–6; Lbib2: 620]

26 *Candida* is shifted to the evening bill at the Court Theatre. [DHL]

30 Shaw lectures on 'Socialism for the Upper Classes' at the Holy Trinity Parish Hall, Sloane Square. ['Bernard Shaw on Incomes', *New York Times*, 23 Dec 1904; DHL]

December

20 In correspondence with Trebitsch, Shaw writes 'I am [in a] very bad temper. I hate Christmas.' He spends Christmas quietly at Harmer Green. [Weiss 76]

27 Shaw writes to Alma Murray about the production of *Arms and the Man*: 'Arms & the Man is off. As luck would have it I took to reading it one day... and was startled to find what flimsy, fantastic, unsafe stuff it is. I countermanded it at the Court [Theatre] then and there, and made them put up You Never Can Tell instead.' [CL2: 473]

1905

In February of this year Shaw is elected to the management committee of the Society of Authors. The first (amateur) production of *The Philanderer* is performed at the Cripplegate Institute in February, as is the first production in England of *How He Lied to Her Husband* at the Court Theatre. On 11 March, a Special Performance of *John Bull's Other Island* is held for King Edward VII. Between March and September, Shaw writes *Major Barbara,* although his dissatisfaction with the ending forces him to rewrite the last act, delaying its completion until October of this year. During the year Shaw also writes *Passion, Poison, and Petrifaction: Or The Fatal Gazogene* which is produced in July. In May, *Man and Superman* premières at the Court Theatre and in June the Shaws' lease on the 'Old House', Harmer Green, expires, forcing them to move back to London. During the months from July to September, the Shaws stay in Ireland. The first American production of *John Bull's Other Island* is performed in October. The first book about Shaw, *George Bernard Shaw: His Plays*, by H. L. Mencken, is published during this year, and Erica Cotterill develops a romantic obsession for Shaw.

February

1 (Wed) Shaw makes a speech at a Queen's Hall meeting on the Russian crisis. [DHL]

14 Shaw lectures on 'What is a School' to the Guild of St Edmund (Educators). Asked how he got the equipment to be a playwright 'save through the help and patience of some schoolmaster', Shaw replied that he had 'no doubt that some schoolmaster had tried to teach composition to Shakespeare and went to his grave claiming credit for joint authorship.' [*New York Times*, 2 Apr 1905; DHL]

17 Shaw takes Augustin Hamon to task for appointing an unapproved translator, Dr Stéphane Epstein-Estienne, to translate *Arms and the Man* into French. [CL2: 512–14]

20 First (amateur) production of *The Philanderer* is presented by Millicent Murby's New Stage Club at the Cripplegate Institute. Shaw, who has directed rehearsals, is prevented from attending the performance by influenza. Only a few weeks previously, Shaw had written to Frederick Kerr (7 January 1905) to discourage

	him from mounting a production of *The Philanderer*: 'It "dates" horribly... let the thing lie where it dropped, unacted and unpleasant. I'm certain I could do better for you.' Kerr was only to perform once in a Shaw play, *Captain Brassbound's Conversion*, opposite Ellen Terry in 1906. [Department of Manuscripts, National Library of Australia; CP1: 134; CL2: 509]
24	Shaw warns Dr Stéphane Epstein-Estienne of the legal consequences of his unauthorized translation of Shaw's plays into French. [CL2: 516]
28	First production in England of *How He Lied to Her Husband* at the Royal Court Theatre. [CL2: 509; Morgan 51]

March

	In an interview for the periodical *World of Dress*, Shaw is asked for his opinion as to what women ought to wear, Shaw replies: 'Anything that will show how they are constructed and allow them the free use of their limbs... A woman is a biped, built like a man; let her dress like a man.' [Maud Churton Braby, 'Dress and the Writer. A Talk with Mr George Bernard Shaw', *World of Dress*, VIII (Mar 1905); I&R 403–4; Lbib2: 621]
1 (Wed)	Shaw invites Lillah McCarthy to play Ann Whitefield in the Stage Society's upcoming production of *Man and Superman*. This is despite having already told Violet Vanbrugh: 'I cannot bear the idea of anybody else in the part' (28 December 1903). [CL2: 518–19; Theatrics 47]
7	Shaw proposes to Vedrenne that the Court Theatre might take up *Man and Superman* after its three Stage Society performances. [CL2: 520]
11	Special Performance at the Court Theatre of *John Bull's Other Island* before King Edward VII. Court legend has it that he laughed so hard he fell off his special chair and broke it. [Pearson 237; Theatrics 62; CL2: 519, 522]
22	Shaw begins writing *Major Barbara*, with Eleanor Robson in mind for the lead female role. [CL2: 524; CP3: 11]

March–June

	The Court Theatre rehearses and produces *How He Lied to Her Husband, John Bull's Other Island, You Never Can Tell, Candida* and *Man and Superman*. Plans are also afoot for Ellen Terry to appear in *Captain Brassbound's Conversion*, and for Johnston Forbes-Robertson in *Caesar and Cleopatra*. [Court 131–9]

April

1 (Sat) – 6	The Shaws visit 'Spade House', H. G. Wells's home at Sandgate near Folkestone, and meet the playwright Gerhart Hauptmann there. [CL2: 648]

12 With Dr Frederick James Furnivall in the chair, Shaw delivers a speech on Shakespeare at the Kensington Town Hall. [DHL]

May

Shaw begins the composition of *Passion, Poison, and Petrifaction: Or The Fatal Gazogene*. The play is written at the request of Mr Cyril Maude, and completed on 4 June 1905. [CP3: 202]

1 (Mon) Yeats drops the Irish National Theatre's claims to *John Bull's Other Island*. The play enters the evening bill at the Court Theatre for three weeks. [CL2: 453; DHL]

2 First of nine performances of *You Never Can Tell* at the Court Theatre. [CL2: 523]

8 Shaw attends a lecture on Jevons by Philip Wicksteed at University College, London. [DHL]

21 First private (Stage Society) performance of *Man and Superman* (excluding Act III) at the Court Theatre, with Harley Granville Barker and Lillah McCarthy. [CL2: 518; CP2: 491; Pearson 226; Morgan 42]

23 First professional (Vedrenne–Barker) production of *Man and Superman* at the Court Theatre with the same cast. The play ran for nine matinées through to 9 June. [CL2: 528; DHL; Pearson 231; Peters 281, 437 n14; Morgan 42]

Summer

Early Robert Loraine meets Shaw at a performance of *Man and Superman* at the Court Theatre, and next day has lunch with the Shaws at Adelphi Terrace. [Winifred Loraine, *Robert Loraine: Soldier, Actor, Airman* (1938), 81–2; I&R 282]

June

26 (Mon) Shaw meets Charles Frohman. [DHL; BL MS Add 56500]

30 The Shaws' lease on the 'Old House' at Harmer Green expires, necessitating a move back to London. [CL2: 533, 535; BL MS Add 56500]

July

6 (Thu) Shaw and Charlotte return to Ireland, staying in Derry in County Cork, where they are joined by Charlotte's sister, Mary Cholmondeley. This is Shaw's first visit to Ireland since leaving in 1876. They remain in Ireland until 29 September, when Shaw departs for London for the rehearsals of *Major Barbara*. Shaw was to recount later: 'I did not set foot in Ireland again until 1905, and not then on my own initiative. I went back to please my wife: and a curious reluctance to retrace my steps made me land in the south and enter Dublin through the backdoor from Meath rather than return as I

came, through the front door on the sea.' [CL2: 536; DHL; Imm xxxiii; Prefs3: 25–6]

14 First production of Shaw's minor play, *Passion, Poison, and Petrification: Or The Fatal Gazogene*, commissioned by Cyril Maude for the Actors' Orphanage, at the Theatrical Garden Party at Regent's Park. [Morgan 102; Hol2: 102]

August

Shaw, frustrated that Ada Rehan is too ill to play in *Captain Brassbound's Conversion*, suggests a postponement of production until she is able to play the part. However, Vedrenne engages Ellen Terry to play Lady Cicely for an immediate start. Eleanor Robson declines Shaw's offer to perform in *Major Barbara*. [CL2: 544ff.; Peters 285–6, 437 n22]

September

5 (Tue) Robert Loraine plays Tanner in the first American production of *Man and Superman* (excluding Act III) at the Hudson Theatre, New York, where it runs for nine months before being taken on a successful seven-month tour. [Pearson 239; Morgan 42; Weiss 93]

8 Composition of *Major Barbara* completed, although Shaw is dissatisfied with the ending. [CP3: 11]

22 First public production of *The Admirable Bashville* at the Royal Theatre, Manchester. [Morgan 41]

28 Shaw responds to a letter from Erica Cotterill, a young Fabian and relative of the poet Rupert Brooke who had become infatuated with Shaw after attending one of his plays. She begins an invasion of his life, first in writing, then by turning up at his house unannounced. [CL2: 562–3; Hol2: 200]

29 The Shaws return to London from Ireland. [CL2: 536]

October

1 (Sun) Shaw reads *Major Barbara* to Gilbert Murray and Harley Granville Barker, and decides to rewrite the third act. [CL2: 565; Hol2: 107]

4 First publication in book form of *The Irrational Knot*. [Lbib1: 63–4]

8 Shaw and Granville Barker call on the Webbs, and, as Beatrice recalls, 'spread out... the difficulties, the hopes, the ridiculous aspects of their really arduous efforts to create an intellectual drama'. Beatrice adds: 'GBS's egotism and vanity are not declining; he is increasing his deftness of wit and phrase, but becoming every day more completely iconoclastic, the ideal derider.' [DBW2: 353–4]

10 First American production by Arnold Daly of *John Bull's Other Island* at the Garrick Theatre, New York. The play survives a mere two weeks. [CL2: 567; Morgan 48]

13 Death of Henry Irving. [CL2: 566–7; Peters 287]

15 Shaw finishes the 'Edstaston MS' of *Major Barbara*, written during a stay at the home of Charlotte's sister, Mary Cholmondeley. [CL2: 524, 565]

20 Publication of a German translation of Shaw's obituary of Henry Irving in the *Neue Freie Presse*. Shaw had instructed that Trebitsch undertake the translation, but a 'bungling hack' causes serious distortions in the printed version. The obituary is then further distorted when retranslated into English, and this version is published in England. Shaw's seemingly disparaging remarks provoke an outcry. [Lbib2: 623; CL2: 566–7; Peters 287; Weiss 90]

27 First American production of *Mrs Warren's Profession* at the Hyperion Theater in New Haven, Connecticut. By order of the mayor, police close the theatre due to the play's 'indecency'. [Hend2: 436; Erv 347; Morgan 18]

30 Sensational opening of *Mrs Warren's Profession* at the Garrick Theatre, New York, staged hastily by Arnold Daly after the failure of *John Bull's Other Island*. Shocked by the threat of police arrest, Daly withdraws *Mrs Warren* after the first performance, substituting *Candida* until the end of the week. Even so, the cast is arrested and tried for 'disorderly conduct'. Shaw did not allow Daly to perform any of the later plays. [CL2: 573–4; Erv 348–9; Hend2: 438; Wall 14]

November

23 (Thu) Arthur Balfour appoints Beatrice Webb to the Royal Commission on Poor Law. [DBW3: 11]

28 First production of *Major Barbara* at the Court Theatre, directed by Shaw and Granville Barker. Beatrice Webb takes the retiring Prime Minister, A. J. Balfour, to the première. Webb comments that 'GBS is gambling with ideas and emotions in a way that distresses slow-minded prigs like Sidney and I'. [DBW3: 12–13; CL2: 583; Annie Russell, 'George Bernard Shaw at Rehearsals of *Major Barbara*' printed in the *Shaw Review*, May 1976 from an MS in the Theater Collection, New York Public Library; I&R 146, 149; Morgan 52]

November–December

Shaw makes two visits (2–3 November and 6–7 December) to H. G. Wells's house at Sandgate. On the first visit he is accompanied by Alvin Langdon Coburn, who photographs Shaw and Wells. [CL2: 648; DHL]

December

Arthur Balfour, in whom the Webbs had placed much of their hope, resigns as Prime Minister. Campbell-Bannerman replaces him. [DBW3: 439]

13	Shaw writes a postcard to Erica Cotterill: 'Patience, dear lady, patience: your turn will come: can I put 48 hours into the day?' [Texas]
16–28	The Shaws make a Christmas visit to Charlotte's sister, Mary Cholmondeley, at Edstaston, Wem, Shropshire. [CL2: 586; Weiss 91]
28	First performance of *Major Barbara,* at the Court Theatre. [DHL]
31	Charles Ricketts records a visit by Shaw and Florence Farr: 'Miss Farr and Bernard Shaw to tea, to discuss the possibility of staging his Don Juan in *Man and Superman*. Shaw has aged, he was voluble and amusing on arrival...' [*Self-Portrait taken from the Letters & Journals of Charles Ricketts, RA* (1939), 127]

1906

During this year, Shaw begins to keep a file on the migraine headaches which have plagued him since the early 1890s, noting the date, effects on his system, medications and their effectiveness, and also to devise a system of postcards to lighten the load of his correspondence. He spends early January in Lancashire, electioneering for Hyndman and Burns. In February the Shaws lease a house at Harmer Green, Welwyn. The first London performance of *Captain Brassbound's Conversion* is performed in March. From mid-April until May the Shaws visit Paris where Rodin does a bust of Shaw. In the early summer, Shaw writes prefaces to *John Bull's Other Island* and *Major Barbara*, and between August and September Shaw writes *The Doctor's Dilemma*. From September until October the Shaws visit Ireland. The first professional production in English of *Caesar and Cleopatra* in New York on 30 October is followed the next month by the first production of *The Doctor's Dilemma* at the Court Theatre. In early November the Shaws move to the Rectory, Ayot St Lawrence in Hertfordshire. During the year, turmoil and disruption occur in the Fabian Society as H. G. Wells tries to push radical reforms. From this time the London Fabian Society began to fragment into subgroups, such as the Nursery, the Arts Group and the Women's Group (of which Charlotte Shaw was a member).

January

The General election brings the Liberal Party into power with Sir Henry Campbell-Bannerman as Prime Minister. Three Fabian Liberals and four Fabian Labourites win seats. The Conservative Party loses seats, and the Labour Party achieves spectacular gains. Of 50 Labour candidates, 29 win seats. These results leave the Fabian Society in disarray, their energies having been expended and apparently wasted on permeation tactics. Many Fabians, including Shaw, begin to feel that a harder, more coordinated party political approach would be more effective. [Pease 152–3]

1 (Mon) The Shaws return to London for a few days before Shaw travels to Lancashire for a week of electioneering, from 4 to 11 January, on behalf of radical candidates including H. M. Hyndman and John Burns. [CL2: 586; DHL; Weiss 93]

3 Shaw takes the chair for G. K. Chesterton's lecture, 'Liberal Watchwords', at the New Reform Club. [DHL]

12 H. G. Wells gives his lecture, 'This Misery of Boots', an indictment of private enterprise which also serves to illustrate his views on the Fabian society's structure and propaganda mechanisms, and by implication is a criticism of Webb and Shaw. [CL2: 648n; Pease 164]

February

5 (Mon) The Shaws take a four month lease on a house at Harmer Green, Welwyn. [CL2: 610]

9 H. G. Wells delivers a lecture, 'The Faults of the Fabian', which argues that the Fabian Society is a 'drawing room society' with little financial or organizational ability: 'Go out to the Strand. Note the size of the buildings and business places, note the glare of the advertisements, note the abundance of traffic and the multitude of people... That is the world whose very foundations you are trying to change.' A Special Committee of Inquiry, chaired by Wells, is subsequently formed to consider Wells's reform proposals, preparatory to the Executive election. [S.G. Hobson, *Pilgrim to the Left: Memoirs of a Modern Revolutionist* (1938), 106–7; I&R 74; CL2: 596; Pearson 256; Pease 165–7]

14 Shaw lectures on 'The Super-Man' at the Unitarian Hall, Plumstead Common. [CL2: 603; 'Man a Failure: Mr Shaw's Pathetic Plea for a Super-Man', *The Tribune*, 16 Feb 1906]

19 Rehearsals of *Captain Brassbound's Conversion* commence at the Court Theatre. [Peters 289; Weiss 94]

28 Shaw and other members of a special committee have their first meeting to consider Wells's proposals. [Pease 166]

March

1 (Thu) Auguste Rodin lunches at Adelphi Terrace with the Shaws, who arrange to travel to Paris for sittings. [CL2: 616; Weiss 96]

12 Publication of an interview, much revised by Shaw, in which he comments at some length on the question of women's rights and the suffragette movement: 'If I were a woman, I'd simply refuse to speak to any man or do anything for men until I'd got the vote. I'd make my husband's life a burden, and everybody miserable generally. Women should have a revolution – they should shoot, kill, maim, destroy – until they are given a vote.' [Maud Churton Braby, 'GBS and a Suffragist', *The Tribune*, 12 Mar 1906; I&R 405–6]

17 — *Arms and the Man* (*Hjältar*) opens at the Svenska Theatre, Stockholm. The cast receive 23 curtain calls. [CL2: 615]

20 — First public London performance of *Captain Brassbound's Conversion* at the Royal Court Theatre, with Ellen Terry playing Lady Cicely. [CL2: 535, 607; Weiss 95; Erv 337]

23 — Shaw gives a Fabian Society lecture on Darwin, part of which is eventually incorporated into the Preface of *Back to Methuselah*. [CL3: 752]

25 — The Wells committee (which includes Charlotte Shaw) submits its report to the Fabian Executive for discussion. [CL2: 611]

31 — First professional performance of *Caesar and Cleopatra*, produced by Max Reinhardt, opens at the Neues Theater, Berlin. [CP2: 159; CL2: 616; Morgan 36]

April

8 (Sun) — The Stage Society produces Charlotte's translation of Eugène Brieux's *Maternité*. [Dunbar 212; Hol2: 180]

*c.*10 — Neville Lytton paints Shaw's portrait. [Wilfrid Scawen Blunt, *My Diaries: Being a Personal Narrative of Events, 1888–1914,* 2 vols (1919–20) II: 141–2; I&R 283–4]

15 — The Shaws leave for Paris where Rodin is to do a bust of Shaw. [CL2: 617]

16 — Shaw begins sitting for Rodin at Meudon. [Siegfried Trebitsch, *Chronicle of a Life*, trans. Eithne Wilkins and Ernst Kaiser (1953), 187–90; I&R 284]

Captain Brassbound's Conversion shifts to the evening bill at the Court Theatre where it runs successfully for 12 weeks. [CL2: 607, 618]

21 — Accompanied by Alvin Langdon Coburn, the Shaws attend the unveiling ceremony in Paris of Rodin's 'Le Penseur'. On the following day, Coburn takes a photograph of Shaw in the nude, in the pose of 'Le Penseur'. (According to Coburn's account in his 1966 autobiography, the idea for the photograph came from Shaw. Archibald Henderson gives two accounts, one in 1911 (quoting Coburn) saying that it was Coburn's idea, another in 1956 saying that Shaw 'offered to sit in the nude'.) [*Alvin Langdon Coburn: Photographer: An Autobiography* (1966), 26–8; Hend1: 224; Hend3: 797; I&R 202–3]

24 — Lillah McCarthy and Harley Granville Barker marry. [CL2: 619; Peters 291]

26 — Poet Rainer Maria Rilke, then acting as Rodin's secretary, reports in a letter that Shaw poses for Rodin 'avec la même énergie et sincérité qui font sa gloire d'écrivain'. [William Rothenstein, *Men and Memories; Recollections of William Rothenstein, 1900–1902* (1934), 108; I&R 284]

30 Shaw and Trebitsch attend a performance at the Théâtre du Grand Guignol, 'that theatre of dread and horror', from which they emerge to find police and cavalry in the streets preparing for a May Day clash with striking workers demanding an eight-hour workday. [Siegfried Trebitsch, *Chronicle of a Life*, trans. Eithne Wilkins and Ernst Kaiser (1953), 187–90; I&R 285–6; Weiss 100–1]

May

8 (Tue) The last sitting for Rodin. Afterwards the Shaws return to London. [Siegfried Trebitsch, *Chronicle of a Life*, trans. Eithne Wilkins and Ernst Kaiser (1953), 187–90; Hol2: 181; I&R 284–5]

23 Death of Henrik Ibsen.

25 Shaw lectures at a Sweated Industries Exhibition in the Queen's Hall; he is listed as a member of the Exhibition's Council. [DHL]

June

Early Shaw writes the Preface to *John Bull's Other Island*. [CL2: 628]

13 (Wed) Expiry of the lease on the Shaws' Harmer Green house. [CL2: 610]

28 Shaw lectures on 'Poisoning the Proletariat' at Caxton Hall. [DHL]

July

3 (Tue) Shaw, Granville Barker, Robert Loraine and Mary Cholmondeley ride for the first time in a gas balloon, the 'Norfolk', piloted by Percival Spencer. The aeroplane crash in *Misalliance* recalls Shaw's balloon landing in the field of an angry landowner. [Winifred Loraine, *Robert Loraine: Soldier, Actor, Airman* (1938), 90–1; I&R 210; CL2: 633–4; *Daily Mail* (London), 19 Sep 1929]

4 Shaw reads *Major Barbara* to actress Eleanor Robson, whom he is trying to convince to perform in it. [DHL]

6 The New York Court of Special Sessions acquits Arnold Daly and Samuel Gumpertz of immorality charges arising out of their production of *Mrs Warren's Profession*. [CL2: 631]

16 July – 3 September

The Shaws stay at Pentillie, Mevagissey, in Cornwall. [CL2: 637; Weiss 107]

August

5 (Sun) Robert Loraine visits the Shaws.

9–17 Granville Barker visits the Shaws. [DHL]

11 Shaw begins writing *The Doctor's Dilemma*, the last play he writes in longhand. [CL2: 639]

September

	The lease on 29 Fitzroy Square having run out, Shaw buys 8 Park Village West, Gloucester Gate, NW, for Bessie Shaw, Arabella Gillmore and Georgina Gillmore, her daughter. The three move from Fitzroy Square under the supervision of Lucy Shaw, who has returned from Germany. [Farmer 146; Hol2: 305]
3 (Mon)	Shaw finishes the first draft of *The Doctor's Dilemma*, but continues revising it throughout rehearsals almost until opening night. [CL2: 639; CP3: 223]
14	The Shaws begin a visit to Ireland, where they stay at Castle Haven Rectory, Castle Townshend until 4 October, at Lismore Castle (also known as Castle Bernard), the Irish home of the Dukes of Devonshire, from 4 to 6 October, and at Mitchelstown from 6–10 October. [CL2: 653; Nicholas Grene, 'Shaw in Ireland: Visitor or Returning Exile?' in SA 46; DHL]
24	Shaw writes to Otto Kyllmann (of Constable & Co.) that the 'Major Barbara preface is set up & complete. Both prefaces [i.e. to *Major Barbara* and *John Bull's Other Island*] are epoch makers'. [CL2: 655]

October

10 (Wed)	The Shaws return from Ireland. [CL2: 653]
20	Shaw addresses the inaugural meeting of the Manchester Fabian Society on the topic 'What is a Fabian?' [CL2: 670; DHL]
21	Shaw delivers an address on 'The Religion of the British Empire' (alternatively billed as 'Realisable Ideals') to the Ancoats Brotherhood in Manchester. [Neville Cardus, *Second Innings* (1950), 110; I&R 73; CL2: 670; DHL]
22	Shaw speaks at the Birmingham and Midland Institute, again on 'The Religion of the British Empire'. His speeches arouse the ire of local church authorities. [CL2: 670]
30	First professional English-language production of *Caesar and Cleopatra* opens in New York at the New Amsterdam Theater, directed by Forbes-Robertson who also played Caesar. [CL2: 530; CP2: 159; Morgan 36]

November

3 (Sat)	The Shaws move into the New Rectory at Ayot St Lawrence in Hertfordshire. Fourteen years later, they purchase the house, which becomes known as 'Shaw's Corner'. The Shaws live there until their deaths. [CL2: 660; I&R 427]
14	A week prior to the opening of *The Doctor's Dilemma*, the *Daily Express* publishes a synopsis and some quotes from the play without Shaw's permission. [CL2: 659]

17 The Granville Barkers spend the weekend with the Shaws at Ayot St Lawrence. [CL2: 660]

20 First production of *The Doctor's Dilemma* at a matinée at the Court Theatre, with Harley Granville Barker as Louis Dubedat and Lillah McCarthy as Jennifer Dubedat. The play runs for eight matinées. [CP3: 223; DHL; Pearson 243; Morgan]

22 Shaw lectures on 'The Religion of the British Empire' at the City Temple in London. [CL2: 663]

23 Shaw lectures to the Fabian Society on 'Socialism and the Artistic Profession'. [CL2: 663]

25 Shaw suggests to Webb that the Fabian Society should establish its own parliamentary party. [CL2: 661–2]

29 Shaw lectures to the Guild of St Matthew on 'Some Necessary Repairs to Religion'. [CL2: 663]

December

6 (Thu) Max Reinhardt's production of *Man and Superman* opens at his new Kammerspiele des Deutschen Theaters in Berlin, despite Shaw's efforts to cancel the contract. [CL2: 629–31]

11 Shaw's first postcard urging members to attend the upcoming Fabian meeting. [CL2: 665]

14 The Fabian Society continues discussing the Wells committee's proposals. According to Beatrice Webb, in the first of six debates, Shaw 'by a scathing analysis of his whole conduct, threw [Wells] finally to the ground and trampled on him, somewhat hardly. With a splutter the poor man withdrew his amendment and announced his intention of falling back into inactivity'. Nonetheless, Shaw acts as Wells's patron and adviser, trying to mould him to take over the reins when the Old Guard is ready to retire. Sensing he would be defeated, Wells withdraws his motion for reform. [CL2: 665, 667; Pearson 258; S. G. Hobson, *Pilgrim to the Left: Memoirs of a Modern Revolutionist* (1938), 106–7; DBW3: 61–2; I&R 74–5]

31 The Court Theatre brings back *The Doctor's Dilemma*, which had opened in November. The play runs for 6 weeks (50 performances). [Court 159]

December 1906 – March 1907

The Fabian Society considers the report of the Wells committee. Against Shaw's resolution to increase the Fabian Executive from 15 to 21, Wells proposes that the existing Executive Committee resign to allow for the introduction of a new three-tiered system: a 'triumvirate' or executive of three, responsible to a Council of 25, responsible in turn to the rank and file members of the Society. Wells also wants the Society to put forward parliamentary candidates. [CL2: 665; S. G. Hobson, *Pilgrim to the Left: Memoirs of a Modern Revolutionist* (1938); I&R 74; DBW3: 61]

1907

The Philanderer receives its first public production in early February of this year, and on the 7th of that month, the first Shaw production in French, of *Candida,* takes place at the Théâtre Royal du Parc in Brussels. The following month *Widowers' Houses* is produced for the first time in America. In late April and early May the Shaws tour in France, visiting several cities associated with Saint Joan. Act III of *Man and Superman,* produced under the title 'Don Juan in Hell', has its première in a matinée at the Court Theatre. On 17 June, *John Bull's Other Island, How He Lied to Her Husband* and *Major Barbara* are published. From July to September the Shaws retreat to Merionethshire in Wales, during which time Shaw begins writing *Getting Married.* On 12 August, Shaw narrowly escapes drowning. November and December see more censorship battles. Membership of the Fabian Society doubles. Shaw and Wells are the dominant figures, rather than the Webbs. The Fabian Executive is expanded from 15 to 21 members, and Shaw engages his cousin Georgina Gillmore ('Judy') as his secretary, a post she fills until her marriage in 1912. Holbrook Jackson's *Bernard Shaw* is published during this year.

January

11 (Fri) Debate continues on Wells's proposals at the Fabian meetings. [CL2: 665]

24 Horace Rayner fatally shoots William Whiteley, Britain's first department store owner, after claiming to be Whiteley's illegitimate son. Rayner's death sentence is commuted to life imprisonment. Shaw adapts this incident in *Misalliance.* [CL2: 675–6]

28 American première of *Captain Brassbound's Conversion* at the Empire Theater in New York, with Ellen Terry playing Lady Cicely in her farewell tour of America. [Wall 104–5; Morgan 39]
Shaw anonymously contributes a playlet to get Winifred Emery into the bill at the opening of her husband Cyril Maude's new theatre, The Playhouse. The work was published in 1927 as 'The Interlude at the Playhouse'. [DHL]

February

1 (Fri) Debate continues on Wells's proposals at the Fabian meetings. [CL2: 665]

5 First public production, for eight matinée performances, of *The Philanderer* at the Royal Court Theatre. [CP1: 134; Morgan 15; Weiss 119]

7 First Shaw production in French – four matinée performances – of Hamon's translation of *Candida* at the Théâtre Royal du Parc in Brussels. [CL2: 642, corrected in CL3: 928; Erv 374]

15 Shaw reminds Wells to make sure he is nominated as a candidate in the March Executive election. [CL2: 673–4]

22 Annual General Meeting of the Fabian Society held, accepting the proposed new executive structure. This clears the way for the election of a new executive. [Pease 179; CL2: 673]

27 Erica Cotterill, now described by Shaw as 'a dreary, DREARY young devil', continues to besiege him with letters. [CL2: 674]

March

H. G. Wells elected to the Fabian Executive, polling the fourth highest number of votes after Webb, Pease and Shaw. [CL2: 650; 673]

Against the Publishers' Association and the Society of Authors, Shaw supports the Times Book Club's highly successful discount marketing scheme. [CL2: 677–81]

Shaw lectures on 'Art and Public Morality' at the Municipal Technical College and School of Art, Brighton. This speech contains Shaw's famous credo: 'My life belongs to the whole community and as long as I live it is my privilege to do for it whatsoever I can. I want to be thoroughly used up when I die, for the harder I work, the more I live. I rejoice in life for its own sake. Life is no "brief candle" to me. It is a sort of splendid torch which I have got hold of for the moment; and I want to make it burn as brightly as possible before handing it on to future generations.' [*Sussex Daily News*, 7 Mar 1907; *Brighton Herald*, 9 Mar 1907; used as an epigraph to Dan H. Laurence, *Shaw: an Exhibit* (1977)]

7 (Thu) First American production of *Widowers' Houses* (revised version) at the Herald Square Theater, New York. [Morgan 13]

8 The last of six Fabian Executive meetings to discuss Wells's Special Committee proposals to reform the Fabian Society. [CL2: 665; Pearson 256]

22 Ellen Terry marries James Carew, the American actor who played Captain Kearney in *Captain Brassbound's Conversion*, when she played the role of Lady Cicely. [Peters 289, 301]

26 Shaw speaks in favour of women's suffrage at a meeting in Queens Hall held under the auspices of the National Union of Women's Suffrage Societies. Having publicly declared his position, Shaw thereafter insists that women, not men, should speak for women's rights. [CL3: 81]

30 The Shaws depart for France, visiting Le Havre, Yvetot, Caudebec, Rouen, Beauvais, Laon, Rheims and Amiens. [CL2: 682]

April

At the poll to elect the Fabian Society executive committee of 21 members, Wells and nine of his supporters are voted in, together with 'Old Guard' members Shaw, Webb and Pease

	and their supporters. The executive is now split roughly in half between new and old factions. [Pease; 179–80]
9 (Tue)	Elizabeth Robins's *Votes for Women!* opens at the Court Theatre. [Peters 307]
11	The Shaws return to London. Later that day Shaw replies to Wells in a discussion of Wells's *A Modern Utopia* at the Fabian Nursery meeting. [DHL; CL2: 682; *New Age*, 2 May 1907]
30	Shaw takes the chair at a dinner held at the Holborn Restaurant to honour Sydney Olivier on his appointment as Governor of Jamaica. [DHL]

May

	Shaw puts up half the money to buy a weekly, *The New Age*, to be run by Alfred Richard Orage, an ex-schoolteacher and Guild Socialist. [CL2: 809; Morgan 9]
15 (Wed)	Shaw lectures on 'The New Theology' at the Kensington Town Hall. [DHL]
27	*Man and Superman* is performed at the Court Theatre with Robert Loraine as Tanner. [Court 168; Morgan 42; CL2: 689]

June

4 (Tue)	Both the 'Don Juan in Hell' scene from *Man and Superman* and *The Man of Destiny* are performed at the Court Theatre. [CL2: 689; Pearson 234; Morgan 42]
16	With H. G. Wells in the chair, Shaw lectures on the Minimum Wage at the Small Queens Hall. [DHL]
17	Publication of *John Bull's Other Island, How He Lied to Her Husband,* and *Major Barbara.* [Lbib1: 77] Archibald Henderson arrives in England on the *Minneapolis*, and at St Pancras Station introduces Shaw to fellow passenger, Samuel Clemens (Mark Twain), who is on his way to Oxford to receive an honorary Doctorate of Civil Laws. A press report of Shaw's meeting with Clemens includes the following detail: '"Do you know", said Mr. Shaw, "these Pressmen were asking me before the train came in if I thought you were really serious in writing the 'Jumping Frog [of Calaveras County].'" Both laughed heartily. "I answered for you", said G.B.S., "and I gave the correct answer."' [CL2: 674–5; Marion Barton, *New York Times*, 19 Apr 1933; I&R 276–7; 'Mark Twain Arrives. Chance Meeting with Mr. G. B. Shaw', *The Tribune* (London), 19 Jun 1907; Archibald Henderson, 'Mark Twain and Bernard Shaw', *The Mark Twain Journal*, vol. IX, no. 4 (Summer 1954)]
27	The Shaws meet novelist George Meredith. [BL MS Add 56500; DHL]
28	Last performances ('Don Juan in Hell' and *The Man of Destiny*) under Vedrenne and Granville Barker at the Court Theatre. [Peters 304]

Shaw is fitted with false teeth. He writes: 'When I spoke at the Fabian on Friday, I had artificial teeth in my mouth for the first time in my life: they had been there exactly four hours. It was awful: the conviction that they would fall out every time I opened my mouth and the impulse to swallow them every time I shut it, made that speech the most agonizing public effort I ever made. But I now understand why Demosthenes practised oratory by putting pebbles in his mouth. It compelled him to make a much greater effort to articulate'. [CL2: 695]

29 Granville Barker and Vedrenne relinquish management of the Court Theatre. [CL2: 702; Pearson 226]

30 Shaw proposes to Dr Julio Broutá that he translate his plays into Spanish, a matter of urgency since Shaw's translation rights are due to expire the following April. [CL2: 695–6]

July

3 (Wed) Samuel Clemens (Mark Twain) and Max Beerbohm have lunch with the Shaws at Adelphi Terrace. [CL2: 696; I&R 276 n2]

4 Auguste Rodin and Yvette Guilbert lunch with the Shaws at Adelphi Terrace. [CL2: 696; BL MS Add 56500]

7 At a dinner held at the Criterion Restaurant in honour of J. E. Vedrenne and Harley Granville Barker, Herbert Beerbohm Tree proposes the toast to 'The Authors of the Court Theatre'. Saluting 'that remarkable man – I was almost saying that remarkable institution – known as Bernard Shaw', Tree accredits Shaw with 'the literary godfathership of the Court Theatre'. [*Complimentary Dinner to Mr J. E. Vedrenne and Mr H. Granville Barker at the Criterion Restaurant, 7th July, 1907*, n.d., 13]

11 Shaw goes to Margate to see a new actor in Vedrenne–Barker's seaside touring repertory performance of *John Bull's Other Island.* [DHL]

15 The Shaws retreat to isolated Merionethshire in Wales, while the Webbs, accompanied by three secretaries, move into Ayot St Lawrence for two-and-a-half months. [DBW3: 76; CL2: 702]

27 Shaw agrees to back Granville Barker and Vedrenne to the tune of £2000 in their effort to invade the West End by undertaking a season at the Savoy. [CL2: 702–3]

27 July – 14 September

While in Wales, Shaw lectures, debates, and gives play readings at the first Fabian Summer School, held at 'Pen-yr-allt', near Llanbedr. [CL2: 702; I&R 197; Pease 199]

August

5 (Mon) Shaw begins writing *Getting Married* (first titled *Any Just Cause or Impediment?*). [CL2: 702–3; CP3: 450]

11	Robert Loraine arrives in Wales by motor car and stays until 28 August. [DHL]
12	While swimming, Shaw and Robert Loraine are carried out to sea by a strong current and narrowly escape drowning. [CL2: 709–10; Letter from Robert Loraine in Hend2: 93–4; I&R 197–8]
24	Shaw travels to Aberystwyth to see a performance of *You Never Can Tell*. [DHL]
26	Shaw begins a tour of Wales, returning to Llanbedr on 8 September. [DHL]

September

	In an interview published in *Cosmopolitan*, Shaw refers to 'that awful country, that uncivilised place called the United States'. ['Bernard Shaw on American Women', *Cosmopolitan* (New York), 43, Sep 1907; Dan H. Laurence, '"That Awful Country": Shaw in America', in SA:279, 295 n1]
8 (Sun)	Having lost his way on a solitary walk on the moors, Shaw is forced to stay overnight at a hotel without a telephone in Dolgelly. An anxious Charlotte organizes a search by torchlight. The London *Punch* later carries a satirical cartoon, prompted by 'The Welsh Vagaries of "G.B.S"'. [DHL; *Punch, or the London Charivaria*, 18 Sep 1907; *Fabian News*, LXIX (Dec 1958)]
16	First professional production in England of *Caesar and Cleopatra*, the play having been transferred by Forbes-Robertson from New York to the Grand Theatre in Leeds. [Morgan 36]
Late	The Shaws return from Wales to London. [CL2: 702, corrected in CL3: 928]

October

7 (Mon)	First public production of *Widowers' Houses* in England by Annie Horniman's Company at the Midland Theatre, Manchester. [Morgan 13; Theatrics 85–6, 94]
24	Publication of a petition by Shaw in *The New Age* protesting against the Denshawai incident and calling for the release of imprisoned Egyptians. Shaw's object is to persuade Campbell-Bannerman to reshuffle his cabinet to the disadvantage of imperialists such as Morley, Grey and Gladstone. [CL2: 712–13]
	Shaw lectures to the Cambridge Fabians. [DHL]
29	Publication in *The Times* of a letter against British censorship signed by 71 playwrights and authors, including Shaw. [CL2: 714]

November

	Granville Barker's play *Waste* is refused a licence. (For Shaw's protest see '*Waste* and the Censor', *The Nation*, II, 8 Feb 1908, 675–6.) [Lbib2: 633; Agits 97; Hol2: 226]

2 (Sat) In a letter to the founder of the Manchester branch of the Independent Theatre, Charles Hughes, Shaw states that he has 'had to put down three thousand pounds' to assist Vedrenne and Granville Barker, and claims 'my sole chance of getting that money back lies with the Vedrenne-Barker Companies in the provinces'. [Theatrics 84–5]

21 Shaw lectures to the Society of Shorthand Writers. [DHL]

25 Forbes-Robertson's production of *Caesar and Cleopatra* opens at the Savoy Theatre under the management of Vedrenne and Granville Barker. It runs for 40 performances. [CL2: 735; Theatrics 64; Morgan 36]

December

4 (Wed) In a letter to opera impresario Henry Mapleson, Shaw declines an invitation (by no means the first) to provide an opera libretto for music by Saint-Saëns. Shaw writes: 'When one is past fifty, and is several years in arrears with one's own natural work, the chances of beginning a new job are rather slender.' [Theatrics 85–6]

19 Shaw lends a further £500 to the Vedrenne–Barker management. [CL2: 742]

1908

On 28 January of this year, Shaw takes part in a copyright performance of Granville Barker's play *Waste* at the Savoy Theatre. He completes *Getting Married* in mid-March, and on 12 May the first production of *Getting Married* is staged at the Haymarket. From 4 July until the beginning of September, the Shaws tour Scandinavia and Germany (during this time they visit Strindberg and attend the Wagner Festival at Bayreuth), after which they stay in Ireland. In November, *The Devil's Disciple* is published in German. On 22 December Shaw takes delivery of his first automobile.

January

15 (Wed) – 16 Shaw goes motoring with Harley and Lillah (McCarthy) Granville Barker to Limpsfield, Horsham, Shulbrede Priory, Petersfield and Luton. [DHL]

26 In a self-drafted interview published in *The Observer*, Shaw reflects on the Vedrenne–Barker partnership, and argues the case for 'a first-rate theatre' endowed by 'the State or the Municipality'. ['Mr Bernard Shaw on the Theatre. Striking Interview. "No More Plans". Tribute to Devoted Actors. Endowed Theatre Wanted', *The Observer*, 26 Jan 1908; Lbib2: 633]

28 Shaw takes part in a copyright performance of Harley Granville Barker's *Waste* at the Savoy Theatre. [Wein3: 51]

March

14 (Sat) Closure of Granville Barker and Vedrenne's first season at the Savoy. Among its productions are *You Never Can Tell, Arms and the Man, The Doctor's Dilemma* and *Caesar and Cleopatra*. The Savoy season proves financially – and, to Shaw's mind, artistically – unprofitable. [CL2: 771]
Shaw finishes writing *Getting Married*. [CL2: 703; CP3: 450]

21 Shaw gives a first reading of *Getting Married*. [DHL]

24 Shaw addresses the Fabian Society on 'Socialism' at the Queen's Hall. [CL2: 763]

April

4 (Sat) Prime Minister Campbell-Bannerman resigns after suffering a heart attack and is succeeded by Herbert Asquith. [CL2: 722]

11 Shaw writes to Trebitsch: 'I write this letter with great difficulty, as I have had a severe attack of influenza – in fact, I am in the middle of it and am unfit for any sort of business.' [CL2: 770]

21 Commencement of rehearsals of *Getting Married*. [CL2: 771]

22 To Erica Cotterill: 'unless you are prepared to treat my wife with absolute loyalty, you will be hurled into outer darkness forever. The privilege of pawing me, such as it is, is hers exclusively.' [CL2: 772]
H. G. Wells walks out of the annual meeting of the Fabian Society, ostensibly over the issue of his support for Winston Churchill. The real cause of his departure is his opposition to the Webbs' gradualist philosophy. [Hol 2: 258–9]
Death of Campbell-Bannerman, one of the Webbs' most valuable political allies. The new Prime Minister, Herbert Asquith relies heavily on Winston Churchill and Lloyd George, who are not sympathetic to the Webbs. The Webbs therefore decide that the Fabian Society should embark on a national propaganda campaign of the kind advocated by H. G. Wells prior to his resignation. (See also Wells, 'What I think of the Minority Report', *Christian Commonwealth*, XXIX, 30 Jun 1909.) [CL2: 722; DBW3: 91]

May

12 (Tue) First production of *Getting Married* opens in a series of six matinées at the Haymarket Theatre, the third West End theatre leased by Vedrenne and Granville Barker. [CL2: 771; CP3: 450; Morgan 58]

25 Shaw calls on Florence Farr at 21 Warwick Chambers, Pater Street, from 3 to 4.30 p.m. [DHL]

June

1 (Mon) *Getting Married* is transferred to the evening bill for nine weeks to 11 July (48 performances). [CL2: 773; DHL]

13 Charlotte Shaw and Judy Gillmore join a Suffrage procession to Hyde Park. Charlotte also joins another demonstration on 21 June. [BL MS Add 56500; DHL]

Summer

Throughout this season, Lucy Shaw attends several of her brother's plays. [Farmer 152]

July

4 (Sat) The Shaws set out by steamer on a two-week tour of Scandinavia and Germany. They visit Gothenberg and Stockholm with Shaw's Swedish translator, Hugo Vallentin as guide. [CL2: 793–4; DHL]

16 Shaw visits Strindberg while in Stockholm. Strindberg accompanies the Shaws to a special performance of his play, *Miss Julie* at the Intima Teatern. [CL2: 802; Gustaf Uddgren 'Om Strindberg och filmen', *Filmjournalen*, no. 6, 2 May 1920; Anthony Swerling, 'Shaw's Visit to Strindberg', typescript of essay sent to Dan H. Laurence, 6 Mar 1980, Guelph]

19 The Shaws sail to Lubeck, Hamburg, Hanover and Coburg, and then attend the Bayreuth festival till 2 August. They then visit several cities in Germany, including Munich, where they see a production of *Candida*. [CL2: 794; DHL]

August

Tolstoy responds by letter to Shaw's gift of an inscribed copy of *Man and Superman*: 'I particularly appreciate Don Juan's speeches in the Interlude... I am pleased by your attitude towards civilisation and progress.' But his letter reminds Shaw that 'life is a great and serious affair' and one 'should not speak jestingly of such a subject as the purpose of human life, the causes of its perversion, and the evil that fills the life of humanity today'. [CL2: 899–900n]

September

1 (Tue) The Shaws embark from Bremerhaven on the *Krönprinz Wilhelm* intending to travel 'to Southampton with a view to the west of Ireland'. [CL2: 794, 809]

7 The Shaws begin their stay in Ireland. Shaw meets Sir Horace Plunkett at Mulranny on 12 October, and visits Dublin for the first time since he abandoned it in 1876. [CL2: 809; DHL]

16 Wells officially resigns from the Fabian Executive. [DBW3: 61]

October

In the foyer of the Coronet Theatre, Notting Hill, the manager, Eade Montefiore told Lucy Shaw that Charles Butterfield 'had been living with another man's wife [the actress wife of Montefiore himself] for ten years in a flat'. [Farmer 166, Hol2: 306]

Judy Musters recounted to Dan H. Laurence that 'Lucy Carr Shaw, on discovering her husband Charles Butterfield was betraying her with another woman, entered the house livid with rage, playing the injured party so completely that her mother, knowing Lucy years before had sent Charles packing, refusing to live with him, burst into roars of laughter and couldn't stop.' [DHL]

4 (Sun) The Shaws return to London from Ireland. [CL2: 809]

8 Shaw lectures on 'Literature and Art' 'from the pulpit' at City Temple, London. [DHL; P&P 41]

17 Shaw, having just purchased a De Dietrich motor car (delivered in December), takes driving lessons. He writes to Vedrenne, 'I was trying to drive a motor car this morning... [and] came within an inch of suicide and murder'. [Theatrics 92; CL2: 822]

26 Shaw urges his sister Lucy Shaw to divorce her estranged husband. Dan H. Laurence points out that a contrary account, given by Farmer, stating that Lucy came to Shaw 'in a burst of fury' saying she must have a divorce [and that Shaw] tried to assure her that she had 'practically divorced him' already, and that any other action was 'superfluous', is largely a fabrication. [CL2: 814; Farmer 168]

November

First book publication of *The Doctor's Dilemma* in German, as *Der Arzt am Scheideweg*. This German translation also appeared serially in *Nord und Süd*, October–December 1908. [Lbib1: 85]

5 Shaw attends a Ruth St Denis dance recital at the Scala Theatre. [DHL]

10 Shaw attends a matinée performance at the Court Theatre of Gilbert Murray's adaptation of *The Bacchae*, having seen a rehearsal of the play at 11 Pimlico Road on 6 November. [DHL]

25 Shaw addresses the Edinburgh University Fabians on 'Socialist Politics'. [CL2: 821]

December

12 (Sun) Shaw writes to Pinero about a proposal by film promoter Karl Strakosch to both Shaw and Pinero which suggests 'the devising and presumably rehearsing [of] a presumably short but intense play [for filming]... I rather think it is implied that the job is

rendered especially easy by the fact that we need not provide thoughtful and witty dialogue.' Shaw points out that 'this cinematograph game is not, like the keeping of oilshops, a matter for a great number of small separate establishments: it is clearly a subject for organization on the biggest scale, by a bloated trust... The Society of Authors should take it in hand, at once.' [Shaw to Pinero, 12 Dec 1908, Texas]

22 Shaw takes delivery of his first automobile, a 28–30 h.p. De Dietrich, built by Todd & Wright Ltd of London. Early in 1909 Shaw, an enthusiastic but erratic driver himself, acquired a chauffeur, Albert J. Kilsby, who accompanied him on numerous motoring tours. A 1910 photograph of the De Dietrich – the first of a succession of fine motor vehicles purchased by Shaw – is reproduced facing page 822 of volume 2 of the *Collected Letters*. [CL2: 822; BL MS Add 56500]

Christmas

Shaw spends Christmas at Ayot St Lawrence while Charlotte visits the Cholmondeleys. [CL2: 822]

Late December 1908 – early January 1909

Shaw joins the Organizing Committee of the Shakespeare Memorial National Theatre and uses the financial losses incurred by Granville Barker and Vedrenne to argue a case for a heavily endowed national theatre. Later he uses this experience in 'A Draft letter to Millionaires'. [BL MS Add 45296 f.20; Hol2: 178–9]

1909

The Admirable Bashville receives its first public performance at His Majesty's Theatre in January of this year. Later that month Shaw is taken ill with kidney stones. From mid-February to 8 March, Shaw writes *The Shewing-up of Blanco Posnet*, a play which causes Shaw great difficulty with the Lord Chamberlain and intensifies his battle with censorship laws. Immediately following the completion of *Blanco Posnet* Shaw begins writing *The Glimpse of Reality*. From March to May the Shaws and Mary Cholmondeley go on a motoring tour of Algeria and Tunisia. During this time, Shaw writes *Press Cuttings*, another play which is subjected to censorship, although it is produced as a charity performance during this year. In early August, Shaw writes *The Fascinating Foundling* and in the same month G. K. Chesterton's *George Bernard Shaw* is published. Shaw manages to outwit the censor with *The Shewing-up of Blanco Posnet* produced at the Abbey Theatre, Dublin, out of the jurisdiction of the Lord Chamberlain. In October the play is also serialized in German translation. Between September and November, Shaw writes *Misalliance*.

January

13 (Wed) Lucy Shaw divorces Charles Butterfield. The case is undefended, Lucy having agreed to ask for no damages or alimony and Shaw agreeing to pay the costs (£91.13.8), but the strain necessitates a trip to Baden-Baden immediately after for her to recuperate. Lucy returns in June, writing to Janey Drysdale from her mother's home on the 21st. [CL2: 814; Farmer 166]

21 Shaw is 'in the thick of rehearsals' of *The Admirable Bashville*. [CL2: 830]

22 Shaw is suddenly taken very ill with kidney stones at a rehearsal. [CL2: 831–2; DHL; BL MS Add 56500]

26 First public performance in London of *The Admirable Bashville* at His Majesty's Theatre. [CL2: 822; Morgan 41]

27 January – 4 February

Shaw attends a Labour Conference at Portsmouth, where he delivers speeches on 28 and 29 January. [DHL]

February

16 (Tue) Shaw begins writing *The Shewing-up of Blanco Posnet* for Beerbohm Tree who wants a play for a benefit matinée at His Majesty's Theatre to aid a children's charity. He lectures to a medico-legal society on 'The Socialist Criticism of the Medical Profession'. [CP3: 671; DHL; P&P 49]

March

5 (Fri) Webb and Shaw speak on 'The Remedy for Unemployment' at a Fabian Society public meeting in St James's Hall. [CL2: 838]

8 Shaw finishes writing *The Shewing-up of Blanco Posnet*, but it is refused a licence by the Censor, as Shaw had anticipated. He immediately begins writing *The Glimpse of Reality*. [CP3: 671, 814; CL2: 835, 855–6]

16 The Shaws, accompanied by Mary Cholmondeley, begin a five-week motoring tour of Algeria and Tunisia. They sail with the De Dietrich motor car on the *Dorflinger* and occupy the captain's suite. Shaw drafts *Press Cuttings* on the way. [CL2: 836–43; DHL; Jerome K. Jerome, *My Life and Times* (1926), 163; I&R 204]

21 The Shaws arrive in Algiers. [DHL]

24 Death of the Irish playwright, J. M. Synge.

c. 27 Shaw commences the composition of *Press Cuttings*. [CP3: 838]

28 The Shaws sail from Algiers on the *Bremen*. [DHL]

May

2 (Sun) Shaw completes *Press Cuttings*. [CL2: 843; CP3: 838]

3 The Shaws return to London from North Africa. [CL2: 836]

13 Rehearsals of *The Shewing-up of Blanco Posnet* begin under Shaw's direction, but the censor refuses to license the play. [CL2: 855]

June

24 (Thu) The Lord Chamberlain's reader refuses to license *Press Cuttings*. [CL2: 843]

27 Publication in *The Observer* of Shaw's vigorous objection to the censorship of *Press Cuttings* on the grounds of its allusions to 'personalities, expressed or understood'. ['Banned Play. Censor's Objection to "Press Cuttings". Special Interview with Mr Shaw. A Barrie Precedent', *The Observer*, 9 Jun 1909; CL2: 886–9]

July

9 (Fri), 12 First performances of *Press Cuttings* by the London Society for Women's Suffrage held privately and by invitation only due to restrictions imposed by the censor. [CL2: 843; CP3: 838; Peters 315–16; Morgan 102]

19 Lucy Shaw obtains her decree absolute from Charles Butterfield. [CL2: 814; I&R 10 n8]

25 Shaw speaks from an open air platform in a Trafalgar Square demonstration by the Labour Party against a visit to England by the Czar of Russia. [DHL]

28 Shaw encourages members of the Dramatists' Club to join the struggle against censorship. [CL2: 851–2]

29 First meeting of the Joint Select Committee of Inquiry into the Lord Chamberlain's censorship powers, chaired by Rt Hon. Herbert Samuel. [CL2: 850]

30 Shaw appears before the Select Committee for the inquiry into censorship armed with his 11000 word submission, published at his own expense, which the committee refuses to accept as evidence. The 'Rejected Statement' is subsequently incorporated into the Preface of *The Shewing-up of Blanco Posnet*. [Prefs1: 471–514; Lbib1: 102; CL2: 850–3]

31 July – 1 August

Shaw spends the weekend with the Granville Barkers at Stanstead. [DHL]

August

G. K. Chesterton's critical study of Shaw, *George Bernard Shaw*, is published. Some years later Shaw was to write to Frank Harris (16 October 1916): 'Gilbert Chesterton has written a book about me which is the last word in the sort of book that can be written about me without reading me. Even you will not be able to beat it.' [Wein4: 53; CL2: 759; Lbib2: 899]

2 (Mon) Shaw sends W. B. Yeats a speech addressed to Dublin Castle about censorship of plays, accusing the Castle of impoliteness and referring to himself satirically as 'a perfectly correct

member' of the Protestant landed gentry 'even to the grace of absenteeism.' [BL MSAd 50553, fols 147–53]

10 Shaw completes a one-act play entitled *The Fascinating Foundling*. Shaw later claimed that he wrote the playlet for a charity performance requested by the Prime Minister's daughter, Elizabeth Asquith. But there is some doubt as to the validity of this claim. Dan H. Laurence states that it was actually commissioned by Winifred Emery for a variety theatre sketch. Shaw writes to Emery: 'You really have no conscience. Of all the nonsensical & ridiculous jobs ever thrust on an unfortunate man of genius at the busiest moment of his life, this is the very absurdest.' [Theatrics 99–100; CP3: 898; Morgan 102–3]

14 The Shaws depart by car from Ayot to Fishguard, cross to Waterford, and then proceed to Parknasilla. [CL2: 858]

17 The censor grants a licence to *Press Cuttings* after Shaw agrees to alter the names of two characters. [CL2: 861]

25 *The Shewing-up of Blanco Posnet* opens at the Abbey Theatre in Dublin, Ireland being outside the jurisdiction of the Lord Chamberlain. Shaw remains in Parknasilla, while Charlotte and Mary Cholmondeley attend the play. The audience finds the play humorous and inoffensive. However, when the intention to produce the play at the Abbey is announced, the Under-Secretary of the Lord Lieutenant of Ireland threatens to revoke the Abbey's licence. Lady Gregory and W. B. Yeats had aided Shaw in his battle against censorship by pointing out in a public manifesto that Irish officials were acting as agents of the British Government Censor. [CL2: 856; DHL; Morgan 60]

September

8 (Wed) The Censor refuses to license a revised version of *Blanco Posnet* for performance at Annie Horniman's Gaiety Theatre in Manchester. Shaw then has the Abbey Theatre company present the play in London on 5–6 December under the auspices of the Stage Society, which remains outside the Censor's jurisdiction. [CL2: 866; DHL; Hol2: 231–2]

Shaw begins writing *Misalliance*. [CL2: 871; CP4: 11]

27 First public production of *Press Cuttings* at the Gaiety Theatre, Manchester. [Morgan 102]

30 H. G. Wells threatens to bring the Fabian Society into public disrepute through his adulterous relationships with Rosamund Bland and Amber Reeves. Shaw acts as an intermediary between Wells and the Webbs. [CL2: 868]

October

18 (Mon) Shaw lectures at the Photographic Salon on 'Photography in its Relation to Modern Art'. [DHL]

25 — *The Shewing-up of Blanco Posnet* is serialized in German translation as *Blanco Posnets Erweckung* in *Der Merker*, 25 October – 25 November. [Lbib2: 639]

November

2 (Tue) — The Select Committee of Inquiry into censorship issues its Blue Book report. [CL2: 850]

4 — Shaw completes *Misalliance*. [CP4: 11; CL2: 871]

8 — Publication of the Select Committee's report into censorship, recommending that the existing system remain in place. [Hol2: 236]

30 — At Oxford, Shaw takes the chair for a Granville Barker lecture on the subject of a National Theatre. [DHL]

December

1 (Wed) — Shaw lectures at Oxford for the National Theatre Organizing Committee, of which he had recently become a member. [DHL]

5 — The Shaws attend the Abbey Players' London production of Yeats's *Kathleen ni Houlihan*, Lady Gregory's *The Workhouse Ward* and Shaw's *The Shewing-up of Blanco Posnet*, sponsored by the Stage Society. [CL4: 576; Morgan 60]

1910

At the beginning of the year, Shaw campaigns in Wales on behalf of Keir Hardie, after which he returns to London for the beginning of rehearsals of his play *Misalliance* at the Duke of York's Theatre. Shaw, along with other playwrights, contributes to this new enterprise – a repertory theatre managed by Charles Frohman which collapses within months. In early March the Shaws and Mary Cholmondeley set out for a driving tour of France, to include Boulogne, Bordeau, Rouen and Biarritz; however, Charlotte and Mary find the trip too difficult and abandon the tour. In response to the collapse of the repertory theatre, Shaw writes *The Dark Lady of the Sonnets* over three days in June, a play intended to support an appeal for a British National Theatre. During August, Shaw writes *Fanny's First Play* and completes *The Glimpse of Reality*. *The Dark Lady of the Sonnets* is produced as a charity matinée in late November, and is translated by Trebitsch and published in German before the year closes. Julius Bab's critical study, *Bernard Shaw*, is published during this year.

January

Early — Beginning of rehearsals of *Misalliance*. [CL2: 894]

4 (Tue) – 5 — Shaw campaigns in Wales for Keir Hardie. [CL2: 890; DHL; DBW3: 440]

February

3 (Thu) At Lady Gregory's behest, Shaw makes a speech at a private fund-raising meeting for the Abbey Theatre. [DHL; L&G 62–4, reconstructed text of the speech]

14 Shaw sends a copy of *The Shewing-up of Blanco Posnet* to Leo Tolstoy. In his accompanying letter he writes of God and the existence of evil, responding to Tolstoy's acknowledgement of his gift of an inscribed copy of *Man and Superman* in August 1908: 'You said that my manner in that book was not serious enough – that I made people laugh in my most earnest moments. But why should I not? Why should humour and laughter be excommunicated? Suppose the world were only one of God's jokes, would you work any the less to make it a good joke instead of a bad one?' Tolstoy replied on 9 May, concluding his letter: '...the problem about God and evil is too important to be spoken of in jest. And therefore I will tell you frankly that I received a very painful impression from the concluding words of your letter...' [CL2: 900–2]

21 Charles Frohman and J. M. Barrie's first season of experimental repertory opens with Granville Barker's production of John Galsworthy's *Justice* at the Duke of York's Theatre in the West End. Shaw has been engaged to write plays for this new theatrical enterprise. [CL3: 905–6; 909]

23 First production of *Misalliance* at the Duke of York's Theatre, with Lena Ashwell. The production survives for only 11 performances. [CL2: 903; DHL; Morgan 62; CP4: 11]

Late Shaw and Granville Barker drive to Adlington, Wiltshire for the opening of Charles McEvoy's Aldbourne Theatre. Shaw formally opens the house with a brief pre-curtain speech. [DHL]

March

30 (Wed) The Shaws and Mary Cholmondeley driven by Shaw's chauffeur Kilsby depart for a motoring tour of France. Life on the road is so fraught with breakdowns and bad weather that Charlotte and her sister abandon the men halfway through their holiday and return to the comforts of civilization. [CL2: 918–22]

May

Frohman and Barrie close the unprofitable Duke of York's Theatre after a short season, the death of King Edward VII on 10 May providing their excuse. Shaw uses the commercial failure of the venture to again argue that a privately endowed National Theatre is needed. [CP4: 260]

2 (Mon) Shaw returns to London from France. [CL2: 918]

6 Shaw speaks at the twentieth anniversary meeting of the Humanitarian League, founded by Henry Salt. [DHL]

June

17 (Fri) – 20 Shaw writes *The Dark Lady of the Sonnets*. [CP4: 267; CL2: 931]

July

23 (Sat) The Shaws leave London for a motoring tour of Ireland via Liverpool and Belfast, staying 12 days (15–27 August) with Lady Gregory at Coole Park. [CL2: 935–6]

26 Shaw writes to Granville Barker: 'From our landing at Belfast on Sunday morning it rained hard for 36 hours.' [CL2: 940; Nicholas Grene, 'Shaw in Ireland: Visitor or Returning Exile?' in SA: 49]

August

13 (Sat) Shaw begins writing *Fanny's First Play*, first titled *Just Exactly Nothing*. [CP4: 343; DHL]

30 Shaw finishes *The Glimpse of Reality*. [CP3: 814]

September

16 (Fri) – 17 Having failed to reach them by yacht on the 16th, the Shaws visit the Skelligs (a group of islands off the west coast of Ireland) by rowboat on the following day. In a letter to Frederick Jackson, Shaw describes Skellig Michael, an island with a remarkable ancient monastery, as an 'incredible, impossible, mad place, which still tempts devotees to make "stations" of every stair landing, and to creep through "needle's eyes" at impossible altitudes, and kiss "stones of pain" jutting out 700 feet above the Atlantic ... I tell you the thing does not belong to any world that you and I have ever lived in: it is part of our dream world.' [CL2: 942; BL MS Add 56500; DHL]

October

Trebitsch's translation of *Misalliance* is published in serialized form between October 1910 and March 1911. This caused the delay of the publication of the first edition until 1911.

1 (Sat) The Shaws motor to Carlow to view the Assembly Rooms and other properties belonging to him, staying overnight at the Clubhouse Hotel. [DHL]

3 After three days' stay in Dublin, Shaw delivers his first lecture in Ireland on 'The Poor Law and Destitution in Ireland'. [DHL; *Irish Times*, 4 Oct 1910]

4 Shaw lunches with author, George Moore. [DHL]

7 The Shaws return to London. [CL2: 935]

11 Shaw drafts a letter for Charlotte to send to Erica Cotterill forbidding further visits to their house. [CL2: 943]

26 In the afternoon Shaw addresses the Edinburgh University Fabians on 'University Socialism'. In the evening he and

Beatrice Webb speak on unemployment and the Poor Law to a meeting sponsored by the Scottish National Committee for the Prevention of Destitution. [CL2: 948]

27 Shaw lectures in Glasgow in the afternoon on 'Public Enterprise and Dramatic Art', and in the evening he and Sidney Webb lecture on the Minority Report of the Royal Commission on the Poor Law at a meeting sponsored by the New Crusade against Unemployment and Destitution. [CL2: 948]

November

3 (Thu) Prince Eugene of Sweden has tea with the Shaws. [DHL]

13 In a self-drafted interview which looks forward to the opening of *The Dark Lady of the Sonnets*, Shaw describes Shakespeare as 'one of the few realities England has ever produced'. This anticipates Ellie Dunn's lament in Act III of *Heartbreak House*: 'There seems to be nothing real in the world except my father and Shakespear.' ['Mr Bernard Shaw and Shakespeare', *The Observer*, 13 Nov 1910; CP4: 328–33; CP5: 165–6]

24 First of two performances of *The Dark Lady of the Sonnets* as a charity matinée at the Haymarket Theatre, London for the Organizing Committee of the Shakespeare Memorial National Theatre. [DHL; CP4: 267; CL2: 931; Peters 320; Morgan 64]

25 Lucy Shaw travels to London from Southsea, where she has been staying since the end of September, to see *The Dark Lady of the Sonnets*. [Farmer 170–1]

28 November – 7 December

In the lead-up to the second General Election in 1910, Shaw speaks in public for ten nights in succession. But again the Liberals win power. [CL2: 957; Weiss 150–1; DBW3: 440]

December

6 Shaw lectures at the London Musical Association on 'The Reminiscences of a Quinquagenarian'. [Lbib1: 282, 430; DHL]

9 (Fri) Influenced by Beatrice Webb's 'Minority Report' on the Poor Law, Shaw delivers a lecture entitled 'The Simple Truth About Socialism'. [L.Crompton (ed.), *Shaw: The Road to Equality: Ten Unpublished Lectures and Essays, 1884–1918* (1971) (MS in British Museum); CL2: 957]

11 Shaw goes to see a German production of Strauss's *Salome* at Covent Garden. [*The Times* (London), 11 Dec 1910; DHL]

24 'Anything to avoid Christmas in England', Shaw declares in a letter to Ernest Parke, before sailing out of Bristol for Jamaica to visit Sydney Olivier (the Governor of Jamaica at this time). [CL2: 958]

25 *The Dark Lady of the Sonnets* is published in German translation as *Die schwarze Dame der Sonette* in the *Neue Freie Presse* of Vienna. [Lbib1: 121, 642; CP4: 267]

1911

During this year the Shaws visit Jamaica – beginning reconstruction after a major earthquake – where their Fabian friend Sydney Olivier is posted as Governor. The two-week journey to Jamaica takes its toll on Shaw, who suffers sea-sickness because of the rough seas. January sees the publication of a collected volume containing *The Doctor's Dilemma, Getting Married* and *The Shewing-up of Blanco Posnet,* first in England and a few weeks later in America. In April *Fanny's First Play* has its première at the Little Theatre, having a run of 622 performances, despite Shaw's name not being linked to the play. In the same month, Archibald Henderson's biography *George Bernard Shaw: His Life and Works* is published, and Shaw resigns from the Fabian Executive. In May *Arms and the Man* opens at the Criterion Theatre, but does not receive the success of *Fanny's First Play.* From June until October the Shaws take a motoring tour travelling through France, Switzerland, Germany, Austria, and Italy. During the year, Shaw is elected to the Academic Committee of the Royal Society of Literature, and to the Academy of Dramatic Art (later RADA).

January

6 (Fri) The Shaws arrive in Kingston, Jamaica, visiting their old Fabian friend, now Governor of Jamaica, Sydney Olivier. Shaw wrote to Granville Barker that 'the trees and mountains look pleasantly theatrical'. Shaw spends much of his time reading Houston Chamberlain's *Foundations of the Nineteenth Century,* which he reviews in *Fabian News* in June. [CL3: 7; BL MS Add 56500; Lbib2: 644]

12 Shaw in a (possibly self-drafted) interview for Kingston's *Gleaner* states that Jamaica should establish a theatre 'with all the ordinary travelling companies from England and America sternly kept out of it, for unless you do your own acting and write your own plays, your theatre will be of no use. It will vulgarise and degrade you.' [Stanley Weintraub, 'A High Wind in Jamaica' in SA 39–42]
The Shaws re-embark for England. [CL3: 7; BL MS Add 56500]

26 The Shaws arrive back in London. [CL3: 7; BL MS Add 56500]

21 Publication of the first English edition of *The Doctor's Dilemma, Getting Married* and *The Shewing-up of Blanco Posnet* in a collected volume. This was closely followed by an American edition on 25 February 1911.

28 Shaw delivers a speech on spelling reform at a Phonetics Conference sponsored by the English Association at University

College London. [DHL; *The Times*, 30 Jan 1911; *New York Times*, 12 Feb 1911]

February

22 (Wed) Shaw has an appointment with J. E. Vedrenne at 3 p.m. 'to wind up V[edrenne] & B[arker]'. [DHL; BLPES]

March

3 (Fri) Shaw informs Edward Pease that he will not stand for re-election to the Fabian Executive, 'all with the view to making room for young men who are not there!' [DBW3: 154; CL3: 12]

5 Shaw finished *Fanny's First Play* for Lillah McCarthy to present in Gertrude Kingston's Little Theatre. [CP4: 343]

8 Shaw gives a first reading of *Fanny's First Play*, for Robert Loraine.

April

Shaw resigns from the Fabian Executive, together with four other members of the Old Gang. But instead of energetic young bloods taking over, mediocre officers are elected, and the Society expends its energies on minor matters. [CL3: 11]

The first edition of *Misalliance* is published in Trebitsch's translation. The edition is dated 1910, full publication was delayed until the serialized version in *Frauen-Zukunft* was completed in March 1911. [Lbib1: 104]

Publication of Archibald Henderson's biography *George Bernard Shaw: His Life and Works* provokes an exchange of quarrelsome letters between Shaw and his biographer: 'You must not fly out at me and smash your idol. There are many things about me that you not only don't know, but can't know, because no matter how explicitly I tell you, you cannot supply the context of the period and movement to which they belong... You may say what you like provided you don't make me say it. The book has been of great service to me in spite of its little aberrations...' [Shaw to Henderson, 7 Jul 1911, Harvard; CL3: 19–22, 35–7; Lbib1: 429–30, 899]

19 (Wed) *Fanny's First Play* opens at the Little Theatre. It runs for 622 performances. Shaw did not admit authorship until the play was published in 1914. [CP4: 343; CL3: 26; Wall 111–12; Peters 321; Morgan 65]

24 The Shaws visit Bertrand Russell at Ely. [BL MS Add 56500; DHL]

May

Publication of Charlotte Shaw's translation (with St John Hankin and John Pollock) of *Three Plays by Brieux*. [Lbib1: 96–7, 429]

14 (Sun) In an interview published in *The New York Times*, Shaw says Tolstoy was a 'prodigious genius' but 'entirely wrong in his analysis of Shakespeare'. In the same interview he castigates Americans as 'an appalling, horrible, narrow lot', and America as 'a land of unthinking, bigoted persecution'; praises the Jewish people as 'intelligent, industrious and hard-working', but criticizes 'the modern Jews' as being 'fond only of music' and says that whereas he thinks the Life Force is God, the English think God is an Englishman. [Herman Bernstein, '"Why Should I go to America?" Asks Bernard Shaw', *New York Times*, 14 May 1911]

18 Opening of Arnold Daly's revival of *Arms and the Man* at the Criterion Theatre in London. [CL3: 26]

26 *Arms and the Man* having failed, Shaw proposes to the Criterion management that either Daly might succumb to a convenient illness or that the play should close altogether. [CL3: 39]

27 Shaw's Collected *Dramatische Werke*, in Siegfried Trebitsch's translations, is published in Berlin, with a Preface by Shaw, 'What I owe to German Culture'. [Lbib1: 104–5]

29 Shaw speaks at a meeting of The Heretics in the Victoria Assembly Rooms at Cambridge on 'Religion and the Future'. Shaw says 'I am, and have always been, a mystic... I believe that the universe is being driven by a force that we might call a life force. I see it as performing the miracle of creation, that it has got into the minds of men as what they call their will.' [Warren S. Smith (ed.), *The Religious Speeches of Bernard Shaw* (1963), 29–37; Hol2: 215]

June

Shaw is elected to the Academic Committee of the Royal Society of Literature. [CL2: 937]

2 (Fri) W. B. Yeats lunches with the Shaws. [DHL]

13 Shaw terminates his professional relations with Arnold Daly who wants to redeem himself by performing in some of Shaw's other plays. [CL3: 41–3]

17 Charlotte Shaw walks in a 'big women's procession'. [BL MS Add 56500; DHL]

19 The Shaws depart for a motoring tour of France, Switzerland, Germany, Austria and Italy, leaving on this date to avoid the just commencing George V Coronation Ceremonies, and not returning until October. [CL3: 28,43; DHL; Weiss 153]

16 July – 8 October

Publication in serial form of *Fanny's First Play* in German translation in the *Neue Freie Presse* of Vienna as *Fannis erstes Stück*. [Lbib1: 108, 644]

July–September

On her return from Germany, Lucy Shaw becomes involved in nursing a number of Gurly relatives. The latter, as was their way, were apparently taking advantage of Lucy's good nature, for each received a weekly or monthly allowance to cover lodging, food, and other expenses, paid by Shaw's bankers. The effort and extra expense falls on Lucy because Shaw is motoring on the continent and, she says, her 'mother lives so completely on the spiritual plane, that nothing mundane seems to touch or disturb her...' As a consequence, Lucy suffers a breakdown in the autumn. [Farmer 173–4; DHL]

August

10 (Thu) – 11 Shaw visits Oberammergau, then meets Siegfried Trebitsch on 17 August in Salzburg. [DHL]

September

Publication in *The Standard* of Shaw's statements about the inevitability of female rebellion, and about 'rowdiness' as a sign of 'new strength in the character of women'. The statements are presented in interview form apropos *Fanny's First Play*, and the rebellious character of the daughter in the play, Margaret Knox. Shaw declares: 'Every daughter, every woman of any character, rebels in time.' [Raymond Blathwayt, 'The Rebellious Daughter. "Finding Out". Mr Bernard Shaw Interviewed', *The Standard*, Sep 1911; repr in *Shaw: The Annual of Bernard Shaw Studies* (1987)]

October

4 (Wed) The Shaws return to London. [CL3: 43]

28 Shaw dines with Wildon Carr at the Savile Club to meet Henri Bergson. [DHL]

November

17 (Fri) Speaking at the Guildhall in Cambridge, G. K. Chesterton replies to Shaw's 'Religion and the Future' with a lecture entitled 'Orthodoxy'. [W. B. Furlong, *Shaw and Chesterton: The Metaphysical Jesters* (1970), 87; Hol2: 217]

30 Public debate at the Memorial Hall between Shaw and G. K. Chesterton, chaired by Hilaire Belloc, on Shaw's resolution 'I assert that a Democrat who is not also a Socialist is no gentleman'. [Bernard Shaw, *Platform and Pulpit*, ed. Dan H. Laurence (1961), 86–93; CL3: 54]

December

4 (Mon) *How He Lied to her Husband* is produced at the Palace, thus becoming the first Shaw work to be performed in a music-hall. [DHL]

Late — Shaw spends Christmas at Edstaston with the Cholmondeleys, returning to London in the second week of January. [CL3: 66; Dunbar 238]

29 — Shaw lectures on art at the Walker Art Gallery, Liverpool. [*Courier* (Liverpool) 30 Dec 1911; DHL]

1912

In January, Shaw begins *Androcles and the Lion*, which he completes on 6 February. The following day he begins work on *Pygmalion*. In April, Charlotte Shaw leaves for the continent. Shaw refuses to go, preferring a motoring tour to Windermere and Carlisle. Both suffer health problems during their tours. In early June, Shaw completes *Pygmalion* (which will have its premiére in Vienna in October 1913, and its London opening in April 1914). On 26 June, Shaw reads *Pygmalion* to, and falls in love with, Mrs Patrick Campbell.

January

1 (Mon) — *Fanny's First Play* transferred from the Little Theatre to the Kingsway Theatre. [CP4: 448]

2 January – 6 February

Shaw writes *Androcles and the Lion*. [DHL correction of CP4: 453]

February

26 (Mon) — The Shaws entertain Sir Winston Churchill and his mother at lunch at Adelphi Terrace. [CL3: 73; Winston Churchill, 'Bernard Shaw – Saint, Sage and Clown', *Sunday Chronicle*, 13 Apr 1930; I&R 494]

28 — A performance of *The Man of Destiny* is given in aid of the Feminist Bookshop in Adam Street, according to Janey Drysdale as a result of Lucy Shaw 'badgering' Shaw on the subject. [Farmer 176]

March

7 (Thu) — Shaw begins writing *Pygmalion*. [CP4: 655]

21 — Shaw lectures at the New Reform Club on 'Modern Religion'. [CL3: 80]

April

7 (Sun) — On this Easter Sunday, Shaw reads *Androcles and the Lion* to the Chestertons at Beaconsfield. [DHL]

12 — Charlotte sails for Rome without Shaw, who had refused to be dragged off on another trip to Europe. [CL3: 82, 99; Dunbar 238]

15 — Sinking of the *Titanic* with the loss of 1490 of the 2201 people aboard. [CL3: 85]

20 Shaw begins a motoring tour of England with his chauffeur Albert Kilsby, his secretary Judy Gillmore, and Harley Granville Barker who joins them at York. They travel to Windermere, Carlisle, Blackpool and Liverpool. Judy Musters (née Gillmore) informed Dan H. Laurence that 'she had sat in the back, with Barker riding alongside Shaw, who was driving. All through the journey the two men chatted and joked and giggled like schoolboys. Then Shaw suddenly threw a Shakespeare quotation at Barker, who threw one back, and they kept shouting quotations rhetorically back and forth, laughing uproariously all the while'. [Guelph; Weiss 161]

28 Shaw writes to Charlotte from Carlisle that he is suffering from migraine and troubled by lumbago. [CL3: 87]

May

2 (Thu) Shaw writes to Charlotte from Windermere: 'The lumbago is still beyond expression.' [CL3: 90]

21 Shaw arrives back in London. [CL3: 82]

22 Shaw meets Charlotte's boat at Southampton. [CL3: 90]

25 Shaw calls on Charles Frohman to discuss the Duke of York's Theatre one-act play season. [DHL]

Lucy Shaw writes that she has been translating plays of Strindberg for the Adelphi Play Society. [Farmer 176]

27 Ann M. Elder (later Jackson) replaces Georgina (Judy) Gillmore (Musters) as Shaw's secretary upon the latter's marriage. Aside from one interruption in 1918–19, Ann remained in the position until her marriage and departure for India in 1920. [Letter by Ann Elder cited in Hend3: 807; DHL; BLPES; I&R 290; Farmer 177]

June

11 (Tue) Shaw advises Annie Horniman about her search for a London outlet for productions of her Manchester Gaiety Theatre repertory. [CL3: 93]

15 (Sat) W. B. Yeats lunches with the Shaws. Shaw visits an aerodrome. [DHL]

16 Shaw reads *Pygmalion* ('just finished') to the Webbs and Robert Loraine at Ayot. Shaw's secretary, Ann Elder, remembered being handed about this time 'a bunch of little hand-made green papers with one word "Pygmalion" written at the top'. This is Shaw's Pitman shorthand copy of the play, and the first she was to transcribe for him. [DHL; CP4: 655; letter by Ann Elder cited in Hend:807; I&R 290]

19 Shaw meets with Arthur Wing Pinero and Dion Boucicault (director) at J. M. Barrie's apartment to discuss the Duke of

York's triple bill performances to be presented by Charles Frohman. [DHL]

26 Shaw declares to Harley Granville Barker that while he was reading *Pygmalion* to Mrs Patrick Campbell, he 'fell head over heels in love with her – violently and exquisitely in love'. [CL3: 3, 95; BL MS Add 56500]

c. 27 Mrs Patrick Campbell to Shaw (postmark 27 June 1912): '...my thanks for letting me hear the play, and for thinking I can be your pretty slut. I wonder if I could please you.' [Dent 12]

July

2 (Tue) Shaw begins writing *Overruled* (initially entitled *Trespassers Will Be Prosecuted*). [CP4: 826; CL3: 112; letter by Ann Elder cited in Hend:807, I&R 290]

Late Mrs Patrick Campbell is injured when her taxi is involved in an accident near the Albert Hall. Bruising forces her to withdraw from her current engagement and, after a short rest, she travels to Aix-les-Bains with Sir Edward and Lady Stracey. [CL3: 101; Dent 23ff]

23 Shaw completes *Overruled*. [CP4: 826]

27 The Shaws and Mary Cholmondeley depart for a motoring tour of France and Germany. [CL3: 101]

30 Mrs Patrick Campbell leaves for Aix-les-Bains in France to recover from her accident. Shaw resists the temptation to detour and rendezvous with her. [CL3: 101; Dent 26–7; Peters 327]

August

Bessie Shaw suffers the first of three paralytic strokes. This one is slight, but the later ones are more severe. Lucy Shaw rushes from the Butterfields' home at Denmark Hill to care for her mother at Park Village West. [Farmer 181]

9 (Fri) Shaw writes to Mrs Patrick Campbell: 'Stella, Stella: all the winds of the north are musical with the thousand letters I have written to you on this journey... Neither [Charlotte nor Mary Cholmondeley]... by the way, is the least ill; but Charlotte wants to get thin; and her sister wants to get plump; so they have both agreed to be asthmatic and have treatments. I have taken the waters myself – one mouthful, which will suffice for the rest of my life...

I am like the brigand in *Man & Superman* with his Louisa (who was our cook, by the way). Still, O Stella, I kiss your hands and magnify the Life Force for creating you; for you are a very wonderful person.' [CL3: 101, 103; Dent 27–30]

c. 13 While motoring through the Tyrol with Kilsby (Charlotte and her sister having been left at Bad Kissingen for therapeutic mud-

	bathing), Shaw's car 'ruptured a vital organ' near an isolated alpine village, leaving Shaw to negotiate rail transportation of the broken car, the luggage, the chauffeur and himself to Luneville in France where the car can be repaired. [CL3: 105, 110; Dent 33]
20	Shaw writes to Ellen Terry about *Pygmalion*: 'I read it to a good friend of mine [Dame Edith Lyttelton], and contrived that she [Mrs Patrick Campbell] should be there... She saw through it like a shot – "You beast, you wrote this for me, every line of it: I can hear you mimicking my voice in it &c &c &c." And she rose to the occasion, quite fine and dignified for a necessary moment; said unaffectedly she was flattered...' [CL3: 110–12]
30	Repairs on Shaw's automobile are completed after several days' delay waiting for delivery of a part. [CL3: 112–13]
31	Shaw and Charlotte rendezvous at Freiburg in the Black Forest and proceed together across northern France towards the coast. [CL3: 112]

September

	Mrs Patrick Campbell's condition having deteriorated upon her return, Shaw attends almost daily at her bedside. Charlotte Shaw is also ill with bronchitis and asthma. Shaw concurrently directs *Overruled* and *Captain Brassbound's Conversion*, due to open on 14 and 15 October respectively. [CL3: 118]
8 (Sun)	The Shaws return to London. [CL3: 112]
16	First American production of *Fanny's First Play* at the Comedy Theater, New York. [Morgan 65]
21	Granville Barker's Shakespeare season opens at the Savoy. [DHL]
29	Shaw praises Granville Barker's experiment with an apron stage for a production of *The Winter's Tale* at the Savoy Theatre: 'Instead of the theatre being a huge auditorium, with a picture frame at one end of, the theatre is now a stage with some unnoticed spectators round it.' ['Mr Bernard Shaw and "A Winter's Tale". What Mr Barker Has Done. Stage Triumphant. Shakespeare and the Critics', *The Observer*, 29 Sep 1912]

October

11 (Fri)	Shaw speaks at a rally at the Albert Hall for a legal minimum wage. [DBW3: 178–9]
14	First performance of *Overruled* in a triple bill with Barrie's *Rosalind* and Pinero's *The Widow of Wasdale Head*. In later correspondence with Frank Harris (16 October 1916) he was to say 'In the tiny one-act farcical comedy I published the other day I actually put the physical act of sexual intercourse on the stage',

but according to Morgan the critics didn't notice. [Peters 353; Morgan 103; Wein4: 54]

15 Following the controversial performance of *Overruled* Shaw again writes to Pinero: 'There is nothing for it but assassination (of Barrie) and suicide. They simply loathed us. They weren't indifferent: we didn't fall flat: they were angrily disgusted: we were trampled on, kicked, and hurled downstairs and out into the street... Did you think my play so very bloody when you read it? How did I miss the horror of yours?... Boucicault wants to consult me about cuts: I have replied that only two cuts are necessary, my piece and yours... I am looking forward comfortably to another failure tonight with that silly old Brassbound. You and I have mistaken our profession. Let's go into market gardening.' [Shaw to Arthur Pinero, 15 Oct 1912, Texas]

25 First performance (with its new 'Ra' Prologue) of *Caesar and Cleopatra* with Forbes-Robertson, in his farewell season, at Liverpool, prior to London. [DHL]

November

Shaw is writing the preface, 'Parents and Children', for *Misalliance*. [CL3: 128]

1 (Fri) Shaw discusses a new weekly (the *New Statesman*) with the Webbs over dinner. [DHL; BLPES]

2–3 Shaw spends the weekend with Harley Granville Barker and Lillah McCarthy at their farmhouse in Kent. [CL3: 119]

3 In a self-drafted interview Shaw advises the 'interviewer' about the prefaces to his plays: 'Get those prefaces of mine out of your head; they were all written two years after the plays were performed, and have nothing to do with their effect on the stage.' ['Mr George Bernard Shaw Tells Why He Continues to Roast the Critics', *The London Weekly Budget*, 3 Nov 1912]

18 Shaw writes to Lady Gregory 'my mother is dying, they say, but *won't* die – makes nothing of strokes – throws them off as other women throw off sneezing fits.' [CL3: 127]

December

Shaw directs a revival of *John Bull's Other Island* due to open in a series of matinées at the Kingsway Theatre on 26 December. [CL3: 133, 135]

1 (Sun) Shaw delivers an address in the Pavilion Theatre, Whitechapel, at a celebration of the jubilee of Prince Peter Kropotkin. The same evening, he makes a commendatory speech at the Trocadero Restaurant on the Shakespearean producer William Poël. [CL2: 128]

2 Mrs Patrick Campbell informs Shaw that her doctors are contemplating surgery: 'I think if you don't come and see me rather soon there won't be me to see'. [Dent 61]

6 Lucy Shaw writes of her mother that 'She is now very near the end. I have been watching her die for five weeks since the last seizure: her body and all her organs are so sound that she seems unable to get away, but it is a question of days and even hours now.' [Farmer 182]

Shaw speaks at a Home Rule demonstration in the Memorial Hall, London, sponsored by the Irish Protestant Home Rule Committee. [DHL; Bernard Shaw, *The Matter with Ireland*, eds. David H. Greene and Dan H. Laurence (1962), 71]

8 Shaw to Mrs Patrick Campbell: '...it is unprofessional to write under the influence of deep feeling...' [Dent 63]

c. 8 Mrs Patrick Campbell admonishes Shaw for his frivolous epistolary gallantries on what is possibly for her the eve of a serious operation. [Dent 65–6]

10 At William Poël's final production of *Troilus and Cressida*, Shaw sees Esmé Percy, who will become one of the most famous, though rather mannered, interpreters of major Shavian roles. [CL3: 133; DHL]

19 First meeting of the Statesman Publishing Company. [DHL]

Shaw dines with the Webbs and Arnold Bennett. [DHL]

26 *John Bull's Other Island* opens at the Kingsway Theatre for a series of matinées. The same day Shaw writes a congratulatory note to Ellen O'Malley who played the role of Nora Reilly. 'A most beautiful, lovely, noble, divine performance.' [Theatrics 115; CL3: 133 135]

1913

In February of this year Shaw's mother Bessie dies. Between July and August, Shaw writes *Great Catherine* and *The Music-Cure*. *Androcles and the Lion* opens in London, *Pygmalion* in Vienna and *The Philanderer* in New York. Augustin Hamon's study of Shaw, *Le Molière du XX siècle: Bernard Shaw* (to be published in London in 1916 as *The Twentieth Century Molière: Bernard Shaw*, trans. Eden and Cedar Paul) is published in Paris. Shaw's attachment to Mrs Patrick Campbell reaches a crisis point when she avoids a planned meeting with him at a seaside hotel, and becomes more difficult for Shaw when Stella begins a relationship with George Cornwallis-West, whom she later marries.

January

7 (Tue) Charlotte Shaw records in her annual summary diary: 'G.B.S. told me about Mrs P[atrick]. C[ampbell].' Charlotte's 1913 engagement diary contains the following entries during the

early months of the year: 'Talk to G.B.S. about Mrs P.C.' (7 Jan); 'Talk to G.B.S. about Mrs P.C. etc' (1 Feb) ; 'G.B.S. decided to go and see Mrs Campbell' (26 Apr); 'Talk to G.B.S.!!' (28 Apr); 'G.B.S not well.' (29 Apr) [BL MS Add 56500; BL MS Add 63190]

12–15 Shaw goes on a short walking tour with Harley Granville Barker, to Bournemouth (by train) then Corfe Castle, Weymouth and Lyme Regis. [DHL]

21 Shaw finishes writing *The Music-Cure*, which was presented a week later to celebrate the one hundredth performance of Chesterton's *Magic*. Shaw commented 'There is, however, no pressing reason why the thing should be performed at all', considering it 'not a serious play'. [CP4: 877–8]

28 Shaw debates with Hilaire Belloc at the Queen's Hall on the subject 'Property or Slavery?' The novelist and playwright Arnold Bennett attends and reports in his journal on Shaw's performance and the progress of the debate: 'Shaw's first [address] was a first-class performance, couldn't have been better: the perfection of public speaking (not oratory); not a word wrong. But then afterwards the impression that it was a gladiatorial show or circus performance gained on one...' [CL3: 128; *The Journal of Arnold Bennett* (1933), 472; I&R 78–9]

February

Early Charlotte to Shaw: 'I never know now where you spend your afternoons. Once I never thought about it – never doubted. Now I always imagine...' Judy Musters reported to Dan H. Laurence that Charlotte was much pained by Shaw's affair with Mrs Campbell, hurt by the publicity but more by being supplanted as the 'NO. 1' woman in his life. She argued that Charlotte was very jealous of her position (for instance, hating Jenny Patterson, whom she had never met, because she had been Shaw's mistress). [CL3: 148; DHL]

6 (Thu) Shaw makes a clandestine visit to Mrs Patrick Campbell at her nursing home and recommends that a plaque be erected there proclaiming 'HERE A GREAT MAN FOUND HAPPINESS'. [CL3: 147–8; Dent 88]

19 **Death of Bessie Shaw**. Shaw's diary records 'Death of my mother'. Lucy Shaw writes that 'The illness was long and trying for the lookers on, although she did not suffer at all from beginning to end. She was unconscious for 16 weeks and passed out in her sleep so quietly and imperceptibly that I could not believe it when they said she was gone.'

Shaw then asks Lucy's friend Eva M. Schneider, who had helped Lucy to nurse Bessie, to act as Lucy's full-time nurse and housekeeper, and engages chest specialist Dr Harold Des Voeux.

[DHL; Peters 340; Farmer 187–8, 194–5; Ervine 452–3; Rat 186; Ross 352]

20 Shaw lunches at the German Embassy with Count Harry Kessler. [DHL]

21 Shaw lunches with Margot Asquith at 10 Downing Street. [DHL]

22 Funeral of Shaw's mother at Golders Green Crematorium attended only by Shaw, Granville Barker and the undertaker. That night Shaw goes to Oxford, as earlier arranged, with Ben Iden Payne and his wife Mona Limerick to see a performance of *The Philanderer*. In the evening, having talked in a detached manner to Desmond MacCarthy about music at funerals, Shaw says 'with a casualness which made a deeper impression': 'You mustn't think I'm a person who forgets people.' [Desmond MacCarthy, 'What the New Statesman has meant to me', *New Statesman and Nation*, 14 Apr 1934; I&R 288 n.2]

March

Shaw is visited by Upton Sinclair, American socialist politician and author. [CL3: 215]

8 (Sat), 9 The Shaws spend the weekend at Beach Head with the Webbs. Shaw secretly leaves to visit Mrs Patrick Campbell at Brighton. [Peters 341; Dent 100]

18 Shaw addresses a suffragist demonstration at the Kingsway Hall against the forcible feeding of political protesters then on hunger strike. [CL3: 158]

20 Shaw takes delivery of a new motorcycle. [CL3: 158–60, 160; Dent 106, 108]

23 *Overruled* is published in German translation as *Es hat nicht sollen sein*, in the *Neue Freie Presse*, Vienna. [Lbib1: 129, 651]

26 The Shaws leave for a two-week stay with Horace Plunkett and George Russell at Foxrock in Ireland. Shaw was to write to Mrs Patrick Campbell that as he drove through Dublin during this visit he 'cursed every separate house as I passed'. [CL3: 161; Nicholas Grene, 'Shaw in Ireland: Visitor or Exile?' in SA 47]

April

12 (Sat) First issue of the *New Statesman*, a new Fabian weekly journal founded by the Webbs and edited by Clifford Sharp. A proprietor and director of the journal, Shaw contributes three articles to the opening number. These are titled 'Wireless Indignation', 'Forcible Feeding' and 'The Muddle over the Irish Grant', and are all unsigned. [CL3: 163; Lbib2: 651]

27 Shaw begins writing *The Music-Cure*. [CP4: 877]

May

Thomas O'Bolger submits his thesis, 'The Real Shaw' for a doctoral degree at the University of Pennsylvania. He declares in the introduction that, in his correspondence with Shaw, he asked 'questions as to his home, his parents, his reading, his studies etc... and Mr Shaw answered with remarkable frankness and generosity'. The thesis was interrupted by war as well as by Shaw's sporadic input and advice. [Harvard]

Overruled is published in the *English Review* and *Hearst's Magazine*, New York. [Lbib1: 129, 651]

Early — In early May, Shaw declares that he will cease contributing to *the New Statesman*. Writing to Clifford Sharp on 19 May 1913, Shaw said, 'I have finally been crushed by Mrs Patrick Campbell, who followed up Miss Lena Ashwell by spontaneously telling me that the last number of *the New Statesman* was a great improvement. Such overpowering hints – unconscious ones too – are not to be disregarded. I retire, superannuated... etc.' He did not, however, cease to contribute. [Cornell; CL3: 176]

Shaw is defrauded of £525 by a confidence trickster passing him a forged cheque. [CL3: 170]

1 (Thu) — Shaw lectures to the National Liberal Club on 'The Case for Equality'. [CL3: 176]

3 — Siegfried Trebitsch visits Ayot for the weekend. [DHL]

24 — Charlotte overhears a telephone conversation between her husband and Mrs Patrick Campbell. Shaw soon takes to meeting Stella at his sister Lucy Shaw's house at 8 Park Village West, Gloucester Gate. [Mrs Patrick Campbell, *My Life and Some Letters* (1922), I&R 174–5; CL3: 181; Peters 342–3]

27 — Lucy Shaw writes that the physician engaged by her brother has admitted defeat in his attempts to cure her by vaccine treatments, and she rejects more radical means: 'I am not going to have any more experiments, and shall eke out what spell of life there is left in me, as far as I can by care and self preservation.' [Farmer 195]

Shaw writes to William Armstrong of *The Music-Cure*: 'I was writing a sketch for you and Mrs Patrick Campbell, your musical accomplishments being indispensable. But the lady is terrified at appearing as a pianist.' [Theatrics 116]

June

Mrs Patrick Campbell, having learned that Lucy Shaw is an invalid, determines to visit her at Park Village West, and does so in the company of Shaw. This was to be the first of many visits, the two women becoming good friends, somewhat to Shaw's discomfort. [Dent 133; Farmer 196–7]

9 (Mon) — Shaw pleads with Mrs Patrick Campbell not to marry George Cornwallis-West 'until I am tired of you.... I will hurry through my dream as fast as I can; only let me have my dream out.' [Dent 131; CL3:184–5]

21 Lady Gregory and W. B. Yeats lunch with the Shaws. [BL MS Add 63190]

24 Shaw meets the Queen, probably at a reception for President Poincaré at the French Embassy. He writes to Mrs Patrick Campbell the following day: 'I was in heaven yesterday. Spoke to the queen. A dear woman, and frightfully beautiful. She just slanged me in the most shocking way for a full hour; and I adore her and burnt endless candles to her all the time. In the end my prayers touched her; and she gave me a little blessing.' [CL3: 187]

Late Shaw and Granville Barker visit Dresden to see Dalcroze's theatre and music school at Hellerau. The Dalcroze is an avant-garde school for children and adults, at which Shaw sees 'one of the best performances of Gluck's *Orfée*... it only needed a few rehearsals by Barker and myself to be perfect'. Hellerau, like Welwyn Garden City near Ayot St Lawrence, was a planned urban development. [Dent 137–40]

July

4 (Fri) Shaw returns to London from Dresden. [Dent 141]

26 Shaw begins an eight-day visit to Harley Granville Barker at Torcross, a small village on the south coast of Devon. He goes motoring and bathing with playwright and designer Dion Clayton Calthrop and his wife. Calthrop recalls: 'Shaw, away from a sycophantic world, was pure joy. He swam, played with the village children, stood on his head, talked seriously, talked wisely, talked wittily to my wife and me...took numerous photographs, went to the local flower show and guessed the weight of a pig.' [CL3: 192; Dion Clayton Calthrop, *My Own Trumpet: Being the Story of My Life* (1935), 210–11; Dent 148]

29 Shaw begins writing *Great Catherine*. [CP4: 896; CL3: 193]

August

2 (Sat) While standing by the sea, Shaw and Lillah McCarthy are hit by a freak wave. [CL3: 193–4; Dent 149–50]

4 Shaw returns with Granville Barker to London. [CL3: 192]

7 Mrs Patrick Campbell warns Shaw she wants to be alone on her forthcoming visit to Sandwich. [Dent 152]

8 Charlotte departs alone on the P&O SS *Morea* for Marseilles, Shaw intending to join her for six weeks at the end of the month. Shaw immediately rushes off to the coast of Kent in pursuit of Mrs Patrick Campbell who is staying at the Guildford Hotel in Sandwich. [BL MS Add 56500 CL3: 195; I&R 175]

10 Mrs Patrick Campbell to Shaw: 'Please will you go back to London to-day – or go wherever you like but don't stay here.' [Dent 152]

11 Mrs Patrick Campbell removes herself from Shaw's unwanted presence by secretly departing from the Guildford Hotel, leaving Shaw feeling bitter and betrayed. [CL3: 195; Dent 153]

12 Shaw to Mrs Patrick Campbell: 'Infamous, vile, heartless, frivolous, wicked woman! Liar! lying lips, lying eyes, lying hands, promise breaker, cheat, confidence-trickster!' [CL3: 196; Dent 156]

13 Shaw finishes *Great Catherine*, and reads it to Gertrude Kingston four days later. [CP4: 896; CL3: 197; DHL]

Shaw returns from Sandwich to London. [CL3: 196]

15 Shaw, the Granville Barkers, and Edward Sillward who is to play the lion in *Androcles and the Lion,* visit the Regents Park zoo to study the lions, Shaw putting his hand into the cage and stroking one lion under the chin. [CL3: 198]

Summer 1913–1914

During this period Charlotte Shaw takes a great interest in the work of James Porter Mills, whom she had met in November 1911 at Lena Ashwell's. [BL MS Add 56500; Dunbar 247–9; DHL]

September

After the jealousies and tensions generated by Shaw's infatuation with Mrs Patrick Campbell, harmony gradually returns to Shaw's marriage during the tour of France. At Orléans, Charlotte proposes that he write a play about Joan of Arc. At Biarritz in early October, Lena Ashwell tells Shaw about the adventures of her seafaring father Captain Pocock, thus planting the seed that grows eventually into the creation of Captain Shotover in *Heartbreak House*. [CL3: 204; Peters 358–9]

1 (Mon) First production of *Androcles and the Lion* at St James's Theatre, London. The play is withdrawn after 52 performances, having incurred a financial loss. [CL3: 202; CP4: 453; 'Memories of GBS and Granville Barker: Hesketh Pearson on the Original Production of *Androcles and the Lion*', *Listener*, 24 Feb 1949; I&R 150; Morgan 10, 67]

6 Shaw departs from London to join Charlotte in France. [CL3: 198]

8 Writing to Mrs Patrick Campbell from Orléans, Shaw declares his intention to write a play about Joan of Arc: 'I shall do a Joan play some day, beginning with the sweeping up of the cinders and orange peel *after* her martyrdom, and going on with Joan's arrival in heaven.' Shaw's treatment of the English in the play, and his use of the story of the English soldier handing Joan a crucifix made out of two sticks, are also foreshadowed in this letter. [CL3: 201; Dent 146]

October

1 (Wed) The Shaws arrive at the seaside resort of Biarritz in South West France, where they are joined by Lena Ashwell and her husband Dr (later Sir) Henry Simson. The Shaws leave Biarritz on 11 October, GBS (driving his car) in the morning and Charlotte by train in the afternoon. [BL MS Add 56500]

16 Première of *Pygmalion*, in Siegfried Trebitsch's translation, at the Hofburg Theatre in Vienna, with Lili Marberg as Eliza and Max Paulsen as Higgins. Trebitsch describes the occasion as 'brilliant and thrilling'. [CP4: 655; CL3: 146; Weiss 17, 169; Siegfried Trebitsch, *Chronicle of a Life* (1953), 174]

17 Shaw arrives back in London. [BL MS Add 56500; CL3: 206; Dent 169]

November

1 (Sat) Shaw speaks at a demonstration at the Albert Hall in support of James Connolly and his striking Irish transport workers. [CL3: 569]

Mid Lucy Shaw flees the London fogs to stay at Walmer, leaving her address for Shaw 'in case he may want to communicate'. [Farmer 203]

18 *Great Catherine* opens at the Vaudeville Theatre, London on a double bill with Hermon Ould's *Between Sunset and Dawn*. [CP4: 896; CL3: 207; Weiss 166; Morgan 103]

28 Shaw lunches with Hugo Vallentin to meet Danish critic and philosopher Georg Brandes. [DHL]

December

1 (Mon) Shaw takes the chair at Georg Brandes's reception by the Royal Society of Literature and his lecture on Nietzsche. [DHL]

6 The Granville Barkers revive *The Doctor's Dilemma* for its first West End performance at the St James's Theatre. [CL3: 217]

9 Performance of Charlotte's translation of Brieux's *La Femme seule* (*Woman on Her Own*). [Peters 359]

11 Shaw takes the chair at a Fabian reception for, and lecture by, Anatole France. [DHL]

20 Shaw begins a walking and motoring tour of Devon and Cornwall with Kilsby, the Webbs and William Mellor, a young Fabian, secretary of the Fabian Research Committee and future editor of the *Daily Herald*. Beatrice Webb's diary entry for 2 January 1914 provides a glimpse of the luxurious style of their travel (made possible by the Shaw motor car) and an intimate comment on Shaw's personal life at this time: 'It has been a delightful and luxurious holiday – our first intention of tramping round the coast, with knapsack and mackintosh being

transformed, by the advent of G.B.S, into walking 10 or 12 miles of picked country with the motor car in attendance to take us when tired to the most expensive hotel in the neighbourhood. Our old friend and brilliant comrade is a benevolent and entertaining companion, but his intellect is centred in the theatre and his emotion in his friendship with Mrs. Pat. He is still fond of Charlotte and grateful to her, but he quite obviously finds his new friend, with her professional genius and more intimate personal appeal, better company.' [DBW3: 194; I&R 214–15; CL3: 211]

24 A wax figure of Shaw is unveiled at Madame Tussaud's Museum.[DHL]

27 First American production of *The Philanderer* at the Little Theater, New York. [Morgan 15]

31 Shaw to Mrs Patrick Campbell: '...you have wakened the latent tragedy in me, broken through my proud overbearing gaiety...' [CL3: 212; Dent 172–3]

1914

Charlotte travels to America to avoid the opening of *Pygmalion*. In April, Mrs Patrick Campbell marries George Cornwallis-West. *Pygmalion* opens in London in April causing a sensation with Eliza Doolittle's famous exclamation 'not bloody likely'. Shaw responds to the outbreak of war by writing his courageous, hard-hitting and highly controversial essay entitled 'Common Sense about the War', published in *the New Statesman* in November. During this year Joseph McCabe's *George Bernard Shaw: A Critical Study* is published. In a letter discussing various biographies that had been written about him Shaw commented: 'McCabe has written a surpassingly bad book about me which shews the extreme danger of dealing with the ideas associated with me instead of the ideas I have expressed.' [Wein4: 53]

Charlotte Shaw's pamphlet *Knowledge is the Door: a Forerunner*, on a religious organization called 'The Fellowship of the Way' founded by Dr. J. Porter Mills, is published.

January

4 (Sun) Shaw returns from Devon and Cornwall to London. [CL3: 211]

7 Shaw (as Jury Foreman) and Chesterton (as Presiding Justice) participate in a mock 'Trial of John Jasper for the Murder of Edwin Drood' at the King's Hall sponsored by the London Branch of the Dickens Fellowship. Shaw declines an American commission to turn the trial into a stage play. [CL3: 215; DHL; Pearson 314]

21 Shaw completes *The Music-Cure*. [CP4: 877]

22 Shaw attends *The Doctor's Dilemma*, now playing at the Savoy. [DHL]

23 Shaw reports that he is 'Prostrate with a blazing headache'. [CL3: 218]

28 First performance of *The Music-Cure* at the Little Theatre, as a curtain-raiser to Chesterton's *Magic*. [CP4: 877; Morgan 103; Theatrics 116]

February

4 (Wed) Shaw attends Wagner's *Parsifal* at Covent Garden, and again on 12 February. [DHL]

19 Rehearsals of *Pygmalion* begin with Shaw's reading of the play at Sir Herbert Tree's His Majesty's Theatre. Shaw directs the play with Mrs Patrick Campbell playing Eliza and Tree playing Higgins. [CL3: 221; DHL]

23 Shaw storms out of the *Pygmalion* rehearsals driven to distraction by the antics of his two stars. [CL3: 221]

24 After a conciliatory letter from Tree, Shaw returns to direct *Pygmalion*. [CL3: 221]

28 Shaw lectures at Oxford on 'The Nature of Drama'. C. E. M. Joad, then an undergraduate, attends, 'glowing with hero-worship', and recalls in detail Shaw's 'melodious voice' and its effects on an audience. The lecture is reported in the *Oxford Times* on 6 March. [C.E.M. Joad, *Shaw* (1949), 29–31; I&R 79–80]

March

27 (Fri) Shaw writes to William Armstrong, advising him about his performance in the revival of *The Music-Cure* at the Palace Theatre. 'Be imposing; and dont be afraid of being dull: they expect high class acting & drama to be dull.' [Theatrics 116–17]

31 American theatrical manager Lee Shubert calls on Shaw. [DHL]

April

Lucy Shaw requests of Ann Elder that 'If the "Super-One" [Shaw] is ever going to see me again, ring me up when I may expect him.' [Farmer 212]

First publication in German translation of *Great Catherine*, as *Die Grosse Katharina*, in the *Neue Rundschau*, Berlin. [CP4: 896]

6 (Mon) Mrs Patrick Campbell marries George Cornwallis-West. [CL3: 226]

8 Shaw having driven her to Southampton the previous day, Charlotte avoids the opening of *Pygmalion* by sailing for America with Lena Ashwell, Dr James Porter Mills and his wife. [BL MS Add 56500; DHL; CL3: 226; I&R 179–80; Dunbar 250]

11 *Pygmalion* opens at His Majesty's Theatre in London with Mrs Patrick Campbell as Eliza Doolittle and Sir Herbert Tree as

Henry Higgins. Furious at Tree's performance, Shaw storms out before the final curtain. In a letter to Charlotte (12 April 1914) Shaw writes: 'The raving absurdity of Tree's acting was quite beyond description. He was like nothing human; and he wallowed ecstatically in his own impossibility, convinced that he was having the success of his life... He did the exact opposite of everything I had warned him to do, not intentionally, but by sheer force of an irresistible genius for bad acting & erroneousness.' [CL3: 226–8; Theatrics 118–9; Pearson 290; Morgan 68]

12 Shaw spends Easter Sunday at Ayot with Mrs Patrick Campbell and her bridegroom. [CL3: 226]

13 Shaw motors over to Filey to visit the Webbs. [CL3: 226]

14 Death of Hubert Bland. Shaw underwrote the education of Bland's son, John who, like his sister Rosamund, was the child of Alice Hoatson, live-in 'companion' of the Bland family. [CL3: 232; I&R 161–2]

20 Shaw returns to London. [CL3: 226]

24 Shaw lunches with H. G. Wells. [DHL]

28 Lucy Shaw returns to London from Walmer. Once back in the city, however, 'most of the old miserable symptoms have returned'. Nevertheless, she sees *Pygmalion* three times and thinks that 'Tree is much better than I expected, and Mrs Pat Campbell not quite so good in some parts.' [Farmer 209–11]

29 Publication in the *Boston Post* of an interview with Charlotte Shaw at the home of Mr and Mrs W. F. Morgan in the Hotel Tudor, Beacon and Joy Streets, Boston. She describes Shaw as a 'thorough feminist', who believes 'all government should be by women [who] are more capable of management than men'. Of herself she states: 'I am a Socialist and a suffragist and devote most of my time to those causes.' [H. F. Wheeler, 'Wife Reveals Bernard Shaw. Noted Englishwoman, in Her First American Interview, Says Husband is Ardent Socialist and Feminist', *Boston Post*, 29 Apr 1914; I&R 179–80]

May

5 (Tue) Shaw calls on Lee Shubert at the Savoy Hotel to discuss the American production of *Pygmalion*. [DHL]

11 Chekhov's *Uncle Vanya* is performed by the Stage Society.[DHL]

15 Charlotte returns from America. [Wein2: 11; DHL]

18 First English language publication, as a collected edition, of *Misalliance, The Dark Lady of the Sonnets* and *Fanny's First Play*. [CP4: 11; Lbib1: 121]

23 With punctuation no doubt reflecting her feelings about Mrs Patrick Campbell (playing Eliza), Charlotte Shaw records in her

diary: 'Pygmalion running at his Majesty's. Saw it on 23rd!!' She and GBS attended the play together in the evening of the 23rd, having been to the cinema in the afternoon. Charlotte saw the play again on 10 June 1914. [BL MS Add 56500; BL MS Add 63190 A-M]

29 The Shaws have Annie Besant to lunch at Adelphi Terrace. [BL MS Add 56500; Peters 398]

June

22 (Mon) Lucy Shaw writes that she has suffered a relapse, mentioning the futility of keeping the spirit 'in a body too decayed to hold it'. [Farmer 215]

24 The Shaws meet Richard Strauss at Lady Speyer's. Strauss's *Der Rosenkavalier* and *Prince Igor* are performed during this month at Drury Lane. [BL MS Add 56500; DHL]

28 Shooting of Archduke Franz Ferdinand in Sarajevo.

June–July

Mrs Patrick Campbell writes to Shaw: 'Lucy sends me a lovely letter – I see her a girl – my heart aches for her – go often to see her now.' [Farmer 213]

July

Shaw attends a Fabian Research Department Conference. [DBW3: 203]

2 (Thu) The Shaws have Rodin, Yvette Guilbert, Lillah McCarthy and others to lunch at Adelphi Terrace. [DHL]

3 Shaw is filmed at a 'cinema supper' arranged by J. M. Barrie at the Savoy Theatre. [CL3: 444–5; Wein2: 16]

4–7 J. M. Barrie and Harley Granville Barker make a film of Shaw, Archer, Chesterton and Lord Howard de Walden acting as cowboys and frolicking about in farcical silent sketches. [CL3: 444–5; Wein2: 17]

8 Shaw visits a performance of *Pygmalion* to find, to his fury, that Tree has falsified the ending by throwing flowers to Eliza. [Wein2: 21]

17 Shaw meets Claude Debussy at Lady Speyer's. [DHL]

24 *Pygmalion* closes after 118 performances. [CL3: 228; Wein2: 21; DHL]

August

4 (Tue) In a hotel in Devon en route to Torquay for a holiday, the Shaws hear that Britain is at war. Shaw telegraphs Siegfried Trebitsch: 'Imagine you and me at war with one another! Can there be anything more senseless? Under all the circumstances you have my most friendly wishes.' Shaw remains in Torquay

	until the autumn, during which time he writes *Common Sense about the War*. [CL3: 243; Wein2: 24, 28ff.]
Mid	Carlos Blacker, a wealthy Englishman who had known Oscar Wilde, lends Charlotte a copy of the manuscript of Wilde's *De Profundis*, which Shaw also reads. [BL MS Add 56500; DHL]

September

	First British edition of *Love Among the Artists*. [Lbib1: 46]
17 (Thu)	Shaw's name is conspicuously absent from a patriotic declaration conceived by Cabinet propaganda chief, C. F. G. Masterman, and signed by 53 prominent writers. [Wein2: 37–8]

October

1 (Thu)	Lucy Shaw to Jancy Drysdale: 'What do you think of the war now?... I am not very happy about it. George is furious about the way we have handled it.' [Farmer 217]
3	Shaw sees Mrs Patrick Campbell off on the *Lusitania* boat train bound for New York to play in the American production of *Pygmalion*. [Wein2: 42]
12	The war having closed down serious theatre in Britain, Mrs Patrick Campbell opens in *Pygmalion* in New York's Park Theater. She does not return to England until early 1916. [Peters 364–5; Dent 185; Wein2: 45]
13	Shaw visits John and Mrs Galsworthy. [DHL]
17	Lucy Shaw to Ann Elder: 'I heard from the "Super-One" a couple of days ago: he seems to be throwing himself, to the extinction of everything else, into a War article. I trust it may not get us all arrested and shot for High Treason.' [Farmer 218]
28	Shaw delivers the first of his six Fabian lectures for the season, on 'Income, Equality and Idolatry' at the Kingsway Hall. [Wein2: 49; DHL]

November

1 (Sun)	Publication of *Pygmalion* in *Everybody's Magazine*, New York and in *Nash's and Pall Mall Magazine*, November–December. [CP4: 655; Lbib2: 657; DHL]
7	Publication in Massingham's *The Nation* of Shaw's 'Open letter to the President of the United States'. [Lbib2: 657]
14	Publication of *Common Sense about the War* as a Special War Supplement to *the New Statesman*. Shaw argues that the war is essentially the outcome of a power struggle between rival European powers and that the German violation of Belgian neutrality was no more than a convenient pretext for Britain's entry into the struggle. He attacks the jingoistic fervour of the recruitment campaigns, and argues that militaristic Junkerism is as

much a characteristic of the English squirearchy as of the Prussian aristocracy. The essay produces an uproar, and over the next several months Shaw is embroiled in debates both private and public about the war. [Lbib1: 123; G. B. Shaw 'Symposium', *Cap and Gown: The Magazine of the University College of South Wales and Monmouthshire*, Nov 1924; I&R 229,352; CL3: 256, 266]

17 First American Production of *The Dark Lady of the Sonnets* at the Little Theatre, Duluth. [Morgan 64]

24 Shaw and the Webbs leave on a ten-day walking tour: 'Tempestuous weather and heated argument' about the war settlement and his proposals for bringing about equality. [DBW3: 221; Dent 191; Wein2: 83]

1915

In the first three months of this year *Androcles and the Lion* , *The Admirable Bashville* and *The Doctor's Dilemma* are all produced in America and in New York's *Everybody's Magazine*, *Great Catherine* is published in the English language for the first time in February. The Shaws visit Ireland during March and in May, Shaw attends the Fabian Society Research conference at Lake Derwentwater, after which he enjoys an eight-day walking tour with the Webbs. In June, *Man and Superman* is performed in its entirety for the first time at the Lyceum in Edinburgh. In the latter months of the year Shaw becomes further embroiled in controversy after expressing his opinions on the war, one example being the Webbs' refusal to publish 'More Common Sense About the War' in *the New Statesman*. The Shaws spend two months in Torquay, where Shaw finishes *O'Flaherty V.C.* and *The Inca of Perusalem*. *Bernard Shaw: A Critical Study* by Percival Howe is published during this year.

January

27 (Wed) First American production of *Androcles and the Lion* at Wallack's Theater, New York. [Morgan 67]

February

Great Catherine is published in New York in *Everybody's Magazine*, the first publication of the play in English. [Lbib1: 655; CP4: 896]

4 (Thu) Lucy Shaw to Ann Elder: 'I have not seen any obituary notice of the "Super-One" in any of the papers, so I presume that he still stalks the earth... I wish I could see the "Super-One": however, my affairs are so trivial compared with his big ones that I don't want to worry him, and this is a nuisance of a place to get to.' [Farmer 220]

8 First American production of *The Admirable Bashville* at the Little Theater, Philadelphia. [Morgan 41]

13 Revival of *Fanny's First Play* at the Kingsway Theatre. [DHL]

March

26 (Fri) First American production of *The Doctor's Dilemma* at Wallack's Theater, New York. [Erv 409; Morgan 55]

31 The Shaws begin a six-week visit to Ireland, staying two weeks with Sir Horace Plunkett, and then proceeding to Lady Gregory's Coole Park, where they stay from 13 April to 9 May. Near the end of their stay, they learn of the torpedoing of the *Lusitania* resulting in the death of Lady Gregory's nephew, Sir Hugh Lane. Augustus John paints six portraits of Shaw (one of which was purchased for the Royal Art Collection and hangs in the Royal Gallery at Buckingham Palace) at Coole Park. John records that in the evenings Shaw (whom he calls a 'Prince of the Spirit') sometimes entertains the company by playing on the piano and singing in his 'gentle baritone', but also complains that the Shaw 'monologues, unenlivened by opposition, gained only in length what they lost in piquancy'. [CL3: 294; Dent 196; Wein2: 95; Augustus John, *Chiaroscuro: Fragments of Autobiography* (1952), 69; I&R 288]

April

16 (Fri) The County Carlow Joint Committee for Technical Instruction writes to Shaw requesting that he present the Carlow Assembly Rooms to them as a Technical School for Carlow 'the consideration offered being that my honoured name will be revered in perpetuity'. Shaw is unable to do so because of lease commitments but early the following year, Shaw writes to the committee informing them that the property is now available and offering to consider their former request. He receives no reply. He attempts to sell the property, unsuccessfully (despite a number of suggestions from Shaw including selling the façade to 'an American millionaire to be re-erected in the United States.'). The property falls into disrepair. In 1919, Shaw again offers the Assembly Rooms to the Technical Instruction Committee and the offer is finally accepted. A partial restoration occurs in the early 1920s with the Carlow Technical School finally moving into the building in 1923. A complete reconstruction occurs in 1934. [Carlow County Library; CL3: 293]

21–25 Shaw attends a Fabian Research Department conference on the war at Barrow House on the shores of Lake Derwentwater, to consider Leonard Woolf's report on International Government, commissioned by the Fabian Society. The report later forms a basis for the setting up of the League of Nations. With the Webbs, Shaw then makes an eight-day walk across the mountains. [Dent 199; Wein2: 96; Weiss 187; DBW3: 231–3]

May

11 (Tue) The Shaws return to England on a ferry transporting survivors from the *Lusitania*. [CL3: 294; Wein3: 95]

June

5 (Sat) Lady Gregory visits the Shaws at Ayot for the weekend. [DHL]

11 First production of *Man and Superman* in its entirety, at the Lyceum Theatre, Edinburgh, directed by Esmé Percy who also played Tanner. The five-hour performance plays to capacity audiences for an extended run. [CL3: 295; Esmé Percy, 'Bernard Shaw: A Personal Memory', *Listener*, 26 May 1955; I&R 143; Wein2: 98; Morgan 43]

26 Charles Butterfield, Lucy Shaw's husband, dies suddenly. She writes: 'Although divorced, we were the best of friends; he lived with his rich brother quite near here and was a constant and regular visitor which was a source of never ending amazement to our relations and friends.' [Farmer 223; Erv 198]

July

3 (Sat) Shaw mails *More Commonsense About the War* to Beatrice Webb, but she and Clifford Sharp think it unsuitable for publication in the *New Statesman*. [Wein2: 102]

9 The Shaws attend a meeting of the Society for Psychical Research to hear author Gilbert Murray's presidential address. [CL3: 300]

19 The interest payment is due on Shaw's £20 000 War Loan bonds. [DHL]

23 Shaw begins writing *O'Flaherty V.C.*, a comic one-act play written for the Irish Players in which the hero reflects critically on the absurdities of patriotism and warfare, but decides that life is more peaceful at the Front than at home with his Irish relatives. Shaw temporarily abandoned the writing of the play, taking it up again in September. [CP4: 984]

31 The Shaws begin a two-month stay at the Hydro Hotel in Torquay. [CL3: 305; Weiss 190]

August

9 (Mon) Shaw finishes *The Inca of Perusalem,* writing it in a few days for Gertrude Kingston to perform in America. This play was one of several minor works Shaw wrote during the war years to exploit the extraordinary popularity of the theatre as a source of light, distracting entertainment, particularly for servicemen. [CP4: 950]

September

3 (Fri) Shaw starts again on *O'Flaherty V.C.*, and completes it on 14 September. [CP4: 984; CL3: 308]

14 Shaw finishes writing *O'Flaherty V.C.* [CP4: 984]

26 Death of Keir Hardie. [CL3: 311]

October

21 (Thu) The Shaws return from Torquay to London. [CL3: 313]

26 Before a capacity audience which includes a large press contingent, Shaw speaks at the King's Hall, Covent Garden, on 'The Illusions of War', opening the Fabian Society's 1915 autumn series on 'The World after the War'. In England reports of Shaw's lecture are suppressed in all but *The Manchester Guardian* and a few provincial dailies which defy the ban. A verbatim report was published in Randolph Hearst's *New York American* on 7 November 1915. [CL3: 315, 334; DHL; R. Page Arnot, *Bernard Shaw and William Morris* (1957), 22–3; I&R 232; Wein2: 123–4]

27 Minutes of a meeting of the Dramatists' Club record that several members object to meeting Shaw because of his attitude to the war. The Secretary, H. M. Paull, is instructed to 'suggest that he should absent himself for the present'. [CL3: 315–16; D. A. Jones, *The Life and Letters of Henry Arthur Jones* (1930), 310; I&R 231; Wein2: 119]

28 Shaw writes to H. M. Paull, rejecting the suggestion that he not attend the Dramatists' Club, and requesting that notices of meetings be sent to him as usual. British Intelligence informs Shaw that the Germans are using his analysis of the war as anti-British propaganda to incite rebellion against the French in Morocco and Algeria. He is asked to write a statement for distribution in northern Africa declaring his fervent wish that Germany is defeated by Britain. [CL3: 315–19]

29 Shaw writes to Henry Arthur Jones expressing the hope that he was not one of 'several members' of the Dramatists Club asking him to refrain from attending. Jones replies on 1 November, saying that he strongly supported the motion and that Shaw's writings 'have done great harm to our cause... Germany is everywhere making use of your utterances to justify her own actions and to befoul and slander England.' Shaw's protest in a letter to Jones on 2 November fails to repair the major rift in their long-standing friendship. [CL3: 320–3; D. A. Jones, *The Life and Letters of Henry Arthur Jones* (1930), 320–23]

November

During rehearsals at the Abbey, Shaw withdraws *O'Flaherty V.C.*, which he had written for the Irish Players. This action is taken on the advice of Sir Matthew Nathan, Undersecretary for Ireland (who feared the recruitment programme might suffer) and of Shaw's Irish theatre associates (who wished to avoid giving the British authorities occasion for closing the theatres). [CL3: 308; Wein2: 129; CP4: 983, 1015–16]

1 (Mon) Henry Arthur Jones denounces Shaw as 'an enemy within our walls'. Shaw announces he will not stand for re-election to the Committee of Management of the Society of Authors. A few days later, Shaw writes to Pinero, who was away at the time: 'It appears that Henry Arthur Jones was the villain of the piece – or the hero to my villain – for he has written to me to say that England is his mother, and that I kicked his mother on her deathbed...' [CL3: 320, 326; Shaw to Pinero, 5 Nov 1915, Texas]

2 Lucy Shaw writes of the difficulty she is experiencing with her health. She has been six weeks in bed with pleurisy after a trip to town in an open taxi, while her nerves have been affected by the Zeppelin raids and the anti-aircraft fire which accompanies them. [Farmer 226]

19 Having successfully challenged the formal impropriety of his expulsion from the Dramatists' Club, Shaw notifies the Club secretary of his resignation. [CL3: 332]

Shaw writes to Lady Ottoline Morrell on the suppression of D. H. Lawrence's *The Rainbow*: 'I am so old and out-of-date that I have never read a word of Lawrence's. He is known to me only as the author of a book that has been solemnly destroyed by the order of a London magistrate... and is therefore presumably a work of outstanding merit. In America he will probably be lynched. Why not open a public subscription for him? He would become rich beyond the dreams of avarice...' [Shaw to Lady Ottoline Morrell, 19 Nov 1915, Texas]

23 Shaw lectures to the Fabian Society on 'Diplomacy After the War'. The lecture, revised by Shaw is published in the *New York American* on 19 December 1915. [CL3: 334; DHL]

December

Shaw writes the Preface to *Androcles and the Lion*. [*Androcles and the Lion* (1946); CP2: 246]

2 (Thu) Shaw lectures, at the request of Sylvia Pankhurst, on 'The Nation's Vitality'. The talk (which was reported in the *New York Times* on 19 December 1915) is given under the auspices of the East London Federation of Suffragettes in aid of Pankhurst's Baby Clinics and a help society called 'Mother's Arms'. [DHL; CL3: 334, 347; CL4: 887]

9 First American production of *Major Barbara* at the Playhouse, New York. The play is produced by William R. Brady for his wife Grace George. [CL3: 334–5; DHL; Morgan 52; Theatrics 123–5]

15 Shaw visits J.M. Barrie to view the cowboy film made at Elstree. [DHL]

19 Shaw to Mrs Patrick Campbell: 'I saw Lucy [Shaw] the other day and was told that it was my first visit for six months, though it seemed to me to be six weeks. She is in bed, frightfully ill: anyone else would be dead after such a relapse; but she will no doubt pull through. She always asks for news of you; and I supply as much as I happen to possess.' [CL3: 336]

Late The Shaws spend Christmas at Ayot. [CL3: 347]

1916

Shaw begins the year by publicly attacking the Conscription Act, introduced by Asquith. In March he begins a play which will eventually be *Heartbreak House*, and in April *Pygmalion*, *Overruled* and *Androcles and the Lion* are published in New York as a collected edition. In June, Shaw embarks on a walking tour with the Webbs, eventually taking accommodation at Wyndham Croft (where he is joined by Charlotte) to enable him to divide his time between walking and his work on *Heartbreak House*. In August, Shaw writes *Augustus Does His Bit* and in September he attends a musical festival, after which he proceeds to a Fabian Summer School in Sedbergh. On the first of October, Shaw witnesses the crash of a Zeppelin a few miles from his home, and elements of this incident are reflected in the last act of *Heartbreak House*. In the same month Shaw resigns from the Board of the Statesman Publishing Company, breaking his alliance with *the New Statesman*. In December, Shaw delivers a lecture on 'Religion,' for the Fabian series 'The World in Chains', and on 7 December he receives a letter from Florence Farr informing him of the illness which will prove fatal for her.

January

3 (Mon) Lillah McCarthy receives Harley Granville Barker's letter disclosing his involvement with Helen Huntington (the 'unspectacular' wife of American millionaire Archer M. Huntington) and asking for a divorce. Shaw finds himself in the awkward position of giving moral support to Lillah while negotiating on Granville Barker's behalf for the divorce. [CL3: 351–3; Wein2: 140]

5 Asquith introduces the First Conscription Act, which Shaw attacks in a letter published in the *Daily News*. [C. Ward-Jackson, 'Mr Bernard Shaw on: Is Conscription Necessary or Advisable?', *New Age*, 16 March 1916; I&R 237; Wein2: 144; Lbib2: 663]

March

4 (Sat) Shaw begins writing a new play first called *Lena's Father*, then *The Studio in the Clouds*, and finally *Heartbreak House*. Shaw's

initial inspiration for the play had come in 1913 from Lena Ashwell's stories of her seafaring father, Captain Pocock. Dan. H. Laurence points out: 'Shaw stated on several occasions that the play was begun before the war, but all surviving evidence contradicts this'. [CP5: 10; CL3: 408; Wein2: 148; A.M. Gibbs, *'Heartbreak House': Preludes of Apocalypse* (1994), 10–11]

28 A great gale strikes Ayot, blowing down hundreds of trees. [BL MS Add 56500; DHL]

April

Shaw engages in epistolary debate in the pages of the *Liverpool Courier* with the Liverpool professor, Alexander Mair, regarding *The Shewing-up of Blanco Posnet.* [CL3: 495]

1 (Sat) Shaw attends a performance of puppets put on by Alfred Powell – an architect active in arts and crafts circles. [CL3: 393]

10 First public production of *The Shewing-Up of Blanco Posnet* by the Irish Players (Abbey Theatre Company) at the Playhouse Theatre, Liverpool. While an application to the Lord Chamberlain to present performances was denied, Dan H. Laurence notes that through 'a strange circumstance the Lord Chamberlain's authority did not extend to Liverpool, and the public performances were offered.' [Theatrics 126–7; Morgan 60]

13 At this time, Shaw is involved in preparations to sell the Carlow Assembly Rooms. Judging from the correspondence involving his tenants, Shaw both revelled in and reviled the role of landlord. He writes to his agent, William Fitzmaurice: 'As to Mrs Aylward, I am beginning to wonder whether she is really a desirable tenant. She apparently made up her mind from the first that she would never pay her rent in full... she now asks me to spend £8.12.6 on internal papering and painting. Is it customary in Carlow for the landlord to pay for internal decorations in an unfurnished house let on lease or agreement? If it is not, and we submit to such a demand, the lady will be asking us next year to pay for her clothes.' [Shaw to William Fitzmaurice, 13 Apr 1916, Carlow County Library]

21 *Pygmalion, Overruled* and *Androcles and the Lion* published. [Lbib1: 128–9; CP4: 453]

Sir Roger Casement lands in Ireland from a German U-boat and is captured. The next day (Easter Saturday, 22 April) he is shipped to London to be tried for high treason and later executed. [CL3: 397]

The Shaws visit Weymouth, Swanage and Winchester to 1 May. [CL3: 395; DHL]

24 Easter Rising in Dublin. Shaw was to say in a letter to H. W. Massingham, 'The Irish business is rather ghastly... Dublin

slums are so damnable that the mere mob part of the business must have been pretty bad... If they send Casement to Broadmoor, no great harm will be done. If they shoot him, he will be canonized with Emmett and Lord Edward, and do mischief for years to come.' [CL3: 397–8]

May

20 (Sat) Distinguished pilot and Schneider Trophy Seaplane Race winner Henri C. Biard takes Shaw on a joy-ride in a two-seater biplane from Hendon Flying School near London. Noting that he did not feel any particular sense of 'invertedness' when flying upside down, Shaw remarked to the pilot on alighting: 'The world is like that, young man.' [H. C. Biard, *Wings* (1934), 56–7; I&R 211; Wein 158]

25 Lucy Shaw writes to Ann Elder that Eva M. Schneider 'has been intending to write to him [GBS] and offer to take half her salary, but now feels [after attending his lecture on 'War Economy'], as one of his most fanatical disciples, that there is nothing left for her but to ask him to double it.' [Farmer 230]

June

1 (Thu) Shaw lunches with Sir Horace Plunkett. [CL3: 402]

2 Shaw begins a walking tour with the Webbs. [Wein2: 162: CL3: 401–2]

6 Shaw and the Webbs arrive at Tunbridge Wells before settling down at Wyndham Croft to divide their time between working and walking. [Wein2: 162]

Mid Charlotte Shaw arrives at Wyndham Croft where Shaw is still working on *Heartbreak House*, called by this time *The Studio at the Clouds*. [CL3: 408; Wein2: 164; DBW3: 259]

17–19 Leonard and Virginia Woolf visit the Shaws and the Webbs at Wyndham Croft, Sussex. This house party influences Shaw in the composition of *Heartbreak House*. In a letter from Shaw to Virginia Woolf (10 May 1940) Shaw writes: 'There is a play of mine called *Heartbreak House* which I always connect with you because I conceived it in that house somewhere in Sussex where I first met you [in 1916] and, of course, fell in love with you. I suppose every man did.

always yours, consequently
"G. Bernard Shaw"'

Woolf replied that 'Your letter... reduced me to two days silence from sheer pleasure. You won't be surprised to hear that I promptly lifted some paragraphs and inserted them in my proofs. You may take what action you like.' [CL4: 557; Virginia Woolf, *The Diary of Virginia Woolf* (1982), vol. IV: 1931–35, eds

Anne Olivier Bell and Andrew McNeillie, 163–4; I&R 442; Dunbar 285; Wein2: 165]

August

3 (Thu) Roger Casement hanged, despite Shaw's contributions to the case for the defence and efforts to have Casement's death-sentence commuted. [Dunbar 285; I&R 229, 240–1; Wein2: 171]

7 Shaw drafts 'My Memories of Oscar Wilde' for Frank Harris, who publishes it in the second edition (1918) of his *Oscar Wilde: His Life and Confessions*. [Lbib1: 434; DHL]

12 Shaw begins *Augustus Does His Bit* 'for Madame Vandervelde, wife of the Belgian socialist minister, to be performed at a matinée in aid of the Belgians'. *Augustus* was Shaw's 'home-front playlet' satirizing wartime bureaucracy, officialdom and the government's call for dramatists to produce didactic theatre pieces to encourage wartime saving. Shaw was to say 'it isn't patriotic. Augustus does his bit energetically; but the consequences are of the most ruinous kind'. [CP5: 200, 227]

14 Publication of Leonard Woolf's book *International Government*. Shaw wrote a Preface to the American edition. Originally published as two supplements to *the New Statesman*, these were Woolf's findings on the causes of the war. Commissioned by the Fabian Society, Woolf's study put forward the first detailed proposal to establish a supranational body, thereby looking forward to the League of Nations. [Prefs2: 265–74; Hol2: 366–7; Lbib1: 130]

22 In a letter to Lady Gregory, Shaw writes: '[Charlotte] has had a brilliant idea concerning the Abbey Theatre… you should break new ground by playing Ibsen… Ibsen has always paid on the Abbey Street scale, though never on the London West End scale. The plays are cheap to stage: all domestic interiors.' [L&G 121]

23 Shaw completes *Augustus Does His Bit*. [CP5: 200]

September

While Charlotte Shaw is in Ireland, Shaw attends Rutland Boughton's musical festival in Glastonbury, then proceeds to the Fabian Summer School at the White Hart Hotel in Sedbergh, where he remains until 18 September. During this time, Shaw wrote to Lady Gregory: 'I refuse flatly to put foot in Ireland without a safe conduct from the present Terrorist Government.' [CL3: 411–18; DHL; Dent 215; Wein2: 173–4; L&G 122]

3 (Sun) Continuing his discussion of Ibsen, Shaw writes to Lady Gregory: 'I am with Synge in thinking that the Irish should do their own Ibsenizing; and in fact all your successes have been

nothing else than that as far as they have been concerned with the works of young Irishmen. But the present crisis has been produced by the drying-up for the moment of that source; and you are going to tide over the famine (mixed metaphor, that) by giving Dublin a turn of foreign work, including mine, of one sort or another.' [L&G 124]

14 Shaw receives news that Janet Achurch has died three days previously. She was buried in the same cemetery as Shaw's sister Agnes. Shaw wrote to Charles Charrington: 'Now Janet is again the Janet of 1889, and immortal. Better than half dead, like me.' [CL3: 415]

18 Shaw spends two days in Birmingham viewing Charles Macdona's repertory production of *Fanny's First Play*. [CL3: 418]

20 Shaw returns to London. [CL3: 418]

October

1 (Sun) At five minutes to midnight, Shaw and Charlotte witness the crash of a Zeppelin at Potter's Bar a few miles from Ayot. Shaw goes to see 'the wreck' on his motor cycle. Aspects of this incident are reflected in the composition of *Heartbreak House*. [CL3: 425–6; BL MS Add 56500; DHL; Wein2: 177–8]

5 Shaw resigns from the Board of the Statesman Publishing Company, alleging that *the New Statesman* has 'turned into a suburban Tory-Democratic rag'. [CL3: 422, 441; Wein2: 186]

A request is made to the Lord Chamberlain by the Plymouth Repertory Theatre for a licence to perform *Mrs Warren's Profession*. When the licence is refused Shaw writes to the Lord Chamberlain: 'About twenty years ago I wrote a play with certain public objects that were then considered quite outside the scope of the theatre... I had to go through the farce of changing Mrs Warren from a procuress to a trainer of thieves like Fagin in Oliver Twist. The play thus became a quite gratuitous Crook Drama, and was solemnly licensed and performed in that state. I think this has been forgotten at the Office, where – to be quite frank – I suspect them of making the point of honor not to give in about this particular play because I did not take its fate lying down.' [Theatrics 128–30]

7 First performance of *The Inca of Perusalem* at the Birmingham Repertory Theatre. [CP4: 950; CL3: 495; Wein2: 175; Morgan 104]

16 In an affronted reply to Frank Harris's suggestion that his plays are not passionate or sexual, Shaw writes: 'take this question of yours about sex. I know of no writer who has dealt as critically with sex as I have. Archer's early complaint that my plays reeked with sex was far more sensible than the virgin-eunuch

theory which the halfpenny journalists delight in... you have not seen my plays nor read them, not to mention their monumental prefaces, which also deal largely with this question of sex... you had better avoid the subject, as you will certainly botch it frightfully.' [Wein4: 53–4]

27 Shaw delivers a lecture on 'Life', the first in the Fabian series on 'The World in Chains'. [CL3: 439; Wein2: 189]

November

6 (Mon) First American production of *Getting Married* at the Booth Theater, New York. [Morgan 58]

18–20 Lady Gregory visiting the Shaws at Ayot St Lawrence records Shaw's reading of 'the first part of a play, very amusing, *The House in the Clouds* [*Heartbreak House*], but says he doesn't know how to finish it, it is so wild'. [*Lady Gregory's Journals 1916–1930*, ed. Lennox Robinson (1946), 202; DHL; I&R 243]

Autumn 1916 – summer 1917

Shaw revival at the Abbey Theatre. A similar revival of interest in Shaw's work took place in Europe and America. [Wein2: 185, 195–6]

December

1 (Fri) Shaw delivers a lecture on 'Religion,' the last in the Fabian series on 'The World in Chains'. [CL 3: 426, 439]

7 Florence Farr writes to Shaw informing him of the breast cancer she has which will eventually kill her. [BL 50533; Wein2: 206]

Lloyd George replaces Asquith as Prime Minister and reorganizes the Coalition. Shaw writes to Sidney Webb 'and Lloyd George is Prime Minister, God help him', adding 'However it is better to have Asquith and Grey in Opposition than where they were...' [CL3: 442–3; DBW3: 442]

23 Shaw gives all the Ayot schoolchildren a Christmas gift of one shilling's worth of credit with Mrs Ward, who kept the shop where sweets could be obtained. [DHL]

24 Shaw has the first of many lunches at Lamer Park, Apsley Cherry-Garrard's home, the grounds of which abutted those of Shaw's Corner. Lady Scott is also a guest. [DHL]

1917

In the opening days of this year Shaw receives an official invitation from Field-Marshal Sir Douglas (later Earl) Haig, Commander-in-Chief on the Western Front, to visit the British Front in France. He accepts the invitation and spends several days visiting a number of sites including Ypres, the Somme and Boulogne. He writes about his experiences in a three-part article, 'Joy Riding at the Front', published in March. During this winter Harley Granville Barker visits Ayot every Saturday. In April, Florence Farr dies in Ceylon, and is cremated according to Hindu tradition. In May, Shaw completes the writing of *Heartbreak House*. In September he meets Charlotte in Ireland, and uses the opportunity to visit Sir Horace Plunkett in an attempt to exert some influence upon the Irish Home Rule Convention held in Dublin that year.

January

1 (Mon) Shaw submits his 'Proposed Manifesto on Republicanism' to the Fabian Executive, calling for European monarchies to be replaced by republics and the formation in Britain of a Republican Party. [CL3: 448; Copy of the manifesto and accompanying letter in Fabian Society file, BLPES]
Shaw begins a new diary, which provides some revealing glimpses of his life at Ayot, but abandons it after 10 January. [D2: 1174–8]

2 Shaw begins writing his article 'What is to be done with the Doctors?' to be published in the *English Review*. [D2: 1175; Wein2: 283]

3 Shaw receives the letter from Florence Farr (7 December 1916) telling him she is in hospital in Colombo awaiting surgery for breast cancer. Shaw writes in his diary 'I began a letter to her, but broke off, resolving to cable for the latest news of her.' [D2: 1175; BL MS Add 50533 fol.111; CL3: 448]

4 Lucy Shaw tells Ann Elder about her wartime circumstances: 'I have got a little house at last [Sussex Lodge, Champion Hill, SE 5]: there is a country lane beside it in which there is a searchlight, so we shall always know when the Zepps are on the way. The light station is near enough to hear the officers giving orders. I am going to grow potatoes, peas and beans, as we shall have nothing to eat by the Summer.' [Farmer 233–5]

6 Shaw receives a written invitation from Field-Marshal Sir Douglas (later Earl) Haig, Commander-in-Chief on the Western Front, to visit the British Front in France. [D2: 1177; Douglas Haig, *The Private Papers of Douglas Haig 1914–1919*, ed. Robert Blake (1952), 194–5; I&R 248; Wein2: 213]

11 Shaw writes to H. G. Wells expressing his anxiety at the prospect of meeting censorship if he accepts the invitation to visit the Front: 'What I want you to tell me is whether they demand any pledges from you as to what you shall say or not say, and also whether the fact of your having been at the Front marks you out for special censorship even in respect of books. If that is the case, I wont go.' [CL3: 449]

21 First production of *Augustus Does His Bit* by the Stage Society at the Court Theatre, staged jointly with J. M. Synge's *The Tinker's Wedding*. [CP5: 200; CL3: 451; Wein2: 211; Morgan 104]

28 Shaw departs for a visit to the Front in France and Belgium. Journalist and author, Sir Philip Gibbs, who suggested the visit, records Shaw's double view of the war as they were going up to the Vimy Ridge: '"Gibbs," he said, "one's thoughts about this war run on parallel lines which can never meet. The first is that all this is a degradation of humanity, a great insanity, and a crime against civilisation....That's the first line of thought: and the second is that *We've got to beat the Boche!*"' Shaw sees his friends Robert Loraine and Sir Almroth Wright on this tour. [CL3: 448; Sir Philip Gibbs, *The Pageant of the Years: An Autobiography* (1946), 195–7; I&R 244, 246–7; Dunbar 253–6; Wein2: 214]

February

1 (Thu) Shaw lunches with Field-Marshal Sir Douglas Haig, who describes him as 'an interesting man of original views. A great talker!' [*The Private Papers of Douglas Haig 1914–1919*, ed. Robert Blake, (1952), 194; I&R 248]

5 Shaw returns to England, after spending the night in Boulogne as a guest of Sir Almroth Wright. [CL3: 448]

16 In a letter to Mary Cholmondeley, Charlotte Shaw relates Shaw's vivid accounts of his experiences at the Front. Shaw is based in 'one of those typical 17th.or 18th. Cent. big French country houses in a kind of park with a great avenue of splendid trees leading up to it'. He is 'very comfortable' there, but is exposed to both danger (from shelling) and extreme cold in expeditions by car to Ypres (where he rides in a tank), Amiens and Boulogne. [Dunbar 253–6; Brigadier-General C. D. Baker-Carr, *From Chauffeur to Brigadier* (1930), 208–9; I&R 246–50]

21 The first (amateur) production of *O'Flaherty V.C.*, probably directed by Robert Loraine, is mounted by officers of the Fortieth Squadron, Royal Flying Corps, on the Western Front at Treizennes in France, in a building christened the Theatre Royal. Shaw had seen a specially called rehearsal of the play on 3 February. The cast included Captain D. O. Mulholland as O'Flaherty and Lady Gregory's son, Captain Robert Gregory as Teresa Driscoll. On the same bill with *O'Flaherty V.C.* was another of Shaw's wartime one-act plays, *The Inca of Perusalem*, which was cast with ordinary soldiers. [DHL; Winifred Loraine, *Robert Loraine: Soldier, Actor, Airman* (1938), 237; Morgan 73]

March

The Russian Revolution.

5 (Mon), 7, 8 The *Daily Chronicle* publishes, in instalments, Shaw's acerbic article 'Joy Riding at the Front'. [Lbib2: 669; CL3: 448; Sir Philip Gibbs, *The Pageant of the Years: An Autobiography* (1946), 195–7; I&R 245, 246]

15 Shaw dines with art critic, Roger Fry. [DHL]

April

Harley Granville Barker and Lillah McCarthy's divorce is finalized, after a prolonged and bitter period of negotiations in which Shaw acts as a go-between. [Wein2: 260]

6 (Fri) America enters the war.

16 The Shaws dine with Lady Kathleen Scott who conveys Brigadier-General Charles Delme-Radcliffe's invitation to Shaw to visit the Italian front. [CL3: 463, 464]

23 Shaw declines the invitation to visit the Italian front. [CL3: 464]

29 Death of Florence Farr, aged 57, in Ceylon where she was Principal of the Ramanathan College. [Henrietta Paget to Shaw, 27 Jun 1917; BL MS Add 50533; Wein2: 206; CL3: 478; Peters 371]

May

2 (Wed) Maxim Gorky cables Shaw inviting him to contribute to a Socialist Russian daily, *Novoye Zhizn* (*New Life*). [Wein2: 240]

11 Shaw writes to his publishers, Constable & Co., suggesting that he had been owed a cheque for £1500 since 25 March. His letter opens with: 'Where's my money? How do you expect a poor author to live?' [CL3: 470]

12 Shaw finishes writing his latest play, tentatively titled by turns *Lena's Father, The Studio at the Clouds* or 'The Hushabye play'. [CL3: 408; I&R 244n]

20 Shaw alters the title of his new play to *Heartbreak House*. [CL3: 408]

21 May – 1 June

Shaw and the Webbs holiday at Logan Pearsall Smith's Elizabethan manor house at Big Chilling, Warsash, Hampshire. [Wein2: 243; DHL; DBW3: 279]

24 Shaw declines Maxim Gorky's invitation to contribute to the new Soviet paper *Novoye Zhizn* (*New Life*) saying 'in England we know nothing of Russia except that there has been a revolution, and that the differences between right, left and centre have created a situation of extreme difficulty and delicacy for the provisional government'. [CL3: 473–4]

June

27 (Wed) Shaw receives news of the death of Florence Farr. [CL3: 478; Peters 371]

July

21 (Sat) Robert Loraine and Robert Gregory drop in to Ayot in a surprise flight, and stay for dinner. [BL Ms Add 56500; DHL]

24 Shaw and H. G. Wells meet Arnold Bennett and Thomas Hardy at the home of J. M. Barrie in Adelphi Terrace. [*The Journal of Arnold Bennett* (1933), 633; I&R 251]

July–August

Having tried unsuccessfully to gain official appointment to the Irish Convention set up by Lloyd George's government to find solutions to the Home Rule controversy, Shaw participates at one remove by corresponding with the Convention Chairman, Sir Horace Plunkett, and his associates. [Morgan 10; I&R 508 n4; CL3: 478–9]

August

O'Flaherty V. C. published in *Hearst's Magazine*, New York. [Lbib1: 138]

4 (Sat) – 26 Shaw lectures and takes 12 dancing lessons at the Fabian Summer School at Godalming: 'Here I am, *only* 61, and learning to dance and tomfool like a youth... My flirtations are scandalous.' [CL3: 483, 503; DHL;Wein2: 260]

29 August–9 September

Shaw represents the Fabian Society at the Socialists' Allied Conference (International Socialist Bureau) held at Westminster, which he calls 'an absurd but international fiasco'. [CL3: 483; DHL]

September

3 (Mon) Shaw speaks to Canadian soldiers on any subject of their choice, their question being, 'Is the church essential to the realization of the Christian ethic?' [BLPES; DHL]

10 Shaw arrives in Ireland to join Charlotte at the Great Southern Hotel at Parknasilla, his plan to attend the International Socialist Conference in Stockholm having been upset by the government-influenced Trade Union Congress decision not to send British representatives. While the Shaws are in Ireland, Adelphi Terrace is damaged by air-raids. [CL3: 483, 505]

27 First American production of *Misalliance* at the Broadhurst Theater, New York. [Morgan 62]

October

2 (Tue) Shaw dispatches to Hugo Vallentin a proof of *Heartbreak House*, 'the first that has left my hands'. [CL3: 505]

13 Shaw moves from Parknasilla to Dublin for ten days' visit with Sir Horace Plunkett at Foxrock before returning to England.

Shaw hopes he will be invited to be one of the proposed one hundred delegates to attend the Irish Convention. He is not invited, and has to be content to 'attempt an indirect influence' while staying with Plunkett, the Convention's chair. [CL3: 505, 517; Wein2: 264]

23 — Shaw and Sir Horace Plunkett are invited to inspect the Royal Irish Constabulary Training Depot and to lunch with a general – an arrangement that does not please Shaw. [Shaw to Rachel Mahaffy, 23 Oct 1917, Trinity College Dublin; DHL]

November

9 (Fri), 30 — Shaw delivers the third and sixth lectures, 'Heredity and Democracy' and 'The Reconciliation of Uniformity with Diversity', in the Fabian series on 'The Britannic Alliance and World Politics'. The former lecture examines issues pursued in *Saint Joan, The Apple Cart* and *In Good King Charles's Golden Days*. [Wein2: 270–3]

26 — Shaw reads *O'Flaherty V. C.* at the Stuarts Hospital (London) to 250 wounded soldiers who 'laughed a good deal; but the best bits were when they sat very tight and said nothing'. [CL3: 517]

27–29 — The *Daily Express* and papers in Ireland, USA and Canada publish Shaw's three-part article, 'How to Settle the Irish Question'. [Lbib2: 672]

December

Early — Shaw directs a production at the Criterion of *The Inca of Perusalem* by the Pioneer Players, a company founded by Ellen Terry's daughter Edith Craig. [Wein2: 275–6; DHL]

3 (Mon) — In a terse reply to a request from Lady Gregory to lecture while in Ireland, Shaw writes: 'As to the lecture, NO. The very words nation, nationality, our country, patriotism, fill me with loathing. Why do you want to stimulate a self-consciousness which is... deluging Europe with blood? If only we could forget for a moment that we are Irish, and become really Catholic Europeans, there would be some hope for us...' [L&G 136]

4–7 — Shaw writes *Annajanska, the Bolshevik Empress.* [I&R 295; CP5: 230]

9 — Shaw spends an evening of conversation and dancing at Lamer Park. Sculptor, Lady Kennet, widow of Captain Scott, who was also present recalls: 'Shaw told stories of his dreams, and how since he was quite little he has always told himself a story each night before he goes to bed, and some, he said, go on as serials, but others he tells himself over and over again. After dinner we danced and Shaw gave a lesson, both practical and demonstrative.' [Lady Kennet, *Self-Portrait of an Artist: From the Diaries and Memoirs of Lady Kennet, Kathleen, Lady Scott* (1949), 160–1; I&R 11–12]

11 First American production of *Augustus Does His Bit* by amateurs at Polio's Theater, Washington. [Morgan 104]

16 At the first performance of *The Inca of Perusalem*, Shaw again meets Ellen Terry. [Peters 386; Wein2: 276–7]

1918

In March of this year Shaw begins writing *Back to Methuselah*. Both Stella Campbell and Lady Gregory lose sons in the war. Harley Granville Barker's second marriage in July, to Helen Huntington, draws him away from his old theatre associates and destroys his friendship with Charlotte Shaw. With the dissolution of Parliament by Lloyd George after the Armistice, Shaw becomes involved in election campaigning on behalf of Labour and Fenian candidates. *Bernard Shaw: The Man and His Work* by Herbert Skimpole (Julius Herman) is published during this year.

At the General Election, Lloyd George's Liberal–Conservative coalition was elected to office. The Labour Party became for the first time the official opposition party, having gained the second largest representation in the House of Commons. Shaw was to cancel almost all engagements as soon as the election was called, and was to assist in both Fabian and Labour campaign meetings prior to the election.

January

7 (Mon) Stella Campbell to Shaw: 'My beloved Beo is killed...' (i.e. Lt-Com. Alan Hugh Campbell, Stella's son). Shaw responded in a letter saying 'Killed just because people are blasted fools.' [Dent 223; CL3: 525; Peters 374]

21 First performance of *Annajanska, the Bolshevik Empress*, directed by Shaw, at the Coliseum Theatre in a variety bill. This is Shaw's last theatre association with Lillah McCarthy. [CP5: 230; DHL; Morgan 104]

February

Food rationing introduced in Britain. [DBW3: 442]

Shaw falls down the stairs while in the throes of ptomaine poisoning, which Weintraub ascribes to an overdose of phosphorus in a synthetic egg compound. [Dent 224; Wein2: 285]

Bertrand Russell is arrested for publishing an anti-war article. Despite Shaw's advice on how to conduct an irrefutable defence, Russell spends the rest of the war in Brixton Prison. [Wein2: 287–9]

5 (Tue) Shaw learns of the death of Lady Gregory's son at the North Italian front. [CL3: 526–7]

15 Shaw speaks in Red Lion Square [Conway Hall?] on William Morris as a Socialist. [DHL]

March

9 (Sat) Shaw calls on Isadora Duncan at 8 Duke St, W1. [DHL]

19 Shaw begins *Back to Methuselah* beginning with Part II, whose working title, *The Adelphians*, he soon changes to *The Gospel of the Brothers Barnabas*. [CL3: 547; CP5: 252; BL MS Add 56500; I&R 295; Wein2: 298]

April

9 (Tue) Shaw completes the first draft of *The Brothers Barnabas*. [Wein2: 298]

May

1 (Wed) Shaw begins revising *The Brothers Barnabas*. [Wein2: 298]

10 Shaw delivers a speech on 'The Climate and Soil for Labour Culture' as part of a Fabian series on 'The Labour Party; Its Program and Its Possibilities'. [Wein2: 290]

16 Shaw completes his first draft of *The Thing Happens* in the *Back to Methuselah* cycle. [Wein2: 304]

22 Shaw writes to St John Ervine after being notified by the chaplain of No. 8 Stationary Hospital in Boulogne that, as a consequence of shell wounds, Ervine has suffered an amputation of a leg: 'For a man of your profession two legs are an extravagance.' [CL3: 551]

31 The Wellses come to lunch with the Shaws. [DHL]

June

21 (Fri) Harley Granville Barker introduces the Shaws to Helen Huntington, his future wife. [CL3: 551]

29 Lady Kennet (formerly Lady Scott) dines with Shaw at Lamer, and is surprised at his singing and piano-playing skills, demonstrated in his rendition of Wagner's *Rheingold*: 'Shaw came to dinner. He amazed me. I have known him for fifteen years, and this was the first time I knew he sang. He went almost all through the score of Rheingold on the piano, singing in a charming baritone voice. He plays amazingly well. He is a marvellous man.' [*Self-Portrait of an Artist: From the Diaries and Memoirs of Lady Kennet, Kathleen, Lady Scott* (1949), 166]

30 The Fabian Research Department, which Shaw chaired, officially dissolved and became the Labour [Party] Research Department. [Wein2: 310]

July

10 (Wed) Shaw addresses an 'at Home' meeting of the Westminster Labour Party. [CL3: 553]

26 July – early September

Shaw sits for ten days for Lady Kennet at Streatley while she sculpts a bust and a full-length figure. He then holidays for ten days (6–15 August) with the Webbs at Presteign in Wales, from where he proceeds to the Fabian Summer School (15 August – 10 September) at Penlee in Devon. On 29 July he makes a mid-summer excursion to London to see a charity performance of Byron's *Manfred* at Drury Lane. [CL3: 561; DHL; Wein2: 312]

31 Harley Granville Barker marries Helen Huntington who draws him away from all his old theatre associates. Shaw knew nothing of the wedding, writing weeks later 'I surmise that you are married, but it is only a surmise.' Judy Gillmore recalls that 'Charlotte's affection for [Granville] Barker turned to hate. After his marriage to Helen and desertion of the Shaws, Charlotte, deeply hurt and frustrated, became violently antithetical – deliberately referring to him as Harley Barker, omitting the Granville. She ordered his portrait to be removed from the wall of Shaw's bedroom at Whitehall Court after discovering Judy had hung it there on the removal from Adelphi Terrace to get it off the floor.' [Guelph; Wein2: 315; Peters 399–400; Hol2: 399; DHL; CL3: 561]

August

8 (Thu) Lucy Shaw is forced to move from Sussex Lodge to Devonshire by the air-raids and by the firing of an anti-aircraft gun situated just outside her garden. [Farmer 237–8]

September

7 (Sat) Shaw rejoins Charlotte at Parknasilla, where he writes the recruiting pamphlet, 'War Issues for Irishmen'. [CL 3: 561; Wein2: 317–19]

October

3 (Thu) – 11 The Shaws visit Lady Gregory at Coole Park (Shaw's last visit there), then proceed to Lucan for nine days before visiting Sir Horace Plunkett at Foxrock, outside Dublin, from 19–30 October. Shaw was to write to Lady Gregory later: 'I found Dublin loquacious as ever, and damnably dull after Coole, as there was nobody nearly as good company as you.' [CL3: 566, 568, 574; Nicholas Grene, 'Shaw in Ireland: Visitor or Returning Exile?' in SA 53]

13 Shaw speaks at a debate in the Abbey Theatre between G.K. Chesterton and Thomas Johnston, Belfast Labour Representative on the Anti-Conscription Conference, on the topic 'That private property is necessary to the welfare of mankind'. [*The Irish Times*, 14 October 1918]

23 Shaw visits his childhood friend Ada Tyrrell (née Shaw), whom he hasn't seen for decades, at 4 Sandford Terrace, Dublin. [DHL]

26 Under the auspices of the Dublin Literary Society, Shaw delivers

a lecture on 'Literature in Ireland' in the Little Theatre, Dublin. He says, among other things, that 'there never was a more tremendous delusion than the Gaelic League is modern Ireland.' [DHL; *Irish Times*, 28 Oct 1918; *Freeman's Journal*, 28 Oct 1918]

November

3 (Sun) Shaw dispatches to the printer his open letter, 'War Issues for Irishmen', written at the request of the Irish recruiting authorities to stimulate voluntary enlistment. The letter was printed but never distributed due to the Armistice announcement. [CL3: 569]

11 The Shaws spend Armistice Day at Ayot. [CL3: 573]

Mid Lloyd George announces the dissolution of Parliament and fixes the General Election on 14 December. [CL3: 574]

21 Lucy Shaw returns to Sussex Lodge, Champion Hill. She writes that 'I only did it by a super-supreme effort of will as... I did not want to die in Okehampton... At present, visitors are forbidden, as I am not able to talk.' [Farmer 240]

27 Shaw dines at the Webbs' where he meets Aleksandr Kerenski – the Russian revolutionary who became leader of the provisional government soon after the revolution took place. [CL3: 574]

29 Shaw delivers his annual Fabian lecture, on the topic 'Jingoism and Pacifism in the New Parliament', published in *The Nation*, 30 November. [Lbib2: 675; CL3: 574]

December

14–28 The Sinn Féin ('We Ourselves') Party wins 73 seats at the Irish election. Boycotting Westminster, they set up their own assembly, Dáil Eireann, in Dublin, representing a completely independent Republic of Ireland.

Early Shaw embarks on a two-week electioneering tour of the Midlands, to speak on behalf of Ramsay MacDonald and other Labour and Fabian candidates. [CL3: 574]

14 Lloyd George's coalition wins decisively in the election. Although Ramsay MacDonald and other Labour candidates lose their seats, Labour becomes the official opposition party.
Shaw attends a requiem for Cecil Chesterton at Corpus Christi, Maiden Lane. [DHL]

1919

Shaw's *Peace Conference Hints* is published early in this year, with the intention of influencing the treaty negotiations at Versailles. With the war finally over, Shaw's plays begin to re-emerge on the English stage, with *Arms and the Man* being his first West End production in five years. Shaw continues to write *Back to Methuselah*, which he does not finish until May the following year. *Great Catherine* and *The Music-Cure* are published in translation in Germany.

January

2 (Thu) Shaw speaks at an Albert Hall demonstration to support Woodrow Wilson and the League of Nations. [DHL]

3 While Shaw is in London, Charlotte spends the weekend with Harley Granville Barker and Helen Huntington at Darent Hulme. [BL MS Add 56500; DHL]

19 January – 23 March

Shaw's *Peace Conference Hints* published in weekly instalments in the *New York American*. [Lbib1: 137]

February

14 (Fri) Shaw completes Act I of *In the Beginning* – the first play of the *Back to Methuselah* cycle. [Wein2: 298]

16 Death of Shaw's old friend, Kate Salt. Shaw responded in a letter, saying 'The loss of one's wife after ten years is only the end of an adventure. After thirty it is the end of an epoch. From that time on it becomes more and more the end of everything.' [CL3: 590]

March

1 (Sat) – 3 Lady Gregory staying with the Shaws at Ayot St Lawrence records Shaw's account on the previous night (2 March) at the Cherry-Garrard house, Lamer, of *Back to Methuselah*: 'A wonderful and fantastic play he is writing beginning in the Garden of Eden before Adam and Eve, with Lilith who finds lonely immortality impossible to face and so gives herself up to be divided into Man and Woman. He read a scene from it [from Part IV] about a thousand years in the future with the Irish coming back to kiss the earth of Ireland and not liking it when they see it.'

At lunch on 3 March Lady Gregory talks of Shaw's writing habits: 'I told G. B. S that I had heard the cheerful little ticking of his typewriter like chickens picking their way out of the egg, and had listened with joy as I used to when I heard a purring from Yeats's room. He [Shaw] composes on the typewriter from shorthand notes.' [*Lady Gregory's Journals 1916–1930*, ed. Lennox Robinson (1946), 202–3; DHL; I&R 302]

7 Shaw attends a rehearsal of two of Sir Edward Elgar's recently completed works, but must leave prematurely to chair a meeting of the Fabian Research executive. [CL3: 592]

12 *Peace Conference Hints* published in book form by Constable. [Lbib1: 137; I&R 352]

April Lucy Shaw has been forced to move from Sussex Lodge when the lease expires, but Shaw bought the lease of Champion Cottage almost opposite it. The move is accomplished, but Lucy is very ill. [Farmer 240]

1 (Tue) Shaw visits Oundle School with H. G. Wells (whose sons attended the school) to see an all-boy production of *Arms and the Man*. [DHL]

26 Shaw spends the weekend with the Wellses at Easton Glebe, and attends a local performance of *The Taming of the Shrew* at 'The Barn'. [DHL]

30 Shaw attends the wedding of Elizabeth Asquith to Prince Bibesco at St. Mary's. [DHL]

May Albert Kilsby having retired in 1917, Shaw engages Fred Day as his chauffeur at Ayot, a post he fills for 31 years. [*Shaw the Villager and Human Being: A Biographical Symposium*, ed. Allan Chappelow (1961), 37–41; I&R 205]

15 (Thu) Shaw lectures in the Hampstead Town Hall on 'The Present Predicament of the Theatre' to aid Norman Macdermott's Everyman Theatre, a venture designed to revive experimental theatre in the suburbs, thus avoiding the prohibitive rents of central London. [CL3: 587]

June

4 (Wed) Shaw threatens to resign from the Shakespeare Memorial Committee if approval is given for Bridges-Adams to play abridged versions of Shakespeare's plays. [CL3: 611]

28 The Treaty of Versailles.

July

4 (Fri) – 26 August The Shaws spend the summer at Parknasilla, Co. Kerry. [CL3: 623, 632–3; DHL]

July

20 (Sun) Shaw writes to Trebitsch, saying 'now that the war is officially over, I have applied to the Board of Trade for a licence to "trade" with you. I doubt whether I shall get it before Austria ratifies the treaty and puts an end to the state of war between us.' [CL3: 624]

August

7 (Thu) Shaw repudiates Thomas Demetrius O'Bolger's account of his early life, especially O'Bolger's vilification of Bessie Shaw. [CL3: 625–31]

27–30 Shaw attends the Glastonbury Music Festival. [DHL]

September

3 (Wed) – 12 While Charlotte remains in Ireland, Shaw travels to Penlee on the Devonshire coast to participate in the activities of Fabian Summer School where he delivers the first public reading of part one of *Back to Methuselah: In the Beginning.* [C. E. M. Joad, *Shaw* (1949), 35–6; I&R 303; CL3: 633; Wein2: 297–8]

16 *Heartbreak House, Great Catherine and Playlets of the War* published in New York. The 'playlets' included in this publication were *The Inca of Perusalem, O'Flaherty V. C., Augustus Does His Bit* and *Annajanska, the Bolshevik Empress.* [CL3: 633; Lbib1: 137]

23 *Heartbreak House, Great Catherine* and *Playlets of the War* published in London. There was a textual variation between the American and English prefaces to *Heartbreak House.* [CL3: 633]

September–October

Publication in Germany of *Die grosse Katharina: fünf Einakter*, containing translations of *Great Catherine* and *The Music-Cure.* [Lbib1: 139]

October

15 (Wed) Shaw declines an invitation to stand for parliament in Northampton. He writes to W. J. Bassett-Lowke, saying 'I am in my sixtyfourth year; and it is now too late to begin a parliamentary career, even if there were any serious likelihood of any borough being wise to elect me.' [CL3: 639]

18 Shaw refuses William Archer's request to help him finish *The Green Goddess*, assuring Archer he is capable of doing a first-rate job on his own. The play was an enormous success both in London and New York, and was twice filmed. [CL3: 639–40; DHL]

20 Shaw delivers an ultimatum to Harper Bros. regarding O'Bolger's book: either drop the book or submit to Shaw's conditions. [CL3: 641–2]

31 During a stay in London, Italian-German composer and pianist Ferruccio Busoni has Shaw to tea (which Shaw does not drink). They discuss Mozart, Wagner, and Shaw's work in progress, *Back to Methuselah.* Busoni finds Shaw witty, lively and sharp, but likens him to Danish critic Georg Brandes in 'excessive talkativeness and the accompanying self-satisfaction', and concludes tartly: 'Shaw loves the people *theoretically* (his telegraphic address is "Socialist", London). He is certainly a great egotist himself. Now he is training to become a second Methuselah, and plays at being a "lively youth".' [Ferrucio Busoni, *Letters to his Wife*, trans. Rosamund Ley (1938), 279–81; I&R 222–3]

November

7 (Fri) Shaw fails to sell the Carlow Assembly Rooms, and is once again embroiled in the problems of landlordism. He plays cantankerous benefactor while paying bakery bills and buying coal for his impoverished tenants. Writing to his land agent William Fitzmaurice, Shaw was to say 'Mrs Aylward is incorrigible. I am repairing her cistern and keeping her roof and gutters in order; and there is no more reason why I should pay for her ~~burial~~ barrel than for her bucket. However, anything for a quiet life.' [Carlow County Library]

9 Lady Gregory visits the Shaws at Ayot St Lawrence, finding the house 'full of comfort and fires'. In the evening Shaw reads from G. K. Chesterton's *Irish Impressions*, which he was reviewing for the *Irish Statesman*. Discussing Dublin statues, Shaw tells Lady Gregory of one of his childhood dreams in which God appeared to him 'in the form of the statue of William III in College Green'. [*Lady Gregory's Journals 1916–1930*, ed. Lennox Robinson (1946) 204; I&R 12; Lbib2: 681]

14 Shaw gives a one-minute filmed interview to Aron Hamburger, managing director of Science and Art Films. [CL3: 644]
Androcles and the Lion revived at the Abbey Theatre. [Morgan 67]

21 Shaw lectures on 'Ruskin's Politics' at a Royal Academy Ruskin exhibition. [DHL]

December

4 (Thu) Shaw attends a Georges Carpentier–Joe Beckett prize fight. His report is published as 'The Great Fight' in *The Nation* (London) 13 December [Lbib2: 681; DHL]

11 Shaw's first West End production in almost five years, a revival of *Arms and the Man*, opens at the Duke of York's Theatre. Although he had staged the production, Shaw had an engagement to lecture elsewhere that night. [CL3: 645, 646]

13 Shaw attends a matinée of Robert Loraine's production *Arms and the Man*, which opened two nights earlier, and is appalled to find the actors visibly intent on scoring laughs. [CL3: 646]

1920

Mrs Patrick Campbell performs in a revival of *Pygmalion* opening on 10 February. In March, Shaw's sister Lucy dies in his arms. *Heartbreak House*, produced by the Theater Guild of New York, makes its world première at the Garrick Theater in New York in November of this year. Shaw finishes writing what he regarded as his 'magnum opus', *Back to Methuselah*, and Henry Charles Duffin publishes *The Quintessence of Bernard Shaw*.

January

	Shaw alienates Robert Loraine by asking whether he was taking morphia while playing in *Arms and the Man*. [CL3: 651–3]
Early	Viola Tree, theatre manager and daughter of Sir Herbert Beerbohm Tree, proposes a revival of *Pygmalion* with Mrs Patrick Campbell at the Aldwych Theatre. Shaw supervises the rehearsals, which begin on 19 January. The first performance is on 10 February. [CL3: 653, 657–70, 661–5; DHL]

February

3 (Tue)	Concerned at mis-interpretation of the relationship in *Pygmalion* between Higgins and Eliza (as had occurred in the 1914 production), Shaw writes a letter to his Spanish translator, Julio Brouta, advising him: 'It is important that the actor who plays Higgins should thoroughly understand that he is not Eliza's lover. You must write a line for him to end the play on. When he is left alone on the stage at the end he should first go out on the balcony and look down, making it clear that he is watching Eliza's departure in the carriage. He then comes back into the room, excited and triumphant, and exclaims "Finished, and come to life! Bravo, Pygmalion!"' [Shaw to Julio Brouta, 3 Feb 1920, Harvard]
4, 5	Shaw is concerned that Mrs Patrick Campbell's arrogant fits of temperament will leave her unprepared for the upcoming opening of *Pygmalion*. He writes several pages of detailed theatrical notes to her. 'Now comes the most important point of all. When Eliza emancipates herself – when Galatea comes to life – she must not relapse. She must retain her pride and triumph to the end. When Higgins takes your arm on "consort battleship" you must instantly throw him off with implacable pride; and this is the note until the final "Buy them yourself". He will go out on the balcony to watch your departure; come back triumphantly into the room; exclaim "Galatea!"... Thus he gets the last word; and you get it too...' [CL3: 662–5; Theatrics 153–5]
10	Opening of the revived *Pygmalion* at the Aldwych. [CL3: 662, 665]
23	Mrs Patrick Campbell visits Lucy Shaw and, shocked by her condition, writes to Shaw: 'Eva seemed to think it would give Lucy joy to see you for a minute. I have hired a car for four weeks so I could take you if [you] cared about my doing so...' [Farmer 241–2]

March

5 (Fri)	Substituting for Gordon Craig, theatre designer, director and son of Ellen Terry, Shaw speaks on 'Art Under Democracy' at an Art Workers' Guild meeting. [CL3: 681]

27 Having attended Lillah McCarthy's wedding in the morning, and Ann Elder's wedding in the afternoon, Shaw is present at the death of his sister Lucy Shaw in the early evening. On the following day Shaw exclaims to Stella Campbell: 'What a day – yesterday! Bride's kisses at 11 (Lillah); bride's kisses at Eliza's church at 3 (my secretary); and at 5 Lucy died in my arms.' [CL3: 672; Dent 236–7; Hend3: 807; Farmer 243; Ross 352]

28 Shaw outrages Edward McNulty by suggesting he sell the piano left him by Lucy Shaw, with whom McNulty had remained close friends since their early Dublin days. [CL3: 673]

31 Funeral, cremation and scattering of Lucy Shaw's ashes. The funeral is well attended despite his having failed to issue invitations, or to place obituary notices in the daily or theatrical press. Shaw improvises a funeral oration, finishing with the dirge from *Cymbeline*. [CL3: 674; Farmer 248–50]

April

2 (Fri) The Shaws leave Ayot by car to visit Sir Horace Plunkett in Ireland. [CL3: 674]

10 The Shaws start for home, spending two days at Lucan on the way. [CL3: 674]

May

3 (Mon) – 7 Shaw attends a British Music Association Congress, and speaks on Municipal Music. [DHL]

27 Shaw finishes his first draft of the pentalogy *Back to Methuselah* which he revises across the summer. [CL3: 687]

June

3 (Thu) Shaw offers Blanche Patch the job of secretary, claiming 'my own has gone and got married on me'. After declining initially, she accepts Shaw's offer, taking up her post in July. [CL3: 676–8]

10 Edward McNulty acknowledges safe delivery to Ireland of the piano Lucy Shaw bequeathed to him, and Shaw shipped from London. [DHL]

18 Shaw debates with Gordon Craig, innovative set designer, on stage decoration and costume. [CL3: 681]

20 Shaw meets Leonid Krassin, head of a Russian trade delegation. [CL4: 103]

21 First American production of *O'Flaherty V. C.* at the 39th Street Theater, New York. [Morgan 73]

July

9 (Fri) Shaw attends Harriet Cohen's private piano recital of music by her lover Arnold Bax, at Swiss Cottage. Shaw and Cohen

become friends and she introduces him to Sir Edward Elgar socially. [DHL]

16 Ann (Elder) Jackson departs from London. [DHL]

19 The Shaws begin another stay at Parknasilla, till 23 September. [CL3: 687; DHL; Weiss 212]

Late Blanche Patch takes up duties as Shaw's secretary, a post she fills until Shaw's death. [CL3: 678]

August

Shaw corresponds with Lee Simonson, scenic designer and a founding member of the Theatre Guild of New York, regarding the set of the upcoming première of *Heartbreak House* in New York. [CL3: 685–7]

August or September

During August or September, Shaw begins 'translating' Trebitsch's play *Frau Gittas Sühne* (*Jitta's Atonement*). Shaw wrote to Trebitsch 'The difficulty has been that I do not know German, and mainly that apparently you do not know it either; for not one of your words could I find in the little pocket dictionary I travelled with… and I had to guess what it was all about by mere instinct.' [CL3: 687–8; CP5: 718]

September

15 (Wed) Shaw says in his letter to Trebitsch: 'At last I have sent the entire work [*Back to Methuselah*] (five plays and a colossal preface) to the printer.' [CL3: 687]

28 Having returned to Ayot, Shaw dispatches a rough draft of Act I of *Jitta's Atonement* to Trebitsch, owning that 'it might be an advantage for the translator to know the language the piece is written in'. [CL3: 690–1]

October

1 (Fri) Concealing his annoyance that Shaw has taken liberties he would not have tolerated from his own translators, Trebitsch permits Shaw to complete *Jitta's Atonement*. [CL3: 691]

15 A memorandum in Shaw's holograph: 'The freehold of the New Rectory [at Ayot St Lawrence] passed to me on the 15th October 1920.' [Cornell (Burgunder Collection); DHL]

21 In response to the New York director Emmanuel Reicher's suggestion of cuts to *Heartbreak House*, Shaw cables 'Abandon play, cancel contract, advance will be returned, writing'. The Theatre Guild backs down immediately. Reicher was immediately replaced by Dudley Digges. [CL3: 694]

30 Robert Bridges-Adams, Shakespearean director, calls to meet Shaw. [DHL]

November

10 (Wed) World première of *Heartbreak House* by the Theater Guild at the Garrick Theater in New York. [CP5: 10; CL3: 694; Morgan 74; Weiss 221; Wall 141]

29 Shaw speaks at the Tolstoy celebration in the Kingsway Hall on Tolstoy as dramatist. [DHL]

Late Lawrence Langner, founder and director of the Theater Guild, New York, which had just staged the world première of *Heartbreak House*, visited Shaw in England with the aim of obtaining a contract allowing the Guild to produce all Shaw's plays in America. [Lawrence Langner, *GBS and the Lunatic* (1964), 29–30; I&R 296–7]

December

2 (Thu) Shaw reads *O'Flaherty V. C.* to Arthur Sinclair and Maire O'Neill, who were to perform it for the Stage Society on 19 December, but O'Neill is replaced by her sister, Sara Allgood. [DHL]

3 Shaw speaks at the King's Hall on the Webbs' *Constitution for the Socialist Commonwealth of Great Britain*. [Weiss 220]

17 Shaw attends a demonstration by Diana Watts, dancer and lecturer on longevity, on 'beauty in movement as a living art'. [CL3: 771]

19–20 First British production of *O'Flaherty V. C.* by the Stage Society at the Lyric Theatre, Hammersmith. [CP4: 984; Morgan 73]

December 1920 – January 1921

Shaw writes an introduction to the Webbs' *English Prisons under Local Government*, an essay later issued separately as *Imprisonment* (1925). [Erv 535; DHL]

1921

In January, Shaw declines Mrs Patrick Campbell's request to play in *Heartbreak House*, and in February *Great Catherine* is revived for a charity performance at the Shaftsbury Theatre. In the first week of April, Shaw begins a two-week holiday in North Wales, which is followed by a four-week electioneering tour which includes Newcastle, where he sees *Man and Superman*. In May, Lady Gregory visits the Shaws at Ayot. In June, Shaw finishes his translation of Trebitsch's *Frau Gittas Sühne* which he entitles *Jitta's Atonement*. In August, Shaw attends the Fabian Summer School in Surrey, followed by the Labour Research Department Summer School in Kent. The London première of *Heartbreak House* at the Court Theatre takes place in October. In December, Shaw is surprised and horrified at Mrs Patrick Campbell's proposal to include his most intimate letters to her in a publication of their correspondence. During the late summer of this year Shaw meets Molly Tompkins.

January

18 (Tue) – 29 Mrs Patrick Campbell pleads with Shaw to let her play in *Heartbreak House*. Shaw refuses. They still write frequently and address each other as 'Dear Joey' and 'Belovedest'. [Dent 250–3]

24 Shaw speaks against the opening of theatres on Sundays in a British Drama League debate. [CL3: 708]

February

10 (Thu) Shaw speaks at a meeting of the Performing Animals Defence League. (He is especially opposed to rodeos and bullfights.) [DHL]

18 Gertrude Kingston revives *Great Catherine* for a charity performance at the Shaftesbury Theatre. [CL3: 705]

April

6 (Wed) – 19 Shaw takes two weeks' holiday, principally at Harlech in North Wales. [CL3: 715; DHL]

20 Shaw leaves Harlech on a four-week electioneering tour which takes him to Shrewsbury, Nottingham, Sunderland, Easington, Newcastle (where he sees a production of *Man and Superman*), Middlesbrough, Edinburgh and Dumfries. [CL3: 715, 723; DHL; Neville Veitch, *Newcastle Journal*, 3 Nov 1950; I&R 107]

Spring

Lawrence Langner, a founding member of the Theater Guild, turns up at Adelphi Terrace proposing to stage *Back to Methuselah* in its entirety at the Garrick Theater. Lawrence [Langner, *GBS and the Lunatic* (1964), 32–55; CL3: 726]

May

13 (Fri) – 18 Lady Gregory visits the Shaws at Ayot St Lawrence. [*Lady Gregory's Journals*, vol. I, ed. Daniel J. Murphy, Coole Ed. XIV (1978), 253–4; DHL; I&R 80]

June

11 (Sat) Shaw writes to Sylvia Beach, publisher of James Joyce's *Ulysses*: 'I have read several fragments of *Ulysses* in its serial form. It is a revolting record of a disgusting phase of civilisation; but it is a truthful one.' [CL3: 719]

16 Shaw sends an inscribed copy of *Back to Methuselah* to Lenin. [CL 4: 103]

July

7 (Thu) Father Joseph Leonard, who later gives Shaw much research assistance with *Saint Joan*, lunches with the Shaws. [DHL]

14 The Shaws attend Robert Loraine's wedding at St George's, Hanover Square. [*The Times*, 15 Jul 1921]

Late summer

Molly Tompkins accosts Shaw outside Adelphi Terrace. Having been invited in for buttered crumpets, she describes her plan to establish a Shavian theatre. [Peters 381]

August

6 (Sat) Shaw completes *Jitta's Atonement*. [CL3: 690]

20–26 Shaw spends a week at Godalming in Surrey at the Fabian Summer School. [CL3: 729]

27 August – 3 September

Shaw attends the Labour Research Department Summer School at Herne Bay in Kent. [CL3: 729]

13 September – 17 October

Shaw directs the Court Theatre production of *Heartbreak House*. [CL3: 736; DHL]

September

18 (Sun) Thomas O'Bolger writes to Shaw, complaining that Shaw caused his publishing problems, and of the limits Shaw had placed on letters etc. that he had placed at O'Bolger's disposal. O'Bolger sends Shaw the manuscript, saying he will: 'turn it over with your approval to the next publisher to whom I submit it, provided only that you do not emasculate it... Failing your liking for either of these plans I shall publish the manuscript myself through the University vehicles...As to your letters, I have tried to protect you on them for nine years for I recognized that there was material in some of them that might not make the most judicious kind of publication. You yourself urged me many times to sell the letters. I shall do so, but I hereby offer you the first opportunity to buy them. It seems to me that if you wish to keep them private this is the best course for you to pursue.' [O'Bolger to Shaw, 18 Sep 1921, Harvard]

October

18 (Tue) London première of *Heartbreak House* at the Court Theatre. '[T]he production was hurried under financial pressure', and interrupted by a mechanical breakdown. The critical reviews were unfavourable. [CL3: 738, 740, 748; Morgan 74]

20 Shaw instructs James Fagan, manager of the Court Theatre, to cut some 65 specified lines from Act III of *Heartbreak House*. [CL3: 738]

November

10 (Thu) The Shaws dine at Adelphi Terrace with the American scenic designer, Lee Simonson and his wife. [CL3: 750]
Shaw writes to O'Bolger, refusing permission for him to publish his manuscript as it stands: 'I was not looking out for any libels on myself; but if you have been half as inaccurate and inventive... you will let your publisher in for fabulous damages. You are quite mistaken in supposing that you have confined yourself to a paraphrase of what I wrote to you. Your imagination has filled up the gaps between my facts in the most amazing manner... [and] its bias has been always disparaging... I should not only be vouching for the accuracy of your history, but sanctioning the attack on my parents.' [Shaw to O'Bolger, 10 Nov 1921, Harvard; CL3: 746]

11 Alice Sharpe (Junior) calls on Shaw. She is the first-born of Shaw's 1880s flame, Alice Lockett. [DHL]

25 The critics attend a specially arranged matinée performance of *Heartbreak House*. Shaw addresses the audience at the end of the play. [T. F. Evans, *Shaw: The Critical Heritage* (1976), 252–5; CL3: 748; Beverley Baxter, *Sketch*, 22 Nov 1950; I&R 297–9]

December

Treaty with Ireland marks the end of Irish unity. [DBW3: 443]

2 (Fri) Overestimating Mrs Patrick Campbell's discretion, Shaw makes a gentleman's agreement to waive his copyright over whatever portion of his letters Stella might judge fit to publish in her autobiography. [Dent 261]

10 *Heartbreak House* closes. [CL3: 748]

24 Mrs Patrick Campbell dispatches to Shaw the letters she intends to publish. Shaw, horrified to see that his most passionate intimacies are included, urges her repeatedly over the coming weeks not to publish them or, if she must, to let him edit them. [CL3: 755–7; Peters 375–6; Dent 266–70]

1922

Shaw begins the year in a frustrating exchange with Mrs Patrick Campbell over the publication of their correspondence. In February, *Back to Methuselah* is presented by the Theater Guild at the Garrick Theater in New York as two three-week cycles, although it runs at a loss due to the size of the theatre. In March, the Shaws meet T. E. Lawrence (Lawrence of Arabia), with whom Charlotte will enter a long-term correspondence. In April, the Shaws visit North Wales and Stratford-upon-Avon, during which time they help edit Apsley Cherry-Garrard's *The Worst Journey in the World*. During this year Shaw is also further engaged in battle with his biographer

Demetrius O'Bolger over O'Bolger's account of Shaw's parental relationship, as well as his own relationship with Charlotte. In July, the Shaws visit Ireland, although Shaw leaves in order to attend the Fabian Summer School and the Labour Research Department's Summer School. In November, Shaw is once more on the campaign trail preceding an election, and in December Shaw makes enquiries of Rev. Joseph Leonard about Joan of Arc.

January

11 (Wed)	Shaw says in a letter to Mrs Patrick Campbell that she will be 'a rotter and a courtesan' if she publishes his love letters. [CL3: 759; Peters 376]
14–16	Shaw edits proofs of his correspondence with Mrs Patrick Campbell, who then accuses him of having 'spoilt my book'. [Dent 276–8]
18	Shaw attends the Molière tercentenary luncheon at the Carlton Hotel, followed by academic papers read in the rooms of the Royal Society. [CL3: 764]
23	Shaw begins a four-day stay with the Webbs in Hastings. [CL3: 760]

February

18 (Sat)	Shaw attends a piano recital by composer and piano virtuoso Ferruccio Busoni at Wigmore Hall. [CL3: 762]
24	Writing to Shaw, Stella Campbell warns: 'I *am* going to publish exactly what I like... Start saying your prayers.' [Dent 281–2]
27	The beginning of two three-week cycles of *Back to Methuselah* presented by the Theater Guild at the Garrick Theater in New York. In the first cycle, Parts I and II were presented from 27 February; Parts III and IV from 6 March; and Part V from 13 March. For the second cycle, Shaw agreed to allow some cuts. The pentalogy was performed 25 times, at a total loss of over $20 000, due largely to the small size of the Garrick Theater. [Lawrence Langner, *GBS and the Lunatic* (1964), 31, 45–50; I&R 304; CL3: 726; Morgan 77]

March

	Shaw and Ezra Pound exchange letters over Shaw's refusal to purchase an expensive subscription to Joyce's *Ulysses*. Shaw writes 'Dont think that you can tell me anything about Joyce and Ulysses. I have been a youth in Dublin, and know every shop he mentions and every street he drags me down. Thank your stars you dont.' [CL3: 763–6]
25 (Sat)	The Shaws are introduced by Sydney Cockerell to T. E. Lawrence (Lawrence of Arabia), then serving in the Royal Air Force. [CL3: 784]

April

5 (Wed) – 22 The Shaws spend two weeks at Malvern, then visit Harlech. They assist Apsley Cherry-Garrard with his book on Scott's Antarctic expedition, *The Worst Journey in the World*. [CL3: 768; DHL]

30 The Shaws visit Mary Cholmondeley at Edstaston overnight, before proceeding to Stratford-upon-Avon. [DHL]

April or May

Stella Campbell to Shaw: 'I am truly dreadfully sorry if Charlotte is distressed, if only she had been kind to me we could have selected the letters together.' [Dent 286]

May

Publication in *St Martin-in-the-Fields Review* of Shaw's answers to a series of questions put to him about religion and his beliefs. He affirms his belief in a purposeful Life Force, but criticizes organized religion, describing the Church of England as a 'Society of Gentleman Amateurs'. But churches are necessary, the only people who can do without them are 'simple materialists' or people like the Quakers, whose 'churches are their own souls'. ['Bernard Shaw on Religion', *St Martin-in-the-Fields Review*, May 1922; I&R 409–11]

Early The Shaws visit Mary Cholmondeley at Edstaston before returning to Ayot. [CL3: 769]

c. 5 Shaw remonstrates again with O'Bolger about his biographical treatment of Bessie Shaw: 'My mother wasn't that sort of woman.' [CL 3: 770]

6 (Sat) Publication in *The Queen* of the first extracts (edited by Shaw) of Mrs Patrick Campbell's autobiography. Extracts were also published in the *New York Herald* beginning in May. The entire book was published in October 1922. [Lbib2: 692; CL3: 770]

21 Shaw writes to G. K. Chesterton 'For a man of your weight, your performance on the thin ice of my loveletters was a marvel of delicate and considerate skating. To me the publication of a love letter is an indecent exposure.' [CL3: 770]

30 In a letter to Diana Watts, Shaw affirms the value of his relationship with Charlotte. [CL3: 771]

June

28 (Wed) Shaw contradicts Demetrius O'Bolger's argument that he married Charlotte for her money. [CL3: 777]

July

Max Beerbohm publishes seven cartoons lampooning Mrs Patrick Campbell and her 'Joey'. [CL3: 770]

12 (Wed) – 24 The Shaws visit Nancy Astor at Cliveden. [DHL]
26–31 The Shaws visit Tenby and Goodwick on their way to Ireland. [DHL]

August

7 (Mon) – 20 The Shaws are in Ireland. [CL3: 778;DHL]
17 T. E. Lawrence asks Shaw to read and evaluate his *Seven Pillars of Wisdom*. [CL3: 784]
19 The Shaws dine with Sir Horace Plunkett and Michael Collins, Chairman of the Provisional Government appointed to implement the Treaty establishing the Irish Free State. Three days later, Collins is ambushed and killed by Irish republicans. [CL3: 783]
20 Leaving Charlotte in Ireland, Shaw crosses from Ireland to Wales to attend the Fabian Summer School at Godalming from 22 to 29 August. [CL3: 782, 784]
30 Stopping for a few days at Glastonbury on the way Shaw travels to Nottingham, Chester and Harlech, and spends five days with the Labour Research Department's Summer School at Cloughton. [CL3: 784;DHL]

September

19 (Tue) Shaw returns to Ayot. (He has not returned to Ireland on 10 September to pick up Charlotte, as he said was his intention in a letter to T. E. Lawrence on 25 August.) [CL3: 784; DHL]

October

The Tories bring the Coalition Government to an end, leading to Lloyd George's resignation and the dissolution of Parliament. [DBW3: 404, 443]
20 (Fri) Shaw lunches with the St John Ervines. [DHL]

November

4 (Wed) – 15 Shaw makes an electioneering tour of adjacent communities, Reading, Luton, Hemel Hempstead, Woolwich, East Ham, then heads North to Northampton, York and Newcastle. [CL3: 787; DHL]
15 The Tories win the General Election. Sidney Webb returned as Labour MP, Shaw having campaigned for him the previous day. [DBW3: 443]

December

Correspondence between Charlotte Shaw and T. E. Lawrence begins. [Dunbar 266]
Shaw works on a Preface and notes to *Immaturity*, to be published for the first time in 1930. [CL3: 801]
11 (Mon) Shaw enquires about Joan of Arc's trial and canonization from Rev. Joseph Leonard, a teacher at St Mary's College,

Hammersmith, whom he had met in 1919 at Parknasilla. [CL3: 795]

15 Shaw has lunch at Robert Loraine's home. [DHL]

1923

The Shaws begin the year with a short stay in Bournemouth. *Jitta's Atonement*, Shaw's free adaptation from the German of Trebitsch's play, is staged in January of this year at the Shubert-Garrick Theater in Washington. In April, Shaw begins to write *Saint Joan* which he finishes on 24 August. In July, the Shaws travel to Wales, and then proceed to County Kerry, where Shaw falls, injuring his back. Shaw returns to England in time for rehearsals of the first British production of *Back To Methuselah* at the Birmingham Repertory Theatre in October of this year. Shaw writes twice during the year to the Prime Minister requesting a pension for T. E. Lawrence in recognition of his services. On 28 December *Saint Joan* has its première at the Garrick Theater, New York.

January

6 (Sat) The Shaws leave for ten days in Bournemouth and Boscombe. [CL3: 806; DHL]

8 *Jitta's Atonement*, Shaw's free adaptation of Siegfried Trebitsch's play, *Frau Gittas Sühne*, first performed at the Shubert-Garrick Theater, Washington. [Lawrence Langner, *GBS and the Lunatic* (1964); I&R 307; CP5: 718]

February

22 (Thu) Shaw delivers a lecture, 'Pity the Poor Rich', at the Emerson Club. [DHL]

March

8 (Thu) Shaw examines the stage lighting at St Martin's Theatre. [DHL]

15 Shaw attends a matinée of *Heartbreak House* in Birmingham. [DHL]

23 Shaw explains to Kathleen Hilton Young (widow of Robert Falcon Scott) Apsley Cherry-Garrard's critical account of Scott's leadership of the Antarctic expedition. [CL3: 814–18]

28 The Shaws proceed via Oxford and Bath to Minehead on the north coast of Somerset. [CL3: 815]

April

1 (Sun) Shaw responds to an invitation from the Manchester *Sunday Chronicle* to write a tribute to Sarah Bernhardt with a kindly but critical piece published under the title 'Handicaps of a Tragedy Queen': 'She had some natural disadvantages to struggle against;

the famous *voix d'or* was produced by intoning like an effeminate Oxford curate; and its monotony was aggravated by an unvarying mask of artificial sweetness, which would have been exasperating in a ballet dancer; yet she forced the public to accept both these faults as qualities.' [*Sunday Chronicle* (Manchester), 1 Apr 1923]

2 April – 7 May

Shaw goes on a motoring tour to Minehead, via Oxford and Bath, Great Malvern and Stratford-upon-Avon. [DHL]

April

29 Shaw begins writing *Saint Joan*. [CP6: 11; *Lady Gregory's Journals 1916–1930*, ed. Lennox Robinson (1946), 211–12, 215; I&R 308; Weiss 242]

May

3 (Thu) Shaw sees a production of *Cymbeline* in modern dress at Birmingham. [DHL]

4 Shaw lunches with novelist Marie Corelli at Stratford-upon-Avon. [DHL]

23 Staying with the Shaws at Ayot, Lady Gregory records in her journal his reading to her of the scene between Joan and Dunois before the Relief of Orléans. She says she suggested the incident of the boy's sneeze when the wind changes. [*Lady Gregory's Journals 1916–1930*, ed. Lennox Robinson (1946), 211]

31 Shaw writes to the new Prime Minister, Stanley Baldwin, in an attempt to secure a pension for T. E. Lawrence in recognition of his heroic undertakings in 1918 in the British campaign against the Turks. [CL3: 828–32]

June

21 (Thu) Shaw notes a performance by Eleanora Duse in *The Lady from the Sea* at the New Oxford Theatre. [DHL]

22 Shaw sits for cartoonist David Low. [DHL]

25 Shaw agrees to the Lord Chamberlain's conditions for granting a licence for the performance of *Back to Methuselah*. [CL3: 840]

27 Shaw asks Ben Turner, Labour MP for Batley and Morley, for published samples of north country dialect for use in *Saint Joan*. [CL3: 842]

29 Travelling by train from Paddington, Shaw keeps an afternoon appointment, probably connected with art collections, at Windsor Castle. [DHL]

July

16 (Mon) On his way to Ireland from Brecon, Shaw writes to Henry Salt, saying 'I have nearly completed the first draft of a play about Joan of Arc'. [CL3: 842]

17 July – 18 September

Shaw travels to Ireland via Wales. [CL3: 842]

August

24 (Fri) Having reached the Great Southern Hotel at Parknasilla, Co. Kerry, Shaw completes the first draft of *Saint Joan*. News of the death of Demetrius O'Bolger inspires mixed feelings of regret and relief. Beatrice Lady Glenavy and her husband, also staying at the hotel, go for boating and bathing expeditions with the Shaws. Lady Glenavy recalls looking at signs of the 1922 'Troubles' and singing Irish political ballads with Shaw. [CL3: 844; Beatrice Lady Glenavy, *Today We Will Only Gossip* (1964), 127–9, I&R 215; Weiss 242]

September

12 (Wed) Shaw falls on rocks on the Kerry coast, injuring his back and ribs. [Tompkins 56; CL3: 850]

18 Shaw leaves Parknasilla and proceeds to Malvern. He never returns to Ireland again. [CL3: 848]

29 Shaw leaves Malvern for Birmingham to advise on rehearsals of *Back to Methuselah*. [CL3: 849]

October

1 (Mon) – 13 Shaw stays at the house of Barry Jackson, Proprietor of the Birmingham Repertory Theatre. [Tompkins 53; CL3: 851]

9–12 First British production of *Back to Methuselah* at the Birmingham Repertory Theatre. Four complete cycles were produced at a loss of £2500. [CL3: 843; DHL; Morgan 77]

13 Shaw motors to Oxford to visit Sir Frederick Keeble and Lady Keeble (Lillah McCarthy). [DHL]

20–22 Siegfried Trebitsch visits the Shaws at Ayot. [Weiss 245]

23 Augustin and Henriette Hamon visit Ayot for lunch. [DHL]

26 Shaw unveils a statue of Richard Brinsley Sheridan at Bath. [DHL]

November

8 (Thu) Shaw lunches at the Bertrand Russells'. [DHL]

12 Shaw writes to the Prime Minister, Stanley Baldwin, for the second time, requesting a pension for T. E. Lawrence. [CL3: 852]

13 Shaw has his first meeting with Italian dramatist Luigi Pirandello. [CL4: 873]

29 November – 6 December

Shaw goes electioneering. [DHL]

Winter

Shaw reads *Saint Joan* to Sybil Thorndike, Lewis Casson and others at the house of Apsley Cherry-Garrard, Ayot St Lawrence.

Thorndike recalls: 'We simply could not believe our ears. It seemed to me the most wonderful first scene that I had ever heard.' [Elizabeth Sprigge, *Sybil Thorndike Casson* (1971), 154–5; I&R 309–11]

December

8 (Sat) The Baldwin government falls and is replaced by Ramsay MacDonald's Labour government.
Shaw begins the Preface to *Saint Joan*. [Hol3: 79]

13 *The Shewing-up of Blanco Posnet* opens in variety at the Alhambra, following a fortnight at the Shepherd's Bush Empire. [DHL]

25 T. E. Lawrence lunches with the Shaws. [DHL]

28 Première production of *Saint Joan* performed by the Theater Guild at the Garrick Theater, New York. [Morgan 10, 82; CL3: 861]

1924

The first production of *Saint Joan* to be staged in England takes place at the New Theatre during this year with Sybil Thorndike in the leading role. The Lord Chamberlain licenses *Mrs Warren's Profession* during this year after thirty years of rejection, leading to the first public performance of the play in England the following year. *Saint Joan* is published in German translation as *Die heilige Johanna* in *Neue Rundschau* from June to September, and during the months from July to September the Shaws tour Scotland. In September, Jenny Patterson dies, and in December, William Archer, journalist and longtime friend and critic of Shaw, also dies.

January

Early The Shaws spend the New Year period at Boscombe. [CL3: 858]

25 (Fri) Floryan Sobieniowski, Shaw's Polish translator, visits Adelphi Terrace. [DHL]

28 Shaw completes the Preface to *Saint Joan*. [Hol3: 79]

February

1 (Fri) Shaw lunches with J. M. Barrie. [DHL]

12 Ralph Pulitzer of the *New York World* calls on Shaw. [DHL]

18–22 The first of four complete cycles of the Birmingham production of *Back to Methuselah* at the Royal Court Theatre in London. Shaw attends the performance of Part IV on 21 February. [CL3: 866]

19 Shaw lobbies for financial support and government recognition of RADA as an educational institution. [CL3: 864]

25 Commencement of rehearsals of *Saint Joan* co-directed by Shaw and Lewis Casson. [CL3: 866]

March

13 (Thu), 22 Shaw seeks advice on the correct pronunciation of 'Stogumber', but does not take it. [CL3: 870, 873]

18 Less than a week before opening night, rehearsals of *Saint Joan* are disrupted by the absence of Ernest Thesiger (the Dauphin) who has the flu. [CL3: 871]

26 British première of *Saint Joan* at the New Theatre with Sybil Thorndike and Ernest Thesiger. [CL3: 867; Dent 297; Pearson 378; Morgan 82]

April

24 (Thu) Shaw is introduced to Laurentia McLachlan (Sister Laurentia, Abbess of Stanbrook) by Sydney Cockerell. In the coming years she serves Shaw ('Brother Bernard') as a spiritual counsellor. [Peters 406–7; CL3: 896; D. Felicitas Corrigan, *The Nun, the Infidel and the Superman* (1965), 45]

29 April – 6 May

Shaw visits Stratford-upon-Avon. He later proceeds to Ely, and then to Norwich to address the local Independent Labour Party. [Tompkins 68–9; CL3: 875]

June

First publication of *Saint Joan* in German translation as *Die heilige Johanna* in the June–September edition of *Neue Rundschau* (Berlin). [Lbib2: 700; CP6: 11]

25 (Wed) – 27 Shaw attends a British Music Society Congress in Liverpool. [DHL]

July

10 (Thu) American novelist and historian Hamlin Garland visits Shaw. [DHL]

13 July – 17 September

The Shaws tour Scotland. [CL3: 882; Weiss 248]

August

Adoption of the Dawes Plan for Germany to pay war reparations to the allied nations, a scheme to which Shaw strongly objected, saying it was 'simply the plunder of the Vanquished'. [I&R 352]

29 (Fri) The Lord Chamberlain having unexpectedly licensed *Mrs Warren's Profession*, 'after thirty years of obduracy', Shaw invites Edith Evans to play the leading role (which she declines). [CL3: 883]

September

10 (Wed) Wednesday and Friday matinée performances of Parts I and V of *Back to Methuselah* begin at the Court Theatre for four weeks. [DHL]

15 Death of Jenny Patterson. [Peters 397]

October

2 (Thu) Hilaire Belloc visits Shaw. [DHL]

7 Shaw describes his system of punctuation in a letter to T. E. Lawrence. [CL3: 885]

16 Sir Sidney Low and his wife Ebba (Shaw's Swedish translator) join Shaw and St John Ervine at lunch. [DHL]

29 Fall of Ramsay MacDonald's Labour government, elected in the preceding January. [DBW4: 9, 43–5]

30 Joseph Smith, descendant of the Mormon leader, calls on Shaw. [DHL]

November

4 (Tue) Stanley Baldwin's Conservative Party returns to government. [CL 3: 864]

14 *The Radio Times* publishes an article about Shaw's forthcoming broadcast (November 20) and quotes a Shavian lecture, in a letter to the BBC, on radio plays: 'You want to broadcast plays; and instead of recognizing that the invisible play is a new thing, and cannot be done in the old way, you persist in asking handsome actresses – and well-known pictorial producers – to get up ordinary theatrical performances and allow the public to overhear the dialogue.' ['B. S. Lectures the B.B.C.', *The Radio Times*, 14 Nov 1924]

20 The BBC broadcasts Shaw's live reading of *O'Flaherty V. C.*, Shaw's first radio broadcast, from 8.30 to 9.15 p.m. [Morgan 10; DHL; CL3: 825, 889]

December

Publication in *The Bookman* of an article by William Archer, which, because of Archer's death later in December, became his public valediction to his old friend, Shaw. The article, partly laudatory and partly highly critical of Shaw, begins: 'The death of Anatole France leaves Bernard Shaw the Grand Old Man of literary Europe. Thomas Hardy, indeed, is an older man; but his fame is comparatively insular.' While expressing admiration for the 'fundamentals' of Shaw's character, Archer also censoriously says of his friend: 'having known him for forty years I say without hesitation that his greatest moral failing…is (or was) a certain impishness, a Puck-like *Schadenfreude*, to which he would sometimes give too free play.' [William Archer, 'The Psychology of G.B.S', *The Bookman*, vol. LXVII, no. 399, Dec 1924; I&R 291]

In an interview published in the same issue of *The Bookman*, Shaw says that he has no new play in mind but is 'getting to work on a little book which I shall call "The Intelligent Woman's Guide to Socialism" – a sort of sequel to the old-fashioned "Child's Guide to Knowledge". It is no use talking to men.' [St John Adcock, 'G.B.S. At Home', *The Bookman*, vol. LXVII, no. 399, Dec 1924]

9 (Tue) – 11 Shaw participates in the first three rehearsals of *Jitta's Atonement*. [CL3: 901]

17 William Archer, about to have an operation for cancer, writes his last letter to Shaw, saying: 'though I may sometimes have played the part of the all-too-candid mentor, I have never wavered in my admiration and affection for you, or ceased to feel that the Fates had treated me kindly in making me your contemporary and friend. I thank you from my heart for forty years of good comradeship.' [CL3: 895]

26 The Shaws sail to Madeira for a six-week holiday, which is described in a newspaper announcement as 'a sun bathing cure'. [*Birmingham Mail*, 23 Dec 1925; CL3: 895]

27 Death in London of William Archer.

30 Arriving in Madeira, Shaw learns of William Archer's death three days earlier after surgery. In a Preface to a 1927 posthumous edition of Archer's *Three Plays*, Shaw recalled that Archer's death 'threw [him] into a transport of fury' (directed, probably injustly as he acknowledges, at the surgeons) and added: 'I still feel that when he went he took a piece of me with him.' [CL3: 895]

1925

The Shaws spent the beginning of 1925 holidaying in Madeira, returning to London in February. In January *Jitta's Attonement*, Shaw's translation of Trebitsch's play, opens at the Grand Theatre, Fulham. In April, Augustin Hamon's translation of *Saint Joan* is produced by Georges Pitoëff at the Théâtre des Arts in Paris. In July, *Mrs Warren's Profession*, written in 1893, receives its first public licensed performance in England at the Prince of Wales Theatre in Birmingham. It had taken more than thirty years for the Lord Chamberlain to grant a licence for the play to be staged. The Shaws spend the months from July to October touring Scotland, the Orkney and Shetland Islands. Shaw spends the closing months of the year concentrating on *The Intelligent Woman's Guide to Socialism and Capitalism*. The Shaws leave London for Cornwall in late December. *Shaw* by John Stewart Collis is published during this year.

January

26 (Mon) Opening of *Jitta's Atonement* at the Grand Theatre, Fulham, for a two-week run. After the tremendous success of *Saint Joan*, Shaw is again very much in vogue, with many producers wanting to stage his plays. [CL3: 901]

30 January – 9 February

Shaw takes eight dancing lessons, including for the tango, from an instructor named Rinder. [DHL]

February

12 (Thu) – 16 The Shaws return from Madeira to London on the SS *Edinburgh Castle*. Another Madeira holiday-maker, struck by Shaw's remarkable physical fitness there, reports that he 'strips like a young man', and that 'to see him take a header from the diving board of Reid's bathing place in Madeira... is to make one reflect that there may be something in vegetarianism after all.' The same observer records that 'Mrs Bernard Shaw is also a gallant swimmer, and she also, after the bathe, loves to sun herself in the perfumed nooks of the gorgeous gardens'. [Marthe Troly-Curtin, 'Genius en Déshabillé. Mr George Bernard Shaw reaches England to-day from Madeira', *Evening Standard* (London), 16 Feb 1925; CL3: 902]
Shaw denies rumours that he has become a convert to Roman Catholicism in Madeira. ['Radio Queries', *Evening Standard*, 16 Feb 1925]

19 Shaw attends the opening of John Barrymore's *Hamlet*. [CL3: 902–4]

February–March

Shaw sits to Sir John Lavery for a portrait. [DHL]

March

28 (Sat) First night of *Caesar and Cleopatra* at the Birmingham Repertory. [DHL]

29 (Sir) Oswald Mosley visits Shaw at Ayot. [DHL]

April

28 (Tue) Opening of the Georges Pitoëff production, in Hamon's translation, of *Saint Joan* at the Théâtre des Arts in Paris. Pitoëff's wife, Ludmilla Pitoëff, takes the role of Joan. [CL3: 890]

June

6 (Sat) – 11 Recovering from influenza, Shaw visits the Webbs at Passfield, returning to London on the 9th for a debate with Hilaire Belloc. [DHL; Weiss 257; DBW4: 50–1]

9 Shaw debates with Hilaire Belloc the question 'What is Coming' at the Savoy Theatre to raise money for the King Edward

Hospital Fund. Shaw says: 'I suggest that one of the things that is going to happen in the future is that we are going to get away from rationalism.' A lengthy account of this debate, with verbatim reports of what the speakers said, is published on the front page of the literary section of the *New York Times*. The debate is broadcast by the BBC. ['Shaw and Belloc Debate "What is Coming"', the *New York Times*, Sunday, 29 Jun 1925; DHL]

20 (Sat) Shaw lectures on 'Nerves' at the Langley Nerve Training Colony, founded by Mrs William Archer. [CL1: 615]

25 Shaw advises Molly Tompkins that her secretary, Molly Little, is trying to blackmail him. [Tompkins 85]

26 Shaw attends a dinner at Lady Lavery's and is seated next to Winston Churchill. Luigi Pirandello is also a guest. [CL4: 873;DHL]

18 July – 8 October

The Shaws tour Scotland including the Orkney and Shetland Islands. During this tour Shaw writes to Lady Gregory: 'Ireland is passing through a series of salutary disillusioning humiliations; and the latest is having her nose put out of joint by the north of Scotland... you will find all the beauties of Ireland without the drawback of Irish inhabitants.' [CL3: 912; Weiss 259; L&G 176]

July

27 (Mon) First (public) licensed performance in England of *Mrs Warren's Profession* by the Macdona Players at the Prince of Wales Theatre in Birmingham. [CL3: 883; Morgan 18]

August

10 (Mon) Shaw begins an epistolary duel about the Paris theatre lasting several months in the pages of *Le Temps* and *Der Jude* with poet-dramatist Henry Bernstein. [CL3: 921; Weiss 278]

15 The Shaws arrive at Shetland on the SS *St Magnus*. Shaw advises the islanders to harness the tremendous force of their tides to produce power, and compliments the people on their 'good looks, good manners, and a very gentle speech'. ['G.B.S. in Shetland', *The Shetland News* (Lerwick), 20 Aug 1925; I&R 216–18n]

October

Siegfried Trebitsch visits Shaw at Ayot St Lawrence. [I&R 439]

21 (Wed) The British Communist Party headquarters are raided and several leaders are arrested, including William Gallacher for whom Shaw puts up bail. [CL4: 101]

23 First London production of *Man and Superman* in its entirety at the Regent Theatre, King's Cross, directed by Esmé Percy who also plays Tanner. [Morgan 43]

November

20 (Fri) The Shaws visit the Webbs. On 22 November, Beatrice writes that Shaw 'is putting in a great deal of work on *The Intelligent Woman's Guide to Socialism*, trying to reduce each thought to its simplest and most lucid expression, "so that any fool can understand it"... GBS never tests or finishes his process of reasoning – it is all brilliantly expressed improvisations to meet new emergencies or carry out sudden impulses, usually dislikes and indignations.' [DBW4: 63–4]

December

7 (Mon) Shaw meets one of Tolstoy's daughters at the Stage Society matinée of Chekhov's *Ivanov*. [CL4: 7]

21 The Shaws arrive in Falmouth, Cornwall, for their Christmas holiday, during which Shaw continues work on *The Intelligent Woman's Guide to Socialism and Capitalism*. [CL3: 925; CL4: 7]

Chronology Part III
1926–50

1926

Shaw begins the year with continued work on *The Intelligent Woman's Guide to Socialism*. In an article in his *Criterion* published in April, T. S. Eliot takes sides with Scottish historian and politician J. M. Robertson in a pedantic attack on Shaw's treatment of the Saint Joan legend in his play. From August to October, the Shaws stay at Stresa, Lake Maggiore. In November, Shaw is awarded the 1925 Nobel Prize for Literature.

January

15 (Fri) The Shaws leave Cornwall, reaching Ayot on 18 January. [CL3: 925; DHL;Weiss 268]

Passion, Poison, and Petrifaction broadcast on the BBC's 2LO. Apart from his November 1924 reading of *O'Flaherty V.C.* this was the first broadcast of a Shaw play. [DHL]

23–25 T. E. Lawrence is a guest at Ayot. [DHL]

30 Shaw writes to Archibald Henderson, promising that he will read through Henderson's revised biography once he has finished his current project. 'I am working hard to get this *Intelligent Woman's Guide to Socialism and Capitalism* through the press. It is a tremendous job of real literary work: not like play writing.' [CL4: 11]

February

12 (Fri) Shaw begins rehearsing *Mrs Warren's Profession*, nominally directed by Esmé Percy. [DHL]

Shaw is filmed in a London studio for a series of short screen studies of noted persons. [*New York Times*, 13 Feb 1926; DHL]

15 Shaw attends the Stage Society's production of James Joyce's *Exiles* at the Regent Theatre. [Richard Ellman, *James Joyce* (1965), 587–8; DHL]

20 Shaw declines an offer of an honorary doctorate from the University of Edinburgh, rebuking the university for 'making a tomfoolery of its graduations'. [CL4: 13]

24 Shaw takes on a rehearsal of *Pygmalion* at the Royal Academy of Dramatic Art. [DHL]

March

2 (Tue) Final dress rehearsal of *Mrs Warren's Profession* attended by an invited audience which Shaw describes as 'horrid'. [CL4: 15]

3 *Mrs Warren's Profession* opens at the Strand Theatre. [CL4: 14]

6 Stricken by influenza, Shaw enters a period of ill-health until 22 March. [CL4: 22; DHL]

19 Shaw writes to Siegfried Trebitsch, who was organizing a German tribute for Shaw's 70th birthday: 'You must not let this birthday business worry you. If the German Nation ... wishes to

celebrate my dotage by all means let it enjoy itself in that strange fashion as much as it pleases...The only condition that I make is that they shall not ask me to join in the festivities... I have been in bed [with influenza] for 10 days & am ten feet long in consequence.' [CL4: 20]

April

1 (Thu) T. S. Eliot's review of John Mackinnon Robertson's *Shaw and the Maid* appears in his periodical, *Criterion*. Eliot's review attacks Shaw, and 'the potent ju-ju of the Life Force'. In 1924, Eliot had acknowledged Shaw as 'the intellectual stimulant and the dramatic delight of twenty years' in London, but described *Saint Joan* (which he later acknowledged having been influenced by *Murder in the Cathedral*) as the 'greatest sacrilege'. [T.S. Eliot, 'Shaw, Robertson and "The Maid"', *Criterion,* IV (Apr 1926); 'Commentary', *Criterion,* III (Oct 1924); I&R 491, 492 n3]

10 Shaw suffers a relapse in health from which he appears to suffer seriously until at least 20 May. [DHL]

May

1 (Sat) Shaw writes to Apsley Cherry-Garrard: 'My dear Cherry, I am half alive: no more ... My inside is deranged.' [CL4: 21]

20 Demoralized by his continuing ill-health, Shaw writes a sardonic note to Kathleen Hilton Young (formerly Lady Scott): 'You can start my monument as soon as you please... the corpse will be ready.' [CL4: 23]

June

2 (Wed) In a written interview with G. S. Viereck, Shaw comments: 'My diet is simply a corpseless (in American, cadaverless) diet. If you think that the world's edible stock consists of corpses and green vegetables and nothing else you are so stupendously ignorant of the subject that you had better not attempt to write about it... All my prefaces are important, especially that to Major Barbara on Poverty. These prefaces have practically nothing to do with the plays, and are treatises of considerable length.' [Cornell]

19–24 The Shaws visit the Webbs. Beatrice Webb reflects that Shaw is a 'somewhat sobered but still brilliant sprite ... He never changes; he never grows old; he has the same delightful personality; he is less vain than he used to be... We four, each one of us, will be saddened by the death of either one of the other pair, and will stand by the survivor.' [DBW4: 87; Cole 104–5]

25 Shaw visits Mrs William Archer before the unveiling on the following day of Archer's bust at the British Drama League. [BL MS Add 56500; DHL]

27 After wrangling about negotiations for a film version of *The Devil's Disciple* Shaw writes to J. E. Vedrenne: 'I think I shall let The Devil's Disciple go if I can guard myself against having it spoiled by turning it into a love story... I am out of sorts and can do nothing today.' [CL4: 23]

July

11 (Sun) Shaw accepts an invitation to join a committee to advise the BBC on Spoken English. [CL3: 24]

15 Shaw refuses to assure the BBC that his birthday speech will be free of political controversy. [CL4: 24–5]

26 Shaw attends a complimentary dinner hosted by the Parliamentary Labour Party, with Ramsay MacDonald in the chair, at the Hotel Metropole to honour his seventieth birthday. The BBC refuses to broadcast his speech, described in *T.P's Weekly* as 'an exposition of the gospel of Socialism'. [CL4: 24–5; *T.P's Weekly*, 14 Aug 1926]

The Everyman Theatre revives *Widowers' Houses* to coincide with Shaw's seventieth birthday. In an article, published the following month. J. T. Grein writes a reminiscence about the first production by his Independent Theatre Society in December 1892, and reviews the revival favourably: 'curiously, in structure and in thought the play seems more up-to-date now than in 1892.' ['G.B.S.'s First Play Revived', *The Illustrated London News*, 14 Aug 1926]

August

4 (Wed) The Shaws depart for Stresa on Lake Maggiore in Italy arriving the following day and staying at the Regina Palace Hotel. Charlotte reports that during this holiday, Shaw enjoys boating, bathing and talking about music with conductor Albert Coates and his circle (Coates had an estate, Villa Intragnola, on Lake Maggiore); and that he also has a figurine and a bust made of him by sculptor Prince Paul Troubetskoy, who 'has a villa on the Lake, a big studio & an astonishing wife'. [Charlotte Shaw to Beatrice Webb, Aug/Sep 1926, BLPES; Dunbar 304; Charlotte Shaw to Apsley Cherry-Garrard, 12 and 20 Aug 1926, Texas; CL4: 26]

7 Cecil Lewis reports to Charles Ricketts about finding Shaw 'installed' on the Coates' verandah at Lake Maggiore, 'as if he had been there for years. He nearly died at the beginning of the journey and felt far better at the end.' Lewis feels uneasy with Shaw: 'He is immensely kind – like God – but no respecter of persons – one feels he would be just as kind to everybody under every given circumstance... He makes no effort, his generosity

and deep humanity seem as much a part of him as his beard...' [*Self-Portrait taken from Letters and Journals of Charles Ricketts, RA*, collected and compiled by T. Sturge Moore, ed. Cecil Lewis, (1939), 354]

27 Shaw writes a letter to Henry Arthur Jones in which he attempts to mend the broken fences of their friendship, and reports that he himself is 'completely done up by work on top of illness'. [CL4: 27]

August or September

First known recording of Shaw's voice, in a 'film interview', consisting of a phonograph recording synchronized with film, made on an Italian movie set. [Lbib2: 871]

September

Death of Charles Charrington [Martin]. [Peters 387; CL1: 215]

October

4 (Mon) The Shaws depart from Stresa, arriving in London the following day. [CL4: 26, 29; Weiss 274]

7 Shaw lunches with Theodore Dreiser. [DHL]

Mid Siegfried Trebitsch visits Shaw at Ayot. [I&R 439; Weiss 275]

November

12 (Fri) **The Swedish Academy announces that Shaw has won the 1925 Nobel Prize for Literature.** Shaw jokingly told Archibald Henderson he presumed the honour had been awarded 'as a token of gratitude for a sense of world relief – as he had published nothing in 1925.' Writing to the Royal Swedish Academy on 18 November 1926, Shaw said; 'The Award of the Nobel Prize for the year 1925 to an English work is a very welcome reinforcement of the cordial understanding between British and Swedish culture established by the famous bequest of Alfred Nobel. It will not be lost on my native country, Ireland, which already claims one distinguished Nobel prizeman [Yeats]. It is naturally very gratifying to me personally that it has fallen to my lot to furnish the occasion for such an act of international appreciation.' Having contemplated refusing the prize money of about £6500, Shaw accepted it on the understanding that it be used to 'encourage intercourse and understanding in literature and art between Sweden and the British Isles', through support of translations into English of neglected Swedish works. Shaw did not go to Stockholm for the presentation ceremonies on 10 December. [CL4: 4, 32–4; Hend3: 838; I&R 491]

24 Shaw lectures to the Fabian Society on 'Cultural Internationalism'. [DHL]

26 James Joyce writes to Shaw congratulating him on being awarded the Nobel Prize and 'to express my satisfaction that the award... has gone once more to a distinguished fellow townsman'. Even though Shaw received numerous congratulatory letters this is the only one he kept. ['Respectful Distance: James Joyce and His Dublin Townsman Bernard Shaw' in Stanley Weintraub, *Shaw's People: Victoria to Churchill*, (1996), 135]

December

2 (Thu) Shaw attends a performance of *The Doctor's Dilemma*, revived on 17 November at the Kingsway Theatre. [DHL]

23 December – 23 January

The Shaws holiday at Port Eliot during Christmas and from 29 December at Torquay. [CL4: 35]

1927

In the early part of this year, Shaw works on *The Intelligent Woman's Guide to Socialism and Capitalism* which he completes in late March. Throughout the year, Shaw's controversial comments about Mussolini fuel a number of public and private debates. From July to October, the Shaws holiday at the Regina Palace Hotel in Stresa, Lake Maggiore where Shaw's flirtation with Molly Tompkins intensifies. In July, the first filming of a Shaw play (a scene from *Saint Joan)* occurs. In October, the first (amateur) production of *The Glimpse of Reality* is performed by the Glasgow Clarion Players.

January

2 (Sun) The *Daily Express* reports Shaw's gift of £5000 to the Royal Academy of Dramatic Art to start a fund for rebuilding the premises in Gower Street. ['G.B.S.'s £5000 Gift. Help for New Dramatic Art Building', *Daily Express* (London), 2 Jan 1927]

13 From Torquay, Shaw writes: 'working hard at the book on Socialism ... it is almost complete now'. [CL4: 37; Weiss 277]

24 Shaw outrages socialists and Italians in exile with the publication of a letter, 'Bernard Shaw on Mussolini: A Defence' (the headline supplied by a subeditor) in the *Daily News*. This controversy initiated an exchange of letters, both public and private, between Shaw and Friedrich Adler, leader of the Austrian Labour Party and Secretary of the Socialist Internationale. [Lbib2: 711; CL4: 41–5; DBW2: 131–3; I&R 353–4]

27 Shaw chairs a debate between G. K. Chesterton and Lady Rhondda of Llanwern on 'The Menace of the Leisured Woman'. [CL4: 45; Lbib2: 711]

February

Having declined to attend the formal presentation ceremony in Stockholm the previous December, Shaw quietly accepts his Nobel Prize medal and diploma in London. [CL4: 33]

March

7 (Mon) D. H. and Frieda Lawrence lunch at Adelphi Terrace. [DHL]

11 Max Reinhardt visits Shaw at Adelphi Terrace, and Prince and Princess [Elizabeth Asquith] Bibesco have lunch with the Shaws. [DHL]

24 Shaw has lunch with Robert Bridges, the poet laureate, at Oxford. [DHL]

Late Shaw completes *The Intelligent Woman's Guide to Socialism and Capitalism*, after three years' work on it. [CL4: 80]

May

5 (Thu) Shaw lunches at the home of Sir Philip Sassoon, politician and trustee of the National Gallery. [DHL]

19 The Shaws lunch with Mme [Thomas] Masaryk, wife of the first President of Czechoslovakia. [DHL]

24 The Shaws spend the weekend with the Webbs who examine proofs of *The Intelligent Woman's Guide to Socialism*. Beatrice Webb comments: 'It is amusing to note that artists like himself are to be allowed to keep their individual gains' despite Shaw's socialist ideal of equality of income. [Cole 143]

30 The Shaws learn that Jane Wells has inoperable cancer and has only a few months to live. [CL4: 53]

June

2 (Thu) Shaw opens Rachel McMillan's new children's shelter at Deptford. [DHL]

22 Shaw purchases in Wigmore Street glasses for seeing the eclipse which occurs on 29 June. [DHL]

July

24 (Sun) The Shaws leave again for Stresa where they stay at the luxurious Regina Palace Hotel on Lake Maggiore. They are joined there in August by Lawrence Langner and his wife, Armina Marshall. (During the Shaws' absence, Judy Musters and the servants arrange, on 28–30 July, the transfer of their belongings from 10 Adelphi Terrace to a service flat, No. 130, at 4 Whitehall Court.) In Italy, Shaw's flirtation with Molly Tompkins intensifies. He takes morning swims with Sylvia Ray, secretary of conductor Albert Coates, who has an estate, Villa Intragnola, on Lake Maggiore. [CL4: 57ff., 198, 354; DHL; Tompkins 122, 124, 131; Lawrence Langner, 'The Sinner-Saint

as Host: Diary of a Visit to G.B.S. at Stresa', *The Saturday Review of Literature* (New York), 22 Jul 1944; Charles Berst, 'Passion at Lake Maggiore: Shaw, Molly Tompkins, and Italy, 1921–1950' in SA 81–114]

27 First filming of a Shaw play, a fragment of a sound scene from *Saint Joan* [Scene 5 of the play] with Sybil Thorndike playing Joan, preceded by a momentary discussion between Shaw and Lewis Casson. The film, which runs for five minutes, was made by De Forrest Phonofilms. [*British Film Catalogue 1895–1985*, by Denis Gifford (1986), entry 08249; DHL; I&R 371]

August

13 (Sat) Publication of an interview (extensively revised by Shaw), 'Shaw Looks at Life at 70' by George Sylvester Viereck. Asked if he himself would become an example of the idea in *Back to Methuselah* of enormous extensions of the human life-span, Shaw replies: 'I can imagine nothing more dreadful than an eternity of Bernard Shaw... If I were like *Ahasuerus* I could think of nothing else except my tragic fate.' [George Sylvester Viereck, 'Shaw Looks at Life at 70', *Liberty* (New York); also in *London Magazine*, LIX (Dec 1927); I&R 421–3]

28 Shaw announces that he is at work on a play about Oliver Cromwell in an interview first published in the Italian journal *La Fiera Letteraria* on 21 August, then subsequently in *The Observer* under the title, 'GBS and the Cat: An Unsuspected Interview'. Shaw's plans for this play, however, were never realized. [Lbib2: 713; CL4: 155]

October

1 (Sat) The Mussolini controversy of February is re-ignited by Shaw who, as Beatrice Webb declaims: 'fortified his admiration of Mussolini by spending eight weeks and £600 in a luxurious hotel at Stresa in continuous and flattering interviews with Fascist officials of charming personality and considerable attainments.' [DBW4: 132]

6 The Shaws return to London, and take up residence at 4 Whitehall Court. [CL4: 57; I&R 200; Weiss 278–9]

7 Shaw views a Gene Tunney prizefight film. [DHL]

8 First (amateur) production of *The Glimpse of Reality* by the Glasgow Clarion Players at the Fellowship Hall in Glasgow. [CP3: 814; Morgan 103]

10 The Shaws attend the funeral of Jane Wells at Golders Green. On 27 October, Charlotte sends a vivid description of this occasion (which was marked by much wallowing in grief and sentimentality on the part of Wells and others) to T. E. Lawrence.

After the ceremony, she reports, 'G.B.S. began to "behave badly" at once, making jokes to everyone, and finally – putting H. G. into his car – he actually got a sort of grin out of *him*. Then we came back here. But I am ten years older.' Gyp Wells records her gratitude for Shaw's advice to follow the coffin into the furnace room (as he had done when his mother was cremated): 'This was a wise counsel and I am very grateful for it....It was indeed very beautiful. I wished she could have known of those quivering bright first flames, so clear they were and so like eager yet kindly living things.' [CL4: 54; Dunbar 288–9; *H.G. Wells in Love*, ed. G.P. Wells (1984); DHL]

13–30 The debate between Shaw and Dr Friedrich Adler is re-ignited with the publication in various British and American newspapers of Shaw's correspondence with Adler about the Fascist regime in Italy. Shaw defends Mussolini and makes public his loss of faith in democracy. This correspondence had been published in the Italian newspaper, *Gazzetta del Popolo*, on 12 October under the headline, 'Shaw Convertito al Filofascismo: Una Lettera del Grande Drammaturgo Inglese'. [Lbib2: 714; CL4: 73–4]

19 The *Manchester Guardian* publishes a critique of Shaw's views on Mussolini and Fascism by anti-Fascist Italian historian in exile, Professor Gaetano Salvemini, later author of *G.B. Shaw e il Fascismo* (1955). In his article Salvemini writes: 'I do not reproach Mr. Shaw with his ignorance of Italian affairs. I only intend to point out his levity in delivering judgement about matters of which he is wholly ignorant, and his callous ridicule of hardships and sufferings which his intelligence ought to understand even if his moral sensitiveness is unequal to appreciating them.' Shaw's defence of his favourable comments on Mussolini, and rejection of the statement that he consorted with Fascists in Italy, is published in *The Manchester Guardian* on 28 October, and Salvemini's retort to this on the 31st. [*The Manchester Guardian*, 19, 28, 31 Oct 1927; CL4: 67]

21 After a lunch with the Shaws, Beatrice Webb reflects on Shaw's strident defence of Mussolini: 'The more uneasy he gets about the validity of his new views, the more he will try to compel us to agree with him... Imagine the hot indignation and withering wit with which the meagrely-fed Irish journalist of the eighties, writing in his dark lodging, would have chastised the rich world-famous dramatist of 1927 defending the pitiless cruelties and bombastic militancy of the melodramatic Mussolini.' [DBW4: 133; Cole 156]

28 Shaw and Chesterton debate in public for the last time, at the Kingsway Hall. The debate was titled 'Do We Agree?' with Hilaire Belloc chairing the debate, and the BBC broadcasting it. A verbatim report appeared in *G. K.'s Weekly*, 5 November 1927 and a more summary account was published as a book in 1928. In his opening salvo, Shaw declares: 'It is my business to tell you... Mr. Chesterton and I are two madmen... we go about the world possessed by a strange gift of tongues... uttering all sorts of extraordinary opinions for no reason whatever.' [Lbib1: 175–6, 715, 865; G. K. Chesterton and Bernard Shaw, 'Do We Agree?' (1928), 8–18, 45; Hol2: 220]

November

5 (Sat) In a letter to Molly Tompkins about their time together in Stresa, Shaw writes: 'I had really a dreadful time in Stresa. I had to preserve the dignity of Mrs Shaw and Mr Tompkins (to say nothing of my own before all the world) as well as the character of Mrs Tompkins, who was determined to throw it all away and lead me captive ... Mrs Tompkins was possessed by seventy and seven devils in addition to being the very devil herself ... I wonder does she ever feel any remorse.' [Tompkins 122]

8–9 Siegfried Trebitsch visits the Shaws at Ayot St Lawrence. Shaw gives Trebitsch directions: 'Go to Kings Cross terminus and take a ticket to Hatfield. The train leaves Kings + at 11.30, and arrives at 12 at Hatfield, where you will find our car waiting for you with a warm overcoat in it.' [Weiss 284]

13 Publication of H. G. Wells's mixture of criticism and praise of Shaw in an article, 'What Is the Good of Shaw?' Comparing Shaw with Russian scientist Pavlov, Wells says: 'To the future, Shaw will have contributed nothing, and yet he may be harder to forget.' [H. G. Wells, 'What Is the Good of Shaw?', *Sunday Express*, 13 Nov 1927; revised version in Wells's *The Way the World is Going* (1928), ch. XXV]

20 First professional production of *The Glimpse of Reality* at the Arts Theatre Club in London. [CP3: 815; Morgan 103]

23 Shaw lectures to the Fabian Society on 'Democracy as a Delusion' in the series on 'Political Democracy: Will It Prevail?' [CL4: 73; DBW4: 133]

*c.*24 After attending Shaw's lecture on 'Democracy as a Delusion', Beatrice Webb remarks that Shaw 'is too old and too spoilt by flattery and pecuniary success to listen to criticism. He has the illusion that he is and *must* be right, because *he* has genius and his critics are just ordinary men.' [DBW4: 133–4; Cole 159–60]

24	In response to a request from Thomas Nelson & Sons for permission to include an extract of *Saint Joan* in a secondary school textbook, Shaw curtly replies: 'NO. I lay my eternal curse on whomsoever shall now or at any time hereafter make schoolbooks of my works and make me hated as Shakespear is hated.' [CL4: 78]
26	Having seen the Movietone *Voices of Italy*, Shaw urges upon Ramsay MacDonald the advantages of the cinema as a medium for political campaigning. [CL4: 79] Shaw records 'Spoken English and Broken English' for the Language Institute. [LBib2: 87]

December

10 (Sat)	The Shaws entertain Lion Feuchtwanger, author of *Jud Süss*, and the Arnold Bennetts to lunch. [DHL]
12	Shaw writes to Stella Campbell: 'Dear Unforgotten...' [Dent 300]
23	The Shaws begin a Christmas visit at Cliveden, the country house of Lady Astor. [I&R 320; CL4: 80, 82]

1928

In January, the first professional production of *The Fascinating Foundling* is performed at the Arts Theatre Club. Also in January, Shaw is one of the pall bearers at the funeral of Thomas Hardy. Shaw's major political tract, *The Intelligent Women's Guide to Socialism and Capitalism* is published in June. From July until September, the Shaws visit the French Riviera and Geneva. In August, Shaw's correspondence with American heavyweight boxing champion Gene Tunney begins. During November and December, Shaw writes *The Apple Cart*.

January

9 (Mon)	The Shaws return home from Cliveden, their stay having been prolonged by heavy snow. [CL4: 83]
11	Death of the novelist, Thomas Hardy. Shaw is one of the pallbearers at Hardy's funeral at Westminster Abbey on 16 January. Shaw writes to Henry Salt (20 January): 'Galsworthy and I played everybody else off the stage... Kipling fidgeted like the devil, and did his best, by changing step continually, to make me fall over him.' To Hardy's widow, Florence Emily Hardy (16 January), Shaw wrote: 'It was a fine show; and I tried to look as solemn as possible; but I didn't feel solemn a bit. I rejoice in Hardy's memory; and I felt all the time that he was there – up in the lantern somewhere – laughing like anything at Kipling and me and Galsworthy and the rest of us... what an adventure it was, wasn't it?

Hooray! It's not proper; but that's how he makes me feel.' [CL4: 84–5]

28 First professional production of *The Fascinating Foundling* at the Arts Theatre Club. [CP3: 898; Morgan 103]

March

1 (Thu) Shaw gives a speech following a matinée of Strindberg's *Comrades* at the Everyman Theatre. [Lbib2: 718; DHL]

2 Writing to Molly Tompkins, Shaw urges her to 'Write oftener, far oftener, even if I cannot answer... I am alone tonight (Charlotte in the country); and if you would just ring at the door – ...' [Tompkins 124]

19 Shaw lectures on 'Ibsen and After' in the Ibsen Centenary celebration of the British Drama League. [*Manchester Guardian*, 20 Mar 1928; Lbib1: 338–9]

31 March – 28 April

The Shaws take a motoring tour in Wales. On 1 April, at the Hand Hotel, Llangollen, he stays in a suite of rooms once occupied by Robert Browning. On 2 April he visits ruins of the famous Berwyn chain bridge recently washed away by floods, and stays at the Oakwood Park Hotel, near Conway. The Shaws' visit to North Wales coincides with the opening on 3 April at the Grand Theatre, Llandudno 'of a nine-day series of the plays of Mr. Shaw by the Macdona Players'. ['Mr. Shaw's Motoring Tour in Wales', *Manchester Guardian*, 3 Apr 1928; DHL]

May

1 (Tue) Shaw dines with Edward Elgar at Stratford. [DHL]

24 (Thu) Shaw dines with the Rakovskys at Claridge's Hotel. Krastyu G. Rakovsky was a member of the Central Committee of the Soviet Communist Party and Soviet chargé d'affaires in London. [CL4: 67, 103]

26 May – 4 June

The Shaws stay with Lord and Lady Astor at Sandwich. [Tompkins 127; DHL]

31 Shaw writes to Molly Tompkins telling her that San Giovanni Island, Lake Maggiore is a place to spend six weeks a year in, not to live in, that she has secured her Ogygia, and is trying to play Calypso to his Odysseus, and adding 'this erotic-romantic attitude to life doesn't make you happy. If only you had a sense of humor!...a te, O cara'

GBS [CL4: 99–100]

June

1 (Fri) Simultaneous publication in London and New York of *The Intelligent Woman's Guide to Socialism and Capitalism*. The book

	attracts 50 000 advance purchasers in America prior to publication. The British edition of 10 000 is also sold out in advance. [Lbib1: 172; Morgan 11; CL3: 900; CL4: 98]
11–13	The first Movietone newsreel of Shaw (with his Mussolini impersonation) is filmed at Ayot after a test made on 9 June. [DHL]
28	Sean O'Casey comes to lunch with the Shaws. [DHL]

July

5 (Thu)	Lady Astor gives a reception for Shaw at her town house at 4 St James's Square. A number of people had been invited to meet Shaw, including A. E. Johnson, a Professor of English at Syracuse University, New York At some point during this reception Lady Astor was heard to remark: '"The trouble with you, G.B., is that you think you're clever; you're not clever, you're only *good*!"...the much-amused Shaw laughingly threw back his head and began to quote Kingsley's famous quatrain: "Be good, sweet maid, let who will be clever!"' [A. E. Johnson, 'Encounters with G.B.S.', in *The Dalhousie Review*, XXXI (Spring 1951); I&R 492–3]
12	Shaw dines at J. M.Barrie's with Florence Emily Hardy. [DHL]
13	American theatre producer-director Ted Harris visits Shaw at Whitehall Court. [DHL]
20	The Shaws begin a seven-week visit to the French Riviera, after five days at Agay. [CL4: 105; DHL; Hol3: 169]
21	Death of Ellen Terry after a stroke four days earlier. In *Ellen Terry and Bernard Shaw: A Correspondence*, Christopher St John notes: 'A few days after Ellen Terry's death, her daughter found a piece of paper labelled My Friends... this role of honour... was of very recent date, the name of Charles Reade was written first. Directly underneath it was the name Bernard Shaw.' [*Ellen Terry and Bernard Shaw: a Correspondence*, ed. Christopher St John (1932), 334; Peters 387]

August

11 (Sat)	Shaw dines with Frank Harris at Nice without Charlotte who refuses to fraternize with 'Frank Casanova'. [CL4: 105–6]
31	Shaw's correspondence with American heavyweight boxing champion Gene Tunney commences with his note to Tunney expressing the hope of being able to 'fix up a meeting' after the Shaws return from a visit to Geneva. (Previously, on hearing of Tunney's 'low opinion' of his early novel about a prize-fighter, *Cashel Byron's Profession*, Shaw had remarked: 'If Tunney said those things, he must have good taste. I'd like to meet the young man.' Their first meeting takes place in November 1928.)

[Gene Tunney, 'G.B. Shaw's Letters to Gene Tunney', *Collier's*, 23 Jun 1951]

September

2 (Sun) The Shaws travel from Cap D'Antibes to Geneva where they stay two weeks, and Shaw attends the League of Nations sitting on 5 September. Shaw's report on his visit to the seat of the League of Nations and the International Labour Organization becomes Fabian Tract No. 226. [CL4: 105; LBib2: 721; Hol3: 170, 396–7; Tompkins 129]

3 Writing to Molly Tompkins, Shaw explains why he has avoided Stresa this year: 'For seven weeks I have been hiding within a day's ride of your Renaud. I shall have left when this reaches you... I am not in the least angry: why should I be? But you should not drive me away to horrible hell-paradises like the Riviera by refusing to behave yourself tactfully.' [Tompkins 129]

12 Shaw dines with the League's Irish delegation. [DHL]

18 The Shaws return to London. [CL4: 107]

22 Ada (Shaw) Tyrrell and her sister Maud Clark come to lunch. [DHL]

26–29 Siegfried Trebitsch visits the Shaws in London and Ayot, and prepares 'Interview mit Shaw', published in the *Bossische Zeitung* on 15 November, as well as 'Mr. Bernard Shaw on Topics I Cannot Resist' on the same date. The same interview was published in the *New York Times* as 'Questions That Shaw Could Not Resist' on 18 November. [Weiss 293]

October

9 (Tue) Shaw declines a request from Marguerite Radclyffe Hall's solicitor, Stanley Rubinstein, to speak in court in favour of *The Well of Loneliness*, her banned novel about lesbianism. He does, however, advise Rubinstein on how to conduct the case. [CL4: 110–11]

25 Shaw guarantees a bank loan for Alice (Lockett) Salisbury Sharpe's husband. [DHL]

26 Shaw dines with Arnold Bennett to meet Sherwood Anderson. [DHL]

November

Shaw corresponds with 'Lewis Wynne' [Lewis Bostock], a freelance journalist claiming to be writing a book about Shaw. Wynne incorporated Shaw's utterances from various sources into a large number of forged letters and MSS, which circulated in the market from 1929 to 1931. [CL4: 120; Dan H. Laurence, *Shaw: An Exhibit* (1977), 26–8]

1 — The Webbs and Virginia and Leonard Woolf lunch with the Shaws at Whitehall Court. [DHL]

5 (Mon) — Shaw begins writing *The Apple Cart: a Political Extravaganza.* [CP6: 247; CL4: 125]

22 — Publication in the *Daily News* and the *Daily Herald* of a letter, 'Book Ban Denounced: Eminent People Defend [Radclyffe Hall's] *Well of Loneliness'* drafted by Shaw and Sir Desmond MacCarthy, dramatic critic and theatre historian, and signed by 45 well-known literary figures, including Virginia and Leonard Woolf, T. S. Eliot and E. M Forster, protesting against the government's censorship of literature. [Lbib2: 722]
Shaw gives a Fabian Society lecture, 'The Future of Western Civilisation'. [DHL]

29 — Shaw completes *The Apple Cart*, and reads it to Nancy Astor and her house-guests at Cliveden over the New Year. [CL4: 125; CP6: 247; Rat 234]

December

13 (Thu) — The Shaws lunch with the Masaryks. [DHL]

14 — The Shaws lunch at Whitehall Court with Gene Tunney and his wife, Polly. [DHL, correcting date in CL4: 130]

1929

In April, the Shaws embark on a continental tour, from which they return in mid-June. On 14 June, *The Apple Cart* premières at the Teatr Polski in Warsaw. By late June, Shaw has completed the draft of his preface to *Ellen Terry and Bernard Shaw: A Correspondence*. In August, the first English performance of *The Apple Cart* inaugurates the Malvern Festival. Shaw attends the festival, staying in Malvern until mid-September. Shaw returns to London and, a few days later, *The Apple Cart* is transferred to the Queen's Theatre, London. In October, the BBC broadcast a speech by Shaw entitled 'Democracy', and *The Apple Cart* is first published in German.

February

2 (Sat) — Shaw reminisces about Stresa, and the walks he used to take with Molly Tompkins: 'You desire to know whether I am Thru with you. At my age one is thru with everybody... I hoarded my bodily possessions so penuriously that even at seventy I had some left; but that remnant was stolen from me on the road to Baveno and on other roads to paradise through the same district. Now they are all dusty highways on which I am safe because nobody can rob a beggar.' [Tompkins 131]

10 — Thornton Wilder, Florence Emily Hardy and Dr Edith Somerville dine with the Shaws. [DHL]

19 Knowing Stella Campbell is in dire financial straits, Shaw offers to pay her electricity and telephone bills. [Dent 312]

February–April

Stella Campbell tries to persuade Shaw to read *The Apple Cart* to her, but he contrives not to do so, knowing she will be offended by his portrayal of her in the character of Orinthia. [Dent 311–18; CL4: 132–3; Peters 391–2; Hol3: 151]

21 February – 6 March

Stricken again with influenza, Shaw is attended by a nurse. [DHL]

March

2 (Sat) – 4 Shaw attends a rehearsal for *Major Barbara* (with Sybil Thorndike in the title role), which opens on 5 March. [DHL]

23 Shaw reads *The Apple Cart* to the Astors. [DHL]

April

5 (Fri) Death of Shaw's sister-in-law, Mary Cholmondeley, at her club in London. [CL4: 133; DHL; Dent 317]

6 In reply to Stella Campbell's comment: 'I ran away from you at Sandwich because I wanted to remain Queen of the Kingdom of my heart…' (5 April 1929), Shaw writes: 'Yes: you were right, Sandwich and all. And wrong, I suppose, to get married.' [Dent 316, 317; CL4: 133]

8 The Shaws attend Mary Cholmondeley's funeral in Shropshire. [CL4: 133]

10 Following a suicide attempt by Molly Tompkins, Shaw writes to her: 'You really <u>are</u> a duffer – couldn't even poison yourself properly!' [Tompkins 133]

14 The Shaws leave for the continent on the Orient Express. They travel first to Trieste, remaining there for two days before proceeding to the Hotel Brioni at Brioni, Istria, a peninsula in the North-East Adriatic Sea and tourist resort, where they stay until 14 May. Shaw spends considerable time at Brioni with Gene Tunney, and writes a film scenario modernizing *Cashel Byron's Profession*. [CL4: 133, 136, 137; Gene Tunney, 'G. B. Shaw's Letters to Gene Tunney', *Collier's*, 23 Jun 1951; Blanche Patch, *Thirty Years With GBS* (1951), 154]

29 Writing to Blanche Patch, Shaw reports: 'I have begun to work at the Ellen Terry preface, but am leaving it to gad about the island at every pretext.' [CL4: 139]

May

15 (Wed) – 26 The Shaws are in Yugoslavia, where they visit Dubrovnik (15th) and Split (23rd), and where Shaw's comments on

Mussolini cause embarrassment to government officials. [CL4: 137; Weiss 299; Hol3: 180–1]

20 Shaw refuses Stella Campbell's request to play 'the Queen' in *The Apple Cart*. [Dent 323–4]

27 The Shaws travel to Venice where they stay for a fortnight before returning to London. [CL4: 137]

June

Labour wins the General Election, and Ramsay MacDonald forms a minority government. [CL4: 141]

13 (Thu) The Shaws arrive back in London. Without yet having read it, Mrs Patrick Campbell resumes her complaints against *The Apple Cart*. [CL4: 137, 148ff.]

14 World première of *The Apple Cart* (*Wielki Kram*) at the Teatr Polski in Warsaw. [CP6: 247; CL4: 146; Hend2: 581; Morgan 85]

26 Shaw completes the first draft of a Preface to the proposed *Correspondence of Ellen Terry and Bernard Shaw*. [CL4: 134; Hol3: 181]

July

1 (Mon) Rehearsals of *The Apple Cart* for the Malvern Festival begin. [CL4: 150]

8 Stella Campbell to Shaw: 'You should have sent me your play to read. You are out of tune with friendship and simple courtesy.' [Dent 329]

9 Shaw attends a reception for Rhodes scholars at Cliveden. [DHL]

11 Shaw cancels an important appointment at the London School of Economics to rush to Stella Campbell's house to read her *The Apple Cart*, hoping to put her anxieties to rest. However, Stella is only upset further by the play's unfavourable allusion to her late son 'Beo'. Shaw removes the offending references to Beo's morals, but Stella still repudiates the play for its 'vulgar' portrayal of the triad of herself, Charlotte and Shaw. [CL4: 151–3; Dent 330]

14 Shaw has tea at Sir Philip Sassoon's where he meets the Duchess of York. [DHL]

19 Actress Elizabeth Bergner has tea with the Shaws. [DHL]

August

6 (Tue) – 31 Shaw at Malvern for the First Malvern Festival. Sir Barry Vincent Jackson, director and theatrical entrepreneur, founded the Malvern Festival, with Shaw as patron-in-chief. The 1929 season, which consisted entirely of Shaw's plays, opened with *The Apple Cart*, followed by revivals of *Back to Methuselah*, *Heartbreak House*, and *Caesar and Cleopatra*. In the 1930s and 1940s, Shaw's plays were the staple dramatic fare of the Festival

with a number of Shaw's plays having their British première at Malvern: *Too True to be Good* (1932), *The Simpleton of the Unexpected Isles* (1935), *Geneva* (1938) and *In Good King Charles's Golden Days* (1939). The film version of *Arms and the Man* (1932) was also premièred at the festival. Having lapsed after the Second World War, the festival was revived in 1977 as the Shaw–Elgar Festival. [I&R 371–2; *The Malvern Gazette*, 19 Aug 1944, 52; DHL; Morgan 23]

19 The first English performance of *The Apple Cart* inaugurates the Malvern Festival. [CL4: 157; CP6: 247; Morgan 85]

September

13 (Fri) Shaw speaks at an International Congress of the World League for Sexual Reform on 'The Need for Expert Opinion in Sexual Reform'. [P&P 200; Lbib1: 445]

17 Opening London performance of *The Apple Cart* which has been transferred to the Queen's Theatre. Celebrities in the audience include Prime Minister Ramsay MacDonald, H. G. Wells, Arnold Bennett, Noël Coward and Anita Loos (author of *Gentlemen Prefer Blondes*). [Erv 518; *Daily Mail* (London), 18 Sep 1929]

October

14 (Mon) Shaw broadcasts from Plymouth where he is visiting Lord Astor (12–16 October) a talk on 'Democracy' on the BBC. The text is subsequently incorporated into the Preface of *The Apple Cart*. [CL4: 164; DHL]

16 The BBC broadcasts *Captain Brassbound's Conversion*, with a live repeat performance three days later. Following the broadcasts Shaw writes to Hilda Matheson, the BBC's director of talks: 'As to the broadcast of Brassbound, its infamy was such that I hereby solemnly renounce, curse, and excommunicate everybody who had a hand in it.' [CL4: 164]

19 First publication of *The Apple Cart* in German translation as *Der Kaiser von Amerika*. The play is published in English in 1930. [Lbib1: 179]

19–21 Lady Gregory spends the weekend at Ayot. [DHL]

24 American dramatist Paul Green lunches at Whitehall Court. [DHL]

1930

In April, the Shaws travel to Edstaston and then Buxton for a short visit which is extended into a month-long stay when Charlotte becomes ill with scarlatina. In May, Edward Elgar dedicates his *Severn Suite* to Shaw. In July, Shaw finishes writing *What I Really Wrote about the War*. The revised version of *Immaturity* is first published in July, the English edition of *The Apple Cart* is published in December, and *The Real Bernard Shaw* by Maurice Colbourne is published during this year. In October, Shaw's first international radio broadcast occurs when he proposes the toast at a testimonial dinner for Albert Einstein. This speech, along with Einstein's response, is broadcast to America by the BBC. During this year, Shaw becomes chairman of the Advisory Committee on Spoken English at the BBC, a post he fills until 1937.

January

18 (Sat) In reply to a questionnaire from Frank Harris, Shaw writes: 'My dear Frank, You really are a daisy... Have you not yet found out that people like me and Shakespear <u>et hoc genus omne</u> have no souls?... You haven't the very faintest notion of the sort of animal I am. If I had time I would tell you the facts just to see how utterly they would disconcert you; but I haven't; so you must drop it.
This is not my humor (you idiot!) but the solid prosaic truth.' [Wein4: 218]

24 Shaw attends a superlative performance by the Hallé Orchestra from Manchester. Sir Hamilton Harty, the conductor, 'was a dripping rag at the end; but he had mastered and was feeling every phrase'. [CL4: 175–6]

February

1 (Sat) – 5 The Shaws visit Lady Astor at Cliveden. [CL4: 176]

6–8 Shaw sits for the American sculptor Jo Davidson at the Savoy Hotel. [CL4: 176]

24 *The Apple Cart* opens in New York. [Erv 518; Morgan 85]
The Dark Lady of the Sonnets and *Androcles and the Lion* are produced as a double bill at the Old Vic. [CL4: 176–7]

28 Shaw calls on C. K. Ogden to view his language experiments. [DHL]

March

7 (Fri) Shaw dines with H. G. Wells. [DHL]

16 Shaw outlines to Lady Rhondda (Margaret Haig Thomas), editor of *Time and Tide* and chairman of its publishing company, who is writing an article on 'Shaw's Women', the dramatic necessity of his characterization of certain women in his plays. [CL4: 179]

April

13 (Sun) Publication in the Manchester *Sunday Chronicle* of an article on Shaw by Winston Churchill. Churchill's discussion of the 'saint, sage and clown', as he calls his subject, begins with the declaration, 'Mr Bernard Shaw was one of my earliest antipathies', and ends with a description of Shaw as 'the greatest living master of

	English letters in the world'. The essay was published again in Churchill's *Great Contemporaries* (1937), and, with some cuts, in the London *Sunday Dispatch* on 2 March 1941. [Winston Churchill, 'Bernard Shaw – Saint, Sage and Clown', *Sunday Chronicle* (Manchester), 13 Apr 1930; I&R 494–5]
16	Shaw sees the John Galsworthy film *Escape*, starring Sir Gerald du Maurier. [DHL]
19–21	The Shaws motor to Edstaston to attend an unveiling of a memorial to Mary Cholmondeley at the local church. [CL4: 182]
22	The Shaws proceed to Buxton where they expect to stay one week. [CL4: 182]
26	Charlotte becomes ill, necessitating an extension of their stay in Buxton, with Shaw commuting to London on 27–30 to attend final rehearsals of *Jitta's Atonement*, which opens at the Arts Theatre on the 30th. [CL4: 185; DHL]

May

1 (Thu)	Shaw finds that Charlotte's illness is scarlatina. [DHL]
5	Shaw engages a nurse to care for Charlotte. [CL4: 185]
14	Shaw dashes off to London, where he attends a Stage Society meeting. [CL4: 186; DHL]
15	Shaw lunches with Nancy Astor and the missionary, Mabel Shaw, at Whitehall Court. The same day he attends a meeting of the RADA council. [CL4: 186]
16	Shaw travels to Birmingham to view a performance of *Heartbreak House* at the Birmingham Repertory. [CL4: 186]
17	Shaw returns to Charlotte's bedside at Buxton. She has her first outing, a drive, on 19 May. [CL4: 186]
21	Shaw sends the car to Nottingham to fetch Lady Astor. [DHL]
25	Shaw accepts Edward Elgar's request to dedicate his *Severn Suite* to Shaw. [CL4: 200]
28	The Shaws leave Buxton. [CL4: 185; DHL, correcting CL4]

June

20 (Fri)	Shaw sends Frank Harris the galley proofs of the autobiographical Preface to *Immaturity*. [CL4: 187–8]

July

3 (Thu)	Sándor Hevesi, Shaw's Hungarian translator, visits Shaw at Whitehall Court, and returns for lunch on 17 July. [DHL]
7	Beginning of rehearsals at the Old Vic for the Malvern Festival, directed unofficially by Shaw. [CL4: 193]
9	Writing to Otto Kyllman of Constable & Co., Shaw reports: 'I have just finished the last stroke of the War Book [*What I Really Wrote about the War*].' [CL4: 193]

10 William Randolph Hearst lunches at Whitehall Court. [DHL]

12 Shaw threatens Elbridge Adams with legal action if he publishes Shaw's letters to Ellen Terry without Shaw's consent. Later in the year, he changes his mind and supports Edy Craig's idea of publishing their correspondence. [CL4: 194, 202–10]

26 Shaw's revised version of *Immaturity* published for the first time as Volume 1 of *The Works of Bernard Shaw: Collected Edition* (1930–8). [Lbib1: 183]

August

1 (Fri) Shaw has a visit from Sasha Kropotkin, whose husband Boris Lebedoff was one of Shaw's Russian translators. [DHL]

c. 1 Shaw negotiates with John Maxwell, Managing Director of British International Pictures, for the film rights to *How He Lied to Her Husband*. [CL4: 195]

10 Shaw departs for Malvern, where he stays until 25 September. [CL4: 193]

September

9 (Tue) – 12 Shaw motors to Hereford for the Three Choirs Festival to hear Elgar's *The Apostles* and *The Dream of Gerontius*, plus Bach's B-Minor Mass. [DHL]

13 Under the heading 'GBS – Beauty Specialist', the *Birmingham Weekly Post* reports Shaw's participation in a bathing party with young Socialists at the Independent Labour Party Summer School at Malvern. Basking happily in the sun, Shaw imparts a beauty hint, telling the company he owes his good complexion to the fact that he 'never used soap upon his face. His morning wash...consisted of splashing his face with cold water, and he proceeded to give the girls a practical object lesson in the art of hygienic ablution.' [*Birmingham Weekly Post*, 13 Sep 1930]

18 Shaw writes another one of his lively replies to Frank Harris's research queries: 'What an impossible chap you are?... I may say that from Ellen Terry to Edith Evans all the famous actresses with whom I had any personal contact have given me their unreserved friendship; but only with one, long since dead, and no great actress either, (she is hinted at in my preface to Archer's plays) had I any Harrisian adventures.

...no biography of me except Henderson's is authorised, and... yours is specially deprecated. And if you publish a word of mine I'll have the law on you.' [Wein4: 237–40]

25 Shaw threatens to sue Simon & Schuster for infringement of his copyright if they publish Frank Harris's biography. The biography misappropriates Shaw's letters and the Preface to *Immaturity*. [CL4: 199]

27 — The Shaws attend the National Brass Band Championship at the Crystal Palace where they hear Edward Elgar's *Severn Suite*, which Elgar had dedicated to Shaw, played eight times. [CL4: 200]

October

28 (Tue) — Shaw proposes Albert Einstein's health at a testimonial dinner for Einstein at the Savoy Hotel. Shaw's speech (and Einstein's reply), broadcast by the BBC to America, is Shaw's first international radio broadcast. [CL4: 210–12]

29 — Charlotte has a fall while shopping in Hanover Street, breaking bones in her shoulder and pelvis. [CL4: 225]

November

14 (Fri) — Shaw addresses the Women's League of Arts at the behest of May Morris.[DHL]

27 — Shaw lectures on 'A Cure for Democracy' at the Kingsway Hall, rounding off the Fabian Society's autumn lecture series on 'The Unending Quest: An Inquiry into Developments in Democratic Government'. [CL4: 214–15]

30 — Shaw proposes to 'bring the Fabian to life again' with a new volume of essays on *The Political Machinery of Socialism*; however, his plan is never realized. [CL4: 215]

December

5 (Fri) — Shaw attends a private showing of Molly Tompkins's paintings at the Leicester Galleries in London. [CL4: 184]

6 — Shaw attends a private screening of *The Love Parade* and meets its star Maurice Chevalier. [DHL]

11 — Publication of *The Apple Cart* in English. [Lbib1: 180]

1931

In January, the film version of *How He Lied to Her Husband*, directed by Cecil Lewis, premières in London. In February, Shaw's article 'G. B. Shaw on Fascism' is published in the *Daily Telegraph*. The early 1930s were an intense period of world travelling for the Shaws. In March, the Shaws embark on a four-week tour to the Mediterranean and the Holy Land, immediately followed by a three-week holiday in Venice and a fortnight in Paris, returning to London in early May. In July, Shaw travels to Russia, followed by the Fabian Summer School and the Malvern Festival. In December, the Shaws sail for South Africa. This period was also a prolific writing period for Shaw. On 5 March, the first morning at sea, Shaw begins *Too True to be Good*. In late August, following the death of Frank Harris, Shaw begins working on the proofs (and rewriting significant sections) of

Harris's *Bernard Shaw: An Unauthorised Biography. Ellen Terry and Bernard Shaw: A Correspondence*, for which Shaw had written the preface, is also published this year. On the journey to South Africa, Shaw begins drafting *The Rationalisation of Russia*.

January

8 (Thu)	Shaw attends a reception for the Bengali poet, Rabindranath Tagore. [DHL]
12	First London showing of Shaw's experimental film of *How He Lied to Her Husband*, directed by Cecil Lewis. [CL4: 286]
23	(Sir) Oswald and Mrs Mosley and the Grigory Sokolnikoffs lunch with the Shaws. [DHL]

February

19 (Thu)	Dean and Mrs W. R. Inge and Sir Robert (later Baron) Vansittart, British Under-Secretary of State for Foreign Affairs, lunch with the Shaws. [DHL]
25	Publication in the *Daily Telegraph* of 'G. B. Shaw on Fascism', Shaw's reply to a question put to him about Hitler and the Third Reich. Shaw states that the rise of the Third Reich 'owes its existence and its vogue solely to the futility of liberal parliamentarism on the English model...we are being swept into the dustbin by Steel Helmets, Fascists, Dictators, military councils, and anything else that represents a disgusted reaction against our obsolescence and uselessness.' ['G.B. Shaw on Fascism', *Daily Telegraph*, 25 Feb 1931; I&R 354–5]
	The Shaws lunch at Lady Astor's to meet Charles Chaplin and the flyer Amy Johnson. Two nights later Shaw attends the première of Chaplin's *City Lights*. [DHL]

March

3 (Tue)	The Shaws leave London for Marseilles to join the Hellenic Travellers' Club tour of the Mediterranean and the Holy Land. Their four-week tour includes Malta, Alexandria, Cairo, Jerusalem, Damascus, Beirut, Cyprus, Rhodes, Eleusis and Athens. [CL4: 228]
5	During the first morning at sea on his Mediterranean tour, Shaw begins writing *Too True to be Good*. [CL4: 241]
29	Shaw lectures on Greek theatre while in Athens. [CL4: 228]

April

1 (Wed)	The Shaws leave the Hellenic Travellers' Club tour to stay three weeks in Venice. [CL4: 235]
22	The Shaws begin their stay in Paris. [CL4: 235]
24	Shaw attends the Pitoëff's performance of *La charrette de pommes* (*The Apple Cart*), and judges it to be 'ugly, silly, and incompetent'. [CL4: 236–7]

30 Ludmilla and Georges Pitoëff and the Hamons are guests of the Shaws at lunch. [DHL]

May

7 (Thu) The Shaws leave Paris for London, their departure having been delayed by Charlotte catching a severe cold. [CL4: 235]

14 Shaw calls on Elizabeth Robins, their first meeting for over 35 years. [DHL]

Saint Joan is broadcast on the BBC. [DHL]

June

7 (Sun) Shaw lunches at Chequers as a guest of Ramsay MacDonald. [DHL]

8 Pleading that 'it is not my subject; and it is not a man's subject anyhow', Shaw declines Muriel MacSwiney's request to support the pro-abortion movement. [CL4: 237–8]

12 Stella Campbell launches another unsuccessful campaign to gain Shaw's permission to publish their correspondence. [Dent 336ff.]

30 Shaw finishes the first draft of *Too True to be Good*. [I&R 328 n1; CL4: 241]

July

18 (Sat) Shaw leaves Victoria Station for a visit to Russia, in a touring party which includes Viscount and Lady Astor, their son the Hon. Francis David Astor (then a student at Balliol College, Oxford), Philip Henry Kerr (11th Marquess of Lothian), newspaper editor and statesman, and Christian Scientist, Charles Tennant. [CL4: 239, 242–3; I&R 320–7; Maurice Collis, *Nancy Astor: an Informal Biography* (1960), 161–8]

19 Early in the morning the party reaches Berlin, departing the same evening on the Moscow–Warsaw night express. [CL4: 243]

20 Crossing the Russian border at 4 p.m., Shaw and his party transfer to a wide-gauge Russian train, where Shaw says he can 'at last stretch myself at full length in my bunk'. [CL4: 245–6]

21 The touring party arrives in Moscow, at the Alexandrovsky railway station. Shaw is greeted by 'a brass band, a military guard of honour ... and a horde of welcoming Russians estimated in the thousands (most of them employees of the publishing house Gosizdat) shouting "Hail Shaw."' After settling in at the Hotel Metropole, he visits Lenin's tomb and the Kremlin, and attends a performance of an adaptation of Bertolt Brecht and Kurt Weill's *The Threepenny Opera* (*Die Dreigroschenoper*) – described by Shaw in a letter to Charlotte as 'an amazing and at points disgusting perversion of The Beggar's Opera' – in the

evening. [CL4: 246–7; H. W. L. Dana, 'Shaw in Moscow', *American Mercury*, Mar 1932; I&R 320–3]

22 Shaw and his party begin their official programme of conducted visits: they are shown an institution for young criminals and a theatre in which a film is being made, and where the audience is instructed to receive Shaw 'with tumultuous applause'. [CL4: 243]

23 A day of sightseeing, meetings and travel to Leningrad. In the morning the visiting party sees 'a huge electric factory' and after lunch they drive to a house in the country where Shaw meets actor, director and producer Konstantin Stanislavsky, who enquires about Granville Barker. In the evening they set out for Leningrad, where they are lodged in 'Grand Ducal suites' at the Hotel de l'Europe. Shaw reports, in a postscript to an affectionate letter to Charlotte that 'Nancy Astor wants to wash my hair with Lux. She says she can do it better than Bertha Hammond.' [CL4: 248–50]

25 Shaw performs informally for a 'Lenin talkie'.[DHL]

26 Having arrived back in Moscow early in the morning, Shaw attends a horse-racing meet in the afternoon (which includes a 'Bernard Shaw Handicap'). In the evening, he attends a dinner in the Concert Hall of Nobles for 2000 people honouring his 75th birthday. [CL4: 250, 253, 254; DHL]

27 Shaw visits art galleries, where he sees works by Gauguin and others. [DHL]

28 Shaw visits model collective farms. [CL4: 250]

29 Shaw visits Maxim Gorky who was too ill to attend the birthday dinner. In the evening Shaw and Nancy Astor have an interview with Joseph Stalin. It is one of the longest interviews ever granted to outsiders, lasting, according to Nancy Astor, an hour and three quarters. Shaw is said to have remarked of his meeting with Stalin: 'I expected to see a Russian working man and I found a Georgian gentleman.' [H. W. L. Dana, 'Shaw in Moscow', *American Mercury*, Mar 1932; I&R 323; 'I Told Stalin – By Lady Astor', *Daily Mail* (London), 6 Mar 1953; CL4: 254, 258]

30 After inspecting the Red Army barracks and making a visit to Lenin's widow, the tourists sets out for home by train from Moscow at 9.30 p.m. [CL4: 250, 258–9]

31 July – 2 August

The tourists travel via Stolpce and Berlin to arrive at Liverpool Street station early on the morning of the 2nd. Shaw is reported as predicting on arrival that 'Russia is Going to be a Roaring Success'. [CL4: 242, 259; '"G.B.S." Back From Russia', *Manchester Guardian*, 3 Aug 1931]

August

6 (Thu) – 7 Beatrice Webb reports that 'tired and excited by his visit to Russia', Shaw attends the Fabian Summer School, and adds: 'It is odd that it is [Russia's] domination by a creed that seems so attractive to GBS; he being that great destroyer of existing codes, creeds and conventions, seems in his old age, to hanker for some credo to be *enforced* from birth onwards on the whole population.' [DBW4: 249–50]

Mid-August–mid-September

The Shaws attend the Malvern Festival, which for the first time presents the works of other dramatists and, at his request, none by Shaw. [CL4: 259–60; V. Elliot, '"Genius Loci": The Malvern Festival Tradition' in *Shaw: The Annual of Bernard Shaw Studies*, vol. 3, ed. Daniel Leary (1983), 206–7; DHL]

August

21 (Fri) The Shaws lunch with the Dean of Worcester. [DHL]

26 Death of Frank Harris. Shaw sets to work immediately correcting the proofs of, and adding embroideries to, Harris's *Bernard Shaw: an unauthorised biography* scheduled for publication in November. [CL4: 259–60]

28 The Shaws take Edward Elgar to lunch. [DHL]

September

4 (Fri) Publication of *Ellen Terry and Bernard Shaw: A Correspondence*, with a preface by GBS, against the wishes of Gordon Craig, Terry's son, who battled Shaw in interviews and with the eventual counter-publication in late 1931 of *Ellen Terry and Her Secret*. During this time, Mrs Patrick Campbell renewed her efforts to gain Shaw's permission to publish their correspondence. [Lbib1: 201–2; Press Release, 'Mr Shaw Explains', G. P. Putnam's Sons, New York, Nov 1931, Cornell 4617 Box 5; CL4: 202, 265; Dent 352]

October

11 (Sun) Shaw's radio address to America about Russia, 'Look, You Boobs', is broadcast. [DHL]

23 The Shaws lunch with the Bertrand Russells. [DHL]

November

At Molly Tompkins's news that she will be visiting London for an exhibition of her paintings, Shaw writes: 'How terrifying! What am I to do with you?' Nevertheless, Shaw meets with Molly and purchases one of her paintings, 'Road to Baveno', which recalled the scene of their walks by Lake Maggiore five years before. [Charles A. Berst, 'Shaw, Molly Tompkins, and Italy, 1921–1950' in SA 109]

6 (Fri) Shaw meets Gandhi in London. Gandhi remarks of Shaw: 'I think he is a very good man... I think he is a very witty man, a lover of epigram and paradox, with a Puck-like spirit and a generous ever-young heart, the Arch Jester of Europe.' [*Collected Works of Gandhi*, vol. 48 (Sep 1931 – Jan 1932), 353; CL4: 267]

26 As part of the Fabian Society's lecture series 'Capitalism in Dissolution: What Next?' Shaw delivers a lecture entitled 'What Indeed?' at the Kingsway Hall. [CL4: 269]

27 Frank Harris's *Bernard Shaw: an unauthorised biography based on first hand information* is published posthumously. Shaw undertook to supervise revisions of the manuscript, rewriting significant amounts of the text and adding a whole new chapter. [Lbib1: 506–7; CL4: 261–4]

December

3 (Thu) Shaw participates in H. G. Wells's BBC symposium on 'What would I do if I were dictator?' [CL4: 272]

10 Lord Olivier comes to lunch. [DHL]

12, 26 Shaw exchanges letters with Rev. Edward Lyttleton in the pages of *Time and Tide* on the subject of 'Moral Detachment'. [Lbib2: 737; CL4: 276]

24 The Shaws sail from Southampton for South Africa on the RMMV *Carnarvon Castle*. During their 17 days at sea, Shaw drafts one chapter of *The Rationalization of Russia*, a book he later abandons. [CL4: 269]

1932

In January and February, an illustrated article by Shaw on Russia is published in New York and London. On 11 January, the Shaws arrive in Cape Town. On 6 February, Shaw gives the first nationwide broadcast in South Africa. The following day, the Shaws hire a car, intending to drive to Cape Elizabeth. Along the way, the Shaws have a car accident in which Charlotte is seriously injured. While Charlotte is recuperating, Shaw begins writing *The Adventures of the Black Girl in Her Search for God*. In March, the Shaws charter a plane and fly to Cape Town where they embark on their voyage home. *Too True to be Good* premières in February at the Colonial Theater in Boston and the film version of *Arms and the Man*, directed by Cecil Lewis, premières in August at the Malvern Festival. In September, Shaw is elected president of the Irish Academy of Letters and sometime during this year, Archibald Henderson's revised and expanded biography, *Bernard Shaw: Playboy and Prophet*, is published. In December, the Shaws set off on more travels, this time on a round-the-world cruise on the SS *Empress of Britain*.

January, February

Shaw's highly favourable illustrated article on Russia published in *Cosmopolitan* (New York) as 'What G.B.S. Found in Red Russia', and in *Nash's-Pall Mall Magazine* as 'Touring in Russia'. [Lbib2: 737]

January

11 (Mon) The Shaws disembark at Cape Town where they stay almost four weeks. During his stay, Shaw is much feted and meets many dignitaries, including Prime Minister James Hertzog, General Smuts and millionaire I. W. Schlesinger. Without using notes, he addresses an audience of 3000 in the Cape Town City Hall for two hours, makes a nationwide radio broadcast and takes a much publicized and photographed flight in a Junkers aeroplane. [CL 4: 269; I&R 327–9]

12 In an interview published in the *Cape Times*, Shaw says that his play of the previous year, *Too True to be Good,* was about 'the breakdown of morality in the [First World] war'. Quoting Milton's Satan, he declares: 'You cannot turn morality upside down for four years and say, "Evil, be thou my good".' ['Breakdown of Morality', *Cape Times* (Cape Town), 12 Jan 1932]

13 Shaw is the chief guest at a University Club luncheon at the Opera House Restaurant, Cape Town. In his address he remarks on the absence of women at the luncheon, and attacks universities for not fulfilling their proper function 'to produce a civilised mentality'. The person usually elected to be a Rector of a University was 'a crude type of politician'. ['"G.B.S" Hits Out Again: The University System Attacked. Turning Out Savages', *Cape Times* (Cape Town), 14 Jan 1932]

19 Shaw has a meeting with Harry Houdini whom he calls in his diary the 'escapologist'. [DHL]

23 Shaw and Charlotte are taken on scenic flights over Cape Town and the peninsula from Maitland aerodrome aboard a Union Airways mail service Junkers monoplane, piloted by Captain R. H. Fry. Shaw is reported as saying 'it was one of the most thrilling experiences I have had'. ['"G.B.S." in the Air: Peninsula Flight Enjoyed', *Cape Times* (Cape Town), 25 Jan 1932]

28, 30 Shaw swims at Glencairn. [DHL]

February

1 (Mon) Shaw lectures to the Cape Fabians on 'The Rationalisation of Russia'. [CL4: 273]

6 Shaw delivers from Cape Town the first nationwide radio broadcast in the Union of South Africa. 'Less surf-bathing and more thinking' was the keynote of his advice to South Africa, in a

wide-ranging, 20-minute talk. Warning that 'saying nice things is not my business', he spoke of Cape Town slums, poor farming methods and of South Africa as a 'sun-trap' for hedonistic pursuits by the idle rich. On race, he said: 'If white civilisation breaks down through idleness and loafing based on slavery, then, as likely as not, the next great civilisation will be a negro civilisation.' ['The Dangers of a "Sun-Trap": Mr Bernard Shaw's Warning to South Africa', *Cape Times* (Cape Town), 8 Feb 1932; CL4: 273; Lbib2: 866]

7 The Shaws set out in a hired car for Cape Elizabeth where they plan to embark for Durban and the homeward voyage up the east coast of Africa. [CL4: 276]

10 Approaching Knysna, with Shaw at the wheel, they have an accident in which Charlotte is injured. Shaw provides a graphic account of the accident in a letter to Lady Rhondda on 15 February, drawing on Mercutio's dying speech in *Romeo and Juliet* and an exclamation from *Hamlet* in his description of Charlotte's injuries: 'I negotiated several mountain ranges and gorges in a masterly manner; but on what I thought a perfectly safe bit of straight road I indulged in a turn of speed and presently got violently deflected into an overcorrected spin. I got out of it by jumping a fence, crashing through a bunker with 5 strands of barbed wire snapping one after another in a vain attempt to restrain me, and plunging madly down a steep place until I had the happy thought of shifting my straining foot from the accelerator to the brake. I got off with a crack on the chin from the steering wheel and a clip on the knee.

But Charlotte!! I can't describe it. Broken head, two black eyes, sprained left arm, bruised back, and a hole in her shin not so deep as a well nor so wide as a church door but – let me not think on't.' [CL4: 276–7]

19 To while away the time during Charlotte's recuperation in Knysna, Shaw begins writing *The Adventures of the Black Girl in Her Search for God*, which he completes in 18 days. [CL4: 280–1]

29 Première of *Too True to be Good* presented by the Theater Guild at the Colonial Theater in Boston. [CL4: 301; CP6: 397; Morgan 87]

March

17 (Thu) Charlotte recuperates sufficiently to allow travel to George where the Shaws charter a Union Airway Junker to take them back to Cape Town and their ship, the *Warwick Castle*. [CL4: 277]

18 The Shaws embark at Cape Town on their voyage home, arriving at Southampton on 4 April. [CL3: 277; DHL; I&R 328]

April

14 (Thu) Shaw sends the MS of 'the Black Girl story' to R. and R. Clark to have proofs printed. [CL4: 288]

18–22 Shaw supervises rehearsals of a revival of *Heartbreak House* to be staged by the Birmingham Repertory Company at the Queen's Theatre in London. He then goes to Stratford for the opening of the New Shakespeare Theatre on 23 April. [CL4: 284; DHL]

20 Shaw replies to Esmé Percy's request for a loan with a gift of £100: 'On your life, don't tell anybody.' [CL4: 288]

25 Shaw returns to London for the opening of *Heartbreak House*. [DHL]

May

5 (Thu) Shaw lunches with the Astors. [CL4: 284]

8 Shaw approaches John Farleigh requesting a trial wood engraving to illustrate *The Black Girl*. [CL4: 295]

21 Sidney and Beatrice Webb leave on a three-month visit to Russia. [DBW4: 286; I&R 497–9]

24 Farleigh's sample proving satisfactory, Shaw engages him to produce engravings for *The Black Girl*. [CL4: 299]

27 Shaw has a meeting with Russian pianist Maria Levinskaya (resident in London). [DHL]

June

2 (Thu) The Shaws attend a lunch party at the home of Maynard Keynes. Virginia Woolf, who is also present, provides a vivid account of the occasion. [*The Diaries of Virginia Woolf 1931–5*, eds. Anne Olivier Bell and Andrew McNeillie (1982), 106–7; I&R 497]

11 Shaw visits Elstree Studios for filming of location scenes for *Arms and the Man*. [DHL]

24 Shaw seeks Sir Almroth Wright's advice on a possible error of medical fact in *Too True to be Good*. [CL4: 299]

July

6 (Wed) Shaw asks Stanley Clench, his accountant and financial adviser, to set up a £10 000 annuity payable to 'my wife during her lifetime and afterwards to me if I survive her'. [CL4: 300]

11 Shaw delivers a radio broadcast on parents and children as part of the BBC series *Rungs of the Ladder*. [CL4: 290]

18 While *Too True to be Good* is in press, Shaw makes last minute corrections of the medical error confirmed by Sir Almroth Wright. [CL4: 299]

23 Shaw visits Elstree again for last-minute additional filming or editing of *Arms and the Man*. [DHL]

25 July – 25 August
Shaw at Malvern. [DHL]

August

Shaw sits at Malvern for his bust sculpture by Sigmund de Strobl. [DHL]

4 (Thu) Shaw attends the world première at the Malvern Festival of the film version of *Arms and the Man*, directed by Cecil Lewis. [CL4: 286]

6 British première at the Malvern Festival of *Too True to be Good*. [CL4: 301]

30 First publication in German translation of *Too True to Be Good* as *Zu Wahr um Schön Zu Sein*. [Lbib1: 208–9]

September

2 (Fri) Shaw visits Elgar in Worcester, and attends the opening service of the Three Choirs Festival on the 4th. On 7 September he attends a performance of Elgar's Symphony No. 1 in A-Flat, and on the 8th *The Music Makers*. [DHL]

13 First night of *Too True to be Good* in London. It survives for only 47 performances. [DHL]

14 In Shaw's absence, the inaugural meeting in Dublin of the Irish Academy of Letters elects him president, an office he fills until 1935, and for an additional year following Yeats's death in 1939. [CL4: 308]

30 Shaw suggests to John Reith, Managing Director of the BBC, that the corporation should sponsor Edward Elgar in the writing of his third symphony. Reith accepts Shaw's suggestion but Elgar dies before the symphony is completed. [CL4: 309–10]

October

10 (Mon) – 18 Exhibition of John Farleigh's work, Shaw having attended a private viewing on the 8th. [DHL]

November

24 (Thu) Shaw lectures 'In Praise of Guy Fawkes' to the Fabian Society at the Kingsway Hall. [DHL; P&P 235]

December

5 (Mon) Publication of *The Adventures of the Black Girl in Her Search for God*, which offended many (including Dame Laurentia McLachlan), but sold 150 000 copies in Britain and America. [Lbib1: 210; CL4: 344, 347, 348; Morgan 11]

16 The Shaws embark at Monaco for a round-the-world cruise on the SS *Empress of Britain*. Sailing from west to east, they proceeded via Naples (visiting Pompeii on the 18th, Vesuvius on the 20th), Athens, Haifa, Port Said and Luxor (with a flight to Asswan on the 31st), through the Suez Canal towards India.

['Shaw in India', *The Independent Shavian*, IV, no. 2, Winter 1965–6; DHL; CL4: 318–22]

1933

Travelling through the Suez Canal on New Year's Day, the *Empress of Britain* proceeds to Bombay, then onto Colombo, Singapore, Bangkok, Manila, Hong Kong, Shanghai, Yokohama, Tokyo, Honolulu, San Francisco, Los Angeles, Balboa, Havana and New York. Throughout this journey, Shaw meets various dignitaries and celebrities including Theodore Roosevelt (Jnr) (the Governor of Manila), Soong Chingling (Mme Sun Yat-sen, one of the famous Soong sisters), Admiral Makoto Saito (the Prime Minister of Japan), Sir Robert Ho Tung (the inspiration for *Buoyant Billions*), William Randolph Hearst, Upton Sinclair, Charlie Chaplin and the daughter of Henry George. During this world cruise, Shaw writes *Village Wooing* and begins writing *On the Rocks*. The Shaws attend the Malvern Festival in August, followed by the Hereford Music Festival in September. In November, *On the Rocks* premières at the Winter Garden Theatre and *Village Wooing* is first published in Germany.

January

2 (Mon) Shaw commences writing *The Red Sea*, later entitled *Village Wooing*. He completes the first draft three weeks later. [CL4: 326; Weiss 334, 335]

8–16 The *Empress of Britain* anchors off Bombay. While the other passengers leave to tour Delhi and Agra, the Shaws explore sites in and around Bombay, including the Jain Marble Temple in the Walkeshwar Hills, where Shaw sees carved images of gods and goddesses. At Aiwan-e-Rafat he sees a performance by sisters Tara, Sitara and Alakhnanada, 'exquisite' dancers from Nepal. (These experiences are recalled in *The Simpleton of the Unexpected Isles*.) [CL4: 320; Hiralal Amritlal Shah, 'Bernard Shaw in Bombay', *The Shaw Bulletin*, I, no. 10, Nov 1956; Atiya Begum, 'Bernard Shaw at Aiwan-e-Rafat', *Dawn* (Karachi), 5 Nov 1950; Valli Rao, 'Seeking the Unknowable: Shaw in India' in SA 181–209; I&R 330–1]

19–23 The *Empress of Britain* docks in Colombo. Shaw tours inland for a visit to Kandy. On the 23rd he visits a cousin, Mary Rhoda Creasy, youngest child of Uncle Henry Shaw. [*The Hindu* (Madras), 1933; 'Shaw in India', *The Independent Shavian*, IV, no. 2 (Winter 1965–6); DHL; Lgen 17; I&R 332–3]

31 As Shaw is leaving Batavia, Shaw learns of the death of John Galsworthy. [DHL]

February

In response to Shaw's censorious comments about Hitler's anti-Semitism on his travels, the opening performance of *Too True to be Good* in Mannheim, Germany is disrupted by Nazi shouts of 'Jew Moissi' (the name of the non-Jewish leading actor) and 'Jew Shaw', until police intervene. Writing to Siegfried Trebitsch on 12–15 May 1933, Shaw said: 'All through my tour the first question put by the press at every port was about Hitler. I said that a statesman who began by a persecution of the Jews was compromised as hopelessly as an officer who began by cheating at cards.' [Weiss 334–5; *New York Times*, 30 Apr 1933; CL4: 336, 338]

6 (Mon) Shaw begins writing *On the Rocks* but does not complete it until after his return to Ayot. [CL4: 326]

9 During the ship's one-day stay in Manila, the Shaws dine with the Governor, Theodore Roosevelt, son of the former President of the United States. They then sail to Hong Kong (staying 11–15 February) and to Shanghai (17 February). [CL4: 325; 'Shaw in India', *The Independent Shavian*, IV, no. 2, Winter 1965–6; Dan H. Laurence, '"That Awful Country": Shaw in America' in SA 282; Lu Hsun, 'Lusin looks at Bernard Shaw', trans. in *Shaw Bulletin,* Nov 1956; I&R 334]

11 Shaw takes a tour of the island of Hong Kong, guided by R. K. Simpson, Professor of English at Hong Kong University. [Piers Gray, 'Hong Kong, Shanghai, The Great Wall: Bernard Shaw in China' in SA 212]

13 Accompanied by Professor Simpson, Shaw visits millionaire merchant Sir Robert Ho Tung at his residence 'Idlewild', and attends a service in the private temple there. Later in the year, Shaw was to write in an essay, 'Aesthetic Science', that: 'I had found it [the service] extraordinarily soothing and happy though I had not understood a word of it. "Neither have I", [Sir Robert] said, "but it soothes me too." It was part of the art of life for Chinaman and Irishman alike, and was purely esthetic.' The temple was later to appear in Act III of *Buoyant Billions*.

In the afternoon, Shaw addresses students in the Great Hall of Hong Kong University. He urges them to be 'revolutionaries at twenty' or risk becoming hidebound in middle age, which is reported as 'incitement to revolution'. [Piers Gray, 'Hong Kong, Shanghai, the Great Wall: Bernard Shaw in China' in SA 213–14; Ritchie Calder, *Daily Herald*, 20 Apr 1933; I&R 340–1; CL4: 764]

17 Shaw in Shanghai, where university students arranging a reception for him are arrested. The Shaws lunch with Soong Chingling, widow of the Chinese revolutionary leader Sun Yat-

sen, and sister of Madame Chiang Kai-shek. The Shaws next travel by train to Beijing for three days, and fly over the Great Wall in an aeroplane. [Piers Gray, 'Hong Kong, Shanghai, the Great Wall: Bernard Shaw in China' in SA 226–35; Ritchie Calder, interview with Shaw aboard the *Empress of Britain*, in *Daily Herald* (London), 20 Apr 1933; I&R 334, 340; CL4: 325–6]

24 Dodd, Mead & Co. publish the first American edition of *The Adventures of the Black Girl in her Search for God*, Shaw having broken with Brentano's, his previous American publisher, who were in financial difficulties. [CL4: 319; Lbib1: 211]

28 February – 6 March

The *Empress of Britain* calls at the Japanese ports of Beppu, Kobe and Yokohama. In Japan, Shaw has a meeting with the Prime Minister, Admiral Makoto Saito, has a two-hour chat with the Minister of War General Sadao Araki, attends a Noh performance in his honour, and addresses delegates from the Socialist People's Party who are confused to find he has changed some of his views between writing *Fabian Essays* and *The Intelligent Woman's Guide*. The *Empress of Britain* then sails to Honolulu and California. [CL4: 326; '"G.B.S." Talks to Japan', *Manchester Guardian*, 28 Apr 1933; I&R 335]

March

16 (Thu) The *Empress of Britain* stops for two days in Honolulu. Shaw explores the city by automobile and attends the world première of Christopher Morley's play *Where the Blue Begins* at the University of Hawaii. [Dan H. Laurence,'"That Awful Country": Shaw in America', in SA 282–3]

24 The *Empress of Britain* arrives at San Francisco, where Shaw is bombarded with questions from newspaper reporters. On the following day, the Shaws are flown from Mills Field to the ranch of William Randolph Hearst at San Simeon, where they stay four days as guests of Hearst and his mistress Marion Davies, and are surrounded by 'a bevy of Hollywood starlets and intimate friends of Davies'. Shaw swims in the two swimming pools and enjoys the Hearst Ranch collection of exotic animals and birds. [Dan H. Laurence, '"That Awful Country": Shaw in America', in SA 284; CL4: 332]

28 Experiencing an alarming forced landing of their aircraft on the way, the Shaws travel to Santa Monica to visit the MGM studio at Culver city where they have lunch in a bungalow built for Marion Davies with Louis B. Mayer, Charles Chaplin, Clark Gable, John Barrymore and others. They afterwards tour the studio, receiving a frosty reception, possibly because of Shaw's

previous caustic remarks about Hollywood. [Dan H. Laurence, '"That Awful Country": Shaw in America', in SA 285]

28 March – 11 April

The *Empress of Britain* sails via Los Angeles (San Pedro) and the Panama Canal to the Caribbean and north to New York, calling at Havana, where again Shaw is besieged by reporters. [DHL]

April

11 (Tue) At 10 a.m. the *Empress of Britain* docks at Pier 61, on West 21st Street. The Shaws are taken on a whirlwind tour of New York City and the Jersey Palisades by Howard Lewis (director of Dodd, Mead & Co.).
In the evening, under the auspices of the American Academy of Political Science, Shaw delivers an address, 'The Future of Political Science in America', in which he publicly criticizes American capitalism and culture for an hour and forty minutes before a not entirely sympathetic 3500-strong audience at the Metropolitan Opera House. The address is broadcast on radio by the National Broadcasting Company. [CL4: 328; Dan H. Laurence, '"That Awful Country": Shaw in America', in SA 286–91; Edmund Wilson, 'Shaw in the Metropolitan', *New Republic* (New York), 26 Apr 1933; I&R 337–9]

12 Continuing his hectic schedule, Shaw breakfasts with Sasha Kropotkin (Prince Kropotkin's daughter), the Lawrence Langners and Robert Loraine, then has brief meetings with his American copyright attorney, Benjamin H. Stern, the publisher William H. Wise, Archibald Henderson and Henry George's daughter, Anna George de Mille, before setting sail for home. [Dan H. Laurence, '"That Awful Country": Shaw in America', in SA 286–91]

19 The *Empress of Britain* docks at Southampton, having sailed from America via Cherbourg. [I&R 330, 340]

28 While Shaw is out on an evening stroll, he encounters Virginia and Leonard Woolf. Chatting about the travels he has recently returned from, Shaw remarks: 'Of course the tropics are the place. The people are the original human beings – we are smudged copies. I caught the Chinese looking at us with horror – that we should be human beings!' [*The Diary of Virginia Woolf*, IV, 1931–35, eds. Anne Olivier Bell and Andrew McNeillie (1982), 152–3; I&R 499]

May

19 (Fri) Shaw pays a condolence call to Olive Galsworthy. [DHL]

June

4 (Sun) Publication in the *Sunday Dispatch* of an interview entitled 'Halt, Hitler! By Bernard Shaw'. Shaw, while saying that 'the

Nazi movement is in many respects one which has my warm sympathy', condemns the 'insanity' of Hitler's anti-Semitism: 'Judophobia is as pathological as hydrophobia.' [Hayden Church, 'Halt, Hitler! By Bernard Shaw', *Sunday Dispatch* (London), 4 Jun 1933; I&R 355–8]

15 Virginia and Leonard Woolf and the Laurence Binyons lunch with the Shaws at Whitehall Court. Virginia Woolf describes Shaw in her diary: 'very jaunty, upright... agility – never to me interesting – no poet, but what an efficient, adept trained arch & darter!... he has the power to make the world his shape – to me not a beautiful shape – thats all.' In the afternoon, Shaw addresses a conference of the Friends of the National Libraries in the rooms of the British Academy, Burlington House. [*The Diary of Virginia Woolf*, IV, 1931–35, eds. Anne Olivier Bell and Andrew McNeillie (1982), 163–4; I&R 442–3]

23 Shaw receives a visit from James J. Walker, former Mayor of New York City. [DHL]

July

4 (Tue) Shaw completes *On the Rocks* which he had begun during the *Empress of Britain* cruise in early February. [CP6: 572; CL4: 326]

13 Dame Laurentia McLachlan of Stanbrook Abbey writes to Shaw asking him to withdraw *The Adventures of the Black Girl in Her Search for God* from circulation and 'make a public act of reparation for the dishonour it does to Almighty God'. Shaw replied on 24 July: 'You are the most unreasonable woman I ever knew. You want me to go out and collect 100,000 sold copies of The Black Girl... and then you want me to announce publicly that my idea of God Almighty is the anti-vegetarian deity who, after trying to exterminate the human race by drowning it, was coaxed out of finishing the job by a gorgeous smell of roast meat.' [CL4: 348–9]

24 July – 15 September

The Shaws attend the Malvern Festival. [CL4: 347–52]

July

27 Completion of *Village Wooing*. [CP6: 536]

August

5 (Wed) In response to a request by William Fraser from the Public Affairs News Service in London for his opinion on Fascism as a political force in Britain, Shaw writes: 'Fascism at present means anything from a mere blind reaction against the futility and anarchy of the British parliamentary system and its Continental and American imitations to the Corporate State as established in Italy. It is useless to criticise a blind reaction: one might as

well criticise an explosion of dynamite.' [GBS to William Fraser, 5 Aug 1933, Cornell 4617]

September

5 (Tue) – 8 The Shaws attend the Hereford music festival. [CL4: 340]

20 Death of Annie Besant. [Erv 144]

23 Shaw speaks at the Charles Bradlaugh Centenary Celebration. [DHL]

October

5 (Thu) German author Werner Krauss and his wife come to lunch with the Shaws. [DHL]

27–8 Shaw is in Edinburgh for a British Drama League Conference. [DHL]

November

23 (Thu) Shaw gives a Fabian Society lecture 'The Politics of Unpolitical Animals'. [DHL]

25 Première of *On the Rocks* at the Winter Garden Theatre. [CP6: 572; Morgan 91; Weiss 336]

December

24 (Sun) First publication of *Village Wooing*, in German translation, as *Ländliche Werbung* in the *Neue Freie Presse*, Vienna. [Lbib1: 215; CP6: 536]

29 The Shaws lunch at the Deanery, St Paul's, with the Inges. [DHL]

1934

In February, Shaw's radio talk 'Whither Britain?' is broadcast by the BBC and NBC, the first English editions of *Too True to be Good, Village Wooing,* and *On the Rocks* are published together in a collected volume, and the Shaws embark on the *Rangitane* for New Zealand. During this tour, Shaw writes *The Simpleton of the Unexpected Isles, The Six of Calais* and the first draft of *The Millionairess*, and *Village Wooing* premières at the Little Theater in Dallas. The Shaws return to England in mid-May. In July, the première of *The Six of Calais* takes place at the Open Air Theatre in Regent's Park. Following this, from late July until mid-September, the Shaws attend the Malvern Festival. Shaw spends October to November working on the screenplay for *Saint Joan*. He collapses from a minor heart attack in late November. In December, *The Six of Calais* is first published in Germany. Robert Rattray's *Shaw: A Chronicle and an Introduction* is also published during this year. Shaw takes a copy with him on his journey to New Zealand. Along with a number of other books, Rattray's work is donated to the ship's library. In June of this year, Shaw sits for a bust by the sculptor Sir Jacob Epstein.

January

13 (Sat) Shaw records a talk for the BBC, as part of the 'Whither Britain?' series, before returning to Whitehall Court for lunch with his guests, Sean and Eileen O'Casey. [CL4: 363; DHL]

Late Shaw gives the Webbs a gift of £1000 to assist recovery from financial difficulties induced partly by Beatrice's illness. Shaw visits Beatrice in the Empire Nursing Home, Vincent Square, on 26 January. [CL4: 363; DHL]

January–February

Having spent a month trying to improve a filmscript of *The Devil's Disciple* written by Lester Cohen of Hollywood's RKO studios, Shaw cancels his agreement to let RKO produce the film. [CL4: 362–3, 365–7]

February

6 (Tue) The Shaws have lunch with Nancy Astor, David Lloyd George and Elisabeth Bergner, a Viennese actress, famous for playing the lead in *Saint Joan*. The BBC broadcasts his recorded talk on 'Whither Britain?', which he delivers live on the NBC network in America on 7 February at 9 p.m. [CL4: 363–4; DHL]

8 The Shaws embark at Tilbury on the *Rangitane* bound for New Zealand via Kingston, Jamaica, the Panama Canal and Pitcairn Island. [CL4: 364, 365; Weiss 340]

15 Publication of a volume of three new plays, *Too True to be Good, Village Wooing* and *On the Rocks*. [Lbib1: 217]

16 Shaw commences writing *The Simpleton of the Unexpected Isles*. [CL4: 370]

21 The Shaws visit Government House at Kingston, Jamaica. [DHL]

23 Death of Edward Elgar. [CL4: 373]

The Shaws disembark at Cristobal and cross the isthmus to Balboa by auto, chauffeured by Ernest S. Baker, steamship agent at Cristobal, who performs the same service on 21 March 1936 but escorts them by train. [DHL]

March

5 (Mon) The *Rangitane* stops at Pitcairn Island at 9 p.m. [DHL]

15 The *Rangitane* arrives in Auckland, where the Shaws are greeted on behalf of the New Zealand Government by Mr D. Ardell and officials of the Tourist Department. Shaw devotes an hour and a half to on-board interviews and photograph sessions. He advises New Zealanders to be less dependent on Britain, and not to be deceived about the amount of interest the British take in the

Dominions. ('Their interest may be guessed from a letter I had before starting from a lady who said she heard I was going to New Zealand and hoped I would stay with her daughter, who has a very nice house in Sydney!') Other topics Shaw talks about include Nazism (explained as a reaction to the failure of democracies), American foreign policy, Russian films and the Roosevelt recovery plan. [*The Auckland Star*, 15 Mar 1934; *The New Zealand Herald*, 15 and 16 Mar 1934]

The Shaws are welcomed to a Vice-Regal garden party lunch at Government House by the Governor-General, Viscount Bledisloe and Lady Bledisloe. In the evening they attend a dinner at the Grand Hotel, Auckland. They meet Mr Leslie Lefeaux, governor of the Reserve Bank of New Zealand, and are welcomed in a speech by the Hon. W. Downie Stewart, MP. In response to a toast to his health, Shaw pays tribute to the social legislation promoted in New Zealand in the 1890s by Fabian Socialist W. Pember Reeves. [*The Auckland Star*, 16 Mar 1934; *The New Zealand Herald*, 16 Mar 1934; DHL]

16 The Shaws lunch at Government House, and are driven round the waterside by Mrs Ernest Davis. [DHL]

17 In the morning Shaw meets a number of Auckland Labour officials and is a guest of the Fabian Club at a private reception in the evening. The Shaws are driven to the West coast by Ernest Davis. [*The New Zealand Herald*, 19 Mar 1934; DHL]

20 Having spent five days in Auckland, the Shaws leave on a three-week tour of New Zealand, first visiting the Waitomo 'Glow Worm' Caves (which Shaw describes as 'an incomparable sight') and then proceeding via Arapuni to Rotorua, where they stay for over a week. [*The New Zealand Herald*, 19 Mar 1934; *The Auckland Star*, 22 Mar 1934; DHL]

28 The Shaws attend a concert of Maori music at the Rotorua home of Guide Rangi. [CL4: 367; DHL]

30 The Shaws arrive at Wairakei, where they stay at the Chateau, before leaving for Wellington. [*The New Zealand Herald*, 19 Mar 1934]

31 Mr R. Cobbe, manager of the Chateau, and Mr G. H. Clinkard, General Manager of the Tourist Department, escort the Shaws on a visit to a country sports and axemen's carnival at Owhango, where a crowd of 2000 gathers. [*The New Zealand Herald*, 3 Apr 1934]

April

3 (Tue) The Shaws leave the Chateau and travel to Wanganui, Palmerston North, Wellington, Picton and Nelson. At Picton, Shaw offends many by saying that New Zealanders went to the First World War

'out of pure devilment'. In Wellington, Shaw meets Sir Truby King, founder of the Karitane hospitals and clinics for infants. [*The New Zealand Herald*, 3, 6, 9,13 Apr 1934; CL4: 368]

8 The Shaws visit Christchurch, where an impromptu reception is held in their hotel lounge. Told at the reception about the New Zealand Moa, a wingless bird, Shaw jokes: 'It sounds like a politician to me. One of those politicians who haven't the slightest knowledge of politics.' Asked about his knowledge of spiritualism, he says: 'I attended my first seance at the age of about six. Why, the first planchette board in Ireland was used in my parents' home in Dublin. The man who used to work it – it wrote very well for him – afterwards went to Australia – not voluntarily though.' [*The New Zealand Herald*, 9 Apr 1934]

10 The Shaws call on the New Zealand Prime Minister, George Forbes. [DHL]

12 At 10 p.m., Shaw delivers a 24-minute radio broadcast from the 2YA transmitting station, Wellington, entitled 'Shaw Speaks to the Universe'. His topics include unemployment, unfinished railways and maldistribution of leisure. The broadcast, thought to be the biggest ever organized in the Southern hemisphere to that time, is relayed throughout New Zealand and picked up by the national network in Australia. [*The New Zealand Herald*, 12 and 13 Apr 1934]

13 Shaw addresses the Wellington Fabians. [DHL]

14 At Wellington, the Shaws re-embark on the *Rangitane* for their five-week voyage back to Britain. Asked if he planned to visit Australia, Shaw replies: 'They have been shouting for me to come. I can't go this time. Perhaps some day or other I might drift to that land.' [*The New Zealand Herald*, 14 Apr 1934]

16 Première of *Village Wooing* at the Little Theater, Dallas. [CP6: 536; Morgan 90]

26 Shaw completes *The Simpleton of the Unexpected Isles*. [CP6: 743; CL4: 370]

27 Shaw begins writing *His Tragic Clients*, later renamed *The Millionairess*. [CL4: 370; CP6: 848]

May

10 (Thu) Shaw completes the first draft of *The Millionairess*. [CL4: 370; CP6: 848]

13 Shaw begins writing *The Six of Calais*, a one-act play which he completes on 16 May. [CP6: 972]

17 The *Rangitane* docks at Plymouth. [CL4: 370]

June

1 (Fri) – 22 Shaw sits for Sir Jacob Epstein. [DHL]

July

12 (Thu) Shaw lunches with physician, psychiatrist and author, Axel Munthe, at Grosvenor House. [DHL]

17 Sydney Carroll produces the première of Shaw's *The Six of Calais* with a revival of *Androcles and the Lion* in the Open Air Theatre in Regent's Park. [CL4: 402; CP6: 972; Morgan 104; Weiss 343]

22 July – 16 September

Shaw attends the Malvern Festival, which is extended from two weeks to four. While driving on a Worcester road, Shaw collides with a motorcyclist and his wife riding in the sidecar. [CL4: 379–80; Weiss 343]

25 In an interview for a newspaper, Shaw makes a tart comment about the English people's awareness of international politics. In answer to: 'South Africa has opened new trading relations with Continental countries, and the Irish Free State is making trade agreements and establishing shipping lines with Continental countries. Do you believe that the English people realise what such movements may mean?' he replies: 'The English people are quite incapable of realising anything except the latest score by Don Bradman.' ['We're on the Rocks', Shaw interview with Andrew E. Malone, *Sunday Chronicle* (Manchester), 19 Aug 1934; Libib2: 747–8; DHL]

October

3 (Wed) Mistaking Dame Laurentia McLachlan's golden jubilee announcement card for an obituary notice, Shaw writes a letter of condolence to the nuns at Stanbrook Abbey. Dame Laurentia answers Shaw's letter of condolence herself, inviting Shaw to resume his visits to the Abbey. [CL4: 379–80]

20 Shaw attends the inauguration of a memorial village hall at Kelmscott opened to honour the centenary of William Morris's birth. [CL4: 391]

October–November

Shaw works on a screenplay of *Saint Joan*. [I&R 393]

November

16 (Fri) Shaw meets celebrated Estonian wrestler Georges Hackenschmidt. [DHL]

23 Death of Arthur Wing Pinero. In a letter to Sir Francis Younghusband, Shaw writes: 'My fellow playwright Arthur Pinero, whose death the other day passed almost unnoticed amid the rejoicings over the royal wedding, once signed a letter to me "with admiration and detestation." That was the truth; but it did not prevent him from treating me with the most

scrupulous consideration... Many ordinary men cannot bear contradiction... but the geniuses... cannot bear agreement, perhaps because it is an assertion of equality.' [CL4: 392–4]

24 Shaw collapses into a faint due to a minor heart attack, after which he sleeps continuously for sixty hours, and is confined to bed for several days. [CL4: 390; DHL]

29 Shaw, 'up but hardly out', issues a report to the *Manchester Guardian* repudiating the Italian censorship exemptions granted on the grounds of his being the 'most anti-British' of British playwrights. [CL4: 371]

December

25 (Tue) Publication of *The Six of Calais* in German translation, as *Die Sechs von Calais* in the *Neue Freie Presse* (Vienna). [Lbib1: 223; CP6: 972]

1935

The Shaws plan to travel to South America but the trip is cancelled when Charlotte becomes ill with blood poisoning. In February, *The Simpleton of the Unexpected Isles* premières in New York. The Shaws go on a short holiday to Bournemouth in early March and, soon after, depart on a voyage around Africa, returning in mid-June. During this time, Shaw revises *The Millionairess* and works on proofs of the Webbs' *Soviet Communism: A New Civilisation?* In June, Shaw completes the screenplay for *Saint Joan*. Shaw travels to Malvern in July to attend dress rehearsals, staying on for the Malvern Festival. In December, Gabriel Pascal unexpectedly drops in for a visit at Whitehall Court. Also, during this year, Shaw is made a Freeman of the City of London and a German language film version of *Pygmalion* is produced.

January

Early Charlotte contracts blood poisoning after re-injuring her old South African leg wound. Her illness, which lasts until the end of February, necessitates the cancellation of an eight-week trip to South America scheduled to begin on 26 January. [CL4: 396] Shaw acquires a Leica camera. [DHL]

February

7 (Thu) Shaw travels to Birmingham to see Reginald Arkell's comic history with music *1066 And All That* (music by Alfred Reynolds) at the Birmingham Repertory Theatre. [DHL]

18 First production of *The Simpleton of the Unexpected Isles* by the Theater Guild at the Guild Theater in New York. The play closes after only 40 performances. [CP6: 743; CL4: 405; Morgan 93]

20 Shaw attends the first meeting of the BBC General Advisory Council. [DHL]

March

3 (Sun) – 10 The Shaws spend a week holidaying in Bournemouth. [CL4: 404–5]

19 In an interview published in *The North Eastern Daily Gazette*, Shaw publicly expresses his approval of Ramsay MacDonald's decision to increase British military spending. [I&R 358]

21 The Shaws sail from Tilbury on the *Llangibby Castle* on a voyage around Africa, taking in Gibraltar, Palma, Marseilles, Genoa, Port Said and Suez, before sailing south to Mombasa, Zanzibar, Beira and Lourenço Marques. During the voyage, Shaw revises *The Millionairess* and works on the proofs of the Webbs' new book, *Soviet Communism: A New Civilisation?* [CL4: 407–8]

April The Shaws are guests at Mombasa of the resident Magistrate, a distant cousin, Bernard Vidal Shaw, son of the famous Sir Eyre Massey Shaw, Chief of the London Fire Brigade. [DHL]

28 (Sun) The Shaws land at Durban, where they spend three weeks, during which they learn of the death of T. E. Lawrence caused by a fall from the motorbike given him by the Shaws. [CL4: 408, 412; Dunbar 299–300; I&R 329; Hol3: 204]

May

5 (Sun) Shaw attends Indian sports at the Jewish Club. [DHL]

24 The Shaws board the *Winchester Castle* at Cape Town, which takes them to Southampton via Madeira. [CL4: 407–8]

June

Shaw completes the screenplay of *Saint Joan* that he had begun the previous year. The producer-director, Paul Czinner, sends the scenario to Monsignor M. Barbera of Catholic Action (an organization which dealt with lay activities of the Catholic church) who subsequently reported on 27 August that the scenario contained 'serious violations of "historical fact" by the "mocking Irishman"'. While Catholic Action was not an official representative of the Vatican, its opposition delayed production until 1957 when Otto Preminger produced and directed the first of several screen versions of the play. [CL4: 428; I&R 393 n3]

10 The Shaws return from Africa. [CL4: 408]

13 Shaw lunches with Colonel Buxton at St Martin's Bank to discuss a T. E. Lawrence memorial. [DHL]

20 Shaw becomes a Freeman of the City of London, as a Member of the City Company of Stationers and Newspaper Makers. [F. E. Loewenstein, *Bernard Shaw Through the Camera* (1948), 15]

21 July (Sun) – 31 August

The Shaws are at Malvern. [DHL]

July

29 Opening of the Malvern Festival, prior to which Shaw attends dress rehearsals. *The Simpleton of the Unexpected Isles* has its British première at Malvern. [CL4: 414; Erv 556; Morgan 93]

September

2 (Mon) First showing of the German film of *Pygmalion* in Berlin. [Weiss 352 n2]

October

22 (Tue) Publication in *The Motor* of an article about Shaw and his new 20 h.p. Rolls-Royce, his first car of that make. Asked if the 'new regulations' about motoring – 'traffic lights, pedestrian crossings, limit signs, and so on' – worried him, Shaw replied: 'Not a bit. I don't take any notice of them.' He also states that he should not be allowed to drive. [Stuart Macrae, 'George Bernard Shaw says – "They Shouldn't Allow Me to Drive"', *The Motor*, 22 Oct 1935]

Publication in *The Times* (London) of a long letter by Shaw in support of the Italian colonization of Abyssinia, and condemning Anthony Eden and the Foreign Office for urging support of Danakil resistance. ['Letters to the Editor', *The Times* (London), 22 Oct 1935]

November

23 (Sat) Shaw declines Harvard University's offer of an honorary doctorate. [CL4: 13]

December

7 (Sat) – 8 Congress of Peace and Friendship with the USSR. Shaw addresses the Congress on the 7th. [DHL]

8 Gabriel Pascal arrives uninvited at Whitehall Court claiming to be 'the young man with the brown buttocks' whom Shaw met while swimming at Cap d'Antibes ten years previously. [I&R 386; CL4: 419–20]

13 Shaw grants Pascal the film rights to *Pygmalion*. [I&R 386; CL4: 420]

1936

The Millionairess premières in Vienna in January. In late January, the Shaws embark on a cruise to the Pacific on the *Arandora Star*, returning in April. During the cruise, Shaw works on prefaces for Dickens's *Great Expectations* and May Morris's biography of William Morris. Shaw also begins writing a play called *The World Betterer* but soon abandons it. In late June, the Shaws attend the Mozart Festival at Glyndebourne. In late July, Shaw is assisting with dress rehearsals at Malvern. He celebrates his eightieth birthday during the Malvern Festival and then proceeds to Penrhyndeadraeth in North Wales in early September to recover from the festivities. In December, Shaw writes *Cymbeline Refinished*.

January

4 (Sat)	Première of *The Millionairess* (in German) at the Akademie Theater in Vienna. In London, meanwhile, Shaw and Gabriel Pascal view Eberhard K. Klagemann's German film of *Pygmalion* in a hired projection room in Endell Street. [Morgan 11, 95; CL4: 420, 422]
10	Shaw lunches with the Aldous Huxleys in the Albany. [DHL]
22	The Shaws embark at Southampton on the *Arandora Star* for a cruise to the Pacific. While crossing the Atlantic, Shaw works on prefaces to the Limited Editions Club edition of Dickens's *Great Expectations*, and May Morris's *William Morris: Artist, Writer, Socialist*, II (the latter preface published separately in the United States as *William Morris as I Knew Him*). [CL4: 419, 425; I&R 319]

February

4 (Tue) – 6	At Miami, Shaw stops at Bernard MacFadden's Hotel and visits the John Kellogg Sanitarium (satirized in the 1994 film *The Road to Wellville*). [DHL]
11	The Shaws' ship passes through the Panama Canal. Shaw begins writing a new play, *Geneva*. [CL4: 426; CP7: 11]
17	Shaw begins another new play, *The World Betterer*, but soon abandons it. The work re-emerges after the Second World War as *Buoyant Billions*. [CL4: 751; DHL]
24–7	The Shaws stop for a short visit in Honolulu. During this stay they have lunch with Charlie Chaplin.

March

6 (Fri)	The Shaws visit the Grand Canyon where they meet J. B. Priestley.
7	First English-language production of *The Millionairess* by Gregan McMahon's Melbourne Repertory Theatre at the King's Theatre, Melbourne. [CP6: 848; DHL; Morgan 95]
10–16	The Shaws visit Mexico: Mazatlan, Guadalajara, Mexico City, Xochimilco, Taxco and Acapulco, where they re-join the ship. [DHL]
17–18	The Shaws remain aboard ship at Guatemala City and San Salvador. [DHL]
24	First English publication of *The Simpleton, The Six of Calais* and *The Millionairess* by Constable. [Lbib1: 227]

April

4 (Sat)	Completion of *Geneva*. The play is revised extensively before it is published in 1939. [CL4: 426]

6 The Shaws arrive back in England. [CL4: 421, 426]

May

22 (Fri) Shaw approaches Edith Evans to play the lead in *The Millionairess*. [CL 4: 431]

June

4 (Thu) Italian actress Marta Abba (leading lady onstage and off to Luigi Pirandello) lunches with Shaw. Pirandello dies six months later. [DHL]

15 Shaw offers financial assistance to the recently widowed wife of G. K. Chesterton. [CL4: 433]

24–28 The Shaws attend performances at a Mozart festival at Glyndebourne of *The Magic Flute, Così fan tutte, Don Giovanni, The Marriage of Figaro*, and *The Abduction from the Seraglio*. [CL4: 432]

July

3 (Fri) The Shaws register as citizens of the Irish Free State at the High Commissioner's Office in London, retaining their British Nationality, the machinery for registration having been set up under the Irish Citizenship and Nationality Act 1935. ['G.B.S. Registers As An Irish Citizen', *Daily Express* (London), 22 Jul 1936; CL4: 396, 725]

9 In an apparently unpublished interview with John Hockin (typewritten questions with Shaw's manuscript replies) on Indian demands for independence, Shaw writes: 'I recognize the existence of an instinct in men called Nationalism which makes them dissatisfied unless they think they are governed by themselves and not by foreigners. They can think of nothing else until this instinct is gratified, just as a wounded man can think of nothing but his wound until he is well.' [Texas]

19 July – 9 September

The Shaws attend the Malvern Festival, after a week of rehearsals at the Birmingham Repertory. While at Malvern he assists with rehearsals and celebrates his eightieth birthday. [CL4: 435–6, 438]

September

Mid The Shaws visit Penrhyndeadraeth in North Wales, 'to shake off maddening Malvern'. [CL4: 442]

October

The Times refuses to publish a letter by Shaw deploring the hypocritical barbarity of flogging anti-British rioters in India. [CL4: 443–4]

13 (Tue) Shaw speaks at a PEN dinner at the Savoy Hotel honouring H. G. Wells on his seventieth birthday (on 21 September). [DHL]

14 Shaw lunches at the Austrian Embassy with the Austrian Minister and Siegfried Trebitsch, six days after they had dined at Whitehall Court. [DHL]

15 Sir William de Courcy Wheeler (Shaw's cousin once removed) and son come to lunch. [DHL]

November

17 (Tue) First British performance of *The Millionairess* by Matthew Forsyth's Repertory Company at the De La Warr Pavilion, Bexhill-on-Sea. Shaw attends a matinée on 18 November. [CL4: 444; DHL]

21 Shaw writes a letter of introduction to Augustin Hamon for Gabriel Pascal who wants to make a French film version of *Pygmalion*. [CL4: 446–7]

24 Hitler, whom Shaw appeared to be supporting to some extent, permits the Nazi authorities in Danzig to sentence a bookseller to three years in jail for selling Shaw's books. In doing so Shaw is effectively banned by the Nazi regime. [*The Western Mail* (Cardiff), 24 Nov 1936]

27 Ann Harding (who was to begin rehearsing *Candida* in December) and Hugh Beaumont come to lunch. She had met Shaw at the MGM studios in 1933. [DHL]

December

Shaw writes *Cymbeline Refinished*. [CP7: 178]

14 (Mon) The first day of rehearsals of a new production of *Candida* starring the Hollywood actress, Ann Harding. After clashing on the first day with the director Irene Hentschel, whom he sees initially as a producer whose job is to implement the author's intentions, Shaw decides not to participate in subsequent rehearsals. [CL4: 451]

1937

The Dutch film version of *Pygmalion* premières in March and *Cymbeline Refinished* premières in November. During the month of May, the Shaws holiday at Sidmouth, enjoying it so much that they return again in August and stay until early October. In between that time, Shaw once again supervises rehearsals for the Malvern Festival. In November, Shaw works on the typescript of his cousin Charles MacMahon Shaw's book about the Shaw family, *Bernard's Brethren*. Some time during this year, Shaw stops driving his car.

January

1 (Fri) Vincent Sheean and his wife Diana Forbes-Robertson lunch at Whitehall Court. [DHL]

23 Former Governor of Hawaii, Theodore Roosevelt (son of the late President) comes to lunch. [DHL]

29 Shaw resigns as Chair of the BBC's Spoken English Committee. [DHL]

March

The Dutch film version of *Pygmalion*, directed by Ludwig Berger, premières in Amsterdam. [CP4: 398; I&R 387]

20 (Sat) The Shaws lunch with the Russian writer Count Aleksey Tolstoy, a distant relation of Leo Tolstoy. [CL4: 462]

23 Shaw sees a private screening of John Drinkwater's Coronation film *The King's People*. (Shaw appears briefly in the film.) [DHL]

April

7 (Wed) New Zealand and Queensland Coronation representatives are guests at lunch with the Shaws.[DHL]

16 Shaw views the Dutch *Pygmalion*. [DHL]

26 April – 31 May

The Shaws holiday at Sidmouth. [CL4: 465–6]

May

The Intelligent Woman's Guide to Socialism, Capitalism, Sovietism and Fascism inaugurates the Pelican series of paperbacks. [Lbib1: 174]

22 (Sat) Shaw dispatches a letter agreeing to let the United States government-sponsored Federal Theater project use as many of his plays as it likes 'as long as you stick to your fifty cent maximum for admission'. [CL4: 464–5]

June

1 (Tue) – 6(?) The Shaws visit the Webbs at Passfield, Shaw assisting with the proofs of their revised edition of *Soviet Communism*, while Sidney Webb helps the Shaws redraft their wills. [DBW4: 389–90; CL4: 466]

11 Shaw makes a BBC broadcast addressed to sixth form students on 'Schools'. [CL4: 468]

19 Sir James Barrie dies. Shaw eulogizes him in 'The Unhappy Years of Barrie'. [DHL; Lbib2: 758]

25 Nellie Harris (widow of Frank) visits Shaw. [DHL]

July

8 (Thu) First Shaw TV production: 'How He Lied to Her Husband' (BBC), with Greer Garson as Aurora. Shaw makes a brief appearance at the end. [DHL]

19–25 Shaw presides over productions at Malvern of *The Millionairess* (opens 26 July) and *The Apple Cart* (opens 28). [Weiss 360; DHL]

26 Shaw spends his birthday at Stratford, viewing *Cymbeline*. [DHL]

August

14 (Sat) Shaw returns his letters from Mrs Patrick Campbell, specifying that they should not be published in his or Charlotte's lifetime. [CL4: 470–2]

22 August – 3 October

Having enjoyed their stay at Sidmouth in May, the Shaws return for a second visit. [CL4: 474]

October

8 (Fri) Shaw proposes to Alfred Douglas a second edition of Frank Harris's book *Oscar Wilde: His Life and Confessions* to aid Harris's widow. [CL4: 475]

November

2 (Tue) Shaw broadcasts a talk, 'As I See It' (better known as 'This Danger of War') on the BBC, opening the 'Empire' series. [DHL; P&P 282]

16 Opening of *Cymbeline Refinished* at the Embassy Theatre, Swiss Cottage, London. [CP7: 178; CL4: 459]

17 Shaw corrects the MS of Charles MacMahon Shaw's book *Bernard's Brethren*. [CL4: 477–83]

December

10 (Fri) Gabriel Pascal visit the Shaws, bringing with him Leslie Howard who is to play Henry Higgins in the 1938 film version of *Pygmalion* and co-direct the film with Anthony Asquith. [DHL]

17 Mathias Alexander, Australian creator of the 'Alexander Technique', comes to lunch. Shaw had undertaken a course of 40 sessions with him in October–December 1936. [DHL]

29 In response to a letter from Margaret Epstein (wife of the sculptor, Sir Jacob Epstein) which claimed that she had heard from A. R. Orage that Shaw did not like the bronze bust which Epstein had sculpted of him in 1934, Shaw wrote: 'What had happened was this. Jacob, as you know, is a savage, always seeking to discover and expose the savage in his sitters and often betrayed by the fact that his sitters are not savages. When he said to me "I will shew you what you really are" I knew quite well that he would do his utmost to represent me as an Australian Bushman. The result was a very remarkable bust; but I am neither an Australian nor a Bushman…' [CL4: 485–7]

1938

Having finished revising the manuscript of Frank Harris's biography, *Oscar Wilde*, Shaw dispatches it to the publisher in late January. In

March, Shaw attends the first day of filming *Pygmalion* at Pinewood Studios. He completes the revisions of *Geneva* in May. A few weeks later, Shaw collapses due to pernicious anaemia and is confined to the house for six weeks. In July, *Geneva* premières in Warsaw. Shaw attends the Malvern Festival for the last time. Following this, the Shaws go to the Worcester Music Festival. In October, *How He Lied to Her Husband* is broadcast on the BBC. In late November Shaw begins writing *In Good King Charles's Golden Days*.

January

	Sidney Webb suffers a stroke which leaves him partially paralysed and impaired in his speech. [CL4: 492]
6 (Thu)	Charles MacMahon Shaw, Australian first cousin of Shaw and author of *Bernard's Brethren* (1939), comes to lunch. [DHL]
25	Shaw dispatches the MS of Frank Harris's *Oscar Wilde* biography to the publisher, Constable & Co. Even though unacknowledged, Shaw had been assisted by Lord Alfred Douglas in revising the preface and amending Harris's text. [CL4: 489]

February

26 (Sat)	In reply to a questionnaire from Hannen Swaffer, a journalist, Shaw writes guardedly about his future: 'I cannot tell you the exact date of my death. It has not yet been settled. When it is, I shall be settled too... how do I intend to leave my money... I do not know how much money I have to leave. Most of my time is spent in earning and collecting money for the government... They do not pay me a commission.' [CL4: 495]

March

3 (Thu)	Theatre critic James Agate visits the Shaws, taking Charlotte a basket of spring flowers. A shaft of sunshine in which Shaw is standing 'stressed [for Agate] the unreality of one who is rapidly turning into a saint... The sun streaming through the white hair made a halo of it, and I thought of Coleridge's "a man all light".' [*Ego 3: Being Still More of the Autobiography of James Agate* (1938), 296; I&R 517–18]
11	Shaw attends a gala luncheon at Pinewood Studios to mark the first day of filming of *Pygmalion*. [Hol3: 390]
13	Hitler announces Germany's annexation of Austria. In the following days, Shaw sends congratulatory cards to his German and Austrian friends, including Trebitsch, hoping to allay possible Nazi suspicions of their race or allegiances. Following Trebitsch's less than enthusiastic response to these actions, Shaw writes to explain: 'I sent you a postcard congratulating you on the glorious achievement of the Anschluss by your fellowcountryman the Führer.

And now you reproach me because I did not write letters pointing out that you are a Jew marked out for Nazi persecution.' [CL4: 496; Weiss 367; 'Bernard Shaw answers Eight Questions', *Daily Express* (London), 26 Mar 1938; I&R 364]
On their way to see a lawyer, Siegfried and Tina Trebitsch are stopped by Nazis. While their chauffeur is being questioned, they open the car door and flee. [Weiss 367, 372]

16 Having obtained Czech passports, the Trebitschs' escape from Vienna to Prague and subsequently to Zurich. [Weiss 367]

18 Shaw informs Stella Campbell of the terms of his will regarding the publishing rights of his correspondence with her. [CL4: 496–7]

31 Samuel Goldwyn comes to lunch. [DHL]

April

22 (Fri) Shaw speaks a brief Preface (seven minutes) to 'The Dark Lady of the Sonnets' for a BBC broadcast, drumbeating for the National Theatre. [DHL]

May

Shaw visits H. G. Wells for lunch. [DHL]

10 (Tue) In a letter to H. K. Ayliff, Shaw announces that he has finished revising *Geneva*. [CL4: 501]

4 June (Sat) – 15 July

Shaw collapses and is diagnosed as having pernicious anaemia. He has a prolonged course of injections of liver hormone and is confined to Whitehall Court for six weeks. He returns to Ayot on 16 July, and does not resume activity in London until 27 July. [CL4: 501; DHL]

15 First American production of *On the Rocks* at Daly's Theater, sponsored by the Federal Theater project of the United States government. [CL4: 464; Morgan 91]

25 Première of *Geneva* at the Teatr Polski in Warsaw. [CP7: 11]

August

1 (Mon) First production in English of *Geneva* at the Malvern Festival. The Shaws attend a performance on 22 August. This was to be the last time that Shaw attended the Malvern Festival. [CP7: 11; CL4: 128, 508; Morgan 11]

18 August – 26 September

The Shaws holiday at Droitwich, with brief excursions to Malvern on 20 August where he sees Bergner in *Saint Joan* (a 'hopeless failure'), and on 28 August for *Geneva*. [DHL; CL4: 508]

26 Lawrence Langner remonstrates with Shaw over his presentation of 'The Jew' in *Geneva*. Shaw makes minor revisions of 'The

Jew's' part to please Langner, and alters the Mussolini part as well. [CL4: 510–12]

September

6 (Tue) – 9 The Shaws attend the Worcester Music Festival. [CL4: 507]

30 Britain, France and Italy sign the Munich Agreement, granting Germany the right to annex the Sudetenland of Czechoslovakia. Shaw agreed with the Chamberlain prewar policy of appeasement towards Germany, saying to an interviewer in July 1939: 'Mr Chamberlain did the right thing at Munich. The alternative was to bomb Berlin and have London bombarded the next day.' [E. M. Salzer, 'Bernard Shaw (Who is Eighty-three Today) says We Will Have Peace', *Daily Express*, 26 Jul 1939; I&R 456–7]

October

4 (Tue) John Farleigh's woodcuts and drawings for *Back to Methuselah* (Limited Editions Club) exhibited at Leicester Gallery. Shaw attends. [DHL]

6 Première of Gabriel Pascal's film version of *Pygmalion*. A press showing on 4 October at 10.30 a.m. was attended by Shaw and Pascal. The New York opening is on 7 December. [CL4: 507; DHL; I&R 371]

Broadcast of *How He Lied to Her Husband* on BBC. In response to the request Shaw had replied (17 August 1938): 'O.K.; but tell the announcer that I am professionally Bernard Shaw and that there will be an additional fee of ten guineas if he calls me George Bernard Shaw.' [Cornell 4617 Box 16]

16 Death of May Morris. [Peters 399]

November

22 *Geneva* opens in the West End at the Saville Theatre, transferring to the St James's in the following January and subsequently touring the provinces. Shaw revises the text to keep abreast of developments in Europe. After seeing a performance, Shaw writes to Ayliffe (11 December 1938): 'What a horrible, horrible play! Why had I to write it? To hear those poor devils spouting the most exalted sentiments they were capable of, and not one of them fit to manage a coffee stall, sent me home ready to die.' [CL4: 518; Weiss 387; Cornell]

Late Shaw begins drafting *In Good King Charles's Golden Days*. [CL4: 522]

December

16 (Fri) Shaw faints (an event described in his diary by the word 'FLOP') at the home of Edith, Lady Londonderry, wife of the

7th Marquess of Londonderry. Attributing his faint to a hormone injection received that morning, Shaw subsequently substitutes a naturopathic treatment, 'Hepamalt' for his anaemia. [CL4: 520; DHL]

1939

In the early part of this year, Shaw's screenplay for *Pygmalion* wins an Oscar at the Academy Awards. In May, he completes *In Good King Charles's Golden Days*. The première follows soon after, in August. During this time, Shaw also writes the final version of the ending to *Pygmalion*. Later in the month, the Shaws go to Frinton-on-Sea for a month's holiday. After the outbreak of the Second World War, Shaw adds a new scene to *Geneva*. In October, his controversial article, 'Uncommon Sense about the War', is published. Also during this year, Charles MacMahon Shaw's *Bernard's Brethren* is published and Shaw joins the Association of Cine-Technicians.

January

3 (Tue) Shaw declines to contribute to the League of Dramatists' fund for Jewish refugees. [CL4: 522]

20 The Shaws lunch with the exiled German writer Emil Ludwig who maintains that Hitler is 'an illiterate semi-idiot'. [CL4: 525]

23 Shaw speaks as a member of a delegation from the Shakespeare Memorial National Theatre to the London County Council Town Planning Committee. [DHL]

February

17 (Fri) Shaw suffers a 'collapse as before' after a hormone injection, lasting several days. [DHL]

20 In a letter to Hesketh Pearson, Shaw writes: 'The word Shavian began when William Morris found in a medieval MS by one Shaw the marginal comment "Sic Shavius, sed inepte". It provided a much needed adjective; for Shawian is obviously impossible and unbearable.' [Texas; Cornell 4617 Box 16]

23 Despite Hollywood's lack of participation in the making of Pascal's *Pygmalion*, Shaw's screenplay wins an Oscar at the Motion Picture Academy awards. [CL4: 494]

March

3 (Fri) Shaw puts in the fire a cheque from Edward McNulty for £100, which McNulty claims is repayment of a debt. [CL4: 526–7]

4 Greer Garson and Gabriel Pascal come to lunch. [DHL]

14 Students at Azhar University, a major Moslem centre of learning, organize a public burning of copies of Shaw's *Saint Joan* because one of the characters (Cauchon, Bishop of Beauvais)

makes insulting references to Mohammed. An exasperated Shaw points out that Cauchon expresses 'the historical view of the Medieval Catholic Church', and adds, 'besides, Mohammed is, and always has been, a hero of mine'. ['G.B.S. Angry at Moslems' Criticism', *News Chronicle* (London), 14 Mar 1939]

April

23 (Sun) The BBC broadcasts Act III of *Geneva* from the stage of the St James's Theatre, preceded by Shaw's reading of a synopsis of the first two acts. [CL4: 524]

27 Shaw visits the National Institute for the Blind to hear the quality of its recordings before authorizing use of his works. [DHL]

May

Before 3 Completion of *In Good King Charles's Golden Days*. [CP7: 202]

5 (Fri) The J. B. Priestleys come to lunch. [DHL]

June

3 (Sat) In a letter to *Picture Post*, Shaw rejects a statement by critic Geoffrey Grigson in a previous issue of the periodical that he was 'disgusted by the unsqueamish realism of *Ulysses*, and burnt [his] copy in the grate'. Shaw replies: 'Somebody has humbugged Mr Grigson. The story is not true. I picked up *Ulysses* in scraps from the American *Little Review*, and for years did not know that it was the history of a single day in Dublin. But having passed between seven and eight thousand single days in Dublin I missed neither the realism of the book nor its poetry. I did not burn it; and I was not disgusted. If Mr. Joyce should ever desire a testimonial as the author of a literary masterpiece from me, it shall be given with all possible emphasis and with sincere enthusiasm.' Shaw did, however, say to Archibald Henderson in 1924: 'I could not write the words Mr Joyce uses: my prudish hand would refuse to form the letters.' ['G.B.S. Was Not Disgusted', *Picture Post* (London), 3 Jun 1939; Archibald Henderson, 'Literature and Science', *Fortnightly Review* (London), CXXII (Oct 1924), 519–21); I&R 508]

13 Death of W. B. Yeats at Roquebrune-Cap-Martin, France.

24 George Arliss and his actress wife Florence are invited to lunch. [DHL]

July

7 (Fri) Marlene Dietrich calls to discuss the possibility of performing in *The Millionairess* for Pascal. Pascal comes to lunch after Marlene departs. [Bernard F. Dukore, (ed.), *Shaw and Gabriel Pascal* (1996), 52–3; DHL]

8 — Shaw takes delivery of his second Rolls-Royce, a 25–30 h.p. chocolate-brown Wraith, with the new Clayton-Dewandre heating in the back seat for Charlotte. To reporters who are present, Shaw comments on Hitler as 'a clever fellow', but adds, apropos, *Mein Kampf*: 'His grammar's bad, though. There isn't a decent sentence in that book.' [Stuart Macrae, 'Mr Bernard Shaw on Motoring', *The Motor*, 18 Jul 1939; I&R 206–8]

13 — In a letter to Trebitsch, Shaw writes: 'I shall not go to Malvern this year. I am quite tired of the place; and I am too old to work at the rehearsals.' [Weiss 388]

14 — Eva Glasgow, granddaughter of Shaw's Aunt Emily (Shaw) Carroll, comes to lunch. [DHL]

26 — In an interview published on his eighty-third birthday, Shaw predicts that mutual fear among the European powers will prevent the outbreak of war. He acknowledges his mistake in a long letter to the *New Statesman* in July 1941. [E.M. Salzer, 'Bernard Shaw... says We Will Have Peace', *Daily Express* (London), 26 Jul 1939; Bernard Shaw, 'My Mistake', *New Statesman*, 5 Jul 1941]

August

4 (Fri),11 — Robert Donat lunches with the Shaws. [DHL]

12 — Première of '*In Good King Charles's Golden Days*' at the Malvern Festival. [CL4: 523; Morgan 100]

19 — Shaw writes the final version of the ending of *Pygmalion* for the Standard Edition. [CL4: 532–3]

21 — Shaw's last letter to Stella Campbell: 'The giant is decrepit and his wife crippled with lumbago... I am too old, too old, too old.' [Dent 385]

29 August – 28 September

The Shaws take a holiday at the Hotel Esplanade, Frinton-on-Sea. [CL4: 534; Weiss 389]

31 — Hitler orders the invasion of Poland. *Geneva* was playing in Warsaw at the time. [I&R 456; Morgan 11]

September

Shaw adds a new scene to *Geneva* to take account of developments in Europe. [Theatrics 208]

3 (Sun) — Britain declares war on Germany. 'War Declared' is Shaw's terse diary entry. [CL4: 534; BLPES; DHL]

5 — Shaw's letter, 'Theatres in Time of War', published in *The Times*. [Lbib2: 767; CL4: 535]

5–17 — Charlotte is bedridden with lumbago, an early sign of the *osteitis deformans* which worsens steadily until her death in 1943. [CL4: 536–8]

20 *The Times* publishes Shaw's letter 'Poland and Russia', in which he describes Hitler as 'Stalin's catspaw'. [Lbib2: 767; CL4: 539]

29 The Shaws return to Ayot from Frinton-on-Sea, and remain there until July, 1943. [CL4: 534; DHL]

October

7 (Sat) Publication in the *New Statesman* of 'Uncommon Sense about the War', which appeared the previous day in the *New York Journal-American*, in which Shaw argues that Stalin will outwit both Allied and Axis powers. The full text is inserted by Congressman John Rankin into the *Congressional Record*, 76th US Congress, 2nd Session, vol. 85. Extracts are read from the floor of the US Senate by Senator Elmer Thomas of Oklahoma on 9 October. [Lbib1: 235, 2: 767; I&R 456 n1; CL4: 539]
Hesketh Pearson writes a questionnaire to Shaw which enquires whether Shaw intends to write a play about Mahomet. 'I have come across several references to Mahomet in your works and letters, from which it appears that you were really keen to write a play on him.' Several months later (14 March 1940) Shaw wrote this reply, probably with the book burning of *Saint Joan* still in mind: 'I certainly should like to write a play about him. But the censorship and the risk of being killed by some Moslem fanatic in the east, are against it.' [Hesketh Pearson to Shaw, 7 Oct 1939 and Shaw to Hesketh Pearson, 14 Mar 1940, Texas; Pearson 366–7]

15 October – 4 November

Shaw records in his diary 'Ayot all the time. C.F.S. ill.' [BLPES; DHL]

December

17 (Sun) John Wardrop, a young Scottish journalist, arrives on Shaw's doorstep in London and is turned away by Blanche Patch. Over the next two years his persistence earns him the position of editorial assistant and proofreader on *Everybody's Political What's What?* [CL4: 636]

22 David Astor visits Whitehall Court

1940

Geneva opens in New York in January. Through most of this year, Shaw is involved with the filming of *Major Barbara* which is completed in October. The war has also begun to intensify with the Blitz on London beginning in September. The Shaws move out of London to Ayot. In mid-September, Shaw's prologue for the American screen release of *Major Barbara* is filmed.

January

11 (Thu) Shaw lunches at H. G. Wells's to meet Wells's son Anthony West, son of Rebecca West. [DHL]

30 After a successful tour in Canada, *Geneva* opens at the Henry Miller's Theater in New York, where it receives poor reviews and survives only for two weeks. [CL4: 550; DHL; Morgan 98]

April

9 (Tue) Death of Mrs Patrick Campbell, impoverished, in Pau, France. This is noted in shorthand in Shaw's diary: 'Death of Stella.'[CL4: 553; DHL]

15 The Roy Limbert and Emile Little production of *In Good King Charles's Golden Days* opens at Streatham Hill. The play is moved to the Golders Green Hippodrome for fine tuning before transferring to the West End. [CL4: 554]

26 Arnold Lawrence, brother of T. E Lawrence, comes to lunch. [DHL]

May

9 (Thu) Opening of *In Good King Charles's Golden Days* at the New Theatre in London. It survives only 29 performances. [CL4: 558]

23 Not having seen the Shaws for two and a half years, Sidney Webb persuades Beatrice to take him up to London to visit. [DBW4: 452]

24 Shaw says Britain must 'die in the last ditch' to resist Germany. ['Mr. Shaw's Advice', *Manchester Guardian*, 24 May 1940]

June

In a facetious letter to Winston Churchill, Shaw writes: 'Why not declare war on France and capture her fleet... before A. H. recovers his breath?' [CL4: 560]

Alfred Duff Cooper, Minister of Information, curtly refuses permission for Shaw to broadcast a talk he had written at the request of the BBC urging the necessity of Britain's fighting to the very end. 'I won't have that man on the air.' [CL4: 563; DHL; Shaw's 'cancelled' lecture, 'The Unavoidable Subject' is reproduced in P&P 286–92]

June–July

Shaw endeavours to keep Gabriel Pascal within his budget and time-limit on the *Major Barbara* film, and to retain his own control over the film's artistic direction. [CL4: 564–8]

July

17 (Wed) Shaw writes a commemorative note for Ellen Terry, which also includes commentary about Terry's various contemporaries. Of Stella Campbell, he writes: 'She was not in love with me nor

with anyone else; but it amused her to give proofs of her power to upset everyone... Yet with all this she had her noble moments, and without being at all extravagant could not keep the money she earned, because she gave too much of it away. She died unknown to our younger generation, and would have died penniless but for an income left her by the late Mrs Bridget Guinness... The two enchantresses enchanted one another; and Mrs Guinness's last request to her husband was... "Let Stella not starve."' [CL4: 568–72]

August

14 (Wed) Shaw attends a performance of *The Devil's Disciple* at the Piccadilly Theatre: 'I left the theatre without saying a word in praise of the performance.' [CL4: 575]

16 Marie Stopes, leading birth control advocate, comes to lunch. [DHL]

28 In a letter to Clifford Bax, Shaw writes: 'Why get out of bed before you are blown out? I slept through the six hours like a baby. My wife dreads shelters more than bombs, and prefers death to getting up and dressing.' [Texas]

September

Shaw visits Feliks Topolski's studio. [DHL]

6 (Fri) Charlotte has a fall at Ayot which restricts her mobility for a month putting an end to the Shaws' regular routine of spending half of each week in London. [CL4: 579]

7 Germany commences the air blitz of London. The previous day the Shaws travel to Ayot where they remain until 12 August 1941 when they visit the Astors at Cliveden to 29 August. [CL4: 577–8; DHL]

11 Blanche Patch joins the Shaws at Ayot. [CL4: 578]

12, 13 Filming of Shaw's three-minute prologue to the American version of Pascal's *Major Barbara*. His conversation with Wendy Hiller and Rex Harrison is recorded (tape held at University of Guelph Library). [DHL; Rex Harrison, *Rex: An Autobiography* (1974), 70–1; I&R 390–1]

18 Bombing of the Leighton-Straker bindery destroying 90 000 sets of unbound sheets of Shaw's works. [CL4: 578]

October

Completion of filming of Pascal's film of *Major Barbara*. [CL4: 585]

23 (Wed) In a letter to Gilbert Murray, Shaw announces that he is 'trying to write a Penguin sixpenny stating the facts that persons ought to know before they are allowed to vote or present themselves for election.' The piece is eventually published by Constable as *Everybody's Political What's What?* [CL4: 583, 585]

November

15 (Fri) A 'grand bombardment' of Ayot occurs because of the presence of an anti-aircraft searchlight in the village. Shortly after the searchlight is removed and bomb attacks on the village cease. [CL4: 594]

17 In an interview in *The Sunday Graphic*, Shaw publicly criticizes the Irish President Éamon de Valera's declaration of Irish neutrality and closure of Irish ports to British ships. [Lbib2: 771; 'Bernard Shaw's Advice to Ireland', *Forward*, Nov 1940; I&R 461]

30 Publication of a Shaw interview 'Bernard Shaw's Advice to Ireland' in *Forward*. While partly supporting the idea of Irish neutrality in the War, Shaw attacks Irish President Éamon de Valera for 'talking obvious nonsense' about Ireland defending herself, and the policy of not allowing the British navy to use the ports it requires. (This interview repeats some points made by Shaw in an interview with W. R. Titterton in the *Sunday Graphic* on 17 Nov 1940). [Lbib2: 771; 'Bernard Shaw's Advice to Ireland', *Forward*, 30 November 1940; I&R 460–2]

December

12 (Thu) Eamon de Valera, publicly rebuts Shaw's views on Irish neutrality in the *Irish News*. [I&R 460–1]

1941

During this year, Gabriel Pascal's film version of *Major Barbara* premières. For the first few months of the year, Charlotte is bedridden. Anxious about Charlotte's health, Shaw's health also begins to suffer, resulting in weight loss and memory problems. On 26 July, his 85th birthday, Shaw celebrates by resigning from the RADA Council and the Executive Committee of the Shakespeare Memorial National Theatre. Also on Shaw's 85th birthday, the Shaw Society is founded.

January

To avoid upsetting Charlotte, Shaw culls newspaper reports of Mrs Patrick Campbell's will which mention his extensive correspondence with her. [CL4: 592]

13 (Mon) Death of James Joyce in Zurich.

30 Shaw records that Charlotte has been bedridden for weeks with lumbago. [CL4: 592]

February

17 (Mon) Feeling the stress of the worsening war conditions, Charlotte's illness and the growing awareness of his own mortality, Shaw writes a melancholy letter to Beatrice Webb: 'I have written nothing for the stage since *Charles* [*In Good King Charles's Golden*

Days], and will perhaps not write for it again... I am very old and ought to be dead. My failing memory plays me the most terrifying tricks. I am losing weight so fast that I shall presently have totally disappeared... I weigh only 9 stone...' [CL4: 595–6]

24 To Otto Kyllman of Constable & Co., Shaw writes: 'I am stoney broke and have paid my January taxes only with the help of the insurance money I got when my books were burnt at Leighton's... Charlotte has been very ill in bed for many weeks, and is recovering very slowly.' [CL4: 597]

April

7 (Mon) First screening of Pascal's film version of *Major Barbara* in London. The film is shot in several locations in Devon, Sheffield and London. During this time, Shaw is also preparing a *R.A.D.A. Graduates' Keepsake and Counsellor* which he has printed at his own expense. He also revises Hesketh Pearson's biography, works on *Everybody's Political What's What?*, and writes a preface for Richard Albert Wilson's *The Miraculous Birth of Language*. [I&R 371, 390; CL4: 594–6]

28 *The Times* (London) publishes a letter to the editor, drafted by Shaw and signed by him and Gilbert Murray, condemning the bombing of cities by both the British and Germans as useless from a military standpoint and destructive of places which 'belong to the culture of the whole world'. ['Bombing of Cities. Military and Non-Military Objectives', *The Times* (London), 28 Apr 1941]

July

26 (Sat) Shaw formally resigns from the RADA Council and the Executive Committee of the Shakespeare Memorial National Theatre on his 85th birthday. [CL4: 607]

Founding meeting of the Shaw Society. [See entry for 14 November, 1941.]

August

Gabriel Pascal's screen version of *Major Barbara* is on show for the first time in Ireland. [*Irish Times*, 18 Aug 1941]

9 (Sat) Shaw writes to his accountant in an effort to devise a tax avoidance scheme. [CL4: 609–11]

12 The Shaws make a three-week visit to Lady Astor at Cliveden. [I&R 518; CL4: 612]

November

14 (Fri) Shaw gives F. E. Loewenstein his written permission to found a Shaw Society, 'but don't bother me about it'. The Society had already been founded on 26 July 1941. Dan H. Laurence writes, privately: 'A report of the 1943 Annual General Meeting of the

Society, signed by the President, Andrew Block, on 26 July 1943, states that the meeting was held two years to the day after the Society's founding meeting.' This tallies with Loewenstein's own dating of the founding in his *Bernard Shaw through the Camera* (1948), 15. [CL4: 621; Guelph; DHL]

1942

At the beginning of this year the Shaws are living exclusively at Ayot. By April, Charlotte's health has worsened to the point where her spine collapses. She is finally diagnosed as having incurable *osteitis deformans*. In July, the Shaws make their final visit to Lady Astor at Cliveden. They return home in August. During this time the BBC broadcast *Village Wooing*. In October, Hesketh Pearson's biography of Shaw is published in New York as *G.B.S.: A Full Length Portrait*, followed by publication in England as *Bernard Shaw: His Life and Personality*. Through much of the year Shaw is slowly proofing *Everybody's Political What's What?*, which is not completed until 1943.

January

4 (Sun) Shaw dispatches the first chapter of *Everybody's Political What's What?* to Maxwell the printer with a request for specimen pages. [CL4: 623]

February

12 (Thu) Shaw records a 'Nasty fall on the ice'. [DHL]

March–April

Charlotte's 'spine has collapsed to such an extent that she cannot stand without hurting herself unbearably by a one-sided stoop'. Her osteopath gives her a reinforced corset but has misdiagnosed her as having arthritis, lumbago or fibrositis. [CL4: 631]

21 July (Tue) – 14 August

The Shaws make what turns out to be their final visit to Cliveden, Lady Astor's country residence. Charlotte is examined by Canadian military doctors stationed there and is diagnosed as having incurable *osteitis deformans* or Paget's disease. [CL4: 631, 668]

July

30 The Shaw's have tea with Nancy Astor's niece, theatrical entertainer, song-writer and mimic, Joyce Grenfell. Grenfell gives a lively glimpse of the Shaws in old age during their visit to Cliveden in the previous year, August 1941, saying that the

85-year-old Shaw 'looks wonderfully pink and white and fresh and beautifully dandified'. [DHL; Joyce Grenfell, *Joyce Grenfell Requests the Pleasure* (1976), 160–1; I&R 518–19]

16 August (Sun) – 1 September

Judy Musters comes to Ayot as substitute secretary while Blanche Patch takes her summer holiday.[DHL]

*c.*25 Shaw writes to the Home Secretary, Herbert Morrison, urging him to seek a reprieve for the six IRA members condemned to hang for killing a police constable in Belfast. Five of the six received reprieves; their leader was, however, hanged. [CL4: 634–5]

28 The BBC broadcasts *Village Wooing*. [CL4: 648]

October

1 (Thu) The first edition of Hesketh Pearson's biography of Shaw, *G.B.S.: A Full Length Portrait* is published in New York. This was followed by an English edition titled *Bernard Shaw: His Life and Personality* published on 26 October. [Lbib1: 511–12]

31 Writing to St John Ervine, Shaw reports: 'Charlotte's *osteitis deformans* is incurable: she is often in pain, and moves about very slowly and not far... We are both deaf; and the number of familiar names that we cannot remember increases; in short, we are considerably dotty... [I] work at my book [*Everybody's Political What's What?*] as hard as I can lest I should not live to finish it.' [CL4: 646]

November

Shaw and Julian Huxley, a biologist and associate of H. G. Wells, begin a five-month exchange of letters in *The Listener* on 'Bernard Shaw as Biologist'. [CL4: 649]

1943

A mournful year for Shaw, heavily overshadowed by the deaths of those closest to him. In February, Sydney Olivier dies, followed by Beatrice Webb's death in April. Shaw's childhood friend, Edward McNulty, dies in May. Charlotte struggles painfully throughout most of the year but finally succumbs in mid-September. Anxious to set his own affairs in order, Shaw offers 'Shaw's Corner' to the National Trust. Meanwhile his writing activities continue unabated, his chief preoccupation being his second large-scale political treatise, *Everybody's Political What's What?*

February

15 (Mon) Death of Baron (Sydney) Olivier. [CL4: 668]

April

30 (Fri) Death of Beatrice Webb. Shaw keeps it secret from Charlotte. [CL4: 668]

May

15 (Sat) Shaw finds out about Edward McNulty's death on 12 May from his daughter, Vera Gargan. [CL4: 670]

July

6 (Tue) Judy Musters again fills in at Ayot as secretary while Blanche Patch takes her holiday till 20 July. [DHL]

26 The Shaws, accompanied by Blanche Patch, return to Whitehall Court on Shaw's 87th birthday. [CL4: 592, 673]

August

Charlotte's mental state begins to deteriorate. [CL4: 679]

21 Shaw is taken in by a confidence trick (unexplained in his diary) apparently perpetrated by a man named Robbins. Detective Sergeant Ottersly of Scotland Yard visits on 23 August. [DHL]

25 John W. Dulanty, High Commissioner for Eire, visits Whitehall Court. [DHL]

September

10 (Fri) Charlotte Shaw experiences a dramatic remission of pain and anxiety. Writing to Lady Mary Murray, Shaw recalls: 'I knew in my soul at once what this meant.' [CL4: 679]

11 In a letter to Lady Mary Murray, Shaw describes Charlotte's final day: 'she looked as she did when I first met her 45 years ago. I stayed with her every moment I could; and she talked to me incessantly... I heaped on her every endearment I could find words for... I was more deeply moved than I had known myself to be capable of being, but not in the least painfully.' [CL4: 680]

12 **Charlotte Shaw dies**. Shaw writes to Lady Mary Murray 'On Sunday morning at a quarter past eight, the night nurse woke me with a cheery shout of "Your wife died at half past two: but I thought I wouldn't wake you". There is always some comic relief on these occasions.' Charlotte's death (aged 86) came after a long and painful illness. Shaw also wrote to H. G. Wells, 'Charlotte died this morning at 2.30. You saw what she had become when you last visited us: an old woman bowed and crippled, furrowed and wrinkled, and greatly distressed by hallucinations of crowds in the room, evil persons and animals. Also by breathlessness...

But on Friday evening a miracle began. Her troubles vanished. Her visions ceased. Her furrows and wrinkles smoothed out. Forty years fell off her like a garment. She had thirty hours of happiness and heaven. Even after her last breath she shed another twenty years and now lies young and incredibly beautiful. I have to go in and look at her and talk affectionately to her. I did not know I could be so moved...' [CL4: 677–8]

13 Following Charlotte's death, Shaw writes: 'On Monday there was nothing but a beautiful wax figure: I could not talk to it: she was gone. On Tuesday it was ready for the Golders Green furnace.' [CL4: 680].

15 In accordance with Charlotte's will, her funeral had 'No flowers; no black clothes; no service', only Handel's music. Shaw (wearing his black suit because Charlotte liked it), Blanche Patch and Lady Astor attended the funeral. 'I was quite happy. All's well that ends well.' [CL4: 678, 680]

27 Shaw writes to Sidney Webb about Charlotte's will. Even during this difficult time, Shaw continues with his characteristic diligence, settling business affairs and working his way through *Everybody's Political What's What?*: 'I am pretty full of business; but the book is getting finished at last.' [CL4: 681]

October

5 (Tue) Shaw offers 'Shaw's Corner' to the National Trust. [CL4: 681–2]

21 Shaw returns to Ayot. Hubert Smith of the National Trust visits that afternoon. [DHL]

November

2 (Tue) Shaw visits Apsley Cherry-Garrard in London for tea. [DHL]

3 Shaw informs William Maxwell that he will appoint the Public Trustee as his literary executor rather than John Wardrop, whom he will appoint as custodian of his papers. [CL4: 683]

23 Shaw completes *Everybody's Political What's What?* [DHL]

25 Charlotte's niece Cecily Colthurst comes to lunch. [DHL]

December

Shaw gives Charlotte's clothing to Blanche Patch, the servants, relatives and the Theatrical Ladies Guild. Shaw's end of year diary indicates Charlotte's tax is £2512.8.4. [CL4: 686; DHL]

1944

In January, 'Shaw's Corner' is finally accepted by the National Trust. He also offers his Carlow property to the Carlow council in May. Towards the end of February, Shaw interviews General Montgomery. In early April, Shaw finishes the proofing of *Everybody's Political What's What?* (completed in November 1943) which is subsequently published in September and instantly becomes a bestseller. Gabriel Pascal's film version of *Caesar and Cleopatra* goes into production in April. Shaw visits the set twice. In late

April, he goes to Denham Studios in London to witness the preparations, and he returns during the filming in late June. At this time, Shaw commissions Loewenstein to compile his bibliography. By the end of the year, Shaw is working on proofs for the Penguin edition of the screen version of *Major Barbara*, and the Oxford World's Classics edition of *Back to Methuselah*. Shaw resided at Ayot for the whole of this year.

January

James Lees-Milne, acting secretary for the National Trust, accepts Shaw's offer of 'Shaw's Corner' for the Trust. [James Lees-Milne, *Prophesying Peace* (1977), 19–23; CL4: 684–5, 691]

February

Early (?) Shaw attends a London Exhibition of Feliks Topolski's Shaw portraits at Burlington House. [DHL; photo in *Picture Post*, 12 Feb 1944]

26 (Sat) Shaw has an interview with General Montgomery while the latter sits for a portrait by Augustus John. [CL4: 700]

March

22 (Wed) Worried that the deeds to 'Shaw's Corner' will not be transferred in time, Shaw writes to James Lees-Milne, acting secretary of the National Trust: 'I am in mortal dread of dying before it is settled.' [CL4: 722]

April

2 (Sun) Writing to Sidney Webb, Shaw declares: 'I am living alone here in Ayot; but I like being alone... I work longer and later than Charlotte would ever have allowed me to... I have finished the book [i.e. the proofs of *Everybody's Political What's What?*] at last... You will find it unreadable, as it contains nothing that you don't know already.' [CL4: 705–6]

27 Shaw visits the Denham film studios where Pascal is preparing to film *Caesar and Cleopatra*. [*Bernard Shaw and Gabriel Pascal*, ed. Bernard F. Dukore (1996), 167]

May

15 (Mon) Shaw offers his Carlow estate as a gift to the Carlow municipality for the common welfare to be administered by the Carlow Urban Council. [CL4: 710]

June

Shaw's London flat is damaged by a German bomb which falls near Charing Cross. Writing to Gilbert Murray, Shaw reports: 'My Whitehall flat has been blasted again, this time by a Robot. A window in my study was shivered into smithereens, my front door blown in, the grandfather clock prostrated, one of

Charlotte's Tang horses shattered, and – *comble de malheur* – Strobl's bust of Lady Astor done in.' This incident drives Blanche Patch back to Ayot. [CL4: 592, 716; Blanche Patch, *Thirty Years with G.B.S.* (1951); I&R 470]

12 (Mon) After several weeks of rehearsals, Gabriel Pascal begins filming *Caesar and Cleopatra* at the Denham Studios in London and on location in Egypt. [Marjorie Deans, *Meeting at the Sphinx: Gabriel Pascal's Production of Bernard Shaw's* Caesar and Cleopatra (1946), 28; I&R 391; CL4: 713]

16 Shaw commissions F. E. Loewenstein to compile his bibliography and perform additional secretarial duties. [CL4: 712]

26 Signing of the deeds transferring 'Shaw's Corner' to the National Trust. [CL4: 722; I&R 427]

July

1 (Sat) Shaw visits the *Caesar and Cleopatra* film set at Denham Studios. [*Shaw and Gabriel Pascal,* ed. Bernard F. Dukore (1996), 169–70]

4 Writing to Gilbert Murray, Shaw announces that: 'My book [*Everybody's Political What's What?*] is printed, and will be published presently if the binders can get the necessary labor.' [CL4: 716]

25 Shaw's house at Ayot has a pane of glass blown out by a German V-bomb which had fallen about half a mile away, on the eve of Shaw's 88th birthday. [Blanche Patch, *Thirty Years with G.B.S.* (1951); I&R 470; Prefs3: 440 n1]

28 First meeting, at 33 Synge Street, Dublin, of the newly formed Shaw Society of Ireland, founded by Shaw's cousin, Horatio de Courcy Wheeler. In order to avoid the acceptance of British standards, subscription was set at 7s. 6d, instead of the 10s. 6d. charged by the London Shaw Society. [DHL; 'An Irishman's Diary', *Irish Times*, 28 Jul 1944; 'Alms and the Woman', *Evening News* (London), 28 Jul 1944; 'Shaw's Boyhood', *Yorkshire Post* (Leeds), 27 Jul 1944]

Shaw writes to Gabriel Pascal: 'Hitler celebrated my birthday by smashing my bedroom window with a bomb; and in the afternoon I had to do a newsreel about it.' [CL4: 721]

September

4 (Mon) Shaw writes a letter to Dame Laurentia McLachlan on the flyleaf of his recently published *Everybody's Political What's What?*, commenting that 'The saint who called me to the religious life when I was eighteen was Shelley.' In reply to a query about his health, Shaw writes: 'deaf, and doddering and dotty as I inevitably am at my age, I am astonishingly well, much weller than I was a year ago.' [CL4: 723]

13–27 Judy Musters substitutes for Blanche Patch. [DHL]

15 Publication of *Everybody's Political What's What?* which became an instant bestseller. [Lbib1: 245;DHL]

19 Alice Laden, who had nursed Charlotte in her final illness at Whitehall Court, takes up the post of housekeeper at Ayot after the retirement of Clara and Henry Higgs who had been employed by the Shaws since 1904. Alice Laden agrees to accept a salary of £143 (£2.15.0 a week). [CL4: 735; DHL]

22 The Higgses depart. [DHL]

October

1 (Sun) In answers to questions put to him by a London correspondent of the Bombay Free Press Journal, Shaw gives his 'views on India' and its struggle for independence. While advising Winston Churchill to keep out of India, Shaw is more equivocal at this time on the question as to whether 'all Asiatic peoples should be free from European domination', saying that 'Europeans can be useful in Asia' and that 'the British Indian Civil Service has had its uses'. In an interview about India published on 12 March 1946, however, Shaw clearly supports Indian independence. ['G.B. Shaw Gives a Tip About India', *Reynolds News* (London), 1 Oct 1944; I&R 473–4; H. C. Miller, 'Shaw on India's Demand', *The Hindu*, 28 Mar 1946]

December

An aversion to cold, isolation and F. E. Loewenstein cause Blanche Patch to leave Ayot and return to London. [CL4: 736]

30 (Sat) Shaw corrects proofs of the screen version of *Major Barbara* published by Penguin, and of the Oxford World's Classics *Back to Methuselah*. [CL4: 732]

1945

Early in this year, Shaw appoints F. E. Loewenstein as his literary executor. Finding that the donation of his Carlow estate has been blocked due to lack of appropriate legislation, Shaw writes to the Irish Prime Minister in May to request the introduction of the Civic Improvement Funds bill to facilitate the transition of his Carlow estate to the city council. The request is granted in June. In August, Shaw resumes work on *The World Betterer*, changing the title to *Buoyant Billions*. The filming of *Caesar and Cleopatra* is finally completed in September and the film premières in December.

***c*. February**

Shaw warns John Wardrop not to build castles in the air about inheriting Shaw's property and being appointed his literary executor. [CL4: 733]

February

17 (Sat) Shaw rejects John Wardrop in favour of F. E. Loewenstein. [CL4: 739]

April

13 (Fri) Shaw expresses his offence at Lady Astor's suggestion that he needs a live-in caretaker-companion. [CL4: 741]

May

5 (Sat) Shaw writes to Éamon de Valera, the Prime Minister and Foreign Minister of the Irish Republic, explaining the legal obstacles to his plans for the Carlow estate, and requesting the introduction of legislation establishing local Civic Improvement Funds to which private individuals could make gifts or bequests. [CL4: 742–4]

7 Germany surrenders.

June

2 (Sat) Éamon de Valera informs Shaw that his request for legislation establishing local Civic Improvement Funds would be granted. [CL4: 744]

July

Mid Shaw makes one of his now rare visits to London for meetings with his accountant, Stanley Clench (19 July) and the Public Trustee, returning to Ayot soon after his 89th birthday. [CL4: 749; DHL]

18 (Wed) Shaw visits the Wallace Collection.[DHL]

25 Shaw visits Doris Thorne, daughter of Henry Arthur Jones. [DHL]

26 On his 89th birthday, Shaw visits the Victoria and Albert Museum to see masterpieces of the National Art Collection. [DHL]

The Labour Party, led by Clement Richard Attlee, wins the General Election in Britain, defeating Winston Churchill's Conservative Party.

August

2 (Thu) Shaw resumes work on *The World Betterer* abandoned in 1936, changing its title first to *Old Bill Buoyant's Billions*, then to *A World Betterer's Courtship* and finally to *Buoyant Billions*. [CL4: 751; Hol3: 485]

6, 9 The United States explodes atom bombs on Hiroshima and Nagasaki. Japan surrenders soon afterwards.

13 The legal conveyance of Shaw's gift to the Carlow Urban Council is completed. [CL4: 748]

September

Gabriel Pascal completes the filming of *Caesar and Cleopatra*. Pascal took nine months longer than scheduled, and ran £1 million over budget, causing Arthur Rank to cancel his contract with Pascal for two more films of Shaw's other plays. Although uncredited, Brian Desmond Hurst, an Irish-born director, had also directed some scenes in the film. [I&R 371, 391; CL4: 736, 802; Hol3: 477]

October

In response to Molly Tompkins's proposal of a visit, Shaw curtly replies: 'I have just received your letter, with its proposal to come across the ocean to live with me... Put it out of your very inconsiderate head at once and forever.' To further forestall any impulsive behaviour, Shaw also sends a telegram forbidding her to come. Molly indignantly responds: 'What a monstrous way to misconstrue my letter. Come and live with you indeed! Do you think I would give up the serenity of my independence to live with anybody on earth... even you? Hell no!' [Peters 408; Charles A. Berst, 'Shaw, Molly Tompkins, and Italy, 1921–1950', in SA 111]

5 (Fri) Shaw's neighbour, Clare Winsten, an artist, persuades Shaw to commission a statue of Saint Joan from her. Finally agreeing, Shaw sends her £50 and writes: 'What an incorrigible megalomaniac you are! Do you suppose I want a white stone ghost of Joan, ten feet high, to haunt the twilight in my garden?' [CL4: 753]

26 In a letter to Sidney Webb, Shaw writes: 'The war and the atomic bomb have produced a situation which is far beyond the political capacity not only of our new rulers but of mankind... My last remaining tooth is to be extracted tomorrow.' [CL4: 757].

November

23 (Fri) Shaw refuses Blanche Patch's request for a pay rise (her first since 1932), and informs her of his intention to turn over to the Society of Authors the duties associated with licensing his plays and collecting royalties. [CL4: 758]

December

6 (Thu) Shaw agrees to let the National Library of Ireland have the MSS of his early novels. [CL4: 761]

13 Première of Gabriel Pascal's film version of *Caesar and Cleopatra* at the Odeon, Marble Arch. This is also the tenth anniversary of the *Pygmalion* agreement between Shaw and Pascal. [Hol3: 477]

1946

In February, Shaw is made a Freeman of Dublin. In April, he hands over the MSS of his novels to the National Library of Ireland. After a long delay, the Oxford World's Classics edition of *Back to Methuselah* is finally published. Penguin Books celebrates Shaw's ninetieth birthday by publishing the 'Shaw Million' and the National Book League presents Shaw's Ninetieth Birthday Exhibition, a month-long celebration. Shaw makes his last trip to London in October for a ceremony where he is to be awarded the Honorary Freedom of the Borough of St Pancras. He falls and injures himself before the ceremony so his acceptance speech is broadcast from his bed at Whitehall Court. In November, he completes *Buoyant Billions*.

January

15 (Tue) In reply to a letter from Sir Robert Ho Tung of 'Idlewild', the inspiration for *Buoyant Billions*, Shaw nostalgically recollects his visit to Hong Kong: 'Nothing soothes me more than the recollection of that service in your celestial private temple and the afternoon we spent together.'[CL4: 764]

February

10 (Sun) Shaw accepts the honour of Freeman of Dublin, conferred on him on 4 February, 1946 by the Dublin City Council. [CL4: 764–5; DHL]

March

28 (Thu) Shaw supports India's demand for independence, saying that 'self-government is... a human passion that demands unconditional satisfaction.' [H. C. Miller,'Shaw on India's Demand', *The Hindu*, 28 Mar 1946; I&R 482–4]

April

Shaw hands over several weighty volumes of bound manuscripts (*Immaturity, The Irrational Knot, Cashel Byron's Profession, An Unsocial Socialist* and the fragment of the unfinished sixth novel) to John W. Dulanty, High Commissioner for Eire, for transfer to the National Library of Ireland. [CL4: 765–6]

27 (Sat) Siegfried Trebitsch visits Shaw. While he is visiting Shaw writes to Tina Trebitsch: 'His visit is an outrageous extravagance in money, but a very enjoyable incident for both of us.' [Weiss 431]

July

18 (Thu) Publication of the World's Classics edition of *Back to Methuselah*. In 1944, Shaw had extensively revised both the preface and the play, and added a postscript. The volume was to have been published in 1945, but publication was delayed until this time. [Lbib1: 148]

26 Shaw orders F. E. Loewenstein and Stephen Winsten to destroy hundreds of unopened birthday cards. ('F. E. L. Throw away all the birthday ones. They make me sick.')
Penguin Books publishes the 'Shaw Million', ten titles in editions each of 100 000 copies. [CL4: 773, 775; Lbib1: 247]

26 July – 24 August

The National Book League presents Shaw's Ninetieth Birthday Exhibition. Having declined to attend the formal opening ceremony, Shaw drops in unannounced in the late afternoon for three-quarters of an hour. [CL4: 769, 772–3]

August

Harley Granville Barker dies in Paris. Shaw hears the news over the BBC. [Peters 400]

13 (Tue) Death of H. G. Wells. Shaw had already written the obituary the previous year at the request of Kingsley Martin. '...an obituary for the Statesman, to be kept in cold storage until he passed out. It also is a delicate job; but I have done it.' [CL4: 756]

17 Shaw's obituary of H. G. Wells, 'The Man I Knew', published in the *New Statesman*. [Lbib2: 792; CL4: 756]

28 The Scroll of Freedom of the City of Dublin, illuminated by Alice O'Rourke, is presented to Shaw at Ayot, with the Roll of Freedom conveyed for his signature by P. J. Hernon, City Manager of Dublin, and T. J. O'Neill, Clerk of Dublin Council. [DHL]

October

3 (Thu) Shaw remonstrates with Peter Watts over his BBC production of *Man and Superman* which was first broadcast two days previously. [CL4: 779–80]

6 Shaw gives Clare Winsten, a cheque for £350 to defray the cost of a statue of Saint Joan for Shaw's garden. [CL4: 780]

9 Shaw makes his last trip to London for a ceremony where he is to be awarded the Honorary Freedom of the Borough by the Council of the Metropolitan Borough of St Pancras. However, Shaw falls and injures his leg before the ceremony. The BBC broadcasts his acceptance speech from his bed at Whitehall Court. A note to Lord Latham, leader of the London County Council, reads: 'I wasn't there; but the mike spoke for me.' [CL4: 781, 789; I&R 68]

Mid Shaw is bedridden for a week after falling from his revolving chair. [Weiss 436]

November

17 (Sun) Writing to Roy Limbert, Shaw announces that he has finished *Buoyant Billions*. 'It is so bad that I ought to burn it.' [CL4: 784]

1947

Early in this year, Shaw joins the British Interplanetary Society. In September, Shaw signs a contract with Irish Productions for the filming of his plays, beginning with *Androcles and the Lion* but, by the end of the year, the project has collapsed due to lack of financing. One of Shaw's few remaining close friends, Sidney Webb, dies in October. Later in this month, Shaw records 'Whither Britain?' for the BBC.

January

Late	Shaw joins the British Interplanetary Society as a Life Member after reading a copy of the Society's *Journal* which Arthur C. Clarke, scientist, explorer and popular science-fiction writer, had sent him. [CL4: 792]

April

19 (Sat)	Shaw's diary records 'Ill this week, "Fibrocitis".'[DHL]
20–27	Shaw has daily electrical therapy for muscular rheumatism as an outpatient at Welwyn Victoria Hospital. [Weiss 439; DHL]
27	Shaw's accountant Stanley Clench visits Ayot. Shaw gives him £25 000 for 'African investment'. [DHL]

Summer

Shaw contributes to a 'Symposium on Capital Punishment' supporting the retention of the death penalty for 'incorrigibles'. [*The Medico-Legal Journal*, vol. xv, Part 2 (1947); Lbib2: 797]

May

1 (Thu)	Gabriel Pascal and Lawrence Langner visit Ayot. [DHL]
5, 9	Siegfried Trebitsch visits Shaw at Ayot. [Weiss 439–41]
14	Lady Astor and Sir Sydney Cockerell visit Ayot. [DHL]

June

4 (Wed)	Shaw writes to thank Jayanta Padmanabha for sending cuttings of *Ceylon Daily News* articles on Florence Farr's last years in Ceylon. 'They have astonished me. I thought that Yeats and I knew her through and through, as far as there was anything to know. I now see that we did not know her at all ... I was the wrong man for her, and I am deeply glad that she found the right one after I had passed out of her life.' [CL4: 795]
14	Maurice Evans visits to obtain rights to *Man and Superman* for a New York revival in October. [DHL]

July

13 (Sun)	Shaw records 'Worldbetterer play [*Buoyant Billions*] finished'. [DHL]
19	Preface to *Buoyant Billions* finished. [DHL]

26 Shaw hears on the radio of the death of Kathleen Lady Kennet (née Scott). [CL4: 798]

August

5 (Tue) Isaac James Pitman, grandson of the founder of the Pitman system of phonography, and chairman of Sir Isaac Pitman & Sons, visits Shaw at Ayot, with the famous phonetician Daniel Jones. [CL4: 799; DHL]

15 India gains independence from Britain; the Islamic Republic of Pakistan established. In an earlier interview Shaw had commented: 'A partition is possible, and may be inevitable, as in the case of Ireland. But India cannot be "divided" by a pair of scissors. Is Pakistan to be an Ulster, a Baltimore or a Canada?' ['G. B. Shaw Gives Churchill a Tip about India', *Reynolds News*, 1 Oct 1944; I&R 473]

September

8 (Mon) Shaw signs a contract with Irish Productions (also known as Irish Screen Art Ltd) allowing them to film his plays beginning with *Androcles and the Lion*. [CL4: 799]
When Gabriel Pascal suggests a visit (after previous visits on 3 June and 20 August), Shaw cantankerously replies: 'I do not want to see you. I do not want to see ANYBODY... Keep away, Gabriel... Come only when there is the most pressing necessity unless you want to kill me.' [CL4: 801]

26 Sybil Thorndike visits Shaw. [DHL]

28 Ignoring Shaw's orders, Gabriel Pascal visits Shaw. [CL4: 803]

October

8 (Wed) *Man and Superman* opens in New York to critical acclaim and runs for 295 performances, before starting a long tour. It is Shaw's biggest box office success in America for years. [DHL]

13 Death of Sidney Webb. In a letter to S. K. Ratcliffe, journalist, lecturer and fellow Fabian, Shaw writes: 'I never expected to survive them [the Webbs].' [CL4: 804]

18 Gabriel Pascal visits Shaw accompanied by his bride, Hungarian actress Valerie Hidveghy. [CL4: 803]

28 Shaw records 'Whither Britain?' for the BBC's Recorded Programmes Permanent Library. [Transcript, Cornell 4716 Box 7]

November

5 (Wed) Shaw records what turns out to be his last radio broadcast, a self-written dialogue between himself and theatre manager C. B. Cochran, which is put to air one week later. [CL4: 804]

December

2 (Tue) Shaw informs Éamon de Valera that the Irish film project has collapsed due to lack of finance. [CL4: 807]

6 A plaque honouring Shaw is unveiled at Torca Cottage, Dalkey Hill. [CL4: 793–4; photo of plaque in F. E. Loewenstein, *Bernard Shaw through the Camera* (1948), 25]

12 The Webbs are re-interred in Westminster Abbey. [DHL]

1948

In July, Shaw negotiates with Dodd, Mead & Co. over the design of *Sixteen Self Sketches*. During this time, Shaw also writes *Farfetched Fables*, completing it in August. In October, *Buoyant Billions* premières in Zurich as *Zu viel Geld* (*Too Much Money*). Also during this year, the Jubilee Edition of *Fabian Essays in Socialism* is published by Allen & Unwin. Shaw contributes an essay, 'Sixty Years of Fabianism', which had earlier appeared in the *Fabian Quarterly* as 'Fabian Failures and Successes'. As a marketing ploy, the editor had wanted to place Shaw's essay at the front of the book but Shaw insisted on it being placed as a postscript.

March

12 (Fri) Shaw writes a reply to an enquiry from Laurence Irving who was working on a biography about his grandfather, Sir Henry Irving. He compares Irving unfavourably with Barry Sullivan. 'H. I. is always described as having succeeded Macready as England's great actor after a long and unaccounted-for hiatus during which there was no great British actor. As a matter of fact this is a cockney mistake. The hiatus was filled by a very great actor: Barry Sullivan, the stage idol of my boyhood…

No two human beings could be less alike than B. S. and H. I. Sullivan's physical endowment was magnificent… He could be majestic, violent, gallant, princely, villainous, agonized, without effort; and always superior and commanding. H. I. had no chest voice, and had to make his head voice resound in his nose: a trick that became a whinny when he tried to rant. This artificial utterance and his walk, which was a shambling dance, was fair game for imitators. Nobody imitated Sullivan. We only wish we could.

…Much as I adored him I never imagined myself writing a play for him.' [Texas]

April

In a series of telegrams, Shaw seeks to deter Siegfried Trebitsch from his annual pilgrimage to visit Shaw at Ayot. [Weiss 444–5]

May

23 (Sun) Following his refusal of Siegfried Trebitsch's efforts to visit, Shaw writes to explain. 'Anyway you are not coming; and that... is a relief. You don't understand the British dislike of Empfindlichkeit [sensibility] and Sentimentalität... I have no patience with it... I can keep my regard for you without seeing you for a hundred years.' [Weiss 444–5; CL4: 818]

27 Shaw attends the film *Les Enfants du Paradis* at Welwyn with Stephen and Clare Winsten. [DHL]

July

4 (Sun) Shaw meets Ghandi's son and his wife, who are guests of the Winstens at Ayot. [DHL]

8 Shaw writes to Siegfried Trebitsch who is busy preparing the world première production of *Buoyant Billions* [*Zu viel Geld* (*Too Much Money*)] in Zurich: 'I have revised B[uoyant] B[illions] drastically, cutting out Thirdborn altogether... Also I have greatly improved the mathematician, and deleted much superfluous dialogue.' [CL4: 825]

12 Shaw negotiates with Dodd, Mead & Co. over the design of *Sixteen Self Sketches*. [CL4: 826]

16 Gabriel Pascal brings Ingrid Bergman to visit. [DHL]

17 July–August

Shaw writes *Farfetched Fables*. [CL4: 869; Weiss 449]

July

27 Gene Tunney visits. [DHL]

September

10 (Fri) Trebitsch arrives for a fortnight's visit to England, his final meeting with Shaw. [Weiss 450]

October

9 (Sat) Tosti Russell, a longtime journalist acquaintance of Shaw, makes an uninvited visit to Ayot. [DHL]

16 Sean O'Faolain, Irish academic and member of the Irish Academy of Letters visits. [DHL]

21 Première of *Buoyant Billions* (*Zu viel Geld – Too Much Money*) in Trebitsch's translation at the Schauspielhaus in Zurich. [CP7: 305; CL4: 825; Morgan 105]

29 A performance of *In Good King Charles's Golden Days* is presented in honour of King George VI and Queen Elizabeth at the People's Palace, Whitechapel. [DHL; Morgan 11]

1949

In January, at the request of the Waldo Lanchester Marionette Theatre at Malvern, Shaw speedily writes *Shakes versus Shav* which premières at the Festival. In July, Esmé Percy, the director of *Buoyant Billions* for the Malvern Festival, and some of the cast visit Shaw at Ayot for directional advice. Also during this year, Shaw completes *Bernard Shaw's Rhyming Picture Guide to Ayot Saint Lawrence*. Originally entitled *Ayot Saint Lawrence: a strip of doggerel verses as written for Ellen Terry*, the guide was a photo album which contained picture postcards of Ayot that Ellen Terry had ordered when passing through on a visit in August 1916. Shaw had written verses to accompany the postcards. This was to be the last book that Shaw worked on before his death. It was published on 14 December 1950.

January

8 (Sat) or 9 Peter Fraser, Premier of New Zealand, is conducted on a visit to 'Shaw's Corner' by John Dulanty, High Commissioner for Eire. [DHL; *South Wales Echo,* 7 Jan 1949]

15 Shaw publishes a letter in *The Times Literary Supplement* about the numerous blunders in Stephen Winsten's recently published *Days with Bernard Shaw*. [CL4: 836]

20 Shaw agrees to write a marionette play to be performed by the Waldo Lanchester Marionette Theatre in Malvern. He completes the play, *Shakes versus Shav* in four days. [CL4: 839; CP7: 468]

February

16 (Wed) Shaw advises the manager of Whitehall Court that as he is unlikely to come to London again he would prefer to rent a much smaller flat in the Court. [CL4: 839–40]

March

11 (Fri) Reading of Shaw's letter on spelling reform in Parliament in support of a Bill which was defeated. [CL4: 842]

30 Shaw writes a letter to Patrick O'Reilly, a Dublin dustman who had spent many years collecting funds for a plaque to be erected at Shaw's Synge Street birthplace. Describing O'Reilly's rather grandiose and patriotic intended inscription as a 'blazing lie', Shaw specifies the inscription to be engraved on a plaque for his old house in Synge Street. 'Bernard Shaw, author of many plays, was born in this house 26 July, 1856.' [CL4: 844]

April

6 (Wed) Frederick Harvey, Shaw's hairdresser, formerly in London now at Peartree Stores in Welwyn Garden City, reports: 'Mr Shaw is

getting a little thin on top now...but is still remarkably thick at the sides. He is wearing his beard a little shorter than he used to. I am not allowed to touch his eyebrows.' His usually good tempered customer likes to be chatted to, 'but when occasionally he starts tapping his finger-tips together, I know the sign, and I shut up.' [*Daily Herald* (London), 6 Apr 1949]

Easter Monday

Inauguration of the Republic of Ireland (formerly Eire). In reply to a letter from Jawaharlal Nehru, India's first Prime Minister, Shaw wrote: 'I am not English but Irish, and have lived through the long struggle for liberation from English rule, and the partition of the country into Eire and Northern Ireland, the Western equivalent of Hindustan and Pakistan. I am as much a foreigner in England as you were in Cambridge.' [CL4: 828]

May

Late — Removal of Shaw's furniture, pictures and books from 130 Whitehall Court, some destined for a smaller flat (No. 116) and the rest destined for auction. [CL4: 849]

July

Early — Esmé Percy, directing *Buoyant Billions* for the Malvern Festival, brings some of the performers to Ayot to hear Shaw's directional advice at first hand. [CL4: 850; Esmé Percy, 'Bernard Shaw: a Personal Memory', *Listener*, 26 May 1955; I&R 143]

14 (Thu) — Shaw writes to his childhood friend, Ada Tyrrell: 'When I was a very small child in Synge Street and news came that my mother's Aunt Ellen was dead I went out into the garden and cried, broken hearted, for a long time... and was terrified by my belief that I should go on crying all my life. I have never grieved since... I never grieve and never forget... I like being alone because I can always tell myself stories, and so am never lonely.' [CL4: 852]

25 — Sotheby's auction Shaw's books and other effects from the old Whitehall Court flat. [CL4: 849]

26 — Writing to St John Ervine, Shaw comments: '93 today... My routine of sleeping and working never varies; and the months pass like minutes.' [CL4: 852–3]

August

9 (Tue) — First performance of *Shakes versus Shav* at the Waldo Lanchester Marionette Theatre at the Lyttelton Hall, Malvern. [Weiss 454; CP7: 468; photo in CL4:between 820 and 821]

13 — The English première of *Buoyant Billions* at the revived Malvern Festival. [CP7: 305; Morgan 105]

December

1 (Thu) Once again trying to deter Siegfried Trebitsch from what Shaw sees as an expensive and wasteful visit, Shaw writes: 'No more of your gottverdammt Schwarmerei [damned gushings].

I do not want to see you.
I do not want to see you.
I do not want to see you.
I do not want to see you.
I DO NOT WANT TO SEE ANYBODY' [Weiss 463]

1950

In April, Jawaharlal Nehru visits Shaw at Ayot. Shaw writes his last play, *Why She Would Not*, during July. Shaw's last interview, 'GBS on the A-bomb', the questions and answers of which were almost entirely drafted by Shaw, is published in August. In September, while attempting to prune a tree, Shaw suffers a fall, fracturing his thigh. The ensuing trauma and illness lead to his death in November.

January

14 (Sat) Eileen (Mrs Sean) O'Casey, and John Dulanty visit Shaw. [CL4: 864]

March

6 (Mon) Six days before Gabriel Pascal is to leave for Mexico to finalize negotiations for a Mexican production of *Androcles and the Lion*, Shaw changes his mind and agrees only that *The Shewing-up of Blanco Posnet* and possibly *The Man of Destiny* might be filmed. [CL4: 860–1]

10 Shaw notes in his diary: '[J] Arthur Rank to pay me £83,705.' [DHL]

April

29 (Sat) Jawaharlal Nehru visits Shaw at Ayot. Later in this year, on the announcement of his death, Nehru pays tribute to Shaw: 'He was not only one of the greatest figures of his age, but one who influenced the thought of vast numbers of human beings during two generations.' [CL4: 828 (photo between 820 and 821); *Daily Telegraph* (London), 3 Nov 1950]

May

1 (Mon) Shaw declines to grant an audience to the Burmese Prime Minister on the grounds of his advanced age and disablement from lumbago. [CL4: 863]

1–13 Shaw undergoes 11 radiant heat treatments for lumbago at the outpatients' section of Welwyn Victoria Hospital, a form of treatment undertaken intermittently since 1947. [CL4: 863]

June

8 (Thu) In a letter to Ada Tyrrell, a childhood friend, Shaw writes: 'Maud [Ada's sister] was wise to die; for old age is bearable only when there is nothing else wrong with one's body... Just now I am recovering very slowly from an abominable attack of lumbago, and laboring at my very complicated last will and testament in daily dread of dying before I have executed it.' [CL4: 867]

12 Shaw signs his final will, and discourages Esmé Percy's plan to stage *Farfetched Fables*. Shaw's will bequeathed his royalties towards establishing a new, improved alphabet. Legally challenged, this bequest was largely put aside in favour of other beneficiaries – the National Gallery of Ireland, the British Museum and RADA. The signing is witnessed by Harold White, a Luton publisher, and his wife. [CL4: 866, 869; Morgan 11–12]

July

17 (Mon) – 23 Shaw writes the first draft of *Why She Would Not* (then called *She Would Not*). [DHL; Weiss 468; CP7: 662; CL4: 87; I&R 396]

26 In his diary Shaw confusedly calls this his '95th birthday'. [DHL]

27 The day following his 94th birthday, Shaw writes: 'Yesterday was simple hell. The Times statement that I was "resting" elicited a yell of rage from me. The telephone and door bell never stopped. The lane was blocked with photographers all day.' [CL4: 872]

31 Writing to Siegfried Trebitsch about his recently completed play, *Why She Would Not*, Shaw announces that the play has just gone to the printers, and vitriolically comments: 'when they send proofs you shall have one unless I tear it up; for it is a pitiable little old man's drivel.' Shaw's fatal accident occurs before the proofs are ready. The play is not published until 1956. [Weiss 468; Dan H. Laurence, 'The Facts about *Why She Would Not*', *Theatre Arts*, XL (Aug 1956), 20–1, 89–90]

August

6 (Sun) 'G.B.S on the A-Bomb,' the last Shaw interview to appear in his lifetime, is published in the London paper, *Reynolds News*. Both the questions and answers were almost entirely drafted by Shaw. In reply to the question whether the use of the atom bomb is ever justified, Shaw says 'in war the word justifiable has no meaning', the only rule of conduct being to kill the enemy

or he will kill you, but 'the bomb is a boomerang, fatal alike to the bomber and his victim'. He publicly defends British rearmament as a deterrent to future world wars, but deplores the Korean war as a crusade against Russian communism. As in previous articles, he argues that in practice Communism and Capitalism are not pure, mutually exclusive systems, and that certain communistic policies and practices, unrecognized as such, are already accepted as natural in so-called capitalist Britain. [Hayden Church, 'G.B.S on the A-Bomb', *Reynolds News*, 6 Aug 1950; I&R 485–7; Lbib2: 809]

21 Alice Head delivers a gold watch from Marion Davies and Randolph Hearst. [DHL]

September

6 (Wed) Sponsored by the Shaw Society, the Watergate Theatre (a private club theatre) puts on 30 performances of *Farfetched Fables*, directed by Esmé Percy. [CL4: 869]

8 Alice Laden leaves for holidays in Inverness. She is called back, arriving on 15 September. [DHL]

10 Late in the afternoon, Shaw falls while pruning a tree and fractures his thigh. [*Shaw the Villager* (1961) 49–50; I&R 526; CL4: 879]

11 Shaw is admitted to the Luton and Dunstable General Hospital where he undergoes surgery in the evening on his thigh. [I&R 526; CL4: 879ff.]

15 Shaw's doctors discover signs of a chronic renal problem. [CL4: 881]

21 Shaw has an operation on his kidney. [CL4: 881]

October

4 (Wed) Shaw returns home from hospital by ambulance, having refused a second kidney operation. He is nursed at home by Sisters Gwendoline Howell and Florence Horan, assisted by his housekeeper Alice Laden. [I&R 526–7; CL4: 881–2]

12 In an interview with a journalist friend, F. G. Prince-White, Shaw remarks, 'I don't think I shall ever write anything more.' [F.G. Prince-White. '"I Would Like to Go into My Garden", said Shaw', *Daily Mail*, 13 Oct 1950; I&R 527; CL4: 882]

25 Lady Astor and Judy Musters, Shaw's former secretary, visit him. [Mrs Georgina Musters to Archibald Henderson, 31 Oct 1955: quoted in Hend3: 665; I&R 396]

c. 26 Esmé Percy visits Shaw. In 'Memories of Bernard Shaw', Percy recounts the visit: 'He told me how he no longer wanted anything but death. "...to have no more control of my bodily functions, to be like a baby in swaddling clothes – no." The sudden, unexpected vehemence and force with which he pronounced the word "no" was startlingly irrevocable.' Around this time, Eileen O'Casey (wife of the playwright Sean O'Casey) also visited Shaw. [Esmé Percy, 'Memories of Bernard Shaw', *British Peace Committee News Letter*, March–April 1956; I&R 528–30; Eileen O'Casey, *Sean*, ed. J.C. Trewin (1971), 209–10; CL4: 882]

31 Shaw is visited by Nancy Astor and Frances Day. [CL4: 883; Nancy Astor to Archibald Henderson, 31 Oct 1955, quoted in Hend3: 874; (1956); I&R 530–1]

November

1 (Wed) Shaw lapses into a coma at 3 a.m. [CL4: 883]

2 **Shaw dies of kidney failure at one minute to five in the morning without regaining consciousness.** [F. G. Prince-White, 'GBS Begged to be Allowed to Die', *Scottish Daily Mail*, 3 Nov 1950; I&R 531–3]

Following Shaw's death, obituary notices and words of tribute fill the pages of international newspapers. When news of Shaw's death is received in New York, shortly after midnight (New York time), all the illuminated signs of Broadway and Times Square are extinguished as a tribute to Shaw. [*Daily Telegraph*, 3 Nov 1950]

5 Shaw's body is transported to Golders Green Crematorium. [CL4: 885]

6 Shaw is cremated at Golders Green Crematorium after a brief non-denominational funeral service attended by three dozen friends and relatives, with a further 500 mourners gathered outside. As Shaw requested, the organist plays a piece from Elgar's *The Music Makers* and 'Libera me' from Verdi's *Requiem*. In between Sydney Cockerell reads the final words of Mr Valiant for Truth from *The Pilgrim's Progress*. [I&R 534; CL4: 885; Wilfrid Blunt, *Cockerell* (1964), 211]

23 Shaw's ashes are mixed with Charlotte's and scattered in the garden at Ayot St Lawrence. [CL4: 886]

A Shaw Who's Who

ACHURCH, Janet (1864–1916), actress and writer of plays and short stories. She was acclaimed for her Shakespearean acting and for her powerful interpretations of leading roles in plays by Ibsen. A member of a Manchester theatrical family, she began her acting career at 19, and later formed a theatrical partnership with her second husband, actor and producer, Charles Charrington. Shaw first met her on 16 June 1889, after seeing her much praised performance as Nora in Charrington's production of Ibsen's *A Doll's House*, in which Charrington himself played Torvald. She successfully repeated the role in the 1890s, and in November 1896 was hailed by Shaw, as one of the three best actresses of her generation, for her performance of Rita in Ibsen's *Little Eyolf*. Shaw refers to Achurch as the 'only tragic actress of genius we now possess' and his letters reveal a fascination with and personal affection for her beyond his high opinion of her acting abilities. He began *Candida* in 1894 with Achurch in mind for the title role, which she played in its first public performance on 30 July 1897, in Aberdeen. Shaw constantly remonstrated with her about drug and alcohol dependencies which prevented full realization of her potential.

ARCHER, William (1856–1924), Scottish literary and drama critic, journalist, translator and defender of Ibsen's plays, author of poems, plays, travel accounts and a novel. He was one of Shaw's closest friends from the time of their meeting in the winter of 1883. He obtained literary employment for Shaw by recommending him for positions as musical critic for the *Dramatic Review* and the *Magazine of Music*, book reviewer for the *Pall Mall Gazette*, and art critic for *The World*. He collaborated with Shaw in 1884 on what eventually became Shaw's first full-length play, *Widowers' Houses*. Although convinced of Shaw's inherent literary ability, Archer repeatedly expressed the opinion that Shaw 'cannot write for the stage'. A lively correspondence between the two was sustained throughout the period of their friendship. Shortly before his death, Archer wrote to Shaw: 'Though I may sometimes have played the part of the all-too-candid mentor, I have never wavered in my admiration and affection for you, or ceased to feel that the Fates had treated me kindly in making me your contemporary and friend. I thank you from my heart for forty years of good comradeship.' When Archer died a few days after surgery to remove a cancerous tumour, Shaw, returning to an 'Archerless London', expressed his grief by way of intense attack on the medical profession. In 1927 Shaw wrote: 'I still feel that when he went he took a piece of me with him.' In his essay, 'How William Archer Impressed Bernard Shaw' (1924), Shaw praises Archer as a poet, translator and 'the most serious critic of his day', and very warmly remembers his friend with anecdotes relating to his personal habits, rational secularism, marriage and visit to India.

ASHWELL, Lena (1872–1957), actress, theatre manager and feminist. She opened and managed the Kingsway Theatre (once the Great Queen Street Theatre) from 1907 to 1915 and the Century Theatre (the old Bijou Theatre, Bayswater) from 1924, and successfully organized acting companies to entertain the troops in numerous countries during and after the First World War, a service for which she received the Order of the British Empire. After the war she managed several companies operating under the name, 'Lena Ashwell Players'. Ashwell represented the Actresses' Franchise League in a Women's Suffrage Deputation to Prime Minister Asquith. Shaw and Ashwell had a close and flirtatious relationship which was threatened briefly by her disagreement with his attitude towards the First World War. She became a close friend of Charlotte Shaw who wanted Ashwell to act in the proposed production of her translation of Brieux's *La Femme seule*. Both women participated in the 13 000-strong procession of suffragists who marched from the Embankment to Albert Hall on 13 June 1908. Ashwell, who first impressed Shaw with her acting at the Lyceum, played Lina Szczepanowska in *Misalliance* (February 1910) and Margaret Knox in *Fanny's First Play* (February 1915). Lena Ashwell's stories about her seafaring father, Captain Pocock, who lived on Tyneside in a sailing ship fitted out as a home, contributed to the creation of Captain Shotover and his ship-like dwelling in *Heartbreak House* (originally titled, *Lena's Father*). Ashwell wrote a number of books including: *The Stage* (1929) and her autobiography, *Myself A Player* (1936).

ASQUITH, Herbert Henry, 1st Earl of Oxford and Asquith (1852–1928), British Liberal Prime Minister from 1908 to 1916; he is caricatured together with Lloyd George in the characters of H. H. Lubin and Joyce Burge in the second play of the *Back to Methuselah* cycle. He is also coupled with fellow British Prime Minister Arthur J. Balfour in the character of Balsquith in Shaw's one-act play, *Press Cuttings*. On 5 January 1916, Asquith introduced the First Conscription Act which Shaw attacked in a letter published in the *Daily News*.

ASTOR, Lady Nancy Langhorne (1879–1964), American-born politician who became the first woman MP to take her seat in the British House of Commons; from 1919 to 1945 she was the Conservative MP for the Sutton division of Plymouth. Astor first became friendly with Shaw in 1927 and became one of his closest friends during the later decades of his life. After 1928 Shaw was a frequent visitor to Cliveden, the Astors' palatial residence on the Thames (where he also met Nancy Astor's niece, theatrical entertainer Joyce Grenfell). He visited Russia with the Astors in 1931. Having completed *The Apple Cart* shortly after Christmas in 1928, Shaw read the play to Lady Astor and her guests at Cliveden over New Year. Lady Astor visited her 'beloved friend' Shaw on 31 October 1950, two days before his death and recorded their exchange of funny stories which were characteristic of the witty banter that had long typified their relationship.

AVELING, Edward Bibbins (1851–98), Fellow of University College, London, journalist, translator of *Das Kapital,* and playwright (under the name of 'Alec Nelson'). He was the common-law husband (while separated from his first wife) of Karl Marx's daughter, Eleanor. Shaw knew him well from January 1885 and wrote: 'He seduced every woman he met and borrowed from every man.' The characterization of Louis Dubedat in *The Doctor's Dilemma* is partly based on Aveling.

AVELING, Eleanor (née Marx) (1855–98), feminist, freethinker, Socialist, translator of Flaubert's *Madame Bovary,* Ibsenite; daughter of Karl Marx; common-law wife of Edward Aveling who was separated from his first wife. Shaw's acting debut was with the Avelings in the Socialist League Production of Merivale and Simpson's *Alone* (January 1885). Having admired her from afar for some months from January 1885, Shaw became her intimate friend, often visiting her at her home across the road from the British Museum. Eleanor committed suicide on 31 March 1898, after receiving an anonymous note revealing Edward Aveling's secret marriage to Eva Frye in 1897.

AYLIFF, H.K. (1872–1949), actor and director who played a leading role in the staging of productions at the Birmingham Repertory Theatre and the Malvern Festival. He directed numerous Shaw plays, including *Candida, Getting Married, Widowers' Houses, Heartbreak House* and *The Admirable Bashville* at the 1930 Malvern festival, and the first British productions of *Back to Methuselah* (1923) and *Geneva* (1938).

BALFOUR, Arthur James (1848–1930), Conservative Leader in the House of Commons and later deputy Prime Minister to his uncle, the Marquis of Salisbury, before becoming Prime Minister himself in the summer of 1902. From 1902 to 1905 the Webbs cultivated his friendship and Beatrice Webb took Balfour to see *Major Barbara* and *John Bull's Other Island* which he liked so much he saw it five times. Balfour resigned in December 1905, the Fabian 'free trade' pronouncements contributing to his political demise. Balfour and fellow Prime Minister Herbert Henry Asquith are combined to form the character Balsquith in Shaw's one-act play, *Press Cuttings.*

BARKER. See GRANVILLE BARKER, Harley.

BARNES, Sir Kenneth (Ralph) (1878–1957), brother of actresses Irene and Violet Vanbrugh, was associated with Shaw through the Royal Academy for Dramatic Art of which he was Principal from 1909 to 1955. Shaw was elected to the 12-member council of RADA in 1911 and resigned from it on his 85th birthday (1941). In 1927 Shaw declined the request to become godfather of Barnes's son Michael on the grounds that he did not fit the job description in the Prayer Book.

BARRIE, Sir James Matthew (1860–1937), journalist, biographer, playwright and creator of the Peter Pan stories. He was partner with Charles Frohman in the 1909–10 scheme to bring experimental repertory theatre to London's West End (the Duke of York's Theatre). Although they were neighbours at Adelphi Terrace, Shaw said he and Barrie rarely encountered each other. He noted Barrie's 'frightfully gloomy mind' but said that they were always on affectionate terms with one another. In 1916, Barrie was the scriptwriter and cameraman for a would-be comic cowboy film in which Shaw appeared with Chesterton, Archer, Frank Harris and Lord Howard de Walden. Shaw declared that the film 'wasn't in the least funny'.

BARTON, Dr J. Kingston (1854–1941), physician, who first met Shaw in October 1879. They became friends and Shaw visited Barton regularly on Saturday evenings until 1885. In 1880 Shaw sought Barton's advice about the accurate portrayal of dipsomania, fainting and death for use in *The Irrational Knot.*

BAX, Ernest Belfort (1854–1926), editor, music critic, author and philosopher. Bax edited *To-Day* magazine with James Joynes and Hubert Bland, which serialized *An Unsocial Socialist* in March–December 1884. He also edited a magazine called *Time* and wrote music criticism under the pen name 'Musigena' for *The Star* until February 1889 when Shaw took over the job under the pseudonym (a little later) of 'Corno di Bassetto'. Bax acted as Hegelian philosopher to the Social Democratic Federation until he and William Morris left to found the Socialist League. Together they were co-editors of *The Commonweal.* Bax was a member of the Hampstead Historic Society, and a close friend of Shaw from the mid-1880s. Shaw acknowledged the influence of Bax in his work and drew attention in the Preface to *Major Barbara* (1907) to his ruthless criticism of current morality. Bax wrote numerous works on Socialism and an autobiographical memoir, *Reminiscences and Reflexions* (1918), in which he fondly remembers Shaw. Bax's *History of Philosophy* was reviewed by Shaw in 1887 in the *Pall Mall Gazette.*

BEATTY, Pakenham ('Paquito') (1855–1930), minor poet and dilettante, born in Brazil to Irish parents. Beatty was an intelligent but extravagant and dissipated young man, who was one of Shaw's closest friends during his early days in London. The two shared an avid interest in boxing and were listed for bouts at the Amateur Boxing Championship at Lillie Bridge Grounds in 1883, although neither competed. It was through Beatty that Shaw met Ned Donnelly, Professor of Boxing at the London Athletic Club, who became a model for Ned Skene in *Cashel Byron's Profession*. Pakenham was attracted to Lucy Carr Shaw and caused trouble by flirting with her. The Captain in *Captain Brassbound's Confession* owes his alias to Beatty's nickname, 'Paquito', and the naming of Mazzini Dunn in *Heartbreak House* recalls Beatty's christening of his son as Mazzini. Beatty's verse tragedy, *Marcia* (1884), was reviewed harshly by Shaw in *To-Day* under the pen name, 'L.O. Streeter'. When stresses at home drove Beatty to drinking bouts, Shaw sometimes came to his rescue. A number of Beatty's lively and friendly letters, addressed to Shaw under various humorous nicknames, survive in manuscript in the British Library, and provide insights into some of Shaw's interests and activities as a young man.

BEERBOHM, Max (1872–1956), essayist, caricaturist, critic, novelist. When he handed over to Beerbohm the post of theatre critic for the *Saturday Review,* Shaw dubbed him 'the incomparable Max'. While in 1903 Beerbohm complained that Shaw only wrote brilliant 'dialogues' and that Shavian figures were not so much characters as mere 'diagrams' only ever so slightly differentiated from their creator, by 1905 he was impressed enough by the performance of a number of plays, particularly *Major Barbara*, to launch a committed defence of Shaw as a playwright ('Mr Shaw's Position'). From 1896 Beerbohm produced over 40 caricatures of Shaw, including a witty set of seven drawings of Shaw and Mrs Patrick Campbell, based on the correspondence published in 1922 (reproduced in *Collected Letters*, volume 3).

BEETON, Henry R., stockbroker and founding member of the British Economic Association. Shaw attended the original fortnightly meetings of the Association at Beeton's home from November 1885 until 1889. He read his papers, 'Unearned Interest' and 'Interest: Its Nature and Justification', at Beeton's house on 1 June and 9 November 1886, respectively. The meetings strongly influenced the development of Shaw's political and economic views. Beeton was the author of *The Case for Monetary Reform* (1894) and *Bimetallism* (1895).

BELL, Chichester (b.1848), physician who gave up medical practice to study physics and chemistry in Germany. Chichester was the cousin of Alexander Graham Bell, the inventor of the telephone, and more importantly for Shaw, nephew of Melville Bell, the inventor of the phonetic script known as Visible Speech. Bell and Shaw met in March 1874 as fellow lodgers at 61 Harcourt Street, Dublin. The two studied Italian together but Shaw confessed to having learned more about pathology and physics. Shaw acknowledged Bell's influence in encouraging his interest in Wagner.

BELLOC, Hilaire (1870–1953), essayist, novelist, historian, biographer, critic, travel writer, and editor of *The Eye-Witness* from 1911. Belloc was involved in the debates, as chair and participant, which took place between G.K. Chesterton and Shaw. Shaw found comic inspiration in what he considered Belloc's naive Catholicism.

BESANT, Annie (née Wood) (1847–1933), freethinker and campaigner for various political, social and spiritual causes. Besant was associated with the Secularist Charles Bradlaugh and his *National Reformer* in the 1870s and in the early 1880s became a Socialist. She was editor and financial backer of the Socialist magazine *Our Corner* which published *The Irrational Knot* between April 1885 and February 1887. Besant first met Shaw in January 1885, and converted to Fabianism in April, serving on the Fabian Society Executive from 1886 to 1890. She considered Shaw a brilliant Socialist writer and became close to him in 1886. In early 1887 (twenty years after her failed first marriage) she presented a common-law marriage contract to Shaw which, upon his refusal to sign, led to a cooling of personal relations. In 1893 she published *Annie Besant: An Autobiography*. She was converted to Theosophy in 1889, and became President of the Theosophical Society in 1907. Besant eventually settled in India where she adopted and educated Jiddu Krishnamurti and established the Order of the Star in the East in 1911 with Krishnamurti as its World Teacher. Mrs Clandon in *You Never Can Tell*, and Raina in *Arms and the Man* are in part based on Annie Besant.

BLAND, Edith (née Nesbit) (1858–1924), poet, and novelist mainly known for her children's stories. Nesbit knew Shaw through the Fabian Society to which she and her husband, Hubert Bland, belonged. In 1886 she became strongly attracted to Shaw who later remembered her as 'a very clever woman and distinguished poetess'. In 1910 Shaw and Edith corresponded on the current topic of whether Bacon had written Shakespeare's plays.

BLAND, Hubert (1856–1914), Socialist journalist, author, Fabian. Bland edited *To-Day* magazine with Belfort Bax and James Joynes, which serialized *An Unsocial Socialist* between March and December 1884. Despite his Conservative and imperialist leanings Bland was a founding member of the Fabian Society and a member of the Executive and Treasurer from 1884 to 1911. Shaw defended Bland's inclusion in the Executive on the grounds of his cleverness, humaneness, individuality and good sense. Although married to Edith Nesbit, he had two children by Alice Hoatson who was

Secretary of the Fabian Society (1885–6), Fabian Executive member (1890–2) and resident 'companion' with the Bland family from 1885.

BRADLAUGH, Charles (1833–91), outspoken atheist and proprietor of the *National Reformer* from 1862; leader of the National Secular Society (1890–1915) where he became a long-time friend of Annie Besant from August 1874. In February 1887 the Socialist League invited Shaw to represent them in a debate with Bradlaugh but the two failed to agree on numerous points and the debate never eventuated. Two years later Shaw gave over the printing of his Fabian Essays to Bradlaugh's son-in-law, Arthur Bonner.

BRIDGES, Robert (1844–1930), poet, essayist, spelling reformer and philologist, who became poet laureate of England in 1913. Shaw had a high regard for Bridges as a phonetician, and in 1910 Bridges sent Shaw a copy of his essay, 'On the Present State of English Pronunciation'. Bridges and Shaw were both on the Committee of English (1921) and on the Advisory Committee on Spoken English formed by the BBC in 1926. In the Preface to *Pygmalion* Shaw confessed that Higgins may owe his 'Miltonic sympathies' to Bridges, but denied explicit portraiture.

BROOKE, Emma Frances (*c.*1854–1926), Fabian, novelist, founder of the Karl Marx Club which was to become the Hampstead Historic Club of which Brooke was Secretary. Brooke was acquainted with Shaw from at least October 1884 when she consoled Shaw by letter over the rejections of his novels for publication. Brooke became involved in the misunderstanding between her friend, Grace Gilchrist, and Shaw in 1888, taking the side of Gilchrist who mistook Shaw's interest in her for wedding intentions.

BROOKE, Rev. Stopford A. (1832–1916), literary scholar, Fabian Socialist, Irish Unitarian Minister at Bedford Chapel, Bloomsbury (1876–95), and founder of the Bedford Debating Society which Shaw attended. In the discussion following Brooke's paper on 'Shelley as Poet and Man', delivered on 10 March 1886 at the Shelley Society, Shaw publicly proclaimed himself to be, 'like Shelley, a Socialist, an Atheist, and a Vegetarian'. Brooke served as one of Shaw's models for Morell in *Candida*.

BURNS, John (1858–1943), MP for Battersea from 1892 to 1914, played a prominent role in the Social Democratic Federation (SDF) and the Trade Union movement, and led the SDF 'Black Monday' demonstration in 1886 and the great Dock Strike of 1892. Burns was the first working man to attain a position in the cabinet (1906). Somewhat of a maverick, he fell out of favour with Keir Hardie and the Webbs. Burns was friendly with Shaw from the early 1880s and Shaw admitted to lecturing often in Battersea because it was Burns's stronghold. In 1903 Shaw told Burns that, ironically, the British workman is anti-Socialist. Burns was a model for the character of Boanerges in *The Apple Cart.*

BUTLER, Samuel (1835–1902), novelist and evolutionary theorist. Shaw was profoundly influenced by Butler's criticism of Darwin's theories of natural selection when he reviewed Butler's *Luck or Cunning?* for the *Pall Mall Gazette* (May 1887). Shaw met Butler on 15 November 1889, and spoke highly of him thereafter as a man of genius in criticism of Darwin and a brilliant writer of oratorios in the style of Handel. Butler declared himself to be both attracted and repelled by Shaw's 'coruscating power', being particularly irritated by the Shavian critical barbs about Shakespeare. In 1901 Shaw introduced Butler to Grant Richards who published *Erewhon Revisited* (1901), and Shaw later assisted Richards with the posthumous publication of *The Way of All Flesh.*

BUTTERFIELD, Charles (1851–1915), insurance clerk turned actor and tenor opera singer who became Shaw's brother-in-law by his marriage to Lucy Carr Shaw on 17 December 1887. The marriage ended in divorce on 19 July 1909. Butterfield's friends and acquaintances knew him both as a likeable wit and as irresponsible with money and alcohol, the latter factors contributing to the demise of his marriage. Butterfield performed under the stage name 'Cecil Burt', and although Shaw's reviews were civil to him, they offered no high praise.

CAMPBELL, Lady Colin (1858–1911), Irish-born playwright, journalist and art critic. Lady Campbell, referred to by her friends (including Shaw sometimes) as Vera, was widely known for the sensational court proceedings which effected her separation from her husband on the grounds of cruelty. Shaw met her on 29 April 1890 when she came and introduced herself to him in the New Gallery. Later that year he sent her a copy of *Fabian Essays.* At Shaw's request Lady Campbell took over his role as art critic for *The World* at the end of 1889. In 1893, she assisted Janet Achurch in her play-writing, advised Shaw to revise act three of *The Philanderer* (which he did), and was interviewed by Shaw for *The Star* (2 June).

CAMPBELL, Stella (Mrs Patrick) (née Beatrice Stella Tanner) (1865–1940), celebrated actress with whom Shaw had one of his most serious extra-marital affairs. She first appeared on stage professionally in Liverpool in 1888 and had her first major success as Paula in *The Second Mrs Tanqueray* in 1893. Having reviewed her acting and met her from time to time in the early 1890s, Shaw fell passionately in love with her in June 1912 when he read *Pygmalion* to her. The affair developed through numerous meetings, love letters and poems until August 1913 when, having seen Charlotte off to France, Shaw followed Stella to the Guildford Hotel,

Sandwich, anticipating consummation of their love. On arrival, he found that Stella had secretly fled. Shaw was deeply hurt and his ensuing correspondence alternately berates her for treachery and himself for foolishness. Shaw's relationship with Stella continued through the stormy rehearsals for the first London production of *Pygmalion,* in which she played Eliza Doolittle opposite Sir Herbert Beerbohm Tree as Higgins. During these rehearsals she married George Cornwallis-West, who left her in 1919. Shaw has testified that Stella was his model for Eliza Doolittle, and she also inspired him in the creation of Mrs George in *Getting Married,* Hesione Hushabye in *Heartbreak House,* the Serpent in *Back to Methuselah,* part 1, and Orinthia in *The Apple Cart.* She strongly urged Shaw to tear up *The Apple Cart* because of its obvious reflection of his relationship with her and Charlotte. Shaw and Charlotte were embarrassed by Stella's publication of some of her correspondence with Shaw (whom she nicknamed 'Joey') in *My Life and Some Letters* (1922). Her will directed that the Shaw letters and poems 'be published in an independent volume to be entitled "The Love Letters of Bernard Shaw to Mrs Patrick Campbell" so that all who may read them will realise that the friendship was *"L'amitié amoureuse"*'.

CARPENTER, Edward (1844–1929), poet, socialist author of *Towards Democracy* (1883), *Civilization: Its Cause and Cure* (1889), *Love's Coming of Age* (1896) and the Fabian Tract, *The Village and the Landlord* (1907). Together with William Morris, Carpenter financed the Socialist weekly, *Justice.* He was strongly influenced by Whitman and Thoreau as to the virtues of the simple life, and after a brief period as a Cambridge don he turned to literary work, market gardening and sandal-making on a small farm near Sheffield. He was associated with Shaw through Kate and Henry Salt. Shaw contributed an essay, 'The Illusions of Socialism', to *Forecasts of the Coming Century* (1897), edited by Carpenter, and used the song 'England Arise!', of which Carpenter wrote the lyrics, at the end of *On the Rocks.*

CASEMENT, Sir Roger (1864–1916), Ulster Protestant and Irish nationalist who, early in his career, was British consul in the Belgian Congo, where he exposed the cruel treatment of Africans by Belgium. Casement later became involved with the Irish National Volunteers and was arrested for treason, on the eve of the 1916 Easter Uprising in Ireland, for seeking Germany's help to liberate Ireland. In response to a plea from Casement's cousin, Gertrude Bannister, Shaw devised a line of defence for Casement (which was gratefully declined), tried to have his death sentence commuted, and drafted the speech which Casement delivered in court after his sentence had been passed. Casement was hanged on 3 August 1916.

CASSON, Sir Lewis (1875–1969), actor and director. Casson's association with Shaw dates from the Vedrenne–Barker season (1905) at the Court

Theatre where, among other Shavian roles, he played Octavius in *Man and Superman*. He played the part of de Stogumber in the first English production of *Saint Joan* which he co-directed with Shaw and in which his wife, Dame Sybil Thorndike, played the lead. In 1927 Shaw was experimenting with a phono-film which would use some dialogue from *Saint Joan* and contain appearances by himself and Casson.

CHAMPION, Henry Hyde (1859–1928), first honorary secretary of the Social Democratic Federation; co-founder of the National Independent Labour Party in the early 1890s; editor of *To-Day* and *The Labour Elector*; and proprietor of the Modern Press. Champion succeeded in achieving acquittal in his trial for sedition in 1886 and went on to lead the pickets in the London Dock strike of 1889. Shaw met Champion at the Georgite Land Reform Union in 1883. The following year, at Champion's invitation, Shaw did some editorial work for the publisher on Laurence Gronlund's *The Co-operative Commonwealth*. Gronlund was so dissatisfied with the result that he published his own edition. In 1886 *Cashel Byron's Profession* was published by Champion's press. Having migrated to Australia in 1893, Champion worked on the *Melbourne Age*, and was appointed Shaw's Australasian agent in September 1911 after Shaw had sacked J. C. Williamson. Champion held the post until his death in 1928, when it was assumed by his second wife, Belle (an Australian), until Shaw's death in 1950.

CHANT, Laura Ormiston (1848–1923), social reformer, temperance lecturer and author. Chant's views on the nature of prostitution and its possible eradication were published in an interview to which Shaw responded in the *Pall Mall Gazette*. Shaw's essay, 'The Empire Promenade' (*Pall Mall Gazette*, 16 October 1894), highlights some problems with Chant's approach, gives his own view and offers advice for the cause of moral reform. Shaw cites Chant as one of his models for Candida.

CHARRINGTON (MARTIN), Charles (*c.*1860–1926), actor, theatre director, Fabian and husband of Janet Achurch. Charrington succeeded J. T. Grein as managing director of the Independent Theatre. He became a member of the Fabian Society in April 1895 and served on the Executive from 1899 to 1904. Shaw met Charrington and his wife on 16 June 1889, after his production of Ibsen's *A Doll's House* in which he played the part of Torvald opposite Janet Achurch as Nora. In 1897 he played Morell, with Janet in the title role, in *Candida*.

CHERRY-GARRARD, Apsley (1886–1959), naturalist on Scott's British Antarctic Expedition of 1910–13 and close friend of the Shaws at Ayot. In 1916 Cherry-Garrard retired, as an invalid, to his estate, Lamer Park, near

Ayot, where he enjoyed a neighbourly friendship with the Shaws from September 1917, by which time he was living alone. Cherry-Garrard wrote his account of the Antarctic expedition, *The Worst Journey in the World* (1922), with editorial assistance from Charlotte and Shaw and some revisionary writing by Shaw who declined any suggestion of co-authorship. The book was successful but Shaw's support of its criticism of Scott's leadership embroiled him in personal controversy with members of Scott's family who argued that he had been uncritically supportive of Cherry-Garrard's biased opinion of the expedition. Cherry-Garrard later wrote the introduction to George Seaver's *Edward Wilson of the Antarctic* (1933).

CHESTERTON, Gilbert Keith (1874–1936), essayist, critic, novelist, biographer and poet. Chesterton engaged in published and live debates with Shaw from 1911 to 1927. Their lively critical engagement elicited from Shaw, among other works, the rebuttal of Chesterton's thesis on 'The Collapse of Socialism' (*Everyman*, 6 and 13 December 1912), and the construction of the mythical beast, 'Chesterbelloc' (*New Age*, 15 February 1908). Chesterton and Shaw both participated in the Dickens Fellowship mock 'Trial of John Jasper for the Murder of Edwin Drood' (7 January 1914). Shaw repeatedly urged Chesterton to try his hand at a play which he duly did in the critically acclaimed comedy, *Magic* (1913). The two appeared together in a cowboy farce scripted and filmed by J.M. Barrie. In 1909 Chesterton's perceptive critical study *George Bernard Shaw* was published. A revised and expanded second edition of this work, which Shaw himself praised, was brought out in 1935.

CHOLMONDELEY, Mary (née Mary Stewart Payne-Townshend) (c.1858–1929), Charlotte Shaw's younger sister whom she called 'Sissy', and who married Colonel Hugh Cecil Cholmondeley in 1885. After Mary's initial dislike for Shaw around the time of his marriage to her sister, the two enjoyed a warmer friendship. Mary was with Shaw on his ballooning ascent in 1906 and accompanied the Shaws on various automobile tours including the French one of 1910. Shaw considered the exhausting effects of Mary's long struggle with asthma to be instrumental in her death. Shaw's *Intelligent Woman's Guide to Socialism and Capitalism* (1928) was initially inspired by Mary's request for some ideas on socialism to present to a women's meeting in Shropshire.

CHUBB, Percival A. (1860–1960), clerk with the Local Government Board of the Civil Service in the 1880s; member of the Fellowship of the New Life and later a founding member of the Fabian Society. Chubb was influenced by Thomas Davidson's teachings of personal and social utopias. He organized a group comprising Ellis, Podmore, Clarke, Champion, Pease and Bland to listen to Davidson at his arrival in London in 1882. Shaw knew

Chubb from at least November 1887 through the Hampstead Historic Club and the two were close through 1888–9. Chubb later moved to the US where he set up Ethical Churches and 'ethical culture' schools.

CLARKE, William J. (1852–1901), political journalist, lecturer, founding member of the Fabian Society and on its Executive from 1888 to 1891. Shaw recalled first meeting Clarke at the Bedford Debating Society. His diary shows he knew him in December 1885 and heard him speak at Bedford on 'The Results of the General Election' on 14 January 1886. Shaw considered Clarke a good lecturer, and was strongly influenced by him. Clarke was sure that, due to its basis in injustice and selfishness, modern civilization was falling apart. His strong religious rationalism and sour temper made him quarrelsome, particularly with Shaw whom he regarded as something of a moral anarchist. Shaw considered Clarke's representation of him in *The Echo* (9 December 1890) an extraordinarily bitter portrait. However, unbeknown to Clarke, Shaw was secretly crucial in relieving his chronic poverty by quietly substituting Clarke for himself as a writer for the *Daily Chronicle*.

COBURN, Alvin Langdon (1882–1966), American-born photographer who settled in Britain. Coburn introduced himself to Shaw by letter in July 1904, mentioning their mutual friend F.H. Evans and requesting a sitting. Coburn dates their friendship from 1 August 1904 and considered it a highlight of his time in London. Coburn made at least fifty photographic portraits of Shaw at various times, and at Shaw's invitation visited Paris in April 1906 to photograph Rodin who was working on the bust of Shaw. He took the famous nude photograph of Shaw in the pose of Rodin's *Le Penseur*. Shaw wrote a letter of introduction to Stella Campbell for Coburn and in it suggested a matching nude shot of her, a suggestion she refused. Although Shaw considered Coburn one of the unsurpassed artistic photographers of the time, he accidentally photographed the wrong house for Henderson's biography of Shaw, a fact Shaw pointed out to the American publishers in 1911.

COFFIN, Charles Hayden (1862–1935), actor-singer of light opera. Shaw frequented Coffin's father's house where a Fabian meeting had been held at which Edward Carpenter read a paper on 'Private Property' (1 January 1886). Coffin had his stage debut in 1885, and in 1886 played Harry Sherwood in *Dorothy*, his song, 'Queen of My Heart', being a highlight of the performance. He maintained the part for 931 performances, including seasons at the Gaiety, Prince of Wales's (opposite Lucy Carr Shaw) and Lyric Theatres. In his reviews of Coffin's performances Shaw consistently praised him and complains that his artistic intelligence was tragically wasted by being allocated inappropriate or minor parts. Coffin was the person who informed Lucy of the death of Vandeleur Lee.

COTTERILL, Erica (1881–1950), author, Fabian, cousin of poet Rupert Brooke and daughter of Fabian schoolmaster Charles Clement Cotterill. Cotterill became obsessed with Shaw in 1905 and, inspired by some clear encouragement from him over following years, wrote him many passionate letters, made uninvited visits to Ayot, and followed him home to Adelphi Terrace from Fabian meetings. She wrote an engaging comedy, *A Professional Socialist* (1908), and published a series of epistolary confessions, most of which were addressed to Shaw. Her autobiographical works, *An Account* (1916), which is dedicated to Shaw, and *Form of Diary* (1939), reveal her creative intelligence and sensitivity as well as her self-absorption. Shaw knew Cotterill had the touch of a highly gifted writer, but confessed that the meaning of her work often eluded him. The disturbance Cotterill was causing to Shaw's marriage resulted in his drafting of a letter (October 1910) for Charlotte to send to her which unequivocally demanded complete cessation of association. The portrayals of Incognita Appassionata in *Getting Married*, and Ellie in *Heartbreak House*, partly reflect Shaw's relationship with Cotterill. As late as 1942, Shaw was still marvelling at her, refusing to consider her mad but noting the fascinating eccentricity of her life and writing.

CRAIG, Edith ('Edy') (1869–1947), actress, and daughter of Ellen Terry and Edward Godwin. Having been involved with the theatre from an early age, she joined the Lyceum company, and played Prossy in *Candida* in the Stage Society's production of 1900. Edith Craig's Pioneer Players presented a single performance of *The Inca of Perusalem* at the Criterion on 16 December 1917. She later left acting to take up costume designing and stage-management. With Shaw's assistance, Edith negotiated the sale of the Shaw–Terry correspondence in her possession to American publisher Elbridge Adams, and there followed a complicated series of negotiations involving publication, copyright, personal interest and misunderstanding which caused a straining of Shaw's cordial relation with Adams.

CRAIG, Edward Gordon (1872–1966), son of Ellen Terry and Edward Godwin, member of Henry Irving's company from 1889, and later a celebrated scene designer. Craig disliked Shaw for his criticism of Irving and for his epistolary philandering with Ellen. After his mother's death he quarrelled bitterly with Shaw over the publication of the Shaw–Terry correspondence, because, according to Shaw, the letters revealed Terry as the powerful woman Craig was always trying to deny and escape. The public antagonism between Craig and Shaw came to a head with Craig's *Ellen Terry and Her Secret Self* (1931) and its accompanying pamphlet, 'A Plea for G.B.S.', and Shaw's subsequent 'Ellen Terry and Her Letters' (*The Observer*, 8 November 1931).

CREIGHTON, Bishop Mandell (1843–1901), Bishop of London; model for the Bishop in *Getting Married*. Creighton's son, Walter, played Juggins in *Fanny's First Play* (1912) and the Emperor in *Androcles and the Lion* (1915). Creighton was a long-time friend of Beatrice Webb and Shaw knew the Bishop's daughter, Beatrice.

CUNNINGHAME GRAHAM, Robert Bontine (1856–1936), biographer, short story and travel writer, and Liberal MP for North Lanarkshire, Scotland from 1886 to 1892. He was a supporter of Socialist causes, and was arrested at the 'Bloody Sunday' demonstration in Trafalgar Square on 13 November 1887, at which Shaw was present. Shaw first met Graham on 25 February 1888 and their active association continued into the 1890s. Graham's celebrated declaration in Parliament, 'I never withdraw', provided a keynote for Shaw's characterization of the cavalry officer, Sergius Saranoff, in *Arms and the Man*, and Shaw borrowed from a work on Morocco by Cunninghame Graham for details of the setting of *Captain Brassbound's Conversion*.

CUSACK, Cyril (1910–93), Irish actor who became established as a leading player at the Abbey Theatre in the 1930s, where he played Marchbanks in *Candida*. Cusack played Louis Dubedat in *The Doctor's Dilemma* opposite Laurence Olivier and Vivien Leigh during the Second World War, at the Haymarket Theatre, but, following a collapse on stage due to the effects of alcohol one St Patrick's Day, he was replaced by John Gielgud. After the war he formed a company of his own which became internationally celebrated in performances of Shakespeare, O'Casey, Synge and Shaw. Cusack's other Shaw roles included the Waiter in *You Never Can Tell* at the Abbey Theatre and Malvern Festival, and the Inquisitor in *Saint Joan*.

DALY, Arnold (1875–1927), American actor-manager who began his theatrical career as an office boy for Charles Frohman. Between 1903 and 1906 Daly staged in New York theatres the first fully professional American productions of *Candida, The Man of Destiny, How He Lied to Her Husband, You Never Can Tell* and *John Bull's Other Island*. In 1904 Shaw contracted Daly to produce his plays in the US. The New York opening of Daly's production of *Mrs Warren's Profession* (1905) was sensational, resulting in the cast being arrested and tried for 'disorderly conduct'. Daly was charged for 'immorality' in staging the production, but was acquitted in June 1906. Shaw became dissatisfied with Daly's presentation of his plays, and concerned about his addiction to alcohol, which probably contributed to his death in a fire which broke out in his apartment.

DAVIDSON, Thomas (1840–1900), Scottish-born philosopher, and founder of The Fellowship of the New Life. His interest in religion, ethics and social reform led to meetings at his Chelsea home from 1881 to 1883 from which 'ethical Socialism' was born. In 1882 the group around Davidson included, with varying degrees of commitment, Frank Podmore, Edward Pease, Havelock Ellis, Percival Chubb, Dr Burns Gibson, H. H. Champion, Hubert Bland, William Clarke, W. I. Jupp, Miss Caroline Hadden, Miss Dale Owen and Mrs Hinton. On 16 November 1883, the charter for The Fellowship of the New Life was resolved. The Fellowship embraced a practical utopian vision characterized by spirituality, wisdom, love and unselfishness. At a meeting on 4 January 1884 the Fellowship gave rise to a new group, the Fabian Society, dedicated to more immediate social objectives. Shaw considered the hard common sense of Hubert Bland to be responsible for leading the Fabian Society into being and out of Davidson's utopian dreams.

DENHAM, Reginald (b.1894), actor, author, director. In 1922 Denham acted in several of Shaw's plays at the Everyman Theatre. When J. B. Fagan appointed him Director of the Oxford Players he chose *Heartbreak House* for the company's first production in October 1923. The performance was hopelessly overacted and Shaw, who was present, saw his 'semi-tragedy' become a 'farcical comedy'.

DEVONPORT, Lord. See KEARLEY, Hudson Ewbank.

DICKENS, Ethel (1864–1936), granddaughter of Charles Dickens, who operated the Type Writing Office at 6 Tavistock Street, Strand. Shaw used this typewriting service for the preparation of prompt-copies of his plays from the drafts. He notes in his diary, for example, that he collected two copies of the *Candida* script from 'Mrs Dickens's office' on 12 March 1895.

DONNELLY, Ned (b.1844), boxing instructor at the London Athletic Club and Shaw's 'Professor of Boxing' in the mid-1880s. Shaw's Ned Skene in *Cashel Byron's Profession* is partly based on Donnelly.

DOUGLAS, Lord Alfred (1870–1945), son of the Marquess of Queensberry. Lord Alfred's father was sued by Oscar Wilde for libel, but the Marquess's defence led to Wilde's arrest and imprisonment in 1895. Shaw met Douglas only once (in 1895), and initially dismissed him as a 'brat' for his behaviour towards Wilde, but the two became regular correspondents in the 1930s and early 1940s (addressing each other as 'St Christopher' and 'Childe Alfred'). Shaw thought that Douglas was politically naive but regarded him as 'a quite considerable poet'. In 1938, urged by Douglas, Shaw attended a performance of Leslie and Sewell Stokes's *Oscar Wilde*, and wrote to tell Douglas he had enjoyed it.

DRYSDALE, Janey Crichton (1861–1949), author, librettist under the pen-name 'Ercil Doune', sister of composer Learmont Drysdale, and friend and correspondent of Lucy Carr Shaw. In the early 1890s she became interested in Ibsen and the Fabian Society. Janey met Lucy in London in 1898 during rehearsals for Learmont's opera, *The Red Spider,* in which Lucy was to star as Honor Luxmore, and the two remained close friends until Lucy's death in 1920.

ELDER, Ann M. See JACKSON, Ann M.

ELGAR, Sir Edward (1857–1934), composer much admired and championed by Shaw. He first met Shaw at lunch in March 1919 after which the two enjoyed a long friendship. Elgar campaigned with Shaw in the late 1920s against the New Music Copyright Bill and dedicated his *Severn Suite* to Shaw in 1930. In 1932, Shaw quietly approached John Reith, Managing Director of the BBC, suggesting that the Corporation sponsor Elgar to complete his third symphony for a commission of a thousand pounds. Reith took up Shaw's suggestion, but Elgar died before the symphony was completed.

ELLIS, Havelock (1859–1939), scientist and writer, famous for his seven-volume study of sexuality, *Studies in the Psychology of Sex* (1897–1928). Shaw was in contact with Ellis from at least August 1888, when Ellis invited him to provide a volume in the Contemporary Science series he was editing. Shaw enjoyed conversation with Ellis in the early 1890s and defended Ellis's publications against would-be censors on the grounds that such authoritative scientific studies were 'urgently needed' in England.

EPSTEIN, Sir Jacob (1880–1959), American-born sculptor who cast a bronze bust of Shaw in 1934. Epstein acknowledged that Shaw championed him in England, but also knew that the Shaws strongly disliked his sculpture. GBS described his image in Epstein's craggy-featured bust as 'Neanderthal Shaw', and Charlotte refused to have it in the house. Epstein nevertheless believed he had captured an essential self of Shaw.

ERVINE, St John (1883–1971), Irish journalist, biographer, novelist, playwright, critic, Fabian and author of a full-scale biography of Shaw. In 1915 he became manager of the Abbey Theatre. Early the following year, attempts by Ervine (and Shaw) to secure a licence for the production of an unexpurgated version of *The Shewing-Up of Blanco Posnet* at the Liverpool Repertory Theatre failed. After the First World War, near the end of which he was wounded by shell fire and had a leg amputated, he acted as theatrical critic for *The Observer, Morning Post* and *New York World,* in which capacity he reviewed *Candida* (1921), *Back to Methuselah* (initiating a recurring debate between himself and Shaw over the play), *Heartbreak House* (1921) and *Too True to be Good* (1932). In 1942, Shaw read a draft of what would become Ervine's biography, *Bernard Shaw: His Life, Work and Friends* (1956).

EVANS, Dame Edith Mary (1888–1976), distinguished English actress, whom Shaw first saw in her London debut of 1912, playing opposite Esmé Percy in *Troilus and Cressida*. After early experience in mainly modern roles, Evans established herself as one of the great actresses of her time in the 1920s and 1930s with some outstanding Shakespearean and Restoration performances. Her acting career extended over sixty years and included the work of Ibsen, Chekhov, Wilde, Fry and Shaw. Evans played the character of Orinthia in Shaw's *The Apple Cart* (1929), and the Serpent and the She-Ancient in his *Back to Methuselah* (1923). She played Lady Utterword in a revival of *Heartbreak House* in 1929, and then Hesione Hushabye in a 1943 production of the same play. Shaw had her in mind for the character of Epifania when he wrote *The Millionairess* in 1934, but she did not play the part until 1940.

EVANS, Frederick H. (1852–1943), London bookseller, pianola enthusiast and amateur photographer. In 1895 Evans proposed the publication, in book form, of Shaw's music criticism from *The World*. Although Shaw showed interest, the project never materialised. The 1902 edition of *Mrs Warren's Profession,* published by Grant Richards, was illustrated with Evans's studio photographs of members of the Stage Society production. On 23 February 1911, Shaw chaired a lecture by Evans at the Camera Club on the topic of the pianola: the presence of the two made for a witty, musical evening. In 1945 Shaw confessed to Blanche Patch that he had paid for the schooling of Evans's son, referring to the educational gift as one of his Pygmalion experiments. Right up until his death Shaw considered Evans one of three unsurpassed photographers (the other two being Mrs Hay Cameron and Alvin Langdon Coburn).

FAGAN, James Bernard (1873–1933), Irish playwright and director, and one of the few members of the Dramatists' Club to support Shaw throughout the First World War. Fagan was manager of the Court Theatre from 1918, where he produced *Heartbreak House* in 1921 with some cuts authorized by Shaw, and founded the Oxford Playhouse in 1923.

FARR (EMERY), Florence (1860–1917), actress, novelist and manager of the Avenue Theatre from 1894. She separated from her husband, Edward Emery, in 1888, and probably met Shaw on 26 August 1890 at William Morris's factory at Merton Abbey. By October, 1890, a love affair had begun between her and Shaw, and by this time she was also involved with W. B. Yeats. Farr played Blanche in *Widowers' Houses* in 1892, and Louka in *Arms and the Man* in 1894. Her novel, *The Dancing Faun*, had a protagonist based in part on Shaw. Shaw's relationship with Farr created tensions in his affair with Jenny Patterson which exploded in a stormy scene at Farr's house on the evening of 4 February 1893. This episode, and the love triangle between Shaw, Farr and Patterson, formed the basis of the first scene of *The Philanderer*. Shaw's intimacy with Farr declined in 1896, as she was becoming increasingly involved in mysticism and the occult society, Golden Dawn. In September 1912 she moved to Ceylon where she later died of cancer.

FOOTE, G. W. (1850–1915), Secularist writer; editor of *The Freethinker* and *Progress;* and lecturer who succeeded Charles Bradlaugh in 1890 as President of the National Secular Society. Foote first met Shaw through William Archer on 26 April 1885. Shaw chaired a debate between Foote and Annie Besant in February 1887 and had a debate with Foote himself in January 1891.

FORBES-ROBERTSON, Sir Johnston (1853–1937), actor, who played Caesar in the first professional American production of *Caesar and Cleopatra* in 1906. Shaw knew Forbes-Robertson from 1895 and read *The Devil's Disciple* to him and Mrs Patrick Campbell in February 1897. In 1899 Forbes-Robertson played opposite Campbell in a copyright performance of *Caesar and Cleopatra* at Newcastle. After years of frustrating indecisiveness about accepting the role, Forbes-Robertson finally played Richard Dudgeon in *The Devil's Disciple* in September 1900. Shaw observed that he was 'cold, very handsome, constrained, and with an air of having been called away from some important business to do something distasteful on the stage. Yet he became our best actor, and indeed is so still.'

FROHMAN, Charles (1860–1915), American theatrical manager, and leading member of a group of managers known as the Theatrical Syndicate. He entered a partnership with J. M. Barrie and embarked in 1909–10 on a scheme to bring experimental repertory theatre to London's West End at the Duke of York's Theatre. Frohman produced *Captain Brassbound's Conversion* in New York (1907) and *Misalliance* in London (1910). He died in the *Lusitania* disaster of 1915.

FURNIVALL, Dr Frederick James (1825–1910), lexicographer, member of the Philological Society from 1847 and founding editor of what would become the *Oxford English Dictionary*. Furnivall coordinated numerous literary societies, three of which Shaw attended: the Shelley, Browning and New Shakespeare Societies. In 1884 Furnivall arranged for Shaw to compile an index and glossary for a new edition of the works of Thomas Lodge, a time-consuming task Shaw gave up and passed on to Thomas Tyler before completion.

GALSWORTHY, John (1867–1933), novelist and playwright, was involved with Shaw and 69 other playwrights and authors in a protest against censorship published in *The Times* (29 October 1907). Although Shaw refused to back Galsworthy's pacifist attempt to limit the manufacture of aeroplanes before the First World War, he respected Galsworthy's work and the two were on friendly terms till Galsworthy's death.

GALTON, Sir Francis (1822–1911), biologist at Trinity College, Cambridge, founder of the quarterly *Biometrika* (1901) and pioneer of the science of eugenics. Shaw attended a series of lectures by Galton at the South Kensington Museum in November and December 1887, and was influenced by his thoughts on 'nature and nurture'. Galton produced a theory, found useful by Shaw, of a class of people who can achieve incredible feats of memory and calculation because they imaginatively visualize diagrams and images. In the Preface to *Saint Joan,* Shaw describes Joan as a 'Galtonic visualizer', her peculiar visionary perception giving rise to extraordinary achievement.

GEORGE, Henry (1839–97), American economist and political reformer; founder of the Land Reform Union. Shaw heard George speak on Land Nationalization and Single Tax on 5 September 1882 and, at the same meeting, bought George's very popular book, *Progress and Poverty,* and read it enthusiastically through September–October 1882. He joined the Land Reform Union at about the same time. Shaw regarded his contact with George as a major turning point in his development as a thinker about economic and political subjects, and as having been a key influence in his conversion to socialism. Shaw probably met George in person through Stewart Headlam on 7 April 1889, and had a shipboard meeting with his daughter in New York in 1933. Shaw's 'Henry George and the Social Democrats' appeared in *The Star* (7 June 1889) and his 'The Hyndman–George Debate' in the *International Review* (formerly *To-Day*) (August 1889).

GIELGUD, Sir John (b.1904), celebrated stage and film actor, and grandson of Ellen Terry's sister Kate. Having joined the Old Vic repertory in 1929, he played the role of Shakespeare in *The Dark Lady of the Sonnets* and the Emperor in *Androcles and the Lion* in the 1929–30 season. In the 1930–1 Old Vic season, Gielgud played Sergius in *Arms and the Man.* He subsequently played Louis Dubedat in *The Doctor's Dilemma* at the Haymarket Theatre, the Inquisitor in a televised version of *Saint Joan,* and Captain Shotover in *Heartbreak House,* also for television. Gielgud recalls Shaw's visits to rehearsals of *Arms and the Man* in his autobiographical work, *Early Stages* (1939).

GILLMORE, Arabella. See 'Ancestry and Family', p. 13.

GILLMORE, Georgina Jane ('Judy'), later MUSTERS. See MUSTERS, Georgina Jane.

GORKI, Maxim (1868–1936), novelist, playwright, author of *The Lower Depths* (1903) which was first played publicly in England on 2 December 1911. Shaw was present at the performance and sent his congratulations to Gorki in a group telegram signed by a number of London drama figures including Harley Granville Barker and John Galsworthy. Gorki corresponded with Shaw in 1915 on the topic of war and invited Shaw to contribute to the Soviet periodical, *Novoye Zhizn,* of which he was editor, in 1917. Shaw visited Gorki on 29 July 1931, during his Russian trip.

GRAHAM, Robert Bontine Cunninghame (1856–1936). See CUNNINGHAME GRAHAM, Robert Bontine.

GRANVILLE BARKER, Harley (1877–1946), actor, playwright, theatre director and scholar, Fabian and friend of Shaw. Barker first met Shaw in the summer of 1900 and was promptly engaged to play Marchbanks in the Stage Society's production of *Candida*. His other Shavian roles included that of Tanner in the 1905 production of *Man and Superman*, in which Lillah McCarthy, whom he married in 1906, played Ann Whitefield. In partnership with J. E. Vedrenne, Granville Barker was the driving force behind the regular staging of new and experimental drama at the Royal Court Theatre, Sloane Square from 1904 to 1907. The Vedrenne–Barker seasons at the Royal Court helped to reshape the tastes of London audiences, alter the practices of dramatists and establish Shaw's reputation as the leading dramatist in England. Granville Barker served on the Fabian Executive from 1907 to 1912. His marriage to Lillah McCarthy effectively ended in 1915 when he fell in love with a wealthy American, Helen Huntington, whom he married in 1918. Shaw considered Granville Barker a brilliant young man and praised his performances in Shavian roles and his Shakespearean productions. His performance as Marchbanks in *Candida* was, according to Shaw, 'humanly speaking, perfect', and his interpretation of Shakespeare led Shaw to conclude: 'it was Barker who restored Shakespear to the stage'.

GREGORY, Lady Augusta (née Persse), (1852–1932), playwright, translator and folklore collector. She became associated with Shaw through the Irish National Theatre Society which she co-founded with W. B. Yeats in 1898. In 1909 Yeats and Lady Gregory successfully joined forces with Shaw to resist the attempts from Dublin Castle to ban the proposed production at the Abbey Theatre of *The Shewing-up of Blanco Posnet*. The Shaws visited Lady Gregory at Coole Park on their Irish motoring tours in 1910, 1915 and 1918, and she frequently visited them for overnight and weekend stays at

Ayot, and for lunches at Adelphi Terrace and, from 1927, Whitehall Court. Lady Gregory's *Journals* supply perceptive comments on Shaw's private readings to her and others of his works in progress, and recollections of other meetings. She greatly enjoyed Shaw's company, describing him in 1915 as having 'a sort of kindly joyousness about him'.

GREIN, Jacob Thomas (1862–1935), Dutch-born drama critic, playwright, and founder of the Independent Theatre Society in 1891. Shaw was one of the founding members of the Society, along with Thomas Hardy, George Moore, George Meredith and Henry James. The Society's opening production was Ibsen's *Ghosts*, in William Archer's translation, at the Royalty Theatre on 13 March 1891. Shaw's first performed play, *Widowers' Houses*, was produced by the Society at the Royalty on 9 December 1892. Grein wrote a recollection of his discussions with Shaw about the production, and the production itself, which was published in the *Illustrated London News* on 14 August 1926. Although never financially secure, the Independent Theatre continued for seven years to produce serious, avant-garde plays as an alternative to the superficial entertainments which made up the greater part of the theatrical offerings of the day. In December 1932 Shaw attended the Critics' Circle dinner in honour of Grein.

GURLY, Walter Bagnall (1800–85). See 'Ancestry and Family', pp. 11–13.

GURLY, Dr Walter John (1831 or 1835–99). See 'Ancestry and Family', pp. 12.

HAIG, Field-Marshal Sir Douglas (1861–1928), Commander in Chief of the British Armed forces at the Western Front from December 1915 to the end of the war. In January 1917 Haig invited Shaw to visit the front lines. In early February, during the course of his subsequent visit to the Front, Shaw lunched with Haig at Montreuil. Haig found Shaw 'an interesting man of original views. A great talker!'

HALDANE, Richard Burdon, Viscount Haldane of Cloan (1856–1928), lawyer and statesman. Shaw dined with Haldane, Asquith and Balfour in February 1896 and used Haldane as a model for the Waiter in *You Never Can Tell*.

HAMON, Augustin (1862–1945), French Socialist editor and author. Hamon first met Shaw in 1894 and, from 1904, became his French translator. Although he tended to get the credit for the translations, Hamon's wife Henriette, who had a better command of English than her husband, was probably the principal translator. Hamon's study of Shaw, *The Twentieth Century Molière,* was published in 1913.

HANKIN, Edward Charles St John (1869–1909), playwright and translator. He was among the dramatists whose works were produced at the Royal Court Theatre in the 1904–7 Vedrenne–Barker period. Hankin translated *The Three Daughters of M. Dupont* to go with two other plays translated by Charlotte Shaw and John Pollock in *Three Plays by Brieux*, published with a preface by Shaw in 1911. He was the model for St John Hotchkiss in *Getting Married*.

HARDIE, (James) Keir (1856–1915), Scottish miners' leader who founded the Scottish Miners' Federation in 1886 and became chairman of the Independent Labour Party in 1893. Hardie was the first Fabian to be elected to Parliament in the General Election of July 1893. Shaw campaigned on his behalf a number of times from 1892 to 1910, and wrote a piece on his death (*The Pioneer*, 9 October 1915).

HARDWICKE, Sir Cedric (1893–1964), actor who played leading roles in many of Shaw's plays including *The Apple Cart, Back to Methuselah, Heartbreak House, Too True to be Good* and *Caesar and Cleopatra*.

HARRIS, Frank (1856–1931), editor, playwright, literary critic, adventurer. Harris edited the *Evening News* until 1886 and the *Fortnightly Review* until August 1894. As early as November 1891 he was asking Shaw for music criticism for the *Fortnightly Review*, but the two did not meet personally till 16 October 1893. From September 1894 Harris became owner-editor of the *Saturday Review* where Shaw took up the position of theatre critic from 1895 to 1898. Harris produced a biography of Shaw, the galley proofs of which Shaw rewrote on Harris's death.

HARRISON, Frederick (1853–1926), manager, associated with Cyril Maude at the Haymarket Theatre from 1896 to 1905. Harrison required such significant changes to the play for a planned production of *You Never Can Tell* that Shaw, frustrated, withdrew it altogether from production during the rehearsal period on 29 April 1897.

HEADLAM, Rev. Stewart D. (1847–1924), Christian Socialist and editor of *The Church Reformer*, to which Shaw contributed. He served on the Fabian Society Executive from 1890 to 1891 and 1901 to 1911. Shaw first met Headlam at the Land Reform Union sometime after 1882 and a lasting friendship developed. It was through Headlam that Shaw met Henry George on 7 April 1889. The character James Mavor Morell in *Candida* was partly modelled on Headlam.

HENDERSON, Archibald (1877–1963), Assistant Professor of Mathematics at the University of North Carolina and Shaw biographer. Henderson's interest in Shaw was sparked in 1903 by seeing an amateur production of *You Never Can Tell* in Chicago. He became an ardent devotee, and first wrote to Shaw in June 1904, asking for information regarding the early publications and stating his intention to write a Shavian biography. Shaw became deeply involved in Henderson's project from 1904, and his generous supply of information and comments on drafts, provided at lengthy intervals during an exceptionally busy period of Shaw's life and over a long period of time, meant the book, *George Bernard Shaw: His Life and Works*, did not come out till 1911. In January 1905 Shaw sent Henderson the first of a series of letters of detailed autobiographical information. As the years went by, Henderson was increasingly anxious to get the book published, but Shaw, impressed with the manuscript and intent on its elaboration, urged patience. In 1907 Henderson finally accepted Shaw's repeated invitations to visit London, and the two met personally for the first time at St Pancras Station on 17 June 1907. Henderson and Shaw collaborated on *Table-Talk of GBS* (1925), and Henderson went on to produce numerous Shavian articles and two more biographical studies: *Bernard Shaw: Playboy and Prophet* (1932), and *George Bernard Shaw: Man of the Century* (1956).

HEWINS, William Albert Samuel (1865–1931), political economist, historian, and first director of the London School of Economics from 1895 to 1903. He was Conservative MP for Hereford City (1912–18), and Secretary (1903–17) and Chairman (1920–2) of the Tariff Commission. In 1898, after the Shaws' marriage, Hewins visited them at Haslemere nearly every Tuesday. He delivered his lecture, 'Foreign Trade and Foreign Politics', as part of the Fabian Society lectures on Imperial Politics between October 1899 and March 1900. Shaw contributed, 'Imperialism', on 23 February, 1900.

HOEY, Frances (Fanny) Cashel (1830–1908). See 'Ancestry and Family', pp. 10.

HOPKINS, Tighe (1856–1919), *Vanity Fair* journalist and novelist. Shaw first met Hopkins at Jenny Patterson's home on 12 January 1886 where they tried to outstay each other, Hopkins being, according to Shaw, 'bent on seduction'. Shaw reviewed Hopkins's novel *For Freedom* in the *Pall Mall Gazette*, 7 May 1888. Shaw made some important statements about his literary aims in letters to Hopkins in the second half of 1889.

HORNIMAN, Annie E. F. (1860–1937), wealthy patron of the theatre who was crucial in the financing of experimental drama at the Avenue Theatre in London and the building and opening of Dublin's Abbey Theatre. *Widowers' Houses* was the first Shaw production at Horniman's newly founded Midland Theatre, Manchester in 1909. At Shaw's suggestion, she applied for a licence to produce the revised *Blanco Posnet* in Manchester, but the application was refused. Annie Horniman later produced a number of Shaw's plays at the Gaiety Theatre, Manchester.

HUDDART, Elinor (b.1839), novelist who published anonymously and also under various pen-names ('Elinor Hume', 'Elinor Aitch', 'Louisa Rouile'). Huddart first met Shaw when she took singing lessons from his mother at 13 Victoria Grove in 1878. Shaw read a number of her books, including *Commonplace Sinners* in 1886, and they frequently corresponded from 1878 to 1894. Only the Huddart letters from this correspondence survive, but they reveal much about Shaw and his literary and intellectual interests in his early London days.

HYNDMAN, Henry Mayers (1842–1921), leading early disciple of Karl Marx and author of *England for All*, originally entitled *The Text-book of Democracy* (1881). A graduate of Trinity College, Cambridge, he founded the London Democratic Federation in 1881 (renamed the Social Democratic Federation in 1884). Shaw attended meetings of the SDF before turning to the Fabian Society in May 1884. In May 1887 the *Pall Mall Gazette* was host to a series of articles in which Shaw and Hyndman vigorously debated Hyndman's presentation of Marxist theories. Hyndman's impetuous character and position as an upper-class radical socialist is reflected in the creation of Jack Tanner in *Man and Superman*.

IRVING, Sir Henry (1838–1905), leading English actor and manager of the Lyceum Theatre in association with Ellen Terry from 1878 to 1902. His knighthood, awarded in 1895, was the first ever to be awarded to an actor. Shaw thought that Irving's domineering style of acting was a hindrance to Terry's artistic maturation and to the development of theatre in London. Terry's enthusiasm for *The Man of Destiny* in 1896 began what became for Shaw a frustrating and eventually vain negotiation with Irving over its possible production.

JACKSON, Ann M. (née Elder) (b.1890), served as Shaw's secretary from 1912 to 1920. Jackson had been recommended by Shaw's previous secretary, Mrs Georgina Musters, and is on record in Allan Chappelow's book, *Shaw The Villager,* as having enjoyed every minute of her time with GBS. In 1920 she married and left England to live in India. Shaw attended her wedding on 27 March, the day his sister Lucy died. On 18 July 1945, Shaw lunched with Ann and Judy Musters at Whitehall Court and then took them to see Wilder's *The Skin of Our Teeth.*

JACKSON, Sir Barry Vincent (1879–1961), theatrical director and entrepreneur, and founder of the Birmingham Repertory Theatre. Shaw stayed with Jackson in 1923 during rehearsals for what was to be the first English production of *Back to Methuselah*. Jackson established the annual Malvern Festival in 1929 with Shaw as leading playwright and patron-in-chief. *The Apple Cart, Back to Methuselah, Heartbreak House* and *Caesar and Cleopatra* were the Shaw plays performed at the 1929 Malvern Festival, which during the 1930s became a regular venue for first performances of new works by Shaw.

JAMES, Henry (1843–1916), novelist, short story writer, essayist, critic, playwright. In a letter of 1909, in characteristically direct and spirited critical style, Shaw rejected James's play *The Saloon* on behalf of the Stage Society. James responded with an indignant defence, and a tussle by correspondence ensued. Although James's play, *Guy Domville,* was disturbed by catcalls on opening night, Shaw's review (*Saturday Review,* 12 January 1895) had good things to say of it. It was at this performance (5 January 1895) that Shaw met H. G. Wells.

JOHN, Augustus (1878–1961), painter who, in May 1915, was a guest with the Shaws at Lady Gregory's Coole Park estate. While there he painted a number of fine portraits of Shaw, the best-known of which is in the Fitzwilliam Museum, Cambridge. John's *Chiaroscuro: Fragments of Autobiography* (1952) includes some warm recollections of Shaw.

JONES, Henry Arthur (1851–1929), a leading London dramatist of the 1890s. Shaw met Jones at William Archer's home on 4 May 1885 and the two became longstanding friends until Shaw's views on the First World War and the Irish question infuriated Jones to the degree that he joined others in seeking Shaw's exclusion from the Dramatists' Club, and would no longer meet with him. Shaw's attempt to renew the friendship when Jones was ill in 1926 was kindly received but unsuccessful.

JOYCE, James (1882–1941), Irish novelist. Shaw read sections of *Ulysses* in serial form before its publication as a book in 1922. His reaction to the novel was heavily coloured by his reading of it as a realistic description of aspects of Dublin life that he preferred to forget. (For his considered opinion about the work, which he thought 'a literary masterpiece', see the Chronology entry for 3 June 1939.) Joyce's 1926 letter to Shaw congratulating him on his award of the Nobel Prize for Literature was the only congratulatory one that Shaw saved. At the age of 93, Shaw tried to read *Finnegans Wake,* but confessed it would take more time to interpret than he had left.

JOYNES, James Leigh (1853–93), poet and member of the Social Democratic Federation. He was a friend of William Morris and Henry Salt (whom his sister married), and co-editor with Belfort Bax and Hubert Bland of the Socialist journal *To-Day* which serialized Shaw's *An Unsocial Socialist* from March to December 1884. Joynes met Shaw in 1882–3 at a meeting of the Land Reform Union and introduced him to Salt. Shaw praised Joynes's *Songs of a Revolutionary Epoch* (1888) and lamented his unnecessary death as the result of 'stupid' medical treatment.

KEARLEY, Hudson Ewbank (Lord Devonport) (1856–1934), Liberal MP from 1892 to 1910; Parliamentary Secretary to the Board of Trade from 1905 to 1909. His appointment as wartime Food Controller in December 1916 was criticized by left-wing intellectuals. Kearley, a personal friend of Lloyd George, was created first Viscount of Devonport in 1917. He was Shaw's principal model for the capitalist Boss Mangan in *Heartbreak House*.

KENDAL, Mrs (née Robertson; later Dame Madge) (1848–1935), comedienne, and one of the premier actresses of the 1870s and 1880s, who was married to William Hunter Kendal, actor and co-manager (with John Hare) of St James's Theatre. In 1884–5 Shaw thought only Janet Achurch and Mrs Kendal to be capable of playing *Candida*. On 16 March 1885, Shaw witnessed Mrs Kendal act in a lamentable *As You Like It* at St James's Theatre (hampered throughout by a cold, she fainted in Act 3), concluding that, with a few tips from himself, she would make a good Rosalind. In 1904 Shaw told Ada Rehan that Mrs Kendal was, at her peak, 'incomparably the cleverest, most highly skilled, most thoroughly trained, most successful actress on the London stage'.

KEYNES, John Maynard, 1st Baron (1883–1946), British economist, and Fellow and Bursar of King's College, Cambridge. Keynes was a member of the Bloomsbury Group and a friend of the Shaws in the 1930s and 1940s. Keynes was among the guests at a lunch party hosted by the Shaws on 2 June 1932. Author and educator Rom Landau, who was also present on this occasion provided an account of it, with a thoughtful comparison between Shaw and Keynes, in his *Personalia* (1949).

KILSBY, Albert James (b.1876), Shaw's chauffeur from 1909 to 1917, who served the Shaws on numerous motoring tours. Kilsby emigrated to Brisbane, Australia in 1917.

KINGSTON, Gertrude (1866–1937), actress, theatre manager, painter, author and political speaker. Having worked with Beerbohm Tree and Henry Irving, Kingston became manager of the Little Theatre, where *Fanny's First Play* was first performed in 1911. Shaw wrote *Great Catherine* for her in 1913 and she acted leads in a number of his other plays including: *How He Lied to Her Husband, The Inca of Perusalem, Captain Brassbound's Conversion, You Never Can Tell* and *Getting Married.*

KROPOTKIN, Prince Peter Alexeivich (1842–1921), Russian revolutionary, social reformer and early follower of the anarchist Bakunin. After being imprisoned in Russia and France he escaped to England where he became a leader of the London anarchist movement from 1886 to 1914. Shaw met Kropotkin on 27 December 1886 through the Socialist League. Kropotkin returned to Russia after the Revolution, leaving his books to exert a strong influence on English Socialists. Shaw spoke at a London demonstration in celebration of Kropotkin in December 1912. Kropotkin's daughter Alexandra (Sasha Kropotkin Lebedeff) and her husband Boris Lebedeff later translated several of Shaw's plays into Russian.

LADEN, Alice (1901–79), Scottish-trained cook-housekeeper and nurse. Having nursed Charlotte in her final illness in 1943, Laden served as Shaw's housekeeper at Ayot from September 1944. She helped Shaw in his last illness, and was appointed curator of 'Shaw's Corner' upon his death. A collection of Mrs Laden's menus and recipes, *The George Bernard Shaw Vegetarian Cookbook,* was first published in 1972.

LANGNER, Lawrence (1890–1962), Welsh playwright, theatre director and patent attorney. Langner co-founded the Theater Guild of New York (a restructuring of the Washington Square Players) in 1918. The Theater Guild staged the world premières of *Heartbreak House,* the *Back to Methuselah* cycle and *Saint Joan.* Langner first met Shaw in late November 1920 when, shortly after the opening of *Heartbreak House* in New York, he visited England to obtain a contract allowing the Guild to produce all Shaw's plays in America. In August 1938 Langner criticized Shaw for his treatment of Fascist ideas in his play *Geneva.* Through September–October they debated by letter Shaw's apparent anti-Semitism and the value of the idea of the 'superman'. Langner's *GBS and the Lunatic* (1964) reveals, through numerous anecdotes, his admiration and affection for Shaw.

LAWRENCE, Thomas Edward (Lawrence of Arabia) (1888–1935), writer, soldier and aircraftman; trained as an archaeologist. He served in the Middle East in the First World War, where he made his name by organizing the Arab revolt which allowed General Allenby's British forces to overthrow the Turks and capture Damascus in 1918. Lawrence was first introduced to the Shaws by Sydney Cockerell on 25 March 1922, and five months later sent one of the eight privately printed copies of his book, *Seven Pillars of Wisdom,* to Shaw to review. Shaw considered the work a masterpiece and noted that an abridged version would have to be made for general circulation. (A shorter version of the work, *Revolt in the Desert,* was published in

1927.) After being discharged from the Royal Air Force in January 1923, Lawrence enlisted two months later in the Royal Tank Corps as Private T. E. Shaw. Shaw wrote to Prime Minister Baldwin in 1923 and 1925 to try to secure a life pension for Lawrence in recognition of his contribution to Allenby's victory. Shaw recalled Lawrence in the creation of Private Meek in *Too True to be Good*. Lawrence had an almost filial relationship with the Shaws, and an extensive correspondence between him and Charlotte reveals much about the private selves of both. A keen motorcyclist, Lawrence died in an accident which occurred when he was riding the Brough SS-100 given him as a present by Charlotte and some other friends (Robin Buxton, C. J. Holland-Martin, Lionel Curtis and Francis Rodd). The Shaw–Lawrence relationship is the subject of Stanley Weintraub's *Private Shaw and Public Shaw* (1963).

LAWSON, Cecil (1851–82), artist. Shaw met the Lawson family on 5 January 1879, and was regularly invited to their Sunday 'at-homes' at Cheyne Walk. Shaw has described his feelings of acute shyness at the prospect of these visits. In the 1921 Preface to *Immaturity*, Shaw praised Cecil Lawson as a truly great artist whose untimely death left the world disappointed of more of his masterpieces. He used Lawson as a model for the artist Cyril Scott in *Immaturity*, but stressed that he really knew nothing about Lawson apart from what he saw of him in the few visits to Cheyne Walk: 'He set my imagination to work: that was all.' The seed for the idea of Mrs Higgins's at-home in her flat on the Chelsea Embankment in Act 3 of *Pygmalion*, where Eliza Doolittle makes her sensational social debut, was probably sown during Shaw's visits to the Lawson house.

LECKY, James (1856–90), musician, writer and civil servant. He was the author of the entry on the 'Temperament' method of tuning keyed instruments in the first edition of *Grove's Dictionary of Music and Musicians*. In March 1879 Shaw met Lecky at Chichester Bell's lodgings. Shaw became interested in phonetics through Lecky, who also introduced him to the philologists Alexander John Ellis and Henry Sweet. Lecky joined the Zetetical Society in 1879, and nominated Shaw for election to the Society soon afterwards.

LEE, George John (later Vandeleur) (1831–86), musical conductor and teacher of singing. He founded an amateur musical society in Dublin in which Shaw's mother, Lucinda Elizabeth Shaw, played a major role. Lee developed a theory of voice production and singing (called 'the Method' by Shaw) which was elaborately expounded, with anatomical illustrations, in *The Voice*, a book first published in 1870. The first and second editions of this book were ghost written. Shaw embarked on, but did not complete, the writing of a third edition. Lee lived in the Shaw household from 1866 to

1873, where rehearsals exposed Shaw to operatic and concert music at a young age. Lee's presence in the Shaw household, as one of a curious *menage à trois,* was possibly a contributing factor in the eventual separation of Shaw's parents. Mrs Shaw's move to London followed shortly after Lee's transfer of his entrepreneurial activities to that city in 1872. Shaw was much influenced by Lee and named him as one of his three 'fathers', the other two being his natural father, George Carr Shaw, and his uncle Walter John Gurly. (Shaw says his idea for a man with three fathers in *Misalliance* came from his own experience.) The speculation that Shaw was the illegitimate child of Lee is based on very slight circumstantial 'evidence' and is unlikely, for several reasons, to have any foundation in truth. After his move to London in 1876, Shaw acted as ghostwriter for Lee's music column in *The Hornet* and also as pianist and helper in concert preparation.

LOCKETT, Alice Mary (1858–1942), nurse by profession, with whom Shaw had his first serious love affair. An attractive and spirited young woman, Lockett met Shaw while he was convalescing from scarlet fever at his Uncle Walter Gurly's house at Leyton in 1882. She later took singing lessons from Lucinda Elizabeth Shaw. The relationship between Shaw and Alice was fraught with numerous would-be terminal quarrels, but continued for many years. Shaw complained that Alice had a dual personality: 'Alice' (romantic and unconventional) and 'Miss Lockett' (proper and respectable). This phenomenon was treated fictionally in Trefusis's description of Gertrude Lindsay in *An Unsocial Socialist*. Shaw's love affair with Alice probably ended in December 1885, but they kept in touch for many years, and Alice borrowed money from Shaw during the First World War when her husband Dr William Sharpe (whom she married in 1890) was in military service. Alice assisted her husband when he operated on Shaw's foot in 1898.

LOEWENSTEIN, Dr Fritz Erwin (1901–69), German refugee who arrived in London in 1933 and established the Shaw Society in 1941. Loewenstein first contacted Shaw in 1936 to request assistance in the compilation of a Shaw bibliography. After Charlotte's death he ensconced himself at Ayot, with the eventual result of driving Blanche Patch and John Wardrop away. While cataloguing Shaw's papers and general effects, he purloined many valuable materials for his own collection. Loewenstein aspired to the role of curator of the 'Shaw Shrine' at Ayot, but the Public Trustee, on the day of Shaw's death, removed him unceremoniously from 'Shaw's Corner'.

LORAINE, Robert (1876–1935), English-born actor, soldier and airman, who established his career on the American stage. Loraine first met Shaw in the Summer of 1905 at a matinée performance of *Man and Superman* at the Court Theatre, and followed this meeting up with a visit to Ayot

St Lawrence. Loraine produced *Man and Superman*, in which he played Tanner, in New York in the autumn of 1905, and toured America with the production. He subsequently played several other Shavian roles, including a superb performance of St John Hotchkiss in *Getting Married* (1908). In July 1906 Loraine accompanied Shaw on a ballooning trip, and left an account of this event in his diary. A year later they had a more serious adventure when a swim they took together in rough Welsh seas nearly became a double drowning. During his visit to the front in 1917 Shaw made a special effort to see Loraine who was stationed at Treizennes. Loraine's war experiences inspired certain aspects of Shaw's characterization of the ex-flying ace turned clergyman/burglar, Aubrey Bagot, in *Too True to be Good*.

MacCARTHY, Desmond (1877–1952), author, critic and theatre historian. He held the post of dramatic and literary editor of the *New Statesman* from 1920 to 1927. MacCarthy first met Shaw in 1906 when Harley Granville Barker invited him to lunch at Adelphi Terrace. In 1928 he and Shaw drafted a letter of protest, signed by many well-known authors and widely published in newspapers, about the banning of Radclyffe Hall's *The Well of Loneliness*. MacCarthy was one of the most acute early reviewers of Shaw's plays but wrote what Shaw considered 'the very worst' review of *Back to Methuselah* (*New Statesman*, 9 July 1921). His Shavian reviews, essays and recollections are collected in his book, *Shaw* (1951).

McCARTHY, Lillah (1876–1960), actress. She made her theatrical debut in 1895, and played major roles in many Shaw plays in the decade following 1905. McCarthy's initial Shavian leading role was that of Ann Whitefield in the Stage Society private performances and in the first public performance of *Man and Superman* at the Court Theatre in May 1905. Thereafter Shaw created a number of his female characters with McCarthy in mind. In April 1906 she married Harley Granville Barker who left her a decade later for the wealthy American, Helen Huntington. Granville Barker sent McCarthy his letter requesting divorce through Shaw on 3 January 1916, and in February Shaw tried, unsuccessfully, to host a meeting between Lillah and Harley. The marriage breakup, during which Shaw offered particular counsel and encouragement to Lillah, was a personal and professional loss and her career never recovered its former momentum. The divorce was finalized in 1918 and four years later McCarthy married Professor (later Sir) Frederick Keeble. Her autobiography, *Myself and My Friends* (1933), contains many reminiscences of her association with Shaw, who contributed a preface to the work.

MACDONA, Charles (1860–1946), actor, theatre manager and director of repertory theatre. In 1921 he formed a company called the Macdona Players, which toured widely with numerous Shavian plays. He also produced *On the Rocks* during the 1933–4 season at the Prince's Theatre, where he changed the composition of theatre audiences – and hence the type of plays demanded – by radically cutting the price of seats in the stalls. Shaw heartily approved of Macdona's experiment, believing it would open the theatres to ordinary working people who wanted an evening of absorbing drama rather than an occasion to make a spectacle of themselves.

MacDONALD, James Ramsay (1866–1937), British Labour Party politician and Prime Minister. He was a dissenting member of the Fabian Society who objected to the Webbs' emphasis on reform from the top down and their founding of the London School of Economics. He was a member of the Fabian executive from 1894 to 1900. MacDonald became leader of the Labour Party and Britain's first Labour Prime Minister in 1924. Shaw spoke on behalf of MacDonald in the campaigns of 1895 and 1918. On 26 July 1926, MacDonald chaired a complimentary dinner in honour of Shaw's seventieth birthday. His suggestions to Shaw that he be honoured with a knighthood and the Order of Merit were both declined. In 1935 Shaw publicly supported MacDonald's view that military spending should be increased so as to keep Britain's defence up to date.

McLACHLAN, Margaret (Sister, later Dame Laurentia) (1866–1953), Benedictine Prioress of Stanbrook Abbey near Malvern. Dame Laurentia first met the Shaws in 1924 after Sydney Cockerell gave her a copy of *Saint Joan*. Over the next seven years Shaw visited Dame Laurentia and corresponded with her regularly, often signing himself, 'Brother Bernard'. In 1931 Shaw sent Dame Laurentia his impressions of the Holy Land and brought her back, as requested, a relic, a gift of stones from Bethlehem. The publication in 1932 of *Adventures of the Black Girl in Her Search for God* so offended Dame Laurentia that relations with Shaw were temporarily severed. The friendship resumed in September 1934 when Shaw mistook an announcement of her jubilee for a funeral notice, wrote a letter of condolence to the sisters at the Abbey, and to his surprise received a reply from Dame Laurentia herself.

McNULTY, Matthew Edward (1856–1943), Shaw's schoolboy friend who became a journalist and whose plays, *The Lord Mayor* and *The Courting of Mary Doyle*, were successfully produced at the Abbey Theatre. Shaw met McNulty at Dublin English Scientific and Commercial Day School in 1869 and their close schoolboy attachment of 1869–70 developed into a lifelong friendship. Their separation resulting from McNulty's new job at the Newry Branch of the Bank of Ireland (1871–4) led to the exchange of lengthy letters between the two young men. Most of this sizeable corpus of fantastic juvenilia has been destroyed at Shaw's request. Over the years, they wrote criticisms of each other's works in progress. Having been rejected by

Lucy Shaw, McNulty married Alice Brennan in March 1883. He wrote an account of his recollections (which Shaw disputed at numerous points) of the early days of his friendship with Shaw in 'George Bernard Shaw as a Boy' (*The Candid Friend,* 6 July 1901), and also composed 'Memoirs of G. B. S', edited by Dan H. Laurence in *Shaw: The Annual of Bernard Shaw Sudies*, vol. 12, 1992.

MANSFIELD, Richard (1854–1907), English actor. After playing minor roles on the English stage from 1877 to 1882, he emigrated in 1882 to New York, where he became a leading actor-manager and the first to produce Shaw's plays in America, beginning with *Arms and the Man* in September 1894, in which he played Bluntschli. Mansfield signed with Shaw to produce the world première of *Candida* in 1895 with Janet Achurch in the lead, but after reading the play (which he considered three long acts of talk) and quarrelling over Achurch's contract, he did not go ahead with the project. Shaw said to Mansfield, after he had turned down the lead role in *The Man of Destiny*: 'Napoleon is nobody else but Richard Mansfield himself.'

MARX, Eleanor. See AVELING, Eleanor.

MASSINGHAM, Henry William (1860–1924), Socialist and editor of *The Star* (1890–1), *Daily Chronicle* (1895–9), *Daily News* (1901–6) and *The Nation* (1907–23). As assistant editor of *The Star,* Massingham hired Shaw in January 1888 for what would turn out to be a very brief stint as political writer. He served on the Fabian Executive from 1891 to 1893, but resigned after Shaw and Webb attacked the Liberals in the Fabian Tract, 'To Your Tents, O Israel'. In 1897 Massingham founded the New Century Theatre Society with Elizabeth Robins, Alfred Sutro and William Archer. He remained, till his death, one of Shaw's most valued journalistic allies. Following Massingham's death, his son edited a collection of Massingham's writings (1925), to which Shaw contributed an introductory essay for the section on dramatic criticism.

MAUDE, Sir Cyril (1862–1951), actor and later co-manager with Frederick Harrison of the Haymarket Theatre from 1896 to 1905. Shaw provided a witty and anonymous commentary on the disastrous rehearsals (which resulted in cancellation of the production) of *You Never Can Tell* for Maude's book *The Haymarket Theatre* (1903). Shaw's comic one-act melodrama, *Passion, Poison and Petrification* was written for charity at Maude's request in 1905.

MAVOR, James (1854–1925), Professor of Political Economy at St Mungo's College, Glasgow, and editor of the *Scottish Art Review* for which Shaw wrote 'The Opera Season' in September 1889. Shaw used Mavor's name for James Mavor Morell in *Candida*.

MORLEY, John (1838–1923), biographer, historian, editor, literary critic and politician. He was MP for Newcastle upon Tyne (1883–95) and Chief Secretary for Ireland (1886, 1892–5). Morley edited the *Fortnightly Review* from 1867 to 1882, and the *Pall Mall Gazette* from 1880 to 1883. After initially encouraging Shaw in 1880 to submit examples of reviews and criticism for publication he concluded that Shaw did not have the knack for journalism and later, on behalf of Macmillan, also rejected *Immaturity*. Although the two parted friends, Morley became one of Shaw's political targets as his series of leading articles in the *North London Press* (1889) illustrates.

MORRIS, May (1862–1938), daughter of William Morris, served on the Fabian Executive from 1896 to 1898. She met and became strongly attracted to Shaw in the mid-1880s. They had a lively friendship and correspondence, but Shaw would not commit himself further. To his surprise, she married Henry Sparling in 1890, but remained fascinated by Shaw. Shaw's lengthy stay in the Sparling house in the winter of 1892–3 probably had a destabilizing influence on the marriage. May's divorce in 1898 may have been an attempt to signal to Shaw her availability but, ironically, it was finalized on the day he married Charlotte. In the preface Shaw supplied for volume two of May's book *William Morris: Artist, Writer, Socialist* (1936), he describes his sense of there having occurred a 'Mystic betrothal' between May and himself in the 1880s.

MORRIS, William (1834–96), designer and craftsman, poet and prose fiction writer, Socialist and proprietor of the Kelmscott Press. He was a leader with H. M. Hyndman in the Social Democratic Federation until early 1885, when he left to found the Socialist League with Belfort Bax, and after that the Hammersmith Socialist Society. Morris's introduction to Shaw was through reading *An Unsocial Socialist* as serialized in *To-Day* in the second half of 1884. By early the following year Shaw was attending Socialist meetings at Morris's Kelmscott House and was becoming a close friend of the family, especially of May Morris. The adjective 'Shavian' was adopted by Shaw after Morris found the marginal comment, '*Sic Shavius, sed inepte*' in a medieval manuscript. In the days following Morris's death Shaw was besieged with requests for articles on the man who had become one of his most respected mentors: he wrote an obituary for the *Daily Chronicle* (6 October 1896) and 'Morris as Actor and Dramatist' for the *Saturday Review* (10 October). In 1934 Shaw attended a celebration of the centenary of Morris's birth and two years later wrote up his recollections under the title, 'William Morris as I Knew Him'. Shaw considered Morris 'a much greater man than his contemporaries'.

MURRAY, (George) Gilbert (Aimée) (1866–1957), classics scholar, playwright and translator. Murray held the posts of Regius Professor of Greek at Glasgow (1889–99) and at Oxford (1908–36). Murray's highly regarded translations of various plays by Euripides had successful productions under the Vedrenne–Barker management at the Court Theatre. On 16 July 1895, at William Archer's suggestion, Shaw met with Archer and Murray to discuss Murray's play, *Carlyon Sahib* (1893). From that time, Shaw began a life-long correspondence with Murray in which he sought Murray's response to his plays and prefaces, commented on his works and posed him questions about literature, history and Greek language. In 1915 Shaw was critical of Murray's book, *The Foreign Policy of Sir Edward Grey 1906–15* (*New Statesman*, 17 July). Murray's generally fond memories of Shaw are recorded in 'The Early GBS' (*New Statesman and Nation*, 16 August 1947) and 'A Few Memories' (*Drama*, Spring 1951). Murray was a model for Cusins in *Major Barbara*, while Murray's mother-in-law, the Countess of Carlisle, was a model for Lady Britomart.

MUSTERS, Georgina Jane ('Judy') (née Gillmore) (1885–1974), granddaughter of Thomas Gurly, was Shaw's first full-time secretary from 1907 to 1912. She married Harold Chaworth Musters on 20 August 1912. From 1912 to 1925 she resided in Egypt where her husband worked for the Eastern Telegraph Company. Later she resided in Folkestone and Farnham. During the Second World War she occasionally acted as relief secretary for Blanche Patch. She communicated recollections of Shaw to Archibald Henderson and Dan H. Laurence. Also see 'Ancestry and Family', p. 13.

MYERS, Frederick William Henry (1843–1901), Fellow of Trinity College, Cambridge, and a founder of the Psychical Research Society in 1882. Shaw attended Myers's lecture on 'Human Personality' at the Psychical Research Society on 29 October 1885, and wrote a response (*Pall Mall Gazette*, 3 November 1885). Shaw's rather belated review of *Phantasms of the Living* (1883), by Myers, Edward Gurney and Frank Podmore, appeared in the *Pall Mall Gazette* on 24 November 1886.

NEWCOMBE, Bertha (1870–1939), Fabian and artist, known for her work in *English Illustrated Magazine*. In 1892 Newcombe painted a striking portrait of Shaw (of which the original is now lost), with which he was very impressed, titled 'The Platform Spellbinder'. She was in love with Shaw for many years from the 1890s, but the feeling was never reciprocated, despite the attempts of various of Shaw's friends, including Beatrice Webb, to promote a match between the two. Newcombe would not fully acknowledge Shaw's marriage to Charlotte and resisted the Shaws' attempts to include her as a friend in the new arrangement.

O'BOLGER, Thomas Demetrius (1871–1923), Irish-American professor of literature who hoped to turn his 1913 doctoral dissertation on Shaw into a published biography. Shaw provided his would-be biographer with copious quantities of written information about his childhood, but was annoyed to find O'Bolger fashioning what he considered a defamatory and inaccurate version of the relations between Vandeleur Lee and Shaw's parents. Shaw suppressed the biography by threatening to sue for breach of copyright which caused O'Bolger's publisher to cancel the contract. O'Bolger revised the biography (for the fifth time) and submitted it to Shaw for approval. Shaw was tardy in reading it and in the meantime O'Bolger died of pernicious anaemia. The unpublished typescript of O'Bolger's work is held in the Houghton Library, Harvard University.

O'CASEY, Sean (1880–1964), Irish playwright. In the mid-1920s a number of O'Casey's plays were performed at the Abbey Theatre, where he was proclaimed a 'genius' by its manager, W. B. Yeats. However, when Yeats rejected O'Casey's *The Silver Tassie* in 1928, O'Casey felt let down personally and disappointed with the Abbey Theatre. Since he was also unhappy with the new Irish State, he moved to London. It was around this time that Sean and his wife, Eileen, whom he had met earlier in London and married in 1927, became friends with the Shaws. They often lunched with the Shaws at Adelphi Terrace and Whitehall Court, and Shaw read all of O'Casey's plays and attended London productions of a number of them. Shaw was struck by the power of O'Casey's work, and wrote to Lady Nancy Astor in 1934 that his plays 'are wonderfully impressive and *reproachful* without being irritating like mine'. In 1932 O'Casey declined the invitation, drafted by Shaw, to join the Irish Academy of Letters founded by Yeats and Shaw. Shaw was delighted when Eileen visited him at Ayot St Lawrence in January 1950, and he had framed the photograph she presented to him of the O'Casey family. Eileen was one of the last people to see Shaw alive and she provides a moving account of her visit to Shaw on his deathbed in her book, *Sean* (1971).

O'CONNOR, Thomas Power ('Tay Pay') (1848–1929), Irish journalist, Parnellite M.P. for Galway, then Liberal MP (1885–1929). He founded and edited *The Star* from 17 January 1888. Although he quite liked O'Connor, Shaw resigned after a short spell as political columnist for *The Star* (January–February 1888) because his Socialist opinions and his attacks on government leaders led to disagreements with the editor and suppression of his articles. He did, however, submit occasional political articles until August 1888 when he began to fill in for the holidaying E. Belfort Bax, as musical critic. With the resignation of Bax in February 1889, Shaw returned to *The Star*, this time as music critic, producing his 'Musical Mems' under the name of 'Corno di Bassetto'. In 1898 Shaw contributed an autobiographical sketch, 'In the Days of My Youth', to O'Connor's magazine, *M.A.P.* [Mainly About People].

OLIVIER, Sydney Haldane (later Baron Olivier) (1859–1943), high-ranking public servant and prominent early member of the Fabian Society. He entered the colonial office after graduation from Oxford, topping the entry competition (in which Sidney Webb came second). He subsequently held many important posts, including Governor of Jamaica (1907–13) and Secretary of State for India (1924). (The Shaws visited the Oliviers for a week in Jamaica in January 1911.) Olivier joined the Fabian Society in 1885, and served on the Executive from 1887 to 1899 and 1921 to 1922, acting as Secretary from 1886 to 1890. Shaw met Olivier in 1883 through the Land Reform Union when Olivier and Sidney Webb were clerks at the Colonial Office. Shaw wrote of him: 'Olivier was an extraordinarily attractive figure; and in my experience unique; for I have never known anyone like him mentally or physically: he was distinguished enough to be unclassable. He was handsome and strongly sexed, looking like a Spanish grandee in any sort of clothes, however unconventional.' Olivier furnished Archibald Henderson with a warmly appreciative recollection of Shaw in the early Fabian days for use in *Bernard Shaw, Playboy and Prophet* (1932).

ORAGE, Alfred Richard (1873–1934), school teacher, journalist and psychologist; exponent of Nietzsche and Guild Socialism, with an interest in Theosophy and the Greek-Armenian spiritual teacher, Georgii Ivanovich Gurdjieff. With the aid of a £500 donation from Shaw, he bought *The New Age* in 1907, which he managed and edited until 1922. Shaw also supported Orage's enterprise by donating over twenty articles free of charge until 1921. Shaw registered amazement at the way Orage managed to keep the chronically insolvent paper running for 15 years.

PASCAL, Gabriel (Gabor Lehöl) (1894–1954), Hungarian-born film director and producer; the major interpreter of Shaw's plays on the screen during the playwright's lifetime. Pascal says he first met Shaw during a nude swim at dawn on the French Riviera in 1925. Ten years later he arrived penniless in London where he requested and was granted the film rights to *Pygmalion*. Pascal produced film versions of *Pygmalion* (1938), *Major Barbara* (1941) and *Caesar and Cleopatra* (1945), each with the addition of new scenes devised in collaboration with Shaw. On 18 October 1947, Pascal visited Ayot to introduce to Shaw the woman he had recently married, Valerie Hidveghy. Throughout the 1940s the friendship between Shaw and Pascal deepened, their collaborative Shavian projects continued, and some months before his death (which he sensed was near) Shaw wrote a touching, fatherly letter encouraging Pascal to seek out 'a young Shaw' for the second half of his career. But the film-maker died a few years after the playwright who had made his name.

PATCH, Blanche (1879–1966), Shaw's secretary from 1920 till his death in 1950. Patch had been introduced to Shaw by Beatrice Webb who had met her at the small town of Presteign in Radnorshire, Wales. For thirty years, Patch, an extraordinarily efficient secretary, practically ran the business side of Shaw's life. Throughout her career, Blanche made a point of declaring how uninterested she was in Shaw and all his works, although on Charlotte's death, the idea of marrying her employer came increasingly to possess her mind, but to no avail. Patch's anti-Semitism found an apt target in the abrasive Dr Loewenstein who was insinuating himself into life at Ayot in Shaw's final years. Patch's book, *Thirty Years with GBS* (1951), was ghostwritten for Blanche by Robert Williamson to whom she supplied memoirs and letters.

PATTERSON, Jane (Jenny) (*c*.1840–1924), an Irish widow who took singing lessons from Lucinda Elizabeth Shaw in London in the early 1880s, and became Shaw's lover in 1885. The first of her many surviving letters to Shaw was written on 28 December 1882. Following a period of flirtation in 1884, a close intimacy between the two developed in the first half of 1885. After a previous declaration of passion from her, and several evenings of gallantry, Shaw finally surrendered his virginity to Jenny Patterson on his 29th birthday, 26 July 1885. A turbulent love affair, from which Shaw made several attempts to extricate himself, continued until 1893. Shaw infuriated Patterson by his flirtations with other women, and the scene in which she burst in on Shaw and Florence Farr spending an intimate evening together became the basis for Act I of *The Philanderer*. Patterson's stormy character is reflected in that of Julia Craven in *The Philanderer* and that of Blanche Sartorius in *Widowers' Houses*. After the affair ended, it was not till 1898 that Shaw saw Patterson again, a surprise visit of hers to his mother which caused him to escape to his study. In Shaw's revised will of 1913 he bequeathed an annual stipend of £104 to Patterson whom he always 'held in affectionate remembrance and honor'.

PAYNE, Ben Iden (1881–1976), actor and manager; associated with Annie Horniman as manager of the Midland and Gaiety Theatres in Manchester, and also managed the Lyric Theatre in the early years of the twentieth century. In 1907 Shaw assisted Payne, who was dealing with him for the rights to *Mrs Warren's Profession*, in his ultimately vain attempt to win a licence for the play. The two had further frustrating dealings with play-examiner G. A. Redford over the licensing of *The Shewing-up of Blanco Posnet* in 1909. In his late years Payne became chairman of the Drama Department of the University of Texas at Austin.

PAYNE-TOWNSHEND, Charlotte Frances. See SHAW, Charlotte Frances.

PAYNE-TOWNSHEND, Mary Stewart. See CHOLMONDELEY, Mary Stewart.

PEARSON, Hesketh (1887–1964), actor and biographer. Pearson played the minor role of Metellus in the first English production of *Androcles and the Lion* in September 1913, and met Shaw during rehearsals for the production. In 1938 Pearson contemplated the idea of a J. M. Barrie biography, but suddenly turned to Shaw. Four years later he produced the well-received *Bernard Shaw: His Life and Personality* (1942), extensive passages of which were supplied by Shaw. In *GBS: A Postscript* (1951), Pearson extended the biography up to Shaw's death, including an obituary written by Shaw himself, and describing how he elicited information from Shaw during their many conversations.

PEASE, Edward Reynolds (1857–1955), a founder and Secretary (1890–1913) of the Fabian Society, which held its meetings in his rooms at 17 Osnaburgh Street. His decision to give up his career in stockbroking and shift to cabinet-making in the mid-1880s was inspired by William Morris and a yearning for a simpler life. In 1916 he wrote *The History of the Fabian Society,* which contains an appendix titled 'Memoranda by Bernard Shaw'. As one of the founding members of the Fabian Society, Pease became closely associated with Shaw.

PERCY, Esmé (1887–1957), actor and producer. Percy first met Shaw in the winter of 1905–6 and from 1911 he played Tanner in several productions of *Man and Superman*. He was the first to produce the full text of *Man and Superman,* playing Tanner and his dream-persona, Don Juan Tenorio, in the Lyceum Theatre production (Edinburgh, 1915). In 1924 Percy was appointed general producer to Charles Macdona's Bernard Shaw Repertory Company in which he played almost every major male Shaw role. Percy wrote 'Bernard Shaw: A Personal Memory' (*Listener,* 26 May 1955) and 'Memories of Bernard Shaw' (*British Peace Committee News Letter,* March–April, 1956).

PERTOLDI, Erminia (1855–1907), prima ballerina at the Alhambra Theatre in Leicester Square; and the model for Mlle Bernadina Sangallo (later changed to Signorina Pertoldi) in Shaw's first novel, *Immaturity*. Pertoldi is possibly identifiable with the enchanting person referred to by Shaw as 'Terpsichore' in early diary fragments (1876–9). Shaw eventually met her in 1888 at Stewart Headlam's house.

PIGOTT, E. F. Smyth (Earl Lathom) (1824–95), the Lord Chamberlain's Examiner of Plays (Censor). Pigott's refusal to license Shelley's *The Cenci* in

1892 sparked Shaw's long battle against government censorship. Shaw celebrated Pigott's death with the article 'The Late Censor' (*Saturday Review*, 2 March 1895).

PINERO, Sir Arthur Wing (1855–1934), actor and playwright. Pinero was one of the leading playwrights of the day in England in the 1890s when Shaw's own career as a dramatist was beginning and he was writing his brilliant *Saturday Review* theatre criticisms. Pinero's best-known play, *The Second Mrs Tanqueray*, in which Mrs Patrick Campbell first played the leading role, was regarded as bringing new dimensions of psychological subtlety to English drama. But to Shaw his work in many ways epitomized the conservative theatrical values which he himself was striving to overthrow. While admiring some of Pinero's works, Shaw wrote scathing reviews of several of the plays, criticizing them for both technical clumsiness and the exploitation of subjects such as the 'New Woman' and the 'Woman with a Past' in ways which endorsed conventional and old-fashioned attitudes. Shaw regarded his early play, *Mrs Warren's Profession,* as a critique of *The Second Mrs Tanqueray* and its treatment of the fallen woman. Despite their professional and ideological differences, Shaw and Pinero conducted a lively and friendly correspondence, and Shaw played an influential part in the awarding to Pinero in 1909 of his knighthood.

PLUNKETT, Sir Horace (1854–1932), founder of the Agricultural Co-operative movement in Ireland. He established an Irish Centre Party, and the Dominion League in 1919, with its journal the *Irish Statesman* to which Shaw contributed. Plunkett first met Shaw in Ireland in September 1908 and thereafter Shaw stayed or lunched with him during Irish trips. The Shaws remained close friends of Plunkett until his death. Shaw described Plunkett as 'the ablest, honestest and whitest man in practical politics at present'. Having failed to gain a place himself on the Irish Convention in 1917, Shaw strove to have his say on Home Rule through conference with Plunkett who had been appointed Convention Chairman.

PODMORE, Frank (1855–1910), author and psychical researcher. He was a founding member of the Fabian Society, and was elected to the Executive Committee in 1886. Podmore was associated with a number of societies including the British National Association of Spiritualists, the Psychical Research Society, the Progressive Association and the Fellowship of the New Life. When Podmore supported the proposals of January 1884 for a separate Fabian society, he suggested the name 'Fabian' and nominated its 'patron saint' as Fabius Cunctator. Following a meeting of the Psychical Research Society on 29 October 1885, Podmore dared Shaw and three others to spend the night at a supposedly haunted house in Wadsworth. Podmore was found drowned on 19 August 1910 in the New Pool, Malvern.

POTTER, Beatrice. See WEBB, Beatrice.

REDFORD, George Alexander (1846–1916), the Lord Chamberlain's Examiner of Plays (Censor). In 'The Censorship of the Stage in England' (1899), Shaw explained the absurdly conservative rules which guided Redford's censorship actions along limited paths to the inevitable exclusion of all innovative art. Redford had rejected the original version of *Mrs Warren's Profession* in March 1898, and was again unmoved in 1907. He followed this up with a refusal to grant a licence to Shaw's *The Shewing-up of Blanco Posnet* (1909). Redford eventually became a film censor.

REEVES, Amber, later Mrs G. R. Blanco White (1887–1981), Treasurer of the Cambridge University Fabian Society; one of the 'younger generation' of Fabians who, led by H. G. Wells, were beginning to influence the direction of the Society in the first decade of the twentieth century. Reeves was involved in an adulterous love affair with Wells which resulted in the birth of a daughter in December 1909. She attempted to contain the scandal by a hasty marriage to George R. Blanco White in July 1909. In 1909 Reeves wrote to Shaw explaining the history of the affair, indeed bragging of it, and claiming that it had taken her a year to wear down Wells's resistance. When Shaw rebuked Wells for his indecorum, Wells responded with 'a torrent of abuse' centred on what he saw as Shaw's conservative values.

REHAN, Ada (1857–1916), famous Irish actress of the New York and London theatrical scenes, and, for twenty years, the leading lady of actor-manager Augustin Daly. Shaw believed Rehan to be one of the greatest actresses in the world and the only Shakespearean rival of Ellen Terry. In 1931 he remembered being enthralled by her beautifully musical pronunciation of Shakespearean lines. In July 1904 Shaw read *Captain Brassbound's Conversion* to Rehan in the hope that she might play Lady Cicely. Despite Shaw's tenacity negotiations dragged on unproductively for over a year and were complicated towards the end by Rehan's ailing health. Eventually, the role was played by Ellen Terry in 1906.

RHONDDA, Margaret Haig Thomas, Viscountess of Llanwern (1883–1958), feminist; founder (1920) and editor (1926–58) of the political review, *Time and Tide*. In January 1927 Shaw chaired a debate between Lady Rhondda and G. K. Chesterton on 'The Menace of the Leisured Woman'. Lady Rhondda wrote numerous articles around Shavian topics for *Time and Tide*, her favourable review of *Too True to be Good* in 1932 receiving high praise from the playwright. Shaw continued contributing material, free of charge, to *Time and Tide* until 1940 at which time their conflicting views on the war forced him to all but cease contribution.

RICHARDS, Grant (1872–1948), author and publisher. Richards published numerous Shavian works and, as time went on, was berated by Shaw for inept business sense, withholding of royalties and failure to advertise. Among other works, Richards published Shaw's first play collection, the two-volume *Plays Pleasant and Unpleasant* (April 1898); *The Perfect Wagnerite* (December 1898); *Three Plays for Puritans* (1901); and a volume including *The Admirable Bashville,* a reissue of *Cashel Byron's Profession* and an essay on modern prizefighting (1901). In the early years of the twentieth century Shaw was only one among a number of angry and frustrated authors struggling to deal with Richards's mismanagement. In a letter of 15 January 1905, he explained to Richards in the plainest terms how he, the author, had repeatedly striven to protect his publisher's business by arranging author–publisher contracts in spite of Richards's cavalier disregard for sensible business agreements. The impending disaster was not to be averted, and by the month's end Richards was declared bankrupt. Richards's recollections of his association with Shaw were included in his memoirs, *Author Hunting by an Old Literary Sportsman* (1934).

RICHARDSON, Sir Ralph David (1902–83), actor. His professional debut was in Lowestoft in 1921, but his reputation was made after his arrival at the Old Vic in 1930. Richardson played Bluntschli in the Old Vic production of *Arms and the Man* in 1930–1. He recalls Shaw's wonderful courtesy in instructing him and other actors at the rehearsals, describing him as 'perhaps the most polite man I've ever met in my life'. In 1932, Richardson's performance of the Sergeant in *Too True to be Good* drew a written note of praise from Shaw. After serving in the Fleet Air Arm until 1944, Richardson returned to the Old Vic to perform Bluntschli again (with Laurence Olivier as Sergius), and later played William the Waiter in *You Never Can Tell* at the Haymarket Theatre in 1966.

ROBINS, Elizabeth (1862–1952), American-born actress, novelist (under the pseudonym C. E. Raimond) and playwright. She was a promoter of Ibsen and experimental drama, and co-founder of the New Century Theatre in 1897 with William Archer, H. W. Massingham and Alfred Sutro. Shaw met her on 21 January 1891 at William Archer's house. Robins mistrusted Shaw and disliked the flattering games he played, which he increased in proportion to her outraged disdain. In February 1893, Shaw's abortive attempt to interview Robins about a production of Ibsen's *The Master Builder* led, through his provocation, to her exasperated threat to shoot him if he compromised her reputation in print. Shaw had at one time hoped that Robins would play the part of Gloria in *You Never Can Tell,* saying that she would 'develop the proud, opinionated, unpopular side of Gloria... in fact, she would be Gloria'. But she never appeared in a Shaw play.

RODIN, Auguste (1840–1917), French sculptor. At Charlotte's instigation, Shaw sat for a bust by Rodin at his studio at Meudon from 16 April to 8 May 1906. Lively accounts of Rodin's 'raging activity... gigantic movements' and not always intelligible exclamations during the execution of the work, have been left by Shaw's German translator, Siegfried Trebitsch, and Rainer Maria Rilke who was Rodin's secretary at the time. Rodin expatiated on Shaw's Christ-like head, declaring it to be '*une vraie tête de Christ*'. The bust was completed in marble, bronze and terracotta.

RUSSELL, Bertrand Arthur William, 3rd Earl (1872–1970), mathematician, philosopher, Socialist, and Nobel Prize laureate in 1950. Russell met Shaw through the Webbs in 1885. In September of the same year, while they were all holidaying together in Monmouth, Shaw and Russell had a spectacular bicycle collision of which Shaw gave an amusing account in his letters. In October 1915 Russell chaired Shaw's lecture, 'The Illusions of War', at the Fabian Society. In 1918 Shaw supported Russell with advice when he was charged under the Defence of the Realm Act for his publication – in the No-Conscription Fellowship's journal *The Tribunal* – of an article stating that American soldiers would be used as strikebreakers in England. In his *Portraits from Memory and Other Essays* (1956), Russell supplied an astringent but kindly pen-portrait of Shaw, including the summary assessment of his achievement: 'As an iconoclast he was admirable, but as an eikon rather less so.'

SALT, Catherine ('Kate') (*c*.1859–1919), wife of Henry Salt and sister of J. L. Joynes, was a close friend of Shaw and intermittently acted as his secretary in the years leading up to his marriage. She had a flirtatious, but not sexually consummated, relationship with Shaw. Shaw called himself her 'Sunday husband' in the late 1880s and they played 'endless pianoforte duets' together. Shaw often stayed with the Salts at their cottage at Tilford, and later at Oxted, in Surrey. When they moved back to London (Gloucester Rd) Shaw continued visiting them until he married.

SALT, Henry Stephens (1851–1939), master at Eton till his resignation in 1884, promoter of animal rights, vegetarian and biographer. Salt was a member of the Shelley and Fabian Societies, and founder, and secretary for thirty years, of the Humanitarian League. He first met Shaw in 1880 through J. L. Joynes and in 1898 was a witness at Shaw's wedding. Salt edited the *Humane Review* which published Shaw's 'The Conflict between Science and Common Sense' (1900) and 'Civilisation and the Soldier' (1901). At Salt's death Shaw told his widow (his second wife, Catherine Mandeville) that he still regarded Salt as an intimate friend although he had not called on him for thirty years.

SCHNEIDER, Eva Maria (1874–1957), friend and nurse of Lucy Carr Shaw. Lucy first met Schneider at her *pension* in Gotha, Germany, in 1904, and they returned to England together in 1908 having become close friends. Schneider assisted Lucy in nursing her dying mother and readily accepted Shaw's request for her to nurse Lucy in her illness following her mother's death. The two were constantly together from 1913 until Lucy died seven years later. After Lucy's funeral Schneider stayed on at Champion Cottage for about a month, at Shaw's expense, but then returned to work, not wishing to be dependent. When she wrote to Shaw after Charlotte's death, he replied that if he had known her whereabouts he would probably have asked her to nurse Charlotte. He left her an annuity in remembrance of her devoted service to Lucy.

SCOTT, Lady Kathleen (later Lady Kennet) (1878–1947), sculptor who made a bust and a full-length figure of Shaw in bronze. Ten years after the death of Lady Scott's first husband, the Antarctic explorer Captain Robert Falcon Scott (1868–1912), she married Edward Hilton Young (later Lord Kennet). Lady Scott met Shaw in 1903 and saw him often from 1917 onwards, sometimes at the home of Shaw's neighbour at Ayot, Apsley Cherry-Garrard. Her relationship with Shaw became complicated by his strong editorial involvement in Cherry-Garrard's critical account of Captain Scott's leadership on his disastrous last expedition, on which Cherry-Garrard had served as naturalist.

SHARP, Clifford (1883–1935), journalist, follower of Sidney Webb and Fabian who served on the Executive from 1909 to 1914. Sharp edited *The Crusade* (a monthly newspaper founded by the Webbs) to promote the ideas of the National Committee for the Prevention of Destitution, and was the first editor of *The New Statesman* from 1913 to 1931. Shaw contributed £1000 of the £5000 of the capital needed to found the *New Statesman,* became one of its directors and contributed numerous articles to its early numbers. Sharp found himself frequently at odds with the content of the Shavian contributions, and he and the Webbs were annoyed at Shaw's refusal to sign them, which defeated the object of using his name to attract a wide readership. Shaw resigned his directorship of the periodical in 1916, disagreeing with the direction it was taking, but remained a shareholder.

SHAW, Charlotte Frances (née Payne-Townshend) (1857–1943), a wealthy Irish heiress born and brought up at Rosscarbery House, Co. Cork who became Bernard Shaw's wife. Charlotte moved to London in 1885 where she met Sidney and Beatrice Webb who persuaded her to contribute towards the Fabian Society and the foundation of the London School of Economics. She was introduced to Shaw by the Webbs on 29 January 1896, and the marriage took place on 1 June 1898. Although she avoided publicity and devoted herself to a supporting role to Shaw in the marriage, Charlotte was very much her own person. She had serious intellectual interests and commitments. She found her own way to the cause of Socialism. She was a committed and active early feminist. She read widely, had a good command of French and developed a deep interest in Eastern religions and philosophy. Her ordinary social letters show her to have been gifted with a graceful natural courtesy and warmth, and more reflective and introspective letters she wrote show her intelligence and insight. There are many testimonies to her social poise and unobtrusive skill as a hostess. She joined the Fabian Society in March 1897, serving on the Executive from 1898 to 1915, and played an active role in the Women's Group established in 1907. In 1922, when T. E. Lawrence sent a draft copy of *Seven Pillars of Wisdom* to Shaw for his comments, Charlotte read it through first and responded enthusiastically. From that time on there developed a close friendship and intimate correspondence between Charlotte and Lawrence. Charlotte kept a commonplace book and her translation of Brieux's play, *Maternity,* was published in 1907. The union with Shaw was probably unconsummated, but on the whole it seems to have been a very successful marriage of companionship. Shaw went through phases of serious discontent with the marital ties, especially during his affair with Mrs Patrick Campbell. But an underlying loyalty to Charlotte, who provided a vital dimension of order and stability in his life, always reasserted itself. After suffering a considerable amount of pain in her later years she died of *osteitis deformans* in 1943.

SHAW, Elinor Agnes ('Yuppy') (1854–76), sister of GBS, See 'Ancestry and Family', pp. 14–15.

SHAW, George Carr (1814–85), father of GBS, See 'Ancestry and Family', pp. 13–14.

SHAW, Lucinda Elizabeth ('Bessie') (née Gurly) (1830–1913), mother of GBS. See 'Ancestry and Family', pp. 13–14.

SHAW, Lucinda Frances (Lucy Carr) (1853–1920), sister of GBS. See 'Ancestry and Family', pp. 14–15.

SHORTER, Clement King (1857–1926), journalist and literary critic. Shorter edited the *English Illustrated Magazine* (1890) and the *Illustrated London News* (1891), and was founder-editor of *The Sketch* (1893), *The Tatler* (1903) and *The Sphere* (1900–26). He was acquainted with Shaw from 1888 through *The Star,* in which he wrote a column of literary gossip. In 1889, Shorter became assistant editor on *The Penny Illustrated Paper,* which published Shaw's column 'Asides'. Shaw submitted articles on music to the

Illustrated London News in 1891–2. Shorter published a 'conversation' with Shaw about his new play, *John Bull's Other Island,* in *The Tatler* (16 November 1904).

SPARLING, Henry Halliday (1860–1924), assistant and protégé of William Morris. He was Secretary of the Socialist League founded by Morris and Belfort Bax, served on the Fabian Executive (1892–4), and was assistant editor of *The Commonweal*. Sparling first met Shaw on 16 September 1885 at a Socialist League meeting. In 1890, to Shaw's astonishment, Sparling married May Morris, who was disappointed that her intimacy with Shaw had not resulted in marriage. Morris and Shaw remained close through the early 1890s and she divorced Sparling in 1898. Sparling later remarried.

STEAD, William Thomas (1849–1912), journalist and editor of the *Pall Mall Gazette* from 1883 to 1890. Stead endorsed spiritualist and pacifist causes, and in 1885 encouraged the introduction of the Criminal Law Amendment Act and exposed child prostitution in England. In 1887, Shaw tried to enlist him and his paper in the campaign to eliminate social injustice and to nationalize land and capital. In July 1894 Shaw passed on to Stead four tickets and some advice for his debut as opera critic. Stead died in the *Titanic* disaster of 1912.

STEPNIAK, Sergius (pseud. of Sergei Mikhailovich Kravchinski) (1852–95), a Russian-born London radical and author of *The Career of a Nihilist* (1889). Shaw often saw him at William Morris's house. Stepniak introduced Shaw to an ex-naval officer who had served in the Serbo-Bulgarian War and was able to set Shaw right about local details to be used in *Arms and the Man*. Stepniak's adopted name of Sergius is used for one of the principal characters in that play. When Steppy, as Shaw called him, was killed by a train while crossing the railway tracks at Chiswick, Shaw helped set up a memorial fund, coordinated by Edward Pease, to help support his wife and children.

STRINDBERG, Johann August (1849–1912), Swedish playwright and novelist. The Shaws visited Strindberg in Stockholm in July 1908 and attended a performance of *Miss Julie* which Shaw found very moving. Shaw recalls that Strindberg terminated a conversation conducted in several languages between himself, Strindberg and Charlotte, by taking out his watch and announcing '*Um zwei Uhr werde ich krank sein!* At two o'clock I shall be sick!' Shaw was one of the earliest active promoters of Strindberg's works in England, a project hampered by the unavailability of English translations of the plays. In 1903 Shaw wrote to Janet Achurch observing, 'Strindberg, who is a great man, is still unexploited in this country.' In 1910 Shaw endeavoured to get Strindberg's early play *Lycko-Pers resa* (*Lucky Peter's*

Travels) produced at the Afternoon Theatre (an adjunct to Sir Herbert Beerbohm Tree's His Majesty's Theatre) as a way of whetting English appetites for proposed future performances of Strindberg's greater works. The treatment of female characters in Shaw plays such as *Misalliance* and *Heartbreak House* was probably influenced by Strindberg.

SULLIVAN, Barry (1821–91), an Irish actor specializing in Shakespearean roles. Sullivan's exciting and forceful style in tragic roles, which drew crowds in Dublin, made him one of Shaw's boyhood idols. Shaw reflected that Sullivan moved with grace, dexterity and power, producing striking performances of Macbeth, Hamlet, Richard III and Richelieu. Shaw remembers how as Hamlet, Sullivan 'killed the king by dashing up the whole depth of the stage... running him through again and again, he was a human thunderbolt'. His Macbeth was so vigorous that in one performance he broke the end of Macbeth's sword and the fragment, 'whizzed over the heads of the cowering pit (there were no stalls then) to bury itself deep in the front of the dress circle'. Shaw recalls that Sullivan's 'superhuman' performances, carried out in a relentless schedule of six a week, ultimately exhausted and paralysed him, leading to his retirement from the stage in 1887 and his death four years later.

SUTRO, Alfred (1863–1933), playwright, and translator of Maeterlinck. Sutro was involved with William Archer, H. W. Massingham, and Elizabeth Robins in setting up the New Century Theatre in May 1897 to promote experimental drama. Shaw first met Sutro on Sunday, 7 March 1886, at Jenny Patterson's house. He was a founding member of the Dramatists' Club which Shaw joined in May 1909. Sutro provides an account of the first performance of *Major Barbara* in his autobiographical work, *Celebrities and Simple Souls* (1933).

SWEET, Henry (1845–1912), Oxford philologist and author of numerous standard works on phonetics and Anglo-Saxon language. He invented Current Shorthand, which Shaw tried to learn but eventually rejected (because it was too idiosyncratic) in favour of the Pitman system. Shaw thought Sweet a brilliant specialist but also 'the most savagely Oxonian and donnish animal that ever devoted himself to abusing other dons'. Sweet's most widely read works include *A History of English Sounds from the Earliest Period* (1874), his *Anglo-Saxon Reader* (1876) and *The Sounds of English: An Introduction to Phonetics* (1908). He was one of Shaw's models for Henry Higgins in *Pygmalion*.

TERRISS, William (1847–97), manager of the Adelphi Theatre and, according to Shaw, 'a good but quite brainless actor'. Shaw wrote *The Devil's Disciple* for Terriss who eventually rejected it. Terriss was stabbed to death by an insane former employee of the Adelphi, Richard Archer Flint, whom Terriss had, on occasion, assisted financially.

TERRY, Dame Ellen (1847 –1928), celebrated English actress who joined Henry Irving's company at the Lyceum in 1878 and soon became his leading lady. She first came into contact with Shaw in June 1892, when he replied to a letter she had sent to *The World* asking that its music critic (Shaw) attend a recital by Miss Elvira Gambogi, a protégée of hers. From 1895, Shaw carried on his famous epistolary romance with Terry (which continued during his courtship of Charlotte Payne-Townshend) but – except for a brief encounter at the Palace Theatre in which Terry did not recognize Shaw as the person to whom she casually said 'Good evening, sir' – did not meet her in person until 16 December 1900 at the Stage Society première of *Captain Brassbound's Conversion.* Terry was a model for Lady Cicely Wayneflete, whom she played at the Court Theatre in March 1906. In a self-drafted interview with G.W. Bishop published in the London *Observer* on 8 November 1931, Shaw said 'Make no mistake about it: Ellen Terry, with all her charm and essential amiability, was an impetuous, overwhelming, absorbing personality.'

THESIGER, Ernest (1879–1961), one of Shaw's favourite actors. Thesiger successfully played the Dauphin, opposite Sybil Thorndike, in the 1924 London production of *Saint Joan.* He went on to play a number of major Shaw roles at the Malvern Festival.

THORNDIKE, Dame Sybil (1882–1976), celebrated English actress. Thorndike's distinguished acting career began under Ben Greet in 1904. In 1908, she joined Annie Horniman's repertory company at the Gaiety Theatre. A year later she married actor-director, Lewis Casson, whose association with Shaw went back to the Vedrenne–Barker season of 1905. Thorndike played the title role in the first English production of *Saint Joan* at the New Theatre in March 1924. The production was co-directed by GBS and Thorndike's husband, who also played de Stogumber. Thorndike responded to the part, the play, and Shaw's direction, with great enthusiasm. Asked what she thought of the role of Saint Joan, she replied: 'I think so much of it that I do not care if I never have another part.'

TOLSTOY, Count Leo (1828–1910), Russian novelist and playwright. In August 1908 Shaw sent Tolstoy a copy of *Man and Superman.* In response, Tolstoy praised Shaw for his perception of social ills but criticized him for reducing such serious issues to satire. Shaw was very impressed by Tolstoy's play *Powers of Darkness* (1889) and, a decade later, reviewed his *What is Art?* In 1910, Shaw sent Tolstoy *The Shewing-up of Blanco Posnet.* Earnest about the seriousness of life, Tolstoy found himself repeatedly prevented from considering Shaw a truly profound writer because he believed he jested too much with important ideas. In a letter to Tolstoy, Shaw provided a memorable response to this criticism with the questions: 'why should laughter and humour be excommunicated? Suppose the world were only one of God's jokes, would you work any the less to make it a good joke instead of a bad one?' Shaw acknowledged the influence of Tolstoy's *The Fruits of Enlightenment* (1891) in the Preface to *Heartbreak House* (1919). In 'Tolstoy: Tragedian or Comedian?' (*London Mercury*, May 1921), Shaw deemed Tolstoy's tragicomic drama, *Light Shining Through Darkness* (1900), his masterpiece.

TOMPKINS, Molly (1898–1960), aspiring American actress who arrived in London with her husband, Laurence, in 1921, with plans to establish a Shavian theatre in the United States. Shaw took her in hand by coaching her and having her trained at RADA where, strong-willed and ambitious, she antagonized her teachers, and soon left. She gave up acting in 1924, and moved with Laurence and a son, Peter, who was five or six at the time, to Italy, where, by the summer of 1926, they had rented a villa on the island of San Giovanni on Lake Maggiore. Shaw was strongly attracted to Molly, and had a serious flirtation with her. He spent a great deal of time in her company in Italy, especially during the summer of 1927, when their affair may have been sexually consummated. Although there was no further development in the romance, Shaw remained on friendly terms with her, and during the Second World War paid university fees for her son, Peter Tompkins. In 1949, a year before his death, Shaw wrote to her fondly, enclosing a poem and a photograph of himself taken the previous year. Shaw's letters to his 'dear Mollytompkins' have been edited by Peter Tompkins in *To a Young Actress* (1960), and her reminiscences of GBS, as recorded by Peter in 1950, were published as *Shaw and Molly Tompkins: In Their Own Words* (1961), a partly fictional work which has been credited with more biographical authority than it deserves. Of possibly a thousand letters from Molly to Shaw, only one is known to be extant.

TOPOLSKI, Feliks (1907–89), Polish artist who moved to London in 1935. Provided illustrations for the Constable editions of *Geneva* (1939) and *In Good King Charles's Golden Days*, and the Penguin edition of *Pygmalion* (1941). Shaw once praised Topolski as 'an astonishing draughtsman: perhaps the greatest of all the Impressionists in black and white'.

TREBITSCH, Siegfried (1869–1956), Austrian novelist and playwright, and Shaw's German translator. Armed with a letter of introduction from William Archer, Trebitsch presented himself without notice at Adelphi Terrace in March 1902. He persuaded Shaw to grant him the sole right to translate his plays into German for stage production and publication in Germany and Austria. Over the next fifty years, Trebitsch promoted Shaw's plays with industry and success in Europe, although his early translations were held up to ridicule by German Anglists, and he several times acted beyond his legal authority by signing contracts with theatre managers and other translators of Shaw's works. Charlotte got on well with Trebitsch and Shaw quickly appreciated his indebtedness to the translator who had made him a famous playwright in Germany before the English had fully accepted him. In the 1930s Trebitsch negotiated on Shaw's behalf with German film producers. Fearing persecution as a Jew by the Nazis, Trebitsch and his wife moved to Switzerland and obtained French citizenship in 1939. After the War Trebitsch made regular pilgrimages to Ayot St Lawrence to visit the Shaws. Samuel A. Weiss's edition, *Shaw's Letters to Siegfried Trebitsch* was published in 1986, and extensive recollections of his association with Shaw and Charlotte were included in Trebitsch's *Chronicle of a Life* (trans. Eithne Wilkins and Ernst Kaiser, 1953). Shaw's *Jitta's Atonement* (1922) is a free translation of Trebitsch's play *Frau Gittas Sühne* (1919).

TREE, Sir Herbert Beerbohm (1852–1917), manager of the Haymarket Theatre and, from 1897, Her Majesty's Theatre. Tree married actress Maud Holt in 1883. Tree was one of the dominant actor-managers of the late Victorian period, and played the original Henry Higgins in England opposite Mrs Patrick Campbell in *Pygmalion* in 1914. During the first run of *Pygmalion*, Tree infuriated Shaw by introducing sentimental stage business into the action.

TROUBETSKOY, Prince Paul (1866–1938), Russian-born sculptor raised in Italy. Troubetskoy created a bust of Shaw at John Singer Sargent's London studio in 1908. Much later at his villa on Lake Maggiore in Italy he produced a statuette (1926) and then a full-length statue (1927) of Shaw. The fine full-length statue is displayed in the Shaw Room of the National Gallery of Ireland.

TUNNEY, Gene (1898–1978), Irish-American heavyweight boxing champion. In October 1927, *The Weekly Dispatch* invited Shaw to a private film-viewing of a fight between Gene Tunney and Jack Dempsey, and then published Shaw's commentary (which favoured Tunney) on the fight on 9 October. Tunney and his wife, Polly, lunched with Shaw at Whitehall Court on 14 November 1928, after which a warm friendship developed between Shaw and the boxer. Through April–May 1929 the Shaws stayed at the tourist destination of Brioni, Istria, a peninsula in the North-East Adriatic Sea. While there, Shaw spent a considerable time with Tunney and amused himself one evening by inventing a boxing film for Tunney. This project was not completed.

TYLER, Thomas (1826–1902), translator of Ecclesiastes, and Shakespeare scholar whom Shaw first met in the British Museum where Tyler was a regular reader through the 1880s. Shaw reviewed Tyler's book on Shakespeare's sonnets (*Pall Mall Gazette*, 7 January 1886) which identified Mary Fitton as the Dark Lady (a motif Shaw later utilized in *The Dark Lady of the Sonnets*). Shaw described Tyler as an uncommercial and perennial scholar whose startling ugliness (due to illness and unfortunate form) confirmed him as a bachelor and pessimist. Tyler completed the Furnivall index of Thomas Lodge which Shaw had begun but relinquished by mid-1885.

VEDRENNE, John Eugene (1867–1930), business manager of J. H. Leigh, amateur actor and proprietor of the Royal Court Theatre. Vedrenne went into partnership with Harley Granville Barker in the project of producing new and experimental drama at Leigh's Royal Court Theatre, in successive seasons from 1904 to 1907. The Vedrenne–Barker enterprise changed the course of English theatre by giving London audiences a taste for serious plays as opposed to the less intellectual, conventional fare commonly offered in London theatres of the day, and by supporting emerging playwrights. Eleven of Shaw's plays were staged at the Court Theatre under the Vedrenne–Barker management and they accounted for over seventy per cent of its nearly one thousand performances. The business partnership went bankrupt early in 1908 when Vedrenne and Barker failed in their attempt to translate Court Theatre success into West End viability. Nevertheless, the project was of great significance in advancing English drama generally and in establishing Shaw's name.

VIERECK, George Sylvester (1885–1962), German-born American poet, journalist and editor. Viereck was ardently pro-German through both wars. He edited *The Fatherland* (which later became *Viereck's the American Monthly*) in New York from 1914 to 1917. Viereck's expulsion from the Poetry Society of America in 1919 over his war stance enraged Shaw, who disliked the fact that what he called 'the Republic of Art and Science' was thus proved not free of politics. But he was also annoyed by Viereck's frequent American publication of so-called 'Interviews with Shaw', cobbled together from half-remembered Shavian comments and pure fiction. The second of these, in July 1927, falsely representing Shaw's view of the British involvement in the First World War, was particularly embarrassing to Shaw.

WALKLEY, Arthur Bingham (1855–1926), drama critic under the pen-name 'Spectator' for *The Star* (1888–1900) and then *The Times* (1900–26). Shaw addressed his Epistle Dedicatory of *Man and Superman* to Walkley, and reviewed his book, *Playhouse Impressions* (*The Star*, 9 January 1892). Shaw thought Walkley's Fabian Society lecture (13 December 1901) on 'The

Modern French Drama' 'a very clever one'. Walkley was humorously satirized as the absurdly conservative theatre critic and exponent of Aristotelean dramatic principles Mr Trotter in *Fanny's First Play*.

WALLAS, Graham (1858–1932), Fabian, political scientist and psychologist; member of the London School Board (1894–1904) and the London County Council (1904–07); lecturer at the London School of Economics (1895–1923) and Professor of Political Science at London University (1914–23). Wallas was a student at Oxford with Sydney Olivier and member of the Fabian Society from 1886 to 1904, serving on the Executive with Shaw, Webb and Olivier between 1888 and 1895. In May 1897 Beatrice Webb's holiday plan to match Charlotte Payne-Townshend with Wallas was shortcircuited by Wallas's late arrival and Shaw's interim entertainment of Charlotte. A year later Wallas was witness at their marriage.

WARDROP, John (b.1919), Scottish journalist who arrived penniless in London from Edinburgh in 1939 seeking his idol GBS. By 1942, Wardrop was serving as Shaw's editorial assistant and proofreader on *Everybody's Political What's What?* He also edited some of Shaw's miscellaneous writings and correspondence. His hopes to serve as Shaw's secretary and literary executor came to an end with the arrival of F. E. Loewenstein. Having been assisted by Shaw to study for a law degree he did not complete, Wardrop finally emigrated to America in 1950.

WEBB, Beatrice (née Potter) (1858–1943), social researcher and author, active member of the Fabian Society from 1903 and on the Executive from 1912. Beatrice Webb first met Shaw in July 1890 after he delivered his paper on Ibsen before the Fabian Society. She married Sidney Webb in 1892, and although Shaw thought she did not value Webb as highly as he did, her marriage was, professionally, a very productive partnership. Differences of character meant that Shaw and Beatrice's relationship, although civil in deference to Shaw's friendship with Sidney, never progressed to easy intimacy. According to Malcolm Muggeridge, she was strongly attracted to Shaw. She was often sharply critical of him in her plain-spoken diaries. In 1895, Beatrice and Sidney founded the London School of Economics and Political Science, and she was appointed to the Poor Law Commission the same year. In May 1909, she founded the National Committee for the Break-up of the Poor Law. In 1913 she established the *New Statesman* with Sidney Webb. It was Beatrice who, in 1920, introduced Shaw to Blanche Patch who became his secretary from then until his death thirty years later. With her husband Sidney, and Shaw as sometime adviser and unofficial editor, Beatrice Webb co-authored numerous books on trade unionism, government, social institutions, capitalism and communism. Shaw said he created Miss Vivie Warren, in *Mrs Warren's*

Profession, in response to Beatrice's call for him to portray 'a real modern lady of the governing class'. He claimed she was the model for this character, and that the play's strong socioeconomic theme was created to please her.

WEBB, Sidney James (later Lord Passfield) (1859–1947), Fabian, lawyer, political economist, historian, social reformer and parliamentarian. Webb met Shaw on 28 October 1880, at a Zetetical Society meeting and he became one of Shaw's closest friends and colleagues until old age. On 1 May 1885, at Shaw's insistence, Webb joined the Fabian Society, rising to the Executive the following year. Outwardly brilliant and composed, Webb suffered from intense feelings of insecurity and pessimism through the 1880s which were substantially alleviated by his marriage. Together with his wife Beatrice Webb he founded the London School of Economics and Political Science in 1895 and *The New Statesman* weekly in 1913. Webb served in Ramsay MacDonald's first Labour Cabinet as President of the Board of Trade in 1924, and was elevated to the peerage as Lord Passfield in 1929. In the same year he re-entered the Cabinet as Secretary of State for the Colonies in MacDonald's second Labour government. Webb dedicated himself relentlessly to the task of social reform, his maxim being, 'never to act alone or for myself'. He felt his association with his fellow leading Fabians (the so-called 'Big Four' were Webb, Shaw, Wallas and Olivier) to be a working epitome of 'intellectual communism', characterized by mutual trust, assistance and obedience. Shaw thought Webb 'one of the most extraordinary and capable men alive', and claimed that while he himself occupied centre-stage, Webb's genius was always feeding him from the side. In January 1938, Webb suffered a stroke, and in his last nine years, Shaw saw him only a few times, but quietly assisted him financially, and after his death encouraged the authorities at Westminster to inter the mingled ashes of the Webbs in the Abbey. Webb was a principal model for the characterization of Bluntschli in *Arms and the Man.*

WELLS, Herbert George (1866–1946), novelist, short story writer and essayist. As a student, Wells attended William Morris's Sunday evening meetings at Hammersmith, where Shaw often spoke, but did not meet Shaw personally until 5 January 1895 at the première of Henry James's *Guy Domville* at the St James's Theatre. After that, they met intermittently until 1903, when Wells joined the Fabian Society. In February 1906 Wells delivered a lecture entitled 'Faults of the Fabian' to a closed meeting of the Society, in which he represented the organization as feeble, inadequate and 'arrested' in its attempts to enact its stated objectives. The Executive began to execute Wells's reforms to extend the Society's influence, financial viability and social effectiveness. However, when Shaw perceived that Wells's agenda could well result in the destabilizing removal from power of the 'old gang', the battle lines were drawn, and, showing characteristic courtesy, Shaw routed Wells in a crucial debate in December 1906. The friendship between Wells and Shaw endured, despite the fact that in 1909 they had another earnest confrontation, this time over Wells's scandalous seduction of two young Fabians, Rosamund Bland and Amber Reeves. The latter relationship, which resulted in an illegitimate daughter, was fictionalized by Wells in *Ann Veronica* and also reflected in Shaw's *Misalliance*. Shaw's kindhearted notice of Wells's death in the *New Statesman* (17 August 1946) was ungenerously repaid by Wells's sour, pre-written obituary of Shaw, published in November 1950.

WICKSTEED, Rev. Philip H. (1844–1927), Unitarian clergyman and political economist. He was a master of ancient and modern languages, Ibsenite, classical scholar, translator of Dante, and leader of the British Economic Association. A follower of the Socialist Stanley Jevons who attacked Marx's theory of value, Wicksteed first came to Shaw's notice with his article '*Das Kapital*: A Criticism' in *To-Day* in October 1884. Shaw initially defended Marx's theories against this attack, but eventually came down on the side of Wicksteed. In November 1885, the Economic Circle meetings, conducted by Wicksteed since 1884, moved to Henry Beeton's house, with Shaw and Wicksteed in attendance. In 1904, Shaw sent Wicksteed a copy of his *Common Sense of Municipal Trading* inscribed 'To my father in economics'.

WILDE, Lady Jane (*c.*1821–96), poet, Irish patriot and mother of Oscar Wilde. Shaw attended Lady Wilde's London 'at homes' in his early twenties.

WILDE, Oscar (1854–1900), Irish playwright. Although Wilde and Shaw were never more than acquaintances, Shaw noted that the often severe, unsigned poetry reviews by himself, William Archer and Wilde in the *Pall Mall Gazette* in the mid-1880s, were often attributed by their victims to the wrong critic. He found Wilde's reviews 'exceptionally finished in style and very amusing'. Shaw admired Wilde's work, and regarded him as an ally in Irish hostility against British philistinism. He did, however, find *The Importance of Being Earnest* a disappointing work, describing it as empty 'froth'. Wilde praised Shaw's intelligence and style in *The Quintessence of Ibsenism* and his realism in *Widowers' Houses*. He sent Shaw a presentation copy of *Salome*. Shaw loved to repeat Wilde's sally that 'Shaw has no enemy in the world; and none of his friends like him.' With the assistance of Lord Alfred Douglas, Shaw revised Frank Harris's biography, *Oscar Wilde,* for its second edition (1938).

WILLIAMS, Harcourt (Ernest George) (1880–1957), actor and theatre director. Williams played Valentine in *You Never Can Tell* and Count O'Dowda in *Fanny's First Play* in London productions before the First World

War. When appointed Director of the Old Vic Theatre in 1929, he successfully urged Lilian Baylis to include Shaw's plays in the repertory.

WILLIAMS, Nurse, Shaw's childhood nurse. Shaw remembers 'the excellent Nurse Williams' as the only good and reliable servant of a number who had responsibility for him and his sisters in Dublin. Williams enforced obedience from her charge by warning him of the cock (which Shaw remembers perceiving as an avenging deity) that would come down the chimney to get him.

WILSON, Charlotte (1854–1944), one of the first female students at Cambridge, hostess to the Hampstead Historic Society and prominent early member of the Fabian Society. She was co-editor, with Prince Peter Kropotkin, of the anarchist serial *Freedom*. Shaw claimed that his essay, 'What's in a Name? How an Anarchist might put it', published in *The Anarchist* (March 1885), was written 'to shew Mrs Wilson my idea of the line an anarchist paper should take in England'. Wilson drafted part of what Shaw considered the deservedly forgotten Fabian Tract No. 4, 'What Socialism Is'. Her early term on the Fabian Executive ended in 1887, but she returned for a second term in 1911 to 1915. Shaw met Wilson through his attendance at the Karl Marx Society meetings (which she founded) held in her home from winter 1884 through to June 1885. The group, with Shaw still in attendance, reassembled to discuss Proudhon, this time in the Hampstead Library, and went on to become the Hampstead Historic Society.

WINSTEN, Clare (1894–1989), sculptor and painter who, during her residence near 'Shaw's Corner', from 1945 to 1949, sketched and painted the ageing Shaw, and secured a commission for a sculpture of Joan of Arc which was erected in his garden in 1947. Although Shaw praised her drawings and paid for the sculpture, he would not buy the portrait which he did not like. Clare illustrated Shaw's posthumously published *My Dear Dorothea*, which was edited by her husband Stephen. Shaw gave £200 for the university education of Clare's son, Christopher, and helped one of her daughters, Theodora, get an assignment as the designer for his late play *Buoyant Billions*.

WINSTEN, Stephen (1893–1991), Shaw's neighbour at Ayot from 1945 to 1949. Shaw considered the Winstens a talented Bohemian family who offered him what no one else in the village could, intelligent conversation. Stephen made a living out of knowing Shaw, beginning with his editorship of a ninetieth-birthday celebration, *GBS 90* (1946) and following up with three more Shavian books, all compromised by plagiarism, errors and deliberate misinformation. Even though Winsten's *Days with Bernard Shaw*

(1948) was so bad that Shaw felt forced to publish a disclaimer in the *Times Literary Supplement* (15 January 1949), he preferred to maintain his relationship with the Winstens, which he enjoyed, rather than destroy it by enquiring too deeply into their debatable usage of him. After Shaw's death, Winsten edited *My Dear Dorothea,* with illustrations by Clare Winsten.

WOOLF, Leonard Sidney (1880–1969), author, journalist and founder of the Hogarth Press with his wife, Virginia Woolf. In 1913 the Webbs pressed Woolf to join the Fabian Society and he soon began writing for the *New Statesman*. He met Shaw through the Webbs and, in his *Beginning Again: An Autobiography of the Years 1911–1918*, he confessed to being fond of the endlessly talking, though always entertaining, playwright. Woolf maintained, however, that for all his warmth and wit, when Shaw was in conversation with someone he saw right through his interlocutor into 'a distant world inhabited almost entirely by GBS'. Woolf was commissioned by the Fabian Society to investigate the causes of the First World War. The first part of his report appeared in a *New Statesman* supplement in 1915 and, together with the second part, was published as a book, *International Government*, the following year, with an American Preface by Shaw.

WOOLF, Virginia (1882–1941), novelist. Shaw first met the Woolfs in 1913 at a lunch party given by Sidney and Beatrice Webb to persuade Leonard Woolf to join the Fabian Society. The Woolfs spent the weekend of 17–19 June 1916 with the Shaws and the Webbs at a house which the Webbs had taken near Turners Hill, Sussex. Brilliant descriptions of Virginia Woolf's later meetings with Shaw in 1932 and 1933 are recorded in her diary. 'What life, what vitality! What immense nervous spring!' she exclaimed about Shaw, as a prelude to less complimentary remarks about him, following a meeting at the house of Maynard Keynes on 2 June 1932. In 1940 Shaw wrote a remarkable letter to Virginia Woolf, recalling their meeting in 1916, and saying that he always connected *Heartbreak House* with her because he conceived the idea for the play at that meeting 'and, of course, fell in love with you'. Two plaques on the front wall of 29 Fitzroy Square, London record the fact that at different times the house had been home to both Virginia Woolf and Bernard Shaw.

WRIGHT, Sir Almroth (1861–1947), Irish-born bacteriologist and Principal of the Institute of Pathology at St Mary's Hospital, Paddington. Shaw had an interesting correspondence with Wright, who served as a model for Sir Colenso Ridgeon in *The Doctor's Dilemma* (1906). On 18 October 1913 Shaw's devastating, though good-humoured, satirical attack on Wright's male chauvinism was published in the *New Statesman*. In 1932

Shaw consulted Wright for assistance in undoing an error he was recently made aware of in the first act of *Too True to be Good*: he had assigned the cause of measles, erroneously, to a microbe. Later, at a performance of the play, Wright whispered to Shaw that every medical student should be made to watch its first act before going into private practice.

YATES, Edmund (1831–94), novelist, journalist and founding editor of *The World* from 1874 until his death in 1894. Shaw first met Yates when he visited the *World* office on 2 April 1886 to examine and review some etchings. Shaw owed his short term as *World* art-critic to William Archer, who also subsequently got Shaw the post of musical reviewer for the same periodical. At Yates's death, Shaw resigned his post as musical reviewer and went in search of an editor of the same calibre as Yates. He found his man in 1895, taking up the position of theatre critic for Frank Harris's *Saturday Review*.

YEATS, William Butler (1865–1939), Irish poet, dramatist, essayist, and founder, with Lady Gregory, of the Irish National Theatre Company. Yeats and Shaw first met on 12 February 1888 at one of William Morris's Sunday evening suppers at Kelmscott House. Their mutual involvement with Florence Farr and her Avenue Theatre led to numerous meetings between Shaw and Yeats in the 1890s. Yeats's play *The Land Of Heart's Desire* was double-billed with Shaw's *Arms and the Man* at the Avenue Theatre in 1894. In his *Autobiographies* Yeats provides one of the accounts of the opening night of *Arms and the Man* and of Shaw's famous retort to the man in the audience, Reginald Golding Bright, who booed while everyone else was cheering and laughing at the author's curtain call. 'From that moment,' Yeats declared, 'Bernard Shaw became the most formidable man in modern letters.' Better known, however, is Yeats's description, in the same passage of *Autobiographies*, of a nightmare he claims to have had in which Shaw appeared to him as a smiling sewing machine. Although they often had causes in common relating to Ireland and other matters, and treated one another as allies, Yeats and Shaw had fundamentally opposed artistic values and ideas about Irish nationhood. Yeats praised Shaw's play *John Bull's Other Island*, but eventually rejected it for the Abbey Theatre, ostensibly on technical grounds, but more probably because of its satirical attack on the Irish nationalist movement with which Yeats had identified himself. Yeats and Shaw were among the 71 playwrights who signed an anti-censorship letter published in *The Times* on 29 October 1907. In 1932 Yeats managed to secure Shaw's involvement in his founding of an Irish Academy of Letters. Shaw held its office of President until 1935 when Yeats took over till his death in 1939, whereupon Shaw served another, year-long, term.

Index